THE BANKER

Books by Leslie Waller

NOVELS: The Banker

Phoenix Island

The Bed She Made

Show Me The Way

Three Day Pass

(with Louise Waller)

Take Me To Your Leader

NONFICTION: A Book to Begin on Time

A Book to Begin on Weather

A Book to Begin on Numbers

A Book to Begin on Our American Language

A Book to Begin on Our Flag

A Book to Begin on Explorers

A Book to Begin on Electricity

A Book to Begin on American Inventions

THE BANKER

LESLIE WALLER

DOUBLEDAY & COMPANY, INC., GARDEN CITY, NEW YORK
1963

Library of Congress Catalog Card Number 63-12961
Copyright © 1963 by Leslie Waller
All Rights Reserved
Printed in the United States of America
First Edition

For the New York newspapermen

who try each day to make sense

out of what happens

THE BANKER

Chapter One

The sun of late afternoon had grown faintly burnt-looking, as though it had now started to consume itself in flame. Aging rapidly, it gave a slightly amber glow to the small, sharp whitecaps that marched jauntily across the waters of Long Island Sound.

"Freshening nicely," Palmer told the older man.

"Nothing short of brisk." The older man handed the tiller to Palmer and, moving forward like a big, agile cat, reefed in a foot or two of mainsail.

Palmer watched him stand up, legs apart, and stare shorewards past the drum-tight jib sheet. Burckhardt's body, lean without real thinness, moved surely with the dip and rise of the boat, planted like a tree on two worn white deck shoes.

"Starboard a bit," Palmer heard him say. "It's that life-guard tower you want."

Palmer nodded, forgetting that the other man wasn't watching. All afternoon, Palmer realized now, the old bird had never once seemed to be watching. And yet, what was this weekend all about if not a personal inspection, pore by pore?

"Just starboard of the tower," the older man was saying, "lies the mouth of the channel."

He turned back to Palmer and his small, milky-blue eyes flicked across the younger man's face. "Take her in," he said then, turning away. Palmer saw him sit down in the shadow of the jib, ream out his pipe and begin loading it as though nothing else could ever concern him.

The offshore wind quickened rather abruptly. Palmer felt the boat heave forward and heel to port. He eased off the tiller. The mast moved slowly to a more perpendicular line.

There was no point, Palmer decided, in finishing off the day by swamping them a mile from shore. If Burckhardt wanted to swim, there was all of tomorrow. Unless the old bird was a proper keeper of the Sabbath.

On the many occasions Palmer had spent in New York he had yet to establish a lucid set of criteria for the people he'd met. Most of them, of course, had been bankers like himself. But he was likely to run up against much more variant types here than he had ever known in Chicago. There were more kinds of bankers in New York, for one thing. There were more of each kind.

And there were more important ones, too. It made the sizing-up process tricky.

Burckhardt was an example, Palmer thought. Outwardly he was fairly standard—if the chairman of a bank as huge as Ubco could be considered in any way standard—and yet there were hints of a certain eccentricity that Palmer had been unwilling to probe, at least not during this weekend, when so much was at—

"We haven't a hell of a lot of time," Burckhardt called. "Take her to starboard and pick it up full."

Palmer nodded, understanding that this was to be the crisis of a crucial weekend. The business background had been checked and confirmed, he had no doubt, by Burckhardt's Chicago apparatus. The family background was already known, although Mrs. B. had gone into it a bit more at lunch today. But now, right now, was the start of the old bird's personality test.

"We're still off a few points," Burckhardt called.

Palmer opened his mouth to call a sarcastic "Aye, aye, sir," but thought better of it. He shoved against the tiller and watched the mast heel sharply to port. The mainsail bellied full with wind. He could hear the sharpened hiss of water, cleft by the bow as it shot more quickly through the rough whitecaps.

The shore grew plainer. Palmer could make out a life guard in a red bathing suit atop the tower. As the boat raced nearer, a knot of children could be seen on the beach. Palmer picked out two striped umbrellas and an inflated swimming tube, but he was damned if he could find the mouth of the channel.

"Just right of the tower?" he asked, shouting against the wind.

"Just starboard," Burckhardt called back.

Palmer's mouth tightened. The old man, he decided, had started marking up the test paper already. And already it was going badly.

The shore moved in on Palmer now. He felt his heart knock sharply, then go on beating at a jagged, nervous tempo. Everything was terribly clear. Tower, children, umbrellas, cabanas, dory. No channel. On Lake Michigan, in his own catboat or the family's 40-footer, everything was known, all landmarks meaningful, all distances remembered. Bringing a boat in, even at this speed, was simple and, thus, satisfying. Here, in alien territory, it was torture.

"Hard port!" Burckhardt shouted.

Palmer let up on the tiller. The boat spun slowly on its stern as the life began to ebb from its sails. In the sudden quiet, Palmer saw the channel mouth quite clearly. A line of rock had hidden it before.

"Take her in," Burckhardt said then.

The boat was beginning to lose way. Palmer picked up some of the breeze again. Correcting his aim from moment to moment, he guided them through the rocky channel mouth and into a long reach of calmer water. To the right, a few hundred yards ahead, he could see the Burckhardt boathouse, a small, neat structure shaped like a miniature Cape Cod cottage, single red pennon taut in the breeze. He waited for Burckhardt to tell him about it, then realized that the whole job from here to tying-up was his alone. He watched the older man strike a match and cup his hands around the bowl of his pipe.

With sudden decision, Palmer picked up the full breeze. Pilings started to fly past, stuttering by like picket fences. If a test was wanted, Palmer decided somewhat grimly, he'd give the old bird a touch of heart failure for his money.

The boat shot wildly through the water. The Burckhardt landing loomed up dead ahead, taller and larger by the instant. At the last possible moment, Palmer yanked the tiller hard starboard and watched the boat swing in a tight circle to port, losing way instantly as the sails fell slack. Dying, the boat's motion became almost imperceptible as its bow turned delicately about and nuzzled the pilings of the Burckhardt landing.

"Nice," the older man said. He got to his feet, line in hand, and made fast to a stanchion. "That's exactly the way I do it," he added, hopping up on the landing dock. "Throw me your stern line, Woody."

They walked slowly up the long gravel road to the main house. Burckhardt had taken off his sweatshirt. Then, after a moment, he had pulled it around him, capelike, the sleeves knotted under his rather prominent chin. "Starting to get chilly rather early in the day now," he muttered.

"You have to expect that, this late in August," Palmer said. He watched a single green oak leaf flutter down onto the road from a giant tree above them. "We usually close our summer place by Labor Day. Edith and the children are still there. This year, we'll close up when I get back home."

"Your idea?" Burckhardt asked, "or your wife's?"

"Mine."

They walked on without speaking for a moment as the grade grew steeper. "Just," the older man went on abruptly, "that if you had to stay East an extra week, she could close up by herself, couldn't she?"

"Of course." Palmer felt his breathing deepen as they climbed the steep road. "Woody's a big help. My eldest. He's fourteen."

"You've got two, haven't you?"

"Two boys," Palmer said, certain that Burckhardt knew but uncertain as to his motives for pretending not to know. "And a girl, Gerri. She's almost eleven. The middle one."

The older man said nothing for a while. Palmer suddenly saw that he was trying to disguise the fact that he was breathing hard. At that moment the road leveled off as they reached the crest of a hill. The Burckhardt place stood some way before them, large, spread-out, but not too large. In the yellow slanting light of late afternoon the blue shutters looked vaguely greenish against the white clapboard. The house had an odd but pleasing style to it, Palmer decided. The central portion was two-storied, with a portico rising the full height. A single-storied wing of rooms on the right was balanced on the left by the garage, separated by a passageway that led to gardens in the rear.

Palmer found it hard to explain the house's delicate elegance of line and, at the same time, conservative solidity of mass. It was probably—

"The only reason I brought it up," Burckhardt said suddenly, his breath fully recovered, "was to make certain that it wouldn't work a hardship on your family if I held you in New York a few more days."

"They're pretty used to fending for themselves."

Burckhardt's sharp little eyes swung toward him for a moment, then looked straight ahead again. "I didn't think your father had you traveling much."

"Off and on, since the war."

"Mortgage stuff?" the older man asked.

"I did appraisal work in the beginning," Palmer said, "but between the end of the war and, oh, two years ago, I was almost entirely in new business. We do our own credit . . ." Palmer let his voice die away, realizing abruptly that he must be boring the old bird.

"I believe you worked in the Trust Department for a while."

"Just before the war, briefly. And for a spell in 1950 and '51," Palmer added, "I did a trick in commodities."

"Your father believed in thoroughness, didn't he?" Burckhardt asked.

Burckhardt stopped for a moment to stare at one pillar of the fieldstone wall that ran along the paved road across the lawn. "Some idiot boy," he said slowly, "has been chucking rotten apples. The damned finial looks as if pigeons had roosted there all year."

"I think it can be hosed off."

"No, damn it," the older man said, "there's an acid in the apples that attacks the stone and discolors it. We'll have to sand-blast or something." He turned angrily away and began walking toward the house again. "You've been doing public relations, too," he said then.

Palmer wasn't sure whether it was a statement or a question. "Just about," he replied, choosing a safe answer.

"I find it hard to believe," Burckhardt said, "that fifteen years ago your father foresaw today's need for proper public relations. But I must say he gave you a thorough grounding for it. There aren't a hell of a lot of men around these days doing bank p.r. with a background that makes any real sense. Newspapermen, mostly. Advertising boys. Not many bankers among them."

"We've got to have those boys," Palmer said, affecting a kind of airiness. "I'd be lost without my specialists."

"Naturally. You hire that kind of thing. Drug on the labor market." Burckhardt held open the side door that led from the garage passage into the house. "But it isn't all that easy to find men with your particular background. Go ahead."

Entering the darkness of the house, Palmer wondered just how specific the old bird was going to get. It wasn't until the end of bargaining, was it, that you admitted your liking for the merchandise?

4

At the back of the house, under a gold-and-black-striped awning, stood half a dozen outdoor chairs of various kinds, grouped loosely around a massive wicker table with a marble top on which sat cigarettes and an ash tray. Showered and changed for dinner, Palmer sat and watched the garden beyond grow dusky-dark, shadows changing from an orangish brown to a greenish black as the sun faded out of the sky. In the chair next to him, Burckhardt loaded his pipe and lighted it, sending almost invisible puffs of smoke into the darkness around them.

The butler placed a tray on the wicker table and then touched a switch somewhere along the wall behind them. Soft indirect light flooded the area. On the tray Palmer saw two whisky decanters, three glasses, a siphon and a wooden ice bucket bound in silver.

"You know," the older man said after they had both settled back with drinks and the first sip had been taken, "people make a hellish fuss about things nowadays. Have you noticed how they apparently go out of their way to complicate the simplest ideas?"

"I don't think it's a new thing," Palmer said, wondering what he was getting at. "I mean, haven't we always tended to do that?"

"Not we," Burckhardt responded, "they. I don't think a banker has any real difficulty keeping things simple."

"If you mean abstract ideas," Palmer said, "they usually seem quite complex to the average person. I don't think we realize how complex they can seem . . . to them."

"I'm talking about concrete things, too," Burckhardt said. "All kinds of things," he repeated in a thoughtful voice. "Marriage. Death. Profit. Power. Work. The price of beans. Whether to wear a belt or braces. Everything and anything. People overcomplicate everything. It's become almost impossible to make any headway against that kind of muddled thinking."

Palmer watched the older man closely now, trying to make out the direction he was taking and the goal in view. The soft overhead light gave Burckhardt's close-cropped gray hair a silvery, unreal look. His sharp, beaky nose stood out strongly over a small mouth and a blunt chin.

Palmer sipped his unlabeled whisky and decided that it must be very old. "I see what you mean," he said then, not seeing it at all. A feeling of being slowly boxed in began to enclose him. It was almost as if, by uttering the kind of lie he had told his father for so many years, he had commanded the swinging shut of a cell door. He took another sip of his drink.

"On second thought," he heard himself say, "I'll be damned if I know what you're driving at." He felt the palms of his hands grow suddenly moist and he realized that he could no more have stopped himself from saying that than he could have brought in the sloop nice-Nelly and slow an hour before. There was something about this man that made Palmer want to set his feet against him and shove. Palmer could not afford to be, with him, as he had with his own father.

5

Burckhardt laughed, the first time Palmer had heard him do so all that weekend. "Woody," the older man said, "for a younger son, your father did a good job on you. You probably don't appreciate it in the least, either." He rattled the ice in his glass. "You don't remember the first time we met, do you?"

"In Chicago?"

"At your father's Winnetka place," Burckhardt said. "It must have been a year or two before the Crash. Your grandfather was still living. You were what? Eleven?"

"Just about."

"You were all together then. Your mother and your brother Hanley and you. Hanley was very much in evidence. You tended to stick in the corners. I remember it very clearly because I didn't see your father again until after the Crash and by then, of course, he and your mother had separated."

"That's right."

"Hanley was what? Fifteen?" Burckhardt mused. "Serious and dedicated. He'd already started working at the bank during summer vacations. But I don't think you shared his enthusiasm, did you?"

Palmer paused before answering. Burckhardt was shrewd, but no one on earth was perceptive enough to grasp the truth about the Palmers, father and sons. "I'm afraid my interest in the bank developed quite a bit later," he said then.

He waited for the older man's reply, wondering how much he had guessed over the years. It was important now that he believe Palmer to have been his father's son, heart and soul, from the beginning to the end.

"You always did have outside interests," Burckhardt said then. "I seem to remember some scrape you got into here in the East. A girl from Radcliffe? Or was it Smith?"

Palmer tried a grin. "That depends," he said, "on which scrape you mean."

For the second time that weekend, Burckhardt laughed. "And then," he said, "you had quite a few close shaves during the war, too. What was it, O.S.S.?"

"Nothing so grand. Army Intelligence."

Burckhardt puffed at his pipe for a moment. "It must have come as quite a relief," he said then, "to be able to settle down after the war."

Palmer took a long sip of his whisky. The danger seemed past. "Yes," he lied, "it certainly was."

"But I still recall you as an eleven-year-old, somewhat quiet, with very definite opinions."

"I don't know any eleven-year-old without them," Palmer said.

"You had built a scale model of Lindbergh's plane, with Hanley's help. I recall it quite well. A damned big model, too. About a yard long or something. And you insisted that you were going to fly it to some place you called the Kee-ber Pass."

6

"Of course," Palmer said. "I'd been reading Hanley's copy of *Lives of a Bengal Lancer*. I remember that year."

"And your mother," the older man went on, "kept saying, 'No, Woody, it's too far away. We'd never see you again.' And you said, 'Nonsense. I'll fly right back the next day.' It's odd how clear a vision of future things youngsters have. And, of course, the future's all come true. But I'm sure your mother still doesn't believe it. Neither did I at the time. It's all seemed to happen overnight."

"Just about overnight," Palmer said. "A few decades."

"You see what I'm driving at?" Burckhardt pounced suddenly. "People complicate very simple matters. It takes a special kind of mind to see things as simply as they really are."

"A special mind . . . either a banker or a child."

The older man laughed again and sipped his drink. "The way people carry on," he said at last. "All these grandiose ideas about Western Civilization and the Free World. It's all you hear today."

"People are concerned, naturally," Palmer said, uneasy again at having lost the old bird's drift.

"No need to be. Not if they stopped complicating simple things." Burckhardt hunched himself forward in his chair and seemed to grow a bit taller and more solid in the process.

"Let's take this Free World business," he went on, staring down at his glass. "That's this hemisphere, and Europe minus the Iron Curtain countries. Is that about it?"

"About."

"All right." Burckhardt straightened up in his chair and his voice grew suddenly direct. "When you say the Free World, you're talking about capitalism. And when you say capitalism, you're talking about the United States, because we run it. And when you say the United States, you mean the banks, because we put up the money for it. Now, when you say the banks, you mean the big ones, because they boss the herd. And when you talk about the big ones, you mean Ubco because it's the biggest." He looked up at Palmer and his small blue eyes became very grave. "But when you say Ubco," he went on in an abruptly softer voice, "you're talking about me."

There was a little moment of silence, during which Palmer heard his chair creak in an odd way.

"Which is what I meant," the old man said then, "about seeing things simply. I need an executive vice-president. When can you start?"

7

CHAPTER TWO

Palmer climbed up out of the Grand Central subway station into the early light of Monday morning and stood for a moment, looking over the heads of people hurrying to work, listening to the sharp tattoo of high heels along the up-swept length of Park Avenue as it rose into the old Murray Hill section of New York.

A low-lying haze blurred the sunlight as it illuminated the inturned, worried faces of passers-by, eyes wide and staring, mouths contorted slightly by private turmoils, women's lips softly red like minor wounds, foreheads wrinkled . . . a collective Monday-morning face, made mercilessly explicit by the shadowless operating-table light.

Palmer hefted his overnight bag and crossed to the west side of Park, looking for a cab. The Fleetwood had dropped both Palmer and Burckhardt some twenty minutes before in the still-dewy softness of Van Cortlandt Park, at the extreme northern terminus of the Jerome Avenue IRT subway, where the two men had boarded an express and sat in silence, each reading the *Times*, until Palmer had got off at Grand Central.

This, Palmer reflected now, was so typical of East Coast bankers as to be almost ludicrous, this oddly Puritan-like approach to matters of comfort. Burckhardt's conscience demanded that the Fleetwood take him only from his Connecticut home to the Bronx, where, for fifteen cents, the IRT brought him downtown to Broad Street.

Probably, Palmer realized suddenly, it had nothing to do with conscience. Burckhardt impressed him as the kind of person who had long ago realized that he could reach the financial district much faster by subway and that, by boarding his train at the end of the line, he could guarantee himself a seat all the way.

Palmer began walking rapidly southward on Park, swinging the overnight bag in a long, carefree arc. As he stopped for a light, the bag nearly collided with the rear of a young woman. Palmer found himself wondering why he had been swinging the bag so freely and had just about decided that it was an exuberance, suppressed until this very moment of leaving Burckhardt, over landing the new job.

The light changed and he found himself dropping behind the woman in order to watch the play of her buttocks as she crossed the street, the alternate

8

swell and slack half-concealed by the dress, her calves swelling as she shifted weight, silken muscle tensing and growing subtly greater, like a heart engorged with pulsing blood.

When she turned west at Thirty-ninth Street, Palmer stood on the corner for a long moment, watching her. He could feel a tightness in his chest that seemed to condense in his throat and push upwards. He closed his eyes and swallowed twice, slowly, feeling the contradictory sensations meet and merge for a moment before, with a dizzying rush, the tension within pushed upward again. His face grew hot. He opened his eyes quickly to stop the sudden sensation of falling, took a step backward to regain his balance. The girl had disappeared.

Palmer took a deep breath and, crossing the street, continued walking southward at a slower pace. He turned west and pushed through the revolving door of the Union League Club.

A calm silence, divorced of auto horns, the gasp of bus brakes and the sharp rat-tat of women's high heels, seemed now to settle over him like a cool, comfortable cloak. He nodded to the tall Negro who, for as long as Palmer could remember, had stood there to the left of the short corridor that led down the steps into the main foyer.

"Good morning, Mr. Palmer, sir."

"Good morning." As if to check the accuracy of the interchange, Palmer glanced at his wrist watch and found that it still lacked five minutes of nine o'clock. He handed his overnight bag to the attendant.

"Room G, sir?"

"I think so," Palmer replied. He followed the man to the elevators, but detoured for a moment to look at the Dow-Jones ticker. Since the market hadn't yet opened—and wouldn't for some time in Chicago—he found himself glancing, without really reading, at a rehash of last week's ups and downs: an abortive rally led by drugs. He entered the elevator and felt its smooth upward surge.

At his floor, the man led the way to Palmer's room, placed the bag on the luggage rack at the foot of the huge double bed and threw open the window. "Will there be anything, Mr. Palmer?"

Palmer started to shake his head. "Yes," he said then, correcting himself. "See if you can dig up a Chicago *Trib* and a *Wall Street Journal*."

"Yes, sir. If you'd care for anything, there's a menu in the drawer of the desk, sir."

"I've eaten, thanks."

"As you say, sir." The man closed the door softly behind him.

Palmer sat down on the bed, feeling again the firm softness of the mattress. He saw that his big suitcase had been unpacked in his absence and both suits had been pressed and hung in the closet in the three days he'd been away from the room. He sat there trying to remember what else he had planned to do during his stay in New York, finding it difficult to think of the other things at all, since the primary purpose of the trip had already been accomplished.

Executive vice-president of Ubco! Palmer leaned back on the bed and stretched out full length. The old bird hadn't been kidding, not really, about the power of his bank. It was undoubtedly the largest and strongest financial operation in the country, with First National City and Bank of America running behind it.

Lying there, he wondered for a moment what the average age of Ubco's previous executive-veeps had been. Fifty-five? Sixty? Palmer closed his eyes and projected across the private screen of his mind the financial-page headlines a month from now when the news was announced: UNITED BANK NAMES PALMER, 44, TO SECOND POST. The Chicago papers would play it up nicely: APPOINT WOODS PALMER JR. UNITED'S YOUNGEST EXECUTIVE V.P.

There was a discreet double knock at the door. Palmer sat up. "Come in."

The Negro entered. "The Chicago *Trib,* sir," he said, "and the *Wall Street Journal.*" He paused for just a moment, then couldn't resist adding: "They just unloaded that *Trib* off the Commodore Vanderbilt, sir. I have a friend at Grand Central brings me one every morning."

"Wonderful," Palmer said. He started to reach into the right-hand pocket of his trousers for some change, but the man nodded, turned and left before he could complete the gesture.

Alone again, Palmer held the newspaper in one hand and let the pages riffle slowly through his fingers. He found himself looking at an automobile ad with a drawing of a girl in a bathing suit that emphasized her bust and hips. He sat there staring at it for a moment, then let the newspaper slide off the bed to the floor.

He picked up the phone. "I want station-to-station, Watervliet, Wisconsin. The number is 559 ring 2." He listened for a moment. "Watervliet," he repeated and hung up the phone.

His heart had started to beat erratically and he took a deep breath to calm himself, wondering as he did so what had suddenly broken into its even tempo. Calling Edith, he told himself, realizing at the same time that he was lying.

He lay back on the bed again and stared at the dark oak beams in the beige ceiling. The bed received him softly, yet kept his body up at the surface of the mattress without enveloping him. What was it, he wondered. What was wrong with him?

It wasn't, Palmer decided, being away from Edith this long, with the sure prospect of at least another week's separation. Since the war he had spent many weeks away from her, traveling the country on business. It had nothing to do with Edith, he told himself, with either her absence or her imminent presence on the telephone.

Then what was it? The new job?

He smiled lopsidedly at the ceiling, understanding how practiced he had become at deliberately confusing himself with terribly sensible suggestions when all the time he knew—with the kind of knowledge that had nothing to do with his mind—why he felt this way.

He could feel the knowledge in the tightness of his throat, in the way his eyes raked the New York pavements, devouring the sight of women with a hunger like a sickness.

It may have begun in the spring in Chicago. At the lake, in Wisconsin, when he had joined his family on weekends during the summer, it had been almost too much, the young girls in their bathing suits. And in the hot, muggy city, perspiring under a heavy blanket of moist air, he had worked late each night in his air-conditioned office until the sun had set and the women, going home from work, window-shopping singly and in pairs, had disappeared from the streets.

It had not made itself plain to him until late August, a few weeks before this New York trip. He had been in conference about the merger with his public-relations staff. Miss Hermann, who specialized in that sort of thing anyway, had been crossing and recrossing her legs in such a way that he had had to shift slightly in his chair to see them. He had felt quite sure, at the time, that what he was doing was baldly apparent to the rest of the meeting.

Male climacteric, he thought. The phone rang.

He sat up on the bed, noting that his heart had slowed to a calm, almost draggy tempo. "Ready with Watervliet," the operator said.

He listened to the familiar double-buzz as the village operator rang the cottage phone. He glanced at his watch. Nine-twenty. Eight-twenty in Wisconsin. Ring-ring. Edith had probably got up with Mrs. Gage, the housekeeper, and the two of them had already had their breakfast. The kids would not yet be up. Ring-ring. Or perhaps they'd all got up early and gone for a morning swim. Except that the lake would have started to turn a bit chilly this time of morning. Ring-ring. Or none of them had yet got out of bed. That was undoubtedly what had happened. Ring—

"Hello?"

"Edith? Good morning."

"Oh, hi, Dad."

"Gerri? Did I wake you up?"

A prolonged yawn directly into the phone. "No," his daughter said after a moment. "There are hornets under the eaves or something. They wake me up all the time. Where are you?"

"New York. How have you been?"

"Fine."

"And Woody? And Tom?"

"Fine."

"Can I talk to Mom?"

"She isn't here."

"Then find her, Gerri. I'll wait."

"I don't know where to look."

Palmer took a quick, calming breath. "Gerri, put down the phone and call her. Call loudly enough for her to hear. All right?"

"I might wake her up if she's still asleep."

"That," Palmer said slowly, "is the general idea. Now, get going, Gerri. This is a long-distance call."

"Well . . ." The girl's voice died away with an indecisive fall. Then, suddenly, with a loudness that hurt his ear, she shrieked: "Mom! Mom! Oh, Mo-om!"

"Not into the phone, Gerri!"

"*Mom!*"

There was a loud bang as the girl dropped the phone on the hall table. Palmer could hear her voice growing fainter as she moved away from the phone, still calling for Edith.

He lay back on the bed and pictured her running through the old house. If she weren't still in pajamas, she was probably wearing short shorts and a halter top into which she had recently begun to stuff padding. Physically, Gerri took after Palmer, which, he reflected now, was probably not the best situation for a girl. She was tall for her age; at eleven years she stood an inch under Edith's 5'7". Her legs were the longest part of her, as they were for Palmer, too, and her face had the narrowness, the almost hollow cheeks under sharp horizontal bones, that characterized her father's face, the skin somewhat too thin-looking, stretched tight over the underlying bone. Deciding that she would probably end up a fashion model, Palmer glanced at his wrist watch and saw that the call had begun nearly five minutes before. He wondered whether shouting into the phone would summon Gerri from wherever she had gone.

The house on the lake had been built by his grandfather shortly after McKinley's assassination, a rambling affair of two and three stories with green copper cupolas and white gingerbread trim across its cedar-shingle façade. A boardwalk led some three hundred feet downhill to the roofed pier. Palmer's earliest memories of the house were connected with the pier at night, ablaze with Japanese lanterns, the music of a three-piece orchestra coming across the water to him as he sat at the window of the room in which he and Hanley had been put to sleep. The women in their short, tight skirts, the faint tinkle of ice in the punch bowl as someone stirred it . . .

He checked his watch again and found that eight minutes had elapsed. Palmer sat up on the edge of the bed and stared impatiently at the *Tribune* lying in a heap on the floor at his feet, the provocative drawing of the girl in the bathing suit looking up at him. He shifted sideways and stared at the wood-paneled wall.

Burckhardt had left him with the thought that the day, including lunch, should be kept clear for discussions with others of Ubco's top brass. At this moment, Palmer thought, the old bird would be trying to get through to him with the final word.

"Dad?" Gerri's voice asked.

"Good grief! Do you realize how long you—"

"I can't find her," the girl cut in.

"All right," Palmer said, the helpless anger hot within him. "Give her this message. No, get a pencil."

"Right."

"Take this down," he said more calmly. "Executive vice-president."

"Right." A pause. "How many 'e's' in 'executive'?"

"For God's sake, Gerri!" Palmer took a steadying breath. "Now put down: United Bank and Trust Com—"

"Whoa-whoa-whoa. United what?"

He closed his eyes. "Bank and Trust Company," he said very quietly. "Read it back to me, please." He listened to her voice for a moment, then nodded. "Tell her I got the job."

"Will we have to move to New York?"

"Eventually."

"Dad!" The girl groaned and made a realistic sound of vomiting.

"Have you ever been hung-up on, young lady?"

"All right," she said. "All right." A deep sigh. "I'll tell her, but nobody's going to like it."

"Good-by, Gerri." He replaced the telephone on its hook. How many "e's" in "executive"? What other way was there to spell it?

He sank back on the bed and covered his face with his hands. Hello, dear, he thought, hello, dear, I am now the second highest officer of the largest bank in the country at the age of forty-four. Hello, dear, I won't have to rot in Chicago with a paper title. Hello, dear, good-by, dear.

He got up from the bed and looked at himself in the mirror over the dresser cabinet. The skin under his rather wide-set gray eyes looked vaguely soft and a little dark, reminding him suddenly that he had not slept well at Burckhardt's home. The almost overwhelming climax of that evening on the patio when, after the prolonged tension of delicate maneuvering, victory had come in instants, had spoiled him completely for sleep.

Palmer walked to the window and looked out over Park Avenue, his eyes feeling somewhat gritty as he watched the people walking. He frowned, sensing something lost, and, as he stood there watching, he realized that the women were missing. It was after nine o'clock. They were all at work. He stood there for a long moment, hoping to see one who was late to work stride past with her—

Palmer felt his throat start to close. He swallowed quickly, turned away from the window and walked to the bed. Looking down at the tips of his shoes, he saw the drawing of the girl in the bathing suit.

The phone rang. He grabbed it up. "Hello?"

"Woody?" Burckhardt's rather deep voice, with its faint crackle of tautness, came through. "What about eleven o'clock?"

"Fine."

"See you," Burckhardt said and hung up.

Opening a bureau drawer, Palmer withdrew a shirt and noted with displeasure that Mrs. Gage had ironed a wrinkle into the collar. Taking another shirt, he unbuttoned it and laid it out on the bed. As his hands went through the motions of stripping off the shirt he was wearing, his mind checked backwards and forwards through the phone call from Burckhardt and the meeting he was about to have. Informal, he decided, introductory, just a few top brass for a quick hello. What problems could be anticipated?

The faculty of anticipation, Palmer knew, was one of his strong points. He hadn't always known this. It had been Harold, his father's executive vice-president, who had pointed it out. Harold had been on the brink of a long-planned retirement. The bank had come to a certain point in its development, shortly after World War II, when its growth had reached a kind of plateau above which it could really not rise under its present management. Harold had seen this more clearly than Palmer's father, who had not, of course, been told about the disease from which he was even then slowly dying. Both men were in their late sixties at that time and Harold had made a strong plea, at one particular staff meeting, for young Woody's promotion from vice-president-secretary to the number-two position Harold was leaving.

"May I remind you," Palmer's father had said then, "that this boy is scarcely thirty-five years old?"

"But he's got your head on his shoulders," Harold had explained, tampering somewhat with the truth. "He thinks like you."

They were discussing Palmer as though he were not in the room. In point of fact, Palmer and the other three vice-presidents were sitting there making every effort to appear engrossed in their own thoughts. No one was under any illusion that, in time, Palmer would not step up into his father's position. It was a simple fact of life. A father builds for his son, simple and unshakable, like the sun's appearance each morning in the east. If the son doesn't want the gift, if he is actually the wrong son, if he is there only because he knows his father is dying, what of it? This is something between the son and his own conscience.

"He anticipates," Harold had said then. "He's got that kind of mind, a banker's mind, the ability to project alternatives endlessly and constantly. He's got it."

In the somewhat embarrassed silence that had followed, Palmer cleared his throat and smiled. "I understand the IBM people are building a machine that can do it a lot better," he had said then.

Slipping on a clean shirt now, Palmer peered at himself in the large mirror over the dresser. The idea of boosting the Crown Prince onto the junior throne at the callow age of thirty-five had appalled his father almost as much as it had appalled Palmer, who secretly wanted none of it. Now he was being dumped feet first onto the junior throne of a much larger kingdom, the empire of United Bank and Trust Company, second to one in a bank that was second to none.

Palmer glanced at his attaché case and wondered if there were anything in the material Meighan had assembled for him in Chicago that might prove useful at this morning's get-together. The invaluable faculty of anticipation.

He unlocked the case and leafed slowly through the "N.Y. Banking Situation" folder, glancing at clippings and typed reports he had read and reread for several days. You could sum it all up, he reflected now, in one good word: "jumpy."

The New York situation, of course, was only as stable as the rest of the country, since it both dictated and reflected the policies of thousands of correspondent banks in every state that had to deal with New York. And everywhere, Palmer decided, the credit cycle showed signs of overreaching itself, like the proverbial hoop snake that almost, but not quite, circled around to swallow its own tail.

There was, as there had been for some time, a desperate need for new money, savings, cash, the green stuff that, taken in over the counter, created even more money in the form of credit the bank could now extend, make-believe money, but eminently spendable.

This was the crux of the credit situation. The whole country cried loudly for more credit, from the machinist who *had* to trade in last year's car on a new rolling pile of rattles, all the way to the Detroit manufacturers who had to convert overstocked inventories into cash in order to buy steel.

Yet in all this, Palmer thought now, where did you find new money? How were people saving? The machinist made $600 a month, $7,200 a year, less income tax, or well under $6,000. His house, built to fall apart in less than a decade, cost him twice what it was worth. At the moment it ate up almost $2,000 a year in payments and taxes. That left him less than $4,000 to live on. But his car and major appliances were costing him another $2,000 in time-payments. On the remaining $2,000 a year, he and his wife were expected to stay alive and happy, while they fed, clothed and educated three children on about $38 a week.

Palmer laid the "N.Y. Banking Situation" folder to one side, wondering when the whole credit balloon would burst. Could it be allowed to explode? Could it, if it came to that, be prevented from exploding?

Opening the "Ubco" folder, he found himself staring for perhaps the twentieth time at a clipping from *Time* of several years back headlined: THE BIG ONE.

The second column of the story carried a biographical digression into Burckhardt's career. A picture of him, looking trim and grim at the helm of a 12-meter yacht, was captioned: LANE BURCKHARDT, CAPTAIN OF

15

UBCO'S FATE. The section began by referring to Burckhardt's experience as a yachtsman and bore down hard on metaphor.

"Back home that September, he doffed his battered blue yachting cap, swung into a no-holds-barred slug fest for control of the ancient (b. 1798), creaking ship of finance known on the Street as Ubco, the United Bank and Trust Company of New York. By Pearl Harbor Day of 1941, control of the bank lay safely in the capable Burckhardt hands.

"The new captain of Ubco's fate had so ably consolidated his control that, as the Frantic Fifties wheeled past and mergers began welding together the top financial institutions, Ubco emerged from the mists of Wall Street bow-to-bow with the Big Two, Chase Manhattan and First National City. The Big Two abruptly became the Big Three, although Californians could continue pridefully pointing to their Bank of America, more mammoth than any of Gotham's Gargantuas.

"This week, Lane Burckhardt and Hudson Trust's Paul Geraghty sat down to a meal at the Union League Club from which Burckhardt arose, having swallowed Hudson, fifty branches and all. In a single spurt, Ubco pulled so far ahead that New York's Big Three were now the Big One Plus Two. Ubco's $12,441,207,353 in assets topped even Bank of America's $11 billion-plus.

"Canny moneymen, never given to displays of public prescience, wondered how much lasting good Burckhardt's meal would do him. Hudson Trust's portfolio, crammed to the lip with high-risk industrial loans in the chancy electronics and rocket fields, looked like a potential case of financial gastritis."

Putting the clipping away, Palmer found himself wondering quite specifically about the questions that had bothered him in a vaguely general way since the day, nearly a week before, when Burckhardt had called him. He got up from the bed, finished dressing and glanced at himself in the mirror before leaving.

He stared into his eyes for a moment, thinking back to the phone call of a week ago. It had been a hot, humid day in Chicago, the sodden sky angry with lightning. He had just concluded the press conference at which he had announced his decision to sell the bank under the face-saving cover of a merger.

He had been feeling oddly light-headed, as though he had brought off a daring coup. And yet he had been careful to follow protocol, allowing more than a year to go by after his father's death. No one could have guessed at his intense eagerness to be rid of the bank and all it had meant to him.

By rights it should have been Hanley's bank, not his. It should have fallen to his older brother, the amenable one, whom Father had always been able to control, not to Woods, the problem son. But Hanley had escaped the old man in early 1941, at the controls of a PBY out of Pensacola that had never returned.

Palmer watched his grayish eyes grow slightly larger in the mirror. He looked away and remembered that sultry day in Chicago a week before. The last reporters had left. He had been alone, feeling a wonderful, almost giddy, sense of freedom. The great stone hulk of his father's bank had been removed from his shoulders and, with it, the dead weight of the old man's hand. After half a lifetime—more—he was his own man again.

The phone had rung, not the office extension but the private, unlisted number. It was Burckhardt, from New York, who seemed to know all about the announcement even before the reporters had filed their stories.

"Woody," the big voice had said, "have you graduated into the major leagues yet?"

"Isn't Chicago major enough?" Palmer had responded.

"Did those casual remarks in recent years mean anything?" Burckhardt had asked, "or aren't you looking for some real action?"

"Could you give me an idea of what you mean by action?"

"Would I do a thing like that over the phone?" Burckhardt countered.

Palmer had paused for a moment, amused by the fact that neither of them would talk except in unanswered questions. Deciding he had let the conversation wander long enough, he laughed softly. "You big-time New York bankers are just too cagey for a country boy like me."

"Hop a plane," Burckhardt had said then, "the 5:40 flight. I'll have you met at Idlewild."

Too fast, Palmer had cautioned himself. "Just like that? I've got things to do, Lane, even in the minor leagues."

"What things?" Burckhardt had asked. "What kind of things has this so-called merger left you with? Pushing papers from 'In' to 'Out'? I'm talking about something real and exciting as hell."

Palmer had paused again. Then, warily: "I don't know. Edith might enjoy a little trip."

"She's always welcome, but not this time. How about tomorrow?"

"I couldn't poss—"

"All right," Burckhardt had broken in, "Friday at the latest. Spend the weekend at my place. Settled?"

"Settled," Palmer had agreed, "but only because you've aroused my curiosity."

"I'll arouse a lot more than that," Burckhardt had said. "Friday, the 5:40 to Idlewild." The line had gone dead.

Watching himself in the mirror again, Palmer recalled the almost unbearable feeling of elation that had taken hold of him after that conversation. He had known, even then, that the job Burckhardt would offer him was a big one, big enough to make up for the years with his father. He had felt the satisfaction of knowing that his hints had created an air of availability even before his father's death and the sale of the bank.

With the goal before him, he had sat back in his Chicago office and felt mounting tension. The close, humid air had suddenly seemed devoid of oxygen. He had found himself breathing with some effort, sucking in the lifeless air and using it up almost at once.

A triumph, a clean, positive triumph. Free of the bank, free of the old man and now, dizzily free of Chicago. Why had he delayed matters until Friday? How could he wait for the end of the week and that final lunge that would win him total freedom?

Staring at his face in the mirror of the Union League Club, Palmer saw his nostrils widen, as if to breathe the new, free air. It had taken so many time-serving years, playing the part that Hanley had been born to play, the right-hand son to a father dying slowly of the thing eating quietly at his insides.

"If it makes you this unhappy," Edith had once told him in those early years after the war, "tell him you can't take Hanley's place. Tell him and leave him."

"I can't. He's dying and he's alone. I just can't."

Palmer turned from the mirror now and went to the door of his room. He felt as he had in those moments during the war when one of the many H-Hours had arrived. There was action to be taken. It was amazing, in a way, that he had not lost the faculty for taking action during the long, dead years after the war when every decision had had to wait upon a cranky, stubborn old man who took such delight in delay.

Palmer opened the door and strode down the corridors to the elevator. The years of waiting seemed to have fallen away. He felt his own man again, the way he had been during the war. It was a strangely buoyant sensation, compounded partly of the illusion of regained youth and partly of pride in having been able to engineer this whole fresh start.

As he waited for the elevator, he recalled the last time he had felt this way, fifteen years before, as the T-Force of jeeps he commanded had roared through Rostock on the bomb-pitted road past Greifswald to the V-2 base at Peenemünde, hurtling ahead, through territory that had not yet heard about the surrender, to kidnap Nazi rocketmen before the Russians did. Overhead, a flight of FW's had howled in at tree-top level with—

"Down, sir?"

The elevator operator avoided Palmer's glance, examining the carpeting at his feet instead. Palmer stepped into the car, watched the doors shut and felt the slight lift under his heart as the elevator sank to the main floor. For an instant, he felt lighter, freer of gravity than he had in fifteen years.

He swallowed once and prepared himself for the action ahead.

Chapter Three

Palmer got out of the cab on Broad Street noting, as he always did on New York trips, how much cheaper cabs were here than in Chicago, and stood for a moment on the sidewalk, looking up at Ubco's headquarters.

The main offices of really important banks, Palmer noted, were nearly always less impressive than any of their far-flung branches. Like a gigantic wheel, the rim always spun faster than the hub and here, before him, stood the hub in all its painful plainness.

Thirty or so years before, when Ubco had caused this building to be erected, it had risen from the earth in full-blown dowdiness. Even then its eighteen stories had been conservative, its decor old-fashioned. Looking at it now, Palmer felt he could read the minds of its board of directors. It would have been after the panic of 1921, not more than a few years, but well into the pre-Crash boom of the later twenties. There would have been hundreds of sketches and elaborate renderings, dozens of bids and estimates. There would have been a small faction of the board that wanted sheer size, as a vote of confidence in the obviously boundless strength of the economy. There would have been the larger faction, Palmer mused, that shoved 1921 under the noses of the optimists. The Carefuls against the Carefrees. And, being a billion-dollar bank, Ubco would have had no real affinity for the big gesture. Ubco didn't need gestures. Ubco, long before the Depression mergers, had for generations been an entity that could stand alone in perfect, dowdy insulation from the society around it.

Palmer noted now that the public banking area, which occupied the ground floor, could be entered by one, and only one, entrance, a rather massive revolving door. He glanced at the small gold clock set into the greenish marble façade above the door and saw that he had less than five minutes before his eleven o'clock appointment with Burckhardt.

He pushed gently against the polished teak frame of the door and watched the heavy plate glass, with its sharply beveled edge, turn slowly. A pencil-thin line of gold leaf, for the electric-alarm system, formed the only other decoration. The door swung silently and he found himself inside.

To Palmer's left, two officers sat at immense teak desks planted firmly in a deep-pile green carpeting. One of them was making notes in a gold-bound calendar pad. To Palmer's right, a wall of greenish marble, flecked with white, was surmounted by the gold wickets of the tellers' windows, twelve of them. Although at this hour not a single customer was to be seen, the tellers busied themselves with their traditional routine that contrived—half in truth and half in pure deception—to indicate that whatever business a customer might bring to them was pretty picayune stuff indeed.

Ahead of Palmer, stretching some two hundred feet, the white marble of the main floor glowed with a kind of golden aura from invisible spotlights recessed in the ceiling three stories above. Palmer squinted up at the dark-green ceiling and noted that the very antique gold chandeliers, with their tiny crystal lights, gave off about as much light as stars would in the night-time sky. Looking down again, he saw that the main aisle was flanked by green leather settees and gold ash trays on small but ornate stands. At the far end two closed elevator doors were attended by a small, thin, gray-haired man who might have been a butler or footman, except for the discreet bulge beneath his green tunic made by a Police Positive .38.

In the gentle silence that only a thirty-foot ceiling can create, Palmer could hear the muted sibilance of an IBM sorter somewhere behind the tellers' line. He listened to the sound it was making for a moment and decided that it was sorting loan delinquencies.

So far no one, neither the officers on the platform, the tellers, nor the guard at the elevators, had actually looked at Palmer. Now, as he walked forward over the golden ambience of the marble floor, he could hear his heels make an alien, flat sound that jarred in his ears.

The guard nodded as Palmer drew near. The old man pressed a button and one of the elevator doors opened. "Eighteenth floor, Mr. Palmer," the guard said.

Palmer smiled and, suddenly caught up in the play-acting, turned quickly on one heel and caught everyone, from the officers to the tellers, watching him closely. Giving them a moment to recover from their surprise, he turned and entered the elevator, pressed a button and watched the doors slide together like the curtains of a stage, bringing to a close Act I. He glanced at his watch. One minute to eleven. Perfect.

As the elevator rose slowly, Palmer reflected on the minds that had, entirely without forethought or training, planned the banking area on the main floor. It was a telling blow for solid conservatism. Hidebound, crusty old fuddy-duddy businessmen had been able to envision a setting that the most sophisticated and cynical minds of stage design and direction could never have equaled.

The sheer inadvertent success of the old birds was stunning. The green-and-gold motif, for example: had they been entirely unconscious when they approved the two colors that in most parts of the civilized world meant money?

The traditional aloofness of the tellers. Never had Palmer seen a more perfect rendition of the part. And yet he knew that no one had ever told any of those men to act that way. It had come down to them by example alone.

Feeling suddenly very happy about working here—as distinct from his first feeling of triumph at the prestige—Palmer smiled to himself. The smile was still on his face as the doors slid open and he walked out onto the top floor.

The girl behind the large desk had bent over to smooth her stockings. Palmer watched the swelling curve of her leg and then looked away. Finding nothing else he could conceivably be watching, he let his glance come back to her as the doors shut behind him. She looked up. "Mr. Palmer?"

He nodded and watched her get quickly to her feet. "This way, please." He walked behind her, trying not to watch her body as she moved along a wide green corridor that led to double teak doors. Palmer could feel his upper lip grow moist. He ran his finger along it and forced himself to think about something else, anything. The fact that Burckhardt didn't believe in an intercom system, that he wanted his guests ushered directly in, was a part of the whole that Palmer had been experiencing. When he watched the receptionist knock at the double doors, he realized that here, too, the solid weight of conservatism had contrived something much more impressive than—

Her weight shifted to one leg and Palmer's glance went down along her flank to— He took a deep breath and closed his eyes, waiting.

Burckhardt's voice came through the thick doors with perfect clarity. "Come!"

The girl opened the door and stood aside for Palmer. "Mr. Palmer is here, sir," she said, closing the door behind him.

Somewhere in the air above his head, Palmer heard a set of bells begin striking the hour. Burckhardt's milky-blue eyes seemed to disappear for an instant as he grinned. "Timing is everything," he murmured in mock admiration. They shook hands and the older man motioned Palmer to one of the green leather armchairs that flanked his teak desk.

Palmer noted that the top of the desk was entirely clear except for a very small gold-bound blotter, a gold clock with a green face and a green marble desk set. Examining these, he was suddenly aware that Burckhardt was waiting for him to speak.

"All right," he said. "I've never been quite so impressed."

The older man laughed outright. "It is quite a show, isn't it?" He leaned back in his chair and sighed. "I'm only here three mornings a week. I have a room in our Fifth Avenue office uptown. This office is for our older clients. You understand."

"Perfectly. And for your newer ones, too, now and then."

Burckhardt nodded. "Now and then. When they need a little reminder of what they're dealing with."

"I've seen the Fifth Avenue office," Palmer said then. "That is, I've seen pictures of it in books on modern architecture. I should think," he went on, "that you'd be able to work a very simple squeeze play between the two. The Fifth Avenue office for go-getting hustlers, to assure them that you can keep step with them all the way. Then, after a few years, when they crave stodgy respectability, a touch of the main office here would reassure them."

He was about to go on, when he decided that he'd said quite enough on the subject for a new man. Shifting ground very slightly, but firmly, he continued: "I imagine most of your branch offices since the war have been patterned on the Fifth Avenue one."

Burckhardt shrugged. "Somewhat. It depends." He got up and went to a bookcase that covered one wall. "When we took over Hudson Trust, we inherited about fifty pretty shabby branches, hardly more than store fronts. But the boys managed to dress them up rather nicely. Formica, aluminum, hot blobs of color. That sort of thing."

He pulled a thick green leather-bound book out of the shelf and brought it back to the desk. "Every branch is in here," he said. "All two hundred of them." He pushed the book across to Palmer. "Take it with you. Look it over at your leisure. Floor plans, color photos, everything."

Palmer took the book, but kept it shut. Something was wrong. He got the uneasy feeling, as he listened to Burckhardt's non-committal voice, that an insubstantial element had entered the relationship between them. It was hard to single out any one thing in Burckhardt's words, any concrete clue to the feeling Palmer now had, but it was there. A certain . . . what? Disinterest? Failure to connect?

Whatever it was, Palmer decided, it wasn't right. Not that he expected chumminess or rapport from the old bird. But, in Burckhardt's own interest if no other, these first few minutes should be used to set up the rest of their life together. Not in so many words, Palmer knew; not by pulling out tables of organization and showing the new man where he fitted in or anything like that. But here, on home ground, Burckhardt should be at work right now setting up the emotional chain of command between himself and his first deputy.

Palmer sat forward in his chair and decided to make a stab at it himself. He cleared his throat. "Something's bothering you," he said in a tone halfway between a statement and a question.

Burckhardt looked up at him, startled. He squinted at Palmer and wrinkled his nose. "I was thinking," he said, and then, surprisingly, sighed heavily and failed to finish his thought. After a moment he roused himself and ran his stubby fingers through his silver-gray hair. "I'd just had a phone call before you arrived. I was thinking about Joe Loomis," he finished. "He's been on my board for damned near twenty years."

Palmer nodded. "Jet-Tech Industries."

"And Vacutherm Electronics."

"He's . . . what?" Palmer asked. "Near seventy?"

"Seventy-one. That's not the problem. Pray you'll have Joe's energy at seventy-one." Burckhardt shook his head. "No, it's something else. He's a trustee of fifteen million foundations and such, plus three other banks."

"I'm worn-out just listening to it."

"One of the banks," Burckhardt added slowly, "is Murray Hill Savings."

Palmer nodded, not sure of what his response ought to be. He watched the older man get up from his desk and go to the big window behind his chair, an opening fully 20 feet wide, but cut into 2-foot squares by polished teak mullions. Standing there, Burckhardt stared out along a narrow slit between two neighboring skyscrapers that blocked the sun. Through the slit, Palmer could see the river sparkling in the late summer sun. As the two men watched, a tanker moved slowly past the narrow aperture.

"You're having a little trouble with the mutual savings banks, aren't you?" Palmer asked then. When he got no answer, he paused for a moment, sorting out his next words from among the several alternatives before him. "It must be a comforting thought," he said then, "to know that you've got a friend in the enemy camp."

Burckhardt turned slowly around and stared at the younger man. "That," he said almost bitterly, "is the way Murray Hill Savings feels about it, too."

When he failed to continue, Palmer stood up and moved to the window. "So your problem is to know which side Joe Loomis is playing on."

"I don't think I made myself clear," Burckhardt said. "He's one of my oldest friends."

Palmer made a face. "That's a tough one."

"Very tough."

Palmer watched the tanker slide past the slit between the two buildings. "What will you do?"

Burckhardt made a sound somewhere between a snort and a laugh. "Nothing," he said at last. "I'm dumping the whole thing in the lap of my new executive vee-pee."

"Thanks."

"In fact," the older man went on, his voice suddenly surer than it had been all that morning, "I'm dumping the whole savings-bank mess in your lap."

"With what instructions?"

"I want every one of them crucified."

Palmer turned away from the window to face him. The morning had taken startling shape, in the space of a few spoken words, and with it the pattern of their relationship. "Beginning when?" he asked.

Burckhardt stepped to a teak-paneled wall and swung open a door. He reached in for his hat and placed it on his head with a sharp downward tug. "Why wait?" he asked then. "Let's go see the smart little bastard who'll help you murder them."

CHAPTER FOUR

Palmer trailed the older man along the corridor past the receptionist, wondering as he did so why none of the other top officers had been brought in to meet him. This was not, officially, his first day at work. He wasn't to start the new job until after Labor Day, but this was his first visit to Ubco and protocol usually called for introductions all around.

The elevator he had come up in was waiting for them as they strode past the front desk. The girl handed Burckhardt an old-fashioned expandable brief case and reached for her telephone. As they entered the elevator, Palmer could hear her calling for Burckhardt's city car. Her eyes lifted for a moment and Palmer found himself staring into them. The doors cut the glance in two as they closed.

"You'll forgive me," Burckhardt said after a moment as the elevator descended, "for not introducing you to a few of the boys."

"I gather this savings-bank thing is urgent."

"It's silly and unnecessary as hell," the older man exploded suddenly. "It's the kind of irrational thing you don't expect from another banker. But for all that, you're right: it's urgent."

"I'm not very well briefed on it yet," Palmer said as the doors opened on the main floor. He was, as a matter of fact, fairly well briefed. Although he'd never had to cope with savings banks in Illinois, he kept abreast of the trouble they'd been giving commercial banks in the seventeen states where they operated. Because most of the money was in New York, the conflict was sharpest here.

"Just what do you know?" Burckhardt asked. They were striding along the golden glow of marble toward the front door, where the gray-haired guard, hand on the revolving door, was poised to start it moving.

"Just that they—"

"In the car," Burckhardt cut in swiftly. He nodded to one of the officers and received a tremendous smile in return, a really thrilling smile, Palmer noted, the kind he had always imagined would be found on the faces of souls at the instant that they discover they have reached, not hell, but heaven.

The gray Rolls stood at the curb, giving no evidence that it had just arrived but rather, Palmer felt, as if the street had been paved especially to receive its tires and no other. He followed Burckhardt into the rear and sat down on the dark-gray leather seat beside him. With no perceptible sound or hint of motion, the car pulled swiftly away from the curb and headed into the heart of Broad Street's traffic.

Burckhardt slid open the plate glass between them and the chauffeur and said: "Fifth Avenue office, Harry." Palmer noted, as the plate glass slid shut again, that the car was equipped with a telephone on a shelf next to the bar.

"All right, shoot," Burckhardt ordered.

Palmer frowned, although it cost him no effort at all to summon up the details. "It's a matter of new money," he said then. "The savings banks are paying a better dividend and they're attracting a lot of new money. The problem is to channel the new money back to us."

"In the nutshell. There isn't a great deal more I can tell you."

"You flatter me," Palmer said. "I don't even know what you've done about the problem so far. I'd have to know that." It was a lie, Palmer reflected as he said it, but it was a lie in a worthy cause. The old bird was so obviously dying to unburden himself that any excuse would be enough to start him going.

"Done?" Burckhardt snapped. "We've sat around diddling ourselves, that's what we've done. For fifteen years we've sat on our butts and let the mutuals snatch every savings dollar out from under our noses because we didn't want that kind of chickenfeed. Now, when we need those dollars, we can't get at them."

"That's the part I don't understand," Palmer lied again. "I mean, what is so mysterious about these mutual banks? What are there . . . a hundred and thirty of them? All over the state?"

"About. With their branches, say, two-fifty."

"Why, Ubco has almost as many branches by itself as their whole system."

When Burckhardt failed to answer, Palmer pressed on, trying to give him another opening to unburden himself. "That's what makes it hard to understand," he said. "Here's a wage earner. He's in debt for about two thirds of his salary. But he puts away, say, ten dollars a week. Say five. It doesn't matter how much. He looks around him for a place to save it. On every corner he finds an Ubco branch, or a branch of Manufacturer's or Chase or First National or Chemical. What I mean is, he has to search long and hard to find a savings-bank branch as convenient to him as a commercial bank. Isn't that so?"

Burckhardt shrugged. "It doesn't explain what's happened," he said, more to himself than Palmer. "It doesn't explain why the mutual savings banks have two thirds of all the savings money in the state. Money we sorely need."

"You make it sound like witchcraft."

"It's plain old American stupidity," Burckhardt retorted. "The mutuals advertise a dividend rate about a half of one per cent higher than we do. One half a miserable per cent per annum. Do you have to have that spelled out for the average saver? It means he gets an extra five bucks on his account each year. If you put it to him that way, he'd see how stupid he was being. But nobody's explained it to him and nobody will." He stopped and turned to Palmer. "Can you guess why?"

Palmer pretended to frown again. "I suppose," he said slowly, feigning deep thought, "everyone's afraid to mention it because it shows just how little your savings earn, whatever bank you put them in."

"Exactly. When people have it spelled out that way, they'll withdraw their money and throw it into mutual funds or directly on the market. Or this other idiocy, real estate syndication."

The Rolls had threaded its way onto the East Side Highway and was now surging uptown at a smooth forty-five miles an hour. Palmer watched the tankers and freight boats on his right for a moment. The river looked sluggish and oily under a barely visible mist. The August sun beat down on its smooth surface and picked out dirty yellow glints among the slow-moving ripples. The car had reached Thirty-fourth Street before Palmer realized that neither of them had spoken for a long while.

He turned to Burckhardt and was surprised to find a look very much akin to pain on the older man's face. The china-blue eyes were almost hidden in Burckhardt's ferocious squint. The corners of his mouth had turned down into deep networks of wrinkles, as if to withstand some intense inner agony. Palmer was about to ask him if he were having some kind of attack, then decided to remain silent. The urge to speak, simply to fill a soundless void, had been one of the hardest of his youthful habits to break. The realization that more trouble was caused by talking than by not talking—a view of life his father had lectured him about since Palmer had been twelve years old— had come very slowly to him in his mid-thirties.

Now, in his mid-forties, he often wondered how sound the idea had been. It was true, he reflected as the Rolls sped northward, that you did avoid trouble by avoiding speech. There was very little question of that. But as he grew older, he had begun to wonder what "trouble" really was and whether, regardless of its identity, it was something to be avoided at all costs.

Sitting beside Burckhardt now, he saw that, in this case, "trouble" was simply a further involvement with the man who was to be his superior for many years to come. Although the nature of the involvement was unknown, was it necessarily to be avoided?

Palmer moistened his lips very slightly. He was about to break training, revert to a habit of his youth, and the anticipation made him feel suddenly uneasy. He turned to the older man and—

"Damned old fool!" Burckhardt burst out.

Palmer blinked and checked back quickly the lines along which Burckhardt might have been thinking. "Joe Loomis?" he asked finally.

"He's a stubborn, senile, fuzzy-headed old coot and I wish to God he hadn't called me this morning."

"What did he want?" Palmer asked.

26

"Why, the earth itself on a silver platter."

"Something to do with this savings-banks business?"

"That's what hurts most, I think," Burckhardt said. "He's a widower now, you know. We may have him out for the weekend once a year. He and I may lunch every few months, if that often. We may see each other at the club for a drink now and then. He may or may not attend an Ubco board meeting. The bulk of our contact is purely social. I don't believe I've ever asked a favor of him that wasn't in his own interest, too, and I'm quite sure that the same applies to those he's asked of me. But, God damn it, today he called me up direct from a trustees' meeting of the Murray Hill Savings Bank and wanted my pledge that we wouldn't oppose one of their bills up at the state legislature this year."

"That's hardly what I call a confidential request."

"Even that doesn't irk me," Burckhardt snapped. "I don't relish the idea of the rest of the trustees sitting around listening to him ask me for such a favor, of course not. But the thing that absolutely violates my . . . my . . ." He paused, struggling for words, and glared angrily at Palmer for help.

Ethics, Palmer suggested silently, conscience, morality, way of life. He said none of these, but waited and endured the glare.

"The thing that angers me most," Burckhardt finished lamely, "is the irrational gall of the man, squeezing me in this impossible position between what I know is right for Ubco and my friendship for him. It's intolerable!"

"What did you tell him?" Palmer wanted to know.

"Tell him? What could I tell him? I stalled."

"You'll have to give him an answer eventually."

Burckhardt nodded and, abruptly, the motion of his head took on an almost savage intensity. His eyes widened and he seemed to be staring at the back of the driver's head as if reading there on the neatly cropped neck and dark-green chauffeur's cap some immense revelation of things to come.

"Oh," he said then, "and don't think I'm Joe's only friend to be asked for a commitment. Nor is he the only savings-bank trustee with commercial-bank friends. All over town they'll be asking this particular favor. It's a completely untenable position and I won't be forced into it."

"What particular bill does he want you not to oppose?"

"I don't even remember," the older man said. The realization seemed to release him from the peculiar trance into which he had fallen, reading, in the entrails of his relationship with a friend, the death of friendship.

"One of their perennial branch bills?"

Burckhardt snorted, then turned slowly to Palmer. "Just how well are you briefed, Woody?" he asked in an irritated tone. "You seem to know as much about this as I do."

"Never. Just moderately up on things."

"You're crapping the old man, aren't you?" Burckhardt's voice had grown very cold. "Let's put it this way, Woody: you're entitled to be ignorant when

27

you really want information. But don't let me catch you faking it just to make me feel good. Understand?"

"I don't—"

"And don't let me catch you lying about it," Burckhardt interrupted. "If I don't have a clear picture of the full extent of your knowledge at all times, I'm working at a handicap. Is that clear?"

"Perfectly. Sorry."

Burckhardt's mouth turned up slightly at the corners. "Finished," he said in a softer voice. "I've forgotten about it."

"I haven't."

"Good."

At Sixty-first Street the Rolls edged smoothly to the left and turned off the highway, sliding west through traffic now as it moved closer to Fifth Avenue.

"As a matter of fact," the older man said after a long silence, "it did have something to do with branches for savings banks. I'm not sure what."

"More of them, no doubt."

Burckhardt shrugged. "In the suburbs, something like that. They can't go out in the suburbs now and it's driving them crazy."

"Their depositors are moving out of the city, I suppose."

"By and large," Burckhardt agreed. "The savings banks have no one to blame but themselves. They've been investing heavily in mortgages since the war. It's the only kind of loan they can make and, of course, they've really plunged into it feet first. They've made it possible for people to move out into the suburbs, but the savings banks can't follow them."

"Then why all the excitement?" Palmer asked. "If they're hoist by their own petard, let them dangle. Why worry about them?"

"Because they don't intend to dangle. They want more rope and they'll move heaven and earth to get it."

Palmer nodded. "Vicious circle." He glanced out the window at the traffic jam that was holding them up. Far ahead, at Third Avenue, a building was being torn down and a line of huge trucks pre-empted all but a narrow corridor along the street as they waited to be filled by an immense bucket that showered debris down into them. The entire corner had been walled off by a plywood barricade on which a series of cartoon figures had been drawn of people hurrying along, smiles on their faces, to a bank teller's window. *It won't be long now,* the sign read. *Another convenient branch of the Murray Hill, paying 4½% to thrifty New Yorkers.*

Palmer smiled slightly and turned back to the older man. "Hold on to your blood pressure as we pass the corner. It's a new Murray Hill branch."

"I know," Burckhardt grumbled. "I pass it every morning."

"I thought they'd been restricted on branches."

"They merged with another savings bank this spring. The merger gives them three more offices. This is one."

28

Palmer whistled softly. "What's to prevent them from—?"

"Nothing," Burckhardt snapped. "They can keep merging just as long as our Banking Superintendent lets them."

The two men looked out the broad side windows of the Rolls. A tall cut-out drawing of the new Murray Hill branch building had been erected at the corner of Third Avenue and, as the car edged with aggravating slowness toward it, Palmer could see that something like a thirty-story office building was being contemplated.

"Odd location for an office building," he murmured, his glance distracted by a woman who was standing next to the sign waiting for the light to change. She was tall and full-breasted, and her long legs seemed to—

"You're thinking of the old Third Avenue," Burckhardt said.

Palmer turned to face him and saw that the older man had noticed the woman too, or rather Palmer's inspection of her. "Bloomingdale's did this face-lifting job after the El came down," Burckhardt was saying, "and it was only a matter of time before the big office buildings came along."

"With money as tight as it is, too."

"That's what hurts," Burckhardt grunted. "Damn it, that's the part that really grinds salt in the wound. These savings banks have the money. They have it right in their hands. Their assets are cash or the next thing to it—governments—and mortgages. It's . . . it's like . . ." He sputtered out.

"Like money in the bank," Palmer suggested with a small laugh.

Burckhardt favored him with a stony glance. "Now, look," he began, "I'm all for a sense of humor, Woody. A man has to have it in the world or he can crack up. But some things are simply no laughing matter. This is one of them."

There was a long silence as the car slid across Third, made the Lexington light and eased to a halt at Park Avenue. Three times Palmer thought of something to say; three times he failed to say it. He sat back on the Rolls' soft leather seat and wondered why he had ever been stupid enough to question a tenet that his whole life had proved right. There were no two ways about it: more trouble was caused by talking than by not talking. Even now, when he felt certain that the old bird would have welcomed talk, was in fact waiting for Palmer to clear the air between them with a few apologetic words, even now there was less trouble in silence than in talk.

"God damn it," Burckhardt murmured, as the car turned south on Park Avenue, "you can see how upset this thing has me. No call to come down like a ton of bricks on you, Woody."

Palmer turned slightly toward him, not eagerly but slowly. "What's more upsetting?" he asked then, "the savings-bank mess or Joe Loomis putting the squeeze on you?"

"You can't separate one from the other. I've lived with this thing for years now. The mutuals are getting desperate and the heat's on. If I do one thing, I lose volume. If I do another, I lose a friend. It's just that brutally simple."

Palmer waited for a moment until Burckhardt, having phrased the problem, saw for himself the only solution he could possibly choose. Then: "That's why you dropped it in my lap, is it?" Palmer asked.

"Partly," the older man grunted.

"There's more?"

Burckhardt shrugged. "Naturally, if anybody has to shaft Joe Loomis, I'd rather it weren't me. But that's only part of the reason." He sighed heavily. "You're about to meet the other part, Mac Burns."

Palmer watched the Rolls swing smoothly west again on Fifty-fifth and head across Madison toward Fifth. "He's a pretty high-powered guy," he mused. "He . . . I heard him at a convention once in Chicago. Good speaker."

"One of the best. Started on the Coast as one of these show-business press agents."

"Now he's a public-relations consultant or something? I think he has some Chicago clients."

Burckhardt sighed. "So the fame of Mac Burns has traveled out to Chicago, has it?"

"What's wrong with him?"

"Nothing. He's just what we need, unfortunately."

"But he's partly the reason you've dumped it all on me."

"That's right," Burckhardt said. The Rolls had slowed to a halt and the driver was holding open the rear door now. "I've got nothing against Greeks or Syrians or whatever Burns is," Burckhardt said, getting out of the car. "It's just that I can't get along with this particular one. So you can have the dubious pleasure of working with Mac Burns or whatever his name used to be." He stood on the sidewalk and waited for Palmer to follow him.

"And one thing more," Burckhardt said *sotto voce*, detaining Palmer from entering the huge plate glass doors of the intensely modern bank.

Palmer turned toward him. "Yes?"

"Burns knows how I feel about him. I can't hide it. That's why you're going to have to get very chummy with him, to counteract me. Can you do it?"

"Why not?"

"It'd better be a damned sight more certain than that," Burckhardt snapped. Then, keeping his voice down again: "You're going to live with this man for quite a while. Can you do it?"

"I can do it."

"Because without Mac Burns, we're dead."

The two men stared at each other without speaking. Palmer found himself wondering whether Burckhardt hadn't gone off the deep end on this savings-bank thing. He turned away from the older man and glanced up at the immense expanse of heavy tinted plate glass and thin aluminum spandrels that encased the façade of the bank. The column of glass shot high into the air above his head, broken at 20-foot intervals by a horizontal silvery slash that seemed too frail to keep that tremendous expanse of glass in check. At any moment, it seemed to Palmer, the whole thing might buckle slowly in the middle and, like a man shot in the stomach, gently collapse in great jagged shards.

Chapter Five

The elevator was unattended, but so mechanized that Palmer decided it would be gross arrogance to call it merely "self-service." As Burckhardt's hand neared the "Up" button, a small disk glowed green and the stainless-steel doors parted in the middle. Palmer followed the older man into the car and noted that as soon as his trailing ankle cleared an electric eye beam, the doors closed at a politely slower rate than that at which they had opened.

The walls of the car were fashioned of a kind of woven metal. Vertical alternating ribbons of stainless steel and copper were crossed by a woof of narrow rods of brass, aluminum and stainless steel. He had the uneasy feeling, as the doors closed, that if, instead of rising, the entire car sank into some briny subterranean branch of the sea, the salt water would cause an immediate chemical reaction and the conflicting metals would produce a great jolt of electricity, killing every human thing within the cage.

He watched Burckhardt's long, thick index finger negligently point at a button on the white formica control panel labeled "PH." This button, too, glowed instantly green and, from a perforated grill in the formica above it, a somewhat human voice stated quite matter-of-factly: "Your next stop is . . . (pause) . . . the penthouse floor."

Burckhardt turned and grinned almost malevolently at Palmer. "We call this the Rube Trap," he said.

Palmer reached past him and touched a button marked "12." The speaker grill clicked twice and its mechanized voice stated: "Your next stop is . . . (pause) . . . the twelfth floor." Palmer touched a button marked "Cancel" and the speaker told him: "Your next stop is . . . (pause) . . . the penthouse floor."

He sighed and stepped back, nodding to Burckhardt. "I'm through playing now."

When the doors opened again, the light pouring in on them seemed almost blinding for a moment. Squinting as he got out of the car, Palmer saw that the extremely high ceiling was made of huge alternate squares of translucent and transparent glass set in mullions of aluminum. Sunlight sluiced down over the two men as they walked along a gray-carpeted floor past white walls on which a number of modern oil paintings were hung. At discreet intervals floor-to-ceiling doors some 5 feet wide chalked bold vertical accents in colors that varied between mustard yellow, deep cornflower blue and a muddy tangerine.

At the far end of the corridor, tiny at first, then growing larger as they approached her, sat a handsomely blonde woman of about twenty-eight who, when she rose, showed that she stood about as tall as her employer. She smiled in a perfectly friendly way and murmured a "good morning" as she moved to another of the immense doors, this one an unflawed sheet of gold-anodized aluminum with a white knob. She held the door open and, as he passed within inches of her, Palmer smelled the same perfume he had given Edith at Christmas.

He found himself wondering whether Burckhardt had hired a woman that tall simply because the penthouse had such a high ceiling. From that thought, he was about to consider the somewhat startling fact that receptionists in New York could afford to buy that kind of perfume, when he got the full impact of Burckhardt's office.

It was not that the room was immense, Palmer decided after a very long look at the place. It was more, he realized, that it had been so frankly and knowingly designed to give an impression of immensity.

Two of its walls were blank white, the shorter being about 30 feet long and the same 12 feet in height as the rest of the penthouse floor. The longer wall stretched for possibly 50 feet and, as it did, the ceiling that met it swept up in a kind of a gull-wing curve so that, where it ended in a single sheet of plate glass, the ceiling hung at least 20 feet above the floor.

Palmer felt as though he had entered the small end of some giant's earhorn. He had the wild thought that if he shouted now, from where he stood, the out-belling shape of the room would magnify his voice so that, as it reached the other end of the megaphone, it would shatter the plate glass with a tremendous bellowing roar.

He resisted the urge to shout and, instead, turned to find Burckhardt's eyes fastened on him. "That window," Palmer said in what sounded like a perfectly calm, perfectly casual voice, "I didn't know they cast sheets of plate glass that big."

"They don't," the older man assured him. "The Corning folks just felt a bit challenged by what the architect called for. They extended themselves. That pane is the fourth they cast. The others shattered during polishing."

"But this one won't?" Palmer started to say and ended by asking.

"The people at Corning guarantee it. Same glass as the Mount Palomar mirror. Same annealing process. Damned thing's an inch thick." He reached out without looking and pointed his finger at a control panel next to the door. The room grew suddenly lighter.

Palmer squinted up at the ceiling in time to see a bank of louvers above the translucent-transparent checkerboard turn slowly and stop, letting the full brilliance of the noon sun wash down into the great room. He stared for a moment at the teak desk that stood a little off-center on the room-sized dark-green rug and, for the first time, saw that someone was sitting in a chair beside the desk. As he saw him, the man stood up.

"Sorry to keep you waiting, Mac," Burckhardt called. He walked forward to meet the man, stopped just short enough of his outstretched hand so as not to have to take it, and turned to Palmer. "Woody, make the quarter-mile dash over here and meet Mac Burns." Then, angling off from Burns to sit on the other side of the desk, Burckhardt successfully avoided giving the impression of having shunned the man's hand.

Palmer walked forward, took Burns's hand and shook it. He found the hand somewhat softer than he had expected. There was a thin, knifelike look about Burns, as seen from a distance, that seemed to evaporate on close viewing. Palmer glanced at his curly hair and wondered how anyone so blond could tan so deeply.

"Mr. Burns, I'm Woody Palmer."

Burns smiled. His intensely sun-tanned face split open to reveal small, well-capped teeth in a thin-lipped, almost feline mouth. "Mr. Burns is my father, Woody," he said. His voice was soft, with a kind of "head" quality to it, not quite nasal, giving the impression that he was chanting his words. "My name's Mac."

"Mac," Palmer repeated, sitting down in an exceedingly plain teak chair of tapered Scandinavian design.

Burckhardt leaned back in a similar chair and smiled somewhat coldly at nothing. "Woody's taking over the number-two spot," he said then. "He's my new exec vee-pee." He paused. "I'll give you a quick run-down on him."

"Lane . . ." The monosyllable hung in the air with a kind of unresolved tone, a subdominant chord waiting for the tonic. Burns left it unresolved as he settled himself in his chair, gently lifting his dark-blue trousers from his kneecaps. Palmer watched him, fascinated at how long the single word could reverberate so silently among the three of them. Burns glanced down at his suit and negligently flicked an invisible mote from his sleeve. The suit was wondrously cut, Palmer saw, in a manner that was not Brooks Brothers or any other recognizable style, but seemed to partake of several influences so that, in almost any company, it would look right. Only the shirt, white with a satiny white pattern of embroidered dots on it, struck a false note.

"Lane," Burns continued then, "what kind of publicist would I be if I needed a run-down from a client? You're a busy man, Lane. Let me give you the run-down on Woody."

When neither man spoke for a moment, Palmer realized with a sudden flash of insight how deeply they resented each other. Burckhardt apparently disliked having to do business with Burns. The other man, Palmer felt, was unhappy at having been kept waiting. Whether the resentment had grown

33

strong enough to be called hatred, Palmer had no way of knowing at this moment. Neither of them looked like the type who would yield easily to the luxury of hatred.

"All right, Mac," Burckhardt said in a mild voice, staring at his desk top. "You're on."

"Woods Palmer, Jr.," Burns intoned, turning his face to Palmer and smiling in an almost self-deprecatory way, as if to say: "You and I hate this show-off routine, but what the hell?" Watching Palmer closely now, Burns went on: "He's going to be forty-five in December. He's married to the former Edith Edison, of Glencoe, Illinois. He has a boy, Woods Palmer the third, a girl, Geraldine, and the baby is Tom, age nine. He reached the rank of Lieutenant Colonel in the Air Force during World War II, and was assigned mostly to intelligence work. He's—"

"Too damned intelligent to be a banker," Burckhardt cut in, trying for a humorous note and not making too much of an effort, "but he may be smart enough to keep up with you, Mac."

"Don't you want to hear the rest?" Burns asked, grinning. "It took my staff all morning to dig it up."

"Anybody can do a job of research," Burckhardt said in a voice so thin as to sound almost angry. "But the thing that interests me is why you asked your staff to do the run-down on him. Not a whisper about him has leaked."

Burns's mouth grew wider and harder as the corners turned down and he shrugged. "Lane," he intoned, and the syllable hung in the air again like a chanted liturgy, "when you hired me, you hired the best. You're not really interested in how I became the best, just that I am."

"Trade secrets?" Burckhardt grunted.

"Does a magician explain his illusions?" Burns countered.

"Am I buying illusions?" Burckhardt snapped, leaning forward now.

"No," Burns agreed. He sat back and smiled pleasantly at the older man. Palmer saw that his eyes were of a brown so light as to be a tawny yellow. "No, you're not," Burns went on. "But, Lane . . ." Again the word shivered above their heads. "Lane, you did hire a magician. Only a magician is going to pull this deal out of the hat for you."

In the silence that followed, Palmer realized that the two men had just reached a new relationship. The luxury of hatred had become a necessity.

Chapter Six

The restaurant was small but terribly ornate. Its single long, narrow room was walled with pink mirrors set in dead-white rococo frames of such a surpassing complexity that, in the dim light, Palmer found it hard to follow their twists and involutions for very long. He blinked, glanced down at his drink and lifted it for a long, slow sip.

Across the table from him, Mac Burns purred almost inaudibly into a telephone the maître d' had brought, with profuse apologies, a few moments before. They had entered the restaurant shortly after one o'clock, been beckoned past a knot of people waiting in the general vicinity of the bar, and escorted with a great deal of bowing to a corner table. They had barely had time to order drinks when the telephone was delivered to the table.

". . . no, sweetie," Burns was murmuring in a voice that showed no great warmth. "Give him the . . ." His words grew fainter.

Palmer sipped his drink and watched Burns, as he was obviously meant to do. The whole performance, from the meeting at the bank earlier in the day, with well-prepared dossier on Palmer, to the choice of this restaurant, so conspicuously organized to impress clients, was fascinating and baffling. Burns was a person of some stature and importance, Palmer knew. Why did he have to restate that importance in such obvious and unworthy ways? Was he really as important as Palmer had had reason to believe? The whole performance made him suddenly doubt Burns's reputation. If he was astute, Palmer wondered, was he not astute enough to realize the unwanted impression he must be making?

Burns had hung up the phone for a moment and glanced at Palmer. "You'll have to excuse me for just another moment, Woody," he said. Then, picking up the phone, he said, without murmuring: "Honey, get me Caracas, Venezuela. The number is San Martin 0040. And while you're at it, give me my office. Thanks, baby."

Palmer gazed down into the amber depths of his Scotch and soda, too embarrassed to look Burns in the face. "This won't take a minute, Woody," he heard Burns say. When he looked up, the man was purring into the phone again. "It's me, tootsie. Let me talk to . . ." His words became indistinguishable above the drone in which they were delivered.

Palmer leaned back against the white leather upholstery of the curved banquette. He closed his eyes for a moment, waiting for the feeling of embarrassment to die away. If it didn't bother Burns, why should it bother him? So thinking, he opened his eyes and watched Burns again.

The man looked to be about Palmer's age, mid-forties, his darkly tanned skin contrasting with the short corn-colored hair. The wavy locks were fairly close cut and combed without a part. This face, Palmer saw, seemed different from moment to moment. Although the raw bone structure of it lay close beneath the skin, any really sharp angles had been subtly padded. Palmer decided that it was the face of a man who had once been a poor boy, poor in a basic way, the poverty of emaciation. Later in life, much more recently it seemed, a thin layer of fat had hidden this childhood shame. But not completely. Never completely. Burns's nose was thin, with long, voracious nostrils set in an unwrinkled face between large yellow eyes rimmed by slightly lighter skin, untanned behind what had apparently been large sunglasses. If anything, Palmer felt, it was the man's mouth that gave his face such a hard-to-pin-down character. Small and hard in repose, the lower lip quite thin, the mouth could take on an entirely different set of characteristics as Burns talked. It could widen and tighten, as it had in talking to Burckhardt. It could quirk and humorously pout, as it had when Burns had begun reciting Palmer's résumé. Now, perfectly relaxed as he murmured to someone he obviously trusted, the lips scarcely moved.

On the whole, Palmer decided then, a man fairly handsome in a stealthy way, but a strange man, as if the series of disguises through which his face went left the real Mac Burns undecided from moment to moment who he was and what he was going to do. Even the blond hair seemed part of a disguise. And yet, Palmer reminded himself, the man obviously must have a core to him somewhere. Despite his little pretenses and performances, Burns could not have got this far without having an inner awareness of who and what he was.

Palmer lifted his drink and found it empty. A waiter appeared at that instant and quirked an eyebrow at the empty glass, as if afraid to break into Burns's telephone conversation by so much as "Another, sir?"

Palmer nodded, falling in with the little charade, and wondering what special quality Mac Burns possessed that made otherwise sane people play parts in the theatricals he rigged around him. "Scotch and soda," he said then, loudly, breaking through his self-imposed trance. He had the pleasure of seeing the waiter flinch.

". . . forget the speech on Sunday . . ." Burns droned, oblivious to the by-play.

Palmer found himself inspecting Burns's cuff links. Each of them was a replica in gold of what appeared on closer scrutiny to be a model of a molecule or atom, the elements of it represented by a brilliant-cut sapphire and four small marquise-cut diamonds not much larger than seed pearls. Narrowing his eyes slightly, Palmer concentrated on the cuff links, trying to decide exactly what they represented.

Burns hung up the phone. "The Caracas circuits are busy," he said off-handedly. "Oh, that? It's my insignia." He shot his cuffs and inspected the links closely. "Carbon," he intoned. "Carbon, without which life itself wouldn't exist," he added piously. "God's greatest gift to man, aside from life, of course."

"Ah," Palmer said. "The sapphire is the nucleus and the diamonds are the electrons."

Burns's mouth, open to speak, closed for an instant, slid into cold immobility and, from there, to a pleased smile. "Lane was right. You're too smart to be a banker. But this thing has another meaning, too." He turned his wrist so that the diamonds shot sharp blue-white splinters of light into Palmer's eyes. "The sapphire is a man, an individual. The diamonds are linked with him for life. Health, wealth, friends and money, the four ingredients of happiness on earth."

"Health," Palmer repeated, not sure he had heard correctly, "wealth, friends *and* money?"

Burns glanced sharply at him. His yellow eyes darkened. "That's right." His mouth pursed for a moment, framing and rejecting several thoughts. Then: "I don't think I have to tell a banker the difference between wealth and money."

Palmer leaned back against the banquette as the waiter brought a second drink for him. Burns's drink had remained untouched. "Money," Palmer said then, "is what if you hold on to enough of it long enough, you've got wealth."

Burns shook his head. "Let me be your financial advisor," he said then. "Money is what I have. Wealth is what I leave to my kids when I pass on."

"Or," Palmer picked up, beginning to enjoy himself, "money is what you spend and wealth is what you save."

"Wealth is what you have," Burns countered, "when you don't spend money."

"No. Money is manure. Wealth is the harvest."

Burns hunched himself forward over the table and the diamonds in his cuff links glittered eagerly. "Tell me, Woody," he said then, "why can't I talk like this to Lane Burckhardt?"

Palmer blinked and sat up straighter. "Can't you?"

"Of course not. We never could. Why is it?"

"Look, you've worked with him a lot longer than I have."

"You've known him since you were a boy," Burns parried. "What's the answer?"

"If I knew, would I tell?" Palmer asked. "No more than you'd tell me how you knew I was the man you had to get a run-down on. Trade secrets."

Burns was silent for a moment. "If I tell you, you'll have to promise never to tell a living soul."

37

"I can't promise that," Palmer replied, amused at the sudden solemnity of the man's voice, like a small boy chanting the initiation ritual of some secret society. "You understand."

"I suppose I do," Burns said after a while. "I suppose I also know why Lane and I can't . . ." He paused and shrugged. Then, with abrupt force: "But let them be the only secrets between us, Woody. I mean it."

The small-boy earnestness, Palmer was surprised to see, had given way to a hardness that seemed almost uncalled-for by the thing they were discussing. Unless, Palmer reflected, he'd entirely missed the real point of what Burns had been saying up to now.

"I'm a banker," Palmer said then. "I have only two commodities to offer: money and discretion. I don't like secrets, but I've had to keep more than my share."

"Not from me, Woody," Burns persisted. "We can't afford it, not now." He took a breath. "Have you any idea of what you've been dumped into? Any idea of how hot things can get before we're done?"

"It's hot enough to have Burckhardt worried."

"Yeah," Burns snapped, "and when Burckhardt worries, I worry double. And when the two of us start worrying, there are a few million people who should be worrying, too."

Palmer picked up his drink and sipped it slowly, determined not to finish his second until Burns had finished his first. "What's good for Ubco," he remarked, "is good for America. And what's bad for Ubco—"

"Exactly. They must have briefed you pretty thoroughly."

" 'It took my staff all morning to dig it up,' " Palmer quoted.

Burns sat back and took a long look at Palmer. His odd face remained without expression, even the mouth immobile. Then he grinned broadly. "Woody," he began then, letting the word hang suspended in the air between them for a while, "Woody, why don't you quit Ubco? I could use an executive vice-president like you."

"Quit? I haven't even started yet."

"You know what Lane would do to me if I stole you away? I might as well cut my throat and have it over with."

Palmer smiled embarrassedly, aware again of the small boy creating goblins to shiver at. "It wouldn't be quite that bad," he said. "You'd still have your cuff links. You could live on those for a few years, I should think."

The second the words were out of his mouth, Palmer was sorry for them. It had not been a nice thing to say, and Burns would have every right to resent the remark. It had all the earmarks of the kind of thing people said about Greeks and Syrians, which made it all the more unfortunate. Palmer glanced up at Burns, ready for any kind of reaction.

The man's eyes widened slightly but, because his mouth was still, Palmer had no idea of what would happen. Then, abruptly: "You really like them?"

Burns asked. He began unfastening the cuff links. "Here, sweetheart, they're yours."

"Now, look, I—"

"Take them, take them. I'm serious."

"I couldn't do anyth—"

"Nonsense," Burns insisted, handing over the jewelry. "They're yours. That's all. Forget it. You'd get a pair at Christmas anyway. But when I like a guy in August, do I have to wait till December to show him I like him?"

Doubly guilty now, at making the statement and at being paid back in such a way, Palmer made some meaningless remark in the "thank you" category and took the cuff links. Burns raised a hand whose fingers ended in immaculate nails, the moons buffed back, the cuticle smooth, the edges pared and sanded into perfect arcs. A faint gloss on the nails made Palmer suspect that clear polish had been applied by the manicurist, a habit he had noted in several New York men he'd met over the years, but one that had never caught on in Chicago. Burns snapped his fingers and the maître d' appeared with genii-like speed.

"Alex," Burns said. Again the word shimmered for a moment above their three heads. "Alex, baby, get a small jewelry box for Mr. Palmer here and, while you're at it, rustle me up a pair of the club's cuff links like a doll, right, Alex?"

Alex nodded and vanished. Palmer and Burns watched each other without speaking for a long moment. All Palmer could feel was a crushing sense of inadequacy at wearing buttoned cuffs today. Had he worn French cuffs, he could have repaid Burns's gesture on the spot.

"So," Burns said at last. "I was wondering when Lane would give me a guy I could work with. But go know he'd have to send to Chicago for him."

"When do we start this work?" Palmer asked.

"We've been working for the past fifteen minutes, sweetheart. Or didn't you notice?"

Palmer smiled slightly. "If this is work, I've been cruelly misled for years. Just what kind of work are we doing?"

"We're getting seen," Burns explained. "Together. In the right places. By the right people. It reminds me of my early days in Hollywood. Don't look around, whatever you do, but in the other corner table on this side there's a man sitting. He's almost finished eating. He'll get up in a minute and, on his way out, he'll stop by to say hello. His name isn't important. He's a bird dog for several columnists. Even that doesn't make him important enough for me to ask him to sit down and have a brandy. His only function is to register us sitting together and report it back."

"What makes us sitting together important?"

"Anybody who has lunch with Mac Burns could be a column item. This guy represents two-bit show-biz types. He's me, twenty years ago. He bird-dogs around town, picking up leads and gags. Then he trades them to the columnists for mentions of his clients."

"Why not just let a columnist see us together?"

"No good." Burns shook his head slowly, almost ponderously. "Woody, I got a lot to learn about banking, but you got more to learn about public relations. You don't bring an item to a columnist on a tray. He automatically suspects it. You leak it to him. Then he comes to you for the real low-down. That way he thinks he's uncovered something. It smells right to him. He prints it." His hand reached across and touched Palmer's knuckles. "He's getting up. Try to act furtive when he shows."

After a moment, a man passed their table, stopped and pantomimed a big-gestured, but silent, "hello." Burns looked up somewhat surreptitiously, then burst into a patently phony smile. "Hiya, Len, buddy."

Len moved in on them, a beefy man in his late fifties with a grayish complexion and an accompanying aura of bourbon. "Macky, honey, *wie gehts?*"

"Same old grind, Lenny-boy."

"Getting much?"

Burns grinned evilly. "You'd think it was a lot."

Len laughed appreciatively, then turned to Palmer. "Len Bannon," he said, extending a hand.

Trying to avoid his glance in a suitably furtive manner, Palmer nodded. "Say hello to Woody Palmer," Burns said. "Then forget you met him here, huh, Lenny-bubbie?"

Len's eyes widened in almost mock surprise. "'S'he on the lam or something?"

Burns smiled, shaking his head. "Len-sweetie, no offense, but it's way over your pointy head."

"Okay, Macky, whatever you say. *Zeit gezündt.*" He extended the already outstretched hand to Burns, who took it and gave it a single shake. The heavyset man started to leave. "Give my regards to Big Vic," he said before he walked away.

As he lumbered out of earshot, Burns muttered: "That'll be the day." He watched the man leave, then turned back to Palmer. "Perfect."

"Except for one thing: who the hell is Woody Palmer?"

"If he doesn't know yet, he'll find out," Burns assured him.

"He'll find out I'm a Chicago banker, if that's what you want him to know. My coming with Ubco hasn't been announced yet."

Burns frowned. "Didn't Lane show you the release?" He reached into his breast pocket and brought out a folded piece of paper. "It went out at noon by messenger to the papers and wire services."

Palmer opened the single sheet of paper and saw that it bore the dark-green-and-bright-gold heading of United Bank and Trust Company. PALMER JOINS UNITED TO HEAD UP STRUGGLE AGAINST SAVINGS BANKS, the neatly multilithed release headline read.

Palmer looked up. "No one showed me this for an okay. Officially, I don't begin work for a month."

"We're in the same boat, Woody. I lifted this copy off that big blonde's desk on the penthouse floor."

"Aren't you Ubco's public-relations counsel?" Palmer demanded. "Wouldn't you be releasing this under your imprimatur?"

"Nobody knows I've been retained. That's why Len Bannon seeing us together was important."

"Then who the hell," Palmer asked, growing suddenly very angry, "sent this out? Ubco's public-relations department?"

"It wouldn't be anybody else."

"Without showing it to me first? That's pretty Goddamned high-handed."

Burns turned his hands palms up and his loose cuffs flopped apologetically. "Is there anything wrong with the release?"

"I don't know," Palmer burst out. Then, realizing that he hadn't yet read the story, he glanced down at it again. "'Lane Burckhardt, president and chairman of the board of United Bank and Trust Company, the nation's largest bank, announced today that the prominent Chicago banker, Woods Palmer, Jr., formerly president of the—'"

The phone rang softly but insistently beside Burns's elbow. Palmer looked up. "Probably Caracas," Burns said apologetically. "Hello?" His mouth, pursed into a tight O, went slack. "It's for you," he said and handed the phone to Palmer.

"Hello?"

"Mr. Palmer, please," an operator asked.

"Speaking."

"I have a long-distance call. One moment, please."

Palmer listened to a dead line for a moment. Then: "Go ahead, please."

"Woods?" Edith asked breathlessly. "Woods, hello?"

"Edith? Where are you?"

"At the lake. The phone's been ringing all— Woods, the papers want to know what— Woods?"

"I'm still here."

"Woods, is it true?" Although her Wellesley drawl could be depended upon to mask almost any kind of inner turmoil, Palmer knew her well enough to recognize the faint signs of something having slipped out of place in the neat little world she created around herself and her family. Someone had thrown a brick through the window and there was glass all over the rug.

"Is what true, Edith?" he asked, wondering why he found it vaguely pleasant to torment her in this small way.

"The new job. They say you— The *Trib* man asked me if— And the *Sun-Times* bureau in New York was— Woods?"

"Didn't Gerri tell you?"

"Gerri?" Her voice lost the faint note of betrayal and took on, instantly, a proprietary tone. One of her responsibilities—the children—was being questioned. "What has Gerri to do with it?"

"I called early this morning, Edith."

"Called? Where? Here?"

"There. You were out and I told Gerri to—"

"I was out this morning? What time was this?" Edith asked.

"Oh, hell. About eight or eight-thirty your time."

"Nonsense, darling," Edith explained, back on firm ground again. "I was here until ten."

"I asked Gerri to look for you. She took her usual good sweet time and then said you couldn't be found."

"You have to expect that in a girl her age, darling." Edith sounded much better now. The original uncertainty and air of betrayal had begun to retreat behind the impressive façade of her usual voice. "All sorts of changes are taking place in her. It's understandable."

"Good," Palmer said. "How've you been?"

"Tol'able." Palmer knew, from her use of dialect, that she was fully back to normal again. "What on earth shall I tell the papers, darling?"

"Tell them to get everything from New York. This thing was prematurely released without my approval and I'm pretty burned about it."

"Isn't it true?"

"Oh, it's true enough."

"Oh. Well, I . . ." Her voice died away as her mouth moved from the phone to address a remark to a bystander at her end of the conversation. "Keep well, darling," she said into the phone.

"How did you locate me here?"

"Yes," she said. "I will. All right, darling. Is it hot in New York?"

"Edith! How did you locate me here?" Palmer felt a surge of unreasoning anger.

"I called the Union League Club. They gave me the bank's number. The girl there gave me this number. It's quite cool here."

"I'm all choked up," Palmer snapped sarcastically. "I'll call you tonight or tomorrow. Good-by."

". . . shell about half a pound, Mrs. Gage." Then, louder: "What, darling?"

"I said good-by."

"Good-by, darling." The line went dead.

Palmer replaced the phone and took a long pull at his drink. He looked up to find Burns watching him with a small smile on his lips, a slightly off-center smile with a peculiarly stealthy look about it. "Well?" Palmer asked challengingly.

"Finish reading the release," Burns suggested.

"The hell with the release."

Burns said nothing for a moment. Then, his mouth motionless, he picked up his drink and held it across the table to clink it against Palmer's glass.

"A toast," he said then, his mouth quirking up oddly at one corner. "I can't drink to health, wealth, friends or money. You've got them all."

"We can always dispense with the toast," Palmer said, still angry at Burckhardt and at Edith.

"The first time I drink with a new friend, I have to have a toast," Burns insisted. "We'd better do it now. There won't be another lunch as loose as this one after we get started with the campaign."

"Let's add another diamond to your cuff links, then," Palmer said, finding it impossible to avoid sarcasm. "What about . . . wisdom?"

"When you have money and friends, who needs to be smart?" Burns asked. "No." The monosyllable hung between them for a long, unresolved moment. His yellow eyes narrowed. "Let's drink to, uh, to love."

Watching each other warily, the two men sipped their drinks.

Chapter Seven

It had been quite difficult, taking leave of Mac Burns. Palmer had found it simple to conclude lunch at the comparatively reasonable hour of two-thirty, but Burns had insisted on taking him to the advertising agency where he headed a subsidiary public-relations firm. This, Palmer had been able to forestall only by promising to meet Burns for dinner that night.

After refusing a cab ride, he left Burns and called Burckhardt from a pay phone, only to find after a great deal of waiting that the man had left the Fifth Avenue office for a tour of branches in Brooklyn and Queens, was out of touch with the home office and could not be expected to return much before five-thirty.

"And when can I expect you here, Mr. Palmer?" the girl asked. "Our interior decorator would like to know."

"Interior wh—?" His time had run out and Palmer fumbled hastily for a nickel to place in the phone slot. "What did you say?" he asked, finally.

"Mr. Burckhardt assumed you'd want your office redone. Our decorator is holding himself available for you any time this afternoon."

Palmer glanced at his watch. "It's three. Let's have him in at four. And I want our public-relations man in at three forty-five."

"Miss Clary," the girl said.

"Pardon?"

"Miss Clary is in charge of our public relations. Miss Virginia Clary."

Palmer sighed. "Let's have Miss Virginia Clary in at quarter to four."

"Thank you, Mr. Palmer. Will that be all?"

"Yes."

"Good-by, Mr. Palmer."

"Good-by. Oh . . . wait! Hello?" The line had gone dead, making it impossible for Palmer to find out where his office was located. Assuming it to be at the Fifth Avenue branch, he left the phone booth and walked to Lexington Avenue, where he paused for a moment in the bright August sunlight and listened to the roar of buses while he thought about Mac Burns.

Although the man was a fairly unstable compound, some of the key elements in him could be separated and identified even at this early stage. Palmer was fairly sure, on admittedly insufficient evidence, that Burns was a romantic of the worst kind. His stratagems and plots, his mythical Caracas calls, his faintly cloak-and-dagger approach to the everyday humdrum of a job, his oaths of secrecy, his fantasies of fear, his mystical belief in signs and symbols, his almost ludicrous generosity—all these added up to a portrait of a full-blown romantic that no bank, and certainly not Ubco, had any business retaining.

So thinking, Palmer began walking south on Lexington past a block devoid of buildings. Behind the blue-painted fence that surrounded the excavation, power shovels and heavy-duty trucks made a clattering racket. He paused at an opening in the wall to let an immense Mack dump truck grind up a sharp incline and enter Lexington, heading somewhere with a pile of old foundation concrete, now shattered into great shards by the wreckers.

Palmer supposed he would have to get used to this characteristic of New York, the incessant demolition and construction, a disease that was rapidly infecting other cities as well. The idea of it was sound enough, if you assumed a stable and expanding economy for the country: tear down undesirable office space at a handsome tax loss and create expensive new office space whose value could be written off for tax purposes under one of the tricky lease-back deals now prevalent in the rarefied heights of big-money real estate manipulation.

He stood there as another truck left the excavation, spewing hot dust on his shoe tips. But the assumed expansion of the economy, Palmer thought, was only assumed, not God-given. Even Vinnie Astor had found that out when he'd started this very demolition job here. The money had run out, new money was too scarce and too expensive, so Astor had unloaded on one of the few investors that could handle the deal, that by-no-means-bottomless wellspring of money, the First National City Bank.

What had begun bravely enough as Astor Plaza would now be known as the First National Building. *Sic transit . . .*

Palmer began walking again. As he reached the corner of Fifty-third Street, he noted that one old building in the entire block-wide area of excavation had not yet been razed. It stood, awkward and alone, like the last thin slice of cake left after everyone else had got his share. Palmer wondered how much the owner was holding out for. Astor might not have been able to match the asking price, but First National would be able to offer inducements. It was just a matter of time.

Smiling to himself, Palmer continued walking south on Lexington. It was somehow comforting to him to contemplate the last hold-out in that empty block of devastation. Not that the owner's motives were in any way exalted. The man had a good thing and he was making the most of it. But the idea that there could still be a hold-out, a single, solitary entity that stood alone against the onrushing steam roller of Big Progress, gave Palmer a peculiar feeling of pleasure.

If Ubco, he reflected now, were to face such a situation, it would be Palmer's duty to crush the solitary hold-out with every means at his disposal. But since it was First National's baby, he decided, it was pleasant to contemplate.

He paused at the corner of Fifty-second Street and wondered what he would tell Burckhardt when he finally got through to him. The release to the press of the appointment, without first clearing with Palmer, had been a disturbing breach of protocol. Miss Clary could supply the details before he went up against Burckhardt, but he had to do it as strongly as possible. Palmer couldn't side-step the issue or water down his position, especially since it could set the tone for his entire future relationship to Burckhardt and the bank. It had to be brought to a head by the end of the day and settled with as much finality as possible.

And while he was putting the question to Burckhardt, Palmer reminded himself now, he would also bring up the question of Mac Burns. What was such a man doing in association with Ubco? When had the bank's situation become so unstable that it had to depend for help on a man like Burns?

There was nothing wrong with Burns, Palmer decided, as long as you didn't think of him in connection with a reputable bank. His kind of person made a lot of sense in other businesses, where outward show was everything. But banking, although it preserved a façade like everything else in this world, was a concept in depth. It began with the most concrete of commodities, money, and built upwards, almost literally, from underground vaults of stability to a superstructure of service. Once a bank's relations with the public lost sight of this concept—as had already begun to happen in many places— it set in motion a process of down-grading, of cheapening, of doubt, that could only end in disaster.

What was Mac Burns, Palmer wondered. How had Burckhardt become involved with him? Through the ad agency in which Burns was a principal? Why was Burckhardt so unwilling to deal with Burns at the personal level, yet so anxious that Palmer establish the relationship quickly? Why had the relationship apparently been kept secret until now? What did Mac Burns have that Ubco needed? And what kind of price—in reputation if nothing else—was Burckhardt willing to pay for what Mac Burns could offer?

Standing now at the corner of Fifty-first Street, Palmer was about to step off the curb when a long black seven-passenger Cadillac turned in front of him, missing him by such a narrow margin that he had to jump back on the curb. He stood there, amazed at himself for having been so deep in thought that he had neglected to watch where he was going. Damn Mac Burns, he thought. And damn Lane Burckhardt with him.

But the fat man in the restaurant had mentioned a name.

Palmer stood on the corner, thinking furiously for a moment. The name had gone right past him in the restaurant and yet had lodged in some inner recess of his mind. It had been a name too gently dropped, a name Palmer had, almost unconsciously, known he should recognize and remember.

He closed his eyes, trying to remember. Someone brushed against him from behind and he had to open his eyes quickly to keep from tripping on the edge of the curb.

Big Vic.

Palmer plunged ahead across the street and along Lexington. Big Vic Culhane. He had already passed the library when he stopped, realizing what kind of building it was, back-tracked and entered the dim, quiet lobby, wondering where one began. Not *Who's Who*.

He asked a librarian for the *Reader's Guide to Periodical Literature* and settled down to the C's. The *New York Times Magazine* had run an article on Culhane, Victor S., in January. *The Atlantic Monthly* had printed a biographical sketch in May under the heading: BIG VIC DROPS THE BIG STICK. In July, both *Newsweek* and *The New Yorker* had done pieces. Palmer glanced at his watch and found that he had half an hour before his first appointment at the office.

Twenty minutes later, he had read enough. The material on Culhane had been the usual stuff, the boy whose Irish father and Italian mother had tried to head him straight for the priesthood, the young man who had entered politics on East 106th Street, bucking the Marcantonio organization in the depths of the Depression, the seasoned young organization hack who had come to city-wide prominence during the overthrow of Ed Flynn and who now, at the same age as Palmer, was popularly supposed to have some of New York in the palm of his hand. None of it was particularly new to Palmer. But in each of the articles, as it dealt with Culhane's career just after World War II, the name of Mac Burns was mentioned.

The *Times* had referred to him, with rather ingenuous simplicity, as "Culhane's public-relations counselor." The *Atlantic* had mentioned him twice, once in connection with an internecine struggle between Culhane and Carmine De Sapio, once all by himself, "Burns, the putative guiding genius behind Big Vic's climb to respectability." *Newsweek* had called Burns "the man who manicures Culhane's cuticles to a shiny gloss." *The New Yorker,* however, had given Burns a rather lengthy paragraph of his own.

"Of the single individual most often credited with being closest to his innermost thinking, Culhane told a recent visitor: 'Mac Burns? A personal friend for whom I have the highest respect. A hell of a guy in every way.' With the sweeping sideways thrust of his hand that has become his trademark in both public and private speaking, Culhane dismissed the often repeated report that Burns, a sleek public-relations counsel, is his personal speech writer and political brains trust. 'Mac's got enough ability and acumen for ten men,' Culhane remarked. Then, waxing even more lyrical, he observed: 'The firms that retain him have got some first-class brains on their team.' Presumably, Culhane was referring to an assortment of blue chip investments that have, at one time or another, retained Burns. The Burns operation, as bitterly summed up by an understandably jealous competitor in the jungles of public relations, went something like this: 'If you want Culhane, you have to retain Mac the Knife. That doesn't guarantee you Culhane, but it's the first step. You'll get there eventually, if your money holds out.' A commendably busy man, Burns is available, if at all, by telephone only. Reached in that manner, his sharp voice, in which the muezzin whine of his native Beirut can still be heard, told one caller: 'You're not likely to find a public servant of Mr. Culhane's caliber growing on the nearest tree. He combines a heightened awareness of social responsibility with a firm grasp of political reality.' Of his reputedly intimate relationship with this socio-political paragon, Mr. Burns's only comment was: 'God gives us but a few precious gifts during this life of ours. One of them is friendship. I am humbly proud to number Victor S. Culhane among my dearest friends.'"

Leaving the library, Palmer tried to piece together the relationship between the savings-bank fight and Big Vic Culhane. He turned west and walked along a cross street to Fifth Avenue, wondering just how strong Culhane really was, how many votes in the legislature at Albany he could guarantee and, finally, whether Mac Burns could really deliver Culhane's support. As he reached the huge glass-and-aluminum bank, he realized that he knew too little about New York politics, city or state, to answer his own questions.

Since the bank was closed to the public at this hour, he knocked at a side door and waved to one of the guards inside, who frowned and strode toward him with a no-nonsense look. As the guard opened the door, however, his face went blank for an instant before a smile replaced the frown.

"It's Mr. Palmer, isn't it, sir?"

Palmer nodded, wondering if his picture had already been circulated throughout the Ubco system, like that of a notorious check-kiter.

"They'll be giving you a key, sir," the guard said, leading him to one of the semihuman elevators. "Just you remind them, sir."

Considering ways to dam the flood of "Mr. Palmers" and "sirs" that had begun to engulf him, and deciding that it would take years before he dared undermine Ubco protocol—by which time he would have begun to like the treatment—Palmer gestured at the sensitive control buttons and watched the "PH" one light up. The car rose and the mechanical voice let him know his destination. Palmer felt a sudden pang of uneasiness. This whole thing was, for the moment, a little too much for him. All of it, the title, the obsequiousness, the politics, people like Mac Burns, the business with the uncleared announcement, all of it gathered itself together for a swift moment of bewilderment and, although he had not wanted it, of uncertainty as to whether or not he had made the right choice.

The doors opened and Palmer squinted against the glare of sunlight through the penthouse ceiling. He walked down the long, wide corridor that reminded him, for an instant, of the approach to an Egyptian throne room. Instead of Horus and Osiris, the figures along the way should be heroic statues of banking's gods: the Ant-god of Accumulation, the Penguin-god of Dignity, the Elephant-god of Stability . . . and what was the god of lending at six per cent?

He pulled his thoughts together as he approached the tall blonde receptionist. She stood up. "Good afternoon, Mr. Palmer," she said, handing him a bunch of five or six keys. "I'm afraid I neglected to give you these this morning."

Almost simultaneously, two thoughts crossed Palmer's mind. The first was sheer amazement at how quickly the guard downstairs had been able to call her about the keys. The other was a hasty analysis of status: the guard called him "sir"; the girl up here called him "Mr. Palmer"; apparently this girl was higher in rank than the guard. At any rate, she was prettier.

Palmer found himself watching, not the keys in her hand, but her rather large bosom, somewhat camouflaged behind a severe black wool dress that hung loosely from her shoulders. No amount of looseness, however, could fully camouflage those— He looked up and saw that she was blushing.

"If you'll let me know which is my office, I'll . . ." He let the thought die away. She moved toward the burnished gold-anodized door of Burckhardt's room. "Oh," Palmer asked, "has Mr. Burckhardt returned?"

"No, Mr. Palmer." She opened the door. "He's assigned his office to you."

In a state halfway between confusion and shock, Palmer followed her into the immense room. A moment later he was seated behind the desk watching her sort out the keys she was giving him. She stood beside him as she spread them out on the polished teak with small, finicking stabs of her very long-nailed index finger. He could smell the perfume he had given Edith. It seemed to fill his nostrils.

"This is for the outside door, the side entrance," she was saying.

She stared for a moment at the other five keys and, leaning over to look more closely at them, her breast brushed softly against Palmer. The perfume was terribly strong. "This is a duplicate," she went on then. "This is, uh, for the elevator. It's locked after six o'clock. This is for the door of your office and this big one, I think, is for the main office door." She picked it up and examined it carefully. "Yes, that's right."

Reaching past him again to a pencil container, her shoulder rubbed against him quite firmly. She took up a black grease pencil and marked each key. "You can rub these off after you become accustomed to them," she said. "The ones marked with a 'five' are for downstairs. Fifth Avenue. The one with the 'E' is the elevator one. 'O' is for your office. 'M' is for main office."

Palmer shifted slightly away from her. "Spelled backwards," he said in a small, faraway voice, "that's 'Moe.'" He could feel himself breathing very shallowly, to minimize the perfume. There was very little resemblance between this girl and Edith, other than the scent. Edith was quite slender, with a tennis player's tightly controlled body. This girl was fleshy without being plump, and didn't seem aware of exactly what her body was doing at all times. Or didn't care.

He watched her walk around to the front of his desk. "Miss Clary can come in whenever you wish," she said then.

"Later."

Palmer watched her leave and wondered why the intricate play of her full rump, only half hidden beneath the loose-fitting dress, failed to bother him. For the briefest moment he wondered if it were Edith's perfume. Then, rejecting the idea as being too damned Freudian for belief, he glanced around the huge room. He saw that the few pictures on the walls had been removed in his absence and two single-shelf bookcases, polished teak on high golden legs, had been installed behind his desk. On what had once been the empty desk top now stood a very discreet dictating machine flanked by the pencil container, a large ash tray apparently made of gold, the small microphone speaker of a remote-control telephone and a flat box with twelve buttons set into its polished gold top.

As he stared at the buttons, one of them glowed green. A faint sound, like that of a very good crystal glass being gently flicked, made him inspect the row of buttons more closely. The lighted one was labeled "Rcpnst," thus saving six letters. Palmer touched the button and, as the light went out, the speaker microphone came alive.

"Miss Clary to see you, Mr. Palmer."

"Later."

As the speaker lapsed into silence, Palmer glanced slowly about the room, feeling an unmistakable sense of possession well up inside him. He would have to pick out a few paintings for the walls. The book shelves needed something useful in them and there had to be one or two more chairs. It wouldn't be wise to put anything terribly big in the room. The essence of it was its bareness.

Looking at the tremendous expanse of plate glass at the far end where the ceiling swept up to its full 20-foot height, Palmer found himself remembering Burckhardt's off-hand reference to the glass being the same as that in the Mount Palomar telescope.

The damned old scoundrel, Palmer thought. Giving up his own office made it a little easier, somehow, for Palmer to swallow the business about the unchecked and premature announcement.

He stared at the bare wall across the room from him and wondered whether he might borrow one of the big Braques in the outer corridor to fill the empty space.

Chapter Eight

The interior decorator had just left. Palmer glanced at his watch and found that it was after five. Had there been anything else to do on this peculiar day?

He sat back at his desk and squinted down the length of the room toward the immense window. It came to him suddenly that he hadn't sampled the view this abnormal porthole gave him. Getting up, he walked slowly, with unusually long strides, toward the great expanse of plate glass. Five . . . six . . . seven . . . eight . . . nine. What would that be? Forty-odd feet? Would anyone believe it?

Palmer stood at the glass and found himself looking north along Fifth Avenue. A few blocks away the Plaza and its fountain broke the even line of buildings. A few hansom cabs stood at the rank, horses' heads drooping in the late afternoon sun. Then, beyond the cabs, the vital green of Central Park began. Some of its details were easy to see: the zoo, the pony ride, cars entering the inner drive at Sixtieth Street. Farther away it blurred into a mass of trees which, at this angle, hid all but a few sharp sparkles of the lagoon.

Palmer raised his glance to the far rim of the park where an uneven row of buildings formed a fringed border. How far north? And beyond, after the land seemed to rise slightly, growing dimmer in the haze, the tiny toy bridge that crossed the Hudson to New Jersey. What was its name?

Behind him the intercom pinged deferentially, like the discreet cough of a butler announcing tea. Palmer turned and walked rapidly to his desk, noting that if it took this long to get back from the window, city-gazing would prove a tiring luxury.

He pressed "Rcpnst" and quenched its well-bred green light. "Yes?"

"Miss Clary is still waiting," the voice told him.

"Good grief! Send her in."

"And, Mr. Palmer . . . ?"

"Yes?"

"Will there be anything else today?"

Palmer glanced at his watch. Five-fifteen. "Nothing. You can go. Thank you." He clicked off, sat down in his chair and tried to arrange his thoughts. It wasn't easy, he found, to reassemble the jagged chunks of anger that had clattered about him at lunch. Some people had the knack of nursing a thing like that for days, years, lifetimes. But then, he reflected, they hadn't been totally and utterly beguiled by a room the size of a tennis court and a view that was good enough to be bottled and sold.

"Mr. Palmer?"

He looked up at the huge open door. On its threshold, dwarfed by the ceiling-high lintel, stood a small, thin woman with big eyes. He forced his face to look blank. "Come in, Miss Clary."

She entered the room, leaving the door open behind her, and advanced toward him on high-heeled black pumps whose needle-thin heels made absolutely no sound in the thick carpet. As she stood for a moment, before sitting down in the chair he had gestured to, she grew slightly in stature. Still a small woman, Palmer noted, she didn't look quite so tiny away from the giant door frame. He watched her sit, cross her legs, make an effort to pull the hem of her skirt over her knees and fail. By the time she looked up at him, however, his eyes were on the desk before him.

"You're our public-relations man," he said then. "I use the term 'man' advisedly," he added, smiling.

She watched him for a moment. Then her rather full mouth bent very slightly upward in a token smile. "Advisedly," she echoed in a nearly flat voice.

Palmer wondered why his first attempt to set her at ease had failed. He realized then, from the motionless way in which she was sitting, back very straight, hands folded on her lap and clenched, that she was expecting trouble, had been kept waiting for it like a child after school. He looked more directly at her and found his glance caught in hers. Her dark eyes seemed much larger at this range, he noted, possibly because she had made them up in the current style—heavily—and partly, too, because they were set in rather deep sockets that cast shadows. He found himself wondering, as he looked at her, whether her eye sockets were really that deep or whether the cheekbones beneath them, jutting out in strong relief, made them seem deeper by contrast.

Her glance broke. She looked away and Palmer could see a faint flush spreading upward along her cheeks and over those highly modeled cheekbones. Then, realizing for the first time that he had been staring at her far beyond the bounds of protocol, he looked down at his desk. He badly missed a few loose papers he might shuffle around.

"I'll tell you," he said then, and stopped. She looked back at him for less than a second, as if afraid of becoming entangled in his stare again, and then glanced away.

"That is, I'll tell you why I called you—" He stopped and edited his words into more politic form. "It's this release," he said then. "That's why I asked you in for a moment."

"The release?" she asked.

"On my appointment."

"That release." She nodded and her black curls shivered slightly.

"What I—" He stopped again. This was going about as badly as possible. She was expecting trouble but, he told himself, she hadn't bargained on a babbling idiot.

"Mr. Burckhardt," she said then, seemingly afraid of another silence, "called me at home on Sunday and had me prepare it." She paused, waiting for him to speak, then pushed on quickly, her voice a rather low monotone. "I read it to him on the phone this morning. He approved it and it went to the newspapers by messenger for immediate release."

Palmer waited for a moment to find out if there was anything more. Then: "In other words, only you and he saw the release before it left the office."

"And Freddie, our multilith boy," she added.

"And Freddie," he agreed, "our multilith boy."

Neither of them spoke for a moment. Palmer found himself examining her general appearance, having learned by now not to get tangled up by concentrating on any one detail. She seemed to be in her mid-thirties, rather pleasant-looking on other occasions, he felt. Right now she was still holding in somewhat tensely.

"Is he cleared for access to classified documents?" Palmer asked suddenly.

"Freddie?" Her huge eyes shifted warily to watch him.

"Apparently this release was highly confidential. An ordinary Johnny-come-lately like me hadn't a prayer of checking it before it went out. I'm glad at least you and Burckhardt were in on it. And Freddie."

Another silence fell around them. Palmer decided that sarcasm, even delivered in what he had hoped was a light, bantering tone, was not going to unfreeze this girl. He knew nothing about her, other than the fact that no bank Ubco's size had ever had a female p.r. director before. She must have come highly recommended and she must have been doing a superior job. But, at the moment, Palmer had no proof of this other than his own deductive logic.

"Say something," he suggested then, smiling again.

She watched him for a moment and then, out of the perfect dead-pan expression she had been wearing, something unusual took shape. One corner of her mouth quirked upward mockingly. "Something," she said.

"There, now," he persisted. "That didn't hurt. Say something else."

"Something else," she said.

"Very good. Now, repeat after me: I will not send out any more releases about Woods Palmer unless he approves them first."

"I will not," she repeated, "send out any more releases about Woods Palmer unless he approves them first. Right?"

"Right. Any questions?"

"One."

"Shoot."

"When are you firing me?" she asked.

Palmer turned his hands palms up on his desk. "Don't you know about bankers?" he asked. "We never strike until the plot demands it. We foreclose on the ranch only after Paw has been shot by rustlers. So, if you play your cards right, you'll get fired about the time you're due for retirement." He nodded firmly. "Saves us all that pension money, you know."

She watched him for a moment, appraisingly, and then said: "I didn't bring my bag with me. Do you have a cigarette?"

"Somewhere." He felt through his pockets, then opened a square box on his desk and removed two cigarettes. "My brand," he said in a suddenly thin voice. A little of the day's anger returned to him. "Everybody in New York knows everything about me, even my brand of cigarette. My life is an open book." As he lighted her cigarette, he tried phrasing his next question in a way that would not reveal how concerned he actually was. "Tell me," he said then, "how good is Ubco's intelligence system?"

"Surprisingly good," she replied.

"I'm not talking about business information," he added.

She watched him light his own cigarette. "I know what you're talking about," she said, her glance dropping to the desk and staying there. "I understand you're no stranger to spy work."

"I have been, for a good fifteen years." He paused for a moment. "But I imagine my dossier gives the exact dates."

She nodded. "Like to see it?"

Palmer sat back in his chair and felt himself relax slightly. "Some other time," he said. "Some rainy afternoon when there's nothing else to do."

"The earliest entry is 1945," she told him.

"It almost looks," he said, "as though you'd been referring to it rather recently."

"First thing this morning."

"Who called who first? You or Mac Burns?"

She smiled softly and Palmer noticed that her mouth grew more attractive as she did so. "I've only been with Ubco a year or two," she said then. "Not long enough to get that corrupt. He called me."

"And you answered his questions."

"Of course." She tapped her cigarette ash on the gold-enameled tray. "He works for us."

"But not everyone knows that."

"I'd have to, wouldn't I?" she asked. "I mean, it wouldn't make much sense if I—"

"Tell me," he interrupted, ready to push on now that he'd found out what he'd wanted to know. "Were you with a newspaper before you came to Ubco?"

"The *Star*."

"Financial side?" he asked.

"To be precise, banking."

"And before that?" Palmer persisted.

"The *Times*. General news."

Palmer frowned. "People usually move the other way, don't they? From the *Star* to the *Times*? Step-up sort of thing?"

"Not everybody," she said in a careful voice. "There was more money in it for me." She stopped for a moment and seemed to take a long breath. "Would you care to see my references?" she asked then.

Neither of them spoke. The immense room, with its far reaches of space, seemed to pad the distance between them with an unnatural silence. Then Palmer smiled. "I've gotten off on the wrong foot again, haven't I?"

She failed to return the smile. "You do very well," she said. "Although you were never a newspaperman, you know how to ask the right questions in just the wrong way. It takes some people years to perfect that technique."

"My wartime training," he said dryly. "May I make a statement?"

She lifted one thin hand, the fingers long and narrow, and made a sweeping gesture that included all the great room. Palmer saw that she wore no rings. "The hall is yours," she said.

"I'm sorry, in a way," he said, "that I had to get what I wanted to know from you. But you were the logical one to ask. In no sense was it personal." He glanced up at her questioningly.

"Yes."

"I've met women in banking before," he went on slowly, trying to think ahead and revise his statement accordingly. "I've invariably found that, just to be hired, they had to be much better at their job than a man in a corresponding position. This is the nature of things. And then, as you know, they still don't get the salary the job calls for."

"I know."

"I've never met a woman doing bank public relations," he continued. "I assume you're much better at it than we have any right to expect." He paused. "End of statement."

She stood up, smoothing her black sheath dress down over her hips. Palmer noticed for the first time that despite her size—5'2''?—she had an extremely well-rounded figure. He felt a vague sense of pleasure. It was interesting, he decided, to find a small woman who didn't have one of these aggressively boyish bodies.

"May I have equal time?" she asked then.

"Proceed."

"I'm sorry," she said, watching him directly now, "that I wasn't—what's the word, 'able'?—able to clear that release with you. We have certain methods of working here that will change, now that you're with us. At least, I hope they'll change. In a sense I'm hoping you'll change them, although I know it can't happen overnight. I can't be more explicit than that."

"I understand."

"As far as Mac Burns is concerned," she told him, "I've known him for a good many years. We've always gotten along because it's his business to get along with newspaper people. That's all there is to it."

"Agreed."

"That's it," she said.

"Very good statement," he commented. "I'll be leaving in a day or two. But when I get back for good, after Labor Day, you'll have to brief me pretty thoroughly on things."

"Will do."

"Thank you," Palmer said.

She turned slightly toward the door. Palmer saw her lips open for an instant, then close, as though she had changed her mind about what she had intended to say. Then she glanced at him and smiled slightly. "You're welcome," she said, and went to the door.

As he watched her walk out of the room, Palmer's glance shifted to her hips, which hardly moved. He had the feeling that she was still very much in rigid control of herself, although he had tried to put her at her ease. There was, of course, plenty of time to do that in the months to come. He found himself wondering how she would talk, and how her body would move, when she was really at ease.

Then he wondered why such a thought had occurred to him. It didn't seem to make much sense.

CHAPTER NINE

That year, Labor Day had come on the second of September, which, as Gerri had thoughtfully observed, really got things going with a vengeance. Mrs.

Gage had been left in Evanston to supervise packing at the house. Edith had closed up the Wisconsin cottage herself and, since they had decided not to sell it for at least a year, it presented no immediate problem. The problem would crop up again in a year, but Palmer felt that he had rather successfully deferred it to a time when they would all be more settled. Although he and Edith had spent two muggy weekends inspecting a list of suburban houses Ubco's mortgage department had drawn up for them, the most attractive thing the department had been able to suggest was a foreclosed brownstone on Seventieth off Fifth Avenue. Normally priced at well over $100,000, the house could be his for half its asking price—"As long as we keep it our little secret," one of Ubco's mortgage officers had said. The immense cheapness of it had faded on inspection, however, when Palmer noted that it would take as much as its cost to repair and remodel. Deciding quickly, however, he had moved himself and his family into a small apartment hotel a few blocks from the house so that Edith could supervise the remodeling. He had enrolled all three children at Bentley and now considered himself lucky to have made the big move with so little trouble.

"It's just as well," he observed to Edith on a morning in early October when the children had gone off to school, "considering that everything else is pure, undiluted trouble."

Edith's rather small eyes, ringed by lashes so light in color as to be almost invisible, moved slowly upwards from the pad of paper on which she was writing. Her glance moved from the paper to the cup of coffee she held in her other hand and then, by shifting focus, to Palmer's face across the table from her. "I've asked them not to make the coffee quite this strong," she said. "We both like it black and, without cream, it's the nearest thing to ink." Then, without a pause: "What trouble, darling?"

"Oh, big things. Coffee too strong, that sort of trouble."

She returned her cup to its saucer with a small, firm click. "What have I done now?" she asked.

"Done?" Palmer sounded too unconcerned. "Nothing."

"To merit the breakfast cup of sarcasm, that is."

He found himself wondering why she couldn't find time in the morning to do something about her eyes. The moment he left, she would work on the lashes and the upper lids until her eyes looked highly presentable. If she could do this for the benefit of the foreman and workmen who were remodeling the house, for the doorman and maids of the hotel and any assorted strangers she met during the course of her day, why couldn't she do it for the husband she would not see again until after seven tonight?

"Do I have a smudge on my forehead, darling?"

"No. Sorry." He swallowed the last of his coffee. "How far along is the carpentry work?"

"They say it's a two-week delay before they can deliver the walnut plywood.

And they still haven't been able to get clearance on that façade grill. Something in the building code isn't quite clear on that point."

"What does the architect say?"

"Says it's approved in Detroit and Cleveland."

"That's some help," Palmer snapped, getting to his feet. "I'll call a man named Feist at Empire Plywood. They bank with us. And Mac Burns can help through his connections, too."

Edith poured more of the too-black coffee into her cup and sipped it thoughtfully. "Is there anything the blond Mr. Burns can't do, darling?"

Palmer, who had started to walk away from the table, stopped in mid-stride and turned back to her. The morning sun came through the window behind her, turning the fine gold-red hair into a kind of nimbus around her head. "For me, anything. The question is, what the hell has he done for Ubco to date?"

"Well, he got the children into Bentley long after admissions were closed for the year."

"That kind of thing is elementary for Burns. Unfortunately, Ubco doesn't retain him for favors like that."

"I wouldn't underestimate favors like that," Edith told him. "It's important to the bank that their executive vice-president's family be educated."

"Favors like that," Palmer repeated the phrase, "come pretty dear at fifty thousand a year."

"Is that all you're paying him?"

"Plus expenses."

"Why, it's cheap, darling. When you think that he found us a contractor who could finish the job in a month."

Palmer glanced at his watch, saw that it was eight-twenty, then walked to the window and looked down at the street below. One of the bank's Sixty Specials was double-parked in front of the hotel. "Edith," he said, turning from the window and starting out of the dining room, "sometimes I wish you had a sense of humor."

"I have a perfectly good sense of humor," she called after him.

He found his umbrella and hat in the hall closet. "Then why don't you smile," he called back, "when you say some of the things you say?"

"I do now and then," Edith said, taking him to the front door. She held a half-full cup of coffee in one hand while, with the other, she tugged the knot of his tie slightly to one side. Knowing that the tie had been squared away before this standard morning attention, Palmer resolved to remember to re-straighten it when he got in the car. It had been all right in Chicago to forget this once in a while. It would not do, in New York, ever to forget it.

He kissed her firmly on one cheek, aware that he was trying to make up in pressure what he lacked in warmth. "What's the schedule tonight?"

"We're seeing the Osborne play."

Without thinking, he delivered a startlingly good imitation of Gerri's pet vomiting sound. "Dinner out?"

"It's easier."

"I'll have to call the kids from the office and say good night."

"I'm afraid so, darling," she said. "Good-by."

"Bye."

As he went down in the hotel elevator, he found himself picturing Edith at her dressing-room mirror, painstakingly strengthening the color of her lashes and emphasizing the sweep of her upper lids. Deciding that he was probably being quite unfair—and thereupon concluding that unfair or not, he was undoubtedly right—he got into the rear of the Cadillac double-parked in front of the hotel. The doorman closed the door smoothly and looked very satisfied at the soft cluck with which the lock caught and held. He was still holding his salute, something halfway between a regulation U.S. Army salute and that of a drunken French *poilu,* when the car pulled away.

"Good morning, sir," the driver said.

Big car sound, Palmer thought. That's what they build into these heavy auto doors. Something in the lock they call "big car sound." Then they build it into Fords and Chevys and Plymouths and people buy the car for the way the door slams. God!

"Good morning," the driver repeated more quietly, as though trying to be only half heard, in case Palmer had already heard the first greeting and was in too foul a mood to answer it.

"Good morning, Jimmy."

The sky, empty of clouds, let the strong October sun slant down in great yellow sheets, casting big warm brown shadows across the street. It was, Palmer noted, a very good morning indeed. He wished, for a moment, that he could summon up some small rag of enthusiasm to match the brightness of the day, then decided that it didn't really matter.

One's frame of mind, he told himself now, was a necessary evil that existed in order to be ignored at the very least, thwarted whenever possible and, in any event, overcome. Otherwise nothing would ever get done. That had always been fairly clear to him: one didn't "give in" to moods. Moods were non-material and nearly always irrational. Life was desperately material and, if not always clearly rational, at least susceptible to logic.

Palmer reflected now that this had been his father's strongest belief; it was now his own, too, along with a number of other deep-seated tenets like voting Republican, living on interest and wearing white shirts. All of them, he decided as the car swung onto Fifth Avenue and started downtown, eminently rational.

He shifted on his seat and eyed himself in the driver's rear-view mirror. The whiteness of his shirt collar was immaculate. He shifted the set of his tie knot to where it had been before Edith disarranged it. Suddenly he became aware that the driver was trying to keep from watching him in the same mirror, torn between curiosity and protocol.

Palmer sat back on the rear seat and looked out the window. He picked up the *Times,* neatly folded on the seat beside him, glanced at the headlines and made a face before returning the paper to the seat.

This was all really impossible, he thought then.

All of it, from the job he was supposed to be doing with Mac Burns, through the children he rarely saw except for a few moments in the evening, directly to Edith herself and the relationship between them, whatever it was. None of it made sense, he told himself, none of it hung together in any kind of natural order and, what was worse, all of it was rapidly degenerating into the most sickening kind of cliché.

Or was the process that rapid? Wasn't it just a neat evasion, he wondered, to try to date the deterioration from the time he had moved to New York? Wasn't it true, in fact, that what he felt now had been building up for several years and that moving to New York had, by placing it all in a new setting, stripped away the camouflage of familiar Chicago background and showed him pretty much the way things were?

It had been so easy back home. The morning scenery from Evanston to the Loop unreeled around him each morning as it had for eighteen years of married life. Even as a single man, he had made much the same trip every morning, except for the years during the war. And, in the evening, the same faces, the same rooms, the same parties and people and chairs and windows and views and talk and talk.

That sort of thing, he thought now, tended to weave a tight little covering over everything important, a (protective?) covering that made it possible, at first, to ignore the important things. Then, as the covering grew thicker with matted-down layers of familiar persons, places and things—it became possible not only to ignore what lay beneath, but actually to forget it existed.

And since what lay underneath was you, Palmer realized suddenly, it became possible for you to die underneath and for the covering (definitely protective) to take your place, for you to become the covering of what used to be you.

You ended up, he thought, as your own shroud.

He sighed impatiently now and picked up the *Times* again, glancing over the same headlines as though for the first time. The Middle East crisis showed signs of easing away from a real show-down. There would be a flurry of selling in the morning's market, Palmer decided, and as prices dropped after lunch, a flurry of buying, but not enough to offset the selling. Cliff Mergendahl, Ubco's securities man, would have a busy day.

The car halted for a snarl of traffic at the Plaza. Increasingly, Palmer thought, it took more and more running just to stay in the same place.

He threw the *Times* on the floor of the car, where it lay in an untidy heap. Wondering whether the driver, noting the flung newspaper, would quickly report that Mr. Palmer was in a rotten mood this morning, spreading the word by phone or E.S.P. or whatever system the Ubco grapevine used, Palmer stared out the window at the fountain across the street in the center of the Plaza.

All right, then, he told himself, one becomes one's own shroud. A convenient, if somewhat too clever, observation solving nothing. There was apparently no clear-cut solution to what had happened to him and to Edith and to the children, because what had happened was in itself not clear, God damn it.

"Sir?" the driver asked.

Palmer stared in sudden alarm at the back of the driver's head. "What?"

"Did you say something, sir?"

Did I? Palmer wondered. Did I God-damn life aloud? What am I really God-damning? Myself, isn't it, and only myself? "Nothing," he said aloud. "Nothing."

The traffic jam broke for several seconds as the policeman on the corner, having let through enough crosstown cars to people the entire borough of Queens, finally allowed the Fifth Avenue traffic to proceed. The Cadillac shot ahead in a rabbit-like fashion more typical of a low-priced car; Palmer's head snapped back against the seat.

"Sorry, sir."

"Never mind, Jimmy. Take it while you can get it."

The driver chuckled for several seconds and Palmer felt an excruciating shame at having to witness the scene of a man pretending to find humor in an off-hand remark of his superior. God damn all of it, Palmer wished fervently. And God damn the false-hearted sunlight on this Godforsaken morning.

Instantly ashamed at having given in so far to his mood, Palmer sat up straight in the car, reached down for the *Times* and neatly refolded it before putting it back on the seat again. Having atoned for the sin of emotionalism, he stared out the window with half-slitted eyes, as if gingerly trying to let some of the sunlight into his brain.

He sat there, as the car drew nearer to his office, picturing the way this intense sun, its rays growing more vertical as the day progressed, would pour down in great sickening cascades through the glass roof of the penthouse floor. Not even the louvers in his immense ceiling would shut it entirely out. If only, he thought, I could condense all of this dull nothingness into a simple headache. It would be a legitimate and understandable reason for hating this morning so fiercely. Two aspirin would set it right.

But where, he asked himself as the car drew up before the side door of the bank, was the aspirin for what really ailed him?

He stepped out of the car, thanked the driver and let himself in the side door with his own key.

CHAPTER TEN

At five minutes to nine, Palmer nodded to the receptionist, entered his office and walked to his desk. He stood there for a moment, watching the row of buttons on the telephone-control panel, each button with a cryptic legend from which all vowels had been excised. They read, in order from left to right: "Rcpnst, Brkhrt, Mrgndl, Scrty, Lvrs." The "Brkhrt" button, he had found from experience, rarely made connection with the old bird when pressed. But when the delicate chime sounded, Palmer could be sure that half the time Burckhardt's button glowed green. "Mrgndl" was Cliff Mergendahl, Ubco's vice-president and secretary, whose primary responsibility was handling the securities portfolio of the bank and some of its larger customers, while supervising the entire securities and trust department. "Scrty" was a line to nowhere, at least not until Palmer found time to interview a girl for the job of what he mentally referred to as "Scairty." The "Lvrs" button controlled the overhead louvers which, after the first week, Palmer had decided to set halfway open and forget about. At the far right of this vowelless line-up that occasionally reminded him of a Notre Dame backfield, were two buttons labeled: "Elder" and "Carse." These, it happened, were the full, true surnames of Ubco's first vice-president, Harry Elder, and vice-president-treasurer J. Phipps Carse.

Palmer now reached under the front of his desk and pressed a hidden switch. The wall behind him hissed briefly, like an awakening serpent, and a small door slid open directly behind the desk. Palmer hung his coat and hat inside, pressed the button again and watched the door close.

The hidden compartment had originally contained Burckhardt's small, almost monklike bar, hardly more than two bottles, six glasses and an ice bucket, together with a tape recorder that was supposed to have been connected, illegally, to the telephone. This had almost taken place during a previous battle with the savings banks two years before when, according to Harry Elder, there had been such an iron reign of secrecy on the penthouse floor here and downtown that for several weeks Burckhardt had had secretaries collecting papers from the waste basket at closing time for incineration in the boiler room. That particular skirmish had been won before the recorder was connected to the phone and, evidently, Burckhardt had thought better of the idea in succeeding years.

Which doesn't mean, Palmer reminded himself now, that he won't get just as manic about it again this year.

Palmer sat down at his desk and, before looking at the morning correspondence, glanced about the room. The Braque from the outer corridor made a strong-colored blotch on the wall opposite the desk, a nice focus of attention when talking to someone on the phone. Toward the giant picture window, at the high end of the room, stood a triple statue in bronze to which a black, rather than a green, patina had been applied.

Now seven years old, the statue dated from a time in Chicago when Edith had become enchanted with the idea of having a permanent record of the children. The boys had been seven and two, respectively, and Gerri had been about four. The sculptor, a raddled old lady in space shoes and a dirty white thatch of hair apparently stained brownish in spots by the cigarettes she chain-smoked, had done the children in the nude, which was perfectly all right at that age, or so Edith had felt. Hannah Kurd was the sculptor's name, Palmer remembered now.

Hannah Kurd had been—and still was, for all he knew—of a nameless school that fell somewhere between the smoothly finished representationalism of the old French and Italian masters and the hacked-out, burr-surfaced abstractions of those who worked with an oxyacetylene torch. Hannah Kurd's figures and busts were recognizable enough for what they were—owls, goats, old women and the like—but their surfaces were finished (unfinished?), Palmer recalled as he looked at the statue, with a kind of horrid super-roughness like sharp-faceted gravel.

Looking at his three children now, he found the harsh surface somewhat to his liking, for the first time in seven years. When Hannah Kurd had completed her work, Edith had been fascinated. But within a year the statue had gone up to the attic, to be loaned out for exhibitions now and then. Woody had found it highly offensive as he grew older. Tom, through it all, had always liked it. Although it had a name, *Youth # 3*, Gerri had dubbed it *The Sea Urchins' Ball*, a name she was fond of repeating in a loud tone while standing next to the statue at a showing.

There was something dancelike in the poses, Palmer decided now. Woody towered over his brother and sister, as he continued to do in real life, looking down at them with an expression that sometimes looked grave and sometimes looked horrified, depending on the way the light struck the gravelly face. Tom appeared to be hopping toward his brother, while Gerri, her eyes closed, was bent back slightly with arms stretched over her head, "fielding a high fly against the sun," as she had once explained. Critics who discussed this particular Hannah Kurd in print usually resorted to phrases like "ineffable searching quality" and "timeless innocence."

Four years before, the Art Institute in Chicago had put a great deal of wonderfully suave pressure on Edith to make a permanent donation of the statue. Her feelings about it had changed so much since its commissioning that she had refused to let it out of the house for more than a few months a year, on the basis that she "didn't want people gawking at the children in the nude, now that they were half grown-up."

Last year, in an evidently desperate move, a New York gallery had offered Palmer $10,000 for the group, about three times what it had cost him originally. Palmer understood from something Hannah Kurd had said, however, that the market value of the statue was well in excess of $10,000. It had been sent to Europe in a State Department batch of art, where the Italian and French critics had alternately jeered at and marveled over it. Publicity alone had jacked-up the reputed value to $15,000.

When Palmer had told Edith that he wanted *Youth # 3* for his office, there had been one of their peculiarly submerged arguments, the kind they had been having now for the past few years, quiet, with the sound of reasonableness, if not the intent. The argument—which Edith called a "discussion"—had run on for several weeks until, moving somewhat secretly, Palmer had recalled the statue from San Francisco, where it was on loan, and had it installed in his office.

Everyone had been pleased—Burckhardt, Hannah Kurd, the Museum of Modern Art and especially Mac Burns, who had parlayed it into a whimsical feature story in the *Times* and a picture in *Look*—except Edith. It had not, Palmer reflected now, resulted in any appreciable coolness between them. It was, after all, fairly difficult to chill the atmosphere much further than it had been without solidifying it.

So thinking, Palmer picked up his morning's mail and tasted again the ugliness of his mood on the ride down that morning. Looking at the statue, and thinking about it, was always a heartening thing to him. It was of his children, although only a father could have recognized them, and it was also, in its own way, a compliment to his changed taste, changed for the better, he really believed. It was a sign of growth, a rare one, and contemplating it usually removed everything from his mind but the most positive kind of thoughts. Now they had evaporated.

He glanced at the top letter and found that a business group in Long Island wanted him to speak on the brewing fight between savings and commercial banks. The second letter was a formal invitation to attend a cornerstone-laying at Columbia. To the third was attached a pair of tickets to a newspaper reporters' annual dinner. The tickets were stamped "Dais," which might or might not mean a speech.

So far, his entire morning's mail had been the product of Mac Burns's campaign to make a public personage out of Palmer.

The telephone chime pealed once, in a refined way, and he glanced at the row of buttons, knowing in advance that "Brkhrt" wanted him. He picked up the phone.

"Good morning, Lane."

"Woody, what's the good word?" The older man's voice sounded enthusiastic, as though a good night's sleep on a clear conscience had somehow made him younger than Palmer.

"You sound pretty chipper," Palmer said. "I'm sitting here looking at a flock of public appearances Mac Burns has schemed up for me."

"Anything particularly juicy?"

"Big one out on Long Island. But it's the wrong audience."

"Any audience is a good one out there," Burckhardt demurred. "It's a crucial area, Woody. The savings banks want to get out there more than life itself."

"Then I should be talking to a different audience. He's got me addressing a pack of businessmen. They're on our side already."

Burckhardt chuckled. "They'd damned well better be."

"What I want," Palmer went on, "is a bunch of uncommitted voters, not people who depend on us for business loans and lines of credit and what-have-you."

"Tell it to Burns." There was a pause. "How're you getting along with him?"

"He'd stick his right arm in fire for me. Right up to here. Told me so himself, so it must be true."

"Seeing a lot of him?" Burckhardt asked.

"I've been a little hard to reach the past week. It was getting entirely too pally. I mean, the man's a business associate, not a long-lost blood brother."

"Don't antagonize him, Woody," Burckhardt said quickly. "I don't want him suspecting anything like that. You know how Greeks can be."

"He's Lebanese," Palmer explained. "Left unchecked, this man would crawl into my pocket and set up housekeeping. It's just too much. Lunch, dinner, theater, night clubs. If I didn't say no, I'd never get a night's sleep."

"Did he offer you girls?"

"Times without number."

"And?"

"And what?" Palmer retorted. "Do you really understand this man, Lane? The way his mind works? It's a sort of cross between an advanced course in political science and a lurid chapter of E. Phillips Oppenheim. He wouldn't be above taking secret photos and filing them away for a rainy day."

"Which is why you said no to the girls," Burckhardt added, too smoothly.

Palmer sighed in exasperation. "It's too early in the morning for either of us to be quite that subtle, Lane."

"I withdraw the remark." Burckhardt paused again. "Woody, I don't want to harp on a point, but I want to be absolutely sure of it: he doesn't feel that you're snubbing him or anything like that."

"No. Certainly not."

"Are you perfectly certain?"

"Of course not!" Palmer burst out. "Look, you're asking too much. I'm reasonably certain. I'm morally certain. But how can I be perfectly certain?"

"I understand," Burckhardt assured him quickly. "Have you met with Culhane yet?"

"Not since six last night, when you asked me that question."

"We're quite touchy this morning, Woody."

"Quite." Palmer was silent for a moment. "I'll be frank with you," he said then. "I realize that an operation of Ubco's size is completely departmentalized under executives who are specialists. It has to be. And yet, I'm not unreasonable in assuming, am I, that the job of an executive vice-president should entail something a little more solid than holding hands with Mac Burns and addressing a series of luncheon meetings."

For a while neither of them spoke. The early morning's ugly mood, combined with Burckhardt's insistence on silly questions, had made Palmer rather incautious. Knowing it now, he nevertheless decided as he waited for the older man's reaction that nothing was to be gained by continuing to suffer in silence. The old bird had to be told, one way or another, and telling him in anger was just as good a way as any.

"What're you doing for lunch?" Burckhardt asked abruptly.

"What else?" Palmer retorted. "I'm eating it with Mac Burns. I've canceled the date three times in the past week. Do you want me to break it again?"

"N-no," Burckhardt said thoughtfully.

"Of course not."

"Then I'll tell you what I have to say straight, Woody, no fancy wrapping paper, no kid gloves. Two things. The first you already know, but you give evidence of having temporarily forgotten. I mean the importance of this savings-bank fracas. It's impossible to overestimate how crucial it is to us, impossible. Which means, quite frankly, that everything's riding on you."

"I don't see it that way."

"Apparently not." Palmer heard a dry bite in the other man's voice. "Let me spell it out in rudimentary terms, then. We commercial banks must win this fight or be faced with the kind of competition that can ruin us. In past years, the savings banks have been a threat, but never as strong a one as this year. They've put everything they have into winning this year—men, money, planning—everything. The commercial banks look to Ubco for leadership. Ubco looks to you. There isn't anything you could do for us, there isn't any amount of papers you could sign and move from 'In' to 'Out' that would equal the importance of your present assignment. Damn it, Woody, this is a real job, not a desk assignment!"

"It's not a banking job, that's certain."

"No, it's not," Burckhardt agreed. "Call it anything you want—public relations, politicking, even cloak-and-dagger stuff—but don't forget that you represent a bank, *the* bank, and to do that properly, you have to be a banker."

"That's a little hard to remember," Palmer said, "sitting in a night club with Burns, turning down an offer of some blonde at the bar."

"Which brings me to my second point," Burckhardt went on smoothly. "We have a certain esprit de corps at Ubco. Every successful enterprise does. It isn't as disciplined as the Marine Corps, for example, or as juvenile as a prep school. But it exists. We expect certain things from Ubco people and they expect to be depended upon for those things."

When he paused, Palmer frowned and leaned forward in his chair. The old bird had paused, it seemed to Palmer, out of a sudden inability to get on with his thought, whatever it was. Unable to lead him to it and, in any event, unwilling to help him out, Palmer sat and waited.

"One of those things, Woody," Burckhardt went on after a moment, "is that we expect our people to leave their personal problems at home."

"Yes?" Palmer said, still not clear about the point.

"We understand that a man can't always do that, but we expect him to try. We're rarely disappointed, I might add."

"Yes?" Palmer repeated.

"Damn it, stop yessing me! You know what I'm talking about."

"I do not," Palmer assured him. Then, abruptly: "You mean I'm bringing a personal problem to the office?"

Instead of answering him, Burckhardt seemed suddenly to veer off on a tangent. "You know, in the old days, when the shop was a lot smaller and the stakes were, too, this speech used to go a different way. I could say: 'Bill, it's none of my business, of course, and don't think I'm trying to meddle, but . . .' That sort of thing. Unfortunately, the shop is big and the stakes are even bigger, Woody. I'm not happy putting it this way, but at least I'm being honest."

"About what?" Palmer asked, completely mystified.

"You see, it *is* my business and I *am* trying to meddle. I can't afford not to. In the old days . . . But this is now and your job is absolutely crucial."

"Lane, will you for God's sake say it?"

"Edith." There was a long silence.

"Edith?" Palmer repeated then.

"You and Edith." When silence fell between them again, Palmer could hear the older man sigh heavily. "This is no good, Woody. Not on the phone. Let's meet at the club for drinks. Five-thirty?"

"Oh no you don't," Palmer said. "I'll meet you, right enough, but you're not signing off this way."

"Five-thirty, then."

"Lane, I—" The line went dead.

Palmer jabbed the "Brkhrt" button so violently that his finger bent backward painfully. He continued jabbing at the button, holding the phone to his ear, until Burckhardt's secretary said: "Yes, Mr. Palmer."

"Give me Mr. Burckhardt again."

"I'll see if I can catch him at the elevator."

"You'll—!" Palmer clamped his jaws down tightly to keep from shouting at the girl. "Never mind," he said then, too softly. "Never mind."

He replaced the phone, stood up and walked to the huge window. On his way there, he stopped for a moment and examined the faces of his three children, pitted and indistinct in the merciless flood of pure, shadowless light.

CHAPTER ELEVEN

Palmer left the bank in enough time to arrive twenty minutes late for his luncheon appointment with Mac Burns.

He walked rather briskly along Fifth Avenue, watching the crisp sunlight flutter among the few leaves that still remained on the cathedral's chestnut trees. The day had turned unseasonably warm, somewhere in the low sixties, and he had left both his coat and hat back at the office, immured in their secret hiding place behind his desk. The air felt bracing as he inhaled it. The middle distance over Fifth Avenue seemed to shimmer invigoratingly. Although he knew it was caused by rising monoxide fumes, Palmer took sudden heart at the sight of it. The girls were all pretty today, their walk both interesting to the eye and satisfying to the soul. The shop windows contained fascinating things in bright, inventive displays. Stepping along at a faster than normal rate, Palmer turned west on Fifty-first and began looking for "21." He had almost reached Sixth Avenue before he remembered that it was on Fifty-second Street.

He stopped, taking the mistake he had made as a kind of warning check, the almost imperceptible tightening of the reins that told him he was being foolish about something.

He stood there at the corner of Sixth and watched the passers-by, noting how different the women were from those only a block to the east. He noted, too, that this was the same sun and air he had loathed in the morning. Coldly now, as if checking back through a column of figures that did not prove, he tried to locate what it was that had led him, through the brisk happiness of a moment ago, to the abrupt mistake.

That he was subject to these suddenly manic moods Palmer had long ago understood. They had been one of the chief things his father had tried to eradicate. "Playing the fool," he had told Palmer at regular intervals, "leads to paying the piper."

Palmer resumed his walk at a much slower pace, moving uptown along

Sixth past shoddy windows filled with surplus merchandise and "Fire Sale" signs. Although there was a pat unoriginality about his father that had always grated on him, Palmer had long ago decided that a cliché was the simplest way of stating a truth and thus, for his father, the most natural means of communication.

He paused at the corner of Fifty-second and glanced about him for a moment. An empty store had been converted, temporarily, into a local campaign headquarters for one of the candidates in the coming city election. Palmer peered through the unwashed glass to see a row of desks, empty at the moment, in a room whose walls were covered with the same campaign poster. Forty identical poster faces stared back at him. The face was that of a man in his middle years, his eyes heavy with retouching, an immense, soul-warming smile disclosing teeth of supernal evenness.

POLITICS IS YOUR BUSINESS! the posters admonished Palmer.

Sighing wearily, Palmer began walking east on Fifty-second Street. His mind returned again to the mood of a few minutes before, the almost gay mood in which he had embarked on his walk. It had not been caused, he reflected now, by joy at the prospect of lunch with Mac Burns. That was certain. Nor had it to do with Burckhardt's pep talk of the morning, the crucialness of the job Palmer was doing for Ubco, for commercial banking, for Western Civilization and the entire human race.

It had to do, Palmer realized suddenly, with Burckhardt's saying that thing about Edith.

He stopped walking and stared at the iron-railed façade of "21" across the street, the mounting line of hitching-post boys glowing in warm colors against the shadows of the building. That was what it was, Palmer decided, Burckhardt's thing about Edith.

He started to cross the street, then stepped back to let traffic rush past him. Burckhardt's tone had indicated something, some disapproval, some lecture in the offing, some painful setting-straight, not only of Palmer's marriage to Edith, but to Ubco as well. How to lead two lives with two wives, Palmer mused.

As he stepped off the pavement and started across the street, he realized that his father's cliché could be made to work both ways. You could play the fool and pay the piper. Or, knowing that your date with the piper was all arranged, you could feel entitled to play the fool, having already contracted for your debt of punishment in advance. It was, Palmer saw now, quite an up-to-date concept: sin now, pay later.

He stood for a moment before the down-dropping canopy of "21" and wondered whether the whole thing was a sign of poor mental health. Was it right to need the advance promise of punishment before you could enjoy yourself? For that matter, he asked himself, was it healthy to believe—to know—that one paid for everything enjoyable?

He walked down the short flight of stairs, pushed open the door and entered the darkened room. "Mr. Burns's table," he told the captain.

"Of course, Mr. . . . ?" The man's face looked completely blank, waiting for the key word.

"Palmer."

"This way, Mr. Palmer." The man smiled brilliantly, bowed and took off for the interior with a graceful body movement reminiscent of the entering step in a minuet. He led Palmer into the inner room, past the bar and directly to an empty corner table. "Mr. Burns is away for the moment," he revealed in a conspiratorial undertone, as though leaking a state secret to the press. "He shall return momentarily."

"He shall, shall he?" Palmer asked, sitting down. "Very dry Martini, lemon peel."

He watched the captain leave and wondered whether he had made a life-long enemy by giving him his order for a drink. One never knew about New York captains and maîtres d'. On the one hand, they had a fierce respect for their own rank while, on the other hand, their obsequiousness before a powerful guest was phenomenal. Palmer guessed that Mac Burns's power would keep the proudest toady in line.

The fact that Palmer was sitting at this particular table, he saw now, had made him the target of a few inquiring glances as the captain had seated him. Who was that at Mac Burns's table? What was the meaning of it? Who was doing what to whom?

Burns slid in beside Palmer and put an arm around his shoulder. "Hello, Woody," he said, squeezing Palmer's shoulder in a friendly way. "Sorry to leave you alone here. I had another client to see upstairs."

"I just this instant sat down," Palmer reported, hoping to puncture Burns's little fantasy.

"Wonderful. What'll you drink?"

"I've ordered."

Burns called the captain's name and hissed twice. "I'll have the same."

"Very good, Mr. Burns."

"And the menu."

"Yes, sir."

"And a pack of Gold Flakes."

"Very good, sir."

"And the phone."

"Immediately."

"Now," Burns added. Palmer saw that his luncheon companion suffered from the necessity to have the last word. It was a state of mind, Palmer knew, that led to a lot of meaninglessly protracted conversations.

"At once, Mr. Burns," the captain assured him, thus protecting his franchise on the last word.

"Good," Burns said.

Palmer saw that neither man realized his own predicament. The clash between any two last-word men was always unconscious and baffling in the extreme. Palmer waited for the captain's next move.

"Anything else, sir?"

Bad play, Palmer noted, since it automatically insured a response.

"Nothing, thank you," Burns lobbed back.

"You're welcome, sir," the captain smashed.

It was a kill. The ball thudded hard against the baseline and Burns was left flat-footed, not even able to bring his racket up to meet it. As the captain strutted off, a yellowish look of frustrated malice came into Burns's eyes. When he turned his glance to Palmer, the look took a long time dying.

"That Long Island speaking date," Palmer said, leaping into the silence as hard as he could. "I'm not sure it's the best audience for us out there."

Burns's eyes looked puzzled for a moment. Then: "Why not?"

A waiter arrived with two Martinis, set them down and left.

"They're on our side already," Palmer explained. "What we want is an audience that needs convincing."

"What makes you think the businessmen are in your pocket?"

A different waiter arrived with the menus and placed them on the table with an elaborate flourish.

"Because the commercial banks have put them there," Palmer explained. "They bank with us. Where else can they open a commercial account? They get their loans through us. They're alive because of us."

"But they live in houses mortgaged by savings banks."

A third waiter arrived with a pack of Gold Flake cigarettes. Burns ignored both it and him.

"That cuts no ice," Palmer said. "A mortgage is a long-term contract. It can't be altered at will. The savings banks can't use it as a club over anyone's head."

"If there's any way for them to use it as a club," Burns assured him, "this is the year they'll try it."

A fourth waiter brought the telephone and plugged it into the wall behind Palmer's head. Burns stared gloomily at the instrument. "Do we have to talk business?" he asked then.

"We have a lot of it to discuss."

"Let it ride a few minutes, Woody. Let's enjoy a drink or three. I'm bushed."

"Hard morning?"

"Hard night. Didn't get in till six, grabbed two hours' sleep and kept a breakfast date with Vic."

"I should think," Palmer said, "that you'd want to be fresh as a daisy for Big Vic Culhane."

Burns winced. "Don't call him that, please? I've been trying to lose that nickname for five years now."

"Negative public relations?"

70

"It's a lousy image. Sounds like a big city political boss or something."

"Well, he's big and he's Vic and he's a political boss."

"That's the trouble," Burns said. "He isn't."

"Come, now."

"Nobody is, any more," Burns assured him. "The breed died out during World War II."

"You aren't serious, are you?"

"Of course I am. Who have you got today to match a Tweed, a Hague, a Pendergast, a Croker? They don't make them that way any more."

"Not as blatantly," Palmer agreed. "But they still make them."

"Who? Jake Arvey in Chicago? Can you compare Jake's power to the kind Ed Kelly or Bill Thompson used to have? De Sapio in New York? His party's chopped right down the middle between the Tammany people and the ADA'ers. Which spells disaster for De Sapio."

"Nevertheless," Palmer insisted, "when you want something done, you go to a man like that. He gets it done and he's the only one who can."

Burns shrugged and picked up his Martini. *"L'chiam,"* he said.

"Cheers." They sipped for a moment.

"I guess . . ." Burns paused and sipped again. "I guess it's about time we started your political education, Woody."

"Am I that ignorant?"

"Not as much as the average person, no. But that's not much of a compliment. The average person is an abysmal idiot who thinks politics is the way governments are run."

"And it isn't?"

"It isn't, no." Burns opened his pack of British cigarettes and took one out, staring at it thoughtfully for a moment. "It's a business. It's a way of making a living. It's a way to become somebody important and get paid handsomely for doing it."

"But, along the way, governments do get run, I should hope."

"That's a by-product of politics," Burns said. "The real business of politics is making a living."

"Pretty cynical."

"All right," Burns agreed. "I don't mind being cynical if it helps me see a thing straight." He shot his cuffs before lighting his cigarette, so that the flame of his lighter twinkled among the jeweled links.

"Like any other business," he went on then, blowing smoke into the air before him and patting it away, "the life blood of politics is the contract. Now, in politics, that word doesn't mean exactly what it means in other businesses. A contract . . ." He paused and squinted out into the dimly lighted room. "When I saw Vic for breakfast, I was carrying three contracts. A young guy from my old district up in the Bronx needed a job. That's one contract. A trotting track is opening upstate next month and they want Vic as a dais guest. That's the second. A friend of a friend is opening a store and needs a license fast. That's three."

"None of them sound too difficult."

"They're not. Now, watch this. Vic hands me two contracts in return. He wants to have a new building at one of the Catholic colleges named after his father. That's one. He also wants to know when a certain stock is going to be dumped so he can dump on time, too. That's the second. You follow?"

"Certainly."

"Stick with me. It gets a little tricky. Now, we've mentioned five contracts. Let's take any one of them. Let's say the stock thing. I now have this contract from Vic. I pick up a phone and ask my broker what he knows. He now has a contract from me. But maybe he can't deliver. My problem is I must deliver. So I make a lunch date with a vice-president in the company whose stock we're dealing with. That's the second phase of the same contract. In order to get the straight word from him, I have to offer something. What? I don't have the slightest idea. The lunch is for the sole purpose of finding out. Maybe he wants special plates on his car. Maybe he wants to be an honorary commissioner. Maybe he wants a season pass to one of the tracks. Maybe he needs a big redhead. Maybe he doesn't even know the answer to my first question, the one I haven't even asked yet. So I also call a market editor on one of the papers. He hears things. But to get information from him, I have to shell out information on something else. You follow this? One of Vic's contracts, just one, leads to at least three others."

"Sounds intricate as hell."

"Oh, this is nothing. Take one of the contracts I gave Vic. Let's say, the guy who wants the license."

"That shouldn't be too complicated for Culhane."

"No? Let's look at his alternatives. First of all, how hard should he try? I've told him it's a friend of a friend who needs the license, but I deliberately haven't told him how badly I need the contract. My reason for not telling him is simple. I happen to need it badly because the friend of mine is a client, a big one, and his friend who needs the license is a good-for-nothing cousin of his wife's who's a millstone around his neck. If the cousin gets the license, he's off my client's neck and my client loves me. And his contract with my firm comes up for renewal next month. And he's a fifty-grand client. But if Vic knows how badly I need this license, it'll go down in his book as a major contract. He'll call it due someday by asking a major contract of me. And I'll have to deliver."

"I had no idea you—"

"Woody," Burns interrupted, "I haven't even started yet. This is all wind-up. Vic has to decide how hard he should try for the license, how much he's going to give away to get me what I ask. I'm a close friend, an old friend. We depend on each other. But my guess is he won't try as hard as he could. He'll try, because we're friends, but he won't try as hard as if I'd made it a major contract."

"Then you might not get the license."

"Possible. Not probable, but possible. I have to take that chance. Owing Vic a major contract is more to be avoided, at this point, than disappointing my client and his nitwit cousin."

"Why at this point?"

"I'll get to that later," Burns assured him. "Now. We assume that Vic decides to give it a good try, but not his best. He has the following ways of doing it. One, he calls his man at the board and asks what stage the license is in now. The board guy tells him and Vic signs off, knowing that his man knows that Vic is interested in speeding along this particular application. So the board guy moves it up a little faster, not much, because Vic hasn't definitely given him that contract, but he does what he can. Two, Vic can call one of his State assemblymen or senators and ask him to put the pressure on the board. That way the assemblyman makes the contract with the board guy. He owes Vic his job as assemblyman, so he cancels part of his debt by building a fire under the board. Now, at some future date, nobody knows when, the assemblyman's contract with the board will have to be paid off. God Himself doesn't know what the board guy will ask for. But the assemblyman will either have to fill the contract on his own, or come running to Vic for help. Three, Vic can call one of the big distributing combines. These outfits live by trucking and being able to park in No Parking zones. They need police protection for their warehouses. They're vulnerable as hell without political help. At the same time, they have a great deal of power. They can make or break a store by the way they handle credit and deliveries. The board tries to keep the stores status quo. They don't like bankruptcies. It rocks the boat. They listen to the big distributors. If one of these outfits takes a personal interest in the license application, it moves up fast. Four, Vic can—"

"Hold up," Palmer cut in. "My head's beginning to swim."

"All right. But Vic has at least six ways of helping that license along without giving away too much leverage. If I'd made it a major contract, he'd have one other way, foolproof." Burns swallowed the remainder of his Martini in one gulp. "That's about enough for your first lesson in politics."

"And you discussed five contracts this morning?"

"Five. By the time all of them have been fulfilled, there'll be a good fifteen more made as a result of the first five."

"A geometrical progression. Where does it end?"

"It never ends," Burns said. "Political contracts hop into bed and breed two or three for every one. I must handle ten a day. In a week's time, that's about sixty. Those sixty breed another, let's say, hundred and fifty. And those hundred and fifty breed at least three hundred. And those three hundred . . . And, mind you, I'm just one guy. I'm a key guy," he added abruptly, "but I'm only one."

73

"Fantastic," Palmer said, sipping his Martini. "Under the surface of this town, more things go on than the mind of man can possibly grasp."

"It's a live little village," Burns agreed. "I put in ten years in an even livelier town, Hollywood, but it was nothing to this." He looked up, snapped his fingers and nodded to a passing waiter. "What's good today, Henry?"

"The boiled beef is very good, Mr. Burns."

"All right. With horseradish sauce. Woody?"

"Lentil soup," Palmer said. "And, uh, oh . . ."

"Roast-beef sandwich?" Burns suggested.

"Might not be bad."

"On rye, Henry," Burns told the waiter. "And two more Martinis."

Palmer sat there and watched Burns play with his cuff links, smooth down his yellow hair, stub out his cigarette, glance at his watch and then make a quick survey of the room. Palmer decided that it wasn't important enough to resent, the suggestion of a roast-beef sandwich and the ordering of two more drinks which would have to be consumed after the food had arrived. The important thing with Burns, he told himself now, was not to let anything unimportant he did bother you. If you got thrown by the trivial things about him that were irritating, you would end up hating him. And that would never do.

He was awfully easy to hate. He was everything—in manner, speech, dress, thinking—that Palmer had been trained never to be. He was full of sudden, somewhat suspect confidences. Palmer's father had done a good job in keeping his son from that kind of indiscretion. Burns was over-friendly in a kind of arm-around-the-shoulder, finger-in-the-ribs, hand-on-the-knee manner at which Palmer had finally steeled himself not to wince. Burns's thinking was intuitive, seldom logical. Or, when it gave the appearance of logic, it suffered badly from a thin glaze of cloak-and-dagger paranoia that Palmer found particularly unsuitable. His appearance, while neat enough, was a little too avant-garde. The lapels of his suit were too narrow. His shirts, always white, usually showed an added pattern of white embroidery that Palmer deemed too much. His hair, of course, was too much of a finishing touch.

Burns was generally too much, Palmer decided. Too much of everything. Too much to be true. He was a man overplaying a part. Palmer quite often found himself watching for a sign that Burns, too, was observing himself and the part he played, the sign of a director hidden within the actor. Burns trotted everything out on the stage: power, money, women. Was there anything else? Oh, yes, God. That completed the script.

"Tell me," Palmer heard himself saying then, "do you believe that people pay for the enjoyable things of life?"

Burns turned to face him. His rather large eyes looked warily into Palmer's. "Pay?" he asked. "I don't get you."

"Nothing. Just thinking out loud."

"Tell me."

Palmer made a meaningless gesture with his hand, angry at himself for having spoken so unguardedly. "It's nothing," he said again. "I just wondered about it, that's all. When you enjoy something in life, you usually pay for it later in some rather dire way. Just an observation."

"Forgive me, Woody," Burns said, touching his arm. "You sound like my father, God rest his skinny soul."

"That's funny. I learned it from my father."

"It's a Moslem idea, you know," Burns said then. "Allah is an angry God."

"So is the Calvinist God."

Burns grinned lopsidedly, as though the two of them had just learned something vaguely obscene about each other. "Sounds like the same God, huh?" He laughed quietly for a moment.

"You still haven't answered my question, though."

"I don't know the answer," Burns responded. "I know what it's like in politics, though. For everything you get, you pay. It's all one big horse trade, Woody. You want something? You have to give the other fella what he wants."

Palmer took one of Burns's British cigarettes and lighted it quickly, before Burns could bring out his own lighter. "Which reminds me," Palmer said, inhaling smoke and finding it so mild that it might have been heated air. "Why don't you want to pin Vic Culhane down to any major contract at this time?"

"I'm saving him, pally."

"For what?"

"For you, sweetheart," Burns said. He sighed and pursed his lips in a most unhappy way. "Just for you."

CHAPTER TWELVE

Palmer had walked from "21" to the East River. Sitting now in a tiny park just north of the United Nations, he realized that his feet ached in a vague but noticeable way.

His lunch with Mac Burns—or what had started out as such—had ended rather abruptly with the arrival of a waiter bearing their food. As he set their plates before them, the telephone had begun ringing and Burns had begun cursing, not vehemently, but enough to demonstrate his chagrin at being interrupted at that point. The call had been important enough for Burns to excuse himself "for not more than half an hour."

Palmer had spent twenty-nine minutes eating his food and had then left the club for the six-block walk to the river. The day had continued to grow unseasonably warmer. A high haze partially controlled the sun's intense light. A light breeze ruffled the fast-running river so that its surface resembled alligator leather. As Palmer watched, a tug hurried past, leaving a frothy wake. The breeze touched the hair at his temples and gave him a feeling of ease.

That it was a false feeling did not, for the moment, bother Palmer. He shifted position slowly, almost luxuriously, and turned his attention to a group of tourists busy taking pictures of each other with the lopsided Secretariat building as background.

In the weeks since he had moved to New York, Palmer reflected now, this was the first time he had deliberately done exactly what he had wanted to do. His working life had been made up of other-planned conferences, lunches, dinners, committee meetings, strategy sessions, interviews, speeches, handshaking and always, always, a great seething flood of talk that washed up over him, over his arms and face, until it threatened to choke him.

His non-business life had been limited to morning-plans conferences at breakfast, the theater and a weekend at the Rockland County home of Edith's Aunt Jane. The remainder of his time had been taken up by that kind of activity that cannot be classified as purely business or solely social, a round of cornerstone-layings, parade-reviewing-stand appearances, outings of various associations, a weekend at the Burckhardts, Kiwanis luncheons, Rotary dinners, award presentations and the like.

He had been able, he recalled now, to take Gerri to the ballet one Saturday afternoon and go riding in Central Park with the boys one Sunday morning on some badly trained horses supplied by a West Side stable. He and Edith had also attended a trustees' tea at the Museum of Modern Art during which time he had discussed Model A Fords with one of the Rockefellers and consumed enough sherry to satisfy any inordinate cravings he might have for the stuff during the next six years.

Other free weekend days, Palmer remembered, had been spent at the brownstone, checking on the remodeling and carefully explaining to Edith why changes made after the architect had turned over his plans to the contractor always cost three or four times more than they should.

Not, Palmer told himself now, that he'd wanted to visit the Statue of Liberty or the Fulton Fish Market or the top of the Empire State Building. But just, he decided, that it seemed fitting, somehow, that one strolled about one's new city and looked at its face and found those parts of it that would be good to revisit during the many, many years to come.

". . . would you, huh?" a woman was asking him.

Palmer blinked and looked up, realizing suddenly that the woman had been talking to him for several moments now. "Pardon me?"

"It's simple. You just look through here and press this button."

He stood up, slowly putting the shreds of the situation together. She wanted him to take a picture of her with her husband and little girl. He nodded and took the box camera from her.

"We want the UN Building in, too," the woman said, hurrying to her family and patting her hair into place as she ran.

Palmer sighted through the view-finder, centered the three people, saw that the building was also displayed and started to press the shutter release. "Wait!" the woman called. "Smile," she said, poking her daughter in the back. "Straighten up and smile."

Palmer waited. The little girl looked pretty fed up with everything, he noted. Her father seemed faintly embarrassed, as if asking to be disassociated in Palmer's mind from the abnormal desire of his wife that the three of them be immortalized before this Cyclopean chunk of architecture.

The little girl managed an unhappy smile. Palmer clicked the shutter. "Thanks!" the woman called. Her husband picked up the girl and used her body to shield his face from Palmer as he muttered his thanks. The woman relieved Palmer of the camera and smiled at him with such patent intensity that Palmer felt suddenly guilty at not being able to match the false gratitude of her smile.

"You're welcome," he said, sitting down on the bench again.

He watched the family move off toward First Avenue, the woman veering at a tangent to the left, urgently pointing toward the United Nations Building, while the man jerked his thumb to the right and continued on his way.

Togetherness, Palmer thought.

He watched the three people disappear into a throng of visitors, still arguing about their destination. The little girl had begun to scream something unintelligible, though piercing. The other tourists took them in like an immense paramecium ingesting several stray amoebae. Where there had been three desperate people trying to inflict their own vision of the future upon each other, there now was a single entity with nearly a hundred legs, the women's in fat-rumped slacks or stockings of a much lighter color than New York women usually wore, the men's in the tired crumple of wash-and-wear.

The legs and arms of the throng pointed here, stepped there, vibrating separately, like the cilia of a paramecium and, similarly, working always to pull toward, take in, swallow and digest all the sights, as though desperate to store up enough of New York to last for long wintry years back home.

Palmer's eyes unfocused slightly. He sighed, turned away and refocused on the river, the smoothly swift flow of green-black water, so rich with sewage that the spume left in the tugboat's wake had not yet dissolved back into the water but rode upon it, like the head on a thick, dark glass of heavy stout.

Togetherness, he thought again. The herd instinct that seeks to make something important out of second-rate material by mounding up as much of it as possible.

It was all growing second-rate more rapidly than anyone imagined, Palmer told himself. All of it was being cheapened and weakened and debased simply to sell more of it. Planned obsolescence for soft goods, for durables, for construction, for everything. And the wonderful thing about it, he saw now, was that nobody complained. Nobody even noticed.

All one had to do, he recalled, was to see the way people tuned in their television sets. It was enough to demonstrate the larger truth. None of them bothered to learn what all the knobs were for. The images were that way, that was all there was to it, ghost-ridden, shifting, dull, out of focus, too bright or too dark, whatever way the receiver had last been turned. All those knobs did something, but when you touched them, you generally lost what miserable image you had, so best to leave them as they were. Next year there would be a newer set anyway, or a gaudier antenna, and what was the use of worrying about it?

Or of worrying, too, about the fact that electric shavers didn't really shave one close, nor were they able to trim sideburns. Or that no one remembered the taste of fresh orange juice any more, or fresh-brewed coffee, for that matter. Or that the wide-screen movies were never truly in focus along their immense width. Or that the new automobiles were crippling to sit in and their windshields distorted everything. Or that frozen prepared dinners tasted of cardboard and metal. Or that cigarettes apparently caused lung . . .

Palmer reached in his pocket and took out a pack of cigarettes, grinning as he lighted one and sent the smoke out into the air before him. The light breeze made the smoke vanish almost as soon as he blew it out.

These moods of his, he decided, were going to have to be controlled. He simply couldn't let himself run on this way.

He stood up, ground out the cigarette with the toe of his shoe, and started walking downtown along First Avenue. He had almost two hours before his appointment with Burckhardt, more than enough time to walk almost anywhere in the midtown area of the city and see almost anything he had a mind to see.

Instead, he ducked inside the United Nations Building, found a public phone and called his office.

"We've been trying to reach you, Mr. Palmer," the blonde receptionist said in a voice that hovered between deference and irritation.

Palmer decided as he listened that he would have to hire his own secretary as quickly as possible, some married woman in her fifties to whom he could give the vaguest of messages and know that she would fend for him the way she had been fending for years. "I've been checking some of our branch offices," he told the girl, wondering why he bothered to lie to her.

"Oh, I'm sorry." The tone in her voice made him realize that she was far happier having a legitimate excuse from him. It kept things fixed in their firmament. "Mr. Burns has called five times," she said then, emphasizing the number in an impressed way.

"He, himself?"

"Every time," she said.

"Next time he calls, explain what I'm doing, tell him I'll try to call him en route and let him know that I can be reached at the Union League Club after, say, five or five-fifteen."

"With Mr. Burckhardt," she added. "Will you want your car?"

"No. Anything else?"

"The second and third mail."

"Anything?"

"I haven't opened it, Mr. Palmer."

"Right. Anything else?"

"A Mr. Loomis called."

"Joseph Loomis?"

"His secretary. They'll call back later."

"Give them the club, too. Anything else?"

"A memorandum from Mr. Mergendahl."

Palmer closed his eyes and remembered not to sigh with exasperation. There was no reason for him to be exasperated with the girl. She was doing everything quite well. "Thank you. I won't call again. You can reach me at the club with anything urgent."

Palmer hung up, put another dime in the phone and called his home. After some six rings a female voice answered. "Edith?"

"Hi, Pop."

"Gerri, where's your mother?"

"Over at Cockroach Castle, managing the serfs and esnes."

"Where, doing what?"

"At the brownstone, telling the workmen what to do."

"Oh." Palmer's mind checked back for a moment through the dialogue. "You don't pronounce 'esne' to rhyme with 'lesson,' Gerri. What are they teaching you at Bentley?"

"Nothing interesting."

"They do that even better in public school, and for a lot less money. Maybe you'd like to be transferred."

"You mean it?" Gerri asked. "All those kooky kids with switchblades and hypodermic needles? Crazy! When do I start?"

"Start by taking down this message. Tell your mother I'll be a little late tonight. I'm having a drink with Mr. Burckhardt."

"Only one?"

"Pop?"—Woody's voice cut in on the extension phone—"how do United's deposits compare with Bank of America's?"

Palmer blinked. "Are you planning to take control of one or both?"

"It's for school. I'm doing a theme for econ."

" 'Banks I Have Known,' " Gerri put in.

"I'm not up to the minute," Palmer told his older son, "but Bank of America holds about nine billion five in deposits. We have, oh, eleven. That's deposits, not assets. In assets we're over twelve."

"And Chase?"

"Almost seven."

"And First National City?"

"Just a bit less."

"And you owe me a dime from yesterday," Gerri reminded her brother.

"What about Manufacturers and Chemical?" Woody asked.

"They're both just under three. How come you're borrowing from your sister?"

"And not paying back?" Gerri added.

"I'm broke, is why," Woody explained. "You'd think, wouldn't you, that the eldest son of the second biggest man in the country's biggest bank would get enough allowance to—"

"Woody's getting sneaky in his old age," Gerri interrupted. "When are you coming home?"

"A little late," Palmer told her.

There was a pause at the other end of the line. Then, thoughtfully: "You know," Gerri said, "I have to be in bed by nine. You'll be home before then, won't you?"

"Long before."

"Crazy!" she yelped. "Bye, Pop."

"Pop," Woody said. "Look, I'm not kidding about—"

"See you later," Palmer cut in. "Good-by."

He stepped out of the booth and stood there for a moment, watching the people move past him in great bunches of arms and legs. Somewhere in this United Nations Building, and the one next to it, highly paid people were going through the motions of preserving the peace of the planet. In little offices and large auditoriums, they were acting out their little playlets, plowing slowly through immense drifts of trivia and somehow coming out at the end of each day that much closer to war, but still at peace. Amazing as it was, it was even more amazing to realize, as he stood here, that this great tourist-paramecium had no thought for anything about these buildings but the celebrity faces it might glimpse, the odd souvenirs it might buy and the pictures of itself, taken before the buildings, that would prove the events of this day to the people back home.

Next stop, Grant's Tomb.

By the time Palmer reached the club—at a little before five—his feet hurt in a very definite, no-nonsense way. He sank down in a padded leather sofa and gave the waiter an order for a Scotch, which, when it came, Palmer proceeded to drown in a great deal of soda. He sipped for a long moment, sighed heavily and settled back in the sofa to wait, as patiently as he could, for Burckhardt.

Although he had been a member of the club since before the war, and had had many opportunities to experience the kind of service it was capable of providing, Palmer had only vaguely guessed at the order and scope of hidden organization necessary to provide that quiet, omniscient service. Like most of the members, he took this effortless perfection for granted. He was not surprised, therefore, when, after sitting for less than a minute, an attendant he recognized from the downstairs area near the checkroom now approached him with five slips of paper.

"Mr. Palmer, sir. Your messages."

Palmer thanked him and looked through the slips of paper. Four of them noted calls from Mac Burns, beginning at 4:40 and ending at 4:55, a moment before Palmer had arrived at the club. The remaining message was from Burckhardt. He would be early for their date because he had had to make another appointment for 6:00.

And so it went, Palmer told himself, stuffing the notes in his pocket. The others had taken over. The others were back in the saddle and driving him again.

He got slowly to his feet, feeling his arches ache protestingly, went to one of the mahogany-and-glass-paneled phone booths and called Burns's office.

"Woody? What's the matter, sweetheart?"

"I'm supposed to ask you that," Palmer responded. "What's up?"

"Up?" Burns sounded puzzled.

"You've been trying to get me, haven't you?"

"Oh," Burns said. Then, with an elaborate display of casualness: "Nothing, Woody. I just thought you were pissed off at me or something."

"Why?"

"For having to bust up our lunch date. When I got back you were gone."

"You said half an hour," Palmer reminded him.

"All right. You can buy me a new watch for Christmas."

There was a rather long pause. Palmer realized suddenly that all Burns wanted to do was shift the blame for a wasted lunch. Feeling guilty about having left him, Burns needed, first, to gauge the degree of Palmer's hurt feelings and, second, to try to make Palmer take responsibility for everything.

"I'm sorry you were called away," Palmer said then. "I understand it perfectly. No hard feelings."

There was another pause. Palmer guessed that Burns would now try to bury the whole thing and let it be forgotten. "It's just too bad," Burns said then. "I mean, I had a couple of fairly important things to take up with you. Now I don't know when the hell we can get together."

"Yes, it is too bad," Palmer agreed. Having guessed wrongly, he saw now that Burns was under some kind of compulsion to shift blame, one of the many little ways he tortured himself. "Don't worry about it, Mac," Palmer added, twisting the knife slightly. "I'm not angry."

For the third time, Burns paused and tried to regroup his forces. Now was the time, Palmer felt, for him to drop the thing quickly. It depended on how strong Burns's blame-shifting compulsion was. "I don't know, sweetheart," Burns said then. "This is a pretty serious thing we're in together. When the heat's on we're going to be going twenty-five hours a day. I just hope we can pull together like a real team."

"Mac," Palmer said, determined not to let the man wiggle off the private hook of his own needs, "today was unavoidable for you. I know that. I also know that when the chips are down, you'll pull your load"—he paused, seeking to scramble the metaphor beyond all comprehension—"like a real trouper," he finished happily.

"All right," Burns pounced. "I have a dinner appointment tonight. Let's meet about eleven-thirty at my place."

"Tonight?"

"Tonight," Burns repeated, "or else not for maybe a week. I'm all jammed up."

"I don't know," Palmer said. "I'll have to call you later. Where can you be reached?"

"When?"

"About eight or nine."

"Chambord."

"I'll let you know," Palmer promised. "So long." He hung up without waiting for a reply, angry at Burns and himself and the silly little games he was being forced to play.

Sitting down on the sofa again, Palmer poured the rest of the soda into his glass and sipped it thoughtfully. The whole trouble, since the beginning, he saw now, had been the problem of authority. Burckhardt had granted him the authority of a second-in-command, without giving him the scope in which to exercise that authority. Apparently it showed enough to tempt Burns into determining which of them would lead the other. It was the kind of game Palmer had seen played by other men all his life, co-equals who simply could not let their equality alone but, like any normal human being, had to test it again and again. Is Smith really on my level? Am I above Jones or below him? Let's find out.

It was a game that Palmer had never before had to play. That was one of the benefits of inheriting one's father's business. But it only looked like a benefit, Palmer decided now. It was like the antiseptic children of the well-to-do, shielded from the bacteria of the street, who became susceptible to almost any disease because, unlike the dirty children of the poor who used the gutters as a nursery, they had never built up an immunity to the more vulgar varieties of germ life.

Palmer sipped his drink, now largely soda, and wondered what it would have been like to build a career solely on one's own abilities. He had never been schooled in the smiling infighting that built a career that way. His little game with Burns was, after all, only a petty clash of wills with nothing more at stake than the protection of an ego. What if a lot more were at stake? What if Burckhardt's obsessive fears were true? What if this savings-bank thing were even one tenth as important as everyone tried to make it?

Palmer sat stock still for a moment, glass halfway to his lips, and remembered that Joe Loomis, Burckhardt's personal nemesis, had called him earlier in the day. Should he mention the call to Burckhardt?

Odd, he thought. Loomis didn't know him at all. He'd probably known Palmer's father, casually, perhaps. His reason for calling Palmer now, his real reason, would have something to do with the savings-bank fight. Peace feeler? Warning? Bribe?

"Woody!" Burckhardt boomed.

Palmer blinked and looked up as the older man sat beside him. "Glad you got my message," Burckhardt went on. "I'm going to have to run along pretty quickly. What the hell're you drinking? Water?"

"Mostly."

"Scotch old-fashioned," Burckhardt told the waiter. "No fruit salad." He turned and banged Palmer's knee. "How was your lunch with Burns?"

Palmer laughed. "Abortive. He had to leave for half an hour when the food came. I ate and left."

"Just like that?" Burckhardt's milky-blue eyes seemed to switch back and forth across Palmer's face, as if raking him with bursts of fire.

"I gave him his half-hour."

"Was he—?"

"Properly contrite?" Palmer cut in. "Guilty, anyway."

"I didn't mean that. I wanted to know if his feelings were hurt. You know how these Greeks are."

Palmer sighed heavily, trying to release some of the sudden anger he felt. "Lebanese. Now, look," he began slowly, keeping his voice down almost to the edge of inaudibility. "That man has the skin of a Sherman tank. When he wants to play sensitive, he can pretend to die on the vine like a morning-glory, but it's all play-acting. Either you let me handle him my way, or you're wasting an awful lot of Ubco's money keeping me in that showroom office of mine. Of yours, I should say."

"I have complete confi—"

"Then try to show it," Palmer interrupted rudely. He paused and shrugged. "I'm sorry. I'm beginning to sound persecuted. Burns has that effect on me."

Burckhardt said nothing for a moment. The silence grew more prolonged with the arrival of the waiter and a drink. Stirring it slowly, Burckhardt remained silent for the purpose, Palmer decided, of milking a more definite apology out of him. Palmer matched silence for silence and waited.

Sipping his drink, Burckhardt turned and asked, "Where were you this afternoon?" When Palmer failed to answer at once, the older man continued quickly, "I'm not checking up just to crack a whip. I really want to know."

"Walking. Sitting on park benches. Killing an afternoon."

Burckhardt grunted and, taking another sip, pulled his chin into his neck, as if he were about to engage in hand-to-hand combat. "You see," he said then, "I haven't opened up this subject a moment too soon."

"What subject are you opening?"

"You and Edith," Burckhardt snapped. His chin dug into his neck. Palmer watched to see if he would hunch up a shoulder and duck his chin behind it in approved boxing stance. "Not a moment too soon," he repeated almost solemnly.

"This is the business over the phone this morning," Palmer said. "This business that wouldn't have been your business in the old days but now everything's changed and it is your business."

"Exactly," Burckhardt agreed, parrying the sarcasm by accepting it as fact.

"Could you tell me what's wrong between Edith and me?"

"Of course not."

"Can anybody?" Palmer asked.

"Only you. Or Edith. And," Burckhardt hurried on, "I'm certainly not about to ask her."

Palmer felt his anger begin to dissolve. There had been something so strait-laced, so antiquated, about Burckhardt's assurance that this was man-to-man stuff that, instead of detesting him for broaching the subject, Palmer abruptly felt sorry for him. The old bird was bothered and unhappy. He had created such an aura of importance around the work he had assigned to Palmer that anything threatening the success of the work had to be examined with the kind of breathless intensity usually reserved for the electrocardiogram, the Dow-Jones ticker or the entrails of an oracular chicken. It was somewhat saddening, in a way, and more than somewhat laughable.

"What does it look like from the outside?" Palmer asked in a more friendly tone. "Pretty bad?"

Burckhardt settled back in the sofa and looked down at his drink. The wrinkled lids of his eyes became smooth as he hid his glance beneath them. "No, nothing like that," he said, addressing himself to his glass. "I realize this must be a particularly sore subject with you, Woody. I knew your dad fairly well, as well as you can know anyone who lives in a different city, and I knew your mother, too, although not as well, of course. I lost touch with her, naturally enough, after the divorce. But . . ." He let the rest of his words die away, having got across his message in an indirect, but definite, way.

Palmer finished the last of his soda and signaled to the waiter, to give himself time to think. Of course, he told himself during the oddly tense little silence that fell between them, of course the old bird's mind would work that way. It was a perfectly obvious way for him to view the matter. Son of a broken home. Trouble in the son's marriage. Simple as a tabloid headline.

"You see," Palmer said after the waiter had brought his second drink, "that really has very little to do with it."

He sat there, wondering what to say after he had said that.

84

Chapter Thirteen

The taproom of the Club had fairly well emptied out except for four men at the bar and a sprinkling of solitary drinkers at widely scattered tables. The remainder of the men had gone home, Palmer decided, or on to another meeting, like Burckhardt, or to one of those peculiarly New York social-business events in which friendship and money wrap their legs around each other and whelp a new race of beings, half human, half dollar.

He made a sour face, unhappy at the way his mind had been working in the last half-hour since Burckhardt had left him. The interview, or heart-to-heart, or whatever it was supposed to have been, had fizzled. Poor Burckhardt. Poor Edith. Poor Ubco.

Palmer sighed and finished his drink, trying to remember whether it had been his second or third or fourth. He got to his feet, looked about the room and suddenly sat down, appalled at what lay ahead of him. He had his choice, of course. None of what was happening to him—none of what had happened over the years—was imposed from on high by a malign being. In all of it choice remained. Take tonight. He had his choice of going home to Edith and, chances were, out with Edith to dinner, an opening, a gathering or something of that nature. Or he had the option of meeting Burns.

That, Palmer told himself now, is Hobson's Choice. What did either alternative have to recommend itself?

He signaled the waiter for another drink (third? fourth?) and began working his way back over the conversation with Burckhardt, wondering whether he had satisfied the old bird that his executive veep was not about to undergo divorce or separation or any other domestic discomfiture that would affect his work at the Shop. He tried to evaluate Burckhardt's somewhat hesitant probing and his own too casual responses, testing the whole thing for the ring of truth.

Had he convinced Burckhardt? Probably not. But had he at the very least calmed his fears? Probably.

The waiter brought his drink and Palmer sipped it slowly, returning to the immediate problem, the choice before him, the alternatives that had nothing to recommend themselves. Which was not unusual, he decided, staring into his drink, merely uncomfortable. Hung juries were an everyday affair. Except that, in his case, he had to decide on something. He got up and carried his drink to the nearest telephone.

As he gave the switchboard his home number, Palmer understood, with the peculiarly heightened clarity that generally possessed him after a certain number of drinks, exactly what he was doing. There came a precious time in his drinking—it usually fell somewhere between the second and fourth drink— a golden moment of perfect objectivity when he could almost literally feel himself lift up, out and away from his regular body so that he could stand to one side and observe with greater accuracy. Aside, he thought now as he waited for the operator to dial his number, and slightly above.

In this wonderful time, he was able to analyze his most cryptic action and the most obscure events. Now, for example. Now, by calling home, he was giving a performance of a man making a decision. Two choices: decisive man; decision coming up.

Not so. Fraud.

He could hear the phone ringing in his apartment. The Palmer who had assumed the watch position apart, above and slightly to one side of the Palmer holding the phone in his hand could read the inner reality of the call being made. He was passing the buck. He was about, Palmer told himself now, to chuck the whole thing into Edith's lap. She would not realize it, of course. But it would be she, and she alone, who would make the choice.

"Hello?"

"Gerri, put your mother on the phone."

"This is her mother. What's the matter, darling?"

"Oh, Edith." Palmer paused and moistened the corner of his mouth. "I'm at the Club."

"I know. With Lane."

"How did y—? Oh, yes. Well."

"And it's dragging on?"

"It's worse than that," Palmer said, shifting the subject slightly to avoid an outright lie. "I'm supposed to meet with Mac Burns tonight, later."

"How much later?"

Palmer shrugged. "I'm not sure," he said, again avoiding a full lie, although by no means even hinting at the truth. "Do we have something on?"

"Not a thing," Edith said somewhat too cheerily.

"Really?"

"I'd planned to let the children eat early so that we could eat much later, alone."

Palmer frowned at the wall in front of him. "No party? No opening? No reception?"

"No." The monosyllable sounded abrupt. Palmer realized with the golden clarity he enjoyed at the moment that he had insulted Edith.

"God, I'm sorry," he groaned. "The one night we had to ourselves. The first in weeks. And I'm about to ruin it."

"I'm sorry, too, darling," Edith assured him. Her voice had warmed up. "But we'll do it some other night. I think," she went on in her busy-planning tone that made Palmer wonder whether his presence at home would have altered any of her evening's routine, "I'll take a long hot bath and go to bed very early."

"Might as well," Palmer said. "I'm not sure when I'll be in."

"Have a good time, darling."

"Thanks. Don't wait up, now."

"I won't," Edith assured him. "Good night."

The line went dead and Palmer hung up the phone. It was not until he had picked up his drink and started back to the sofa that he remembered how much he had wanted to say good night to the children.

He sat down and placed his glass very carefully in the center of the low magazine table before him. The Palmer that watched him now wondered just how much he had wanted to say good night to the children. Enough, for example, to go back to the phone and make the call again?

The moment of crystalline insight suddenly shattered. Palmer grunted inarticulately, a sound somewhat akin to clearing his throat but more violent, strong enough, in fact, to dispel the sharp-eyed Palmer who had been watching him. There was no point, the entire Palmer now told himself, in getting so damned discerning about oneself that one began prying up stones best left unturned.

At any rate, one thing had been accomplished. Edith had decided his evening for him. She had done it, all unwittingly, by the simple act of not making a fuss. By realizing the importance of Mac Burns to the family's well-being. By allowing her husband to preserve that very sacred division between Home and Shop that Burckhardt had plumped for. By being, in short, an understanding wife.

Struck by the irony of it all, Palmer got to his feet, rather ostentatiously ignoring the nearly full glass on the table before him. He walked slowly to the elevator, wondering how he would spend the hours between six-thirty and whenever he met Burns, wondering why he had allowed himself not to spend them at home.

He could stay here, he thought, have some dinner, read a few magazines or even take a short nap, and then go to meet Burns. The elevator door opened and Palmer got in the car.

"Down, Mr. Palmer?"

"Down," he agreed.

Although it was still quite light outside, the air had turned rather cool. Palmer walked up Park Avenue for a few blocks, watching the traffic snarl itself in tight, honking knots at Fortieth Street, where the tunnel led up to the ramp that ran around Grand Central Terminal. When he reached Forty-second, he walked west to Fifth Avenue and stood looking at the façade of the library, wondering whether it might be nice to sit on a bench in Bryant

Park and watch the night overtake the city. Deciding that it was too cool for that, Palmer began walking uptown, aware that he was drawing closer to the bank. He had never been the kind of man who returned to his office in the evening except under the most extreme kind of provocation, nor had he ever worked late at his desk.

People did, of course, and increasingly so, Palmer reflected as he strolled north along the Avenue. Some of them did it to impress the people above them. Some simply to get through a temporarily unwieldy workload that could not be processed in the normal day. Some because they hadn't the intelligence to do their work in the regular time allotted them and had to make up for lack of quality by heaping up quantity. And some, Palmer recalled, stayed late because they had nowhere better to go at the end of the day.

He paused before the great glass wall of the bank and peered inside. The ceiling, a glareless sea of light, poured down on an emptiness of lobby. Somewhere inside that building, Palmer thought, was the place where he went through the motions of being a banker. But it had been several months since he'd done any of the work of a banker.

He decided to go up to his office and take a look at the statue of his children, telling himself that it was one way he could get to see them when all others failed. It was a form of atonement for not going home or talking to them on the phone, he supposed as he let himself in the side door, and it was an amazingly inexpensive way of allaying his guilt.

He let the outer door lock itself behind him. He stood for a moment in the glass cubicle between the street entrance and the inner night safety door, to which no one had a key. Palmer began to grow impatient, wondering whether the electrical system had failed to alert the nightman to the fact that someone had opened the outer door. But then, Palmer told himself chidingly, I have no reason for being in a hurry.

The nightman's face peeped out at him from behind a chin-high cabinet, observed him warily for a moment before emerging into the open. Buttoning up the flap on his side holster, the man produced a broad, welcoming grin as he opened the safety door from inside.

"Working half a day, eh, Mr. Palmer, sir?" he asked.

"Half a day here and half a day there," Palmer mumbled, trying to match his joking tone. He gestured at the semi-human elevator button and its doors opened immediately. Getting inside, he touched the "PH" button.

". . . still," the nightman called.

"What?" Palmer asked. The door slid shut on the nightman's reply. Instead, the mechanical voice of the elevator let Palmer know where he was going. He got off at the penthouse floor and stood for a moment, admiring the look of the late evening sunlight and the darkening sky through the glazed ceiling. Then, walking along the corridor, he entered his room and switched on the lights. A hidden trough that circled the perimeter of the ceiling bathed him in the shadowless synthetic warmth of pale-pink and white fluorescent bulbs.

He walked to the statue and saw that, in this almost sourceless light, all character had been sponged out of the faces and figures. They looked pretty much to him like pitted metal chunks and husks, an illustration in some welding shop's brochure, perhaps the "Before" photo. "Don't Let Shoddy Workmanship Botch YOUR Next Welding Job. Let Acne Welders Produce Results. Established 1931."

He pressed the button on his desk which opened the wall compartment behind his chair. Back in a far corner stood a half-full bottle of Old Fitzgerald. Palmer watched it for a long moment and then heard a woman giggle.

He whirled. No one stood at the door of his immense office, watching him with high amusement. But a woman had giggled.

He walked to the door and stood in the threshold, listening to voices from an office at the opposite corner of the penthouse. Moving silently on the carpeted floor, he made his way to the door of the Public Relations Department and peered in.

The lights—no one had bothered to conceal them in troughs or recesses—flared a bluish-white that made Palmer squint for a moment. The room was exactly as large as his office, except that eight people worked in it. One end contained an empty office that pre-empted a third of the space and all the windows. In it the vice-president in charge of public relations and advertising was supposed to work. There was no such person; Burckhardt deemed it unnecessary in view of Palmer's experience. Miss Clary, who had no rank at all, served as acting supervisor of the department, with two other professionals, two secretaries, a multilith boy who also handled mailings, and a messenger.

Virginia Clary was sitting there now on the edge of a desk, giggling at something one of her girls—a Miss Rawlins or Frawley or Hawkins—had said. Apparently neither one of them had heard the elevator bring Palmer up to the penthouse.

"That's almost what happened to me," Miss Clary was saying. "Except that it wasn't Scotch, it was one of those horrid blends."

She stood up and smoothed her black wool skirt down over her hips. Then, bending over the other woman's typewriter, she said, "You're going to be late if you don't leave soon."

Palmer stood just beyond the edge of the door and watched the two women. He could see only the back of the girl's head, but he could see all of Virginia Clary, not that there was much. She was slight in stature, her face narrow and rather nicely modeled, considering that there was very little flesh on it. Because her face was so thin, Palmer decided now, her eyes looked much larger than they probably were, great dark eyes in great deep sockets under rather heavy black brows and a mop of short black curls that gave the impression of having just been combed by a high wind.

She knew every reporter and editor on the banking and business desks of every newspaper and magazine in town. This made it necessary to pay her $11,000 a year, but did not, and never would, give her any title higher than assistant secretary. At the moment, of course, she hadn't even that. It would take her years to achieve it, probably . . . unless she changed sex.

". . . right," she was saying. "You read it to me and I'll check the master copy. Then you can go."

"'From,'" the other girl began reading, "'the United Bank and Trust Company, New York City. Contact: Virginia Clary, Extension 4108. For Release Wednesday, October 7, A.M.'"

"No," Virginia Clary cut in. "We'll take out the 'A.M.' No need to get fancy on a routine story. Give me the headline."

"'Savings Banks Promote Creeping Socialism, Palmer Tells Long Island Leaders.'"

"Go on."

"'So-called mutual savings banks,'" the girl read from the paper multilith plate, "'are promoting a form of creeping socialism at the expense of private initiative, was the charge leveled last night by Woods Palmer, Jr., executive vice-president of United Bank and Trust Company, before a capacity audience of nearly a thousand business leaders in the Nassau-Suffolk area.

"'Sounding a warning that the savings banks, with their "protected and preferential tax coddling," were undermining the entire financial structure of New York State, Palmer termed their continued expansion a "major threat to economic prosperity and an open invitation to nationalize the banking system of the country" as a first step down the road to socialism.

"'He reminded Long Island businessmen that the entire growth of the United States had been founded on the kind of private initiative which had made their own business success possible. "But the savings banks," he pointed out, "are owned by no one. There are no stockholders. No private capital is being risked. Instead, a self-perpetuating clique has free rein to expand across the face of the land like some bloated fungus, gobbling up all new money within reach and channeling it into such a limited sphere of activity that every kind of business suffers."

"'Palmer termed recent rumors that the savings banks would once again ask Albany for increased branch privileges "the kind of maneuver we must expect from a faceless, ownerless entity that, like a cancer, lives only to grow." Text of speech follows.'"

Virginia Clary was silent for a moment. "I don't know," she said then. "What's an easier word for 'entity'? Uh . . . 'being'? Something not as fancy. 'Individual'? Uh . . . 'faceless, ownerless monster.' Right. Perfect."

"'Monster' and 'cancer' in the same graph?" the girl asked.

"Why not?"

"I don't know," the girl said, making the change on the plate. "It's pretty rough."

"You're right," Virginia Clary agreed. "There are millions of savings-bank depositors who'll get angry if . . ." She paused and thought for a moment. "What's bad about that?" she asked then. "They get angry. Then what? Who do they get angry at? Palmer? Who's Palmer to them? They get angry at the thing they're connected with, their own savings bank. They ask nasty questions next time they make a deposit or a withdrawal. It figures."

"You're talking to yourself," the girl said as she got up and stretched. "It's all words to me."

"Um." Virginia Clary ran her fingers through her dark curls. "It isn't easy getting anybody excited about a fight between different kinds of banks. It's a big yawn to most people. They can't even tell the difference between one kind of bank and another. But they've heard of socialism. They don't know what it is, but it's like monsters and cancer. Bad."

The girl laughed and picked up her handbag. "I'd hate to have you mad at me, doll. You're a dirty fighter."

She started for the door. Palmer realized that he had no time to retreat out of sight along the corridor. He took a breath and walked in the door. "Working a half-day, eh?" he asked, smiling.

The girl (Frawley, Rawlins?) let loose a shrill yip and clutched her breast. Then, recognizing him, she sighed heavily. "Don't ever *do* that, Mr. Palmer," she pleaded, trying to smile. "Good night." She left for the elevator.

Palmer watched Virginia Clary, who hadn't moved an inch during his entrance. She looked up at him, and, before either of them could speak, the clearly audible whisper of the elevator doors opening and closing set a kind of full stop to what had gone before.

She moistened her lips and Palmer saw that they were fuller than he remembered. "We don't often see you here on the late, late show," she said then.

"I like to tiptoe noiselessly along corridors spying on the help," Palmer said.

"For a moment there," she said, "I thought you were a savings-bank spy. I was about to crush a cyanide tablet under my tongue."

"Good show."

"Then I saw you weren't wearing a long, dirty beard, and I knew you must be one of ours."

"I haven't checked lately," Palmer said. "I suppose I still am." He picked up the paper multilith plate she had been holding. "Pretty brilliant speech I made next week." He put the stencil down and looked at her. At close range, he saw that she had drawn a thin line of blue-green above her eyelids and slight upturning flecks of black at the outer corners of her eyes. He had never been this close to her before. In the vast immensities of his office, one never got within yards of anyone else.

"Are you writing it?" he asked then. "I understood Mac Burns was in charge of that work."

"I do the first drafts," she said.

"Odd he's never mentioned it." Palmer grinned then. "I suppose between the two of you there isn't enough knowledge of banking to fit on the head of a pin."

"Well, as Michelangelo or somebody once put it, 'I don't have to be a cat in order to draw one.'"

"Doesn't sound like Michelangelo." He sat down on the edge of the desk and looked at a bulletin board on which press clippings were pinned. "What if we were in a different kind of business? What if we made serums, antibiotics, that sort of thing? And here you were, you and Burns, working on the Michelangelo principle and making small errors in fact and judgment and treatment. Only this time someone could get hurt."

She was silent for a long moment. Palmer saw that, far from being unkempt, her hair was actually a carefully arranged sequence of curls and wisps. "Well," she said at last, "isn't it lucky we're not druggists."

"You know," Palmer replied, "I get the strong feeling that you don't set much store by banking."

"The romance-of-the-counting-house sort of thing?" she asked. "But we can't afford to kid ourselves. Banking is just moneylending. No matter what form the loan takes—mortgage, commercial credit, factoring, bond buying, you name it—it's all moneylending. And the big secret of moneylending is that you have it to lend out, you charge as much as you can and you make sure you get paid back."

"Right." Palmer got to his feet and walked to the bulletin board. He pretended to examine the clippings there for a moment, but their headlines were an unfocused blur. "Right," he said again. "But moneylending isn't 'just' moneylending."

"I imagine that a profession this old has quite a mystique built up around it."

"You're baiting me."

"A little," she admitted, glancing at her watch.

"I'm sorry," Palmer said quickly. "I've been keeping you here."

"Nothing of the kind."

"You looked at your watch."

"Sheer nervousness," she said. "You make me nervous. That's why I was baiting you. Also, I have to run this thing off."

"Doesn't What'shisname do that? Freddie?"

"This has to be in the mail tonight. I've always assumed that you pay me three times Freddie's salary because in a pinch I'm expected to do three times the work he does."

He lifted his hands and then let them drop to his sides. "Your understanding of the executive function," he said then, smiling to make certain she was not offended, "is only matched by your vast knowledge of banking."

"If you'll leave me alone with a revolver, I'll do the decent thing."

He made a face. "No profit in it. We moneylenders like to squeeze our little profit out of everything."

"Truce."

"I'm seeing Burns later tonight," Palmer said. "As a matter of fact, I'm just killing time before I see him. I think I'll ask him what he plans to have me say out in Long Island."

"Are you trying to play us off against each other?" she asked. "It can't work. I'm too small and he's too big. Besides, that socialism line was his idea in the first place."

"It's exactly the kind of idea that someone with a basic contempt for banking, or a basic ignorance of it, would invent."

She tilted her head sideways on her rather long neck and watched him closely with her terribly large eyes. "You're really angry," she said then. "You're being very polite and matey, but you're angry as hell."

He shook his head from side to side. "Not at all. No harm's been done. You haven't even gone through the trouble of running off that release, which I would have had to kill tomorrow morning when I saw it."

"Oh," she said. "It penetrates my skull. New release. I get it." She sat down at the other woman's desk and rolled a piece of paper in the typewriter. "Shoot."

"I'm not writing your releases. You've got the three of us confused."

"Three?"

"Yes, I'm Palmer. I don't write releases. You do. You're Virginia. You don't run the multilith. Freddie does. After you learn that, you'll know why they pay me my salary, why they pay you yours and why Freddie is making seventy a week."

She stared at him for a long moment and then burst out laughing. Getting up, she went to her desk and rummaged around on top of it for a pack of cigarettes. She held them out to him. "Um?"

"Thanks, no." He took one of his own and lighted both.

"All right," she said after a moment. "I know all about the executive function. Now tell me all about banking."

"It's moneylending. I thought you knew."

"Just moneylending?"

"Not just. That's where you go off," he objected. "It's like saying we breathe just air or eat just food. Money is a necessity of life. Modern man can no more live without money than he can without air or food or water."

"It's that way, is it? I'm impressed."

"But not convinced."

"No, I'm impressed by you being convinced," she said.

"Well, that's a start."

He looked for an ash tray and finally found one among the papers on her desk, beside a silver triptych of photographs that stood by itself to one side near the telephones. The pictures were somewhat old-fashioned in appearance, sepia-toned and vignetted to a hazy white around their edges. One showed a thin-faced woman in her sixties whose eyes were, if anything, even larger than Virginia Clary's. The second was of a young man in his early twenties, wearing the uniform of a World War II Army Air Force navigator.

The third photograph showed a child so young it could have been either a boy or a girl. It was a pretty child, in either case, with a narrow face and large eyes.

"Mother?" he asked.

"Right."

"Uh . . . brother?"

"Husband." She paused for a moment. "And daughter." She paused again. "Only my mother's still alive."

He straightened up, holding the glass ash tray in his hand, and offered it to her. She tapped some ash into it. "It happened during the war," she said.

"We were driving from Lubbock, Texas, to Tonapah, Utah," she said in a thin voice without any quality to it. "A staging area, shipping out to the Pacific. A truck hit us. I know," she went on quickly. "I keep promising myself to put the pictures away in a bureau drawer at home. I know all about that." She took the ash tray from him and walked toward the center of the big room. "Tell me all about banking. Sort of standing on one foot, as it were."

Palmer looked at his cigarette. "I wish I could." He watched her for a long moment, seeing her at this distance the way he usually saw her, small, attractive-looking without being beautiful, a pleasant cog in the intricate mesh of the Ubco machine. It was wrong to hold up a magnifying glass to any part of the machine. You saw too much too quickly and nothing had the same bland pleasantness again.

She was glancing at her watch once more. "Seven-thirty," she announced. "I don't know when your date with Mac Burns is, but you probably have time to eat dinner with me."

His father had dinned it into Palmer's head: more trouble came of talking than of remaining silent. He had talked and now he was in trouble.

"Or some other time," she said then, letting him well off the hook. "I've been ignorant this long. My enlightenment can keep for a while."

He shook his head. "I'm sorry," he said, "but there isn't a moment to lose."

CHAPTER FOURTEEN

After the first dinner he had ever eaten at Schrafft's, Palmer sat back and sighed, not so much in appreciation of the meal, but in silent recognition of the fact that millions of people regularly ate such meals and, apparently, came back for more. He had agreed to Schrafft's, on Virginia Clary's suggestion, in simple accord with the unspoken fact that it would be impossible for him to run into anyone he knew there. At the time, her choice had seemed an admirable compromise between the need to be fed and the need to minimize, without any outright intrigue, the fact that they were eating together.

"That look on your face," she said after the waitress had cleared away their dishes. "After all, I warned you you'd be better off with the Tom turkey."

"With pineapple-and-chestnut dressing?" Palmer asked in a semi-stricken voice. "My father warned me never to eat turkey before Thanksgiving or after Christmas. Unfortunately, he had nothing to say on the subject of chicken loaf."

She smiled and sipped her water. Palmer noticed that in the somewhat subdued lighting of Schrafft's, with its faintly rosy tint, the deep shadows in which her eyes were set seemed less stark, more becoming. Although she could not be considered beautiful, he told himself now, she was certainly attractive enough, in a small, intense way.

"That's the third time," she said then, "that you've quoted your father."

"He turned out a tremendous number of quotations in his time. Should I apologize?"

"I think it's old-fashioned and charming," she said. "People who haven't yet learned to hate their parents are quite rare in New York."

"You even have your mother's picture on your desk."

"She lives with me. Or vice versa. I'm never sure. Not," she went on hurriedly, "that we're devoted to each other or anything like that. I wouldn't want to seem un-chic."

"Of course."

"We keep a kind of armed truce. She's never really forgiven me for going to work at a bank."

"Bad as all that?" he asked.

"A bank foreclosed our house in Hollis in 19—oh—31."

"Your mother can't forgive that?"

"Neither would you if the house meant to you what it did to my folks. We'd lived most of our lives in the upper Yorkville section, the part they call Spanish Harlem now. When my father managed to make the downpayment on that bungalow in Hollis . . . I tell you, it was Hallelujah Day. And then, after only three years, to . . ." Her voice died away. "But then," she went on more strongly, "we had a lot of company in 1931. All our neighbors were foreclosed, too."

"It was quite a year."

"What happened to you in 1931?" she asked.

Palmer shrugged. "Nothing much. I think it was my freshman year at college. Well insulated from the outside world, to say the least."

"Class of '34?"

"Yes. Another great year."

"I was class of '34 at Barnard," she said.

Palmer's eyebrows went up slightly, then came slowly down. He wondered whether she had seen the movement, decided that she undoubtedly had and then, suddenly, wondered why he had bothered to try concealing it. "I'd never believe it," he said then. "You don't look old enough."

"I'm a few years younger than you, at any rate," she said. "I was ahead of my class at Holy Name. Graduated when I was fourteen with a scholarship to Marymount, but we couldn't afford me living out of town. My mother wouldn't hear of me at a co-ed school like C.C.N.Y. I was just about to matriculate at Hunter when this Barnard thing came through, thanks to Paddy Culhane."

Palmer sat forward slightly. "Why is that name familiar?"

"He was our old district captain in East Harlem."

"Any relation to Big Vic Culhane?"

She looked at him in vague amazement. "His father."

"Did you know Big Vic?"

"Of course," she said. "He went to the boys' part of Holy Name."

"Ever seen him since?"

She frowned. "Many times. I used to be a newspaper gal, you know. Is something wrong?"

Palmer shook his head. "Not at all. Quite the contrary, if anything."

She watched him for a moment, then sat back and folded her hands in her lap. "Anyway," she said then, "that's all there is to the history of Virginia Clary. Except that I'm working on my mother every spare moment I get, trying to wean her from this unreasoning hatred of banks."

"You could have lied to her, told her you were working in a house of ill fame."

"I thought of that," she said. "But then she'd insist on me going to Mass every morning. It's easier this way."

Without warning, the waitress plopped menus in front of them with the question, "Dessert?"

"Just coffee," Virginia Clary said.

"The same."

"You get dessert on the dinner," the waitress reminded Palmer.

"I know."

"Loganberry shrub, luxuro peach smash, kumquat supreme, huckleberries in wine."

"Just coffee," Palmer said, trying not to wince.

"I may have some peanut-butter snowball left."

"Just coffee, please."

"Yes, sir."

They sat in silence until the waitress had moved away. "It is not true," Virginia Clary said then, "that they launder the food in Oxydol before serving it."

"You're certain of that." He offered cigarettes and lighted them. "Do you eat here much?"

"Most of the time." She examined her cigarette. "It's close by and it's quick and it's clean and, really, the food is quite all right, for lunch, anyway. Better than eating at your desk." She inhaled a great deal of cigarette smoke. "My mother insists on my not eating at my desk."

"My father had a maxim about it, too, I think."

"Your quotable father. I have to keep remembering," she said, "you're a second-generation banker."

"Third. My grandfather founded the bank."

"None of us were quite sure why you were chosen over the heads of some of the old-timers around the shop, or a man from another New York bank who knew the local set-up. But I begin to see the logic of the choice."

"The usual move," Palmer explained, "is to pick a man who's a senior partner in the law firm that represents the bank. The future of the world belongs to lawyers, anyway."

"They picked you against a trend?" She thought for a moment. "I doubt it. I think they wanted somebody with banking in his blood."

"I imagine I'll have to take that as a compliment." He sighed. "There are a lot of things about being chosen by Ubco that still haven't been answered to my satisfaction."

"Such as?"

Palmer shrugged slowly. "Technical things," he parried, unwilling to let the matter go any further. It was easy enough, he told himself, to let pleasant conversation with an agreeable dinner partner spill over into the exchange of confidences that weren't meant for exchange. He glanced up at Virginia Clary. Not, he decided, that she'd divulged many confidences about herself. She looked too intelligent for that.

"If you'd—"

"Which reminds me," Palmer cut in, determined to get away from his previous words, "we haven't even begun making a dent in your colossal mound of banking ignorance."

Her eyes widened in mock chagrin. "I'm beginning to feel like a terrible liability to the firm."

"Take comfort from the fact that you probably know more than most of the people in the shop."

"I know about interest rates and personal loans and amortization and the Federal Reserve and like that," she rattled off. "What am I missing?"

"As we say in public relations, the Big Picture."

Palmer looked up as the waitress brought their coffee. He watched Virginia Clary add cream and sugar and stir it with slow, full sweeps of the spoon. "Something I said before," he began then. "About money being as important to modern man as air and food. That's the frame of reference you have to understand."

"Believe me, no one has to explain the importance of money to me."

"Let's call it the necessity of money," he amended. "There are still places on earth where you can trade a dozen spearheads for a side of dried beef. But they're not the places where history and progress are being made."

"These miserable bartering folks have no A-bombs or moon rockets."

He looked up at her. "You're baiting me again."

"Sorry. Mother's influence. I really do want to know."

"Fine." Palmer sipped his coffee and found it good. "As we get a more highly organized society, money begins to become more important than anything else. Eventually, we reach the stage we're in now. Money buys a man the food he eats, the clothes on his back, care when sick, the roof over him, his education, his recreation, everything. Without money, he can't even die properly, unless he wants to lie in Potter's Field. It's become that sharp a definition: without money, man cannot live or die with decency."

"Is that good?"

"Probably not," Palmer said. "But we're not philosophers, we're bankers. We supply, safeguard, control and define the most precious commodity of life—money."

"More precious than anything?"

"Suggest some other commodities."

"Health?" she asked.

"Preserved and recovered through money."

"I see. And things like, oh, love or hate. Money buys them."

Palmer hunched himself forward until both his elbows rested on the small walnut table. "Try to understand that we're not conducting a philosophical analysis. A man can live without love or hate. Without friends. Without the gratification of desires. But he cannot live, on the material plane, without money."

"That's only one plane of living," she demurred.

"It's the life-or-death plane."

"Yes, but I want to get that on the record. It's only in the material scheme of things that money is the most important."

"All right. Granted."

She eyed him closely. "You're patronizing me," she said then. "You don't for a moment grant that life has any other plane than the material one."

"Not for the purposes of this discussion, at any rate."

She shook her head almost sadly. "You're a very hard man to trap," she admitted. "I'd hate to interview you for a newspaper." She watched him for another moment and then gave up. "All right," she said. "We're bankers. We aren't interested in anything but the material world. Go on, please."

He sipped his coffee and sat back in his chair. "What do banks do with money? We keep it in vaults where it can't be stolen, except occasionally. We invest it in bonds and stocks and mortgages and business and personal loans. We handle it. We channel it. We tell it what to do. We mold it and teach it. We create it."

"Money? What do we do, print it?"

"Almost literally," he said.

"Is that legal?"

"Perfectly," Palmer assured her. "As a Federal Reserve Bank, we create a brand-new dollar out of thin air for every four dollars we take in."

"Is that good?"

He slapped his hand palm down on the arm of his chair. "Stop asking philosophical questions. It probably is the worst thing that could happen to the United States of America and our great-grandchildren will pay for it dearly. But right now it's the money that makes our particular mare go."

"In other words, we're responsible for printing money that isn't based on silver?"

"In other words, we're creating inflation," Palmer told her. "But inflation is what the American people want."

"You don't really believe that."

"It's not a question of belief. It's a fact. People want to buy all kinds of gimcracks, twenty-one-inch color television sets, two-door refrigerators, over-powered automobiles. They refuse to wait until they've saved up money. Like little children, when they want something they want it *now*. All right, behind every automobile and television set stands a man willing to sell it on credit. But he can't wait thirty-six months for his money; when he sells something, he wants to be paid *now*. So, behind him stands a finance company, an acceptance corporation or an accounts-receivable factor. They pay him the money and get paid for the favor by charging his customer carrying charges. But they need their money *now*, too. Where do they get it? Most of them don't have enough money to cover the tremendous amount of time buying that goes on. So, behind them stand the banks, providing the money, and more money, and more money still, until the supply of money begins to run a little short. You wonder where it's all coming from. But you know where it's coming from. It's rolling off the printing presses."

He stopped, suddenly aware of the fact that his voice had grown in intensity until a man two tables away glanced at him. In the odd silence that followed, Palmer stubbed out his cigarette and wondered why he had got so excited.

"You were beginning to sound like a philosopher there for a second," Virginia Clary said then.

"I do have a philosophy about money," Palmer admitted. "It's an archaic one that would probably wreck the country inside of a week if we ever put it into effect. It's a banker's view of money with centuries of banking behind it."

She leaned forward toward him, watching very closely now. "Tell me this explosive philosophy."

Palmer laughed briefly, without much joy. "Don't spend what you don't have," he said then. "So simple. So impossible." He laid his hands palms up on the small table between them. "When you see a lovely gimcrack, resist the urge to own it at once. Save for it. Then buy it. Chances are, by then the urge to own it will have passed, anyway."

Her rather full eyebrows drew together in an expression of pain. "Oh," she said, "what a terribly limited way to live. I wouldn't like it at all."

Palmer shrugged. "If by limited you mean disciplined, yes."

"Disciplined? Does that sound any better?" She shook her head. "It's a bleak, stark, cold way of life. No adventure, no excitement."

"No problems, no crises."

"You see?" she pounced. "It isn't a way of life at all. It's a preview of death."

"Nonsense."

"What is life all about?" she asked. "Problems and crises. Seeing something lovely and wanting it now and taking it and paying for it later."

"Whose life are we talking about?" Palmer wanted to know.

She frowned again. "Yes," she said, "that's right, isn't it? Not everybody wants to live that way. I forgot."

Neither of them spoke for a moment. Palmer watched the upturned palms of his hands, then turned them over on the cool table top. His palms felt moist and he wondered why. "At any rate," he said, "no matter whose life we're discussing, the philosophy is mine."

Her great eyes opened as wide as they could and she seemed to be taking a deep breath. "If you'll forgive me for saying so," she said, "it's the philosophy of a man who's never wanted for money."

Palmer sat perfectly still for a moment, then withdrew his hands from the table and placed them in his lap. "You're probably right," he said after a while in a voice that sounded to him entirely devoid of any feeling. "The whole idea of deferring desires comes easily to someone who's never had to."

She looked down at the place on the table where his hands had been. "I didn't mean to imply," she said in a deliberately slow manner, "that having money automatically gratifies all one's desires. I don't for a moment think there are things money can't buy. Goodness, no. But, having bought them, they don't always gratify the buyer. Everything is for sale, apparently, but when you get it in your hand, it isn't always the same as it looked in the shop window."

"If you'll excuse me for saying so," Palmer said, in a parody of her former remark, "that's the philosophy of a dyed-in-the-wool mystic."

"Yes," she agreed. "I'm a Celt and I'm fey and I'm a card-carrying mystic. I might even be a witch, if I could ever buckle down and put my mind to it."

"That would be interesting. We'd probably have to double your salary to keep you on our side."

She began poking in her bag for something. "Just what is 'our' side?"

"Cigarette?" He offered one and she took it. "Just a figure of speech."

"No, it's more," she said, getting a light from him. "Mr. Burckhardt talks about 'our' side as though we were at war."

"With the savings banks? We are."

"Yes, but that doesn't make any sense. We're all banks. Some of their people are on our board of directors, or vice-versa, whatever way you look at it. They use us as a correspondent bank. We sell mortgages to them. We're all doing the same thing—banking. But there's our side and their side. Why?"

"Do you know the difference between a commercial and a savings bank?"

She nodded, blew out smoke and waved it away in a business-like manner, as if disposing of the question. "They can't make business loans."

"That's a by-product of the real difference."

"Which is?"

"Which is shrouded in the mists of time," he explained. "Back, oh, about a century and a half. Right after the turn of the nineteenth century. Poor people could do only two things with their money: hide it under the mattress or spend it. It wasn't safe under the mattress, so they spent it on the thing that would let them forget their poverty: whisky."

"Ah, well I know the feeling."

"The do-gooders of the day were appalled. Drunkenness was all about them. So they imported an idea developed in Scotland by a dominie. Ministers, philanthropists, educators, reformers . . . they began organizing savings banks to accept the savings of poor people."

"Sounds pretty dastardly."

"Terribly. The regular banks of the period wouldn't touch anything but business deposits or the estates of wealthy men. But the savings banks would accept anything, a penny a week, whatever a wage earner wanted to put aside. And the really dastardly thing was that they invested those pennies and paid back interest to the wage earners as an incentive to save more."

"Criminal!"

"No, the worst part hasn't been explained yet."

"What could be worse?" she asked.

"Just this: these savings banks were mutual. They had no stockholders. They were owned by their depositors. They made money only for their depositors. Nobody skimmed a profit off the top. All the earnings went right back to the wage earners who deposited their pennies in the savings bank."

"Sounds downright socialistic."

"It is," Palmer told her. "But, you see, Karl Marx was only eight years old when that Scottish minister had his brainstorm."

"Oops."

"In any event, our brand of savings bankers were pretty true-blue. They usually invested their funds in government bonds and such. Highly patriotic. Highly stable, too. Almost none of their banks ever failed, which is more than you can say for . . . well, anyway, time passed."

"A century of it."

"A century and more," Palmer said. "Things happened to the wage earner. He became unionized. He got Social Security, old-age benefits, health insurance, life insurance, welfare funds, pensions, everything. The commercial banks stopped turning up their noses at him. They welcomed his savings. He was banking's darling now, secure whether he worked or not, whether he was healthy or sick and with his family provided for when he died."

"Which has what to do with savings banks?"

"Exactly. It has nothing to do with them. They've outlived their usefulness. Nobody needs them any more."

"Oh," she said, "that's a shame. Really?"

"Seriously. What do they provide that isn't available to the wage earner from five other sources?"

"But it's sad," she objected. "All those ministers."

"I'd never have told you if I'd thought you'd crack up."

"I'll get over it in a moment," she said. "See? I'm over it already. Tell me, has anyone mentioned this to the savings banks? They're cruising right along as though they still served a purpose."

One corner of Palmer's mouth turned up in a wry expression. "That's the whole problem."

"No one's told them, huh?"

"Here's what's happened," Palmer said. "Those ministers planted a seed that grew into a tree. Nobody needs the tree, but it keeps right on growing. Savings banks give jobs to tens of thousands of employees, from the presidents on down to the clerks. True, there aren't any stockholders. But the employee corps has a stake in making sure the savings banking system keeps flourishing."

"Why not let them? I mean, people like to save at savings banks."

"I'll tell you why," Palmer said. "That tree, the one that kept growing? It has deep roots. They've spread out and they keep spreading. And they're stealing the nourishment from the ground on which *we're* planted. Does that make it clear to you?"

"All of a sudden, yes." She sat back and stubbed out her cigarette. Then, looking up at him in a wary way, her eyes half hidden behind her long black lashes, she asked, "What are you going to do about the tree?"

Palmer looked at the table. "Prune it . . . drastically."

Virginia Clary pushed back the sleeve on her left wrist and glanced at her watch. "Hadn't you better call Mac Burns now?" she asked in a perfectly calm, perfectly civil tone.

Palmer frowned. "I . . . uh, is it that late?" He looked at his watch and found that it was after nine. "You're right," he said then.

They sat watching each other for a long moment, neither of them speaking. Palmer started to go back over the conversation to recall what he had said that had chilled the air between them, but the hour was late and he had promised Burns and, besides, what was so important to him about the way Virginia Clary felt?

CHAPTER FIFTEEN

Edith Palmer pushed back the long, loose sleeve of her pale-blue dressing gown and consulted the wrist watch on her left arm. The motion caught Palmer's eye. He looked up from his breakfast coffee and watched the way the horizontal morning sun made the fine blonde hair on Edith's forearm shimmer with light. Having seen that, and evaluated the gesture that had drawn his attention, he cleared his throat and asked: "Eight-thirty?"

"Almost. Woods, spare me five or ten minutes now, will you?"

"Is the car downstairs?"

"Of course it is. You can be five or ten minutes late." She glanced at him with imperfectly concealed annoyance. "Or tell the driver to speed."

Palmer finished his coffee and touched his napkin to his lips. "If we get a ticket," he said in a parody of her tone which was lost to everyone but him, "Mac Burns can always fix it for me."

Edith frowned. "Five or ten minutes," she repeated.

"Right."

She got up and led the way into the quasi-library the apartment hotel had provided them in lieu of a study or den or something. At the moment it was cluttered with several dozen oil paintings, still in their burlap wrappings, and some wooden crates that contained his father's collection of rare books. As he always did at the sight of this gypsy-like impermanence, Palmer winced. "Well?"

"Here." She strode to the inadequate desk near the windows and began unrolling architect's drawings. The ozalid paper crackled with a richness that suggested parchment. "It's this third-floor thing I need to discuss with you."

"By all means. I'm in favor of having one."

She closed her eyes for a moment. "Not this early in the morning, please." Her long, narrow index finger, tipped by a carefully natural nail, touched an area of the plans labeled STUDY. She glanced up at him for a moment. "Your study, that is," she said. "I have to know how you feel about the position of the desk and shelves and all that."

He glanced over her shoulder and managed to determine that in a room about 14 feet square one wall had been tentatively given over to book shelves. "Put the desk on the opposite wall from the shelves."

"Do you want your back to the wall or the room when you work?"

"What sort of work am I supposed to be doing here?"

Edith shrugged. "I haven't the faintest idea, darling. All I know is that you had a study in Chicago and, by George, you'll have one in New York."

"What role am I supposed to be playing here, Edith? The kindly old family banker? The dynamic young tycoon?"

"We can begin by crossing off 'kindly,'" she retorted.

Neither of them spoke for a moment as her finger traced a line on the plan. "Hold on," she said then, "it can't go here. It's a built-in, you know."

"The desk?"

Edith's pale-blonde eyebrows drew together and a faint line showed between them. "Just a second, darling," she mumbled, paging through the plans until she came to a blueprint that bore a great number of additional pencil markings on it. As she pulled it out of the stack of sheets, a fine plaster dust flew up from its surface and made a whitish spot on the hotel's rug. "This isn't a load-bearing wall," she announced then, tapping the blueprint. "Not enough studs. Will it be all right if we hang the desk from the rear wall there?"

"Just as long as it's a load-bearing desk." He watched her speculatively. "When did you learn to read a blueprint?"

"About a month ago."

"Why?"

"I accused the foreman of putting a wall in the wrong place. So he took out an hour and showed me how to read a blueprint."

"That was darned democ—"

"The trouble is," Edith cut in suddenly, "that your working light gets reoriented if we have to hang the desk on the back wall. The light from the windows will glare in your face."

"Edith," Palmer said rather heavily, "perhaps it doesn't make any difference. Let's first answer the question of what I'm up to in this study. Maybe I'm only there at night anyway."

"That's true." She turned to look at him. "Well?"

"What? Me answer? I thought I was asking the question."

She watched him silently for a moment, with that look she had of outguessing not merely him, but everything in the world. "Of course," she said, "the children will use it, too, from time to time. All the reference books will be there."

"Ah. Now we begin to make progress. My study, but the children will use it. From time to time."

"Every day, probably. Don't forget, we'll have the encyclopedias there, and the dictionaries, and all your banking and economics texts, and . . ." She stopped and glanced at him again. "What else do you want? *Polk's Directories? Who's Who? Thesaurus? Bartlett's?*"

Palmer brushed aside some of the white dust on the blueprint and sat down on the edge of the desk. "What in God's name would I want with *Bartlett's?*"

"All these speeches you're starting to make."

"I don't write them."

She stood motionless for a moment, looking at the floor. Then her light-hazel eyes came up slowly to meet his, not with the outguessing look, but with a frank request for information. "You don't?"

"A corps of writers works on them."

"Who?"

"Who?" he echoed. "Well, Ubco people, Mac Burns's people. I don't even know who they are, most of them." Sensing that there was something not quite right about admitting a thing like this, Palmer stood up and walked halfway toward the door. "The five or ten minutes are up, Edith."

"Yes, I know." She continued to stare at him. "Woods," she said then.

"What?"

"Tell me: if you don't write those speeches, what on earth do you do all day at the bank?"

Palmer gestured abruptly and was shocked to see how openly the movement expressed both annoyance and a desire to hit back in advance of the attack he could feel coming. "That's a damned silly question," he said.

"I'm sure it is. But you've taken to telling me so little that I'm forced into these damned silly positions."

"I haven't forced you into anyth—"

"Like not knowing what you'll do in your study," she went on quickly. "It is pretty silly, isn't it? If I were a professional architect or decorator, you'd make it your business to give me a thorough briefing. Would it make things easier for you if I dropped out of this remodeling and called in some professionals? Could you manage to spare them the information you can't spare me? Then, perhaps, I could come around and pry it out of them. At least I'd know what you were—" She stopped herself in mid-phrase and stood there without speaking, her lower lip drawn tight as if to bar any further words.

After a moment, she turned back to the plans. "Your car's waiting," she said then in a perfectly normal tone. "It's eight-forty now."

"Yes." He stood there without moving. "Look, I'm sorry I've upset you. That question of yours was just too damned ingenuous or something."

"What question?"

"About what I did all day at the bank."

"I'm sure you work hard," she said, still in that calm, reasonable voice. "It wasn't a fair question."

"Oh, yes, it was," he said bitterly. Then, turning to go: "I'll call after lunch and let you know my schedule."

"Dinner with the Grahams," she reminded him as he walked out of the room.

"Right."

"And, Woods?"

"Um?" He paused at the front door.

"When you work out an answer to the question, let me know?"

He slammed the door as he left. Not as hard as he wanted to. Not hard enough to excite the attention of the hotel staff. But hard enough to let her know, he told himself as he went down in the elevator, that she'd scored a hit.

CHAPTER SIXTEEN

Palmer stood at the immense window, seeing the small spots of brown and red leaves among the trees of Central Park. A change had come over that great expanse in just the last few days. The green, once so lush it seemed to vibrate in the sun's rays, had grown dusty almost overnight. It was as if the city itself, an unbreathable caldron of soot and fumes, had finally beaten down exuberant nature after a summer of struggle.

His intercom tinkled softly and he turned to face his desk, at the far end of the long room. Leaving the window unwillingly, he repaid whoever had broken his moment of peace by moving very slowly to answer the summons. Still standing, he touched the green-glowing "Scrty" button. "Yes?"

"Miss Clary to see you, Mr. Palmer."

"Right."

He sat down on the edge of his desk. As she came into the room, leaving the door open as usual, he saw that she was wearing dark red today, a smooth-textured knitted fabric that hugged her small waist and the outward curve of her hips.

"I have the material you asked for," she said, her face immobile under his examining glance.

He blinked and looked up at her. "Good morning." He thought for a moment. "What material was—? Oh." Getting up, he walked to the door and closed it firmly. "You kept it all very quiet?" he asked, returning to his desk and sitting down behind it.

"Very discreet. Through an old friend on the *Star*." She handed him a folder, sat down, started to cross her legs and stopped the movement, planting her heels firmly together on the thick pile rug.

Palmer leafed through the folder and found a thick collection of negative Photostats whose black pages seemed to cover at least half a century of the life and times of Joseph Loomis. "Have you looked it over?" he asked.

"I checked the chronological continuity."

Palmer's eyebrows went up slightly. She was at her most formal today, partial repentance for their informal dinner of the night before. "Read any of it?"

"The material that gives his business affiliations." She gestured stiffly, a truncated version of the fuller movement she normally used. "I've put it all together on a typewritten sheet at the back of the folder."

"Fine."

"The ones with asterisks are companies in which he no longer has an interest, firms that have gone out of business through merger and so forth, or ones in which he has resigned any active participation as a director."

"Very good."

"If you look at the sheet," she said then, "you'll see that, for him, he's leading a rather inactive life at the moment. Only about a dozen business affiliations."

"Is he equally devoted to all twelve?" Palmer asked.

She shook her head. "As far as my friend could see—and I've checked this with some other people—Mr. Loomis devotes most of his energies to Jet-Tech International."

Palmer nodded. "Devoting yourself to Jet-Tech is like playing handball with an octopus."

Virginia Clary raised her chin, as if pointing with it. "If you look at the other typewritten sheet, you'll find a list of all Jet-Tech's subsidiaries, affiliates, spin-offs, joint ventures and firms in which it maintains a stock position."

Palmer let the folder fall flat on the table as he glanced up at her more directly. "I must say," he said, "that I have seen efficiency before without understanding the meaning of the word till now."

"Thank you."

"And, after all, this isn't even your proper work," he continued. "I mean, our credit department is really the place to go for material like this."

"If you want to spend a few weeks waiting," she amended.

For the first time that morning they smiled at each other. "I have to call Loomis today," Palmer said, "not two weeks from now." He looked down the typewritten sheet of business names. "Some of these are new to me."

"I don't know all of them either, but . . ."

He read through some of the names to himself. "This Wilmington corporation, J-T Industries. That's the basic holding company?"

"As far as I can tell."

"Then Jet-Tech International is a wholly owned subsidiary," he mused. "And it controls what? Hi-Thrust Manufacturing Corporation. That would be rocket engines. And this one? Consolidated Energy Company. Which does what?"

"High-octane additives," she explained. "Solid propellants. Exotic fuels. Liquid oxygen. Hydrazine. Energy cells. Ion motors. Also makes a consumer line of flashlight dry-cells and storage batteries for the automobile people."

"Nice match," Palmer said. "Consolidated fuels Hi-Thrust's rockets. Here's a subsidiary in micro-relays. What else do they make?"

"Transistors," she told him, "diodes, rectifiers, condensers, resistors, printed circuitry, memory drums and discs."

"That's another pretty match," he said. "They pair off with the automation concern. I've dealt with them. Very big in computers and test equipment."

Palmer continued reading the list in silence. "Now here," he said then, "this affiliate produces typewriters and adding machines. They also have a strong position in similar firms abroad, Germany and Italy. They probably make the electric typewriter read-outs for computers."

"They own about forty-five per cent of a vending-machine company," she volunteered, "that makes robots for controlling atomic reactor work."

"Which brings us," Palmer said, "to this separate atomic-projects firm. It's operated directly by the Wilmington holding company. Are they doing anything at Oak Ridge?"

She shook her head. "That's Union Carbide."

"They must be out in Washington State, then, or New Mexico." Palmer frowned slightly as he reread the list. "What other firms have we got now? Missiles here. Ground-support equipment here. Aluminum here. Some copper and zinc holdings in Chile and Peru. Caribbean bauxite. Uranium. Some oil, not much. Sulphur in Louisiana. Machine tools in Aliquippa. Rubber in Canton. Here's a little transducer firm in Burbank and a lumber company in Tacoma. What's this? Bicycles?"

"Why not?" she asked.

"Bicycles," he repeated in a thoughtful tone. "What in God's name is something called Co-ordinated Western and United Company?"

She thought for a moment. "I believe," she said, "that they try to sort of co-ordinate and unite Western-type stuff."

Palmer nodded and closed the folder with a loud smack. "Well, Miss Clary," he said after a moment, "I hope you are properly humble at this moment."

"Practically speechless."

"I trust you realize that we are sitting here before an entity at once unique in its scope and typical in its inner meaning. In short, that latter-day miracle, the New American Business."

"I am devoutly impressed."

"How long did it take them to put together this jigsaw puzzle?"

She shrugged. "It's all post-war. In fact, it's all since 1952, when Loomis' group took control after a very hush-hush proxy fight."

"You're missing a few other things about 1952," Palmer pointed out. "Little things like Korea and Eisenhower getting elected." He opened the folder and studied the typewritten sheet again. "I wonder," he said at last, "how much of this empire is nothing but paper. Are some of these companies simply tax-loss situations? Or were they turned around and put in motion again? Is Jet-Tech for real?"

"It better be," Virginia Clary said. "We hold enough of their paper to reach from here to the planet Mars."

"That a fact?" Palmer mused. "Did we inherit it when we merged with Hudson Trust?"

"I don't really know," she explained. "But downtown it takes an assistant vice-president and a staff of two to handle the Jet-Tech paperwork alone."

He glanced at her and was pleased to see that she had relaxed in her chair and seemed much more at ease now. "You may not know too much about banking," he said, "but you have an eye for the significant details."

"As I said once before, you don't have to be a cat to draw one."

Palmer nodded. "You may sell me that little motto if you keep trying long enough."

She watched him for a second, then looked down at her knees. "How long does it take to sell you something?"

"It depends on who's selling. And what's being sold."

"I don't think you buy very easily," she said, still not looking up at him. "Anything. From anybody."

Palmer was fascinated by the way she avoided his glance. Her large eyes were half lidded as she watched the hem of her skirt, riding up over the soft roundness of her knees. Palmer looked at her legs, rather slim, with calves that swelled slightly before narrowing to thin ankles. She kept her feet close to-gether. Palmer could see a slight ripple in the rug where her high heels had dug in tensely and pushed the heavy fabric forward.

"I have been known," he said, "to make up my mind—" He stopped him-self and forced his glance to the folder in front of him. He found himself un-able to let the sentence remain unfinished. "—rather quickly," he said. "On occasion," he added somewhat lamely, wondering why he had had to finish the sentence and then carefully hedge it.

Virginia Clary stood up. She seemed suddenly taller than she really was. Palmer got to his feet, not sure whether he was being courteous or simply trying to readjust their heights in his favor. "In any event, thank you for this very thorough research job."

"I hope it solves whatever you needed solved." Their eyes met. "Before you call Loomis, that is."

"Partly."

"If there's anything more you—"

"Thanks. No."

"Well," she said. "I'll be getting back to my desk."

"Thanks again." Palmer could feel his cheeks growing warm. His mouth tightened and he forced himself to move toward the door. Opening it, he nodded in her direction, careful not to look directly at her. There had been too much of it already.

She moved past him and out the door, leaving a faint, smoky scent in the air, not enough for Palmer to know exactly what he was smelling. It was a suggestion of a scent, he decided, a sketch of the real thing. She turned in the corridor outside and looked past him into his room. Her eyes flicked across his face. Then her full lower lip curved upward at one corner in a kind of smile. It bore the same relation to a real smile, Palmer found himself thinking, as her scent did to real perfume.

She walked down the hall, turned a corner and was out of sight. Palmer closed the door and sat down at his desk. His finger went to the intercom buttons, guided by a kind of subconscious memory of what he had planned to do. Instead of pushing a particular button, however, his finger lightly touched each in turn without pressure.

Palmer blinked. He sat up straighter, glanced at the intercom and resolutely punched the "Elder" button. It glowed green for a moment until the speaker grill rasped with sound. "Yep?"

"Harry? Palmer. Got a second?"

"Shoot." Harrison Elder had a hoarse, high voice that had probably sounded in his youth as it did now that he had almost reached retirement age. It was a weather-beaten kind of voice, Palmer reflected, a boy soprano with a bad cold.

"What can you tell me about our Jet-Tech business, off the top of your head?"

Elder chuckled for a long moment, a startling sound, especially when filtered through the innards of the intercom. "Twenty-five words or less?" he asked, still wheezing.

"How much are they into us for?" Palmer persisted.

"Hard to tell. Paul Geraghty used to handle them personally when Hudson Trust had the account. Let 'em get away with murder."

"How much murder?" Palmer asked.

"Let 'em do business with the bank under every corporate name in their books."

"We inherit a headache?"

"A profitable one," Elder amended. "I never bothered to put it all together. No need to. You want to know, I can put a boy on it. Take about a week."

"Give me an educated guess."

Elder chuckled again. "Hell, who's educated?" He was silent for a moment. "Let's see. The holding company banks in Delaware, token account. Jet-Tech International has seven open-end plant improvement loans with us. We're factoring accounts receivable on some of the subsidiaries. Of course, we're the stock and transfer agent for all the companies. Atomic Projects has a whopping big R and D loan outstanding at twelve per cent. We've set up lines of credit for most of the affiliates doing business abroad, which is damned near all of them. God, Woods, how close do I have to come?"

"Somewhere in the neighborhood, Harry, anywhere remotely nearby."

The intercom gave off a high, hoarse grumbling sound. ". . . funded indebtedness on Continental Equipment," Palmer heard. "Let's just say," Elder spoke up then, "in very round figures, give or take the usual margin, about, oh, make it maybe eight hundred million."

There was a long silence. The intercom's last words seemed to radiate into the immense room and lose themselves in the farthest corners. "Woods?" Elder asked. "Hello?"

"Thanks, Harry."

"It's a very rough guess."

"I understand."

"I could be off as much as twenty-five per cent, Woods."

"I get the picture, though." Palmer sighed. "Even if you're that far over, they represent five per cent of our business. But if you've underestimated by that much, we do ten per cent of our volume with Jet-Tech."

"That's about the range."

"Which makes them our biggest customer?"

"Right."

"Thanks again, Harry."

"Pleasure." The intercom went dead.

Palmer sat still for a moment, staring at the row of buttons. Then, reaching across the desk, he pulled yesterday's telephone message forms from a spindle and leafed through them until he found Loomis' call. The number was obviously a private one; it didn't end in a double zero. He pushed the button that gave him a direct outside line and slowly dialed the number.

After four rings, an old man's voice answered. "Mr. Loomis?" Palmer asked. "This is Woods Palmer."

"I'm sorry," the elderly voice told him. "Mr. Loomis has left town. He'll be back next Monday, Mr. Palmer. This is his secretary. Would you care to leave a message?"

"Just that I returned his call."

"Certainly."

When the call was over and he had replaced the telephone in its cradle, Palmer found that the palm of his hand was excessively moist. He sat there, grateful for the delay in reaching Loomis, and wondering what on earth he would have said to the old man.

He stood up and began moving slowly toward the big window, his mind edging back and forth rather cautiously through the mass of information he had got. Something didn't make sense. Loomis' loyalties should lie with the bank that held his notes, not with a mutual savings bank in which he had no monetary interest.

Palmer stood at the window and watched the hansom cabs at the Plaza move up one place in rank as a man and a girl got into the first cab and were driven away.

The girl wore a red suit. Her hair was black. For a moment Palmer thought it might be Virginia Clary. But that, obviously, wasn't possible.

Chapter Seventeen

The elderly bellhop had finished clearing away dinner. Palmer sat back in his chair and watched the old man wheel away the soiled dishes with their domed silver covers. He found himself wondering, as often happened, whether this gypsy-like existence annoyed Edith as much as it did him. He lighted a cigarette and, under cover of the flame and smoke, watched her pour second cups of coffee for both of them.

She looked as competent as ever, Palmer noticed, although she had, for the occasion, put on what he referred to as her "public" look, a kind of glossy finish that turned her natural blonde good looks into the brittle fashion-model beauty of a cold-hearted mannequin on a page in *Vogue*. Every hair had been smoothed into place. Her eyes had been increased in size and presence by what was, for Edith, a lot of make-up. The skin of her cheeks and nose looked like very fine-grained velvet. Palmer itemized the "public" look for another moment and remembered how badly he had reacted that morning to her "private" look.

What was it, he wondered; why couldn't he be satisfied with the way she was? Could nothing she did please him?

Or was it, he reflected, just that he knew her too well? She could no longer do anything mysterious and there was nothing to replace the lost mystery. But why should he expect replacements?

She had noticed his examination of her. Her eyes came up to meet his glance. "Coffee?" she asked, extending a full cup to him. "What on earth were you thinking about?"

Palmer's mouth tightened. "Nothing."

"I didn't know nothing could be quite that deep."

"I was thinking," Palmer said, deciding to try part of the truth, "how nice you looked tonight."

Her eyes widened. In the artificial light, their hazel irises looked faintly gray. "Why, darling, what delightful nonsense," she said. "As a matter of fact you were cataloguing what you call my 'public' look and wondering why I'd bothered."

"I was not."

"When what you should have been wondering," Edith went on smoothly, "was how I'd found time to bother, after a full day with the builders and an evening devoted to squaring away the children for bed."

"That hadn't occurred to me either."

"The reason," she continued, "since you ask, is that this is our first dinner at home together in I have no idea how long. A week? So I bothered."

"And I'm happy you did," Palmer said, wondering whether she would catch this lie, too.

"Oh, drink your coffee." Edith sipped hers for a long moment. "I had a horrible experience today. One of the workmen fell from the scaffolding."

"How badly is he hurt?"

"Nothing broken. The foreman sent him home," Edith said. "I insisted he see a doctor first. He said he would, but, of course, I have no way of knowing whether he will or not."

"The contractor's insurance covers him."

"That's not the point, Woods," she told him. "I thought that kind of thing happened only around big projects, skyscrapers, bridges. It's damned disconcerting when they happen in your own house."

"That kind of thing happens all over."

Edith sighed impatiently. Her hand darted across the table to take a cigarette from Palmer's pack. "That isn't the point, either, darling," she said then. "I'm not really sure what the point actually is. All I know is that I'm still not over it."

He struck a match and held it for her. "You want immunity," he said, watching her get the cigarette started. "Everybody does. You can't have it any more than the man who fell today or the man who gets run over by a truck tomorrow or the girl who gets attacked in Central Park tonight."

Edith made a face and studied the burning tip of her cigarette. "I'll tell you what I want," she said, finally. "I want to live with a little less violence around me. This town is filled with it."

"Just this town?"

She waved one long, thin hand, as if to brush away his meaning. "It's not so much for me," she explained. "But I don't like it at all for the children."

Palmer smiled slightly. "They've adjusted pretty well to the change." He paused, then decided to finish the thought. "I don't think you have, yet."

To his surprise, she nodded. "I haven't," she agreed. "I suppose I shall, in time. But I don't view the period of adjustment with any joy. I'm not an eleven-year-old, like Gerri. I'm forty. Forty doesn't take kindly to sudden changes."

"Fortunately, you can pass for thirty-uh, three?"

"Not this morning," she said. "Not the way you were watching me."

"When you get in one of your mind-reading moods, I—"

"Anyway," Edith interrupted, "the point is that we really don't know any-one in New York and the prospect of building new relationships is not one I would voluntarily choose."

"We see all kinds of people. Too many, in fact."

"Courtesy acquaintances," Edith said. "They invited us because, oh, for many reasons. Mutual friends, mostly. And we haven't invited them because we have no home as yet. When we do, the return invitations will begin. The prospect is disheartening."

"They don't seem that much different from our Chicago friends."

Edith sighed. "Friends are friends," she said, "and people we've met once are not friends. Not to me, at any rate. I suppose that kind of thing is considered friendship in New York."

"I had no idea you were so unhappy with New—"

"I'll get over it," Edith cut in again. She got to her feet. "If you're finished with your coffee, let's go over the plans."

He glanced down at his full cup. "I'll take it with me," he said, rising. "Tell me more about this thing you have for New York."

Saying nothing, she led the way to the little room the hotel hopefully called a library. Dusting off the seats of two chairs, she drew them up to a table, removed a carton of books from it and unrolled a set of blueprints.

"Are we going through that business again about load-bearing walls and what am I supposed to do in my new den?" Palmer asked. "Because, if we are, I—"

"That question," Edith snapped, "was settled, by me, at two this afternoon. The work's already done. They'll plaster that room tomorrow."

"Good. What's the agenda for tonight?"

Edith sat down slowly in one of the chairs and stared for a long moment at the blueprints. Her mouth took on a thin, downward twist, as if she were watching some unhappy event.

"Woods," she said then, "sit down."

He did so, placing his cup and saucer on the blueprints. "I am not," Edith said slowly, "a figure of fun. I will not be treated as one."

"What are—?"

"I know what a figure of fun is," she went on. "I used to be one, a gawky towhead too tall for my age. But I haven't been one since the year I came out. And I refuse to have you treat me as if I were."

"I don't consider you a figure of fun," Palmer assured her.

"This snide comment about an agenda," Edith continued. "It isn't lost on me. I'm well aware that you take a dim view of the way I keep things organized. I'm also quite sure that if I didn't, you'd have to and you wouldn't like that, either. I'm damned if I do something for you and damned if I don't. Not a very happy position, is it?"

"No, not if I'd really put you in that position. But I haven't."

"For a man with such an unruffled exterior," she pointed out, "you maintain an unusual collection of inner contradictions, don't you?"

"I'll be happy to rule on that," Palmer said, "if you'll be good enough to explain it."

Edith pushed his cup and saucer aside and studied the top blueprint for a moment. "Do you want to keep the Kurd sculpture at the office?" she asked then, pointing to the floor plan. "If not, I want to plan on it for this corner here." She turned to face him. "The reason I ask is not to torment you, but because I'll want recessed ceiling spots put in. And the wiring starts next week."

"I'd like to keep it at the office."

She turned back to the blueprint. "Along this wall," she said, "I thought we'd hang the modern paintings, all but the still lifes. Agreed?"

Palmer narrowed his eyes to read the floor plan. "What is that, a hall?"

"Part of it," Edith said. "The rest is foyer wall. Agreed?"

"Agreed."

"Mother's Constable will go here, then," she said, indicating a position. "And the Ingres here. Lots of space around them. I can't lump the Ernst with the other moderns. What if we hang it here?"

"Fine."

"And the still lifes reserved for the dining room. Yes?"

"Yes."

"I'm relegating prints to other rooms. The Frasconis and Pierces in the guest rooms, for example."

"Except for that fishing one," Palmer objected. "I'd like that in the study."

Edith turned to him again. "What did I do? Strike a nerve? Up until now I had the distinct impression that I was boring you to tears."

Palmer stood up. "Edith," he said, "I have no idea what's behind all this, but I can't take too much of it."

He watched her eyes widen slightly as she stared, unseeing, into the darkened corner of the room. He had the feeling that she was not, as he had, going back over their conversation this evening, testing the individual parts of it as he had done. Instead, she seemed to be listening for something else, something neither of them had said that night, an overtone perhaps, inaudible to the common ear.

Finally, she shook her head slowly from side to side. "You're right." She glanced up at him. "I'm not sure what's behind it, Woods. But sit down and help me a little longer, will you? I'll be good."

He sat down and sipped his coffee. The single lamp overhead laid a small circle of light around them on the floor, touching the surface of his coffee with a yellow highlight and illuminating the mass of her blonde hair so that it put her face in shadow.

"What did you mean before?" he asked then in what he hoped was a neutral, friendly voice, "about my collection of inner contradictions?"

She shrugged. Her wide, thin shoulders moved unevenly beneath the white silk of her long-sleeved blouse. "I suppose it's just the way I look at them," she said in a tone something like his. "You are a much more complicated person than you realize. And I'm much simpler than I'd like to admit. You are able to keep all kinds of contradictory things whizzing in the air like a juggler. I can't."

"What sort of things?" he persisted.

"Oh." She looked down at her hands and twisted one palm up to examine the cuff link. The small single gem shot a bluish flash of light into Palmer's eyes.

"You didn't seem that way when we were engaged," she said then. Her voice was so quiet that Palmer had the sudden idea that she meant him not to hear. He sat forward in his chair.

"You were somewhat different from the rest of the boys I knew. Somewhat less solemn. Mocking things they didn't mock. You had a terrible reputation. Three different colleges. Some story about a girl back East." She was silent for a while, turning her wrist this way and that, making the cuff link flash again and again, like a hypnotist might.

"But still, despite all that," she said, "you didn't seem complicated. I don't suppose you really were. Then Hanley was killed."

Palmer nodded. "You picked the right event."

"But even then nothing changed overnight. Even in the Army, on passes and furloughs, you were still much the same. How long were you in Europe? Two years?"

"Eighteen months."

"When you came back I could see the changes." She looked up at him for a moment. "You didn't really have to take Hanley's place at the bank. Your father didn't ask you to."

"He didn't have to."

"Contradiction number one," Edith said. "The first of many. There is something very different about you, Woods. I'm just beginning to realize how different you are from . . ."

He waited for her to finish, then quickly added: "From normal people?"

Edith smiled wryly. "I'm only trying to answer your original question. It isn't easy, when one doesn't really have the answer."

"Let's let it rest, then," Palmer suggested.

She shook her head. "This year brings all the contradictions up so sharply. After your father died, when you sold the bank, I might even have predicted it, I suppose. But I couldn't have predicted this new job. It's almost as though you had resurrected your father and begun the whole thing all over again in New York."

Palmer sat back in his chair and kept himself from replying. It was one thing for them to talk, in reasonable tones, about a personal thing. It was another for her, under the cover of sweet reason, to lance out at him in such a vicious way. But, instead of hot answers, he forced himself to say: "I'm not sure I follow you."

"It's the same relationship, Woods," she said. "Burckhardt is the same overweening, dominating type. And you've already become just as unhappy in New York as you were in Chicago."

Again, he held himself in check. "What makes you think I'm unhappy?" he asked in a tone of almost disinterested curiosity.

"Nothing but the things you say and the way you behave." She studied his face for a moment and then touched his cheek with one cool finger. "Don't be angry, darling. I'm not being—" She checked herself and her eyes shifted sideways across his face. "But you think I am, don't you?" she asked in an abruptly toneless voice. "You think this is all malice, all viciousness." She paused, waiting for an answer. "Don't you?"

Palmer moistened his lower lip and tried to relax his posture in the chair. "Has it occurred to you," he began in as quiet a voice as he could, "that unhappiness can come from a source other than my job?"

"It has." She reached for his coffee and sipped some. "It can be the way we've been living, in this ungodly hotel. It can be this town, even though you'd never admit it, and the strain of breaking with the old life. It can be the peculiarities of this job, which has so little to do with banking. No dearth of reasons."

"But of all, you choose the most devious and Freudian."

"You seem to consider those words synonyms," she countered.

"I consider your thinking devious," he amended, "and the suggestion Freudian. I suppose it's really a tribute to my celebrated complexity."

"Are you trying to masquerade as a simple type?"

"I am trying," he said, suddenly aware of the ludicrous element in their argument, "simply to preserve a shred or two of ordinary dignity in the face of a wife turned analyst before my eyes. If I closed them for a moment, I would confidently expect to find that you'd donned a long, fake beard."

She continued sipping his coffee for a moment. "All right," she said then, "but tell me one thing. Not because I'm entitled to know, but just for the flaming hell of it. Why did you take this job?"

Palmer started to answer, then paused, wondering how he could tell her so that it would make sense, so that his motives seemed reasonable and clear. Were they? He sighed softly.

"I should begin," he said, "by telling you something. For almost five years now, I've been going out of my way, in as off-hand a manner as possible, to interest Burckhardt in me. I knew Father was dying and I knew that I had to be ready, the moment I was free, to make my move. You've seen the results."

Edith had paused, coffee cup halfway to her lips, all motion frozen. Now she smiled faintly. "Oh, yes," she agreed. The cup remained motionless.

"I'm now working backward," Palmer went on, "to the time right after the war when I decided to stay with the bank until Father died. Moving back before that, we get to the war, where I found I liked myself when I was out from under Father's thumb. Does all that hang together?"

Edith nodded. Even the movement of her head failed to disturb the rock-steady poise of the coffee cup.

"If you understand that, you understand why I took this job," he explained. "Why I schemed, if you will, to get this job."

"No, I don't," she said. Palmer looked down into the cup, as she held it in mid-air, and saw that the surface of the coffee was perfectly smooth, perfectly free of ripples. "You've explained how you did it," she told him, "but not why."

Palmer's hand shot out, palm up, in mute appeal. Wasn't it possible, he wondered, for one person to explain himself to another? Communication couldn't be all that difficult, could it?

"All right," he said. "Let me put it this way: I am not content, I never was content, to be another Woods Palmer in the image of the Original. He was a mean-spirited, small-minded man with a narrow view of life. If he had a motto, it was 'No.' He could go through a whole day, functioning with brilliant success according to his own lights, on just that single word. He said no to his wife, no to his sons, no to friendship and, I suppose, no to life. It wasn't possible to hate him, because hate is an emotion. It was possible only to outlive him. Or, if you were so inclined, to try it Hanley's way in a plane that never returned. I wasn't so inclined. Do you follow all this?"

Edith cleared her throat softly. "Yes."

"Now, to outlive him," Palmer went on, "you had to find a good reason that would sustain you during the process. Not a negative reason, either. You had to fix something positive as your goal. I wasn't able to do that until the war. Until then I was still too much his boy. During the war I found I was my own boy and a pretty capable one at that."

He stopped, trying to evaluate what he had said, trying to test it. But Edith's eyes, fixed on the cup, suddenly swung up to look at him. "What was the goal?" she asked.

Palmer took a breath and held it for a moment. "To be useful," he said then. "Just to be useful."

Edith's fine, light eyebrows drew slowly together in a frown. "Now I'm not following you," she admitted.

"When he died," Palmer said, his words coming faster now, too fast to be studied the way he liked to, "a hundred fellow bankers, political hacks and business leaders laid his body to rest with the traditional pieties. He had devoted his life to service. He had given unselfishly. He had been a good citizen.

You heard them. Did you wonder why so many second-rate fakers thought so highly of him? Second-rate praise is more damning than insult."

"But he'd led a useful life," she said.

"You mean he gave money," Palmer retorted.

"Money, to people who need it, is useful."

"Giving money is a cheap way out," Palmer snapped. "It doesn't engage any part of you but your checkbook. And that," he added in a much louder voice, abruptly seeing a way to explain himself, "is exactly what I mean."

Edith shrugged lightly. "I'm lost, darling."

"He gave money," Palmer said, forcing himself to speak more slowly. "To be useful means to give of yourself, not just of your checkbook."

"You want to . . ." she hesitated for an instant ". . . give of yourself?"

"I can do things in my own right," he told her, "as myself, a private, particular person. I want to be myself, doing those things, not my father's son, spending his money. That's what I mean by being useful. That's what all of this is about."

Neither of them spoke for a moment. Palmer looked down into the cup she was holding and, to his surprise, saw that the coffee was no longer still. An unsteady tremor kept its surface agitated. He glanced up at Edith's face. It was blank.

"You understand me," he said then, trying to reach past the mask on her face. He tapped the blueprints on the table. The thick paper crackled as if in flames. "All the work you're pouring into this remodeling job. It's something you can do, something useful, something of yourself."

Her hazel eyes shifted from his hand to his face. "Woods," she asked softly, "I . . ." She stopped and considered for a moment. "You're right, in a way," she went on then. "It's something useful and I enjoy doing it. But enjoyment isn't a reason. It's a result. And the reason I'm pouring myself into this remodeling, as you put it, is that I . . ." She stopped again. "Is that I haven't anything else to do in this unfriendly, utterly false-hearted city."

"Edith!"

"I don't know anyone," she continued, her voice still soft. "I don't want to know anyone. I am no one to them. I mean less than nothing in the scheme of things. And I'm selfish enough to remember that I meant something in Chicago. I was a medium-sized frog in a medium-sized pond. Here, I'm . . ." She gestured meaninglessly. "Oh, hell," she said gloomily, "I swore a tremendous oath never to tell you any of this."

When he said nothing, she pressed the half-full cup of coffee on him. "Anyway," she said then, "it's a temporary condition. I'll get over it. When we begin to entertain, it'll all come right. I'm old enough to know that it's temporary."

She waited for his response. Then, getting none, she said: "Your condition, however, is permanent, darling."

He frowned. "Meaning?"

They watched each other. The light from the overhead fixture touched the very edges of her eyelashes, making it impossible for Palmer to see into her eyes. He felt at an uncomfortable disadvantage. She could see much further into him.

CHAPTER EIGHTEEN

The man to his right hadn't spoken to Palmer all during dinner, for which Palmer was grateful. He turned slightly, as the waiter bent obsequiously to serve a wedge of ice cream, and looked to see if his right-hand neighbor had fallen asleep. It was that kind of dinner.

In his short, but busy, time in New York, Palmer had attended a dozen dinners, all of which seemed to fall into a very limited number of categories. The political dinner was designed to raise money and provide a way, for those who had contributed, to demonstrate by their physical presence how loyal they had been. Since the same businessmen, with some exceptions, showed up at both Democratic and Republican affairs, it was not so much their loyalty, Palmer recognized, as their perspicacity that was on display. The testimonial dinner, of course, was never found in its pure state, a tribute to a man and his achievements. Palmer had quickly learned that such dinners honored someone, to be sure, but only *on behalf* of something else, nearly always a something in need of funds. The charitable dinner was also, Palmer had found, inextricably mixed up with something else, usually a religious cause, rarely Protestant. Somewhere, he knew, the Protestants were busy raising money as Protestants always do, but in New York nearly every religio-charitable dinner was in aid of a Catholic or Jewish cause, whether a general fund, a hospital or a children's camp.

This, tonight, was a charitable dinner. Palmer sat watching his wedge of white ice cream—he knew from experience that it might not be vanilla, despite its color—and wondering why, as he grew more familiar with New York public dinners, he found it increasingly harder to separate them into their respective categories.

Tonight's affair, for example, was nominally in aid of a parochial school on the Upper East Side run by a particular order of teaching priests and brothers with whom Palmer was totally unfamiliar. He knew, because Mac Burns had told him so, that although Vic Culhane hadn't attended this particular school, it was in his territory and had become known as one of Big Vic's pet projects. As a result, Palmer realized now, the charitable dinner, with its religious overtones, took on a strong political coloration. And, since there was indeed a guest of honor—an alumnus of the school who had grown big in asphalt—the whole event partook of the aura of a testimonial as well.

As he sat there sorting out the threads and wondering which one led to the heart of the matter, a second waiter in the resplendent maroon-and-gold livery of the hotel bent low beside him and spooned out a great gob of viscous dark-brown sauce that sank into the softening ice cream like crank-case grease over a hot bearing.

Once again Palmer refused to believe the color of the food. Dark brown was not always chocolate. In this town, he knew, it might be coffee flavor or even a concoction of cinnamon, nutmeg and other spices, darkened to conceal the fact that it was plain, ordinary hard sauce.

He picked up one of the four dessert spoons left of the mighty array of silverware that had been spread before him and managed to lift a tiny bit of ice cream to which a stray drop of sauce adhered. He tasted it. He nodded. Pineapple ice cream with a kind of puree of walnut poured over it. He pushed the plate a discreet three inches away from him and lighted a cigarette.

He glanced about this place, the hotel's grand ballroom, an immense area containing dozens of round tables, each seating ten people. High on the walls curved a horseshoe balcony at which tables for four were arranged. At the far end, on a kind of stage platform, sat a five-piece band which had played through dinner what seemed in retrospect to have been a non-stop medley of popular songs exactly two years past their prime. During the main course— rare roast beef—they had played several choruses of "Tenderly," evidently the leader's time-honored attempt at levity. There was to be dancing later, Palmer knew from the invitation, and some kind of floor show featuring a master of ceremonies he had never heard of, but who Virginia Clary remembered as very big in the Mountains. Since this had meant nothing to Palmer, she had explained that these Mountains were the Catskills, where summer resorts employed both the kind of comedian and the style of floor-show act that these dinners seemed to keep alive during off-season months.

Palmer looked for her now. She was supposed to be at the Ubco table, Number Six, with Harry Elder and a group of the boys from the press.

He tried to make out the table numbers but, from his seat on the dais, flooded with light, he could see very little of the darkened room. Before dinner he had verbally okayed ordering as much liquor as Virginia thought she would need for the table. Palmer squinted now, trying to find a table with at least six empties on it, but quickly saw that nearly all the tables had several bottles of whisky. The dais guests' reception before dinner, in a room separated from the much noisier and obviously happier general reception, had been a dull, almost drinkless affair. The number of priests, politicos and other dignitaries hadn't held down the drinking, Palmer reflected. It had been, instead, the knowledge in the minds of all of them that they had a two- to three-hour stint ahead of them under lights that pitilessly revealed their smallest action. They had to remain relatively sober, all of them.

And so, at a signal, when they had filed out one behind the other in a kind of lock-step to take their places on the dais before a seated throng, the special guests had all been uncomfortably aware of the fact that, with a few exceptions, they were the soberest men in the hall. Standing at his chair for the "Star-Spangled Banner" and for the benediction by one of the school's priests, Palmer had tried to locate a captain from whom another drink might be got. There was no help for it, however, nor through the whole long meal. Dinners like these called for a great deal of drinking from their common guests, but demanded a dais of upright, clear-eyed, exemplary leaders of men.

Now, as he watched his ice cream settle slowly into its plate like a deflated balloon, Palmer tried to accustom his eyes to the darkness beyond the dais. Some of the guests were on their feet, that much he could see. They moved slowly in the narrow spaces between tables, bending over to shake a hand here, pat a shoulder there, linger for a whispered conference, then inch their way crabwise to another table, another handshake, another exchange of whispers.

At that moment someone rapped sharply on the speaker's microphone standard, a clanging, hollow sound that echoed through the room. Palmer heard a throat being cleared on mike and turned to see the dais master of ceremonies, as distinct from the floor show's moderator, rustle through a sheaf of exceedingly noisy papers.

"Ladies and . . ." The man stopped talking and began searching through his papers for, Palmer felt sure, the missing word. Having found it, the master of ceremonies, a short, squat man named Groark, cleared his throat again.

"Ladies and gentle—" An agonized howl drowned out his words as the public-address system developed an attack of feed-back. Groark rattled papers and looked despondently at the man on his right, Vic Culhane, who sitting down was almost as tall as Groark standing up.

"Friends!" Groark attempted. The word fell like an immense papier-mâché boulder among the tables in the darkness before him. "Before we hear from some of our distinguished and honored guests tonight, which I know we're all waiting and anxious to hear from, it is my distinct and very pleasant honor to introduce Rabbi Ben Chaim Feitlebaum, who will do us the invocation."

The news was greeted by a wave of chair-scraping and coughing from the almost invisible audience as table-hoppers found seats and the more responsible guests began shushing the more inebriated among them.

Rabbi Feitlebaum, in the sudden piercing glare of a spotlight thrown on his face, looked all of eighteen years old to Palmer. His ritually unshorn sideburns were so short that he seemed not yet to have begun shaving—anywhere, let alone his sideburns. Then Palmer noticed a soft, full, light-brown and very wavy mustache. He revised his estimate of the Rabbi's age upwards to, possibly, twenty-five.

"My very good friends," Feitlebaum began.

Palmer immediately amended the man's age to the mid-thirties. No one younger than that could have gained enough churchly experience to invest a monosyllable like "good" with such wondrous unction. He reminded Palmer at once of his old minister at St. Paul's in Chicago who could do much the same thing with the word "blood," creating three distinct vowel sounds to replace the mingy original one, all of them produced just above the pharynx with the kind of gloating throatiness that Palmer had always imagined came from having a dumpling stuck in there.

"My very good friends of every faith," Feitlebaum continued. "We are gathered here tonight in the sight of the Almighty on high and in the spirit, the word and, yes, the deed of lovingkindness and eternal brotherhood to celebrate and to exalt with our common understanding, our mutual devotion and our everlasting humility a cause which has found a chosen place at the very center and core of our being, so central to our philosophy, so deeply and so fundamentally imbedded in our immortal souls that it has become a part and a portion of the daily existence which, under Divine sufferance and in the spirit of most holy and reverent works, we are given to enjoy."

Palmer saw a man tiptoe past the Rabbi, bend over Big Vic Culhane and begin a long, whispered conversation complete with gestures. Palmer sat forward, so that the overhead floodlights cast a shadow across his face, and closed his eyes for a moment, hoping that everyone's attention was on Feitlebaum. He tried to recall the roster of speakers, mentally assigning an outside limit to the length of their remarks. He arrived at a total of one solid hour of speech-making. Sighing softly, Palmer sat back in his chair and held his cigarette before his face to hide his still-closed eyes.

". . . shine down Thy radiance upon our works here tonight and in the tonights and todays that shall follow," Feitlebaum was saying, "and touch with Thy goodness and inspiration the deeds that we shall make possible."

Palmer opened his eyes and turned to the Rabbi, noticing as he did so that the hair of the man whispering to Culhane was a brilliant yellow, Mac Burns's shade.

". . . altogether fitting and proper that we shall do so," Feitlebaum went on, "and that a representative of the Senior Faith, such as I, shall be called upon and summoned forth to join shoulder to shoulder in such a worthy cause."

The black satin skullcap on the Rabbi's head moved gently forward and back as he spoke, alternately revealing and hiding Mac Burns. Culhane himself seemed not to be talking. Motionless, eyes straight ahead, he sat there while Burns poured out a torrent of muttered words from a mouth that moved as little as did Culhane.

Palmer found himself wondering what could possibly be quite so important that Burns could not wait until after the Rabbi had concluded. Then he realized, with a slight shock of recognition, that he knew too much about Burns to be that naïve. Almost any moderately interesting chitchat would do in a situation like this, Palmer understood. It was not what Burns was telling Culhane, but rather that he actually was doing it, in front of several thousand people, during a preternaturally solemn moment.

The great thing in politics, Palmer decided, was appearance. Everyone knew that Burns was Culhane's intimate. But Culhane had other men close to him, too. Burns had the job, therefore, of constantly reminding all to whom such matters were important that he, Burns, and no one else, stood so closely to Culhane. Palmer had seen Burns stage much the same kind of scene at other of these dinners, Culhane unmoving, eyes staring out into the audience, Burns's hand on his shoulder or arm, the other hand gesturing, pointing, making motions of smoothing, of stirring, of pushing away, of beckoning. The free hand, as eloquent as a dancer's entire body, managed to catch the audience's attention, divert it from the speaker and concentrate it where it belonged, on the tiny, intense scene between Damon and Pythias.

". . . full measure of devotion," Feitlebaum was saying, "in Thy hand and with Thy guidance, O Lord. *Boruch atoh adonai, elochainu melach hoalom. Hamotseh lechem min haorets. Au-main.*"

Several guests in the audience echoed the Hebraic amen, their efforts partially smothered under another outbreak of chair-scraping, throat-clearing and the beginnings of conversation.

"Thank you, Rabbi Ben Chaim Feitlebaum," Groark said, rising to his feet and moving in on the microphone until the public-address system squealed again. He backed away to a more proper distance. "And thanks for the prayer in Gaelic," he added, winking at the audience.

After allowing a moment for laughter, Groark settled down to a rather dry summary of the school's financial situation a quarter of a century before, contrasting it with its current condition. Palmer watched Burns conclude his one-way conversation with Culhane. The public-relations man never ceased to impress Palmer with his intuitive grasp of rather complex situations. If Burns had stopped talking when the Rabbi had, it would have been seen as a kind of vaguely insulting act, and irreligious, to boot. This way, by being rude to both Feitlebaum and Groark, he depersonalized the situation and at the same time took it out of the religious realm.

Culhane nodded twice, somewhat thoughtfully, and Burns straightened up, sidled past the gesturing Groark and made his way off the dais. He paused for a moment behind Palmer and bent down, his long, narrow nostrils flaring triumphantly.

"Full house, Woody," he whispered. "They had to set up half a dozen extra tables. Great, huh?"

Palmer felt his cheeks grow warm. The experience of his adult life could not quite overcome the training of his childhood: he was embarrassed. He understood everything Burns was doing—and doing for him—by linking him with Culhane in the minds of the audience. But he could not help blushing both at contributing to an act of rudeness and at being the center of attention.

"You look like you could use a belt, buddy," Burns murmured. He patted Palmer's shoulder and, with his other hand, started to help him rise.

"Look," Palmer started to say.

Burns's thin mouth began to frame a series of soundless sentences, delivered with great urgency. His hand darted out in front of Palmer, pointed to a corner of the hall. His head nodded vehemently. His yellow eyes glittered. The whole pantomime indicated that Palmer's presence was vitally needed elsewhere. Palmer felt himself get to his feet and follow Burns off the dais and into the welcoming dark of the ballroom floor.

After they had threaded their way between a seemingly endless number of tables, they reached a side door and left the hall. Immediately the air was cooler. The sound of Groark's rather hoarse voice faded to a mumble as the door swung shut behind them.

"Boy, did you need rescuing," Burns said, grinning.

"What's supposed to be happening?" Palmer asked. "I mean, what terribly urgent thing needs my attention out here?"

Burns shrugged. "This character Groark has oral diarrhea. Isn't that enough of an emergency?"

Palmer smiled slightly. "Do you think anyone there missed seeing you talk to Culhane and then to me?"

Burns's eyes narrowed for a moment, then widened as he laughed. "You're learning," he said. "We just gave heart attacks to half a dozen savings bankers in the audience."

"It's still a Republican majority up in Albany," Palmer mused. "I don't think any of our thrifty friends will lose much sleep, even over a Democrat of Culhane's rank."

Burns's eyes darted sideways for an instant and Palmer had the odd feeling that what he had said was like a blow to the man, the rapid eye movement Burns's way of making sure no more blows were forthcoming. "Sweetheart," Burns said then, "show me where, in what book, it is written that the Republicans are unanimously sewed up in favor of the savings bankers? Have I been asleep lately, while maybe Moses came down from the mount and knocked off an eleventh commandment?" He chuckled softly and the somewhat moist sound made Palmer realize that Burns had had quite a bit to drink.

"It's common knowledge," Palmer replied. "Are you implying it isn't so?"

Burns shrugged elaborately, at the same time putting out a hand to pat Palmer's forearm. "I'm implying nothing," he said with sudden forcefulness. "Anything I tell a friend I say straight out."

Palmer grinned. "So tell," he said, resorting to New Yorkese.

"This whole cat fight at Albany," Burns explained, "is shaping up as strictly nonpartisan. You know what that means?"

"It means nobody's given any orders yet."

Burns frowned. "Such cynicism," he responded. "No, sweetie, it doesn't mean that. It simply means that when bankers start fighting with bankers, the legislators smell money."

"I'm afraid I get it," Palmer said.

Burns nodded. "By making it a nonpartisan issue, the boys at Albany will be able to milk every cent they can. They've laid it out as a real gravy train."

"In other words," Palmer said, knowing he shouldn't, but unable to resist extending the culinary imagery to infinity, "they'll be eating high on the hog."

Burns stared almost muzzily at him for a moment, sensing the sarcasm, but unable to locate it. "Listen," he said then, the sibilant juicy, "after this wake is over, I'm having some of the right people up to my apartment. Come by for a little plasma."

"When?"

"Elevenish," Burns said. "Too early?"

"Early?" Palmer asked. "I was wondering how I could survive till elevenish."

Burns's golden eyebrows went up and down several times. Then he winked broadly. "Anyone for tenish?"

Inside the grand ballroom there was a loud burst of applause.

Chapter Nineteen

After half an hour at the hotel bar, Palmer made his way back to the grand ballroom in time to hear the end of Big Vic Culhane's speech.

". . . today as in countless centuries of time past," the big, somewhat nasal, typically New York voice was saying, making the glottal stop in "coun-less," clipping the next word down to "cenchries," turning time into "toym," and doing something to the a in "past" that moved it almost across the ocean to London, but not quite.

". . . we cherish and revere the memory of those to whom we owe so very, very much," Culhane went on with his choppy, forceful delivery, "and we face the fragmentary future unafraid, unawed by its immensity, bold in attack and reluctant to retreat. It is not for us to judge, lest we be judged, the full meaning of our generation's misleaders, the despoilers of our national honor, the ravishers of our global glory. Let history judge the small, petty, picayune and infinitesimal minds who betrayed our birthright for a mess of pottage. But let history also note, and note it well, I say, that there were those among us, as there are today—and as there are here in this room with me tonight—good men and true who faced the task with courage and resolve, who . . ."

Palmer sidled into the darkened room and scanned the audience for Table Six. He hadn't the courage or resolve to walk back up on the dais, he decided now, and resume his rightful seat.

". . . place in the sun," Culhane bellowed, "the free birthright of every . . ."

Place in the sun, Palmer amended silently, locating Table Six. He side-stepped his way there and slipped into an empty chair beside Virginia Clary.

She hadn't heard him. She sat with her profile turned toward Palmer, her eyes on Culhane. Palmer watched her. He realized that he hadn't been this close to her before, only a foot away if that. In profile her high cheekbones were rounded by flesh and her mouth looked full. Her thin, somewhat long nose was turned up slightly at the squared-off tip. It struck Palmer that in profile she was beautiful while, seen full face, she was only pretty. She sat up very straight to the table, her breasts rising high under the low-necked white gown she was wearing, a kind of sheath with very thin straps. From where he sat, slightly behind her and taller in his chair, he could see the bare curve of her breasts as they entered the dress, making a dark triangle of warmth between them.

Palmer sat back in his chair and felt his cheeks grow hot. He stared at the dais. It seemed to tilt slightly for an instant. Palmer closed his eyes and waited for the tightness in his throat to subside.

". . . characterized by abnegation, capitulation and prevarication," Culhane thundered. "But the catalogue of a demagogue is a tiresome one. Let me say, instead, that . . ."

Opening his eyes, Palmer found himself staring into those of Harry Elder, his first vice-president. He winked. Harry winked. Then Elder's eyes glanced at the square bottle of Scotch before him and his eyebrows went up questioningly. Palmer nodded. He watched the older man take an empty glass filled with ice cubes and pour it almost to the top with whisky. Harry handed the glass to the man beside him, pointing to Palmer. The man, who was either from the *Times* or the *News*—Palmer couldn't remember which—silently passed the glass along.

The motion caught Virginia Clary's eye. She turned to see Palmer. Her mouth curved up in a smile. She took the glass from the newspaperman and gave it to Palmer, murmuring: "Confusion to the enemy." Then she resumed the listening pose, profile to Palmer again. He saw her sit up still straighter. The soft curving mounds of bare breast above the dress swelled slightly.

Palmer sipped his whisky, trying to remember whether this would be his third or fourth. He decided that, the way Harry Elder poured, it didn't pay to keep track.

". . . secure in the knowledge that not might, but only right, and right alone, can ever make true right," Culhane concluded. "I thank you."

The great room burst into crashing waves of applause. Culhane gestured happily and sat down, immediately turning to the man beside him, Carmine De Sapio, and beginning a rather lengthy conversation. Chairman Groark got to his feet while the applause continued to resound, and tried a few gestures of his own which, to Palmer, seemed evenly divided between motions tending to call for order and those hoping to whip up another round of clapping.

Palmer sat back in his chair, where he could see only the back of Virginia Clary's carefully tousled black hair and the smooth, faintly olive skin of her neck and back, modeled by her shoulder blades and the incurving valley of flesh that extended downward from her neck out of sight.

He sat there, alternately listening and not listening, as the speaking ground slowly on to its conclusion and the final prayer by one of the priests. (Palmer had paid so little attention that he had got the impression the clergyman was Anglican, in the dim light, until the final *"In nomine Patri, et Filii et Spiritu Sancti,"* at which point Palmer shrugged and continued sipping whisky.)

Matters progressed as they generally did after that. The comic who led off the floor show produced a firecracker string of off-color jokes, pausing momentarily between each to cover his mouth in mock embarrassment at having uttered such witticisms in the presence of the clergy.

". . . without further ado, ladies and gentlemen, I give you my favorite blonde, although I hear if you get to the bottom of things she ain't, and a really terrific little singer, ladies and gentlemen, none other than that real-life star of everybody's 'Pajama Game,' ladies and gentlemen, I give you pretty Kitty Kane. Givera big *han'!"*

A dispirited blonde with an immense rear end and a smile that had nothing to do with her eyes sang several songs of the same carefully controlled vintage that the band had been playing throughout the evening.

A ballroom dance team, the man at least ten years younger than the woman but making up for the difference with a scowl of heroic proportions, then performed two versions of "Temptation," one at slow bolero tempo, the second in what seemed to be stop-time. They finished several bars before the band did and the music vaguely petered out without reaching its conclusion, except for the accordionist, who played several chords before he realized that he was alone.

A tall, muscular tenor was allowed to sing exactly one full chorus of "The Rosary" before the comic interrupted and the two men went into a tangled routine in which the comic seemed to be impugning the tenor's masculinity and hinting at a variety of perverse tendencies while, at the same time, apparently propositioning the singer without luck. Palmer tried to follow the number for a while, just to see if the viewpoint ever cleared up, but eventually turned away and favored Virginia Clary with a broad, fake grin.

"Direct from a triumphal European tour," he remarked.

"Before the crowned heads of?" she asked.

"Drowned heads," Palmer muttered. "Isn't it eleven yet? Why isn't it eleven yet?"

"Only ten-thirty."

"Because I can leave at exactly elevenish."

"Can or must?" she wanted to know.

"Can and must."

"You turn into something pumpkinish?"

Palmer shook his head. "The word is 'pumpkinesque,'" he explained.

"What is so special about elevenesque?"

"You're drunk," Palmer told her. "I thought I recognized you."

"Not wounded, sire, but dead. You have no idea how Mr. Harrison Elder pours drinks."

Palmer lifted his empty glass. "Haven't I?" He glanced down at it and frowned. "Burns write that speech for Culhane?"

"Definitely."

"'S'he always so purple?"

"With Culhane," she said, "the mauver the better."

"Put them all together," Palmer mused, "they spell mauver." He sighed.

The comic relinquished the stage to the tenor, who launched a fiery rendition of "Temptation," evidently under the assumption, rightly or wrongly, that the audience couldn't get enough of the tune. It soon developed, however, that he was the hapless victim of special material, in that he was actually singing a medley of "Temptation," followed by "Jealousy" and concluding with *Besame Mucho*, all delivered to a rock-steady fox-trot beat from the drummer. The audience applauded fitfully, glumly endured another bucket of offal from the comic and then brightened as he announced dancing.

The ballroom lights went up. People got to their feet, squinting, and looked around them. The dais, no longer so brightly illuminated, seemed to dwindle in importance. Half the chairs along it were empty, notably those in which clergymen had been seated.

Harry Elder stood up and patted his paunch. Several of the newspapermen, without a word, made their way over to Culhane. Elder twinkled brightly at Virginia Clary. "If he won't ask you," he announced in his high, hoarse voice, "then I will."

Sitting there, Palmer had no idea what he was talking about for a moment. Then, getting the idea, he stood up and bowed slightly to Virginia. "May Mr. Elder have the honor of this next dance?" he asked politely.

"Charmed."

Palmer sat down again and watched them make their way to the dance floor, already crowded with couples. He watched the way her buttocks moved under the tight whiteness of her dress. Then he glanced at his watch and saw that, unfortunately, he had all the time in the world before his elevenish meeting. He reached over for the square bottle and poured Scotch over the half-melted ice cubes in his glass. Sitting there, he decided on this one for the road and then, whatever time it was, a quick departure. If need be, he could walk the dozen or so blocks to Burns's apartment and waste time that way. From time to time his attention was caught by a glimpse of the white dress on the dance floor. He sipped his whisky.

They returned to the table laughing. Palmer stood up and indicated her chair. "You're next, Woody," Elder rasped. "It's one of these fast tunes."

The three of them stood for a moment. Then Virginia took Palmer's hand and led the way back to the dance floor. She paused at the edge of the cleared space and turned to him. "It isn't really fast," she said, "just Latinesque."

He took her in his arms and led them slowly around the edge of the floor, doing a rhumba to what was, he supposed, something else, a mambo or cha-cha-cha, perhaps. Palmer was over 6 feet tall and, he knew, Virginia could not be much over 5 feet. Yet she seemed taller to him as they danced. He kept her body slightly away from him, on the traditional assumption that it was her prerogative to close the gap, not his. The music changed to a slow fox trot, an old Gershwin tune Palmer remembered very well from college, when it had been played much faster.

" 'Treat me rough,' " he quoted, " 'Muss my hair.

" 'Don't you dare to handle me with care.

" 'I'm no innocent child, baby.

" 'Keep on treatin' me wild.' "

They both laughed softly and continued dancing through the next chorus. "You go a long way back," she said.

"My dancing does."

"How many thousands of songs have you committed to memory?"

"I didn't even know I'd committed that one," Palmer explained. "It just sort of popped out of the nowhere into the here."

"Know any more of it?"

"Not a line."

They continued dancing. Palmer noticed suddenly that the gap had been closed. Her breasts moved slowly across his chest. He automatically began to take the necessary step back and restore the space between them. Then he decided not to.

The band lingered on the tune, moving into the verse. He could hear her as she began singing in the middle of the song's verse:

" 'Tutors and headwaiters fawned on me;

" 'Life was just a bore until it dawned on me:

" 'The cushy, sheltered way of life was really no fun;
" 'From now on some manhandling must be done.' "

Palmer tried to turn and see her face, but it was buried in his shoulder. He could feel her body down the length of his. He wondered, as he always did when dancing with someone not his wife, how much of this kind of contact meant something and how much was unconscious. He decided, as he usually did, that very little that any woman did was unconscious.

The ballroom lights had been lowered again for the dancing. Behind him, waiters were clearing tables. It was past elevenish, but Palmer had forgotten to look at his watch.

CHAPTER TWENTY

It was a much longer walk than Palmer had anticipated. The hotel had been in the Times Square area and Burns's midtown apartment was in the East Fifties. Since Virginia's apartment was on the way, or Burns's was on the way to hers—at this point Palmer was not taking tremendously great pains with details—she had offered to accompany him part of the way.

The east side of midtown Manhattan had begun to churn with people getting into and out of cabs, into and out of night clubs, bars, apartment houses and the like. The theaters to the west had brought down their curtains. The out-of-town clients and their hosts were migrating eastward.

As they stood for a moment at the corner of Park Avenue and Fifty-second, Palmer and Virginia saw two small Puerto Rican boys who looked about six years old dash up to a long, black Fleetwood and wrestle to open the door of the still moving car as it drew to a halt before a restaurant. One of the boys stumbled. His legs shot under the car.

"*Cuidado!*"

"Stop, mister! Stop!"

The other boy pulled his companion free just as the rear wheels of the car were about to roll over his ankles. The doorman of the restaurant deserted his post on the run. He dashed into the street and shoved both boys into the opposite gutter. Then, straightening up, he raced back to the pavement in time to open the Fleetwood's rear door. Even at this distance, Palmer could see his broad, welcoming smile.

"There's a really big man," Virginia muttered.

"They aren't hurt," Palmer said. "See?"

The two boys lay back against the edge of the gutter, laughing breathlessly. Virginia watched them for a moment. "It beats crying," she said then.

The light turned green and she led the way across the street. Neither of them spoke as they passed the stark, dusty vertical columns of the Seagram Building, its entire window-wall façade glowing yellowly from within.

"Violent town," she said after a moment. "Violent people. Violent things happening. Violent contrasts all over."

Palmer sighed. "Are you one of those who bleed over street urchins?" he asked.

"Not me," she said. "I used to be one. But in my day it was a respectable calling. Nowadays it's just another desperate way to be, one among many."

Palmer walked along for a moment in silence. "Those two kids didn't seem desperate to me."

"Oh, look," Virginia said.

"Oh, look, what?"

"It's too long a story."

"I'm listening," Palmer said. "And since we seem doomed to walk these streets for all eternity . . ."

"You won't like it."

"Perhaps. Tell me anyway."

"You have to understand what's working for and against those two boys," she began. "For them is the fact that they have a pretty good location. There's one fantastically expensive restaurant and two very posh celebrity-type supper clubs in that block, plus a hotel further along. And it's their block. Any other kid who tries to work it gets taken apart."

"By them?"

"If it's good—and it is—it's worth defending," she explained. "At least until somebody bigger or stronger realizes how good a block it is and takes it away from them. Why, from midnight on, they must clean up five bucks apiece."

"Opening doors?"

"Looking poor enough to kick. The guests who frequent that block are afraid to kick a poor kid, so they do the next best thing, toss him a quarter."

"What about all the doormen?" Palmer asked. "Don't they chase the kids away?"

"When somebody's looking, yes. Or if the kids get too obnoxious. Otherwise it's live and let live. After all, the kids are an outlet for the aggressions of the guests. They earn their money. It's what you might call a symbiotic relationship."

"I might? You're sure of that?"

"The other thing they have working for them," she went on, "is their pride. They will not cry in front of Anglos. That's all there is to it. Laughter has to express everything for them."

Palmer turned slightly as they walked along and caught sight of her profile.

Her mouth had thinned out to a tight line. "It's a limited vocabulary," he said then.

"Very. Now, then, working against them are a number of things. Time, for one. If they grow too big, the doormen get worried and chase them for good. Who wants a big Puerto Rican kid panhandling the block? Switch-bladesville. So their laughing, golden earning years pass pretty quickly.

"The second thing against them," she said, "is what they do with the money. If they bring it all home, they're in pretty good shape. But what kid can resist the temptation to hold out a few bucks? So many things happen with those few bucks. A kid can get his head kicked in and have the money stolen. Or he can buy pot and graduate, eventually, to horse. A full-time junkie. Or he can save up for a gun."

"Or," Palmer put in, "he can buy some clothes, see some movies, grab a hamburger now and then. Why must there be only disastrous ways he can spend money?"

She stopped walking and turned to him, her arm still slipped inside his. "I said you wouldn't like it, my square friend."

"I'm simply pointing out alternatives."

"Drawn from your own youth, probably," she said. Her large, dark eyes examined him in the light from a foreign auto display window. "You simply can't understand the way it is for a street kid in New York, can you?"

"I'm trying."

"Or what money is to him? You once told me all about money, remember? What a basic fact of life it was?"

"True."

"For these kids," Virginia told him, "money buys a way out. Release. It's spent fast because their need for escape is a pressing one. They are small, insignificant ciphers. Money makes them big, significant figures. Money is a gun that makes them taller than anyone. Or it's a pint of cheap wine spiked with methyl alcohol. Or it's a reefer or a fix. It is not a hamburger, a coke and a banana split."

"Oh, nonsense," Palmer said, trying to stare back into her deep eyes. "What were those kids? Six years old? Seven?"

She shook her head. "One of them was ten and the other slightly older. Eleven or even twelve."

"I find that hard to—"

"It's true," she interrupted. "I don't know about that particular pair, but kids their age have had it all, including sex."

"At ten?" An open Mercedes convertible, white with creamy leather upholstery, cruised slowly past. The tall blonde who sat next to the driver turned and frowned at Palmer.

"At ten years of age?" he asked in a more reasonable voice.

Virginia's mouth twisted sideways in an odd smile. "I finally shocked you."

"I'm not shocked," Palmer protested. "Awed, maybe."

133

"Comparing it to your own tender years," she suggested. She began walking again. "Don't. You and I were very late blooms, I have a feeling."

"In my day, eighteen wasn't late for that kind of thing."

"In my day, eighteen was downright early," Virginia said.

"Do you mean to tell me I wasted eight big years?" Palmer demanded, "eight years in which, had I but known, I was in my true prime?"

They turned down a side street and began walking toward the East River, crossing Lexington and stopping for a moment at the corner of Third Avenue. "I leave you here," she said then. "You keep walking east until just before your hat floats. It's the brand-new building on the right-hand corner. White brick."

For a moment, Palmer wondered whether he should ask her how she knew the location of Burns's apartment. In the distance a siren whined, growing louder. He turned in time to see a prowl car tear past, followed by a large green police ambulance.

"Somebody," Virginia said in a thin voice, "somewhere, didn't get pulled out from under the Fleetwood in time."

They stood and watched the rotating red light of the ambulance until it disappeared along the uptown stretches of Third Avenue. Without thinking about it, uttering it the instant it popped into his head, Palmer heard himself say:

"Let me walk you home."

She shook her head slowly. "I thank you," she said, "but I have a mother who watches out the window on salubrious nights like this. There would simply be too much to explain. You have so many strikes against you as an escort for her daughter that I'd never hear the end of it."

"What kind of strikes?"

"Too numerous. You're my boss, you're married. Eventually she'd worm out of me that you aren't even a Catholic."

"If I attend enough of these dinners, I'll end up taking instructions. Meanwhile, you could lie to her."

"I did that once. No good. She found out."

"That he wasn't Catholic?" Palmer asked.

"That he wasn't single. Good night."

There was an awkward pause. "Imagine," Palmer said then, "letting your mother worm a thing like that out of you."

"It's nothing," she said after a moment, "to his letting his wife worm it out of him. Really good night."

He stood there, watching the way she made no move to leave. "You struck me as someone who was pretty good at keeping secrets."

"My mother would strike you as someone who was pretty good at learning secrets."

Once again, Palmer heard himself speaking before he had thought about it. "Why don't you drop up to Burns's with me?"

"I would be sensationally out of place there tonight."

"Why? We're all working together on this thing."

"I would clash," she said, "with the other girls."

Palmer frowned. "Nobody said anything about girls."

"No one has to."

"It was explained to me as a sort of business thing. Are you sure?"

"I am not sure. Just handicapping on form alone."

Palmer nodded. "He called them 'right people.' Who do you think they'll be?"

"They'll be right, all right. Trust the old Lebanese libertine. It won't be a wasted evening."

Palmer made a face. "Be serious. I'm talking about the men."

"Eminently right." She smiled at him. "Righteously right. My, you look upset. Is this the first time Burns ever invited you to one of his gatherings?"

Palmer grinned wryly. "If what you suspect about this gathering is true, I have turned down the invitation several dozen times."

"Why?"

He watched her for a moment, his mind starting to side-step along the intricate mazes that her question opened up. Then he shook his head, declining the opening. "Why what?" he parried.

She made a face. "As an interviewee," she said, "you manage to keep several paragraphs ahead of me. I'm sorry I asked. It was a very silly question."

"No, it wasn't." Palmer heard his own words and felt his jaw clamp tight. He sensed that even the slight movement was too apparent and he tried to relax his face with a small smile. "Not always."

"Not always in general or not always in your case?"

He sighed. "I decline to answer on the grounds that it might incriminate or tend to incriminate me or not incriminate me as the case may be."

"You're among friends," Virginia said. She stood there silently for a moment. "It isn't necessary to invoke the Fifth among friends." When he failed to speak she moistened her lips slightly. "If you are among friends, that is."

Palmer realized that he had had a lot to drink. It was causing him to read too much into everything, to guard against non-existent dangers, to exercise super-caution in the absence of normal, non-alcoholic judgment. She was his friend, he supposed, if anybody was in this town. But instead of saying something like that, he heard his voice again:

"Am I?"

She took her time answering. Palmer saw now that his question had been a minor kind of insult. He understood that he had unconsciously done what he generally did, keep people at arm's length. But, in this case, did he really want her that far away?

"I don't know," she said at last, "if that deserves an answer." She paused and looked off up Third Avenue, as if to find the revolving flare of the police car again. "Friends don't exist in units of one," she said in a thin, thoughtful

135

voice. She glanced back at him and whatever she saw on his face impelled her to add one more thing: "At any rate, I am trying to behave as a friend would."

Palmer nodded. "I know that."

"There aren't . . ." She paused, then decided to go on. "There aren't any strings tied to it. As you said, we're all working together on this. We can work as friends. That's really all there is to it."

"I know," he said. "And I app–app–" He blinked, horrified at the sudden stammer. He took a quick, silent breath. "I appreciate it. Thank you."

She reached out and touched one long, thin finger to the center of his cheek. He was surprised at how warm it felt. "You really had a hell of a time with that word, didn't you?" she asked, smiling.

Palmer nodded twice, unable to talk.

"Never mind," she said, keeping her tone light. Her huge eyes swung slowly back and forth across his face. "If it's that hard for you to express, I take the whole thing as a great compliment. Good night."

She turned and walked away up Third Avenue.

CHAPTER TWENTY-ONE

The building in which Mac Burns had his midtown apartment was one of the newer, fashionable developments on the extreme East Side, a mammoth 18-story white brick edifice studded with dangerous-looking terraces set at an odd angle so that most of the tenants had a kind of view. It was built directly over a major traffic artery as the result of a daring new concept in city financing by which the air above public property was offered for sale.

Some previous city administration, more attuned to the times than its predecessors, had awakened to the wonderful possibilities involved in selling air. Palmer stood at the very edge of the river and stared up at the immense building, wondering as he did how much the contractor had paid for all that air. Had it been more expensive than other air around town? Had the city bothered to launder it, like a conscientious seller, to remove the soot and corrosive fumes before handing it over in good faith? How far above the city did such salable air exist? What if some of this expensive air drifted eastward over the Atlantic beyond the 12-mile limit? Worse yet, what if it drifted west to New Jersey, where the city fathers of Weehawken could auction it off to the highest bidder?

Genuine, natural Manhattan air. Bargain prices.

Palmer stared at the building and found it strangely menacing, the wicked-looking terraces with their sharp angles like the armed knuckles of a great mailed fist. What kind of people, he wondered, lived in this castle in the air?

He had a vivid idea of the cost of living here, either on co-op or rental basis, since Ubco held mortgages on many such properties. On a rental basis each room began at at least $1,000 a year. A small five-room apartment with a poor view thus cost well over $400 a month but, since most apartments had terraces, their cost was quite a bit higher. Four hundred a month entitled you only to the Tobacco Road section.

Palmer walked slowly along the sidewalk that led to the recessed porte-cochere, noting that when one arrived here by taxi the driver was able to swing in off the street and deposit you directly under the huge glass canopy. He found himself wondering whether the lowly $400-a-month tenants were entitled to have their cab drivers execute this dashing maneuver. But then, of course, impoverished types like that would not be able to afford cabs.

Two doormen, one in an overcoat and cap, the other in a jacket, hovered inside the glass vestibule. Both beige-and-red uniforms closely resembled that of a colonel in the French Foreign Legion. The man in the coat and hat watched Palmer's approach with grim attention, while the man in the jacket, lounging idly against the building's telephone switchboard, neglected even to look up.

Just as Palmer reached for the door himself, the man in the coat almost reluctantly swung it open for him. "Good evening?" he asked, as if genuinely concerned about the condition of the night.

"Whom did you wish I should announce you?" the man in the jacket inquired in a bored way.

"To or as?" Palmer asked.

The man looked up quickly and then managed to shove himself erect. "Pardon me?"

"Fine," Palmer responded.

"I mean, who'd you want to see?"

"Mr. Burns."

The man's eyes widened. He was now standing at attention. "Mr. Burns. Yes, sir!" He wheeled and yanked at a switchboard cord, searching for a hole in which to plunge it. His lips moved slowly for a moment until, with a sudden dart, he stabbed the plug home. "Whom shall I say is calling, sir?"

Palmer smiled slightly. "Woody."

"Yes, sir, Mr. Woody, sir." He waited, holding the telephone to his ear. "Mr. Burns, sir? A Mr. Woody to see you, sir." He listened, then frowned. "Name of Woody, Mr. Burns, sir." Then he nodded happily. "Yes, sir, Mr. Burns, sir. Right away, sir." He extracted the plug and turned to Palmer. "This way, Mr. Woody, sir."

As he followed the man to an elevator, Palmer reflected that Christmas was as yet too far away to inspire this kind of abject servility. It was also true that money alone could not, in any case, draw from such a healthily hostile man so inspired a quality of abasement. It had to be, Palmer decided, that Burns was not simply fawned on but also feared. To get a man to toady this low, one first had to scare him silly.

The foyer through which he now walked, feeling his feet sink at each step into a carpet with such a deep pile that it coated his shoe tips with dust, seemed to extend into the dim reaches of infinity. Mirrors along the walls, their faces etched in frondlike patterns, only served to heighten the vast spaciousness of the place out of all scale to the human body. As if to make certain this inhuman scale did not go unnoticed, a reflecting pool at least 50 feet in diameter now lay directly in Palmer's path, forcing him to detour around it. At the center of the pool, placing the official stamp of non-humanity on the surroundings, was a heroic-scale statue of an impossibly thin woman (since she had no breasts, Palmer was forced to make assumptions based on the excessive length of her hair) bent back at an angle that would permanently damage a human sacroiliac. She had somehow got her hand entangled in the kelpy meshes of her hair and, whether she was struggling now to free it or to relieve the pressure on her back, she was definitely in trouble. To add to her problems, Palmer noted, a triple jet of water shot up from the pool, spurted with a kind of homosexual obscenity ceilingward between her thighs and mushroomed above her head into a furious down-dropping barrage of rain. As the drops hammered on her bronze face and shoulders, they merged in rivulets that coursed down her body, creating the illusion, to Palmer at least, that the muscles of her pelvis and thighs were twitching with passion or sheer fatigue.

He was ushered into the self-service elevator with a cryptic direction: "Eighteen H north, Mr. Woody, sir."

Palmer nodded, pressed the "18" button and felt his stomach lurch as the car shot skyward. On the eighteenth floor, he wandered around in the gun-metal gray corridors for several minutes before reaching an open door through which Mac Burns's hand beckoned. Even at a distance of several yards, there was no mistaking the high gloss of the fingernails or the brilliant twinkle of the atomic cuff links.

"The man said 'Woody'?" Burns asked, grinning lopsidedly. "Aliases, yet?"

"Sorry I'm late," Palmer said, taking the offensive from him.

Burns stood leaning against the frame of the door. His suntanned cheeks looked particularly rosy, as if he had just run quite a distance. "You're early, sweetheart," he assured Palmer. "Welcome to my little shack on the river."

"Am I the first?" Palmer asked, moving slowly past him into the room.

"Not exactly." Burns chuckled loosely. "But, man, you're the most."

Palmer winced. "To think I walked all the way over here."

"Baby, you shouldn't have," Burns said. He had been drinking enough so that his normally fast, crackling voice slurred the words into a mere sketch: "Bay, y'shoun've."

"I had company." Palmer stood there in the entry foyer, eying himself in an immense pier glass of very dark mahogany and antique glass. The foyer itself seemed to have been done in a kind of Miami Regency style keyed to the pier glass. From the room beyond, he heard low voices speaking rapidly.

"The bewitching Miss Clary," Burns surmised. He laughed softly. "The boys all starey at Virginia Clary. Man, this chick is put togethairy."

Palmer made an is-that-so face. "Very bright young lady."

"Bright?" Burns seemed to consider this. "Yeah, bright." He nodded vehemently. "Bright. But put together like a telephone exchange, you know?" He poked a finger into Palmer's chest. "Every line busy?" He dissolved helplessly in mirth.

"I invited her up here," Palmer added, "but she refused."

Burns thought about this for a moment. Then: "Bright."

"Why?"

Burns shrugged. "This wasn't the time to play around with a chick, Woody-baby. She dug that. She's bright."

Palmer's mouth flattened. "I didn't invite her here for that."

Burns chuckled again. "You got another pad for playing around, huh? But, look, Woody, what's mine's yours. You need a pad, you got the run of this one. I mean it. 'S'yours. Don't even have to ask. Just lemme know so I don't bust in unexpected."

Palmer opened his mouth to say something as cutting as possible. Before he got the words out, however, Burns took his elbow and guided him quickly into the living room.

Miami Swedish, Palmer noted. The decor seemed overloaded with blond and teak colors of wood, thin upholstered squares in monotones of white, gray and black, and lighting fixtures composed almost entirely of oddly blown glass shapes held together or apart by intricate wickerwork. A large deep-pile, free-form white rug dominated the center of the perfectly square room. In the center of the rug stood a free-form cocktail table with a glass top at least two inches thick. On the table, in various degrees of fullness, sat large squat glasses with ice and amber liquid in them.

"That rug," Burns murmured in Palmer's ear, "has a thick foam-rubber backing. Take the table off it, Woody-boy, and you got the greatest, biggest, roll-aroundest humping-type bed in town. Dig?"

Palmer had begun to take in the people there, nodding to them in turn. None were strangers to him. In the far corner, next to a stainless-steel, free-standing fireplace, sat Big Vic Culhane. Despite the slump of his massive body in the low-slung chair, it was impossible to miss the size of him. His heavy legs were crossed in front of him with a solidity that resembled a bridge over a major river. His broad trunk increased in dimension from his hips to the wide shoulders that always seemed about to pull a button loose from his jacket. Culhane's rather small, regular head, with its olive Mediterranean skin and neat Irish nose, was topped by another of his political trademarks, the GI-type crew haircut he had brought back with him from World War II. Watching him, Palmer was impressed all over again by the physical power of the man which, even in repose, gave an immense, bulky solidity to everything he did. The long-lashed green-blue eyes flicked up at Palmer. Culhane winked solemnly in greeting, then glanced sideways at the man beside him, Augie Prince.

Although not an unusually small man, Prince looked tiny beside Culhane. He was, Palmer noted, as carefully dressed as ever, in a narrow-trousered, high-cuffed, skimpy-jacketed style. As if to complete the job, Prince wore a burnt-orange shirt with a faint checked pattern of brown and a tie in which the colors were painstakingly reversed. His body was narrow, no matter from what angle one viewed it, Palmer realized, with that bony kind of slimness that conferred no grace at all.

Prince was sitting forward in his chair, ankles crossed, as he continued a story he was telling Culhane about a newspaperman both of them apparently detested. Prince himself was a political reporter on a kind of roving assignment which took him from City Hall to Albany and, occasionally, to Washington, with some regularity.

Behind Prince, hunched over a corner bookcase in which Burns had installed some very current approved titles, stood Al Conn, one of the most ordinary men Palmer had ever met, of middle age, of medium height, of nondescript brownish-grayish hair, of undistinguished face, except for the eyes. They gave him away.

As Palmer watched, Conn's remarkable eyes, heavy-lidded and large, raced back and forth over the pages of a book he had opened. Palmer wondered whether Conn suffered from a form of hyperthyroidism that made his already huge eyes bulge slightly, as if straining against the lids that held them in place. They were exceedingly hungry eyes, Palmer decided, devouring whatever was placed before them. In public, Conn wore large, thick-rimmed spectacles, as if to mask the voraciousness of his eyes. Among friends, however, he seemed to see perfectly well without glasses. He had a lot of friends, Palmer reflected, in many walks of life.

Conn was known as a construction man, with interests in a general contracting firm and several real estate offices. But Palmer also knew that he was a major stockholder in private bus and cab fleets, a director of a structural steel concern, an insurance firm and several interstate trucking companies. He was also, and not incidentally, one of the most successful money raisers for the local Democratic Party committee, single-handedly amassing most of the funds for each election campaign. To his face, his many friends referred to him with loving ease as Al. Behind his back he was sometimes called The Invisible Mayor and, in lighter moments, King Conn.

". . . about what happened last week up at the radio station," Augie

Prince was saying. "We decide to rib this disc jockey so solid he'll never live it down, see? So we bring this chippie up to the studio after midnight when . . ."

Palmer nodded to Conn and allowed himself to be led to the corner bar, where Burns gestured to an array of expensively labeled bottles. "Name it, Woody."

Palmer shook his head. "My colleagues at the dinner table were dealing with a heavy hand. I'll pass."

"Y'gotta have something. Seltzer?"

"Uh, ginger ale."

". . . wait till he's got this ten-minute news break, see?" Prince was saying. "He's got to keep talking and the minute he starts we pull his jacket down over his arms and tie him into his chair. He keeps talking on mike. Get the picture? Then we pants him and he's sitting there naked from the waist down, gassing away about the latest news. But already he's got like a desperate tone in his voice, see? We bring in the hooker. She starts to work. And the disc jockey's still got maybe eight minutes more to . . ."

Conn turned toward Augie Prince. His peculiar eyes relinquished the pages of the book he was holding and swiveled slightly to devour the anecdote. Culhane, feeling the pressure of those avid eyes, turned slightly and winked at Conn. Burns pressed a large, squat glass in Palmer's hand.

"You're the first banker I ever met," he murmured, "who ever turned down a belt of booze."

"That's possible," Palmer granted.

". . . worked on him pretty good," Augie Prince was saying. "Real sense of timing. He had about maybe forty seconds to go when . . . voom! You should've heard what he did to that last news item. Right on the air! I tell you we were laughing so hard we nearly missed it. Then we grab the chippie and beat it out of the studio before they spin the next platter. Laugh? Shees!"

Culhane's big chest expanded still further as he laughed. Expecting a bellow, Palmer was surprised at Culhane's soft, controlled chuckle. "Augie," he said finally, "could we pull that on some speaker at a dinner?"

Prince's high-pitched cackle hurt Palmer's ears for a moment. "I'd be afraid to, Vic," he said, gasping slightly for breath. "This disc jockey is so mad at me I been avoiding him all week."

"Wants to get even, huh?"

"Wants the name of the chippie," Prince said. "And I won't give it to him."

Palmer winced as the combined laughter volleyed across the room. Burns, at his side, was howling joyously. Conn's sharp laugh, like the yip of a small, aggressive dog, seemed to climb through and above Prince's squeal of delight. Beneath all of them, like the steady banging of a bass drum, Culhane chuckled in that same measured way.

"Augie," Al Conn began, "if you—"

"You don't get her name neither, buddy-boy," Prince shouted.

Palmer chose this moment, amid renewed laughter, to cross the room and sit in a chair facing Culhane. It was as if a minister had entered the room, a minister or somebody's wife. The silence grew in intensity for a moment, during which Palmer reflected that there were advantages to being the relative stranger in a gathering. It gave one a kind of veto power.

The four men watched Palmer, sensing the social tension and unable for a moment to ease it, despite their experience. Then Conn laughed again, in a reminiscent way, as if Prince's anecdote had been told hours before. "I tell you," he said in a heavy, sententious tone, "as long as you can laugh, life is worth something."

As host, Burns now moved to the center of the stage, taking Conn's inanity for what it was, the lowering and raising of a curtain. "I would like to remind you humorists," he said then, "that we are exactly six weeks away from the opening of the next legislature at Albany."

Culhane lifted his heavy arms in a helpless gesture. "*Oi, g'valt,*" he muttered.

"Mac's right," Conn said staunchly. "In six weeks we gotta come to grips with this thing one way or the other, fish or get off the pot."

Palmer felt himself warming to the man with the greedy eyes. Anybody who could mash two prickly metaphors into one soggy malapropism could not be all bad. "As far as I can tell," he began, "the first thing—"

"Augie-honey," Burns cut in, "you got a deadline to make somewhere?"

Prince got up from his chair in one smooth motion, responding so rapidly to the suggestion that Palmer felt certain the reporter had been expecting it.

"It's Thursday, Macky," Prince said, moving toward the door. "I got a whole heap of things to take care of."

"Right." Burns took the reporter's elbow and moved him out of sight into the foyer. After a moment, Palmer could hear their voices raised slightly, not in argument but in some minor disagreement. Palmer stood up and went to the bar, ostensibly to add ice to his ginger ale. From the bar, he could see Burns gesticulating, a large black pin-seal billfold in one hand. Then Burns shrugged, removed a bill and handed it to Prince, who tucked it away in a wallet of almost identical design. Palmer put another cube of ice in his drink and returned to his seat.

"As far as I can tell," he began again, "the thing we have to do first—"

Culhane's head shook slowly from side to side. He grinned softly at Palmer and raised his rather heavy eyebrows several times, as if flagging a speeding train.

A door closed in the foyer and Burns returned to the living room, replacing his billfold as he did so. "All alike," he muttered, sitting down next to Palmer and laying his hand on Palmer's knee. "Can't trust 'em."

"Even if they're on your payroll?" Palmer asked then.

The silence was broken, at last, by Al Conn's high, barking laugh. "The man's waiting for an answer, Macky-boy," he said.

Burns grinned with mock sheepishness, half proud, half pretending chagrin, his narrow nostrils twitching. "To me," he intoned, his voice getting the echoing quality at once, "there is no lower form of life than a newspaperman. There are a few honest ones, sure. But when you talk about corrupt cops, corrupt politicos, corrupt businessmen, baby, the newspaper guys wrote the book."

"That's an odd thing for a public-relations man to say," Palmer observed. "Are you implying that most of them can be bought? Or are you suggesting that you've bought most of them?"

"That," Burns said, "would be telling."

"I'm interested as a banker," Palmer responded. "I know what we're paying you and I'm beginning to worry that with so many incidental expenses you aren't holding on to any of the fee."

"Don't worry about Mac Burns," Conn said. "This lad is a cat. He lands on his feet."

"Don't forget the nine lives," Culhane added almost somberly.

"I'm still interested," Palmer persisted, trying to sound equable and friendly, "in why you're so down on the press. Are they all corrupt? And if so, why?"

Burns began by shaking his head from side to side. He continued the motion as he spoke: "Damn few of 'em you can't get to, somehow, some way. Why?" He stood up and began pacing on soft, sure feet. "Know what these guys make a week? Even under the Guild contract?"

"There are a lot of underpaid people in the world," Palmer pointed out, "not all of them totally corrupt."

"And not all of them have the power newspaper guys have," Burns added. "That's what makes corruption, sweetheart. Not only the need for money, but the ability to deliver something valuable for it. Cops have that power, too. But cops are high-school stuff. On the papers, now, you're getting college men, some of 'em with two degrees. A cop will take a sawbuck bribe and run like a thief, but a newspaper guy has delusions of grandeur. He looks to better things. You can't always buy him just with money. Newspaper guys have three things going that make it impossible to resist temptation: money-hunger, power and ambition. And of the three, ambition eats them out fastest. I mean, what is a newspaper guy, way down deep? He saw too many movies and read too many stories and he's in love with one of the crumbiest businesses in the world. As long as he's in love that way, he'll never grow up. And as long as he doesn't grow up, the ambition eats away inside him. He sees guys his age making it big, famous, wealthy. He's tied to a one-fifty-a-week job. And what is this job? Cleaning out the lint from other people's navels and making it look fancy on Page One. Tipping over other people's spittoons and drawing pictures in the slime. And if he ever gets hold of a real story, he can't print it. He knows that. His advertisers will kill it. So there he is, with a kid's dream turned sour. Frustrated. Envious. Scrambling for status. No wonder he's corrupt."

None of them spoke for a moment. Then Culhane chuckled softly. "Jesus, Mac," he said, "you make him sound just like everybody else in the world."

CHAPTER TWENTY-TWO

Al Conn had left shortly after midnight, pleading that he was too old for these sorts of games although, in point of fact, he was probably no more than five years older than any of the rest of them. "Besides," he had said, raking them with his hungry eyes, "the less I know, the less I have to deny."

After that, and until about one-thirty, Burns and Culhane had continued drinking. At some point Palmer had returned to drinking Scotch because he had begun to feel lonely as the only comparatively sober man there. The talk had woven in and out of the various people and committees in Albany, tracing a complex course only a professional could follow. At one point a kind of archetypical phrase had fallen from Culhane's slack lips which seemed, to Palmer, to epitomize the whole thing:

"Mouse-trap it out of Banking onto the floor with Bernie and Jim fronting and Old Iron Ass keeping Rules under wraps."

To which Burns had responded: "If Ham can meld the two entries fast enough."

Which seemed to dispose of that point.

Shortly after one-thirty, however, the talk had become less arcane. "I hear," Burns said, his words about as slurred as they could get without being completely unintelligible, "that Murray Hill Savings Bank holds a mortgage on Harry's house and two of his farms." He turned slowly to Palmer. "Zat so?"

"If it's the Harry I'm thinking of," Palmer responded with equal slowness, "I wouldn't know. But one of our big upstate commercial banks retains him as an attorney."

"So which," Culhane demanded, "outweighs which? Which way'll Harry jump? To save the house and farms? Or the cushy lawyer's fees?"

Burns shrugged. "The Murray Hill bank can't foreclose his house and farms. Harry isn't in arrears or anything." He wheeled ponderously on Palmer. "Zat so?"

"I wouldn't know. I suppose I could find out a little about him through the clearinghouse credit office."

"Not Harry," Culhane said. "He's solvent."

"The big *gonnif*," Burns mused. "If anybody's solvent, Harry's solvent. Zat so? Woody? Huh?"

"What's a 'gonnif'?" Palmer asked.

"I mean," Burns amended, "I don't mean solvent like, solvent with whisky and cab fare, but solid solvent is what I mean. Zat so?"

"All kinds of solid solvents," Palmer murmured, listening lazily to the way his words had begun to wind in and out. "Some solids are insoluble. Some solvents are liquids."

Culhane nodded understandingly. "You are drunk," he informed Palmer.

"Zat so?" Palmer asked brightly.

Burns thought for a moment. "We got all the business out of the way? Huh? Any left?"

"No," Culhane assured him.

"Sh'I call up the broads?" Burns asked.

"Not for me," Culhane said. "Didn't I tell you I was studying to be a priest? Took both vows. Chastity and poverty."

"Keeping 'em both, too," Burns mumbled. "Goo' boy." He turned to Palmer again. "Broads, Woody?"

"He doesn't want any either," Culhane announced.

"Let the man talk for himself," Burns said.

"Took both vows," Palmer explained, raising his right hand. "Solemnly swear to tell the truth."

"Plead the Fifth," Culhane advised him.

"Cannot tell a lie," Palmer continued. "Devout, non-practicing heterosexual male Caucasian."

Burns pulled over a white phone and dialed a number. "Peachy?" he asked after a moment. "Mac. Wake y'up?"

"Don't take Peachy," Culhane warned Palmer in a stage whisper. "Too fuzzy."

". . . party going here," Burns was saying. "Couple, three guys."

"You don't want any of Mac's broads," Culhane said then. "There isn't one of them under five-ten and weighing one-sixty. You never saw such big broads, all of them. Mastodons. Not worth it, Woody."

". . . real swinging blast, Peachy," Burns was saying.

"He likes 'em that way," Culhane went on. "He used to get 'em for me, because with my size I can handle a big broad like that. He got the taste for 'em, too, out in Hollywood. He's hooked on mammoth mamas. You'd think there weren't so many monster dames that size. But he digs 'em up out of the woodwork somewhere. Any of 'em hit town from the Coast, they call him." Culhane sighed and stood up. He took a step toward Burns and snatched the phone out of his hand. "Peachy?" he yelled into the phone, "you stay up this late you'll stunt your God damned growth! G'night, doll." He hung up the phone.

"Jeez, Vic," Burns said accusingly, "I had her all ready to—"

"Big day tomorrow," Culhane said, towering over him. "I gotta blow, kid. Lunch, maybe?"

Burns stood up in a futile attempt to equalize their relative heights. "Go, already. Wife and kids bit." He watched Culhane move with surprising grace to the door. "Lunch," he called after him.

"Right," Culhane responded. "You better blow, too, Woody. Don't take any of his wooden tomatoes. Night." The door closed softly.

Burns dialed 211. "Mobile operator, please." He waited, then gave the operator a number. He waited again, examining his fingernails as he did so. "Timmy? He's on his way down. Start the motor. Night."

"Culhane's chauffeur?" Palmer asked.

Burns nodded. "Don't you dig mammoth broads?" he asked then. "Ever try one?"

"Not in a long time."

"Great sensation, buddy. I mean, you really know what you got ahold of."

"That," Palmer said, "figures." He stood up slowly, feeling little shooting pains in his knees. "Cabs hard to get this time of night?"

"What cab?" Burns asked. "I'll have my boy drive you home."

Palmer looked at his watch. "He can't be awake this late."

"My boy goes to sleep when I go to sleep," Burns said. He laughed in a meaningless way and looked around him at the glasses. Then he sat down rather hard in a chair, grunting as he did so. He stared at Palmer's tie for a moment and then up into his face. "Hey, fella," he said then.

"Time for you and your driver to go to sleep."

Burns shook his head slowly. "Tell me, sweetheart, when you get home this late, what does the Mrs. think?"

Palmer stood there indecisively for a moment, wondering whether to answer him or firmly say good night and leave. For no reason he could put a name to, he found himself saying: "I have no idea. She's always asleep."

"Never waits up f'you?"

"Not unless she knows I'm coming home at a reasonable hour."

Burns smiled. "Next morning, you never get the old third degree?"

"Never."

"Never once's she asked you where the hell you were until yay A.M.?"

"Not that I can remember."

Burns sighed. "Doll," he said, his voice taking on that chanting kind of head tone, "you have got it made."

To his surprise, Palmer found himself sitting down again. "Got what made?"

"A wife who isn't suspicious, and he asks what he's got made."

"She's used to odd hours," Palmer explained. "I've always had a lot of functions to attend."

"Woods Palmer, Jr.," Burns intoned. "Can you be as square as you come on?"

Palmer sat silently for a moment. "If I get your drift," he said then, "and you make it hard to miss, you're suggesting that infidelity would be a lead-pipe cinch for me."

146

"Made in the shade," Burns agreed. "Isn't a married guy in this town wouldn't envy the husband of a wife like that. So tell me, sweetie, how come you don't take advantage of it? Make the adultery scene? Go the Cheatsville route?"

Palmer laughed slightly and leaned back in his chair. Now was the time to say good night and leave. Definitely. "I'll tell you," he heard himself saying, "it just never entered my mind."

"Horse crap."

"I wouldn't even know where to begin."

"More horse crap."

"All right," Palmer said, starting to get up.

"Man, the sparrows will eat hearty tonight," Burns said. "Woody, this is Uncle Mac. I got eyes. I got eyes that watch your eyes. I see you measuring the chicks. I don't know what you think you got, buddy, but if it ain't a letch, I'm a Trappist monk."

Palmer sat back and reached for a glass half full of whisky. Without stopping to determine whether it was his or not, he took a long sip of it. He told himself, first, that Burns's observation had to be a shot in the dark, a lucky one. Burns simply wasn't that observant, nor had he had that many opportunities to observe. Then he realized there was nothing he could say to disarm Burns, or turn him off the track. Silence was his best weapon, a poor one at that. Silence: Father's weapon.

"No comment?" Burns asked after a moment. "None needed." He sighed. Then, grunting, he reached over and patted Palmer's knee. "I dig, Woody," he said then. "I dig the whole thing. But, baby, it's nothing to feel down about. It's not a bad thing. It's a sign you're alive, that's all. The best sign there is."

Palmer stirred slightly. He felt his lips move, stop. He moistened them by sipping more whisky. "I'm all right," he said slowly, in a very low voice, "as long as I keep that under control."

The words seemed to buzz in his head long after he had stopped speaking. He felt the usual sense, for him, of being in two places at once, the effect of drinking. He could see himself lolling in the chair, hear again what he had said and feel uneasy about having confessed such a thing. At the same time, he could feel inside himself, saying the words, and not giving a damn.

"Very odd," he muttered.

"You know what happens," Burns said, "when you tie down a safety valve so it won't work? Huh? The whole boiler blows up is what happens. I mean, control is great. I mean too much control is bad. Huh?"

"I'm all right," Palmer heard himself repeat, "as long as I keep that under control. Just that."

Burns shook his head sadly. "You banker guys. You Midwest guys. I don't know what does it. You're all hung up on sex. Instead of it working for you, all it does is bug you."

Palmer started to lift his hand and found that he couldn't. At the same time, watching himself from another part of the room, he saw the weakness of the gesture and knew he was suddenly much more drunk than he had suspected. "Control," he said, "is the whole secret."

"Release," Burns said, "is the whole secret. A guy isn't made to be that controlled." He shifted in his chair somewhat nervously. "Your married life is your own business, Woody. She's a fine-looking woman. What I'm saying has nothing to do with her or you or anything but just the plain facts of life."

Palmer tried to lift his hand again and this time got it several inches off the arm of the chair. "Enough," he grunted.

"I said it wasn't personal," Burns reminded him in a hurt way. "Men are different from women. Women have the kids and make the nest for 'em. All that crap. They're stable. They stay put. I don't mean the wild ones or the pros. I mean the average decent woman. Sexville, U.S.A., has only one location for her. But men are built different. They're hit-and-run artists. It's in the nature of the machinery, Woody. You look at the way a guy is put together and the way a chick is put together, and you know one thing is meant to stay put and the other is meant to move around. It has nothing to do with people. It has to do with the plumbing inside people. And conquisently . . ." He paused and frowned. "Conquisently . . ." He wiped the back of his hand across his thin-lipped mouth with a hard motion. "Consequently," he finished, "no matter how good it is at home, a guy still wonders. And if it turns not so good at home, he stops wondering and starts roaming around, finding out. Some guys have it good at home and good outside, too. It's no judgment on them or their wives. Got nothing to do with the case. It's the plumbing, the machinery. That's all."

Palmer sat motionless for a long moment. He felt enough at ease to fall asleep. At the same time, watching himself, he saw that he presented a picture of slovenly weakness. With a great effort, he straightened up slightly in his chair.

"Horse crap," he said then.

Burns laughed. "The sooner you realize I'm telling the truth, sweetheart, the sooner you'll ease up and live a little." He reached for the telephone again. "Lemme call Peachy, huh?"

Palmer closed his eyes. "No Peachy. No Creamy." He opened his eyes and slowly pushed himself out of the chair, feeling the strain in his shoulder muscles as he shoved down against the arms of the chair.

"What is it gonna hurt?" Burns asked. "This is an absolutely clean chick. During the day she's a ticket clerk at an airlines office. Now, you *know* she's gotta be clean. Huh?"

"Do the cabs cruise by here this late?" Palmer asked, moving toward the entrance foyer.

"Woody, slack off. Get out and meet the people. Mix it up a little. Get with it. How rough can it be?"

Palmer heard Burns stumble to his feet and follow him to the front door. "'Treat me rough,'" Palmer muttered, "'muss my hair. Don't you dare to handle me with care.'"

"Wha'?"

"'I'm no innocent child, baby,'" Palmer said, opening the door. "'Keep on treatin' me wild.'"

"You're bombed, Woody," Burns warned him. "Lemme get my car for you." He followed him along the corridor.

"Bombsville, U.S.A.," Palmer said, punching the elevator button twice before connecting with it.

"Can you make it?" Burns sounded concerned and vaguely irritated at the same time. "I'll go down with you and find a hack."

"No hack, Mac," Palmer said. The elevator doors opened. "Mac, the Knife."

"I'm coming down with you." Burns got into the car with Palmer and pushed the ground-floor button.

"'Fancy gloves has Macheath, dear,'" Palmer quoted softly, "'so there's not a sign of red.'"

"Look," Burns said gloomily as the elevator car went down, "when we hit the lobby, try to stay clammed up. I grease those doormen regular, but they got big eyes just the same."

"And Macheath spends like a sailor," Palmer whispered. "Did our boy do something rash?"

"How many did you have before you got to my place?" Burns asked.

"Puh-lenty," Palmer said. *"Ist nichts gut, Macky Messer?"*

"You *sprech* a *bissle Deutsch?"*

"Learned in the line of duty." Palmer felt the car abruptly slow to a stop. As the doors opened on the ground floor, his stomach grew queasy. "I was the guy who nabbed those rocket scientists. Me. That was *die alte krieg.* World War *Zwie."* He took a deep breath and walked into the lobby.

"Feeling okay?"

"Keep your hands off me," Palmer said in an undertone.

"I was just sort of steering you."

"And keep your women off me."

"Easy, buddy," Burns whispered. His eyes narrowed to yellow tiger slits. They were approaching the main entrance. The single doorman on duty stood up and nodded politely.

Palmer stood straighter, nodded coldly and walked by the man out into the cool night air. He continued walking toward the street. "'Tutors and headwaiters fawned on me,'" he announced to the empty street. "'Life was just a bore until it dawned on me.'"

"This way," Burns said, guiding him north on Sutton Place. "See the Eldorado under that tree?"

"Hands off."

"Ooh, you are so stoned."

"I don't want your car," Palmer insisted. "I don't want your women. You are not going to do this to me. Understand?"

"Forget the women. But take the car."

"'The cushy, sheltered way of life was really no fun,'" Palmer said. He shrugged away from Burns's hand on his shoulder, turned and began running along the street, past the long, low, black Cadillac.

At the corner he turned and ran west along a cross street until he reached First Avenue. Then he stopped, out of breath, and leaned against a rough brick wall. "'From now on some manhandling must be done,'" he said under his breath, gasping for air.

After a moment he felt the perspiration spill out on his forehead. Panting, he slumped there and felt in his pocket for a handkerchief. He could hear the snapping sound of high heels approaching. As he mopped his face, he saw a man and a woman turn the corner. They walked past him without a glance. Some drunk. Lush in a dinner jacket.

He watched the woman's buttocks sway slightly as she walked away from him. For a moment, then, he closed his eyes, turned his head away, opened his eyes, saw a cab cruising slowly up First Avenue, top light on. Stumbling slightly, he ran toward it, ran out into the street, waving one hand, running, running, furiously running.

CHAPTER TWENTY-THREE

The day had started badly. Edith had been awake at her usual hour, six-thirty, to supervise getting the children off to school. When he had finally awakened, Palmer felt the headache even before he moved his body. Wincing, he reached across to his wrist watch on the bedside table and saw that he had overslept until nearly eight o'clock. As he sat up on the edge of the bed, coming awake much too quickly, he realized that he had missed seeing the children, would get to the office late and had a miserable headache, all in one unfortunate lump, so to speak.

At breakfast, matters grew no better. Two aspirin had failed, as yet, to make much difference in the headache, but the tension he felt between himself and Edith was, in any event, increasing the headache's pain. Or so it seemed. He watched her covertly, trying to determine if only he were tense, projecting his sense of stress into the atmosphere between them. He found himself wondering what could possibly cause such tension.

"There's a very sketchy report of the dinner in the *Times*," Edith announced. "Hardly worth attending, it seems."

"None of them are," Palmer muttered.

"Then, why—?"

"My motives," he cut in, "are somewhat different from those of the *Times* reporter. He was looking for news. He found none. I was there to be seen. I was."

"Mission accomplished," Edith said in a flat tone.

"Exactly."

When she fell silent, scanning the paper again, Palmer felt unspoken thoughts hovering in the air between them. She had seemed ready to continue talking about the dinner. For some reason she had stopped herself. Wasn't that it? He sipped his coffee.

"Of course, I wasn't there the whole evening," he said then, consciously digging into the matter once more.

"I shouldn't think so."

"Burns invited me to meet some people."

Edith nodded and returned to her reading. Palmer finished his coffee and was about to reach for the pot when, without looking up from her paper, Edith lifted the pot and tipped the spout over his cup.

"Watch it," he warned her.

Her eyes flicked up, not to the cup but to his face. "Am I spilling any?"

"I didn't—" He sighed and stopped talking.

She finished pouring the fresh cup of coffee. "You're very jumpy today, darling."

"Had a lot to drink at Burns's place."

Her glance returned to the newspaper. "Lot of people?"

"Not many. Eventually just Burns and Culhane and me."

"Cozy."

Palmer decided to stop trying to read her face. "Eventually Culhane left."

"And Burns did his best to keep you there a while?"

"Yes. How'd you know?"

Edith shrugged very slightly. "He impresses me as a person who hates to be alone for too long, especially late at night." She frowned at something. Then she folded the paper and pushed it away from her. "Of course, he also impresses me as a person who'd much rather have female companionship than yours."

Palmer nodded and tried to smile. "You've about summed it up."

Edith lifted her cup and looked into it for a moment. Palmer watched her pale eyes survey the dark liquid. Wellesley sybil. "It must be a bit uncomfortable at times," she said then. "He's overfond of women, isn't he?"

"He is. But why should it be uncomfortable?"

"To another man, I meant."

"I don't follow you."

"To another man like you," she amended.

"Oh."

"He does try to include you in his plans," Edith said. There was a slight questioning edge to her words, but they remained a statement. "He strikes me as the kind who would. Aunt Jane's second husband was that way. Always trying to organize jolly little orgies." Her glance lifted from the cup. She smiled slightly at him. "But he was from the East, like Mr. Burns. Easterners are notorious."

"Mac is from the West Coast," Palmer pointed out. "Notorious for what?"

"Since when is Beirut on the West Coast? For being different from Mid-westerners. About sex."

"Pretty much what Burns was telling me last night." As he sipped his coffee, Palmer subdued the urge to glance at Edith and read her expression.

"The poor man just doesn't understand you, darling," she said.

"You could compile quite a book just of things Mac Burns doesn't understand."

"About you."

"About a lot of things," Palmer said, but too late to soften the point she was making.

Later, in the car going to the office, Palmer had rerun the conversation in his mind, trying to determine why it had seemed so fraught with hidden tension. At first it had seemed clear that only he had struggled to command composure. She had seemed perfectly at ease. Then, as he played back the conversation again, he got the uneasy feeling that everything she had said was teeming with second meanings.

At the office, irritably working his way through the meaningless contents of his "In" box, Palmer tried to dismiss the entire thing from his mind. This seemed to increase the severity of his headache. When Virginia Clary came in to him at ten o'clock, he was pleased to see her. But, after a while, she too began to add to his irritability.

". . . had a profitable evening with Brother Burns," she was saying.

"Dull, stale and profitless," he grunted. "You were wise to stay away."

"Women are always well advised to give Mac Burns a wide berth."

He looked up, frowning, from the papers she had given him to read. "What's that supposed to mean?" he snapped.

"Ee. Never mind."

Palmer stared at her for a moment, still frowning, watching the smooth curve of her high cheekbones and the untroubled clarity of her huge dark eyes. He wondered why her good spirits and obvious good health should gall him so. "Just exactly what kind of reputation has he got, anyway?" he demanded.

"Where women are concerned?" she parried.

"Yes," he said wearily, "where women are concerned."

"His private life," she told him, "is reliably said to rival the plots of a dozen stag movies."

"My God!" Palmer burst out. "What in hell possessed Burckhardt to—?" He stopped, realizing too late that he had no business criticizing the old bird before his employees. "It doesn't matter," he finished in a tired voice. "Forget it."

She said nothing for a moment, eying him, then looking down at her lap. Despite his headache, Palmer could see that she no longer sat across from him the way she once had, tense and wary. She seemed to be at ease, which was all to the good. Or was it? What purpose was served in allowing anyone around him to . . . He shook his head, as if to clear it, but only succeeded in sharpening the pain for a moment.

"I'm sorry," he heard her say.

"About what?" His voice sounded thin and peevish to his ears.

"About the way you feel."

"Um." He looked down at the papers she had brought and once again failed to get past the first few words. He heard, rather than saw, her stand up.

"Will you do me a favor?" she asked. "I told you last night that I was trying to behave as a friend. If you'd rather I didn't, please tell me."

He glanced up at her. "I'd rather you did," he said, trying to smooth out his voice and keep it from sounding pinched and irritable. "I thought I'd said as much last night."

She nodded. "But people sometimes change their minds."

"People," he said, trying to smile. The effort did something painful to the hinges of his jaw and he realized that all morning he had unconsciously been clamping his teeth together. "But not me," he added as the smile finally came through.

"What, never?"

"No, never."

She sat down, returning the smile, and watched him for a moment. " 'Then give three cheers and one cheer more,' " she quoted, " 'for the single-minded captain of the Pinafore.' "

"Wrong. I'm the first mate." He sighed, finding that, after all, he was going to discuss Burckhardt with her. "The captain, on the other hand," he said, "employs idiots like Burns and drops them in my lap for care and feeding." He shook his head sadly. "What could have possessed him to retain anybody like that?"

"Oh, come on," Virginia Clary said. "Secretly you like Mac."

"Give me one good reason."

"Because he's likable, in a horrible way. Because he's useful. Because you need him. That's three," she said. "Shall I continue?"

"What makes you say he's likable?"

"He is," she persisted. "That lunatic way of his. His play-acting. His acutely bad taste. His supreme nerve. His complete inability to understand anything about people except their basest motives. The way he looks. That hair. And, after all of that, the way he's able to kid the whole thing."

Palmer watched her and was pleased that she didn't look away, as she had in the past. "You seem to know him pretty well," he said.

"Women can read him fairly easily."

"I've noticed that." Palmer sat back in his chair and closed his eyes for a moment. "Is there anything stronger than aspirin around here?"

"How strong?"

"Stronger."

"Ever try a tranquilizer?"

He opened his eyes. "For a headache?" he asked.

Her mouth twisted up at one corner. "I can't tell you how much well-bred shock you just managed to convey. I withdraw the suggestion."

"The implication is what bothers me," Palmer said. "Tranquilizers are for tension. What I have is a plain, garden-variety hangover."

"I may have some codeine in my desk," she said.

"Thank you." Palmer swiveled in his chair. He felt the tension recede slightly. He wondered whether her reference to it, having brought it out in the open without putting it in so many words, had somehow eased the tightness he felt. Perhaps it was the promise of codeine. Perhaps it was the easy way they were able to talk.

"I'm better already," he said then. "How do you do it?"

"I am a witch," she explained. "Your ordinary witches are usually gypsy types. For high-class witchcraft, you have to take from a Celt. Accept no substitutes."

The intercom on his desk emitted its soft, clear ping. "Excuse me." Palmer pressed a button. "A Mr. Loomis for you, Mr. Palmer."

"Put him on." Palmer sat forward and raised his eyebrows. "A Mr. Loomis," he echoed to Virginia Clary. "Are there two of him?" He picked up his phone and waited.

"Palmer?" An old man's voice, but terribly strong.

"Mr. Loomis," Palmer responded. "I'm sorry we've been missing each other the last few weeks. It's good of you to call back."

". . . till it drops another point," he heard the old man saying to someone at the other end of the phone. "Hello, Palmer? I was wondering what you were doing for lunch."

"Today?"

"I'd like to send my car for you. We could eat down here at the Club."

Palmer closed his eyes, trying to concentrate. Loomis was apparently calling from the downtown financial district. "I think I can make it," he said then. "About what time?"

"I eat early," Loomis said. "My man will come by around twenty to twelve, if that's all right with you. He'll have you down here by noon or so and back uptown by one-thirty."

"Fair enough." Palmer paused. "Anything . . . ?" He paused again, trying to phrase the thing properly. "Shall I bring anything along?" Once he had asked it, the question sounded silly.

"Purely social. Eleven-forty."

"All right. I—" Palmer heard the line go dead. Rude old bastard. He hung up the phone. Immediately a sharp pain seemed to stab inward and down from a point on his skull above his left eye. He could feel it lance its way into his brain with a kind of swift brutality. He glanced at Virginia. "Codeine," he said. "Please."

After she left, he sat there and massaged the back of his neck. He wondered how it would feel to have someone else do it for him. It would be terrible to have to depend on someone that way. Or would it?

Clasping the back of his neck, he closed his eyes again and sat quietly, enduring the pain, waiting for Virginia Clary to come back.

CHAPTER TWENTY-FOUR

Of all the luncheon clubs in the financial district, only a few could trace their history as far back as this one. Most of them, Palmer reflected as he got out of Loomis' small black Oldsmobile, were post-war creations, a result of the phenomenal increase in the district's population. The buoyant upward swing of the market since the war, despite momentary reversals, had attracted tens of thousands of new bees to the old hive. Established firms burgeoned. New firms popped into existence like maggots multiplying in rich offal. Every public eating place—and the dozens of new ones did little to ease the over-crowding problem—was so jammed to capacity that companies released their employees for lunch on shifts.

But the Club had been in existence long before the stock market became a plaything for housewives and garage mechanics, long before the ownership base of American capitalism—as the brokerage publicists put it with such a fine marriage of patriotism and greed—had been broadened to include vast hordes of people who had nothing to lose but money.

Unlike the newer luncheon clubs, which provided a place for junior partners, customer's men and the younger securities analysts to eat without being jostled by filing clerks and errand boys, the Club also offered its members a billiard room, a lounge bar and a card room. Fiske had been a member, and Gould and Morgan. Not Baruch, nor Otto Kahn. The Club was that way.

Palmer's father had belonged, too, and he had somewhat foolishly enrolled his first son, Hanley, on his birth. He had never, somehow, got around to enrolling Woods.

Palmer walked into the lobby of the narrow old office building in which the Club was located. Long ago, he thought as he waited before the iron grillwork of the elevator shafts, a building this antique would have been razed to make way for one of those wedding-cake granite monstrosities they used to build in the thirties, all setbacks and stainless-steel moderne gingerbread. And that building, he told himself now, would in turn have been demolished during the past five years for one of the all-glass fish bowls they built nowadays.

He stood there, listening to the creaking of an elevator as it made its leisurely way down the open shaft, protected only by the lacy wrought-iron grillwork. It seemed obvious to him, although he couldn't be sure, that the Club owned the building. Considering the individual power of the Club's membership, it was easy enough to understand why the building had withstood so many onslaughts of progress. By now, a creaky, cranky classic, it was probably a certified landmark.

The elevator arrived. After a moment of fumbling with the ancient latch, an operator easily seventy years old managed to slide back the door. Palmer stepped inside.

"The Club, please."

He watched the fine white hair on the back of the operator's head. After a moment, the door slid shut and the car rose through the shaft, accompanied by strange clankings and a persistent gurgling sound. Palmer frowned. Surely this building wasn't so old that it used water-ballast elevators?

"Is that the ballast I hear?" he asked the operator.

The old man turned his head slightly. "The what?" he asked.

"Nothing."

They moved slowly upward, neither speaking, as if the noises of the elevator were a concert they had both bought box seats to hear. On the twelfth floor the operator stopped the elevator too soon, then overshot his mark and had to settle the car in place with a series of crashing jerks that worried Palmer.

"Visitors to the desk," the operator said, opening the car door.

Palmer reported there, found no one and rapped the counter bell. It emitted a low peal, more like that of a gong. Time passed. Palmer glanced around him. No one built things this way any more. The ceilings were easily 15 feet high. A natural oak dado, much waxed, ran around the walls, dividing them into a lower section of virulent bottle green and an upper section of dusty ecru. Every chair in sight had also been made of a particularly light-colored oak, fashioned in a spindle-back captain's-chair design with heavy arms and a dark leather cushion. Palmer lifted one. It weighed at least 50 pounds. He found himself wondering when the chairs had been made. Half a century ago? Seventy-five years? It would be almost impossible to get them duplicated today at a reasonable price. But then, of course, chairs like this simply didn't break down and need replacement.

"Yes, sir?"

Palmer turned to find an elderly gentleman in light-gray trousers and black serge jacket addressing him. "Mr. Palmer to see Mr. Loomis."

"Yes, Mr. Palmer. He's expecting you. This way, please."

Palmer followed him along a rather narrow corridor that seemed to run half the length of the building until it opened into an immense room containing some twenty round tables. A wall of windows, the old-fashioned double-hung sash kind, let in most of the room's light. Palmer could see the river, but not much of it. An immense shaft of greenish glass and anodized aluminum blocked most of the view. He smiled slightly, trying to picture the indignation of the membership when the intruding building had gone up.

He found himself standing before a table in the far corner of the room, around which more than the normal amount of space seemed to have been left. He nodded politely to the thin old man sitting there. "Mr. Loomis?"

"Palmer, sit down. We'll order, Henry."

Palmer glanced at his watch and saw that it was just noon, which accounted for the fact that they were practically alone in the big room. He watched Loomis and hoped his examination wasn't too obvious. One didn't often get this close a look at a classic fully as creaky and cranky as the building itself.

The first impression most people got of Joseph Loomis was usually an accurate one, unchanged by closer inspection. He had probably looked this way for the past thirty years and his photograph was familiar to anyone who followed the financial news. A long, narrow head, wide through the temples and exceedingly narrow through the jaw, was topped by fine, sparse white hair that he carefully combed across his skull. His eyes were large, Palmer saw, as large as Virginia Clary's, but they rested in a fine, complex network of folded skin like two rare gems in crumpled tissue. Loomis' Yankee nose looked less sharp in real life than in photographs. It was true, Palmer noted, that his nose had an edge like a knife, but its tip was fleshy enough so that it seemed to droop slightly over the large, thin-lipped mouth and calm, false-toothed smile.

"Glad you could come," Loomis said as the waiter arrived with small leather folders in which someone had painstakingly calligraphed the daily menu. Palmer admired the delicate strokes of the pen, now thick, now hair-thin. He held the menu at a slight angle to let the light hit the paper. Yes, hand-written in thick ink. Probably a hand-trimmed goose quill, too.

"Have the roast beef," Loomis advised him. "The emince of chicken is for old codgers like me."

Palmer smiled politely, noting the strong Parisian nasality of "emince." "I remember the chef here doing something rather unusual with his *sauce naturel,*" he said to Loomis, giving the words their French pronunciation. Then, to the waiter: "Does the roast beef come that way today?"

"Always," Loomis said. "All right, Henry."

"Yes, Mr. Loomis," the waiter responded, turning away.

"A drink, Palmer?"

"Not especially."

"That's it, Henry," Loomis said. He waited until the man was out of earshot. "Flattered you like our cooking," he said then. "The last time you were here would be . . . ?" His eyes tightened thoughtfully in their bed of wrinkles. "Three years ago?" he said then. "You were here with your father. Sorry to hear about him. Thought a lot of him. Cancer, they said. Cancer?" His eyes opened very wide. Palmer stared into their hot, hazel irises.

"That's right."

"Knew he had it, I suppose."

"No. He—"

"Kept it from him, eh?"

"More or less."

"Probably wouldn't've believed it, anyway." Loomis nodded several times. He looked down at the backs of his long-fingered hands. Small brownish age spots made an irregular pattern on the thin, veined skin. "Nobody does," he added then.

An odd silence settled down over the two men, as though the reaper with the great, gleaming scythe had passed between them. Palmer felt the skin across his shoulders prickle. He wondered how he would handle the subject when he got to be Loomis' age. If.

But then, he told himself, old men live with it, sitting there in the coffins of their bodies, wondering as they got up each morning whether the clothes they put on this day would bring them home safely again tonight. He found himself thinking of Burckhardt, chunky and powerful, but only ten years younger than this man here. How soon would the muscle grow lax and stringy? How quickly the sharp blue eyes veil and grow aimless?

He watched Loomis' eyes for a moment, noting absolutely nothing aimless in their glance. The older man was examining his hands, as if for portents. Then he sighed very softly, a sound Palmer had probably not been meant to hear.

"How's Burckhardt treating you?" Loomis asked then.

"Leaving me pretty much alone."

"Ha." The monosyllable was not a laugh, but a word. "Lane leaves nobody alone. I imagine he warned you I'd turned renegade, eh?"

"He didn't use exactly that word."

"Too weak, eh? Turncoat? Traitor?"

"He told me about what I suppose a lot of people already know. Your loyalty to Murray Hill Savings."

"Can't figure it out, I imagine," Loomis said, smiling slightly. "Lane has a sharp mind for corporate structures and such. But he's poor on people. Can't read them the way he ought to. Or won't take the trouble, more likely."

"I really haven't noticed that."

"Seems pretty astute to you, eh?" Loomis asked.

"Yes."

"Why? Because he hired you?" Loomis smiled thinly again. "Sound judgment, eh?" The older man nodded several times. "All right. But he also hired Mac Burns. Eh?"

"And?" Palmer parried.

"Ha." Loomis closed his menu with a sharp slap and pushed it away from him. "You're about as close with words as your father before you. I'd heard there was another son."

"Hanley. Two years older than me. He died in the war."

Loomis looked down at his hands again, this time his palms. They looked pink and fleshy, as though they didn't belong to the bony, blotchy backs. "You're the last of the Chicago Palmers, eh?"

"Not quite. There are cousins and such. As a matter of fact, there's a whole other Palmer clan in Chicago to whom we're not even remotely related."

"Last of the banking Palmers, then."

"I'm afraid that's true enough."

"You have two boys, though, eh?"

"And a girl."

"Making bankers of 'em?" Loomis' whitish eyebrows wigwagged for a moment.

Palmer grinned. "Not if I can help it." He paused and cleared his throat. "About this Murray Hill Savings business."

"Yes, all right."

"The whole savings-bank thing, really," Palmer amplified. "Does it have to be as serious as it seems to be?"

"Seems to who?" Loomis asked dryly. "Lane Burckhardt and who else?"

"You'll have to forgive me there," Palmer said. "I'm a country boy, still. I'm not as up on things as I'd like to—"

"Palmer," the older man cut in. "Every time a man tells me he's a country boy who isn't up to our big city ways, I always finish without my wallet. Now, then. I will do you the favor of being entirely candid. I know the job you've been assigned. Will you be equally candid and stop pretending this fight with the savings banks is a holy crusade?"

Palmer smiled. "It's refreshing to hear you say that."

"Eh?" Loomis stared at him, then nodded by way of acknowledging the evasion. His large eyes scanned the room behind Palmer. "All of us here," he said then, "understand that it's a grab for cash. The savings banks now get more of the cash and the commercial banks want a bigger share than they've been getting. In a situation like that, nobody profits."

"Except the public."

"Exactly." Loomis nodded again several times. "There are certain battles the public watches with ill-concealed glee. Any kind of retail price war, for example. The public couldn't care less who wins. They simply step in and buy at the lowest prices they can find. What we have here is much the same thing. Bankers at each other's throats? The public loves it. And, meanwhile, they shop around for an extra quarter of a per cent per annum as though it would make them all rich as Croesus. Who gains? They, not we. Are we agreed?"

"Agreed."

"A man with your particular background," Loomis went on quickly, "doesn't have to be told that bankers, of all people, can't afford to wash their dirty linen in public. Am I right?"

"You are."

"It may be somebody's meat," Loomis added, "but it's our poison. Is that correct?"

"Correct."

Palmer settled back in his chair, enjoying the flow of clichés. Rich as Croesus, he mused, dirty linen, another man's poison. Had Joe Loomis really got so far, traveling on such well-worn ideas? No fuel like old fuel.

". . . time we settle the whole mess out of court, so to speak," the older man was saying, "before it gets started at Albany. Once the legislature gets its hands on it, we'll all be in the stew."

Palmer nodded politely, waited a second and then asked, with as little ingenuousness as he could muster: "Do I understand, then, that you'd be willing to withdraw your branch bill?"

Loomis sank back in his chair and, for a moment, Palmer thought he had scored a point. It was an interesting game, now that he knew the name of it. But Loomis' retreat had only been for the purpose of giving the waiter access to the table. He served their lunch and immediately retired. Palmer watched the older man poke his bits of chicken about the plate for a moment.

"You understand nothing of the sort," Loomis said at last. He glanced up at Palmer. "They warned me you were bright," he added in a quiet voice and looked down again.

"It's just," Palmer went on, "that it will be difficult to settle things out of court as long as the savings banks pursue their branch bill."

"And if we withdrew it?" Loomis' glance lifted from his plate to fasten on Palmer.

"Then there'd be nothing to battle about."

"Is this your view, or Lane's?"

Palmer shrugged and began cutting his beef. "Anybody's, I should think." He tasted a morsel of meat and found that the sauce was as good as he remembered. "No branch bill, no branch battle."

Loomis nodded. "You have an odd idea of a compromise, eh? Nothing less than unconditional surrender." He placed a bit of chicken in his mouth and chewed vigorously for a long moment. "I really wish Lane hadn't found you, young man. You're as intransigent as he."

"Not really."

"Perhaps more so, since you are, as you say, new to the situation. One expects a wait-and-see attitude from a new man."

"Actually, wait-and-see is my attitude," Palmer said.

"Let me tell you something about Lane Burckhardt," Loomis began. "He fancies himself a leader. He is, too. He has all the physical qualities of a great line officer: bearing, gusto, presence, style, dash, all the outward qualities. He seems born to deliver the line: 'Follow me, men!' As head of Ubco, he adds something else to his natural attributes: great financial power. You would think, therefore, that he should be, and therefore is, the leader of the commercial banks, eh? But he is not. No one is. Each bank follows its own destinies. After all, they compete with each other, as well as with the savings banks. What's good for Ubco isn't always good for its sister commercial banks. And when something's bad for Ubco, not all of Lane's immense personal qualities of leadership will convince his rival banks that they, too, are suffering. They may be. I should think they are, as a matter of obvious fact. But they would suffer still more if they had to submit to Lane's leadership, because they would be abdicating a piece of their own autonomy by so doing. You'll find that the chief spokesman for the commercial banks in this state will always be some gentleman from a smaller bank, preferably upstate, who has been carefully chosen to head their trade association because, in real life, he is a pygmy among giants. The giants endorse him because they obviously surrender nothing by so doing. When Lane jumps into the situation, they flinch. They retreat. And that leaves Lane so far ahead of the parade that he can't hear the music."

Palmer smiled, not so much at the thought, but at the fact that Loomis had been effortlessly able to express it without clichés, unless you counted the parade-music thing.

"I think that figure with the baton out there in front all by himself," he said, "isn't Burckhardt. It's me."

For the first time since they had met, Loomis' mouth split into a real, full grin. "Now we're talking," he said. "I wondered if you'd understood just what Lane was doing to you."

"But you're not going to like this next thing," Palmer said. "You see, the business of being a whatayacallit? Cat's paw? Stalking horse? It may all be true."

"I assure you it is," the older man said.

"But it doesn't bother me in the least."

Palmer watched him sit perfectly still for a moment. Then Loomis nodded twice. "I see," he said, finally. "I was afraid of that."

CHAPTER TWENTY-FIVE

The rest of the lunch, Palmer reflected on his way back uptown, had been a rather perfunctory brush-off, conducted by Loomis with only barely concealed haste. The sense of it could be summarized by Loomis' parting:

"I'm driving uptown in forty minutes. I don't suppose you'd care to wait?"

And Palmer's: "Thanks, no."

Now, as his cab zigzagged through East River Drive traffic, Palmer tried to sort out the somewhat meager events of the luncheon and make sense of them.

Loomis had been right, of course. Palmer's attitude was too intransigent. But it seemed clear enough to Palmer that anything less than intransigence would be taken as weakness. And, whether Burckhardt's view of the situation was exaggerated or not, Palmer understood a man like Loomis too well to show weakness.

His father had been much the same sort, although less successful than Loomis. Whether it was a game of tennis or a business battle, they both had the single-minded dedication to winning that took all joy out of opposing them. They lived by the same motto: "It isn't how you play the game as long as you win." And very possibly they were right.

Palmer shook his head. He watched the sprawling complex of Bellevue buildings move past on his left, the old, grimy hospital surrounded by steel-and-glass match boxes. Had anything been accomplished by the meeting he'd just left?

The passing reference to Mac Burns had not gone unnoted. Loomis had played that card deftly, a throwaway card, indicating specific information and implying much vaster general knowledge.

The implication that Loomis knew exactly the assignment given to Palmer, however, was either a confession of ignorance or a true statement of fact. In either case it was unimportant.

The diatribe against Burckhardt, Palmer decided now, had two purposes: to undercut his own confidence in the old bird and, at the same time, to indicate dangerous disunity among the commercial banks. In retrospect, neither bothered Palmer very much. He wasn't quite sure why, and he deliberately postponed finding out.

But the crux of the interview, he felt, had come when he admitted to being in a highly exposed position, a position in which Burckhardt had placed him, a position the old bird had carefully avoided for himself.

Palmer grabbed for a hand strap as the cab veered sharply right into a lane full of cars in order to stay clear of the ramp leading out to Forty-second Street. For a moment, Palmer caught a hectic glimpse of the United Nations Building before his cab plunged into the underpass beneath it.

Palmer let go of the strap and tried to relax in the back seat. What possible difference could it make to him, he wondered, if he were put to the job of snatching Burckhardt's chestnuts out of the fire? Why should Loomis think it mattered? Palmer was a salaried employee, not a major stockholder, of Ubco. His personal financial situation was surely known to Loomis. One didn't liquidate majority holdings in a medium-sized Chicago bank without taking home something more than cigarette money. Surely Loomis understood that Palmer was working for the pleasures of working, such as they were or someday would be, and not for the pay involved. Did Loomis seriously think that placing oneself in an exposed position was anything but a risk calculated to increase those pleasures?

As the cab slipped off the Drive and headed across town, Palmer nodded, pleased with himself for having put the thought that clearly. It was the first time he had been able to do so. He'd failed completely in trying to explain the thing to Edith. But, when put this way, it began to make sense. He tried to picture himself explaining it again to Edith:

Palmer: It isn't the money, as you know. It's the chance to do what I do best, on my own.

Edith: A chance you had in Chicago, too, after your father died.

Palmer: Not surrounded by an orderly army of his ghosts. But here, here I am, exposed, way out in the thick of a big, disorderly fight. It's a chance I'd never have in Chicago. Only here.

Edith: Here under Burckhardt's thumb.

Palmer: Beyond his reach, far beyond. So far beyond that he can repudiate me if he wants to. He planned it that way, I'm sure.

Edith: A thoroughly charming old man.

Palmer: Forget what Burckhardt is. What I am is all that counts. And I am a young man burning to act, to use power, to create, to do.

Edith: Forty-five is no longer young.

Palmer: I'm forty-four until December.

Edith: The insurance actuaries call you forty-five, and for their rather grim purposes, they're right.

Palmer closed his eyes hard and squeezed the trembling lids so tightly together that a tear oozed out the far corner of one eye. Why, he wondered, did he always cast Edith in this carping role? Why had it become so difficult for him to feel anything about her but these negative qualities? She was never this completely negative in real life, was she?

He felt the cab slow to a halt and brush against a curb. Opening his eyes, he looked at his bank, seeing it distorted for a moment by the smear of moisture across his corneas. He flicked away the tear, paid off the driver and entered the bank.

To the guard's greeting, Palmer merely nodded on his way, head down, to the elevator. Later, walking along the top floor beneath the glare of the ceiling, down the long hall of pictures toward his office, Palmer fastened his glance on the dark-green carpeting, with its flecks of metallic gold. He strode past the blonde, big-breasted receptionist.

"They're all in your—"

He was halfway into his room when he suddenly understood what she had started to tell him. The office, for all its immense size, seemed cluttered with people. Harry Elder sat on the edge of Palmer's desk, his thin white hair glowing in the diffused sunlight from the translucent ceiling. In one of the chairs before his desk sat Virginia, the only one watching Palmer, as if she had sensed his arrival. Mac Burns stood at the vast expanse of plate-glass window, pointing out something on Fifth Avenue below to a man Palmer didn't know. Examining the Hannah Kurd sculpture with a bewildered, if superficially practiced, eye stood another stranger, this one with a Rollei and flash gun slung over one shoulder.

"Woody," Mac Burns's voice intoned. Although the word gave him little to work with, he still managed to invest it with a kind of ringing aftertone that shimmered in the air for an added second or two.

"Woody, say hello to Jim Steckert, of the *Star*. And this is Mr. Kessler, his photog. Gentlemen, Woods Palmer, Jr."

Palmer moved across the expanse of carpet, shaking hands with each man in turn. Steckert was slight with a sallow face and wary eyes. His smile had a mechanical, an almost electronic, quality to it, as if controlled by relays and servo devices. A man who gives nothing away, Palmer thought. Kessler, the photographer, he soon noted, was a different proposition.

"You do this?" Kessler asked, jerking a thumb at the sculpture.

"A woman named Hannah Kurd."

"What's it, anyway?"

"My three kids."

"Shees! It's so wild it must've set you back a bundle."

"You are so right," Palmer said gravely.

Kessler turned his back on Palmer to resume his study of the sculpture. "Kooksville, U.S.A.," he muttered.

"Mac," Palmer began, "don't you think it's time to let me in on the reason for this get-together? Or am I supposed to guess?"

"Didn't you get my—?" Burns stopped, frowned, pursed his lips and ended by chewing thoughtfully on a corner of the lower one. "I'm really very terribly sorry," he said then. "I thought you— I thought I'd— Jim Steckert is on the city side of the *Star*, Woody. He's—"

"I may be new to town," Palmer cut in, "but I know Mr. Steckert's byline well enough." He turned to Virginia Clary and Harry Elder. "Will some-one . . . ?"

"Talk to Mac," Virginia said, smiling somewhat tightly. "This is all ex-ceedingly Greek to us."

"I've got it!" Burns burst out. As soon as everyone had turned to look at him, he continued: "He's forgotten what day this is. It's as simple as that. After fifteen years, he's forgotten."

"Fifteen years of what?" Palmer asked.

"Don't be so damned modest, Woody," Burns countered. He turned to the man from the *Star*. "Ever see anything like it?"

"Sure," Steckert snapped. "Every time you forget to brief a client." He turned to Palmer and switched on the smile again. "According to this character," he said, jerking his thumb at Burns, "it's the fifteenth anniversary of your entry into Peenemünde." Smile out.

Palmer frowned. "Is it? Good God, it may be at that." He moved toward his desk and sat down behind it. "Fifteen years."

"Then Burns is leveling with me?" Steckert demanded.

"I can vouch for the fifteen years," Palmer said, "but I can't give you the exact day."

"That's all right," Steckert said, sitting down across from Palmer. He pulled out a wad of yellow flimsy sheets, folded twice into a fat bundle, and produced a thick black pencil with almost no point.

Palmer watched him for a moment, wondering whether everybody was operating on clichés today, or whether he was simply being picky. He decided that if Steckert had kept his hat on, and were now to tilt it still further back on his head, the picture would have been complete. But men from the *Star*, he reflected, always remove their hats indoors.

"Just start anywhere, Mr. Palmer," Steckert said.

"How about the beginning?"

"Fine. Fine."

"You know where Peenemünde is?"

"Germany somewhere. On the water?"

"Right. The farthest east you can get in Germany, right at the border of Poland, actually a big island in the Baltic where the Peene River empties into the sea. To the northwest is the Pomeranian Bay and, on the mainland, the German town of Greifswald. To the south and east is the Stettin Lagoon and a place in Poland called Swinoujscie. S-w-i-n-o-u-j-s-c-i-e. Pronounced Svin-of-ski. Right?"

"Right."

Palmer was careful to keep a straight face as he watched the last lingering shreds of doubt in Steckert's face disappear. The reporter's pencil began to mark up the yellow paper. Nothing like a barrage of facts to dissolve doubt. He noted, too, that the photographer had abandoned his art appreciation and was listening intently. For that matter, so were Virginia Clary and Harry

Elder. Mac Burns had turned to look out the window again. But Palmer could see a faint smile at the corner of his thin-lipped mouth.

"We were a T-force of two jeeps, an armored command car and a truck carrying a squad of infantry," Palmer went on. "The boys had M-1's, bazookas and a flock of riot guns with tear-gas cartridges. I was a major then, with a lieutenant and a sergeant. The rest of the non-coms were with the platoon, not part of the T-force."

"Can you explain what a—?"

"Yes," Palmer interrupted. "It's a small, highly mobile S-2 group with very specific instructions. It avoids enemy encounters, ignores civilian resistance and moves right to its objective, which is usually the gathering of intelligence. In our case, however, we were sort of an advance movement for a larger unit following up about twelve hours behind us. My C.O. was Eddie Hagen. General Edward H. Hagen. The Russians had a main group much nearer Peenemünde than we. Hagen was sure they'd get there first, but in case they hadn't thought of making their move yet, we hoped a really fast-moving unit might pull in ahead of them."

"Which is what happened."

"Not exactly," Palmer said. "Some of the German rocket scientists had already started off toward the Russian lines. Some had gone to meet us and, of course, weren't rounded up for days afterwards. We might have gotten there almost a day sooner, but we'd been strafed several times. My lieutenant, my driver and three infantry boys were wounded. We carried them in the command car, because it had the softest springs. What they really needed was to be sent back to a medical base. But we couldn't. Hagen's orders wouldn't let us. We started from Hamburg and moved east to Rostock, about a hundred and twenty miles. It was sixty more to Greifswald, where we finally left the command car hidden in a grove of trees. The boys couldn't take the jouncing at high speeds. From Greifswald it was twenty miles to Wolgast and five more to the island of Peenemünde."

"How many Germans did you capture?"

"Technically, none. It wasn't a troop capture, you understand, just the business of taking them into custody without much in the way of security because we were thoroughly outnumbered. The only reason we could control them is because they let us disarm them."

"What about some of the better-known scientists there? How did they react? What did they have to say?"

Palmer shrugged. "They were fairly chipper, the more intelligent among them. Some of the subordinates—mainly the political spies—were glum. After we'd rounded up all of them, about a week later, let's say, we realized that we'd missed a few good ones. But we had Von Braun and Ehricke and Gauss, which wasn't to be sneezed at."

"Gauss?" Steckert asked.

"Heinz Gauss. The booster expert."

"What ever happened to him?"

"Gauss is here," Palmer explained. "He came over with the rest. He's . . . I don't know, with one of the aero-space firms. There was something about him in the papers a few months back. In the *Star,* if I remember correctly."

"Jim just writes it," Burns murmured, grinning, "he doesn't have to read the damned paper."

"In connection with what?" Steckert persisted.

"I'm not sure," Palmer said. "Some sort of exotic-fuels propulsion unit that exploded on the test stand. You could look it up."

"Do you ever run into any of the men you captured?"

"We didn't capture them," Palmer replied. "Our job was to get to them before the Russians did. The ones we got had already decided to let us get them."

"But do you keep in touch with them?"

"Not at all. Hagen and I keep touch, of course. We're still pretty good friends." Palmer glanced at Burns and then smiled at Steckert. "I think you'd get a much better story out of the Germans, or Eddie Hagen. He's a civilian now, with one of the big companies."

"That isn't your whole story," Burns said, moving toward Palmer's desk, but keeping his eyes on the reporter.

"I was about to ask," Steckert began. "With this sort of background, how did you get into banking?"

"I was already in it."

"All right. With banking as a background, how did you get into cloak-and-dagger work?" the reporter asked.

"There isn't any real—" Palmer began.

"There are a lot of ways to serve your country," Burns cut in heavily, his voice louder than usual. "Some people grow wheat to feed the nation. Mr. Palmer is another kind of specialist. He's a commercial banker. That means he . . . safeguards the nation's money and . . ." He paused and moistened his lips.

"Finances the nation's industry," Virginia Clary added in a slow, deliberate voice, her eyes on Steckert's note pad. "And does it within the framework of the nation's philosophy, free enterprise and private ownership. A lot of institutions will safeguard your money for you. But only a commercial bank is a privately owned, profit-making organization in the traditional American way. The rest of the places you might go to are modeled after other ideas, public ownership, no profit incentive, the kind of thing you might find in Russia, where they—"

"Where the rest of the Peenemünde scientists are," Burns interrupted. "You see the connection, Jim? Nothing strange about a commercial banker playing the kind of role Mr. Palmer did in the war. It all fits together, part of one picture, the protection of typical American ideals."

Steckert's pencil moved on rapidly for a moment, then more slowly. He glanced up at Palmer. "Is that the way you see it?"

"Good grief, no."

The pencil halted in mid-word. Steckert's eyes widened. "How's that?"

"The kind of things Mr. Burns and Miss Clary have been talking about have absolutely nothing to do with the orders I was carrying out at Peenemünde. In a war you live from minute to minute. You do what you have to do. You never bother wondering why. You just—"

"What he means," Burns blurted out, "is that you haven't time to think when the shells are bursting around you and—"

"Nonsense," Palmer cut in. "There was a lot of waiting in war. You seem old enough to remember, Mr. Steckert. When you got a free hour, you slept. A lot of waiting, but damned little thinking."

"I am," the reporter said. "I didn't get any farther east than Remagen, but I remember." The corners of his mouth went slowly up and something unusual happened to his eyes. He glanced sideways at Burns and then fully at Palmer. For the first time, his smile looked real.

Palmer looked down at his desk. It had been a close call. The kind of half-baked idiocies his public-relations people had tried to graft onto the story would have killed it. Any editor would have deleted such obvious editorializing, especially at the *Star*. But this way, with his disclaimer on the record, Steckert might be able to get some of the idiocies in print, if only to give meaning to the disclaimer.

(Mr. Palmer modestly denied any connection between his wartime experiences and his present work as a commercial banker. Asked if he saw any similarities, he dismissed the idea that . . .)

". . . line up a shot over here," the photographer was saying.

"Not next to the statue," Palmer objected.

"Over here," Burns said. He was standing at the window again. "You've got one hell of a view of the city here, and especially the park."

In all, Kessler took a dozen shots, using the available light that flooded down from the ceiling. As he posed, Palmer continued answering Steckert's questions until the reporter nodded and put away his pad of yellow paper. At the door, as they left, Kessler squinted at the statue.

"Can I come back some time and take another look at that thing?"

"Any time," Palmer offered.

"I don't get it. It bugs me, but I can't keep my eyes off it."

"I think that makes it a success, wouldn't you say?"

"I wouldn't know what I say," Kessler admitted. He pumped Palmer's hand. "Except that anybody who can face it eight hours a day has a lot of guts." He turned to Virginia Clary. "See you, Ginnie," he said, and followed Steckert out of the room.

In the silence that followed, Harry Elder closed the door, walked back to the empty chair beside Virginia Clary and collapsed in it. He blew out a big sigh. "Me, too," Virginia said.

"You're a fine pair of opinion molders," Palmer began bitterly as he sat down behind his desk. "Did you think anyone would actually swallow that hogwash?"

"Woody," Burns intoned. "Woody, you fielded it perfectly."

"Is that what you're paid to do?" Palmer asked, "smash line drives at me?"

"You're kidding, aren't you?" Burns retorted. "Why do you think I opened up that whole line? I wanted to hear you deny it. Steckert ate it like popcorn." He chuckled softly. "That kind of stunt goes over big with the reputable press. The human angle. The added dimension. The body behind the stuffed shirt. 'See, he doesn't buy that crap, either. He's a regular guy, just like me.' They love it at the *Star*."

"You do that very well," Palmer said. "Somebody who didn't know you would never suspect you'd just thought of it."

"I'm stabbed," Burns complained. "Tell him, Ginnie."

Virginia Clary nodded. "He's on the level. He really did plan it that way."

Palmer turned to Harry Elder. "Say something."

Elder blew out another breathy blast of air. "'S'true," he said in his scratchy, high-pitched voice.

Palmer watched each of them in turn for a moment. Look at me, he thought, the young man burning to act, to create, to use power. Did someone that vulnerable always end up being used? Manipulated?

His glance dropped to the desk. And why was it, he wondered, that the only one he really felt betrayed by was Virginia?

Chapter Twenty-six

"No," Palmer was saying as he made a second pair of drinks in Burns's big, hand-blown glasses. "You'll have to wait till the wily Lebanese gets here. I'm not going to give this lecture twice."

He turned and brought the drinks back across Burns's living room, feeling the heavy pile of the free-form white rug snatch at his heels as he walked. He handed Virginia her drink and sat down opposite her. "The only reason we're not having this session at my office," he continued, "is that I don't want any of this leaking out. And, once I get started, I have the feeling that I may raise my voice."

Virginia stared into her drink. The indirect lighting overhead reflected from the surface of the liquid into her huge, dark eyes, an up-from-under illumination that gave her an oddly gypsy look. "Which particular part of it angers you most?" she asked then. "The fact that it happened at all, or that I should have warned you in advance?"

"I'm planning to tell you both in no—"

"Because," she went on, "I'm well aware of being remiss in my duty. When Mac trooped in with the *Star* squad right after lunch, I should have gotten on the phone to you somehow."

"You couldn't have reached me. I was in a cab."

"I could have had you stopped in the lobby of the bank," she offered.

Palmer suppressed a smile. He had never seen her contrite. He had the strong conviction that very few people had ever had that privilege. "You could have," he agreed in a stony voice.

"But, honestly, it never occurred to me that Burns would pull this without discussing it with you first."

"Oh, we discussed it," Palmer admitted.

"I thought—?"

"We discussed it at well after two this morning, both of us the worse for wear," Palmer explained. "That is, I mentioned that Peenemünde thing. I see now that I shall have to be especially careful with Burns. One stray word and the whole New York *Star* descends on me."

"Did you ever think," Virginia said, still watching her glass without drinking from it, "that if he'd tried to clear the idea with you, you'd have stopped him?"

"Of course I would."

"Then it's just as well that you—" She stopped herself and looked up at him, putting her drink on the table beside her chair. Without the light from below, her eyes looked even darker, more shadowed. She seemed to be watching him out of two caverns. "I suppose," she said then, correcting herself, "that I should first ask if you think a *Star* story will help the cause. I have the feeling you don't think much of it."

"Personal publicity can't help the fight with the savings banks," Palmer said. "What on earth's difference does it make if I was at Peenemünde or Timbuctoo during the war?"

"It helps build an image."

Palmer made a face. "Talk English."

"We flacks have a language all our own," she said, picking up her glass. "But 'image' really means something, you know. The public has a mental image of you, the part of it that knows you're alive. After the *Star* runs the story, many more people will have your image in mind. The image will be a more detailed one. And the detail will be positive, strong stuff, a man of action, an intelligent man who's fast on his feet."

"Is that a true image?"

As soon as Palmer asked the question, he wished it were possible to reel it back in and bury it. He realized, however, that something had changed, probably permanently, between himself and Virginia Clary. It had changed when they danced together and when they walked home. But the change, he saw now, had really been in her.

As he sat there in momentary silence, afraid to look at her face, he recalled quite clearly that they had always been interested in each other. That was natural enough, since she was directly under his supervision. The night they had dined at Schrafft's, however, Palmer had got the clear feeling that by the end of the meal her interest in him as a person had cooled. Only the professional relationship had remained, which was good. But after last night that coolness had disappeared. He found it impossible to ignore the change. That, he reflected now, was the worst part of relationships between people. You couldn't, for long, ignore that kind of interest, keep up a pretense of professional detachment. And once you warmed to the other person's warmth, you found yourself committing hideous errors in judgment, like asking what your true "image" was.

"It is a true image," she said at last, in so grave a tone that Palmer was forced to look at her. She had leaned back slightly in her chair and her eyes were no longer watching him out of hollow caves. The light from the ceiling made her high cheekbones seem rounder than before. "It's a true image," she repeated, "of one of the Woods Palmer, Jr.'s, I've seen."

"The schizophrenic Mr. Palmer."

She shook her head. "The complicated Mr. Palmer." She sighed and sipped her drink. "Very strong," she commented. Then she sipped again. "Very good Scotch."

"Naturally."

"Meaning that on what we pay him," she said, "Mac can afford the best."

Palmer stood up. "He was supposed to be here at five-thirty." He looked around him for a phone, located it and dialed a number.

"As a matter of fact," Virginia said, "I think he represents the importer of this brand. Probably gets it free."

Palmer heard an operator answer the call. "Is Mr. Burns there?" he asked. "This is Mr. Palmer." He listened, thanked her and hung up. "I thought switchboard operators could lie better than that."

"He's out at a very important meeting?" Virginia suggested.

"And when he calls in, she'll give him my message," Palmer finished. "She doesn't know what the message is, of course."

"A terse one?"

"Practically monosyllabic."

She giggled and sipped her drink. "I think you get along amazingly well with him, considering what you are and what he is."

"All right."

"That's it? Just 'all right'?"

"Should there be more?"

She lifted her drink at arm's length and smiled at it. "You ought to get some sort of medal as the wariest conversationalist east of the Mississippi. Twice now you've managed to avoid hearing what I think about you."

"Should I?"

"Why not?"

"Why?"

"I asked first." She sipped her drink again. "I happen to be a compulsive opinion-giver. And when the object of my opinion shows no interest, it acts on me the way a match affects kerosene. I burn to issue opinions. I thirst for words to be uttered."

Palmer stirred uneasily in his chair. "I am nothing if not a gentleman," he said then. "The thought of keeping you in such distress pains me deeply. Yet I still have to know why you must offer opinions."

"I suppose," she said, more to herself than aloud, "for the same reason that you refuse to."

"Do I?"

"You dislike committing yourself."

"That's somewhat true."

"I am uneasy until I can let everyone know precisely how I feel."

"Everyone?"

"Everyone that matters."

Palmer nodded and took a long pull at his drink. After a moment he managed to quell the odd sensation of dizziness he had felt at hearing her words. After all, he told himself, a lot of people matter to her. I matter because I'm her boss. There's nothing more to it.

He drank again, set down the glass and went to the picture window that led onto the terrace. Like the other terraces in this building, it was set at an obtuse angle to the building, so that everyone might have a view of the river. He stared out at the water, darkening quickly at this hour, the lights of the Queensboro Bridge flickering endlessly in it. Behind him he heard the ice clink in her glass. A moment later he heard her put the glass down. Then she was standing at the window next to him.

"It can look much better than this," she said.

"How?"

"I'll show you."

She left and, a moment later, the room lights went out. Then she rejoined him at the window. "No inside reflections now," she said. "Everything's much clearer. In a little while the last sunlight will be gone, except for a glow in the sky. If we're lucky you'll see a boat or two come by. I mean a real ship, not barges or tugs. If it were warmer, we could watch it from the terrace."

Palmer found himself wondering—with the fatal ability to evaluate that made him a good banker—how she knew all this about the view from Mac Burns's window. He had just begun to suppress the question, when he found himself asking about it.

"Been here often before?"

"Not often. Just before."

"I didn't realize you'd known Burns personally before you came to Ubco."

"Yes, I did. A lot of newspaper people do."

"I can believe that."

"He has his private briefing sessions here for Vic Culhane. It's a tradition. Everything informal and off the record."

"I see."

She turned slightly to watch him. "Do you?"

"Certainly."

"Of course," she said then, answering Palmer's unspoken question, "I couldn't do much river-watching on those occasions. But I have one or two other friends with views of the river. And I live only a block from it myself. It makes a nice walk in the evening. I manage to keep tabs on it throughout the year."

"That's . . . uh, good."

"The wonderful thing about you," she said suddenly, "is that I can't tell whether you're relieved to hear all that, or bored to tears. What a face."

"Silent, inscrutable."

"A perfect face for a banker . . . or a gambler."

Palmer nodded. Then: "Where in God's name is Burns?"

"He'll be along."

"Did you two plan this scene?" Palmer asked. "Scenic view, strong drinks, soften up the boss, ease up on the lecture?"

"I had the distinct impression that you made these drinks."

"That's true. I'd forgotten."

"I need another. I think you do, too."

Palmer went to the bar. The half-light from the window was just enough to let him find his way. "I don't need another," he corrected her, "but I will have another nevertheless."

"Because a gentleman doesn't let a lady drink alone."

"Because I'm not a gentleman and you're not a lady," he said, fixing new drinks. "I'm a banker and you're a p.r. man." He handed her a drink and went to the phone. "Turn on a light, will you? I can hardly see to dial."

"You're not going to leave Mac another message."

"I—" He put down the phone. "I suppose not." He returned to the window. "There's a ship!" he said. "Freighter? Look at the size of her."

The phone rang. Virginia immediately picked it up. "Mr. Burns's residence," she announced. "You mealy-mouthed bastard, where are you?"

"Give me the phone," Palmer demanded.

She held him back by placing her hand on his chest. "The Waldorf? Mac, this is serious. You were supposed to be here an hour ago." As she listened, her hand moved to Palmer's lapel and brushed something from it. "Nine-thirty!" she burst out then. "What do you expect us to do till then, sit around here discussing operations?"

"The phone," Palmer said.

She shook her head. "I think I have a right to be angry," she said into the phone, "but it's nothing compared to how Mr. Palmer feels." Her hand moved slowly back to Palmer's chest and stayed there, exerting a soft pressure. "What nonsense," she said then. "We'll just go home. But he wants you in his office at nine tomorrow. Even if you have to skip bed to make it."

Palmer took her hand and removed it, holding it at her side while he reached for the phone. "Just a second. He wants to talk to you," Virginia said.

"What's the delay?" Palmer asked, holding his voice far down in tone.

"Woody-sweetie," Burns began in what *The New Yorker* had called a "muezzin whine," "I'm so upset my stomach's in knots. I've got the top three guys from my biggest account. We're huddling on major across-the-board product price changes. I just ducked into another room to call you. But, honestly, Woody, I can be there by nine-thirty at the latest."

"Nine A.M. tomorrow will do," Palmer said coldly. "We'll have our discussion then. And, at that time, you'll be able to tell me which of your accounts is that much bigger than Ubco." He let the phone drop slowly into its hook.

"It's twenty below on that telephone line," Virginia murmured.

"Let him freeze. The odd thing is, I don't believe him. Why's that?"

"Because Mac lies. I doubt if he's lying now. But you're right to wonder."

They stood there, thinking, for a moment. Palmer abruptly realized that he was holding her wrist. He started to let go, then checked the movement as being too quick, too obvious.

"That's all right," he heard her say. "You can drop it."

"What?"

She turned to watch him in the gathering darkness. "Nothing," she said, moving toward the window and breaking his grip by walking away. "Nothing."

He watched her hazy-edged silhouette against the twilight. A trick of the faint light made her seem taller there than when she stood beside him. After a moment he joined her. "You have to understand," he said, facing the window, not her, "that Chicagoans lack many of the social graces."

"They seem to lack a number of things."

"Including . . . ?"

He heard her inhale slowly. "Heart," she said then.

"We have the usual quota."

"One each. But some of you seem rather deaf to it."

"You mean because I was cool to Burns?"

"Nothing of the kind." She leaned forward, her high forehead against the cold windowpane. "Sometimes I think you have to be that way to become a successful New Yorker."

"I'm totally lost now."

"Look at that river," she said. "All glitter. Dark, swift, hidden currents with wicked rocks just under the surface and secret paths through the danger. It occurs to me now and then that the only way you succeed in this city is to have a cold core of imperturbable steel."

"I haven't looked at any X-ray photos lately, but . . ."

Neither of them spoke for a long moment. "I have," she said then. "There are several people mixed up inside you. It's a double-exposure sort of thing. There is a warm man in there and a cold one."

"In everyone."

"Is that true?"

"I believe so." He turned slightly toward her and was surprised to see that she had been watching him all along. "The warm one gets you into trouble. The cold one gets you out."

"Trouble?"

He gestured vaguely. "Complications. Contradictions. Quandaries."

"That isn't trouble," she said softly, "that's merely life."

"If you're right, then life is a messy business."

"It is."

"Disorderly," he added.

"Very."

"Upsetting."

"Always."

"I find that hard to believe," he said. "It's . . . it's . . ." He gestured again. In the darkness he felt his hand brush against hers. Then he felt her fingers take his hand.

"Confusing," she said. "Shall I hold her hand or let it go? Shall I let it go fast, like a hot potato, or play it cool? The two men inside can't make up their minds. And the peculiar thing is that the mind has nothing to do with it."

"That's hard to believe, too."

"You don't easily surrender to emotions, do you?"

"I don't ever," he corrected her.

"What, never?"

He laughed quietly. "The only times I have, I've been sorry."

"That's terrible." Even in the darkness he could see her turn to face him directly. The lights of the bridge outside struck tiny sparks in her great eyes.

"Perhaps. But true," he said.

"It's the most depressing thing anyone's ever said to me."

"I am not what you'd call a barrel of laughs at any time. And tonight I'm probably at my worst. I don't like being stood up by anybody, much less Mac Burns."

"What do you like?" she asked suddenly.

"Peace and quiet. Orderliness."

She nodded. " 'The grave's a fine and private place,' " she quoted, " 'but none, I think, do there embrace.' "

He sighed. "All day long people have been bludgeoning me with clichés. And now you quote Marvell at me."

"It's never been a cliché to me."

He listened to her voice, normally low, go somewhat lower, and realized that he had been unkind. "I didn't mean—"

"I know you didn't," she assured him. "But whatever Marvell meant, I mean." She took a breath. "And I meant it for your edification, not mine." He felt a fine tremor in her hand for an instant. "Not that I have any business lecturing. I'm supposed to be on the receiving end, aren't I?"

"Tomorrow. Nine A.M." He squeezed her hand very slightly. "You'll be there for window-dressing. It's Burns I'm really lecturing."

"Thank you." She paused a moment. "Are you always so precise in handling people? The master chess player and all that?"

"Not always."

"Only when you can keep emotion out of it?" she asked in a teasing tone.

He dropped her hand by almost throwing it from him. "That's enough," he snapped. "You're pressing on nerves."

"All right."

"You've been doing it for the last few minutes."

"I'm sorry." She stepped away from him. "It's late. Let's go."

In the darkness of the room, with the city far away outside the window, he felt an abrupt sense of isolation. She had not been touching him, except his hand, but by stepping away she had left him painfully alone. And now they were leaving.

"No," he said. "I'm sorry. That was the cold man talking."

She stood completely motionless, her eyes unblinking. "What does the warm man say?"

"He . . ." Palmer could feel his throat constricting oddly. "He doesn't . . ." He cleared his throat, but found the tautness still there. "He doesn't t-talk," he heard himself say, finally, in a pinched voice he could hardly recognize as his own. The stammer seemed only to tighten his throat still further. He closed his eyes for a moment and concentrated. "He doesn't talk," he managed to repeat then.

"Ever?"

"He seems . . ." Palmer stopped and took a long, hard breath. The tension in his throat seemed to spread downward into his lungs. He found it hard to get enough air. He opened his eyes slowly. Holding himself very erect, as if to brace himself, he took another, almost gasping, breath and said, quickly:

"He s-seems to have d-died."

"I—!"

"Long ago," he finished. The words came out in a racking exhalation that sounded like a sob.

He reached out in desperate haste as he felt the second sob building at the base of his throat. He grasped her forearms. Her skin felt warm beneath his cold fingers. He pulled her in to him and the faint, smoky scent of her perfume seemed to engulf him. Her lips were soft and, when they opened, gave him the smoky taste of Scotch. Then her arms closed around him and he began slowly, then quickly, to drown.

Chapter Twenty-seven

The first clear perception of reality came coldly, much later, with the startling realization that Mac Burns seemed to have silk sheets on his bed.

Palmer rolled sideways and stared at the sheet beneath him. In the darkness it was hard to tell. A faint light shone through the bedroom window to his left, some sort of light from an apartment across the court, perhaps, a source several floors lower which projected a small square of light on the ceiling over his head. Palmer's fingers stroked the sheet for a moment, testing the elegant texture. Then he sighed and rolled on his back again, his head propped on one misshapen pillow. He stared down at his body. He had not contemplated it in leisure for many years.

He decided that his legs were too thin. Or else, he told himself dispassionately, his trunk had thickened in recent years to the point where the legs—still the limbs of his youth—no longer matched. He stared past the dark blond patch of pubic hair to his feet, flexing his toes slightly. Damn Burns. One could get used to such Levantine luxuries as silk sheets.

Her feet could not be seen. She lay on her stomach to the right of Palmer, breathing so slowly that he felt certain she must have fallen asleep. In the faint light, the two mounds of her buttocks swelled like a pale yellow-pink confection, spun sugar, before they narrowed into the thinness of her waist. The cleavage between the mounds, deep and dark, grew shallow as his glance moved upward. The same cleft, like the bed of a river, reappeared above her waist and began to deepen until it reached her shoulder muscles. Again the indentation disappeared. Because her dark hair had tumbled sideways, he could see the nape of her neck for an inch or two and there, once more, lay the cleft, flowing upward into the great mass of tangled curls.

Palmer propped himself on one elbow, sitting up in the outsized bed to look at her from another angle. "Mhn?" she mumbled, her mouth pressed against the sheets. "Time?"

Palmer looked at his wrist and was surprised to find that he'd removed his watch. He glanced at the luminous face of the traveling alarm next to Burns's bed. "Half-past eight," he said. His voice sounded much too deep. It crackled faintly, an instrument too long unused, then used too much.

177

She sighed and turned her head to face him. "He'll be here in an hour."

"Uhn."

"Damn him." She reached out to rub the palm of her hand across his chest. He could hear the hairs rustle slightly. "I know," she said then, coming fully awake.

She shifted across Palmer, her breasts rubbing slowly over his chest as she reached for the bedside phone and picked it off its cradle. "Dial Eldorado 5-3110."

As he did, Palmer felt her push the phone receiver under his ear. Then she nestled her head against his, imprisoning the phone between them. "Waldorf Towers," he heard an operator say.

"Mr., uh, Carmody's suite," Virginia said.

After a pause, the operator replied: "Mr. Carmody is away this month."

"Then let's have, uh, Mr. Dreschler."

"One moment please."

They listened to the suite being rung. After a long moment, the phone was picked up. "Yes?" a man asked.

"Is Mr. Burns there?"

"I don't know. Who's calling?"

"Miss Clary, of United Bank and Trust Company."

"Hold on."

They lay together on the bed, waiting a much longer time, until they heard Burns say: "Doll, how'd you track me here?"

"I see you're still at the Waldorf. What was all that stuff about getting back to your place by nine-thirty?"

"You still there?"

"I've been home for an hour and I'm going out now for the rest of the evening. I just called to tell you, pal to pal, that you pulled a boo-boo tonight."

"Palmer's pissed off, huh?"

"His type just congeals. Everything he touches turns to ice. Wear a heavy coat when you show up tomorrow morning."

"The deep freeze?"

"Siberia." Her hand moved down Palmer's chest until it reached his navel. "This is a very chilly cookie." She poked her forefinger in Palmer's navel and wiggled it for a moment.

"I couldn't help it, sweetheart," Burns insisted. "Besides, Palmer needs me more than I need him."

"Wrong. He does very well by himself." She pushed down hard on Palmer's belly for a moment, but relaxed the pressure before he reacted. "Anyway, next time you spend all night with another client, think twice."

"Who's spending all night?"

"You, now that Palmer isn't waiting for you."

"Truth is, I couldn't have made it by nine-thirty. I'm just as happy he canceled. We've been at this since six and we're only half through."

"I wish I had your money, Mac."

"I wish I had your looks, kid."

"Do yourself a favor," she said. "Show up on time tomorrow. And admit you were wrong. It'll make things a lot easier for everybody."

"You're a pal, pal."

"Happy meeting." She started to put the phone away. Then they heard his voice, faintly.

"What, Mac?"

"I asked how the two of you got along together at my apartment."

Her hand moved up to cover Palmer's left nipple. "I already gave you the word," she said, rubbing the nipple from side to side. "Siberia."

"Too bad."

"For who?"

"Who else?" Burns chuckled for a moment. "Palmer's missing a real dish, doll."

"What would you know about it, doll?"

"I can dream. See you at nine A.M. sharp."

"Bye."

She reached across Palmer and hung up the phone. Then, as her face came back on a level with his, she gently bit his lower lip. "We have hours, yet," she murmured. "You heard the man."

Palmer nodded. "I don't think I've ever been party to a conversation exactly like that."

"It had its odd moments," she said, her voice half muffled in his mouth. Then she sat up and examined his face at arm's length. "You look tired."

"But happy."

"But tired."

"But of course," he said. "I'm not that much out of practice. It's only that I haven't been in special training."

"If you're trying to shame me, it's impossible."

"Women are different."

"You noticed." She ran her hand down the side of his torso. "You don't feel too much out of training." She reached his midriff and squeezed the slight bulge there. "This is particularly choice right here."

"Corn-fed."

Her hand moved slowly downward. "Prime quality," she said after a moment. They were silent for a while. Then she lifted her hand from him and reached behind her for the cigarettes on the table at her side of the bed. "Yes?"

"Please."

She lighted their cigarettes, inhaled on hers and blew smoke at the square of light on the ceiling. "I can see things no ordinary mortal can see," she said then.

Palmer shifted to a more comfortable position, reclining full length on the bed again. He felt the soft, pleasant ache in his legs and the tenderness of the muscles across his abdomen. "Tell me."

"I see that this is very new to you."

"Would you define 'this' a little more fully?"

"This . . . situation. This . . . relationship."

"Not new," he told her. "Unfamiliar."

"How unfamiliar? How long ago?"

"You're the seer," he pointed out.

"The crystal ball is cloudy. But the image is clearing. The date is hazy. But it is some time before your marriage."

He turned away from her and watched the greenish numbers on the face of the clock. Then he closed his eyes. "That's a damned astute crystal ball," he admitted.

"I'm sorry."

"Why?"

"Because I've upset you."

"How did you do that?"

"I'm not sure." She sighed unhappily and stubbed out her cigarette. "I'm no good at this sort of thing," she said then. "Out of practice and training both." She reached for his cigarette and inhaled briefly on it. "I'm pretty good at stand-up repartee, but I haven't done enough of it in bed to get the real knack."

"There, now," he said, turning to see her. "Both our shameful secrets are a matter of record."

"What?"

"That this is my first adulterous relationship. That you're not much of an expert either."

She made a face and gave him back his cigarette. "You bankers don't mince words."

"Right."

"But you have to admit," she said thoughtfully, "that we both gave polished performances. Then, what—?" She stopped herself and thought for a while, frowning.

He blew smoke at his feet. "I keep wanting to make a speech," he said. "I can't find the words for it, but the need to say them is very real."

"What sort of speech?"

"About what's happened."

"I don't require a speech."

"I do," he insisted. "Can you wait?"

"Indefinitely."

"Good." He stubbed out his cigarette and slid further down on the bed until his head was on the mattress, face tilted up at the ceiling.

"Please don't fall asleep," she asked.

"I won't."

"You seem about to. You're all limp and lazy and passive."

"Not all of me. Only choice parts."

"Very funny."

"I'm thinking, that's all," he assured her.

"Bad habits are hard to break." She turned on her side to watch him. "You're not thinking," she said. "You're worrying."

"Not at all."

"Guilt has set in."

"Not yet."

"Soon."

"I suppose so," he agreed. "Does it always?"

"Yes."

He opened his eyes. "Really?"

"Yes."

"Why must you feel guilty?" he asked.

"Many reasons."

He looked at her and found that he had slid down so far on the bed that her head was above his. He watched the rise and fall of her breasts, the faint tremor that shook the wide, brownish-pink aureoles. He reached up slowly and touched one nipple. As he did, it grew firm beneath his fingers.

"We can always do our thinking later," she said.

He grasped her breast and felt its warm softness surge to meet his fingers behind the hard point of the nipple. She shifted position and rolled on top of him. Her breasts were hot against his face, her legs smooth and cool, her belly moving slightly, steadily on his. He felt a pleasing ache in his groin that quickened to fierceness almost before he knew it.

"It was the cold man who died," she whispered in his ear, "not the warm one."

His hands stroked down along her sides until they reached the narrow waist. Then he felt his fingers close over her soft, firm buttocks and once again, gasping for air, he began to drown in the rich, dark sea of her body.

Chapter Twenty-eight

When Palmer woke up, the luminous clock face stood at nine-thirty. He turned to touch Virginia and found no one beside him.

Sitting up, he looked about the darkened room. Then he heard the sudden shutting-off of a shower somewhere in the apartment and, a moment later, the squeal of a sliding door, which he took to be that of a shower stall. He swung his feet over the edge of the bed and stood up. He immediately sat back down again.

Grinning lopsidedly, he stood up more slowly this time, feeling the long sweep of soft pain along the muscles in his thighs and back. He looked about him for his underwear shorts, found them finally under a black slip and put them on. Then he padded on bare feet into the living room, located the bathroom and knocked on the door.

"Decent?"

"Always."

He opened the door and stood there, admiring her body as she dried herself. In the pale light of the bedroom she had looked soft and yielding, all smoothly joined curves and swelling mounds. Here, in the bright glare of fluorescent fixtures, he saw the delicate ridges of ribs under her breasts, and the play of muscles in her forearms and calves.

"I would like to bottle that look of yours," she said, stopping for a moment. "I would like to cork the bottle and open it only when I needed moral support."

"There is nothing moral about my support."

"Exactly." She finished drying her legs and straightened up. "It's a little late to ask," she said then, "but I take it you like me."

"Yes, I do."

Her eyes widened. "You said that without stammering."

He frowned. "Don't be incisive, on top of everything else. You've done enough for me this evening, without that."

Her head tilted slightly, as if straining to hear the words correctly. "And here I thought all along that you were doing something for me."

"Oh, look," he began, "there must be a dozen other men in your life who'd jump at the chance to—"

"How do you know so much about me," she cut in, "and the dozens of men in my life?"

"I don't. But you're very attractive."

"Thank you." She turned to the medicine-cabinet mirror over the sink and began to fluff out her hair with her fingers. Palmer's glance met hers in the mirror. "I'm going to astound you," she said.

"Again?"

"Look," she began, "I . . . What do I call you? In the office, I know what to say. But what about here?"

"For a long time I was called Junior," Palmer said. "Don't ever try it."

"Look . . . Woods," she said then. "Woody?"

"Go on. Suffer."

She turned to face him, smiling. "Woods, I have this astounding confession. At least it's astounding to me. I calculated it while I was showering. This hasn't happened to me in almost two years."

"You're right. It's astounding."

"Isn't it? And it wasn't because I didn't want to, several times."

"What a judgment on New York men."

She nodded. "I'll tell you about the New York men I've met sometime." She came to him and put her hands on his shoulders. Her body felt cool and very firm. "But not now. I have the feeling we ought to vacate the premises."

"Separately."

"Very separately," she agreed. "I'll go first. I'll clean up the place a bit before I do."

"No. I'll do that."

"It's all right."

"I'll do it," he insisted. "I'm much better at it than you."

She watched him for a moment, puzzled. Then: "The former intelligence officer. Do you really remember all the training you got?"

"It wasn't training. It was brain-washing. You just don't forget it."

Her fingers tightened on his shoulders. "One kiss this way," she said. "When I'm dressed it won't be the same."

After she had gone from the apartment, promising to leave by a different entrance from the one she'd arrived at, Palmer stood in the middle of the living room for a minute, trying to analyze the peculiar sensation he felt. He got it after a moment: relief.

He realized then that, no matter how safe they had felt, it would have been total disaster for Burns to have walked in on them. Not that it wouldn't be as disastrous right now. But at least the first phase of putting the place to rights had already ended with her departure.

Palmer checked the glasses and ice bucket, deciding that nothing there gave away any secrets. He returned to the bedroom and snapped on a light. The appearance of the bed dismayed him. He took all his clothing to the bathroom, returned and stripped the bed down to the mattress. Then he substituted the upper sheet, relatively smooth, for the badly wrinkled sheet that had covered the mattress. He counted on the fact that the next person to use the bed could examine the bottom sheet almost without trying, but that the sheet beneath the blanket was practically invisible. After he had turned the pillow cases inside out, plumped up the pillows and smoothed down the spread, he carried the two ash trays into the living room and added their contents to the big ash tray there. Then he cleaned the bedroom ash trays with a wet Kleenex and flushed it down the toilet. When he had returned the ash trays to the bedside tables, he checked over the room again, even kneeling to look under the bed for a possible stray earring.

S-2 had trained its people in the art of creating what it called a "clean house." This meant that all rooms were free of listening devices, phones free from taps and windows arranged to make outside surveillance impossible. It also referred to the condition in which an agent left his place when he abandoned it, for an hour, a week or permanently. Nothing must be left behind that hinted at anything but normal occupancy. Finally, it covered the technique of entering an enemy agent's clean house, inspecting it and leaving it without clues to the unauthorized inspection. As a discipline, it left little to be desired. Palmer was especially grateful for it now, because it relieved him of the necessity to think.

He turned off the bedroom light and stood at the door for a moment, trying to remember whether it had been open or closed earlier in the evening. Things had happened quickly. He couldn't really remember when they had moved from the couch to the bedroom, but he seemed now to recall that the door had been closed. So be it.

He walked into the bathroom and felt the towel Virginia had used. It was not quite damp to the touch, which meant that if Burns returned by midnight, the towel would feel dry. It also meant that Palmer could not shower if he wanted to keep the towel this way. Moving quickly, he spot-washed himself and dried off with Kleenex. Tiny shreds of it clung to his skin. He rubbed them off and hurriedly dressed.

An oddly compelling sense of urgency drove him to move faster yet. The odds, he knew, were against Burns's returning this soon. But odds can be upset. In a sense, too, the picture of himself and what he was doing had begun to emerge more clearly with each minute, fighting for recognition against the S-2 routine which saved thinking. The whole thing was a little hard to believe, he realized as he sat on the toilet and knotted his shoe laces. He hadn't done anything like this since before the war. And the idea that his S-2 training would one day help him hide the evidence of an illicit meeting from a man who not only didn't care, but had urged him to do just this thing, would become wildly incongruous as soon as he really thought about it.

As he straightened out the towel, he found himself beginning to wonder whether anything was worth all this. He avoided the thought.

He turned to leave the bathroom, then wheeled and went to the shower stall. Grimacing, he reached for a handful of Kleenex and carefully mopped the sliding glass door, dried the soap, then sponged up as many of the droplets on the shower floor as he could. He dropped the soggy paper in the toilet and flushed it.

Kleenex. Kleenex. Palmer turned out the bathroom light, closed the door (Yes? Yes.) and stood for a moment in the center of the living room, the thick white rug beneath his feet. As he did so, the ability to postpone thinking failed him.

Was anything worth it?

By his father's standards, he knew, all of this was simply the act of a damned fool. It would never have begun, by his father's standards, because when his father had wanted to bawl out an employee, he had done it in as public a manner as possible. The very idea that a separate, private meeting should have been called would have seemed the utmost cowardice. But then, he reflected, his father had never employed anyone like Mac Burns.

Palmer looked at the two glasses on the cocktail table. One showed a bright arc of lipstick on the rim. He reached for the glass, intending to wipe off the stain. Kleenex. Kleenex.

Palmer's hand stopped in mid-air. He recognized a sign of panic, the attempt to destroy evidence that Virginia had been there, when Burns already knew she had. And if it were panic, what was the cause?

Palmer sat down and took Virginia's glass in his hands. He could feel the shifting flow within him, the hidden river of guilt bursting up into the light and flooding across his soul like a great tide of bitter green water, choked with wrack and yellow, dying spume.

Too much, he thought. I'm not really made this way. She'd been wrong. The cold man hadn't died. The warm man had done all this. And the warm man was really not him.

He turned the glass slowly in his hands, watching the way her lipstick mark appeared and disappeared.

"What do I call you?" she had asked. "In the office, I know what to say. But what about here?"

What about here? Why should she assume that they might ever be here again? She had no idea of what the cold man could do. Anything. Fire her. Anything. Get rid of her, erase the whole thing. What was it, anyway, but a casual business, a physical business, a matter of accidental propinquity.

He watched the lipstick mark appear again as he rotated the glass. He lifted it slightly to examine it and, as he did so, he got a very faint sensation of odor, a vague perfume, the scent of her lipstick. He brought it to his nose and inhaled slowly, deeply. Then, suddenly, he found himself tasting the rim of the glass with his tongue. He closed his eyes and sank back in the chair.

The warmth, the sheer remembered warmth of her overwhelmed him. The taste of her lipstick on his tongue closed his throat with longing. From somewhere far away, he heard the sound of a car changing gears. Reluctantly, he opened his eyes and put down the glass. As he hurried out of the apartment he rubbed the tip of his tongue in hard strokes across the front of the roof of his mouth.

When the self-service elevator arrived, he took it to the basement, got out and made his way through a labyrinth of corridors to an entrance marked for employees only.

He tried to remember the corridors he had taken, because he knew he would be using them again.

Chapter Twenty-nine

Palmer got out of the cab in front of his hotel, ignored the doorman and walked quickly through the small lobby to the elevator. He had, almost from the first day they'd moved into these temporary quarters, disliked the place. Now, as he stood before the elevator and watched the arrow over the doors swing slowly in an upward arc, he felt it in his heart to hate the entire hotel. It was a confining place, confining in its vistas of old age, of meaningless retirement, confining in its constipated decor, a kind of imitation French Provincial in more tones of brown than he ever knew existed.

Tonight, as he stood there impatiently and waited for the idiotic elevator to complete its stupid upward trip, he felt particularly hostile toward this tasteless, stultifying pile in which he was forced to live. He loathed the doddering old people living in it and he detested the cheeky subservience of the help. He felt almost certain that the doorman, seeing his cab pull to the curb, had instantly sent the elevator operator up the shaft on a nuisance call.

Palmer watched the needle of the indicator hover at the top floor, twelve, and come to rest for a long, maddening moment. There was, of course, another elevator. It stood where it always stood, at the lobby floor, open, empty and dark.

Palmer turned away from the elevators and forced himself to appear—to the eyes of the help, all of them, he was sure, focused on him, enjoying the scene—completely indifferent to the situation. He kept himself from glancing at his watch. He reached in his pocket for cigarettes, found none. Out of the corner of his eye, he saw the needle tremble again and begin its downward arc.

The moment was at hand, Palmer realized suddenly. Instead of being grateful for the delay, he had been impatient to speed the moment. Now that it was within reach, he dreaded it.

Virginia had been very nearly right, he reflected. Nothing like this had happened to him during the eighteen years of his marriage. Not precisely like this, that is, he amended. There had been that one time in Los Angeles almost ten years ago when Eddie Hagen had decided at three in the morning, after a tremendous drinking bout, to summon two professionals to Palmer's hotel suite. The whole thing had been somewhat hazy, even while it happened, except that Palmer could clearly recall the clinical, the almost therapeutic atmosphere of the thing, as though he had been suffering from grave impurities in the system and the girl had solemnly set about effecting total catharsis. She had been very beautiful, Palmer remembered now, but as Hagen had assured him, "The most beautiful whores in the world work here." She had also been doggedly thorough. No one had ever done so much for or to Palmer before. His primary reaction had been a kind of hazy surprise. When he'd seen Hagen peel off two $100 bills for the girls as they left, some of the surprise vanished.

The difference between then and now, Palmer decided, hearing the elevator stop at another floor on its leisurely descent, was that in Los Angeles he hadn't sought out sex—it had come by accident and he'd had little choice in the matter—nor had there been any relationship between him and the girl except the purity of professional and patient. And a week had gone by before he'd returned to Chicago, a week during which his hazy recollections could be given a coat of camouflaging paint and locked in a distant room of his emotional attic. He'd been able to face Edith with virtue and loyalty intact.

Tonight had been different.

The elevator door opened, revealing no one but a smiling operator. "Yes, Mr. Palmer, sir."

Tonight had been entirely different, Palmer mused as the elevator car moved upward. And he'd had no time to get his emotions in order.

Too quickly, they reached his floor. "Here you are, sir."

Palmer walked toward his apartment suite. His training was such that his pace did not slow appreciably as he drew closer to the door. But his mental processes seemed to shift into low-low gear, the first forward speed on a Jeep transmission that applies tremendous torque to the wheels, but very little speed. His thoughts, as he selected the proper key on his ring, were strong, slow thoughts, suitable for climbing out of axle-deep mud. He opened the door and walked in.

"Hello?"

"Hello, Edith," he said, closing the door firmly behind him.

"It's not Edith. It's Gerri."

Palmer leaned back against the door and closed his eyes for a moment. "Where's your mother?"

"She waited as long as she could," the girl said, approaching along a corridor. He could hear her bare feet thump on the floor as she walked, as always, hard. "Then she took off."

He opened his eyes to look at his daughter. She now stood, at the age of eleven, even in bare feet, some 5′6″ in height. In the pale light of the entrance foyer her blonde hair looked darker than it really was, parted in the middle and swept down straight on each side in that pre-Raphaelite manner the more knowledgeable teen-agers affected at the moment. The fact that Gerri was eleven, Palmer thought, didn't stop her from considering herself

187

a teen-ager. Although she had her mother's pale coloring, and freckled easily in summer, she had Palmer's facial bone structure, long, narrow and sharp-cheeked. Her eyes, he saw, as he had often seen before, were entirely her own creation, wide-set like his, hazel like Edith's, but with an odd heaviness to the outer curve of the upper lids that gave her an almost Oriental look.

"It's after ten o'clock," he said.

She nuzzled in against his chest and, linking her thin arms around his waist, squeezed hard enough to make him catch his breath. "Woody's still up," she said, her voice muffled.

"And Tom?"

"Asleep."

"And lucky Gerri's in the middle, neither awake nor asleep."

"Wide awake," she said, stepping back to look at him. " 'S'matter with your tie?"

Palmer glanced down and saw that his tie was hanging to one side. He'd forgotten to pin it. With a sudden, sick feeling, he knew that his tie pin was somewhere in Burns's apartment. A moment later he realized that even if Burns found the pin, it would mean nothing to him. Just a plain pin, a bit longer than the ordinary straight pin, with a small white ball for a head. Burns had never seen it, because Palmer inserted the pin from behind his shirt front, pushing it down through a fold of tie and sticking it back into the shirt to make an invisible connection. As for the pin itself, you could buy it by the box in any stationery store.

"The pin must have worked its way out," he said then.

"Better pick up another and take off," Gerri informed him. "You were due at the Burckhardts' an hour ago."

"What?"

"Don't go senile on me."

"Good God." Palmer turned to look at himself in the foyer mirror. He saw a tall, thin man with a furtive face. But the clothing was unruffled, he noted. Pulling off his jacket, he dashed for the bedroom, stripping off tie and shirt as he moved.

"That's my pop," Gerri said, trotting after him. "Fast on his feet."

As he put on a fresh shirt, Palmer became slowly aware that someone else was watching him. He glanced at the bedroom doorway and saw Woody, his eldest, standing there with a dreamy, inward-turning look. "Ever see Pop move this fast?" Gerri asked her brother.

"Dad," the boy began, "what's commercial paper?"

Palmer frowned. "Your sense of timing is impeccable," he said, struggling to push cuff links through the fresh, unyielding buttonholes. "Will it wait till the weekend?"

"Huh?" Woody asked.

"First you have to explain what 'impeccable' means," Gerri suggested.

"I'm pressed for time." Palmer looked over his tie rack, then realized that he should arrive at the Burckhardts' wearing the same tie he'd had on during the day. It made a better story that way. Already the double life had begun.

"Im-pec-cable," Gerri was saying. "Free from sin."

Palmer darted a glance at her and saw that she was looking at her brother. He looped the tie around his neck and, for the third time today, knotted it. He found himself wishing that either of the boys had Gerri's mind. They needed it badly and she, with too bright a mind, would eventually find it a liability. They could also use some of her powers of observation. She had too many of these, too. But perhaps she would grow up pretty enough to keep such dangerous attributes from mattering. One always made allowances for beauty.

He finished knotting his tie, tucked in his shirt and put on his jacket again. "Just to avoid arguments," he said as he walked toward the door, "I'm giving Gerri an extra half-hour to stay up, Woody. And I'm lopping half an hour off your bedtime. In other words, you both hit the sack at ten-thirty on the dot. Understand?"

"I dig," Gerri said.

"I don't," the boy insisted.

"I'm serious," Palmer said.

"How do you do, Mr. Serious," Gerri began. "I'd like you to meet Mr. Dubious. Dubious, meet Serious. Serious, meet—"

"Ah, knock it off," Woody interrupted. "You get to stay up late and I have to suffer for it." He turned his sulk in Palmer's direction. "It isn't fair, Dad. She always gets everything her own way."

Palmer watched his eldest son, nearing his full growth now at just a shade under six feet, with cheeks already fuzzy enough to shave if he were a brunette and a voice almost as deep as his father's. He found himself wondering how long, if ever, it would take Woody to grow up. Immediately, he realized he'd been caught in the same trap he'd always stumbled into. Because Gerri was quick and glib and fearless, he expected Woody to surpass her because he was almost three years older. Palmer had to keep reminding himself that they could only be judged by different standards.

He smiled at the boy and then clapped him on the arm. "I'm only giving her the half-hour because she'd take it anyway."

"You know it," Woody agreed. "How come the clean shirt?"

"The boss is having a party."

"But the old one's hardly even dirty."

"Ooh," Gerri moaned. "With that for company, I think I'll go to bed right now."

They walked him to the door, where Gerri hugged him again, presenting the top of her head for kissing. As always, in the last few years, Palmer was afraid to kiss Woody good night. It was a reflection of the boy's own unspoken fear that his father might once, absent-mindedly, forget himself. They nodded to each other over the girl's head and Palmer winked, feeling about as insincere as it was possible to feel. He compensated for this by giving Gerri an extra-hard squeeze.

She backed away and grinned at him. "You look special tonight," she said. "How come? What happened?"

On his way to the elevator, he glanced at his watch. He was now an hour late for Burckhardt's affair. In the cab, Palmer realized how lucky he had been, after all. He was getting additional time to arrange himself in his new posture of adultery. In her most intuitive moments, Edith was no match for her daughter. And, by the time the evening was over, Palmer told himself, that special look Gerri had seen would undoubtedly wear away.

CHAPTER THIRTY

The Burckhardt town house was a modest duplex on Central Park South in a rather narrow old building that had once housed artists' and musicians' studios. The bank had acquired it by foreclosure in the 1930's and had broken the long, floor-through apartments into smaller ones, all except the top floor, with its slanting two-story windows overlooking the park. Palmer rode up in the self-service elevator with a small, dark, thin man in his mid-fifties who seemed very familiar. He appeared, by the more-than-normal length of his black hair and the color of his vest—which contrasted with his suit—to be anything but a banker: art dealer, impresario . . . ? They nodded politely to each other as it became clear that both were destined for the penthouse duplex.

"Mr. Palmer, isn't it?" the man asked in a low voice with a strong touch of British accent. His large, dark eyes regarded the younger man with unnatural steadiness.

"Yes." Palmer's hand went out. "Mr. . . ?"

"Nicos." They shook hands.

"I remember now," Palmer said. "Almost five years ago, wasn't it?"

"In Chicago?" Nicos suggested.

"At the meeting with Harris Trust," Palmer responded.

This, he reflected, would have to be Archibald Nicos, the younger of the two brothers who controlled Lionel Nicos and Sons, the fantastically complex investment banking house that had put together, some five years before, an industrial loan with Harris Trust of Chicago and several other local banks, including Palmer's father's. There had been something more about the deal that Palmer now tried to remember, but the elevator came to a halt before the thought returned to him.

Arriving with Nicos, he saw now, made his lateness pardonable. It also gave, or seemed to give, Edith the idea that the two of them had been involved together. At any rate, her greeting seemed sincere enough. He stood beside his wife and nodded to each of the party in turn. He knew them all, it seemed, and all of them knew him.

At the far end of the high-ceilinged room, wedged into a chair that sat in a corner where two bookcases met, was Harry Elder. Standing in front of Harry, deeply involved in some lengthy explanation, was Cliff Mergendahl, Ubco's number-three man, whose specialty was investments. Palmer watched Nicos make his way to them with purposeful directness.

At the opposite corner, under the high, slanting windows, stood a long couch of French design, its embroidered white upholstered ends curving up and out. On it sat Mrs. Mergendahl, a plump redhead some fifteen years younger than Cliff, talking with a tall man named Winthrop Skipworth who had two distinctions: he was the chairman of one of the oldest and smallest banks in town and was the only man Palmer knew who answered to two nicknames, Winnie and Skippy. Both had the effect of diminishing him slightly, a fact that had never seemed to bother Skipworth in the slightest. Seated next to Edith, on the long side wall of the room, was Grace Burckhardt herself, in one of what Palmer had come to call her "rare public appearances."

He managed to keep up his end of the inconsequential conversation she was holding with Edith and him, while at the same time examining her rather closely. The stories about Grace Burckhardt were fairly unenlightening. Gossip of the meaty, malicious kind didn't exist. She spent nearly all her time at the Connecticut place, even in the worst months of summer, coming to town no more than half a dozen times in a year. Why tonight was one of those times, Palmer could not tell.

Grace Burckhardt was a small, wiry woman of about Burckhardt's age, mid-sixties. Her skin was frail and bluish-white, where his was rough and reddened. Palmer saw that she had had her gray hair blued slightly, with this unfortunate result: it almost matched her skin. He found himself wondering if perhaps she suffered from some illness that produced a kind of cyanotic hue to the skin, then decided that the color was not pronounced enough. In any event, her general pallor did not indicate general debility. She chattered away at a great rate, moving surely and swiftly from the servant problem to the upbringing of children, the latest fashions, the misfortunes of friends and the health of her husband.

". . . amazing in a man his age," she was saying.

"Any age," Palmer put in, noting with horror the sleazy ease with which he had insinuated the compliment.

"I dare say you're right about that," Grace Burckhardt agreed. "I've seen him do those whateveryoucallems of his, those pull-ups, are they? No. He calls it chinning himself. Chin-ups, I believe. I've seen him do that with a man twenty years his junior and, of course, the younger man has to stop long before Lane is tired."

"I've often thought that Woods ought to take an interest in an athletic club," Edith said then. "In Chicago he avoided them like the plague. If only he'd put on a few pounds I might be able to convince him. But . . ."

The two women turned to stare at Palmer, examining him from head to toe, their glances lingering on his midriff. "Much too thin," Mrs. Burckhardt decided. "What is that about lean and hungry men?"

" 'Yon Cassius has a lean and hungry look,' " Edith quoted without hesitation.

" 'Such men are dangerous,' " Grace Burckhardt finished. She frowned at Palmer. "But he has a sweet expression, nevertheless," she added, smiling.

"Ladies," Palmer began, "you overwhelm me." He bowed slightly and moved toward the bar, where an elderly Negro in a dinner jacket and black tie was polishing glasses with a soft white towel.

"Your pleasure, Mr. Palmer?"

"Scotch and ice. Chip it up a little, please."

"Scotch Mist?" the bartender asked.

"Fine."

"Twist of lemon?"

"Fine."

Palmer sighed and tried to keep the sound from matching his great impatience with the overcomplications of life. A simple drink had become what amounted to a theatrical production. A business gathering had been tricked out as a social evening, complete with wives. And whatever seemed to be going on was only camouflage. He accepted his drink and stood for a moment at the bar, trying to understand what was really happening.

The discussion between Harry Elder and Cliff Mergendahl had ground on for a few moments after Nicos had joined them, almost as though the subject had gained a stodgy momentum of its own that had been difficult to stop. But when it dawned on the two Ubco men that Nicos had made directly for them, they jettisoned the discussion and put themselves at his service. As soon as they had done so, Burckhardt's eyes fixed on the three of them and never wavered for an instant, even though he was standing in the center of the room, directly under the downward glare of a recessed spotlight, supposedly talking to a man of Palmer's age named Archer, a partner in the law firm that handled most of Ubco's work.

In many ways, Archer resembled Palmer. They were both in their mid-forties, fairly tall and thin, with intelligent faces and close-cropped hair. Archer had become a partner in the law firm his father had founded at the turn of the century, another point of similarity with Palmer. There the resemblance ceased. Archer's complexion was almost olive in its darkness; his black hair held faint blue highlights. And, Palmer recalled as he watched the man with Burckhardt, the intelligent look was sheer façade. The Archer mind was barely good enough to limp through law school and pass the bar exam. His strength lay in his family and business connections.

Whereas I, Palmer reflected, am about the most brilliant monkey ever to dance on the end of Burckhardt's string.

Taking a long sip of his drink, Palmer moved purposefully past Burckhardt toward the three men in the far corner of the room, sensing that his employer would stop him in mid-journey.

"Woody," Burckhardt's thick, crackling voice said, "you remember Jimmy Archer." His big, knobby hand gripped Palmer's arm just above the elbow.

"Jimmy. You're looking very fit."

"Just back from Buenos Aires."

"Lovely," Palmer said. He eyed his employer. "You look disgustingly fit. Your Mrs. was describing how you shame young men with your prowess on the chinning bar."

"Not recently I don't," Burckhardt snapped. His grip tightened slightly, then relaxed. "I don't fool around with that any more, Woody. Too damned strenuous."

Palmer touched his chest on the left side. "Still ticking like a jeweled movement?"

"Ha. Never fear." Burckhardt's small, milky-blue eyes narrowed slightly. He seemed to be grimacing into intense sunlight. He drew his hand away from Palmer, made a fist and punched him on the forearm. The movement was small in scope and the older man seemed to put almost no strength behind it. But it stung.

"Easy," Palmer murmured. "Mustn't abuse the help."

Burckhardt continued to face Palmer, but his eyes moved sideways to Archer. "You ever notice," he asked, "how solicitous a number-two man always is about your health?"

"I can think of better ways to waste my time," Palmer said, "than waiting around for you to crack up."

"You know it," Burckhardt agreed, too heartily, it seemed to Palmer. "Oh, do you know it."

"How many executive vee-pees have you buried, Lane?"

"Only the ones that deserved it."

Palmer laughed softly. "Touché." He nodded to the three men in the corner. "I think I'll go talk shop."

Burckhardt's powerful fingers closed over Palmer's arm again, directly on the flesh he had just punched. Palmer's muscle began to ache slightly. "What d'you think we're talking here?" Burckhardt demanded.

"Damned if I know," Palmer said. "You make yourself so scarce around the shop I've forgotten how to talk to you."

"You don't need me looking over your shoulder, Woody. I understand you're doing fine."

"Who told you that?"

"My morning papers. You're in every third day or so."

"If you mean I've occupied dais chairs at every public dinner, yes."

"I wouldn't push ahead too fast," Burckhardt said.

"I'm talking in Syracuse next week. I imagine that's progress."

"Where else?"

Palmer frowned. "Buffalo the week after. Then Brooklyn, Utica and Rochester, within ten days." He waited for the older man's grip to relax. "Jimmy, did you ever hear my little speech?" he asked then.

"What's that, Woody?"

"My banking-type speech. You haven't heard it?"

"I'm not sure if I have."

"It's a very clever little production," Palmer explained. "Ostensibly, I'm giving them a fascinating glimpse into the history of banking, from the dawn-of-time sort of thing. Babylonian corn factors. Egyptian investment trusts. Down through the ages. That takes all of five minutes, including jokes. Then I find myself in the modern era, the bitter pill beneath the sugar coating. And we're off on a hell-for-leather attack against the savings banks. It's a gem."

"I didn't know you wrote speeches, Woody."

"I don't. They're written by—" Burckhardt's grip grew suddenly fierce. Palmer winced and stepped away from him, breaking his hold. "I'll let you know when I make an appearance in town, Jimmy. You have to catch me. I'm a smash."

"I understand," Burckhardt said with a heavy kind of emphasis, "that you're polishing up the act out of town before bringing it in for the money audience."

"Very well put."

"But the advance notices are raves," Burckhardt added, smiling at Archer.

Palmer watched the older man's small eyes swing back halfway to watch the three men in the corner again. Without excusing himself, Palmer walked away from Burckhardt and joined the other group in time to hear Archibald Nicos saying:

". . . the very essence of today's economy."

"You're right, of course," Cliff Mergendahl said. "But in the present condition of the market, an unsecured loan of that size, at that low a rate, isn't something you can decide on overnight."

"And," Harry Elder chimed in, "when you add the extreme length of the loan's term, you've got a hell of an iffy proposition."

Nicos' smile remained fixed as he swung about to include Palmer in the discussion. "But surely," he said, "Palmer here will agree that the public image created by such a transaction is in itself almost a form of collateral."

"What transaction would that be?" Palmer asked.

"The—" Nicos stopped himself. His big eyes looked vaguely worried for an instant.

"Woody doesn't bother himself with moneylending," Harry Elder said in his scratchy, hoarse voice. "He's too busy with this savings-bank mess to get much time for briefings."

"I see," Nicos replied. He stood silently for a moment, then smiled. "You have a very charming wife, Mr. Palmer."

The change of subject was like a slap. Palmer smiled back at the smaller man. "Thank you. I haven't been filled in," he admitted, returning instantly to the previous subject, "but I can pretty much put together the details from what I've just heard. The only thing I can't guess is the amount."

"A half-billion," Mergendahl said in a somewhat peevish tone, as if resenting the unbusinesslike immensity of the sum.

"At what rate?" Palmer persisted. "Five? Six?"

Harry Elder chuckled raspingly and winked at Nicos. "He's too smart for any of us, Archie."

"Five and a half," Mergendahl said, in a voice that again complained of heterodoxy. "It's a VA mortgage rate, for Pete's sake."

"And the term's more than twenty years," Palmer surmised.

"Just twenty," Mergendahl amended. "You don't need any briefings."

Palmer shrugged and addressed himself to Nicos. "You're right about one thing. It's unusual enough to make headlines. But I'm not sure that Ubco is accepting publicity as collateral these days."

"That was an unfortunate figure of speech," Nicos began quickly. "The image created here is not really a headline sensation. It's a vote-of-confidence sort of thing. At this particular time, it would be especially opportune for—"

"Say," Burckhardt's voice boomed out from the middle of the room. "We're all due at the Waldorf. The floor show goes on in fifteen minutes."

The sound seemed to increase in volume behind Palmer as people got to their feet. He looked down at his drink and took another long sip of it. "The thing I'm not clear about," he said to Nicos, raising his voice to be heard, "is who we're expected to do this favor for?"

"Don't play dumb, Woody," Harry Elder said. "After that quiz session you gave me the other day?"

Palmer stared at him for a moment, trying to understand what he had said. "No, really," he went on after a moment. "I'm serious."

". . . and phone downstairs for the cars," Burckhardt was saying behind him.

Nicos seemed ready to use Burckhardt's announcement as a handy diversion. He smiled and nodded to Palmer as he began to sidle past him. "Tell me," he said, "who are we seeing at the Persian Room tonight? Belafonte?"

Palmer shrugged and turned to Harry Elder. "What firm, Harry?"

"I thought you knew, Woody."

"I don't."

"It's Jet-Tech International."

Later in the evening Palmer tried to decide why it was that as Harry spoke, the room grew abruptly quiet. Perhaps people had stopped talking as they were helped into their coats. Perhaps some of them had already started for the door. Whatever it was, Harry's words fell upon almost silent air.

Palmer felt the coldness of the glass in his hand. A faint line of chillness shot across his shoulder blades. "Jet-Tech?" he echoed.

Much later, as they sat around a ringside table at the Persian Room, Palmer found himself running the scene through his mind once more, doggedly trying to get at the inner sense of it, the meaning that had sent a peculiar chill across his back.

He watched the singer without hearing the words of the song, and wondered why he had, for a moment in Burckhardt's duplex, felt the sharp chill of a sensation like vertigo. It was almost, he reflected, as if an immense pit had opened up at his feet.

Chapter Thirty-one

It had all the earmarks of a bad morning. Palmer had awakened with a totally uneasy feeling, part hangover, part the same nameless suspicion he had had the night before, the whole complicated by Edith's determination at breakfast to discuss at length the howling inanities of Burckhardt's party.

Now, seated at his desk in the office, the great overhead louvers shut tight against the brilliant winter sunlight outside, Palmer finished his second complete trip through the information Virginia Clary had compiled about Joe Loomis and Jet-Tech International. From the moment he had arrived this morning, Palmer had resisted the urge to talk to her. He had even postponed his promised lecture to Virginia and Mac Burns. Yet he badly needed to discuss the Nicos proposal with someone he could trust.

Now, as he put down the sheaf of papers and stared blankly at the wall opposite him, Palmer realized that he didn't want to see her because he had no idea of how she would act toward him. At the same time, he knew that he had no one else to talk to about this, not yet, anyway, not until he had groped his way to some kind of understanding.

Palmer watched his hand move toward the intercom buttons. With a detached feeling, he saw one finger press the "Scrty" button. When she answered, he cleared his throat—trying to minimize the sound as a possible confession of nervousness—and said:

"Ask Miss Clary to come in, please."

As he waited for her, Palmer realized that all his usual executive-style tricks had deserted him. He had many papers on his desk that he could examine, shuffle through, tap, frown at, shift from place to place, unclip, reclip, annotate and otherwise play with. The morning papers, neatly folded by his secretary to the business-financial pages, lay near at hand. He also had his unread copy of the *Wall Street Journal.* But instead he sat without moving, his eyes on the closed door. When it opened, he found himself standing up.

Virginia nodded as she sat down across from him. "Good morning."

He watched the way she arranged her body, both feet planted together on the floor, hands folded palms-up in her lap. After a moment he realized that he hadn't responded to her greeting.

"Good morning," he said hastily. "Tell me . . ." He paused and tried to think. "Tell me," he went on, "were you with Ubco when this savings-bank fracas began?"

She shook her head. "That was nearly ten years ago. I remember the circumstances, but not from the Ubco viewpoint."

Their glances met. Palmer regarded her face, with its high, rounded cheekbones and large, dark eyes. "You look disgustingly healthy this morning," he murmured.

She glanced over her shoulder at the closed door, then turned back and smiled. "You don't."

He nodded and offered her a cigarette. "If I were the nervy type, I wouldn't have slept a wink."

"But you did, of course," she said, refusing the cigarette.

He nodded again. "Uneasily."

"Conscience?" She frowned softly. "I'm sorry."

"No." He realized that they were each talking about different reasons. He also saw that if he corrected her at this point it would be in the nature of an insult. Naturally, he reflected, she would assume that his nervousness came from guilt. She had no way of knowing that he had yet to feel anything strong enough to go by that name. Nor could she know what had happened after he'd left her last night.

"Not conscience?" she asked then.

"I meant," he said, "no, you're not to be sorry."

"I can't help the way I feel."

"If I'm not sorry, neither should you be."

"All right," she agreed. "As a matter of fact, I'm glad." Her eyes grew bigger suddenly. "As a matter of fact," she went on, her voice dropping almost to a whisper as she watched him, "I have never been gladder of anything I've ever done. Now." Her voice went up in volume and became quite businesslike again. "What about this savings-bank thing?"

Palmer settled back in his chair, feeling a sense of relief so great that it had an almost physical force, like a hand stroking his body, smoothing away tension. "Look," he said then, "I want to ask you mysterious questions, only because I need your unedited answers. Tell me exactly how this savings-bank battle first began."

"With an Assembly bill at Albany about ten years ago, authorizing savings banks to have branches outside the county in which their main office was located."

"Who introduced the bill?"

She shrugged. "Some downstate assemblyman. From here in the city, I think."

"What happened to the bill?"

"It died a small, unheralded death."

"Just like that? No struggle?"

"None." She thought for a moment. "If the banks had spent in that first year all the money they've since spent on branch bills, they'd have bought victory the first time. But nobody was bold enough for that kind of tactic."

Palmer nodded. "That part's been explained to me already. By Burns. He claims the branch bill, in its various disguises over the years, has become a gravy train for the legislators. Tell me: when did the thing become an open fight? What year?"

"It's gotten bitter on several occasions. Eight years ago. Five years ago. And, of course, it hit its peak last year. You look very different this morning."

Palmer frowned. "How different? What way?"

"Slightly shook up." She paused and shook her head. "Wrong topic. I'll have to watch that. Now, then, the savings-bank battle."

"Yes. Why did it get so acrimonious last year?"

"Partly because the savings banks pushed harder than ever," she explained. "Partly because they took off the kid gloves and began attacking the big city banks like Ubco. And, partly because Lane Burckhardt decided they were attacking him personally. When he waded into the fray, it became a Donnybrook."

"Now, this is the crux of it," Palmer said. "Why did Burckhardt decide to get into the fight?"

She shrugged again. "It was almost a repeat of this year's opening round. Joe Loomis asked him, on behalf of Murray Hill Savings Bank, to stay out of the fight. So Burckhardt decided he'd have to do just the opposite."

"He and Loomis are old friends, old associates, not old antagonists. Why would Burckhardt react that way?"

"For just that reason," she said. "He felt his friendship was being imposed on. He felt that the enemy considered him a key factor in the fight and was taking unfair advantage of the Loomis friendship to immobilize him."

"All right," Palmer said. "How do you know all this?"

"Some of it Burckhardt hinted at. Some of it he flatly stated to me or in my presence. The rest I picked up from newspaper guys."

Palmer started to light a cigarette, then offered the pack to Virginia again. When she refused, he lighted his own. "Now tell me: is Burckhardt's stubbornness legendary? Doesn't everyone in the industry know that about him?"

"If they don't, I'd be quite surprised."

Palmer nodded. "Next question: how was the branch bill defeated at the last session? How much credit could Burckhardt take for the victory?"

"Gee, you ask sticky questions."

"I'm trying to unwind a particularly sticky ball of twine."

"I would say . . . um, what would I say?" she wondered. "The legislature was almost equally divided on the bill last year. The vote could have gone either way. The issue wasn't split along party lines, but the opposition was mostly upstate, and thus Republican. The savings-bank forces were mostly downstate and Democratic. And then . . ." She paused and thought.

"And then?"

"And then one of the boys got up and called for party unity. He pointed out that since savings banks were little people's banks and the Democratic Party was the party of the little people, then, by God, let's unite against the unholy commercial bank-Republican alliance and push this bill through."

"What effect did the outburst have?"

"It suddenly made a party issue out of a nonpartisan one. The few Republicans who had been for it pulled in their horns and voted against it in a solid GOP phalanx. They had no choice, once the speech was made."

"Would you say," Palmer persisted, "that the speech was ill-advised?"

"Spectacularly."

"Would you characterize it in any other way?" he asked.

"Damned peculiar."

"You wondered at the time why a supporter of the bill would so stupidly sabotage its chances?"

"Very well put, chief."

Palmer made a face. "Will you cut out the 'chief' business?"

"Yes, boss."

"Please."

"Sorry." She started to giggle, then stopped. "Very sorry. It's just that I'm prickly with curiosity. Won't you please tell me what you're driving at . . . Mr. Palmer?"

"All in good time," he intoned piously. "A few more prickly questions. How did you know that Joe Loomis triggered the whole thing off again this year with another request to Burckhardt?"

"Burckhardt's made no secret of it. He was fuming about it just after you joined our happy throng."

"Fuming and vowing a fight to the finish?"

"Exactly."

"At the time, last year, when this peculiar party-unity appeal was made, did anyone here suggest a reason why one legislator should have decided to wreck the whole campaign?"

"I believe the commonly held theory was that he was stinking drunk."

"Was he?"

"He was known to imbibe," she recalled. "But he'd been imbibing freely for several decades without pulling a boo-boo like that one."

"Any other theory?"

"That someone on our side had gotten to him with a number of large, coarse notes."

"Any truth to it?" Palmer asked.

"Look, I'm a poor working p.r. girl, not a tea-leaf reader."

"I understood you were a genuine Celtic witch."

"Only after dark."

"Yes. I remember now."

"Umm."

They were silent for a moment. "Oh, yes," Palmer said then. He sighed and then grinned at her. "I think I now have the end of the ball of twine in my hand. If I give the whole thing a sharp shake, it may unwind like a conjuring trick."

"Proceed, maestro."

He reached for his intercom and pushed the "Elder" button. After a moment, Harry's hoarse voice came through the loud-speaker. "What's up, Woody?"

"I have to be discreet, Harry. Give me an idea of when last night's glamour deal was first offered to us?"

"The twenty-year—?"

"Discreet," Palmer interrupted.

"Oh. Well. I'd have to think. And it's so early in the morning."

"Be my guest."

"Think," Elder rasped. "Think. Think. Got it."

"Yes?"

"It came up about eighteen months ago in connection with some renegotiated plant financing. At the time nobody seemed serious about it."

"Least of all Lane Burckhardt?"

"Especially Lane. He thought it was the silliest deal he'd ever heard of."

"Everyone treated it as a joke?" Palmer asked.

"Not our long-haired friend of last night."

"Of course. And when did he frame the deal in its present form?"

"About a year ago. Maybe less."

"But Lane still thought it was a joke."

"Not by then," Elder said. "He saw it was serious. So, very seriously, he turned it down cold. With the approval of the board, by the way."

"And now it's come up again?"

"Fresh as a daisy. Only the sum is larger this time."

"Oh?" Palmer thought for a moment. "You'd almost think they wanted to guarantee another turn-down by us."

"That isn't it," Elder said. "It's just that a year's gone by. Their plans are bigger and they need more money. I can understand that, can't you?"

"I guess so. Well, thanks, Harry."

"What'd you think of that floor show last night?" Elder asked.

"I liked the show at our table better."

"Woody, you have turned into a suspicious young man. That's worse than a suspicious old man, you know."

"I'm not suspicious. Just nosey."

"What do you know that I don't?" Elder wanted to know.

"Not a thing."

"Don't kid a suspicious old man, Woody."

"Wouldn't think of it."

"Next time you have another of these talkative fits, let me know." The intercom went dead.

Virginia Clary watched the silent loud-speaker box. "What was all that?"

"More mysterious questions."

"You and Elder were out somewhere last night?"

"With Burckhardt and Mergendahl and our respective ladies and a few more guests."

She continued watching the intercom, but her eyes had narrowed slightly. "You lead an awfully eventful life, Mr. Palmer," she said then.

"I arrived at the party late. I'd forgotten about it completely."

"Really?"

"Really. Something had happened earlier in the evening to drive it out of my mind."

When she failed to speak, Palmer sat forward and pushed all the papers away from the center of his desk. "Say something."

"I will, when I think of it." Finally she turned her glance to him. He saw that she was puzzled enough to be on the verge of anger.

"I mean it," he said. "I had forgotten all about the party."

After a moment, her face went blank. She looked away and sighed. "I'm being a fool," she said. "And I don't even know why I'm upset. Isn't that silly?" She glanced sideways at him, then away again. "Ignore it, please?"

"Will you?"

"I will," she promised.

Neither of them spoke for a long moment. "Damn it, but I'm sorry," she burst out then. She sat up straighter and tried to smile. "All right," she said. She took a breath and nodded firmly. "All better. Now, about those mysterious questions." She nodded again, encouragingly, as if to reassure him that she was fine once more.

"Yes." He stared at the cleared space before him on the desk. It looked as bleak and forlorn as the idea he had now come to believe. Almost unconsciously he shoved a few stray papers into the cleared space, filling it again.

"I'm considering a concept so devious and so reckless that I'm not sure I'm in my right mind even to entertain it."

"Try me."

"You're about the only person I'd dare try it on." He rubbed his face slowly. "What would your reaction be if you heard that Jet-Tech was trying to negotiate a loan from us for a phenomenal amount, at a low rate of interest and a very long term?"

"How phenomenal an amount?"

"For your own sake, I can't tell you. Or the rate, either. Do you understand that?"

"Yes. What I don't know I can't be accused of leaking."

"Exactly."

"Well, then," she said, "I'd assume that they weren't going to get it, from your talk with Harry Elder."

"And what would your reaction be?"

"I'd . . ." She looked blankly at him for a moment. Her eyes widened slowly and her mouth parted. "I'd ask myself . . ." She shook her head. "No."

"Go ahead."

"I'd ask myself about Joe Loomis," Virginia said at last in a thin, wondering voice. "I'd ask exactly what it meant that he was behind both Jet-Tech and the savings-bank branch bill."

"And what answers would you get?" Palmer asked.

"I . . . I don't know," she said. "I honestly don't know."

"Neither do I." Palmer's voice sounded heavy in the big office. He cleared his throat. "Yet," he added.

The word reverberated slightly in the far corner of the huge room. After a long moment Virginia stood up. Her face looked almost blank, as though absolutely nothing had been said. Palmer recognized it for something else, however, the false blankness that tries to pretend nothing has happened. Sympathetic magic. He smiled very slightly and the effort stretched the skin of his lower lip almost painfully.

"So," he said, simply to say something.

"Can I help you with the answers?" she asked then.

"Not just yet. You already have, of course."

"I want to help."

"I'll ask. Don't worry."

"That's a promise?"

"Yes," he assured her.

"Then I'll go back to my typewriter," she said. "Oh."

"Yes?"

She reached inside the neckline of her dress. "Something," she said. "Here. Something of yours." She drew out his missing tie pin and held it to him.

"Good grief." He took it from her. "Thank you."

She nodded. "I was going to keep it."

"Not in there. You might have gotten hurt."

She nodded again. "I know." She turned slowly and walked to the door. " 'Impaled' is the word." She opened the door and left.

Chapter Thirty-two

It was not until noon that Palmer's secretary finally found Burckhardt for him. "Lane," Palmer said into the phone, "join me for lunch?"

"I'm downtown, Woody."

"I'll meet you there."

"I don't want to draw you off base, Woody."

"Not at all." Palmer watched the fingers of his left hand roll the tie pin back and forth. "Half an hour?"

Burckhardt hesitated for a moment. "I'll hop up there, then."

"As you wish."

"Twelve-forty. Union League."

"No," Palmer said. "Some place that isn't crammed with financial types."

"Secrets?"

"Nothing so elaborate," Palmer assured him. "It's in the nature of a progress report. I'm going to be away quite a bit for the next few weeks. There are a number of things I want to clear with you."

"Woody, you don't need any clearance from me. You know that."

"Let's get off the beaten track. There's a steak place on Second Avenue in the Forties."

"That's about as far off the track as you can get," Burckhardt said. "All right, Woody. I guess you've just never outgrown the cloak-and-dagger stuff."

"Does anybody?" Palmer asked. He broke the connection before Burckhardt could answer. Then he punched the button for his outside telephone line, the one that didn't go through a switchboard, got a number from information, called the restaurant and made a reservation.

He glanced at his watch, saw that he had plenty of time and sat back in his chair. Too much time, he reflected. He could feel the peculiar sensation of pre-combat tension, the heightened reaction to everything, the formless, aimless series of small actions, diversionary tactics, anything to keep the mind from leaping ahead. He put down the tie pin and watched it roll in a broad arc, turning swiftly on the white ball that formed its head. Then he pushed it and watched the pin roll back again.

He wondered, as he had all morning, if he would be right to put the idea point blank to Burckhardt. How much did the old bird know? If he knew nothing yet, would the sudden knowledge infuriate him, force him to some impulsive action that might harm the situation? If he knew something, or sensed it, would Palmer's suspicions unnerve him? Or would they seem so far-fetched as to turn him against Palmer?

They were, of course, about as far-fetched as any set of suspicions could be and still make sense, Palmer realized now. But the damnable part was that they did make sense.

He picked up the tie pin and tried to decide what to do with it. One just like it was holding down the tie he wore. He might slip the loose one in his desk, or pocket. Or he might just throw it in the waste basket. Why not? It was only a bit of metal with a tiny ceramic ball head. If he were silly enough to keep it—as a memento? God!—he would soon confuse it with the other tie pins and the whole thing would become ludicrous.

She had thought of keeping it. Why?

Palmer dropped the pin in his breast pocket and stood up. He paced quickly to the immense window and stared at the sunny winter day. Central Park, even with bare-branched trees, looked calm and orderly and as supremely natural as only carefully planned artifice can be.

Palmer watched a tall, blonde girl in a bright fuchsia coat stride out of Bonwit's and head north toward the Plaza. From this distance she looked almost 6 feet tall. If it were not for the color of her coat, she might have been Edith. She had the same lean, greyhound stride, the same light-blonde hair, the same angular swing to her arms. She looked remarkably exciting.

Palmer found himself wondering how he might feel if she turned out, after all, to be Edith in a new coat. Hastily, he checked the height of her heels. At this great distance, even with his sharp eyesight, it was almost impossible to tell. But something about the way she walked convinced Palmer that she was wearing fairly high heels, at least as high as those Virginia Clary wore. And Edith, of course, rarely wore any higher than two inches. So she wasn't Edith. But she was exciting.

Damn the whole thing, Palmer thought, turning abruptly from the window. He was trying to think about too many things at once.

He put on his coat and left the building, heading east until he reached Second Avenue. In that way he had a long, straight walk before he reached the restaurant, long enough to find out if he were being followed.

The air was mildly cool, but it hit Palmer's face in chilling gusts that made his eyes water. He stopped at one point in mid-block and, under the pretense of looking into a window, checked the people behind him. A block later he repeated the action.

It was the kind of sharp, sunny day that had brought a lot of people into the streets. They walked to and from lunch with quick, energetic strides, enjoying the clear sky, the sparkle of mica in the cement sidewalks, the glinting flashes from passing car windows, the wind whipping skirts. Palmer felt none of this.

He had begun, instead, to feel unsure of himself. As he ran his suspicions back and forth through his mind, testing them for flaws, for hasty conclusions, for signs of stupidity or even downright paranoia, he began to realize that he had very little to substantiate his basic idea. And if this were so, he had no business putting it before Burckhardt. What he needed was one solid piece of proof. So thinking, he stepped inside a corner telephone booth and called his broker. Their conversation was brief but educational.

Half a block from the restaurant, Palmer checked his trail again and found nothing unusual. He realized, as he did so, that if his suspicions were right or wrong he was behaving like an idiot. In this particularly dour mood, he entered the restaurant, got his table and ordered a Scotch.

By the time Burckhardt arrived, Palmer had started on his second drink. Although he was angry with the older man for being late, he kept the preliminary conversation easy and meaningless. The restaurant itself was a cramped affair, cut up into two long rooms like the legs of an H, with a narrow passage connecting them in the middle. The walls, at some time in the far past, had been painted with cartoons of literally hundreds of people. The allusive legends that accompanied the drawings made it no easier to identify any of the subjects. Palmer knew none of them and assumed, wrongly, that one would have had to be a New Yorker to recognize the people involved.

". . . but this is sensational roast beef," Burckhardt was saying.

"Harry Elder mentioned this place," Palmer explained. "I thought you'd know it."

"Of it. Never ate here before." Burckhardt cut a large bit of beef, doubled it over with his fork, speared it, swished it through the clear reddish gravy in his plate and ate it. "Umm."

"It is good."

Burckhardt chewed vigorously, swallowed. Then he put down his fork and stared at Palmer, his light-blue irises seeming larger than normal around the tiny black pinpoints of his pupils. Palmer caught himself wondering, as he often did, why Burckhardt had this perpetual look of being under a bright sun with a sharp wind in his face.

"Start talking, Woody. I'm due downtown at one-thirty."

"I'm sorry I dragged you uptown if your schedule's that tight."

"Nonsense. What's the secrecy stuff for? Give."

Palmer sipped the dregs of his third Scotch. "I think I told you there was nothing secret about it," he explained. "It just occurred to me that we always eat in the same places, and . . ." He shrugged. "I wanted to give you the strategy of my speaking tour. Mac Burns's strategy, I should say."

"Things working out between you?"

"Fine."

"Glad to hear." Burckhardt was speaking with a full mouth. "I knew you had enough flexibility to work with that little Greek."

Palmer ate some of his roast beef in silence. Then: "Lebanese. If you think of him that way, why in God's name did you ever hire him?"

"Had to. He's the key to the Democrats."

"The Democrats are solidly pro-savings bank and against us. No key can unlock them."

Burckhardt shook his head and swallowed a mouthful only half-chewed. "Don't believe it. If they were, why would Joe Loomis try to hire Burns himself?"

"When was this?"

Burckhardt waved his hand expansively. "I got wind of it last spring. Joe was going to retain Burns for the savings-bank fight. If the Democrats are so solidly for the savings banks, why would Joe waste money sewing them up even tighter? Besides, Burns operates the p.r. subsidiary of our own ad agency. So what could be simpler?"

"Who told you Loomis wanted to hire Burns?"

"Never mind." He cut and began chewing another mouthful of beef. "What the hell, you might as well know. Archie Nicos let it slip."

Palmer sat forward and watched his employer more closely. "Is Nicos that reliable a source of information?"

"God, yes. Safe as Gibraltar."

"He's as close to Loomis as he is to you."

"That's what I mean," Burckhardt assured him. "When he tells you something, it's got to be straight." Burckhardt stopped chewing. "What's the matter, Woody?"

"Just curious."

"You're implying." Burckhardt shook his head slowly. "These international operators have only one commodity to offer: reliability. If they began to play games with a big bank like Ubco, where would they get funds for the next deal they put together?"

"There are other banks. And insurance companies. And welfare funds. The country's full of money looking for the right deal."

"Woody, grow up. How long could Archie Nicos last if he diddled his prime money sources? What the hell are you getting at, anyway?"

"I told you. Just curious. Curious to know why you hired Burns."

"Now you know. To keep Loomis from hiring him."

"And to put him in our corner?" Palmer asked.

Burckhardt nodded. "Satisfied?"

"As much as I'll ever be. Look," Palmer went on, "during my speaking tour there'll be no more Marquis of Queensbury rules. I'm going to throw anything

I can at the savings banks, as long as it's hard and lumpy. Before I begin, I have to know, from you, how far I can go."

"As far as you want." Burckhardt's milk-blue eyes narrowed as he bared his teeth in a grin. "After all, I can always fire you."

"Specifically," Palmer continued, as though he hadn't heard, "where do our directorates and their boards of trustees overlap? If I let fly with a brick, is it going to hit one of our people on the head?"

"Possibly. I don't really care."

"What about our stockholders?" Palmer persisted. "I have your assurance on our directors, but what about the celebrated widows and orphans who own us?"

"No problem."

"I like your attitude," Palmer said. "The fight manager who tells his boy 'they can't hurt us.' Just who holds the big blocks of stock?"

Burckhardt finished off the last of his beef and leaned back contentedly, chewing more slowly now. "It's a matter of public record, Woody. Don't tell me you haven't checked it."

"Who's had time?"

Burckhardt shrugged. "Ubco is a blue chip. Everybody owns a hunk of us. I've got about ninety thousand shares. Harry and Cliff and some of the other vee-pee's have some. The big mutual funds and investment trusts hold a lot. What can I tell you, Woody? A blue chip is held by anybody who can afford it. Other banks own Ubco stock. Insurance companies, too. Brokerages always maintain a position because their customers ask for it. Trust funds. Pension funds. There's a block of twenty thousand shares owned by some burial fund for the widows of missionaries. Ubco's damned good stock. It hasn't passed up a dividend since the bank holiday of 1933. And the dividend's gone up about sixty per cent since World War II. We even split the shares in 1954. If you had a hundred bucks' worth of Ubco in 1945, your stock'd be worth two-forty today. Everybody buys Ubco. It's one of the least volatile issues on the market. How can I tell you who you'll hit when you start chucking bricks? All I can say is, it doesn't really matter. Our base of ownership is so broad you can't alienate any segment large enough to cause trouble."

"What you mean is, take a gamble and see what happens."

"All right. Put it that way. But what I don't understand is why you're so nervous about this? Why now? Why suddenly?"

Burckhardt's eyes opened wide and, in the instant before the pupils shrank under the increased light, Palmer thought he had caught a glimpse of something else besides bluff confidence. Or had he heard it? Was Burckhardt protesting too vehemently? Or was Palmer himself, as he groped for evidence, finding clues where none existed?

Instead of replying, Palmer pushed his plate away from him, sat back and lighted a cigarette. "I've been watching the market action for some time," he lied, depending on what his broker had just told him. "You know," he said, "I try to take an interest in as many of Ubco's activities as I have time for. I check the shares traded every day. There's been a slow, steady rise in activity."

"You've sharper eyes than I do," Burckhardt snapped.

"You haven't seen it?"

"I've seen a generally active over-the-counter market. Ubco shares trade as actively as anything else. But everything's brisk. It has nothing specifically to do with Ubco."

"I'm not so sure."

"Woody." The older man put down his fork so sharply that the noise was startling. "What in the hell are you driving at?"

"If you tell me the activity's not abnormal, I take your word for it."

"You do like hell," his employer retorted.

"All right," Palmer conceded. "Let's take the last few months. Stock prices have trended downward slightly. Volume of trading has fluctuated. Some days high. Some weeks high. But plenty of lows. It's an unsteady market. Bullish, now and then, because so many half-baked amateurs are in it. But the bears are still active and they've got occasional situations to their liking. A lot of short sales, if you study the reports. No clear trends except two that I see. No matter what the market does or where the week's trading leads, you can always count on a slight increase in the number of Ubco shares traded. A few months ago the daily norm was about three thousand. Yesterday six thousand were traded. That's one trend. The other is our price. A few months ago it was steady at a seventy-two. Yesterday it closed at seventy-eight."

Burckhardt threw up his hands. "I just got through telling you we're a defensive element in the market. Why do you think we're in so many fund portfolios? Ubco's a stable security. If it moves, it moves up. Slowly, but steadily. Now, will you stop all this horse shit and get to the point?"

Palmer's mouth flattened into a narrow line. "Don't try to holler me down," he said in a cold voice. "It can't be done."

Burckhardt watched him for a long moment. Then something changed in his face. The tanned wrinkles around his eyes deepened slightly. Palmer could see the big muscle in his temple bunch up as Burckhardt's jaw tensed. "Talk," the older man said in a tight, congested tone. "Go ahead. Talk."

"I've said my piece. It's your turn."

"What do you want me to say?" Burckhardt asked. There was a muted, plaintive note in his voice. "Tell you you're right? Maybe you are."

"Then tell me what it means," Palmer suggested.

"If I knew that . . ." Burckhardt sighed softly. "All right. I noticed it about three weeks ago. I checked back, the way you did, I suppose, and saw that it'd been happening for some time. I called Cliff on the carpet right away. He's supposed to keep on top of those things and alert me the second he sniffs anything. Cliff was as surprised as I'd been."

"Does that make sense? Shouldn't he have known?"

"Theoretically, yes. But, in practice, he felt sure it was a normal trend."

"All that rationalization you were giving me a moment ago," Palmer said. "That was the gospel according to Cliff Mergendahl."

"More or less. And it still makes sense."

"Sure it does," Palmer agreed. "Except that you have a funny feeling at the back of your neck and so have I."

Burckhardt smiled wryly. "You tell me your twinge and I'll tell you mine."

"My first feeling is that I'd like to know why Cliff didn't have the same twinge."

"Forget it," Burckhardt said. "I'm interested in what you think is behind this business."

"It's either something, or it's a normal pattern. If it's normal, good. If it's something else, then it's somebody else. That's as far as logic can carry me. From there on, I need facts I don't have. But you do."

"I do?"

"Of course you do," Palmer said in a flat, authoritative voice. "You can give that somebody a name. A list of names, at the very least, from which we could cull the name. I can't do that. But you can."

"I can't even begin to." Burckhardt sat back and stared at the cartoon on the wall beside him. It depicted someone named Charley shinnying up a pole to reach a girl, seated on top, named Ginnie.

"Can't," Palmer asked, pressing the older man, "or won't?"

Burckhardt's eyes swung sideways to glare whitely at him. The muscle in his temple kicked. "Watch it, Woody," he said in a low, harsh voice. "Watch that mouth of yours, boy."

"I'm not trying to insult you," Palmer said angrily. "I'm trying to help you."

"I don't remember issuing an invitation."

"Am I supposed to wait for one?"

"You're Goddamned good and right you are," Burckhardt rasped. "When I need help I'll ask for it. And if I ever need it from a new boy, then I'll know I'm in big trouble." He got to his feet slowly, controlling himself because they were in a public place. "Now, look," he said. "You have spoiled a perfectly good lunch. I'll let that pass. You've talked a lot of nonsense. I'll let that ride, too. But one thing I'm making clear: nobody helps Burckhardt across any crowded streets. When I need a Boy Scout, I'll call for one. Till then, go make your speeches and leave the rest to me. Understood?"

Palmer stood up. "It's your bank."

"Now you've said something," the older man told him, "something you'd do well not to forget." He held out his hand. "Nothing personal, Woody."

Palmer took his hand and felt the powerful pressure of the rough, thick fingers. "If you say so."

"Right," Burckhardt said. "Got to run. Talk to you later. Or tomorrow." He waved and went to the cloakroom, pulled his own coat off a hanger and tossed the surprised girl a quarter as he walked out of the restaurant.

Palmer stood there for a moment. He caught a glimpse of Burckhardt's stocky figure outside as he put on his coat. He waved at something. Palmer watched Burckhardt dash across Second Avenue, through moving traffic, to meet his Rolls as it pulled up on the opposite side of the street. He jumped in, slammed the door and was gone. Palmer calculated that from the time Burckhardt had shaken his hand to the time he had disappeared in his car barely thirty seconds had elapsed.

Fast. Indomitable. Self-reliant. Imperturbable.

Except, Palmer reflected, that he had been good and perturbed when he'd learned that someone else had noticed the action of the stock.

Palmer looked about for his waiter, failed to find him. He sat down, lighted another cigarette and stared at the new glowing ash. He was getting a little tired of rough, tough old men who didn't need any help. He'd always given in to his father on a point like this and left the matter alone. But that was another time and this was now. This time he was not going to leave the matter alone.

CHAPTER THIRTY-THREE

Palmer sat alone in the little room the hotel called a library. The children had gone to bed an hour before. He could hear Edith somewhere in another part of the six-room suite. The "library" was totally empty now of the stacked paintings and cartons of books Edith had not trusted to be left in storage after the move from Chicago. The men had come that afternoon, apparently, and had taken all the Palmer possessions from the hotel suite, except for one change of clothing. The whole thing had been worked out in advance. Edith and one of the hotel maids had packed all the suits, dresses, shirts and so forth in plastic bags, leaving just enough in the closet and bureau drawers to outfit the family for the next day. As he sat there under the dim light of what the hotel called a reading lamp, Palmer wondered idly what ensemble his wife had chosen for him to wear tomorrow.

He was, of course, grateful to her for the planning that had gone into the Chicago-New York move, and now this move from the hotel to their new home. He could not have supervised the remodeling of the house himself. He also understood that not just any woman could have planned the entire thing with as much success as Edith had.

Having realized all this, Palmer's mind shifted slightly—but not by much—to a different set of thoughts, his own sins of omission.

He had not, for example, visited the site of the remodeling in nearly a month. As a matter of fact, he had seen the house exactly twice: once on the day he and Edith had decided to buy it and a second time when the interior demolition had been completed. In other words, he told himself now, he had completely neglected the place since the work of construction began. He had no idea, except from Edith's blueprints, just what had been built there, or what it looked like or whether it suited him or not.

All of which meant, he recognized now, an indifference to the house which bordered on callousness.

Edith had not directly accused him of this. In the last few weeks, as the big outlines of the remodeling work had been refined into an infinite series of small details—that dado in the dining room: walnut or teak?—she had had little time in the evening to do more than learn his preferences. Random-width oak in the large living room. Hand-drawn, not motorized draperies. Edge-cut maple on the kitchen counters. No vinyl-asbestos tile in the children's rooms. (Too cold for bare feet; try oak.) Ten-second delay on the automatic elevator door? All right. Yes.

As he sat in his hotel-suite library, Palmer knew that Edith had done, in the two months the job had taken, the work of a general contractor, an interior designer and part of the work of an architect as well. For all these things, he told himself, he was grateful.

He didn't really feel grateful, he decided now, but he recognized the suitability of such a feeling. It was not only expected but earned.

So thinking, Palmer squinted slightly under the weak light and tried to pick up his reading where he had left it. The sheaf of papers, all legal-sized 13 inches in depth, was bound in a blue folder by chromium-plated clasps at the top. Palmer flipped through several more pages before his attention began to wander again. There was something lethal to the attention span in a list of names and addresses. Burckhardt had been right. Everybody who could afford Ubco stock had, most evidently, bought some. The list of stockholders he held in his hands weighed at least a pound.

It was actually two lists bound together. One detailed the situation as of six months ago. The other was current, or as nearly current as Harry Elder had been able to provide, which meant no more than thirty days out of date.

When the activity of a stock went up, Palmer knew—because more shares were traded each day. One could expect a natural flow of shares from the few big holders to a lot of small ones. A mutual fund, he assumed, with tens of thousands of shares, might be moved to unload Ubco for the last quarter of the year. These thousands might eventually find their way into the portfolios of several hundred individual buyers.

This was the logical expectation. But, as Palmer compared the lists, he saw that during the past six months more shares were held by fewer hands. This was contrary to expectation.

He sighed and let the heavy sheaf of papers drop to his lap. He had spent the last half-hour ticking off names on the new lists that hadn't shown on the older one. He could summarize the situation very clearly: in half a year, about 200,000 Ubco shares had been transferred, through purchase, from some 3,000 individuals to approximately 25. He failed to recognize any of these 25 new names. No pattern was discernible. Even the addresses were scattered over most of the country.

Palmer yawned and closed his eyes. He could hear Edith moving about fitfully in another room.

Edith. Palmer tried, in his drowsy state of mind, to check back over the last two months, searching for the times when he had complimented Edith on the job she had been doing. Had he ever said as much to her? What had he said? Had he made any comment at all, beyond conventional interest in specific problems? Had he at any time expressed an opinion on the total situation? Had he, in fact, said anything at all to her about it, except in response to questions?

Palmer's eyes opened quickly. He stood up and laid the sheaf of stockholder lists on the chair. Then he walked into another room, looking for his wife. He found her in the kitchen, staring at the open refrigerator. The up-from-under light emphasized the rather long, sharp chin in her narrow face. Without make-up, dressed in a nondescript short-sleeved white blouse and narrow-legged khaki slacks, she would not, Palmer decided, have passed as a banker's wife. His glance moved up the long line of her slacks, over the boyish hips to the waist, cinched in by a black leather belt.

"No ice-box raiding allowed," he said.

She stood there without turning around. "Darling," she said, "what a dead giveaway of your age. 'Ice box,' indeed." She bent down to remove something from the refrigerator and Palmer noticed that, even in that posture, her buttocks remained flat and lean. "I'm just seeing what non-perishables I can pack tonight."

"When do they come for the rest of the stuff?"

"Five minutes after you and the children leave tomorrow morning."

"Timed that close."

"That's nothing," she said, straightening up. "The afternoon schedule is the real split-second wonder. The children's rooms have to be habitable by three P.M. Ours can wait."

"I hope you've got work for the kids to do."

"Lots." She turned slightly, without looking at him. Her body was silhouetted against the refrigerator light, the small, high breasts outlined, the stomach so absolutely flat that the belt buckle jutted out as a distinctly added feature.

"I wouldn't like to think of them lolling around just watching the men work," Palmer added. "They have little enough to do as it is."

"They'll be busy." She paused for a moment. "When can I expect you tomorrow?"

"The . . ." He paused, too. "I'm not sure. If you want me to, I'll make a special effort."

"I wish you would, within reason."

He nodded, then realized that she couldn't see the movement because she still wasn't looking at him. "Special chores for me?"

"Mrs. Gage is arriving tomorrow, you know."

"Early?"

"She's due at Idlewild by noon. I've told her to take a cab directly to the house. If the three of us devote an evening to it, we can have the books installed, the pictures placed and all the occasional furniture where we think it looks right."

Palmer groaned softly. "An evening of hanging pictures. Marvelous."

"Not hanging. Placing. You don't really think I'd trust the hanging to amateurs?"

"Doesn't your master plan have all the art placed?" Palmer asked. As soon as the words had been said, he sensed the not-too-veiled sarcasm. "I mean," he hurried on, "aren't the ceiling spotlights already installed?"

This time she turned to face him. With the light behind her, Palmer found it difficult to read the expression on her face. "Woods," she said in a quiet voice, "they are movable spots. They can be aimed almost anywhere we choose."

"Oh, I didn't—"

"Never mind," she cut in. Her hand moved up in the beginnings of a gesture of helplessness, then stopped. "Just never mind." She turned her back to him and stared into the refrigerator again. "But please try to get home for dinner. It's our first in the new home."

"Of course."

He waited for her to say something more. When she failed to, he tried to think of something he could say to round out the interchange in a pleasant manner. He watched her at the refrigerator and, suddenly, realized that she was quite upset. There was no other way to account for the fact that she had left the refrigerator door open this long. Edith's training had been of a peculiar kind: the usual amenities from her mother and governesses, the usual from Wellesley, but from somewhere Palmer had never been able to locate came an odd streak of atypical information. For example, Edith knew a great deal about electricity. She was the only woman he had ever met who understood that you couldn't plug in an electric heater, a vacuum cleaner and a floor lamp on the same wall outlet without running the risk of blowing a fuse. She also understood how long it took a refrigerator to re-establish the same degree of cold it had created before its door was opened. And yet the door had been open now for several minutes.

"I'll go back and finish my work," he said then.

"All right." She glanced at her wrist watch. "I hope to be in bed soon."

"I'll be along as quickly as I can."

"Fine."

He turned to leave, then stopped, remembering his original mission. "Look," he said slowly, "you must be tired as hell. Why don't you go to bed right now."

"I will."

"These last two months have really been something, haven't they?"

He could see the small of her back, just above the black belt, tighten slightly under the thin white blouse. She wheeled halfway to her left, a peculiarly rigid movement, as though her spine were locked in position. "Yes," she said in a guarded tone, "they have." She looked down at the floor.

"I mean, all the planning and supervision," he went on. "It's been quite a job. I guess you're happy to see it end."

"Yes. I am."

"Look, I . . ." He stopped and moistened his lower lip, glad that she wasn't watching to see him do it. "I haven't said much about it before. But I'm really very grateful for everything."

She nodded. Her glance was fixed on the floor near the tips of the soiled white sneakers she wore. "I know you are," she said at last.

"I don't know how you could be," he said, trying for a light, chaffing tone, "when I've been so Scotch with my gratitude."

Edith shook her head. "It's not that," she said. "It's that you're a logical person. And any logical person would see what you've seen. And feel . . ." She paused. Palmer could see her lips move silently for a moment. ". . . grateful," she said, finally.

"Well, I do. Very much so. And I . . ." He gestured, trying to eke out the thought without further words.

"And you wanted to get it on the record," she supplied for him.

"I suppose."

Her eyes swung up and sideways to look at him. "The record is very important to you, Woods. It's a thing bankers live by, isn't it?"

"In a way. Yes."

"The record," she repeated, her eyes on him. "That's the summing up, really. I mean, that's the, uh, balance sheet. What do you call it? The bottom line?"

"The bottom line. Yes."

"And, actually, nothing matters but that bottom line," she said, her voice so soft Palmer had to lean forward. "It sums up everything. What comes before could be anything, anything at all, good, horrible, delightful, agonizing, anything. But if the bottom line is in black ink, the whole thing is good."

"Well . . ." He let the syllable hang there in the air for a moment, not sure of what she was getting at, but damned sure of its hostile intent. "I've never heard the debit and credit process described quite so poetically, but I'm afraid you're right. Nothing does matter but the bottom line."

"And nothing's more important than having it show a credit."

"Yes."

She nodded. "All right. Your bottom line's black, darling. Good for you."

"Edith." He watched the way her spine straightened still more tensely now, as if pulling in for protection against imminent attack. "All I wanted to do was tell you how I felt."

"You have."

"And . . . ?"

"And thank you, darling." She was watching the floor again. "I mean that. Thank you."

"You don't have to thank me. I'm the one thanking you."

She laughed, a short, abrupt sound. "Alphonse and Gaston?"

"Talk about giving away one's age."

The line of her back softened and she turned to face him. He thought he could see a smile on her face. "I've just figured out what we're suffering from, darling," she said. "It's the New York disease. The symptoms are total lack of communication. And the causes are overwork."

"You might have something there."

"But after tomorrow," she continued, "or, at any rate, after the week's over and we're really settled down, I intend to relax. Just relax. What about you?"

"Not just yet. A little matter of a speaking tour."

"Ugh."

"And more of the same till the legislature adjourns in Albany."

"Which is when?"

"March? April? I'm not sure."

"Darling, that's more than four months away."

"I know."

She stood there without speaking for a moment. Then she frowned, reached behind her and slammed the refrigerator door shut. "I'm sorry," she said then. "Maybe you can do some relaxing over the holidays."

"I hope."

"All right. Finish your work and come to bed."

He tried a small grin. "Right. See you later."

"Not too much later."

Palmer walked back into the library and sat down in the chair again. Odd that she'd deliberately built up tension and then washed it away. Almost as if she'd been on his side, an ally, not an enemy.

He leafed through the lists of Ubco stockholders until he came to the sheet of scratch paper on which he'd made some of his calculations. At least, he found himself thinking, he'd gone on the record as being grateful. But the way she'd taken it had all but robbed the gesture of any meaning.

He settled back in the chair and began to copy down page numbers from the list. Tomorrow morning he'd have a secretary list the names and addresses of the twenty-five recent buyers of Ubco stock. Or could she be trusted to do that without Burckhardt finding out?

Palmer realized that literally no one in the bank could be relied on for that. Except, of course, Virginia Clary.

He heard Edith open the refrigerator door again. He looked up and peered into the darkness around his chair, suddenly tense, alert for something without a name. He sat that way, waiting, for a long moment. Whatever he had expected had not come. Yet.

CHAPTER THIRTY-FOUR

Palmer waited at a table for four in the far corner of a seafood restaurant on West Forty-fifth Street. He looked at his watch and then at the clock on the wall, hoping to find a discrepancy. Both told him it was one o'clock and, by inference, that Mac Burns and their newspaperman guest were half an hour late.

Palmer watched the waiter ceremoniously tie paper bibs around the necks of two people at the next table who had just been served lobsters that were unusually large for a midday meal. The live crustaceans had been offered for inspection some fifteen minutes before, claws still shifting faintly with the last mortal twitches of life. Now, scarlet in death, they were being attacked with a variety of lethal implements.

Like some Midwesterners, Palmer had no taste for seafood. Shellfish of any kind were faintly disgusting to him. Lobsters, prawns and crabs seemed to resemble the giant insects of a raving nightmare. Oysters and clams, on the half-shell, reminded him too vividly of clotting phlegm. Like many Midwesterners, too, he had never accustomed himself to the fact that the time of a New York appointment, particularly one involving a social activity like lunch, was far from precise. An after-dinner party scheduled for eight did not begin until at least nine. And a twelve-thirty luncheon date, Palmer told himself now, merely meant that any time after one would do.

At that moment he saw Virginia Clary burst into the restaurant with a man in tow. She glanced quickly about the room, found Palmer and bore down on his table.

"Sorry we're late," she said, gasping slightly for breath. "Mac called me fifteen minutes ago and said he couldn't make it. So I tore over to the *Star* and picked up George myself." She stepped aside to reveal George.

Palmer stood up. "Mr. Mallett," he said, extending his hand.

George Mallett took Palmer's hand and gave it a firm, ceremonious shake. He looked about him for a moment, then took off his coat and draped it over a chair before sitting down.

Mallett was a youngish man, under forty, Palmer noted, with a stocky body of medium height and a perfectly round head. His cheeks looked unusually red, but whether they always did, or were the result of the December weather, Palmer didn't know. Mallett's eyes, of a blue almost as light as Burckhardt's, were restless, but not in an aimless way. They seemed to take in something through short bursts of furious inspection, then move on to the next object. And no object about him, Palmer realized, was beneath Mallett's inspection, whether it was Virginia's hands, folded on the table before her, or the salt shaker, or the bibbed lobster eaters at the next table or the points of Palmer's collar. The eyes, for all their inquisitiveness, surmounted a nose of no particular shape, faintly bulbous, though small. It was, Palmer decided, as if the ordinary nose had been hired to camouflage the querying eyes. Mallett's mouth was small and full and placid in repose. He opened it now to ask in a husky, confidential tone, "What are we drinking?"

Palmer laughed and waved to a waiter. "It's turned unseasonably cold," he said. "What sort of anti-freeze would you like?"

"Scotch. Any kind." Mallett turned to Virginia. "Mac crumped out, huh? I didn't think he'd have the nerve to eat lunch with me."

"Why?"

Mallett made a brushing gesture, as if waving off a noxious odor. "That guy loused me good last week with a phony stock tip." He hunched forward in his chair and propped himself on his elbows, while his voice lowered. "What a pipe dream. Supposed to declare a dividend increase and take off like a bird. Supposed to double in two weeks. Eighty-million-dollar government contract announcement, all that jazz. Real sex appeal."

"I hope you didn't buy any," Virginia said.

Mallett shook his head and smiled. "Honey, if I ever bought stock on tips I especially wouldn't buy stock on Mac Burns's tips. He expected me to give it a write-up. The write-up was supposed to move the stock. The usual razzle-dazzle. Very funny." He made a face.

"Such a thing has never happened," Virginia said very gravely, "in the entire history of New York City journalism."

"Yeah. Ha. But at the *Star* we try not to get euchered into those deals."

"It's those crumbs on the other papers who play tricks like that, huh, George?"

He gave her an up-from-under look. Then he turned to Palmer. "You got yourself a sharp little cookie here. She'll end up owning the bank."

Palmer gave their liquor order to the waiter. "Somebody will," he said then.

Mallett's eyes zeroed in suddenly on Palmer's. "Pardon?"

Palmer shook his head. Then, to Virginia: "What excuse did Mac give? Cowardice?"

"He was making a one o'clock flight to Albany."

"That's Mac Burns," Mallett confided. "By the time you get to the airport and take one of those two-engine clunkers to Albany and get from the airport to the heart of town, you could have taken the train. But not Mac."

"Speed itself," Palmer said, "isn't always as important as the illusion of speed."

"And the illusion," Mallett added, "is always more important than the reality, if you're Mac Burns."

A small silence engulfed them. Just as he could feel himself drowning in it, Palmer said: "I'm curious. If you feel that way about Mac, how could he possibly entice you to lunch today?"

Mallett pointed a broad-tipped finger at Palmer. "I'm here to see you," he said in his low, confiding voice. "Frankly, I'm just as happy Mac the Knife is winging his way to Albany."

The drinks arrived. Palmer lifted his. "Confusion to the enemy."

Mallett smiled sweetly. "Whoever he may be."

"What can I tell you?" Palmer asked then.

"You have to understand," Mallett began, "that our regular banking guy is on vacation. I'm normally on another financial beat. Just filling in for this interview. But I have a small list of several thousand questions."

"With what theme?"

"How you plan to beat down the savings banks' branch bill."

"For publication?"

Mallett spread his hands out, palms up. "That's what they pay me for."

"That's not what they pay me for," Palmer reminded him. "I'll be happy to talk about some of it, off the record. But what I could tell you for publication would hardly make a paragraph."

"Let's start with the paragraph."

Palmer sipped his drink. "We intend to press the point home, as aggressively as we can, that at this stage in our nation's economy, the savings banks constitute a dead end for money. That savings are a good thing, but that more savings are not necessarily a better thing. That, in fact, the unchecked accumulation of savings tends to hamper the natural growth of the economy. And that, therefore, the expansionist demands of the savings banks are not in the public interest."

Mallett thought for a moment and then lifted his glass. "I don't mean to be snide or anything," he said, looking at the whisky and ice, "but I would not call any of that particularly hot news."

"I know," Palmer assured him, "but I can't go any further unless it's off the record."

Mallett sighed. "Then let's go off the record. If I see anything good, maybe we can rephrase it and put it back on the record. Okay?"

"Let's try it, anyway."

Mallett nodded and turned to Virginia. "Refreshing, for a banker." Then he turned back to Palmer with his same sweet smile. "Off the record, do you believe any of that bilge you just pumped up?"

Palmer grinned. "Off the record, 'bilge' is the wrong word. 'Poison' is more like it. But, still off the record, what I said is considered gospel truth in Washington and other lofty places where economic policy is created."

"As a banker, how do you feel about the unlimited extension of personal credit?"

"You don't have to be a banker to resent it," Palmer said. "Any human being with a feeling for the welfare of the country knows it's insane. He also knows," he added, "that if we clamped down on credit, we'd go into an economic tailspin that would make 1929 look like a slow waltz. It's too late. Once you grab the tiger's tail, you can't let go."

"Very good," Mallett said. "Quotable?"

"Hardly."

"That tiger's-tail bit cuts several ways," the reporter went on. "For instance, what about a bank that plays footsie with the Tammany tiger? Even with Mac Burns as go-between."

Palmer raised his eyebrows. "Could you define 'footsie' a little?"

"I withdraw the word," Mallett said. "Let's say a bank that uses Tammany power to gain its own economic ends."

"You'd have to ask Mr. Burckhardt about that, I'm afraid. Mac Burns was retained long before I arrived on the scene."

"If I asked Burckhardt," Mallett said, "he'd only yell at me. I'm asking you because you seem reasonable. You project a modern image," he added, winking at Virginia, "with strong overtones of co-operation and a generally high I.Q."

"Flattery will get you anything but a story," Palmer told him. "Again, off the record, I inherited Burns and the Tammany affiliation. It makes a certain amount of sense. It's just that Ubco should never conduct itself in a manner that leaves it open to questions like the one you raised."

"In other words, you don't approve of the Tammany tie-in?"

"I don't disapprove, either. I simply accept it as one of the ground rules in this game."

"Shees!" Mallett breathed. He turned to Virginia again. "Next time I interview him, remind me to leave my pencil at the office."

"Don't ask such blunt questions," she suggested.

"We're off the record," he said. "The sky's the limit. Right?" he asked, looking at Palmer again.

"Keep asking."

"I know." Mallett laughed. "How else am I ever gonna learn anything?"

He hunched forward on the table, cuddling his glass of whisky next to his chest. "How's this one: do you trust Mac Burns?"

"Shouldn't I?" Palmer parried.

"The bankruptcy courts are loaded with guys who did."

"I understood most of his clients were fairly affluent."

"The ones you hear about," Mallett said. "Not the smaller schnooks who went to Mac for political influence. He milked them unmercifully and if more than one per cent ever got a government contract, I'd be surprised."

"Your heart doesn't bleed for them, does it?" Palmer asked. "The essence of a con game is that the sucker has to be larceny-minded from the start."

"True. That's what bothers me about Ubco."

Palmer summoned the waiter again. "Another round?"

"Fine," Mallett agreed.

"Pass," Virginia said.

"But let's order," Mallett added. "I'll have a medium lobster, broiled, and a green salad. Ginnie?"

"Lobster Newburgh."

"Small steak, medium," Palmer said. "Anything to start?"

"Not me." Mallett cocked his head sideways. "You know, after he takes our order and leaves, I'm still going to ask the same question."

"That's what I was afraid of. Virginia?"

"Nothing but the Newburgh, thank you."

"All right, waiter." Palmer watched him leave. "You suggest," he said then, "that Ubco has larceny in its soul?"

"I suggest it's making motions as if it did."

"I'm surprised you'd think that about a bank. Don't you know banking's the only legal larceny known to man?"

Mallett smiled in a dogged way, pursing his small, full lips. "You want to joke your way out of it?"

"All right. Let me put it this way: in previous years at Albany, the up-state legislators favored the commercial banks. The legislators from New York City favored the savings banks. If we can, through Tammany, swing a few of the city boys into our camp, is that larceny?"

"It depends on how Tammany swings them."

"That's Tammany's problem."

"Ah," Mallett pounced. "We have arrived at the nitty-gritty of the question, as a colored friend of mine says. You supply the cash for Tammany. But you claim you're not responsible for the way they use it."

"What cash? We pay Burns a respectable retainer. But it's hardly enough to buy any legislators."

"Did you ever—?" Mallett stopped and shook his head. "Of course you didn't. Nobody has. I was about to ask if you'd ever seen Mac's private ledger books. I don't suppose he'd even show them to his mother. But if you could take a look, you'd find he has a partner whose silence outdoes anything a clam can offer. This silent, invisible, nonexistent partner takes a healthy chunk off Mac's profits. No one will ever be able to prove it, but the unnamed partner is Victor Salvatore Culhane."

Palmer shrugged. "You're entitled to think so. But why should this be anyone's concern, other than Mac Burns's?"

"You don't shake easy, do you?" Mallett said admiringly. "Doesn't there seem to be something even slightly reprehensible in the idea of paying money to a man so he can buy the votes of representatives elected by the people?"

"Of course," Palmer agreed. "There is something very reprehensible about it, and about war, famine and pestilence. But all these are facts of life. Reprehensible, but real."

"I hadn't heard," Mallett said dryly, "of Ubco underwriting any wars, famines or pestilences lately."

"And we aren't underwriting Tammany, either. Would it interest you to know," Palmer went on, trying to keep his voice level and noncommittal, "that the savings banks were about to hire Mac Burns? Before we beat them to it?"

Mallett fell silent. He accepted a fresh drink from the waiter and sat there, pushing it around on the tablecloth with his stubby forefinger. Finally he looked up, a darting glance that bounced quickly between Virginia and Palmer several times. "That's very interesting," he said then in a low tone of voice.

"Why?"

Mallett shook his head several times. "Let me do the interviewing."

"It's just that the news seemed to throw you."

"No. Just interest me." Mallett laid his hand over Virginia's. "Doesn't it interest you, too, Ginnie?"

"Ah, come on, George, stop playing hard-to-get." She put her other hand over Mallett's. "If you know something, be a pal."

The reporter cocked his head sideways again. "Hear that?" he asked Palmer. "'If you know something, be a pal.' I couldn't have put it better myself."

Palmer was silent for a long moment. Now was the time, if ever, to suggest the thing that would win Mallett's confidence. But even suggesting it was dangerous. Mallett could be trusted with something as hush-hush as this, but only if assured that he could print it first, once it could be printed at all. And, at this stage, Palmer realized he didn't know enough about the situation even to promise that it might one day be printable. Besides, he reflected, why talk? What ever came from talk but trouble? And there'd already been too much talk as it was.

"I'd like to help you," Mallett said then. "But you don't make it easy."

Virginia cleared her throat. "This impossible man," she said to Palmer, "is one of the few people who could help."

Palmer lifted his new drink, decided not to have it and put it down. As if to enforce his decision, he pushed the glass several inches away from him.

"I have to know this first," Palmer began. "Let's suppose I told you something in confidence that might never be printable. Let's suppose either that it could not be proved or that I was dead wrong about it. And let's suppose, too, that what I have to tell you is incomplete with further work on your part. Would you feel justified in doing that work even if the story might not be printed?"

Mallett's small, soft mouth pursed into a mock-sweet smile. "I just love to work on unprintable stories," he said. Then, seriously: "Give me an idea of the thing. If it's big enough, I'm willing to invest time in it."

"Off the record."

"Off the miserable record," Mallett agreed.

"I have reason to believe," Palmer began quickly, knowing that if he stopped to choose his words he might never get them out, "that an outside group is seeking control of Ubco."

Mallett whistled soundlessly. His eyes flicked sideways to Virginia. "On the level?" he murmured softly.

"You heard the man," she said.

The reporter sat back in his chair, slowly, until he was sprawling comfortably. "Am I glad Mac Burns had to go to Albany."

"Why do you say that?" Palmer asked.

"Because if he were sitting here, you'd never've told me."

"True. But what makes you think so?"

"Come on. Mac Burns may wear those gorgeous two-hundred-buck suits of his, but to me he still looks like a wooden horse, Trojan style."

"Now that," Palmer said softly, "is the most interesting thing I've heard today."

None of them spoke for a moment. The silence grew longer. Into the middle of it, the waiter now lowered three dishes. He began transferring Lobster Newburgh from a marmite to Virginia's plate with finicking gestures of a fork and spoon, held pincer-wise in that unnatural, inefficient way that waiters in higher-priced restaurants use to clarify the status of the place and confirm the large dollar amounts printed on the menu.

Mallett sighed, his eyes following the movement of the waiter's fork and spoon. "Read any good books lately?" he asked no one in particular. Palmer watched Mallett's fingers drum impatiently on the white tablecloth.

After the waiter had served the rest of them and left, Mallett's fingers relaxed. "We were talking about something, weren't we?"

"We were talking about whether the story was big enough for a hot-shot scribe from the *Star*," Virginia suggested.

"Even if it turns out to be a pipe dream," Palmer added.

"And you had just plunged a dull dirk into the spine of one Mac Burns," Virginia went on.

"Me?" Mallett spurned the bib the waiter was trying to tie around his neck. "Me do that to Honest Mac?" He watched the waiter retreat. "I simply indicated," he said then, attacking the lobster with deft precision, "that as a reliable political fixer he made a good double-cross artist." He lifted a large shred of lobster, dipped it in melted butter and conveyed the morsel to his mouth. As he chewed, his eyes shifted abruptly to Palmer's face. "Did you say something?" he asked then.

"I merely choked," Palmer said, cutting into his steak. Instead of a medium broil, the chef had simply charred the outside and left the center raw. "Look at this," he complained.

"Looks yummy," Virginia said. "But it's Friday. I have to go the seafood route."

"How can anybody in his right mind call this medium?"

"Little rarish," Mallett agreed. "Send it back."

Palmer shook his head and began eating the more well-done portions of the steak. "You haven't told us yet whether the story interests you in working on it."

Mallett continued eating for a moment. "It's a little hard to explain," he said then. "In fact, it's damned near impossible."

"Not interested?"

"Very interested."

"Then . . . ?"

Mallett's mouth flattened as he tore free another shard of lobster. "I'm not sure I should even explain this," he said.

Virginia Clary put down her fork. "Oh, no," she said. "Don't tell me."

Mallett nodded. "Yeah."

Virginia turned to Palmer. "What this character means," she said in a low tone, "is that someone's already given him the story. Someone from the other side."

Palmer stopped chewing. He sat back in his chair, his eyes fixed on the reporter. After a moment he swallowed his mouthful of steak, but made no effort to cut another bite. "Then why," he asked at last, "did you seem so surprised when I told you?"

"I had been assured, one, that nobody at Ubco suspected anything and, two, that they never would . . . until the ax fell."

"I'm not too flattered at someone's opinion of me."

"It's their opinion of Burckhardt, the fossil that walks like a man," Mallett said. "You see, I got this lead before you ever came to New York."

Palmer nodded. "I knew the grab had been going on awhile. How many shares do you think they've assembled?"

Mallett frowned as he dipped lobster in butter. "You forget. This was given me in confidence."

"George," Virginia said, "what kind of pal are you?" When the reporter continued eating in silence, she went on: "The thing I really don't understand is why this is all so hush-hush. Other management battles are way out in the open. Proxy fights. Headlines. This one is so secret I'm still not sure I believe it."

"Believe it," Mallett told her.

"A bank isn't just any corporation," Palmer explained. "When someone tries a coup to gain control of a bank, he can't afford to do it openly. That kind of publicity might not hurt the average business. But it's been known to start a run on a bank."

"It's been known," Mallett echoed, "to gut a bank so completely that the new management inherits nothing but a headache."

Again a silence dropped about them. Palmer looked around the room to see if anyone had been listening. He caught sight of a teen-age boy in a leather jacket, standing at the cashier's counter and talking to the maître d'. After a moment, the boy handed an envelope to the man.

"All of which," Mallett said abruptly, "leaves you where?"

Palmer looked into the reporter's eyes. "With information you can't help me develop."

"That's right. If you'd come to me first, I'd be able to do something. This way, my hands are tied."

"But not your mouth," Virginia put in. "The ethics of the thing might now suggest you run back to your original source and report that Ubco's wise to the deal."

Mallett looked as hurt as a man can who is happily chewing a morsel of buttered lobster. "I resent that," he said at length. "You gave me your news in confidence."

"Thank you," Palmer said. He watched the maître d' heading for their table. "Is there any way we can enlist you on Ubco's side?"

"A *Star* man?" Virginia asked in a shocked tone.

"Look at it this way," Palmer said. "The more we know, the hotter a fight we'll put up. And the bigger a story you'll get."

"Machiavellian," Mallett pronounced. "You Chicagoans have the true killer instinct."

The maître d' arrived at the table. "Mr. Palmer, sir?" he asked, no longer sure which man was Palmer. "Ah, yes, sir." As Palmer nodded, the man gave him the envelope.

It was a long, plain, unmarked white envelope, sealed and double-sealed with Scotch tape. Palmer turned it over and saw that there was no way of knowing who it came from or for whom it was meant. He tore it open and found a small slip of stiff white paper to which a key had been taped. On the paper, in red pencil, was this note: "Won't be back from Albany for ten days. Be my guest." Palmer looked up to see both Mallett and Virginia watching him. Fortunately he hadn't held the paper so that the key showed. He pocketed the note and key, against his better judgment, simply to get them out of sight. Nothing about the note identified either the sender or the recipient.

Palmer found himself wondering how Mac Burns would have done in intelligence work. Too well, probably.

He smiled at his luncheon companions. "The true killer instinct," he said slowly, "has no geographic limits."

"Meaning?" Mallett asked.

"That origins tell you nothing. After all, Joe Loomis is from Ohio, if I remember correctly."

Mallett's small mouth twitched slightly. "Uh-huh."

"And Archie Nicos, I believe, originally comes from London."

"Um."

"And Mac Burns, so they tell me, is a product of Beirut and Hollywood."

"Unh."

"Say something in English, George," Virginia urged him.

Mallett chewed and swallowed. "All I can say," he announced then, "is that wherever they come from, now that I've met a country boy from Chicago, I pity 'em."

CHAPTER THIRTY-FIVE

As he stood at Mac Burns's window overlooking the East River, Palmer realized that Burns could not really be trusted in anything, especially the length of time he had announced he would be in Albany.

A man trained by several disciplines to check his facts, Palmer had done what he could to substantiate the ten-day period Burns had mentioned in his note. A call to Burns's office had helped. His secretary didn't expect him until the day before Christmas, which was eleven days away. Palmer had also called Culhane, on some trifling matter, and managed to learn that the politician didn't expect Burns back in New York for at least ten days.

Standing at Burns's window now, as the headlight beams of auto traffic along the East River Drive blurred into a steady stream of yellow-white against the darkness of the unseen river, Palmer wondered why he found it so easy to dismiss Burns's possible treachery. It was not that he discounted the idea of betrayal. It was that he could, with very little effort, put it to the back of his mind.

In fact, Palmer reflected now, nothing he himself was doing, or about to do, seemed to bother him terribly. He was not, he told himself, so driven by hot desire that everything else faded into insignificance. The prospect of the evening before him did not fill him with the choking kind of tension that blocked off other considerations. As a matter of fact, as Gerri might put it, he seemed to be playing the whole thing very cool.

Three taps on the door.

Palmer went to the door and opened it several inches. Virginia Clary smiled at him from the corridor. He opened the door, let her in, closed the door and locked it. Then he turned around to face her. She stood there in the half-dark, eyes shining, a faint brightness on her high cheeks, her mouth still parted in the smile with which she had greeted him. Palmer knew that he had the same smile on his own face, a broad, silly, what-ho kind of grin.

"I rushed," she said.

"You didn't have to."

"I had to. I didn't even fix my lipstick."

"It's mostly chewed away."

"Usually is by sundown," she said.

"Drink?"

"Immediately." She led the way to the living room. When Palmer started for the bar, she stopped him and pointed to the long sofa. He sat down and watched her make drinks. "Ice in the bucket," she murmured. "Some men think of everything."

"It's what my father used to call the all-important power of anticipation."

She brought the drinks to the sofa and sat down beside him. They touched glasses. The room was lighted by a small lamp on the far window wall. Palmer had planned it that way: enough light for the two of them, not enough for anyone watching from a window across the way. The position of the lamp, too, made observation almost impossible. It lighted up the translucent draperies, setting a shield of whiteness between an outside observer and the people in the room.

Cool, he thought. Why so cool?

"And what," Virginia asked then, "would your father call this?"

"Idiocy."

She nodded. "I'm with him."

"Then let's drink up and leave. I'm not all that certain Mac is really in Albany."

"I am."

"How?"

"I called him in Albany just before I left the office," she explained. "Legitimate reason. I also had a legitimate reason for asking to see him tomorrow. He told me he wouldn't be back for ten days. Q.E.D."

"Why'd you double-check?"

"It seemed sensible."

"Worried?"

She nodded gravely. "Scared stiff. I have so much to worry about. I'm single.

I have money in the bank. I could get a newspaper job again any time I needed to."

He smiled. "Which bank do you keep your money in?"

"Secret." She sipped her drink. "Do you have a lot of money, Woods?"

"Why?"

"Enough to weather a big, messy scandal?"

"Yes."

"Then neither of us has anything to worry about." She touched her glass to his again. "But next time, I'll still double-check." She sipped her drink and put it down on the big, heavy glass cocktail table. "The funniest thing happened to me this afternoon. A man in my office stopped by my desk. While we were discussing something else, he showed me a slip of paper with a key taped to it. He didn't refer to the paper or the key and neither did I. Do you think he was trying to tell me something?"

"Off-hand, I'd say yes."

"Have you any idea what he was up to?"

"No good."

"And if you think that was funny," she went on, "what I did next was hilarious. I called a man who had invited me to dinner tonight. I told him I was indisposed."

"You shouldn't have done that. I mean it."

"I know you do."

"Don't do it again."

"Why not?"

"It . . . it isn't fair to him, whoever he is."

"I'm not concerned with him," she said. "I'm trying to decide about me."

"I thought you'd decided. I believe you agreed it was idiocy."

"Yes." She sat up straighter on the sofa and watched him more directly. "And I think I suggested that we drink up and leave."

"I ignored the suggestion."

"It's still open."

She took his hand. Her fingers felt small and warm. "Let's not talk about it," she said. "Let's just not talk. For a while." She turned his hand over and looked at his palm for a moment. Then she lifted it to her lips and kissed it.

He put his arms around her as she leaned over, slowly, and settled her upper trunk in his lap. He kissed her cheek and then her mouth. He could feel her lips open under his. She bit the tip of his tongue very softly, then harder. He began to stroke her side, his hand moving down into the soft indentation where her trunk flowed into her hip. Her mouth was hot now, moving. She rolled slowly into his chest and his hand began to caress her buttocks. She said something unintelligible, the syllable lost in his mouth, and the crook of her arm that cradled his head suddenly tightened, pulling his mouth against hers with a force that cut his lip. He was stroking her thigh now, from the round softness of her hip to her knee. After a moment she relaxed her arm. Their mouths parted.

"No talking," she said breathlessly.

He took his hand from her thigh in order to touch his lip. He looked at his finger but could see no blood.

"Why did you do that?" she asked then.

"Hm?"

"Take your hand away from there."

"Good God, did I?" He placed his hand on the inside of her knee and slowly caressed the underside of her thigh. In the silence of the room he could hear the crackle of his hand against the nylon stockings. His hand moved higher.

Cool, he thought. It was as if he did this sort of thing every night of his life. It was true, he supposed, that no one really needed much practice at this, but still and all . . .

"Um," he said aloud. "Here is this lovely thing here."

"Yes, it's there."

"How is it these days?"

"Just the way you left it."

After a while he found himself, eyes closed, lying on his back on the thick pile of the white rug. She had wandered off somewhere. He could hear her making a drink. He opened his eyes to see her standing over him, the drink in one hand. She was still wearing her blouse, unbuttoned, but nothing else. She stood there in the half-darkness, watching him and idly tracing a pattern on his abdomen with her big toe. "You're quite hirsute, for a blond," she said then.

"I try."

She planted her foot on his chest and shifted some of her weight onto that leg. "Hurt?"

"No."

"Now?"

"If you hear a sharp twang, it's a rib breaking."

"Chicken." She took her foot off his chest and walked to the sofa. He watched the play of muscles in her rump and thighs as she moved away from him. She returned with two small pillows. "Prop up your head," she suggested. "The rug isn't all that soft."

After he had done so, she sat down on his belly and slowly tilted the drink against his mouth while he sipped. "Thank you," he said at last.

"If I get too heavy . . ."

"You won't."

She smiled at him and put the drink down on the floor near his head. She started to say something, then stopped. "Tell me," she said, finally, "are you the result of sedulous practice? Or are you just a natural?"

"How's that?"

She wriggled slowly. "Don't be dense."

"Oh, that. Well." He made a what-can-I-tell-you face. "It isn't practice."

"The thing I love most about you is your modesty."

"I'm trying to tell you in as modest a way as I can," he insisted. "But the question doesn't really lend itself to modesty. Anyway, it works two ways. What's the secret of your fantastic success?"

"To coin a phrase, it isn't practice."

"Then what?"

"Ah," she said, "I can tell you. In fact, I can answer both questions. The reason I'm good is you. And the vice is versa."

"Very adroit."

"Don't carp," she warned him. "You're in no position to." She lifted her legs from the rug and crossed them tailor fashion, on his stomach. "Heavy enough?"

"What do you weigh?"

"One-five. All pressing on your innards."

"Gee."

She uncrossed her legs and returned them to the rug, lightening the pressure on him. "That's what I meant when I said you were in no position to carp."

"I had a useful thought," he said. "Exercise for tightening the abdominal muscles. I need a girl who weighs about one-five. Are you interested?"

"No."

She leaned forward and spread herself along his body until her face was pressed into his neck and her toes were touching his. "Notice what happens?" she asked then. "You hardly feel me now."

"You're so wrong."

"I mean my weight."

"Oh."

"As a couch, you leave a lot to be desired."

"Nag. Nag."

"You're too bony," she said. "And there are these protuberances."

"Probably a spring worked loose."

"There must be some way to fix it."

"There must."

"Ah," she said, gently biting his chest, "I know."

"How?"

"Watch."

It was shortly after nine that the telephone rang. Palmer had been sleeping on his stomach, his face half buried in the rug. He stirred slightly, then came fully awake, staring at Virginia. She put her finger to her lips. They waited, watching each other intently, as the phone rang seven times. In the middle of the eighth ring, it stopped.

"Outside call," she said. "Not the house phone downstairs."

"Time's it?"

"Nine-ish. Hungry?"

He shook his head. "What've you been doing while I snoozed on?"

"Watching you."

"And?"

"And thinking." She handed him the cigarette she was smoking. "About sex."

He inhaled smoke and returned the cigarette. "What'd you find out?"

"That none of us will ever understand it."

"I'm sorry to hear that."

"Don't be," she said. "I've reached the conclusion that sex is one thing you absolutely don't have to understand. It's like looking at a tree."

"Not everybody feels that way."

"I mean, look at the two of us. If we stopped to work out the whole thing, with all the various names of the sins and the degrees of guilt and the areas of furious tension, we'd soon stop enjoying it."

He propped himself up on one elbow. "You're missing the point."

"Not very often tonight."

"The point," he said sternly, "of your observation."

"Ah. That point."

"To wit: that we successfully avoid naming the sins and pinpointing the guilts. How do you account for that?"

"Beginner's luck. I expect the whole load will tumble in on us some night."

"And we'll suddenly stop enjoying this?"

She sighed. "I'd like to talk about something else."

"You're a very odd person, aren't you?"

"Yes. Half nymph, half old maid."

"Horrible thing to say. False on both counts."

"All right. You've entered your objection, like a gentleman. Now let's talk about something else."

He settled back on the rug, cradling his face in his arm. "I think I missed something while I was asleep. Did they proclaim this Be Unkind to Virginia Clary Week?"

"Oh, screw it."

He closed his eyes. "Nag. Nag."

"I wish to hell," she mused, "that we could be like ordinary illicit lovers. The girl falls asleep. The man tiptoes about the bedroom, getting dressed. In the morning, she awakes to find him gone and money on the dresser. Instead, you kip off and I'm left to examine my own entrails."

When he failed to respond, Palmer could hear her inhale on the cigarette and blow out a great quantity of smoke. After a moment, he could smell the smoke. He said nothing, but continued to lie there with his eyes closed.

"I mean, it isn't fair," she went on after a while. "I've led a calm, ordinary life. My sins are pretty much under control. The cardinal ones have been spaced at decent intervals. I haven't been to confession in so long, I feel like a Methodist. I'd managed, not without a lot of trouble, to relegate sex to the position of a dispensable necessity, like a mink coat. Nice on other women; too rich for my blood. The first miserable moment I laid eyes on you, I knew you were someone I had to be especially careful about. It's not your appearance. I don't run to any particular physical type. It's just something about the way you look at me. You emit signals. My radar picks them up. And I suppose I emit a few signals of my own, or something. I don't really pretend to understand the mechanism. But, my God, Woods, I tried, I really did. Everything about you is wrong. Married. Children. My boss. The night we danced at that dinner, remember? I could feel all my good work gurgling down the drain. When we walked across town that night I tried to be honest and just say it, in a nice way, but unmistakably. I even tried to end it with a little bit of a quarrel. I couldn't. You don't remember. It's all forgotten now. But, anyway, at the time you thanked me. It kills you to thank anybody. You couldn't get the words out without stammering. It was that damned stammer that finished me off. It showed me how you were inside, a little of you, anyway. And it turned my own insides to cream cheese. So here I am, tumbling all over Mac Burns's fancy rug with you, when I should be looking for a job somewhere else and trying to forget all about the whole thing."

She fell silent. After a moment, Palmer lifted his face from his arm. "Finished?"

"Utterly."

"I have a question."

"Yes?"

"How do you manage to get so worked up and still look so beautiful?" She glanced up, startled. Then: "Are you sure you aren't Irish?"

"Come over here."

"Coming."

"So soon?"

CHAPTER THIRTY-SIX

Palmer leafed through the Seventh Sports Final edition of the *World-Telegram* until he reached the financial section. As the bank's Sixty Special Cadillac moved smoothly up Park Avenue in the six o'clock darkness, Palmer switched on the reading light and examined the closing prices on bank stocks. Ubco's price was up a quarter and the number of shares traded had risen slightly.

Deciding that whoever was buying still had a long way to go before they owned a controlling interest, Palmer folded the paper and let it drop on the seat beside him. He stared at the back of his driver's head for a moment. After a while an odd sense of isolation crept over him. Although the driver was only a few feet away, Palmer felt totally alone. He rather liked the sensation.

It was probably, he thought, the fact that he was seated here under the soft white dome light, like an object in a store window, alone and somehow singled out, while all around him the city slipped by in darkness like an unseen audience. Palmer watched the illuminated Christmas trees move past in stately rhythm. Park Avenue at night, ordinarily, was dotted with small, fierce red dots, the taillights of cars. Because of the tree lights, he saw now, the whole scene became Christmasy, taillights and all.

The driver signaled a left turn in the Seventies and Palmer leaned forward. "Jimmy, make a U-turn and let me off at the corner. I'll walk the rest of the way."

"Yes, Mr. Palmer. And thanks."

Palmer frowned. What merited thanks? He'd cut, at the most, five minutes off Jimmy's return-trip time. Was five minutes that important?

"Got something special on?" he asked.

"Tree-trimming at home, Mr. Palmer. I been putting it off and putting it off and I've got only six days left. So, before the kids murder me . . ."

The car swung smoothly in a tight circle and edged against the curb, facing downtown. Palmer turned off the dome light and picked up his paper while Jimmy got out and opened the door for him. "Have a *Telly*," he said, handing the paper to the driver, who, he knew, preferred the *Journal-American.*

"Thanks again. And good night to you, sir."

"Night."

Palmer took a deep breath of the cold air and looked up at the sky as the big car pulled away. So clear was the sky overhead that he could even see one or two stars, an unusual event in smoky Manhattan. He looked down the sweep of Park Avenue and tried to count the Christmas trees. After a while they merged into a single blurry line. He gave up.

Turning east now, Palmer walked briskly to his house.

Edith's plans for it had been brilliantly executed. In a block characterized almost entirely by large, wide three- and four-story buildings erected at the turn of the century, the Palmer home was unmistakably distinct. The absolute limit to which any of the other owners had gone in remodeling consisted of a thorough sand-blasting or a painting of the stone façade, or an installation of continuous casement windows. In one case, a daring innovator had installed a new façade of faked Roman brick. Not so Edith.

Palmer had seen buildings with pierced-screen façades before. They were usually built in hot climates. The United States Embassy in India, he recalled, used a modern version of the technique. Since Manhattan was tropical only on occasion, Edith's reason for a pierced-screen façade, she said, was privacy. She had therefore caused to be erected, some 10 precious feet back from the sidewalk, a towering wall of curved and spiky cast-concrete forms that linked together in a kind of lattice.

This cement lacework admitted light and air but, by casting a complicated shadow not unlike the dazzle stripes of a camouflaged warship, contrived to hide the house proper from vulgar view in the daytime. Behind the façade, recessed a few more expensive feet of space, stood the house itself, a four-story front entirely fashioned of 4-by-6 panes of plate glass set in aluminum mullions. Up the inside of the pierced-screen façade, Edith would eventually train ivy.

Palmer let himself in through the plain black door in the outer wall and paused a moment to stare straight up the narrow space to the sky. Yes, a star. One.

He unlocked the plain black inner door and stepped inside his new house. Far off, somewhere in the still unfamiliar arrangement of floors and rooms, he could hear Gerri and Tom arguing fitfully. Woody's record-player, muted by doors and walls, introduced a hectic note of Dixieland jazz. Palmer could smell the faint spicy odor of fried bacon.

He removed his coat and hung it on one of the thick unvarnished oak pegs Edith had had installed in the entry. He took off his hat and placed it on the narrow oak shelf over the pegs. Then he moved through the small foyer to stand at the entrance of the two-story main living room.

There was no question about it, Palmer told himself, this was a gorgeous house. Although he viewed some of its elements—like the pierced-screen façade—with amusement, he understood that Edith had created a masterpiece.

Palmer frowned, remembering that the word had already been devaluated. It had been used to describe the house by a twittery pair of photographers and a heavy-set, elderly lady editor from one of the magazines. He had come home the previous night to find them still there, equipment packed and ready to leave. "A true masterpiece," one of the photographers had said.

"So rare these days. A charming *pied à terre*," the other had chimed in.

"It's a town house," the tired lady editor had told one of the photographers. "Just a plain ordinary English phrase."

"Yes, ma'am."

Remembering last night, Palmer wondered now when the photographs and story would appear in the magazine. He was familiar enough with deadlines to know that magazines often worked six months ahead of publication. But if they decided to run the story before the legislature adjourned, the whole project might turn into a liability.

The wives of state senators and assemblymen would read the article, pore over the pictures. Somehow, in a dozen negative ways, they would convey to their husbands a lively sense of dissatisfaction with their own living arrangements and an even livelier suspicion of any family who lived in the style reported by the magazine. Last night, Palmer remembered, he had been quite angry with Edith for letting the magazine use the story. He'd said nothing at the time.

Palmer walked slowly up the curved double flight of stairs to the second floor. The sounds of music and argument grew clearer. "Hello?"

"Hello, darling." Edith came to the door of their bedroom and waved. "Dinner in ten minutes. Tell Mrs. Gage." She disappeared.

Palmer walked up another flight to look in on his two younger children. They glanced up as he stood at the door of Gerri's bedroom, then continued their argument without a pause.

"*I* didn't say you could have it," Gerri insisted.

"You didn't say I *couldn't*," Tom said.

"I said you *might*, but not *now*."

"Why *not* now?"

"Because *I'm* using it."

"You *are* not."

"I most *certainly* am."

"You most certainly are *not*, you liar."

"Don't you call *me* a liar, you stupid idiot."

"At least I'm not a liar, like you."

"You are so."

"I—"

"Halt," Palmer croaked hoarsely. He cleared his throat. "Hello, children," he said in a falsely sweet voice. "So nice to see you dear little ones enjoying yourselves."

"He's a dirty little liar."

"She's a *big*, dirty liar."

"And good evening to you, too, dear children," Palmer responded. "I always look forward to your evening greeting because you do it so well."

Both children paused, giggled and jumped to their feet. They launched themselves at Palmer on two levels, Tom at his groin and knees, Gerri at his chest and arms. Within the next few seconds, Palmer was buffeted, squeezed, kicked, hugged, kneed, tickled, stepped on, pinched, prodded, butted and accidentally scratched.

"All right!"

While he disentangled himself with some difficulty, Gerri surveyed him critically. "Those dark things are under your eyes again."

"What do you mean, 'again'?" Palmer asked.

"They're always there," Tom volunteered.

"Only sometimes," Gerri said. "At the end of a day sometimes."

"A long, hard, grueling day," Palmer amended, "over a hot, grueling desk."

"I'm starving," Tom announced.

"How do you do, Mr. Starving," Gerri began, "I'm glad to—"

"Enough," Palmer cut in. "You've worn that poor, miserable joke to a nubbin. Pick a new joke."

"What did one wall say to another wall?" Tom asked.

"Meet you at the corner!" Gerri shrieked.

Palmer placed his hands over his ears. "Gerri," he said, "calm down."

"What looks like a box," Gerri asked, "smells like a lox and flies?"

"A flying lox-box!" Tom shouted.

Palmer closed his eyes in pain. When the noise died away, he opened his eyes and asked: "What's a lox?"

Gerri shrugged. "Some kind of fish. Smoked fish."

"Nah," Tom told her. "Lox is liquid oxygen. They use it to fuel rockets."

"A girl at school," his sister explained, "the one who told me the riddle, said lox was smoked fish. Smoked salmon."

"She's nuts," Tom stated.

"Either way," Palmer pointed out, "what's funny about the riddle?"

Both children thought for a while. "You don't understand," Gerri said at length.

Palmer nodded. "Dinner in ten minutes." He walked down the hall to Woody's room. As he stood at the closed door, he could hear a sharp, high, jittery trumpet, interwoven with looping arabesques of low clarinet notes. Woody's taste ran to the absolutely authentic. The band he was listening to, in *echt* New Orleans tradition, used a tuba rather than a bass viol. Palmer felt the beginnings of a hemicranial headache over his left eye.

He knocked on the door, waited, knocked again more loudly. After a while he opened the door and found his eldest son hunched over his desk working with a slide rule. Palmer strode to the record-player and cut down the volume with one sharp twist of the knob. "How in God's name can you concentrate on anything?" he asked.

Woody looked up slowly. "Oh, hello."

"Dinner in ten minutes. Five."

Woody nodded. "Look," he said then, "how much do you know about interest?"

"Everything."

Woody looked dubious. "You know what I mean . . . on loans and stuff?"

"I know what you mean," Palmer assured him patiently. "What do you want to know?"

"I'm supposed to do a report on installment buying."

"Is this for math?"

"Social studies."

Palmer pushed aside half a dozen records and sat down on Woody's bed. "What example did they give you?"

"He wouldn't do that," Woody complained. "I had to make one up myself."

"Give out."

235

The boy sighed heavily and a faintly sullen look settled on his face. "Man buys a three-thousand-dollar car," he began in a singsong monotone, trying to demonstrate how boring the whole thing was to him. "Trades in his old car for a thousand. Pays off the remaining two thousand in two years. The loan is for seven per cent. Seven per cent of two thousand is a hundred and forty bucks. For two years. So the car costs him two-eighty in interest. Right?"

"Yes."

"Okay, thanks, Dad."

"What have all those figures got to do with social studies?"

Woody's sullen expression shifted slightly toward extreme boredom. "Search me."

"Why were you supposed to work out a problem? To prove you can do simple arithmetic?"

The boy shrugged. "Satisfy Old Filmer, I guess. It's his idea, not mine."

Palmer started to snap back at him, then restrained himself. "All right, get that bored look off your face and listen to me."

"Yeah."

"When you borrow money and pay it back by the month," Palmer went on, "what happens to the principal?"

"The what?"

"The original amount of money you owed. Does it get larger?"

"Smaller." Woody frowned, then brightened. "Sure, smaller."

"Right. Now, if you went to a bank for a two-year auto loan of two thousand, you would sign a note for two thousand, two hundred and eighty dollars. In other words, they'd hand you two thousand in cash, but add on the full two years of interest. Do you follow me?"

"Sure. Makes sense."

"Does it?" Palmer asked him sharply. "Think about it. You'll be paying out close to nine dollars a month for two years. Each time you pay, you reduce the principal by that much. But you're still paying interest on the whole two thousand because it's already added on."

"So?"

"Doesn't that seem odd?"

The boy shrugged again. "It's the system. What's odd about it?"

Palmer's headache grew slightly more painful. He rubbed the skin over his eye and continued: "Let's suppose you could get a different kind of loan, like a mortgage, in which you paid interest only on what you actually owed. The first month you'd owe two thousand. But after a year of monthly payments you'd only owe a thousand. Suppose each month, as the amount you owed grew smaller, you paid interest only on that amount. Do you have any idea what you'd pay, at seven per cent, for the use of two thousand dollars?"

"Two hundred and eighty. I told you."

"No. You'd pay about seventy dollars."

"You're kidding."

"I'm serious."

Woody stared at his father for a long moment. "You *sure* you're right?"

Palmer stood up. "Yes," he said with icy calm. "I'm sure."

"But then . . . the other way, you're paying four times as much interest."

"Ah," Palmer breathed softly. "The dawn."

"Think Old Filmer'll believe all this?"

"Try him." Palmer went to the door. "Dinner in one minute."

"Cool," Woody mumbled, his slide rule working again.

Palmer walked downstairs to the kitchen and looked in on Mrs. Gage. The smell of fried bacon was stronger here. Some fourteen years ago, when Woody was born, Edith's mother had suggested she "give" Mrs. Gage to them. Mrs. Gage was a thin, bony widow with a gaunt face whose down-turned mouth, close-set eyes and sharp nose seemed perpetually to utter a silent moan of pain. Her mouth and chin were bracketed by deep-cut vertical lines so that, when she talked, the lower part of her face swung up and down like the hinged jaw of a ventriloquist's dummy. Despite all this—and her rheumatic joints and her touch of asthma and her bunions—she had turned out over the years to be a reliable and efficient housekeeper who could, in an emergency like the present one, double as a fill-in cook, at least until Edith found a real one.

"Ten minutes ago," Palmer told her now, "I was supposed to tell you to serve dinner in ten minutes."

"Surest thing you know," Mrs. Gage said. "Get Gerri in here to help and we're ready, Mr. Palmer."

"Right."

Palmer returned to Gerri's room and looked in on his two younger children. "Go ahead," Gerri was saying. "But I'll never, *ever* speak to you again as long as I *live*."

"I'm scared," Tom retorted. "Look. I'm *shaking* I'm so scared."

"You'll be worse than scared, if I—"

"Still at it?" Palmer interrupted. "Gerri, help Mrs. Gage. Tom, show me your hands."

The boy proffered them, palms down. "They're clean."

"Turn them over."

"They're clean," he insisted.

"The original Typhoid Mary," Gerri murmured.

After a long moment of silence, Tom sighed heavily and went to the double bathroom at the end of the hall. Palmer watched him for a moment, noting that, for a boy with skinny parents, his rear end had grown un-precedentedly plump.

Palmer found his way down the stairs to the second-floor family dining room. He switched on the lights and saw that the table had already been laid. He tried, unsuccessfully, to light the candles with his cigarette lighter, then found some matches in a drawer of the sideboard and completed the job. Surveying the table, Palmer decided to cut down on the overhead illumination. He dialed a lower setting on the wall rheostat and stood there in the half-dark, watching the odd things that happened to the colors in the big Shahn across the room. He twisted the rheostat higher. In the sudden flare of light, he saw the painting as he was used to seeing it, two men at a sparse table, holding their spoons tightly as they stared with a kind of baffled helplessness at the plates in front of them. Watching closely now, Palmer cut down the lighting again. The helplessness in the men's faces seemed to churn up into glaring anger. Odd.

He glanced at the opposite wall, next to the small fireplace of random old brick, and examined the face of the man in the Buffet. He, too, sat at a table, with the spiny remains of a fish on the bare wood in front of him. His face held nothing, in the half-light, but the hollow, dark-lined look of hunger. Palmer turned up the lights and saw that nothing changed in the man's face. No one would ever know if he'd already eaten the fish or was looking at the ghost of someone else's dinner.

On the other side of the fireplace hung a small, early Braque, a still life of cheese, two apples, a knife and a wine bottle. Palmer slowly turned down the light and noticed that, of all the objects, only the knife was now visible. Strange. He wondered for a moment if he'd discovered something new about the paintings. Had the artists themselves known about this? He could hear Gerri and Mrs. Gage in the other room, rattling dishes.

He left the ceiling lights turned low. Moving swiftly out onto the landing, he stared down the curving double flight of stairs that led to the entry foyer. Each tread was a 3-by-10-inch plank of oak some 6 feet long, unstained and treated with a plastic preservative that sealed the surface but left it unshiny. There were no risers. Palmer wondered for a moment what it would be like to mount those seemingly insubstantial stairs late at night, in the dark, drunk.

So thinking, he started to descend the stairs, one hand on the railing. He got exactly the feeling he had envisioned. Placing one foot carefully before the other, locating the plank before trusting his weight to it, Palmer got the immediate sensation of descending through nothing but air. He reached the bottom and turned to where he remembered the master light-control panel would be. He squinted at the dials and switches, finally locating one marked "Stairwell." He pressed the button. A down-dropping shaft of light from a recessed cluster of spots on the second-floor ceiling turned the twisting stairway into modern sculpture. Palmer smiled as he examined the stairway. Dramatic. Effective. Striking. Yes.

He turned back to the control panel and twisted the dial for the main living room. Soft indirect lighting slowly flooded the area. This was the only room that, when he'd first looked at it, Palmer had not liked. For one thing, it was much too big. The entire ground floor of the house, an area about 25-by-60 feet, was more or less given over to the living room and its subsidiary roomlets. The foyer took a small corner out of it. The stairwell, too, used some of its area, although it had been designed as a feature of the room itself. At the back of the ground floor a series of smaller rooms ran the width of the house: liquor and wine closet, bathroom, serving kitchen connected by dumb-waiter to the main kitchen above. The result was a room about 25-by-50 feet, with a ceiling another 25 feet above its random-width, pegged oak floor. The glass front wall was totally uncurtained. The aluminum mullions cut it into squarish oblongs of glass through which the exterior pierced-screen façade could be seen. At night, passers-by could—and did—peer through the interstices in the façade. Once the ivy and shrubs were planted, Palmer realized, this goldfish-bowl effect would be mitigated. Until then, he supposed one could learn to rise above it. Or not use the room at night.

The long far wall, as he stood near the stairwell, was dominated by the fireplace, a modern adaptation of a colonial hearth with an opening so wide and deep that several people could stand inside. Plain black andirons and a grate almost 2 yards wide had been placed at the exact center of the hearth. Several logs sat on the grate, flanked by hearth tools and a black iron Cape Cod lighter pot.

"The damned thing is dangerous," he had told Edith.

"It's been used for more than a century," she had said.

"The one we have?"

"Yes."

"Hasn't anything newer been invented?"

As he surveyed the room now, Palmer once again missed the element of color. The floor was fine, he reflected, since he shared Edith's preference for unvarnished oak. But all the walls were white, as was the interior of the hearth. The doors to the little back rooms were black and so were the fireplace fixtures. It was true, he noted as he examined the room again, that the paintings did something to help matters. Each of them had been positioned under its own spotlight, which had the effect of playing down the white walls and picking up the intensity of the oil colors. But the rest of the room did little to help matters. A grouping of low chairs and divans was upholstered in an oaklike tan, black and white. The few green-leaved plants stood in wooden tubs painted either white or black. The tubs had been mounted on casters and could be moved about.

When he had mentioned the lack of color, in a very mild, off-hand way, to Edith, she had taken the observation as a compliment. "That's right," she had said. "It's worked out so that the people in the room add the color."

"You mean the women."

"I suppose," she said, "I could get a few smallish rugs in solid colors."

Overhead now, Palmer heard the sounds of his family coming to the dining table. He returned to the master control panel, switched off the lights and mounted the now invisible stairs.

The same sense of isolation he had felt in the car coming home tonight he now felt as he paused for a moment at the mid-point of the great twisting upthrust of stairs. He listened to a brief discussion between Edith and Mrs. Gage, hearing the voices but not the words. As he did so, Palmer was suddenly aware of another sensation, one almost as strong as the feeling of isolation.

He could find no name for it at first. It was part of the isolation, yet separate, a sensation strong enough to make the aloneness pleasant, even exciting.

Then he realized what it was. He had for all these months in New York led a rootless existence in the hotel. This had changed and solidified when they moved into the house. Now he once again had the role he had always played, the father of a family in a house of its own, the master of the house, if only in a legal sense, the male figure encumbered with responsibility and property. With this role, at least as it had been played in Chicago, went certain other things: the helping with homework, the constant if unconscious inventorying of the house, the giving or relaying of orders to Mrs. Gage and the children.

In other words, Palmer decided now, he had been completely reinstalled as *paterfamilias*. But the thing that gave all of it a new dimension was Virginia Clary.

For the first time he saw that the role was just that. And he understood, now, that it was one of two roles. He was, in fact, leading a double life, like an actor on a stage. As long as there were two roles to play, neither could be real. Life—all of it—had become fiction.

Palmer smiled lopsidedly in the darkness. Now he understood both sensations. The isolation was that of the actor. And the other feeling was one of being on exhibit.

Paterfamilias. Lover. Not everyone could handle the roles, he saw now. Not everyone could play both the character man and the juvenile. He wondered, abruptly, if anybody ever could.

"Woods, darling?"

"Coming."

He started up the stairs, slowly at first, unsure of the hidden treads. Near the top, where the light was brighter, he put on speed. He stopped at the entrance of the dining room. Edith had turned up the lighting. The room looked brilliant, the children's faces upturned and almost clean.

Curtain up!

CHAPTER THIRTY-SEVEN

Every seat in the club car was filled by the time the train pulled out of 125th Street in Manhattan and rumbled north on the run to Albany. Palmer had been one of the few people to reserve seats in the car. The rest had drifted in gradually, with that false casualness Palmer had often noted on trains and—for the first day, at least—on ocean liners, too. There was a certain studied off-hand quality to the movement of people into a club car, an as-long-as-we-seem-to-be-here-let's-have-a-drink attitude that masked, they hoped, their real motives.

Palmer sipped his Scotch and watched his fellow travelers over the rim of his glass. It was clear enough, he decided, that not many of them actually needed a drink badly. On planes, of course, liquor was the great tranquilizer for nervous passengers. But here in the club car, Palmer saw, the attraction was, simply, the possibility of talking to other people and a freedom to move about, even in a limited way, which was denied them in the day-coach seats. Faced with the prospect of four hours with nothing to do, Palmer realized, Americans would prefer almost anything to sitting in one place.

After all, he reflected, when you sat still in one place you were immediately thrown back on your inner resources. This meant you found yourself thinking.

Palmer smiled slightly as he continued sipping his drink. If there was anything Americans made a practice of avoiding, it was thinking. The newsstands at train depots and airports shouted this fact. Tons of paper and garish ink had been lavished on magazines and paper-bound books, all time-wasters guaranteed to fill the dread hours of inaction, the long, lethal hours when hideous thought pounded at the door of the mind.

Palmer turned in his chair to look out the window. The last light of the winter sun was dying quickly. The landscape, for one more moment, stood out in bold yellows, sharp blacks and a faint roseate haze. Then the western sky faded into the same darkness as the sky overhead. Contrast disappeared. The hilly view flattened into night and small, brilliant sparks picked out the places where houses and crossroads had once cast shadows.

Palmer sighed very softly. He had counted on a few minutes more of light. He had been told by someone—Virginia?—that the Hudson Valley route was very pleasant. At the moment, and from here to Albany, it gave him nothing but selected samples of rural night. He closed his eyes and, eventually, dozed.

In the ancient station at Albany, a Negro chauffeur in dark-blue uniform touched the brim of his cap. "Mr. Palmer, sir?"

Palmer let him take his one bag, then followed him along the steamy open platform and down a flight of concrete steps that reeked of old urine. A long, gray Fleetwood stood at the curb. Palmer was ushered inside. He found the interior of the car uncomfortably warm.

"Mr. Burns suggested we go right to the Fort Orange Club, sir," the chauffeur said, putting the car in motion.

As the Fleetwood sped along a wide avenue, Palmer tried his best not to give in to the same feelings of impatience that had unsettled him since Burns's long-distance call that afternoon. His plane tickets had already been bought, New York to Syracuse and return, for tomorrow. Instead, Burns suggested, Palmer would be well advised to leave a day early and spend the extra time with him in Albany. He had offered to drive Palmer to Syracuse the next afternoon in time for his speech, then drive him back to Albany for more conferences.

Actually, Palmer decided now, since he had no idea of Burns's reasons for suggesting the change in plans, he had no business resenting the idea. He could, however, resent the loss of a day in New York. Was it, Palmer asked himself now, that he would lose an evening with Virginia?

Or was it, he thought, that the change in itinerary would get him back to New York on Christmas Eve, with barely enough time to join in the family festivities, whatever they might be?

Or is it, he mused as the big car swept around in a U-turn and parked on the opposite side of the avenue, that I resent saying yes to Burns about anything?

The Fort Orange Club, its several stories of McKinley Gothic a dark, irregular mass against the night, was alight in every window. Palmer followed the chauffeur inside and paused in the wide foyer, uncertain of his next move. An elderly man approached him from the corner desk.

"You're expected, Mr. Palmer," he said in a high, cracking voice.

Palmer tipped the chauffeur and dismissed him. "I understand Mr. Burns has reserved a room?"

"It's Two B, Mr. Palmer," the attendant said. "I'll take your bag up, if you wish. Mr. Burns is waiting in the lounge."

Palmer turned away and started up the stairs. "Tell him I've arrived," he said, hiding his smile.

"Right away, sir." The man scurried to pick up Palmer's bag, then paused and shifted from one foot to another, unable to decide which duty came first, taking the bag or notifying Burns. "Right away, sir," he repeated, in an agony of false starts. "Right away."

Palmer turned and frowned at him, projecting the expression as strongly as he could from his position halfway up the broad stairs. The attendant noted the frown and scrambled up the stairs to lead the way.

"Can I tell Mr. Burns you'll be right down?" the man asked after he had opened the room and deposited Palmer's bag on the luggage rack.

"Just tell him I've arrived."

The attendant left. Palmer stood in the middle of the room and wondered why he couldn't have had a modern suite at the De Witt Clinton or the Ten Eyck or one of the other downtown hotels. It was like Burns, of course, to stay here at the Club because the place was frequented by politicians and visiting dignitaries. But why, he asked himself, do visiting dignitaries have to suffer along with the politicos?

Although the room was quite large, the abundance of oversized furniture, an overpowering arrangement of fumed oak and dark leather upholstery, made the quarters seem cramped. The wide bed's brass head- and footboards were separated by a roundish, plump mattress Palmer suspected of being that abomination, a real featherbed. To sleep in one was like falling into some primordial womb.

Palmer inspected the bathroom and found it almost as large as the bed-room, its fixtures massive with a kind of elephantine elegance that almost transcended the crazed porcelain and tarnished faucet handles. He made note of the fact that he could take a bath but not a shower. Then he returned to the bedroom, stripped off his coat, jacket and shirt. He was washing his face in the bathroom when he heard a knock on the outside door.

"Come in."

"Woody-baby?"

Palmer dried his face and came out to greet Burns. The two men stood there for a moment without speaking, Palmer in his trousers and undershirt, his hair rumpled; Burns in one of his narrow-cut Italian suits and white-on-white shirts, a white tie that featured silvery embroidery, his yellow hair brushed to a dull gleam. He carried drinks in both his hands. As he extended one to Palmer, his cuff link twinkled.

"Cheers, old buddy."

Palmer took the drink and lifted it silently, then sipped it. "Sit down while I get dressed." He put aside his drink and began rummaging through his bag for a clean shirt. When he found one, he noted that Mrs. Gage had once again pressed a wrinkle into one point of the collar.

"Woody." Burns let the word reverberate in the air for a moment. "Woody-doll. You're a sight for sore *augen*, sweetie. Nice trip?"

Palmer shook his head. "I'd have preferred to fly into Syracuse tomorrow afternoon and fly back the same night. What was so pressing here?"

Burns sighed and sat down in an immense leather-covered armchair that immediately dwarfed him. As he got into his shirt, Palmer watched the other man and saw that he looked extremely tired.

"Rugged-looking, huh?" Burns asked then, with the actor's immediate understanding of his own appearance. "I been wheeling and dealing for you, Woody-honey. I been hatching and scratching for Ubco. In the last eight days I got maybe an average of let's say three-four hours a night sleep. When I got it at all, I mean."

"I'm sorry to hear that," Palmer said, tucking his shirt into his trousers. "But, I repeat, what was so urgent about my coming here?"

Burns squinted at him. "Something wrong, sweetheart?"

"Nothing beyond intense curiosity."

"You sound pissed-off at me."

"That's not it," Palmer lied. "I'm never at my charming best after a train ride. Especially when I don't quite know why I've made it."

"Lots of reasons," Burns said. "Just having your body here is almost as important as any of the other reasons."

"Be seen with the right people? That the reason?"

"Only part of it, Woody. We'll drop down to the lounge and belt a few with some of the Democratic leaders. That'll look good. Later on we'll drift over to a shindig one of the Republican bigwigs is having at the Ten Eyck. But being seen is only part of it. I need you with me to back up what I've been selling these boychiks all week."

"I shouldn't think many of them would be around this soon before Christmas."

"They'll leave tomorrow. That's why I asked you to make it now. Tonight's the last night for this kind of stuff. And, after the holidays are over, voom, it's the start of the session. So it's tonight or never."

Palmer chose a new tie from his bag and stared at himself in the high, dull mirror over the dresser. "What sort of things have you been peddling around town?"

"Dreams. What other business am I in?"

"What kind of dreams?"

Burns shrugged. The movement caught Palmer's attention in the mirror. He watched the other man for a moment. "Anything concrete?" he asked.

"A few of the downstate boys, the ones we need as friends, are lawyers and such. I pointed out to them that savings banks couldn't do a damned thing for any of their clients whose businesses needed financing. Only a commercial bank could help there."

"You make any commitments?"

"For votes? Too early."

"For loans, I mean."

"Loans? Me?" Burns's hands turned palms up. His fingers swiveled in to touch his chest. "Me commit Ubco to loans? What do I look like, some kind of nut?"

"Just checking."

"Woody." Again the word hovered over their heads for a long moment.

"Woody-baby," Burns continued then, "you are honest-to-God pissed-off at me. Admit it."

Palmer made a face in the mirror, annoyed at himself for so easily demonstrating his distrust of Burns. He carefully knotted his tie before replying. "Mac," he said then, "I trust your discretion implicitly. I trust your judgment, your political acumen, your loyalty, your energy. But one thing I do not trust is your ability as a banker. You'd make a rotten one. That's why when you tell me you're talking business loans, I get somewhat curious."

Burns's narrow face split into a smile, his thin lower lip curling outward with pleasure. "A banker I'm not. Believe me, baby, I know it. But stupid I'm not, either. I leave the financial details to you."

Palmer turned to face him directly. "Is that why I'm here? To talk lending?"

Burns's long, bony hands shot out, palms facing Palmer in an ecstasy of denial. "Never. Woody-sweetheart, would I put you on the spot like that? It's a simple case of if Mac Burns hints at loans, why believe him? But when Mac Burns and Woody Palmer are knocking around Albany together, then you believe it. It may never come true in a million years, but you believe it. Like I said, Woody, I peddle dreams."

"As I said, Mac, that's why you'll never be a banker."

Burns was silent for a moment. "Thanks," he said then.

"You shouldn't regard it as a compliment."

"Not for that, for the correction in my grammar."

"What correction?"

"Don't play dumb, Woody," Burns said. "I said 'like I said.' You said 'as I said.' *As* I said, Woody, stupid I'm not. And thanks for the tip."

"It wasn't meant that way. Now who's angry at who?"

Burns watched him noncommittally for a moment, his tawny eyes level and very calm. Then he smiled slightly. "Sorry, old buddy," he said then. "When I know you better, I'll explain what something like that does to me" —he tapped his chest—"inside."

Palmer smoothed his tie down along the buttons of his shirt and carefully inserted a white-headed pin from behind, holding the tie in place. He found himself wondering what would have happened if Burns, not Virginia, had found the tie pin he'd left at Burns's apartment. Then he shook his head, as if to shunt his thoughts back on the main track. "I have got a tip for you, however," he said then.

Burns's face went dead again. "Yes?" The monosyllable came out flat, not yielding an ounce of shading.

"Stock tip. You want it?"

Burns grinned. "Any time, doll."

"This is going to sound funny," Palmer began. "Perhaps 'funny' isn't the word. Self-seeking. The stock is Ubco common."

Burns laughed. "Some tip. It's been climbing for months."

"Slowly, though."

"You predicting a big jump?"

"When it makes its move," Palmer said, "it should be good for ten points over two days of trading."

Burns's eyebrows drew slowly together. "Why?"

"No comment. Just the tip."

"All right. When?"

"That's the only thing I'm not certain of."

"That's funny, you not knowing."

"If something I was about to do were the factor that caused the jump," Palmer explained, "then I'd be able to time it for you. But I'm not responsible. No one at Ubco is."

Burns sat forward in his chair. "Then who?"

Palmer shrugged. He picked up his drink and sat down in an armchair across the bed from Burns. His bag lay on the luggage rack beside him. He lifted his glass and said: "To an unknown benefactor."

Burns automatically lifted his glass, then forgot to drink. "Woody-baby, don't play games with me. What did you get wind of?"

Palmer drank slowly, then reached inside his bag and drew out several legal-length folders. "Transaction lists," he said. "As of October thirtieth. Who sold. Who bought. It's all here."

Burns stood up and circled slowly around the foot of the bed. Palmer watched the path he took, a devious one designed not to betray his sudden interest in the lists. "What's all there?" Burns asked then.

"Who sold. Who bought."

"Yeah, yeah. But what does it tell you?"

"Nothing."

"At all?"

"Conclusively nothing."

Burns cocked his head. "You putting me on, Woody?" He returned to his armchair and sank down into it. Palmer noted that there was no more interest in the transaction lists.

"Have we got time for a story?" Palmer asked.

"Five-ten minutes."

"You remember the big battle when Robert R. Young took control of the New York Central?"

"Do I? Who doesn't?"

"My father was a fairly large stockholder, in his own name, not the bank's. He was loyal to the White administration and he was absolutely certain Young couldn't take the Central from them. When the big proxy fight started, he followed it blow by blow. And when it was all over, and Young had won, my father still couldn't believe it."

"It was pretty surprising."

"For all his experience, my father had no idea of how a top-level management battle is won these days. He thought the noise and struggle of the proxy fight was Young's big bid to buy up a whole flock of shares."

"Wasn't it?" Burns asked.

Palmer smiled into his drink as he sipped it. "We'll never really know. You see, nowadays, by the time it gets to a proxy fight, everything's over but the shouting. Before the fight becomes public knowledge, there is a period in which it's a deep, dark secret. The management in power sits there calmly going on about its business, totally unaware that a fight's brewing. They hear noises from time to time. Dissident stockholders sound off. That sort of thing. But they don't notice what's really happening. Very quietly, in small lots, shares are being bought up wherever they're available. A hundred here. Five hundred there. A thousand now and then. It all looks like normally active trading. That's what it's supposed to look like."

Burns shook his head. "At that pace, it would take somebody a lifetime to get control."

"Sometimes these quiet maneuvers take years. You can't hurry them. Too much activity would look suspicious."

"I get it." Burns glanced at his watch.

"If we have to rush," Palmer said, "I can finish this story some other time."

"No, no. Go ahead."

"I'm not boring you?"

"I dig this high-level chicanery, Woody. You know that."

"I'll bet you do." Palmer sipped his drink. "Well, then. Another reason you can't hurry this patient assembling of shares is that it can cause a sharp price rise in the stock. You can't have that. Makes the whole thing too expensive too soon. The essence of success is that the price stays pretty much where it belongs, give or take a few points. Then, when you publicly uncork your proxy fight, you offer a ten-point premium to anyone who'll sell a sizable block to you. You've already assembled as much as you can at market prices. Now you up the ante and start pulling in shares in five-thousand chunks. The technique has worked half a dozen times that I remember. But it's failed, too, whenever somebody got careless. Whenever the price rose too quickly, or the management in power got wise. Or the bunch seeking power ran out of money."

Burns, his narrow face blank, was apparently watching nothing. Palmer had stopped talking for nearly a minute before Burns suddenly realized that the story had ended. He looked up quickly, lifted his glass and made quite a business out of taking a long series of sips. Then he got to his feet and walked to the bureau mirror. He stood there, staring at himself, touching one of the dark pouches under his eyes. He frowned at his blond hair and pressed it flatter with the palm of his hand. After a moment, he walked into the bathroom. Palmer heard water running, then stop. Burns returned with his glass full of water. He stood there sipping it, his yellow eyes moving slowly along a line of engravings on the wall. He sighed then.

"Let me see if I get this straight," he said at last.

"Certainly."

"You're telling me that somebody's making a bid to oust the Burckhardt administration? That's why the stock is inching up? That's why it'll take a ten-point jump one of these days?"

"If all goes well for our secret bidder, yes."

Burns gestured at the lists on Palmer's lap. "Can't you figure out who it is?"

"Now, wouldn't that be stupid of him? These are names no one's ever heard of. They're distributed over most of the United States. And you can be sure they're attorneys for obscure corporations, retired investors, small private funds and pension plans, brothers-in-law, nephews, maiden aunts, secretaries and God knows what else."

"How would they get these people to buy?"

"That's the easiest part. The group bidding for power guarantees that the stock will go up. It has to, by the very nature of the operation. They don't want to repurchase these shares. They just want them in the hands of close-mouthed investors loyal to their bid for power."

"I understand that," Burns assured him. "What I really don't dig, Woody, is why anybody would want to take over Ubco. Who needs it? And, what's more, who's got the money to buy a controlling interest?"

"You can always find the money if you seem to have a chance of winning."

Burns shook his head slowly, sadly. "Bad business," he muttered. "Bad."

"Which part of it, Mac? Someone trying to do this . . . or me finding out too soon?"

Burns stared at him. "What's that supposed to mean?"

"I'm not sure. Perhaps nothing. At any rate, just a shot in the dark."

Burns continued to watch him for a long moment, his eyes very alert, unmoving. Then his glance wavered. "Ah, well, I guess it's old hat to money guys like you."

"It's never old hat when it's happening to your own company."

"I suppose. What do you plan to do about it?"

Palmer finished his drink and stood up. "I don't happen to own any Ubco shares. I'm just a hired hand. It's Burckhardt's problem."

"Does he know?"

"About the maneuvering? He ought to. I told him."

"Oh?" Burns's forehead wrinkled in thought. "Well, anyway, old buddy, it doesn't change our mission up here tonight, does it? We still have some savings banks to scalp."

"That we do." Palmer put on his jacket and started for the door.

"Unless this changes the situation," Burns added in a cautious voice.

"Why should it?" Palmer stopped and faced him. "One thing has nothing to do with the other, does it?"

He watched Burns pause, uncertainly. Palmer tried to read the other man's hooded expression. He'd deliberately fed Burns the whole stock situation as if

it were a self-contained maneuver. And he'd plainly indicated that the struggle for control of Ubco had nothing to do with the savings-bank branch fight.
Actually, Palmer reflected, both were one and the same maneuver. You didn't
gain control of a corporation as big as Ubco just by buying stock. Burns was
right in one respect: not everyone had that kind of money.

But money wasn't the only weapon in such a battle, Palmer thought. If
you could discredit the management in power, you could influence major
stockholders to side with you. It didn't matter, in the final analysis, how
much stock you actually owned. What counted was which side the big stockholders would choose to support. If you could make Lane Burckhardt look
like a paranoid, dithering with his self-chosen savings-banks vendetta and,
eventually, losing in disgrace, then you had a weapon worth more than
money.

"Let's go downstairs and politick," Palmer said at length.

"Right." Burns was searching slowly around the room. He stepped into the
bathroom, came out a moment later with a puzzled expression. "You got any
Kleenex, old buddy?"

"I don't think so."

"I got the tail end of a cold and I've run out of them."

"They're sure to have those little packs downstairs at the cigar counter."

"Sure." Burns joined Palmer at the door. He smiled softly at him. His tiger's
eyes looked bland for a moment. "I was sure you'd have some Kleenex, Woody-
baby."

"Why me?"

"I don't know." The smile broadened slowly. "I just had the idea you used
a lot of them."

Burns opened the door and walked out of the room.

CHAPTER THIRTY-EIGHT

Although he had left a call for ten o'clock, Palmer was still in bed at eleven
the next morning. The desk had phoned him at ten and he had asked them
to hold all further calls. For the next hour he dozed fitfully, the kind of
nervous sleep that produces short, tension-wracked dreamlets almost indistinguishable from real life.

In one of these, shortly after ten-thirty, Palmer was lunching with Burckhardt. In the midst of their argument, Palmer lifted his napkin and found it

to be a thin wad of Kleenex. He awoke, turned over and lay for a while before sleep overtook him again. His final dream evolved after a long period in which he wandered through a crowd of people, a normal lunchtime crowd on Fifth Avenue, all moving in one direction while he moved in the other. He found himself somewhere south of St. Patrick's Cathedral, and north of the Public Library, standing before a travel agency or airline office. In the window he saw the reflection of a woman who had stopped behind him on the street. He turned and greeted her effusively. They embraced. She had no arms.

Palmer immediately awoke and began trying to explain what the Kleenex dream meant. His recollection of the armless woman grew vaguer as he determinedly suppressed it. By thinking about the Kleenex dream, which really needed no interpretation, he finally forgot the other.

He sat up in bed, wide awake now, and wondering why he had felt the need to sleep this late. Burns had brought him back to the Fort Orange Club at two that morning, after a dull party at one of the downtown hotels. Then there had been a small group in the club's lounge with whom Palmer had had several drinks. He had been in bed, he recalled, no later than three. Probably earlier.

Thinking about last night, Palmer remembered the party at the hotel best. It had been made up almost entirely of men, a handful of wives and several unattached women. Palmer could not recall any of the women saying much. The conversation had been dominated by the men, old ones, middle-aged ones, thin ones, gross ones, men with flat, nasal accents from the western tier of New York counties where the speech was almost indistinguishable from that of the Midwest, men from downstate, with the glottal stops and mushy sibilants of New York City, important men, party hacks, men of influence, men seeking favors.

They are not, Palmer told himself now, my kind of people.

Worried by the snobbery in his thought, he lay back in bed and tried to justify it. Were politicians real people? Wasn't there something basically false about a man taking money from his neighbors in order to represent their wishes at the capitol? Or did the falseness come from the many ingenious ways in which they failed to represent those wishes?

Wasn't it, he asked himself, a certain kind of person who decided to make a living by running for public office? He knew for a fact that it took a certain type to become a model bank employee. Devoting one's life to a bank was a schizoid retreat from the harsher cruelties of life. The bank employee was only a notch above the civil servant who, in turn, ranked only slightly higher than the peacetime regular Army man. All bought permanent security by sacrificing ambition. All surrendered the risky business of chasing dreams for the solid comfort of a life without surprises.

The politician, then, Palmer decided, whatever reasons he advanced for his choice of career, was essentially the airiest of the *Luftmenschen*. The commodity he dealt in was faith, surely the most fragile of all. The buying and selling began early, when he bought the faith of his constituents with promises. His career advanced on faith in the men with whom his deals were made, faith in their ability to deliver, their faith in his ability. Not deals, Palmer corrected himself. What did Mac Burns call them? Contracts. Yes, a word borrowed from commerce to give some flesh and blood to this nebulous bartering of faith. And over the whole market place where faith was merchandised lay the pervading atmosphere of a general faith in the democratic process. It was this faith, for which the only name was "blind," that kept the electorate returning to the polls again and again, despite betrayals, despite disillusionment. Tired but hopeful, they made the painful return journey to the ballot box, past the decaying corpses of old promises.

Palmer sat up in bed and swung his feet to the floor. The tubular brass headboard rattled slightly with a muted clinking, as of tiny finger-cymbals. Lebanese? He stared at one of the leather-upholstered armchairs, wondering how many betrayals had been consummated in its depths.

He stood up and went to the window. Why had he let Burckhardt push him into the same arena with these political animals? Had the promised excitement of the job meant so much that he could stomach even this? Once he'd learned what Burckhardt expected of him, why hadn't he resigned? Instead, he had elected to inflict on himself such evenings as the one he had just spent, amid aliens not only to himself but to the human race, with their alien chatter of contracts, their ceaseless trading of faith, like apes in a cage exchanging fleas.

It was true, Palmer told himself as he stared out the window, that some of politics was exciting. A man like Culhane, for example, with his immense power, could be stimulating to watch and to deal with. But the run-of-the-mill nonentities he had been with last night, in the interests of backing up whatever items of faith Burns had peddled to them, were dull, vaguely reprehensible people, not vicious, not depraved, yet all the same the leisurely gravediggers of the democratic process.

Was it any accident, Palmer wondered, that so many major political figures in recent years were political amateurs? Yes, there was Truman. But death had put him in the White House. Roosevelt and Rockefeller and Kennedy had been proven vote-getters. But their wealth—their wealth alone, if nothing else—made it impossible to call them professionals. The professional politician earned his living at it. It was a small sign of hope that some of the voters could no longer tolerate such a man in the higher elective offices.

Palmer turned abruptly and went to the phone. "Mr. Burns, please. Wherever he is."

It took almost five minutes for the desk to locate Burns, who was evidently somewhere else in town. "Woody-baby, wide awakey now?"

"Mac, you don't have to drive me to Syracuse. I'll pick up a Hertz car here and fly back from Syracuse to New York after the speech tonight."

"Sweetheart, it's a pleasure for me. I'm happy to do it."

"No need to. I've accomplished what you wanted of me here in Albany."

"That's no way to talk."

"I mean it sincerely. This way you can get back to New York today and so can I. The other way we'd have to drive back from Syracuse to Albany tonight and get to New York tomorrow."

"Um. Makes sense. But I wanted to chat some more with you."

"We have all kinds of time after Christmas, Mac."

"Not as much as we need, doll. Lot of loose ends to tie up. And you'll be all over the state on your speaking tour."

"We'll get together."

There was a pause at Burns's end of the line. "Gee, sweety, I don't know. How's it look, the executive vice-president of Ubco driving a rented heap?"

"Don't talk nonsense."

"I mean it, Woody. At least let me lend you my car and driver. He can come back to Albany for me after he drops you in Syracuse. You like?"

Palmer thought for a moment. He had noted the "8Z" prefix on the limousine's license plate, indicating that it and its driver had been rented. Could he afford to let Burns get away with the bluff?

"Mac," he said then. "It'll cost you more to rent the limo those extra hours than it will if I use a self-drive car." Palmer tested the words and decided that he had hit just the right note of man-to-man understanding.

"Oh?" Burns paused for only an instant, then picked up smoothly. "Woody, when a banker tells me to economize, I listen."

"Good man. I'll catch up with you in New York this weekend."

"Right. Give 'em hell in Syracuse."

Palmer called the local rent-a-car office, gave his credit card number and identified himself as being from downstate.

"Would you like me to reserve hotel accommodations in Syracuse?"

"That won't be necessary," Palmer assured the reservation clerk. "I'm flying back home tonight."

"In that case, I can reserve you a seat on a flight."

"Yes? Fine. Something about midnight."

"That would be flight fifty-three, non-stop to New York."

"How long will it take me to drive to Syracuse now?"

"Two hours."

"Um. Better reserve a hotel room after all. I'll have a lot of time to kill."

"Just turn in your car at our office in the hotel. They'll have your plane tickets by then."

Palmer hung up. He began getting washed and dressed. The thought of not seeing Mac Burns any more on this trip made him whistle softly as he took a bath. Burns was always hard to take in large doses. But now that Palmer suspected him of being involved in the plans to gain control of Ubco, Burns became almost intolerable.

He had been fairly cool about the whole thing yesterday, Palmer reflected.

Hadn't referred to it again all evening. Of course, that remark about Kleenex had not gone unnoted.

Palmer stopped drying himself and stood there on the bath mat, thinking. How much could the Kleenex remark have meant? At worst, it meant only that Burns suspected Palmer of . . . what? The disappearance of a large quantity of Kleenex meant nothing in itself, did it? Was Burns incisive enough to begin thinking about the Kleenex, testing possibilities in his mind, creating possible situations that might have called for the use of a lot of Kleenex?

Palmer sat down on the edge of the tub and tried to place himself in Burns's position. What facts did Burns have about that night, the first time Palmer and Virginia had used his apartment? He knew, of course, that they had both been there, at least for a while. Arriving home, he may eventually have noticed that a large quantity of Kleenex was missing. He may then have remembered that neither Palmer nor Virginia had a cold. Why would either of them, or both together, have used that much Kleenex? Something had spilled? Why not use a paper towel from the kitchen, assuming there were paper towels there?

Was it possible, Palmer wondered, for a bright person like Burns to argue backwards in time, postulating that one or both people had washed themselves, had considered this fact incriminating, had therefore not used a towel, but disposable Kleenex instead?

Palmer decided that it was simply not possible. There were too many gaps in the chain of deductive logic. He dressed himself and stood in front of the dresser mirror, tying his tie.

Of course, he thought then, if Burns had suspected anything at all, he might begin searching the apartment for other clues. He would find evidence of drinking, which meant nothing. He would look at the bed and see that it was smoothly made. He would eventually pull back the covers. But if he were tired and ready to go to sleep, he would probably notice nothing.

Palmer glanced at his face in the mirror. The man there looked furtive and worried.

Palmer tried a smile, succeeded. He broadened it to a grin. Whatever Burns suspected, he had no way to prove it. And, just as he had not responded to Palmer's hints about the plan to buy Ubco stock, so Palmer had not responded to his hint about the Kleenex. It was a stand-off.

Still grinning, Palmer folded the remainder of his clothes into the small bag, glanced quickly around the room and left.

CHAPTER THIRTY-NINE

"I want to make it absolutely clear," Palmer said, his voice magnified and deepened by the loud-speaker system and the acoustics of the hotel ballroom, "that savings banks are a positive force for good in the life of the family and the community. No one questions this. But—and you know I didn't come all the way up here to Syracuse without bringing along my but—" He stopped and waited for the chuckle. It came as a solid laugh instead, which pleased him. He grinned as he waited for the laughter to subside.

"But," he continued then, "as responsible citizens, the businessmen of the nation, like you here tonight, see the economy of the United States as a single entity. We all agree, I believe, that anything which contributes to a long-term weakening of that economy—no matter its short-range or local effects—is a danger to the nation at large.

"That, I submit, is precisely the effect the savings banks have had, continue to have and will increasingly have on the economy of the nation. Let me make my position quite clear. There are many ways Americans practice thrift. Savings banks provide one of those ways. I am not arguing against saving money, but rather against the attempts of the savings banks to get all the money in their vaults.

"Consider what happens to a dollar deposited in a savings bank. By law, that bank is forbidden to invest in anything but government bonds, a very limited number of securities, and mortgages. As a matter of fact, it is forced to keep a significant amount of its deposits in cash. Once again, let me point out that there is nothing wrong with such safeguards. If they were restricted to a few banks handling modest amounts of money, the effect on the economy would not be noticed. But . . ."

After a few more minutes of speaking, Palmer paused and took the opportunity to glance to the left and right. The ballroom was filled, a good sign. The dinner had been fairly jovial and his listeners were in a receptive mood. He had hammered away at their profit potential until, he felt, they were now on his side. There remained only the job of assuring them that neither Ubco nor the other commercial banks had a selfish motive—God!—for opposing the savings-bank branch bill.

"If I were one of these carnival pitchmen," Palmer began now, "this would be the place where I held up the bottle of snake oil and guaranteed it would grow hair on a billiard ball." Some laughter. Not much.

"Unfortunately, gentlemen, I have nothing to sell. My bank doesn't do business in Syracuse, except indirectly with your fine local banks. And we wouldn't dream of rustling any of you dogies off the local range." Laughter, again. A bit more.

"I can't talk for your local commercial banks," he went on, "but I am quite sure they have all the business they can handle. Syracuse is a prosperous, expanding community. There's enough banking here for everybody. You're getting your business loans, your lines of credit, your payroll service, your credit information, your trust-fund stewardship, your investment-portfolio help, your loans for autos, homes, major appliances, remodeling, your financing for revolving credit plans and all the rest of the services that only a commercial bank can offer.

"But I ask you to look not only at the economy of Syracuse. I ask you to examine . . ."

When he ended his speech, Palmer stepped back from the lectern and listened to the applause. He hadn't given enough speeches yet to be able to read applause accurately. But it sounded strong enough and it lasted almost a minute. He turned to the chairman to accept the ceremonial handshake. The rest was epilogue.

Later, as he left the dais by a side door, Palmer glanced at his watch. He had wanted to check the time for the last fifteen minutes, but he knew that a speaker made a bad impression that way. He saw now that it was just eleven o'clock and that he had an hour before his plane left. In the lobby of the hotel he accepted the congratulations of several other committee members, two local commercial bankers and an elderly man who claimed to have known his father. Then he went upstairs to the room he had rented for a nap earlier in the afternoon. He picked up the phone. "Can you tell me when the limousine leaves for the airport?"

"Eleven-fifteen, sir. One moment please."

The line went dead. Palmer waited impatiently. "Mr. Palmer?" the operator cut in again. "A phone message while you were in the ballroom." She gave him a local number without knowing the name of the person who had called him. Palmer hung up, frowned, then zipped his bag closed, picked up his coat and left the room. Whoever had called him could wait until he was back in Syracuse again, some day.

Palmer went downstairs and walked to the side entrance, where a blue neon sign indicated the airport limousine stop. A handful of people looking as tired as he did, probably, stood or sat near the door. A bellhop walked slowly past muttering: "Mr. Marmer. Mr. Marmer, please."

Palmer stopped him. "Palmer?"

The bellhop nodded slowly. "Just pick up that phone over there." He waited for a moment. "Thank you, Mr. Marmer."

255

Palmer blinked. Then he dug out a quarter, handed it to the bellhop and picked up the phone. "This is Mr. Marm— Palmer."

"One moment, please." Clicking.

"Good evening, Mr. Palmer," Virginia Clary said. "This is the Commercial Banker Crocheting and Tatting Sodality, Syracuse Chapter."

"Are you the one who called before?"

"Right. I thought you—"

"What are you doing in—?"

"—might like to see some of the Syracuse scenes while you were—"

"I'll be damned," he said.

"I'm glad you're not at the airport," she said. "I would hate to have to page you there."

"I should hope so. Or not, as the case may be."

"Instead of the limo," she suggested, "you really ought to take a cab."

"Because it's more expensive? Keep-money-in-circulation-type thing?"

"Because," she said, "a cab could take you to the intersection of Hill Avenue and Western Highway. It's, uh, number seven."

"Number seven what?"

"You'll see."

"I have a feeling this may make me late for my plane."

"This may do a lot of things for you, including that."

"Um. We creatures of habit hate to have our plans changed." The line went dead in his ear. "Hello? Hello?" Palmer glanced around to see if anyone were watching. Finding that he was safe, he softly replaced the phone, picked up his bag and crossed the lobby to the front entrance. "Cab, please," he told the doorman.

The intersection of Hill and Western was several miles outside Syracuse, surrounded by small clumps of trees and isolated houses. As the cab drew to a halt, Palmer saw the long, low main building of a luxury motel. It looked like a very posh ski lodge, all redwood, fieldstone and brick. "Number seven," he told the driver.

The cab swung into a curving inner roadway that led past a semicircle of detached cottages, each a smaller replica of the main building. The cottages were arranged, Palmer saw now, around a small artificial lake, not yet frozen over. Some of the pines planted along the rim of the lake had been decked out with Christmas lights. Although number seven, like all the rest, presented a large picture window to the lake, it was impossible to see any light inside.

"Number seven," the driver announced. He accepted Palmer's five-dollar bill and returned a dollar's worth of silver to him, which Palmer indicated he was to keep. "Thanks. Have a ball, Mac. Have two." The driver threw the car in gear and roared off to town. Palmer walked to the door of number seven and knocked twice.

"It's open."

Palmer entered the darkened room. "Hello, whoever you are."

"Listen." He saw her standing in the middle of the room, faintly illuminated by the light from outside. "I've had second thoughts."

Palmer took a step toward her. "Fine time for that."

"It seemed like a great idea when I thought of it after dinner in New York tonight. I just hopped a jet. But I've been thinking." Palmer took another step toward her. "No, just stand there. Look, we're only half a mile from the airport. You can still make your plane."

"And leave you standing here?"

"You didn't ask me to show up. I brought this on myself."

"That's true."

He took another step. She was a foot or two away from him now. In the darkness her eyes looked enormous. "What're you wearing?"

"A silly, Goddamned peignoir. Go back to New York."

"I don't believe I've ever seen you in one of those. Can we pull the curtains and turn on a small light?"

"Please, Woods, what I'm saying is that I shouldn't have done this and it's perfectly all right with me if you take off. You can still make your plane."

"You said that before." He put down his bag.

"Don't do that. You were right. It isn't smart to change plans suddenly. It's dangerous."

"Out here? Nobody but the cab driver knows."

"Anybody could find out if they wanted to."

He reached for her hand. Her fingers were cold. "I'm not expected in New York until noon tomorrow. That's when Burns would have gotten me back by car."

"Where is he?"

"Probably flew to New York this afternoon."

"Is he likely to call you tomorrow?"

"It's Saturday. He'd have to call me at home."

"That's bad. Get your plane. Go."

"Burns wouldn't call me at home."

"Why not?"

"I'll explain it some time." Palmer pulled her to him. She came reluctantly. He dropped her hand and grasped her gently by the waist, rubbing his hands upward under her armpits, then down along her back to cup her buttocks. The soft film of fabric gave her flesh a kind of supple depth that slid sensuously beneath his fingers and palms. Her face came up slowly. Digging his fingers into the warmth of her rump, he pulled her body in to him. They kissed briefly.

Instead of going around him, her arms came between them for a moment as she unbuttoned his coat. "I am such a fraud," she said then, more to herself. She slid his coat off his arms onto the floor and began to unbutton his

257

jacket. "In the plane coming here I got the most awful attack of fright." She dropped his jacket on top of his coat and began removing his tie. "Then, when I arrived, I was all right again. I called your hotel. When you didn't call back, I thought I'd missed you, that you were on your way back home. It was such a relief for a moment."

"Here." He finished taking off his tie.

"It's really very warm in here," she said. "Have you got some kind of robe in your bag?" When he nodded, she began to unbutton his shirt. "But I told myself I had to call again, once more, just once. And they found you. So that was all right. And the minute I hung up, I was frightened again. Such a fraud."

"I'm glad you caught me."

"Are you? I think you're just being amenable."

"Yes. Very."

"You don't have to be. Be honest instead."

"I'm being honestly amenable. I mean," he said, "this isn't exactly hard to take, you know."

"I thought about that, too, back in New York. At La Guardia, I kept asking myself what kind of person I was, throwing myself at you this way. How easy can a woman make herself? All that. But then I decided I was past that. There simply isn't any such thing as half an illicit affair, is there? What I mean is, once it starts, that's it, and it doesn't matter where it takes place or who goes to who. So then it all came down to how much I needed this. That was the general drift of things at La Guardia, waiting to board the plane. Did I need this? Was it something I wanted? Was it good for me? All that."

There was a little pause. Palmer smiled at her. "Tell me," he asked, "whatever happened?"

"You know what I decided?" she asked him. "I find this hard to believe. I decided it wasn't good for me but it was something I wanted. Just like that. Bad for me, but I needed it. Does that make any kind of sense?"

"It doesn't have to."

"I suppose not. Will you do that to my back again, please?"

"This?"

"Oh, yes. That."

"You've stopped talking," he pointed out after a while.

"Look at the lake." She broke away from him and led him by the hand to the window. The Christmas lights on the pine trees had been turned off. In the faint moonlight, the trees were silhouetted against the sheen of the water. "Amazing how much better it all looks without those tatty lights."

Standing behind her, he undid the cord of her peignoir and began to stroke the fair firmness of her belly. Warm air rose from a kind of register at the base of the picture window. The glass itself was cold to the touch and seemed to be covered by a thin layer of chill air, in odd contrast to the warmth from below. Palmer pulled her back a step from the window. He cupped her naked breasts and felt the nipples grow suddenly firm and pointed. She murmured something and reached to the side for a hanging cord. When she pulled it, an opaque curtain slowly closed off the lake, the trees, the window and its frail shell of chillness. Heat engulfed them. He lifted her off the floor, one arm under her shoulders, one under her knees. He rubbed his face slowly in the hollow between her breasts. She felt very light to him.

"It's the biggest bed I've ever seen," she whispered in his ear. "Right behind us, through that open door."

He carried her into the other room and put her on the bed. Then he undressed and knelt over her, his hands moving slowly up and down her thighs. He began to kiss her body. Her arms tightened around his neck, pressing his face into her. She was moaning softly as he began to nibble her flesh, gently biting his way down the inward sweep of her waist. When the midnight jet howled overheard, rending the night, neither of them heard it.

CHAPTER FORTY

For reasons Palmer did not at first understand, Vic Culhane made his headquarters in a rambling suite of rooms at a small midtown hotel. His law offices, which he visited no more than once a week, were downtown on Broad Street in the financial section. His political headquarters were uptown, in the same building on East 116th Street where his father had been district leader almost since the turn of the century. But the place Culhane was most often to be found, Palmer had learned, was the midtown suite that had no real connection either with his private business or his public service.

Burns had tried to explain the situation once, without really doing so. "It's a question of availability," he had put it. "Downtown he's available to his legal clients. Uptown to his constituents. You wouldn't want the man to get the two groups confused, would you? And the midtown office, well, it gives him room to maneuver, without mixing into his other affairs."

Palmer had suspected, after some reflection, that what Burns meant was simply this: Culhane practiced the business of politics at the midtown hotel. The business, of course, was the trading of favors, as distinct from the ostensible mechanics of politics, which Culhane practiced uptown in full view of his constituents.

This morning, two days after Christmas, as Palmer walked up a flight of stairs to Culhane's suite, he saw that his suspicions were well founded. Even the corridor that led to Culhane's office was crowded with people whose patient air of waiting, combined with their touching attempt to look as if they really didn't need to be here, marked them immediately as favor seekers. Their eyes darted sideways as Palmer passed them. He could almost hear their thoughts, so obvious was their attention. Who's he? Politico? Don't recognize him. Who's he know? What's he here for?

Palmer paused at an open, unmarked door and looked inside at a waiting room where more than a dozen men, standing and sitting, bided their time. An attractive girl sat at a desk, doing her best to avoid the glances of the waiting group. She looked up, saw Palmer and moved her head sideways several times in an almost imperceptible negative. "Next door to the right," she said.

Palmer walked on. Behind him, in the room, he heard someone say: "Honey, is he gonna see me or isn't he? My appointment was for . . ."

Palmer knocked at the next door, waited, then twisted the knob. The door was locked. He stepped back. A faint buzzing sounded. He turned the knob again and this time it opened the door. He found himself looking in on Culhane, at his desk.

"Step in and shut the door fast, friend," Culhane said, getting to his feet. "Otherwise we have half the hotel pouring in here."

The two men shook hands. With Culhane, Palmer always felt dwarfed. The man was only a few inches taller, perhaps two at the most, but his bulk, without fat, was massive. The politician sat down behind an immense desk covered with papers, leaned back in his chair and smiled. "Where's Mac?"

"Supposed to be here." Palmer glanced at his watch. "I'm due at a meeting soon. You give me what you have and, if necessary, I'll pass it along to Mac later on."

Culhane turned his hands palms up, as if emptying himself. "Nothing but good news. My man in Syracuse called me Friday midnight to say that everybody bought you. Liked the speech, liked the ideas. Which means you'll go over even bigger in Buffalo next week. These things tend to snowball. Word-of-mouth-type thing."

"Good. I don't suppose he'd had a chance to sound them out on the savings-bank branch bill?"

"No. But if they're for you, they're against the bill."

"Not always. I didn't make a straight-out pitch for support. I don't think we should do that, anyway. And I especially don't think a total stranger should try it upstate."

Culhane nodded. "My man will beat up some reaction in the next few days. Say a week at the most and we'll know how we stand in Syracuse. Again, these things snowball. Syracuse may hold off making up its mind until it hears from Binghamton and Utica and Rochester and such."

Palmer lighted a cigarette. "I didn't realize there was such a grapevine among upstate businessmen."

"It's not a grapevine, exactly. But they do a lot of criss-cross socializing. You've got your Kiwanis, your Rotary, your Lions, your various fund drives, your Junior and Senior Chambers of Commerce, your church groups, your K. of C., your business associations and, this time of year especially, you've got your politicians mixing and mingling all over their bailiwicks, trying to sound out sentiment before they head for Albany. In summer this kind of criss-crossing breaks down. People are away on vacations and such. But in winter, around the holiday season, right before the opening of the legislature, you get a real bush telegraph going."

"All right," Palmer said. "Now tell me about your own bailiwick."

Culhane stared down at the palms of his hands and shrugged. The gesture made his chair creak protestingly. He scratched his close-cropped hair and smiled a wry, lopsided smile. "You know, upstate was never in doubt for you. They're solid behind the commercial banks. Down here is another matter. But we're making progress. Mac tells me you two did a little politicking in Albany."

"True. And mostly with downstate people."

"Then you can tell me more than I can tell you."

Palmer started to respond, then thought better of it. Men with Culhane's power, who pretended not to know the outcome of an issue in an area they controlled, usually angered Palmer. The pretense they made of being in doubt, of deferring to public opinion, of having no control over their people, usually meant one of two things: they really hadn't got to work on the project or, more often, they wanted more concessions. In Culhane's case, Palmer decided now, this was further complicated by the fact that he was probably in with Burns on the Jet-Tech plot.

"I'm so involved in other things," Palmer said then, "that I really haven't been paying too much attention."

Culhane looked surprised. "I thought your only assignment was this savings-bank business."

"We've got an inside thing at the bank," Palmer said. "Something's happening to the stock."

Culhane sat forward. "Something good?"

"For outsiders, yes. By the way, you might make a note of it: I expect our shares to take a sizable jump soon."

Culhane pulled a pad of paper toward him and picked up a pencil. "What kind of jump? How soon?"

Palmer watched him for a moment, trying to evaluate the politician's reaction. Was it an act? "Ten points wouldn't surprise me," he said at last. "As to timing, I've no idea. Within a month? I don't know."

"When will you know?" Culhane asked, making a note on his pad.

"Can't say. You might ask Mac, though."

"Mac? What the hell would he know about your stock?"

"More than I."

Culhane put down the pencil with slow deliberation. He leaned forward across his desk, propped his head up on his hands. "I don't get it."

"I don't either," Palmer assured him. "But I'm quite certain he's in on it, with an outside group."

"Doesn't make sense. Nobody has enough leverage to manipulate a bank stock. The damned things just don't move that easily."

"Granted. But this one will."

Culhane shook his head ponderously. "I stopped relying on Mac's stock tips a long time ago. I won't say he's always wrong. It's just that you have to grill him pretty closely before you can make your own interpretation. I'll never forget one he gave me on a client of his. They were going to announce that they'd be leasing their equipment, not just selling it. Big shift in policy for them, although the rest of the industry'd already done it. Mac figured them for a five-point change. He was right. Damned stuff dropped five points. Their announcement was a confession that their previous policy'd been all wet. So instead of boosting the stock, it depressed it." He chuckled softly. "Poor Mac. He went for a bundle on his own tip."

"I'm surprised he hasn't told you about Ubco."

"I'm not. I told him last year to peddle his tips somewhere else. I'm not a rich man to begin with, but I'd be a lot poorer if I played all his hunches. If he gave you the tip on your own stock, I'd ignore it."

"The tip came from another source." Palmer ground out his cigarette. "Mac given you any other market news lately?"

"I discourage him. The market isn't my style, anyway. First of all, you have to report how much you made or lost. The income tax people play it cozy. You want a deduction for your losses, you have to report your profits. Me, I hate reports." Culhane leaned back and winked.

Palmer grinned at him. "You run a strictly cash operation."

"Not always. I'll take stock if I have to. But, by God, I'm running out of dummy names to put on the certificates."

The two men laughed. Palmer found himself wondering why this man's open confession of corruption didn't bother him at all, compared to the veiled, nebulous aura of venery that surrounded the politicians he'd met at Albany.

Perhaps it was, simply, that he was not really an elected public servant. His district leader's post, it was true, was elective. But the outcome of any balloting was never in doubt. Even when an eager reform group opposed him, Culhane always managed to be re-elected by phenomenally wide pluralities. His was a poor district. A little help went a long way. A job for this one and that, a yearly outing, baskets at Christmas and Thanksgiving, college scholarships for a few deserving kids . . . the cost was low, but the returns were high.

After all, Palmer reasoned, what more would any of Culhane's people expect of their political boss? He saw to it that relief rolls were maintained at a high level in his district. He was available three nights a week. He spoke Spanish, Italian and enough Gaelic to blarney the older Irish folks. From what Palmer had learned of him, he handled his large Negro bloc with consummate skill. His right-hand man had, for many years, been a Negro. Culhane gave him absolute authority to administer and hand out jobs. It was widely rumored that the Negro assistant was worth more, in cold cash, than Culhane. As a matter of fact this might even be true. In any event, it was believed. Several years before, according to Burns, one national company had found itself suffering from a Negro buyer's boycott, a result of the fact that it employed white salesmen exclusively. Through Burns, the concern had got to Culhane's Negro assistant. In a matter of weeks, the entire city north of 110th Street was handled by no one but Negro salesmen, even for white neighborhoods. Sales returned to normal, or better. It was a peculiar example, Palmer reflected, of the quick results civic corruption could achieve while the N.A.A.C.P. limped slowly after. There were many paths to social progress but, in Culhane's district, the back-alley short cuts were faster.

Culhane's secretary came in with a brown paper bag and put it on his desk. "They were impatient to begin with," she said. "Now they're getting hungry, too. Some of them have been waiting since before breakfast."

"Won't be long," Culhane said, opening the paper bag and removing two foil-wrapped sandwiches. "Want one?" he asked, offering it to Palmer.

"Thanks. I've eaten." He glanced at his watch. "Two o'clock? My meeting's at two-thirty. It looks as though we'll have to dispense with Mac's presence."

Culhane began to munch industriously. "I don't know why those people out there get here so early. They know I don't even wake up till nine A.M. I can't get here before ten. Crazy people."

"Hungry, too." The secretary left them alone again.

"As far as dispensing with Mac," he said, around bites of a bacon, lettuce and tomato sandwich, "we haven't needed him for weeks. His job's done, right?"

"He brought us together. That what you mean?"

Culhane finished off the sandwich in two more bites and turned to his second one. "That was his contract with you," he explained when his mouth was clear. "You and I have a different contract. I've never led you to believe, have I, that I could guarantee results?"

"Not in so many words."

"Consider them said, then. Some things I can guarantee. Not this. We have a pack of prima donnas downstate. I can guarantee the hacks. But we have a bunch of reform boys and a whole group sitting on the fence. In a million years I could never convince them that what's good for the bloated commercial banks is good for their voters. Unless I can make it good for them, personally. You got any ideas?"

"The usual. We always need outside attorneys, insurance brokers, realtors."

"That's chicken-feed," Culhane said, chewing his second sandwich, "and you know it."

"Each retainer is a small one but we have a lot of retainers to hand around. It's more than the savings banks can offer."

"You think a downstate senator's interested in that kind of crud?"

"May be crud to you," Palmer responded, paraphrasing an old joke, "but it's his bread and butter."

Culhane's face grew red as he laughed. After he had subsided, his face grew grave again. "I'm serious. Unless you have something bigger in the carrot line, the donkey won't budge."

Palmer looked blank for a moment. "I don't know what to say," he said then. "If it comes to that, what's in it for you?"

"Ah. That's another contract. Between Mac and me."

"Which you're not about to disclose."

"I'd tell you in a minute if I knew." Culhane rooted around in the paper bag and drew forth a container of coffee and a bagel. "But at this point I honestly don't know."

"Is that possible? I thought—"

"Both sides of a contract had to be specified?" Culhane finished for him. "No. Mac and I have been through a lot together. If he tells me it's worth my while, I buy it. Another guy, I might not be so trusting. But I trust Mac right down the line."

"Except on stock tips."

"Except on stock tips." Culhane chewed off a bite of the bagel and sipped his coffee. "We go back a long way, the two of us. Almost anything that could happen to two guys in politics has happened to us. There aren't many surprises left. Mac is the only friend I have in politics. That's saying something."

There was a long moment of silence. Palmer wondered whether Culhane's frankness would extend to any equally frank discussion of Mac Burns's general loyalty. Probably not. Nevertheless . . .

"I'll be frank with you," Palmer began. "I was a little wary of Mac when I first met him."

"He's not your type. The two of you are entirely different kinds of people."

"How different? People don't really vary that much when they reach a certain level of achievement. Are you and I that different?"

"Are we?" Culhane finished the bagel. "Oh, brother, are we."

"I don't think so," Palmer persisted.

"Look." Culhane reached in the bag and drew out a small container of ice cream. "It's a question of background. It's a question of money. My old man didn't do too badly. He had seven kids and they all finished college. Maybe that's why you don't see the difference between you and me. Now, Mac's old man, as near as I can figure it, was a chicken butcher in Beirut. You wouldn't know the routine. You spend a lifetime gutting chickens and arguing price with customers as poor as you are. Your kid's there sticking his bare hand inside the hot guts and ripping them out. Before he's five years old, yet, he's in there with you, killing and flicking and gutting and everything is all mixed up with the smell of blood and poor people. Finally the whole family got to the States. Mac never made it through college. You'll hear him talk about Harvard. What he means is he took two years of night classes at U.C.L.A. and had to quit to take a night watchman's job at one of the studios, on top of the day job. Later, after he bleached his hair and hit it big in public relations, he once attended a three-day summer seminar at Harvard, representing his company. So now, put it all together. That's why I say Mac and you are different kinds of people. Which is why you don't trust him."

"I didn't say that."

"That's right, you didn't. I said it." Culhane was eating ice cream with a flat wooden spoon. "And, by the way, you may be right not to."

"Now I'm totally confused."

"I'm much closer to Mac. I didn't grow up his way. I was born here but plenty of kids I know came over from the old country. I have an inkling of what goes on inside him. I know how a man like that can hate."

"Hate me?"

Culhane paused, started to say something, then looked helpless for a moment. "You're a smart man. Did you ever bother to figure out why you were hired?"

Palmer nodded. "Several reasons. But since we're talking about Mac, one reason I was hired was because Burckhardt couldn't stand him."

"Head of the class. Now, put yourself in Mac's position. What do you think he feels for Burckhardt, and every other Burckhardt in this great big country his old man busted a gut to get into?"

"I see."

"You see because I've painted you a picture." Culhane hunched forward. "But you don't feel. How could you? You're closer to the Burckhardts of the world than I am to Mac."

"So, really, all of this adds up to a warning," Palmer said slowly.

"I'm his best friend," Culhane said. "But I can't answer for all the dark little corners inside him. Hell, I've got my own dark corners. Plenty of Burckhardts have crapped on my head, too. You know, combining two races is always a tricky business. But when the two are Irish and Italian, friend, look out. They almost equal one Lebanese."

"Um." Palmer nodded, then glanced at his watch. "Our Harvard graduate isn't going to show."

Culhane laughed boisterously. "Don't you ever let on I told you that bit about Harvard." He stood up.

"Fair enough." Palmer got to his feet. "Don't you ever let on I told you about the Ubco stock. But buy some."

"Sold." They shook hands.

As Palmer started to leave him, Culhane sat down and poked his hand in the brown paper bag. After a moment he found and drew out a candy bar.

Chapter Forty-one

Palmer arrived at the bank with a minute to spare before the meeting began. Because he had not been invited to attend, he wanted to arrive well after it started. Therefore he spent some time in the public lobby of the bank, looking at the promotional booklets in the little racks, watching customers and, until they noticed him standing there, observing his tellers. Certain standards of behavior were expected of all Ubco employees, but the ones picked for this showcase branch office were supposed to meet even higher criteria. They had, for one thing, to be physically attractive. For another, their voices were expected to be well modulated and as cultured as could be hired at $80 a week for the women and $110 for the men. Finally, they were supposed to represent the New Banking, the Open Society of Money, the postwar revolution in customer relations which had torn down the bronze wicket barriers and moved the bank a step closer to the friendly supermarket.

At two-forty, Palmer took the elevator upstairs and headed for Harry Elder's office. Today's meeting, he knew, had an added item on the agenda, a discussion of tactics in relation to the Jet-Tech application for what Harry privately referred to as "that Great Big Loan in the Sky."

Because he was supposed to be preparing himself for his speech in Buffalo, or dealing with Mac Burns or something or other, Palmer had been asked by Burckhardt to "skip this one, Woody. Waste of your time."

It was for that reason, Palmer saw as he entered the room, nodded to the men at the table and sat down, that Burckhardt stopped talking in mid-sentence and failed to pick up the threads of his thought for several seconds. When he did, Palmer realized that the Jet-Tech application had been placed first on the agenda, which pretty much meant that the other items were expendable.

"As I said," Burckhardt continued, "hi, Woody, the Jet-Tech task force hits town tomorrow. We're lunching them in the big room downtown; Irma, you needn't write down any of this, and it's going to be sticky from the soup to the dessert."

His secretary put down her pencil and sat there with an abstracted look on her face, her eyes fixed on nothing in particular, unless there was something utterly fascinating to her about the area of teak table between Palmer's ash tray and Mergendahl's brief case.

Clifton G. Mergendahl, vice-president and secretary of the bank, had several responsibilities, none more important than his expert reading of market trends. In co-ordination with his research department, he was supposed to see to it that none of the trust-fund portfolios administered by Ubco made any fatally bad investments. A man not much younger than Burckhardt, Cliff Mergendahl had come to Ubco shortly after the war from a position as a partner in a Wall Street brokerage. He, Burckhardt and Elder were directors of the bank and he himself apparently held more of its stock than any other officer, except Burckhardt. Watching him now, Palmer was immediately aware of Cliff's main strength and reason for success. His small, somewhat narrow face, topped by a sideways swash of fine, white hair, was the most confidence-inspiring sight outside of Gibraltar. Cliff's wide-set, dark-gray eyes were round, unblinking and calm. If anyone in the world ever really had an honest face, it was Cliff. You would trust him, Palmer decided, with your money and your life. He was, in short, too good to be true.

"It needn't be all that sticky," Cliff was saying in his calm, soft voice. "Everyone's acting in good faith. We can say that we've considered the application at some length and we regretfully feel that due to the uncertain et cetera et cetera of the general economy and in particular of the aero-space segment of et cetera et cetera."

"Barney Kinch and Joe Loomis will nod politely," Burckhardt snapped, "kiss your shoe and silently fade into thin air."

"Not Barney," Harry Elder said. "You'll be in for quite an argument from that one. He'll arrive all primed for it. Cliff, you've seen how he does it. Joe Loomis just sits there quietly. But Barney's got his charts, graphs, blown-up photos and the testimony of his experts. He'll bring along his controller, that German research head and half a dozen intricate working models of weird electronic gizmos that will revolutionize civilization. And these little dohickeys will hum, buzz, give off light and do everything but dance a buck and wing. By the time you've watched them for a minute or two, you're hypnotized and your head is going up and down. Yes, Barney. Who are we to keep America off the moon? We wouldn't want to hand outer space to the Russians. Half a billion, Barney? Sign right here."

"I remember one time," Burckhardt said, laughing, "when Barney and that Whatshisname, his technical director, the German, anyway, the two of them had this dingus that sent a beam of green light across the board room. Barney talked in one end and I could hear him through some headphones at the other end. His voice had been sent over the beam of light. Damned thing nearly blinded me."

"Laser," Palmer said.

Burckhardt squinted at him. "I think you're right," he said at last. "Anyway, that little green light was going to cost seven million to develop, and then there was that toy thing that crawled around on the table. Remember, Harry? Looked like a steel crab? It bumped into an ash tray and before we knew what was happening it'd eaten two cigarette butts and given us a detailed chemical analysis of them. Five million dollars, as I recall, to find out what cigarettes are made of."

"Supposed to work on the moon's surface," Palmer said. "Apparently it does. Or will." He took a long breath. "You know what I'm wondering?" he asked then. "Why do we have to turn down their application? They're a solvent bunch and God knows the stuff they do is important."

No one spoke for a while. Then, in a tired voice, Burckhardt said: "Woody, are you suggesting we put half a billion eggs in one basket? For twenty years? At five and a half per cent? You know that's madness."

Palmer shrugged. "Make them use a bunch of baskets. Say yes in principle, but demand that they do it in stages, segregating groups of subsidiary companies and borrowing so much on each group. That way we spread our risk and they get their money."

Harry Elder shook his head. "We told Barney Kinch that a year ago. He won't do it. Jet-Tech's a publicly held company. The details of these loans have to be reported. So Jet-Tech's competition can immediately determine, by how much was borrowed on what group of subsidiaries, what the expansion plans will be. They'll know what lines of effort are being cut, where the big push is being made, everything."

"It's worse than that," Mergendahl added. "The Russians can figure out exactly the same things from a cluster of loans. No. Jet-Tech wants an unearmarked lump sum."

"So you see," Burckhardt said, for Palmer's benefit.

"Afraid I do."

"All right," the older man continued, "let's talk tactics." He turned to Mergendahl. "Clifton," he said, "give us a reading on the current state of mind of Archie Nicos."

Palmer listened to the words, repeating them again in his mind while Mergendahl prepared himself to answer. Nobody at the bank called the man Clifton. Palmer had never heard Burckhardt use the full name before, either. Was it a delicate touch of irony? Was it even delicate? And, if it was irony, was it a signal to Palmer, a sign that Burckhardt no longer trusted Mergendahl? Was it Burckhardt's way of saying he now agreed with Palmer's conclusion that a power fight was brewing? If so, did the old bird consider Palmer an ally? If he did, why hadn't he invited Palmer to this meeting?

". . . as I can tell," Mergendahl was saying at last, "he's remaining very neutral, very friendly on both sides, very hopeful the loan can be made, very understanding if it can't."

"What is that 'if'?" Burckhardt asked. "Archie knows for a fact the answer's no. He was told that some time ago."

Mergendahl nodded. "He wouldn't be Archie Nicos if he didn't try to keep the door open a wee bit."

Harry Elder's cracked, high-pitched voice was louder than usual. "Archie only wants this loan okayed as much as life itself. The last thing in the world he is is neutral. And don't tell me he hasn't mentioned that, in view of our reluctance, as he usually puts it, he's been forced to investigate other sources of financing."

"Oh, he's mumbled a little about that," Mergendahl agreed.

"What other sources would there be?" Palmer asked. "Who else has that kind of money?"

Burckhardt's laughter rumbled for a moment. "I know for a fact that Archie's European sources are always ready to listen to business."

"Where would you find that much loose capital floating around Europe?" Palmer wanted to know.

"It can be found," Burckhardt assured him. "Archie can put together a Common Market syndicate. They're all itching to get chunks of our businesses anyway. Imagine a European-controlled Jet-Tech." He started to laugh again. "Imagine Joe Loomis and Barney Kinch having to swallow that."

"Exactly," Palmer said. "They want U.S. money, ours."

"Well, we haven't got it for them," Burckhardt retorted. "That's all there is to it. Have you any idea how much more we could earn with half a billion if we let it out in hundreds of thousands of small consumer loans? The whole idea's ridiculous."

"Not to Kinch," Mergendahl said. "He needs the money. Badly."

"How badly?" Harry Elder asked. "What kind of trouble's he in?"

"None that I know of," Mergendahl said quickly.

"Badly enough," Palmer suggested, "that he'll let us up the rate?"

"To what?" Burckhardt burst out. "Six per cent? Seven? To cover our risk we'd have to shoot into the twelves. Can you see Loomis or Kinch paying twelve? Usury!"

Mergendahl picked up his pencil and tapped the nail of his thumb with it. "If it's tactics you want," he said, "the most important thing with Kinch is to give him an out, a refuge, a place he can retreat to and still negotiate."

"Barney doesn't negotiate, you—" Burckhardt stopped himself from calling Mergendahl a name in front of the secretary. "Loomis does the negotiating. Barney's the charm boy with the charts and graphs and mechanical whatsits. And why in hell should I worry about giving Joe Loomis a hole to run into?"

"We seem," Harry Elder observed, "to be getting nowhere. Your idea of tactics is to holler no and walk away."

"Maybe so," Burckhardt mused. "Maybe so. And if I do, I'll have my reasons."

"Not good enough," Mergendahl said in his low-pitched, pleasant voice. "I know you. You're going to go in there and play it by ear. After a little while, you'll get angry at Joe Loomis and that's the ball game."

"The ball game," Burckhardt said, his teeth clamped together between each slowly spaced word, "is already over. There are no extra innings. Get that through your head, Clifton."

"Look," the other man pleaded, "it goes against reason, against form, against good business procedure. We have the potential of making a tidy sum with Jet-Tech. You just don't slam the door in their face."

"If I do," Burckhardt said in that same slow, gritty manner, "you can be sure they'll stand on the other side and wait. We hold tons of their paper, Clifton. They are into us for a major bundle. So whether I close the door gently or slam it hard, they'll stand there like good little boys and wait for me to open it again sometime. Which I will. When I'm Goddamned good and ready."

Mergendahl dropped the pencil on the table. "It's hopeless," he said, mildly.

"An accurate observation," Burckhardt agreed.

Mergendahl picked up the pencil and pushed it inside the open mouth of his brief case. He started to speak, then stopped and got out a cigarette. As he lighted it, Palmer saw that the man was teetering on the edge of some decision. He took too long with lighting the cigarette, his mouth too tight, his eyes too steady, his manner too controlled. The thatch of white hair over his forehead had worked loose. A lock dipped down.

"Now, look," Mergendahl said at last in a reasonable tone, blowing out smoke, "put yourself in Kinch's shoes. In Loomis', if you will. What would you do if you got that kind of a turn-down?"

An odd silence settled around them. Irma, the secretary, shifted slightly in her chair and shoved an ash tray in front of Mergendahl. Her shorthand pad was still blank.

Burckhardt snorted softly. "Fight," he said.

"How?" Mergendahl asked quietly.

"Dirty."

"Meaning what?"

Burckhardt waved a burly hand in front of him, sweeping away the question. "My business," he said. "Let's get on to the—Irma, start taking notes, the rest of the agenda."

Mergendahl began to say something, then thought better of it, shrugged and opened his brief case. He brought out a sheaf of papers. "I'll start with the weekly deposit total," he said.

"Just a second, Cliff," Palmer said.

He watched them all turn toward him, even Irma. "Before we leave this point, give me a minute more on it."

"One minute," Burckhardt promised grimly.

"Despite what you've all said," Palmer began, "I'm still for giving them the loan. I'm for saying yes and then working out the details to the best advantage we can get, even if it's only to bump the rate to seven, or cut the term to fifteen years. Something. Anything. But I feel we should make this loan."

"That, if I may say so," Burckhardt grunted, "is the coward's way out."

Harry Elder's eyes opened wide. "What kind of remark is that?"

"Woody knows what I'm talking about," Burckhardt assured him. "Don't you, Woody?"

"I think so. And you're wrong. I have something else in mind, something entirely different, when I suggest that we give them their money."

"You notice that, gentlemen?" Burckhardt asked. "Give this man one minute and already it's 'their' money."

"This whole thing goes deeper than anybody recognizes," Palmer said. "A moment ago you mentioned the profit we'd make out of small consumer loans. There's nothing wrong with a profit. But I happen to feel some kinds of consumer-lending are an indecent way of showing a profit. You get all these little five-thousand-a-year wage earners on the hook for every cent they earn. I don't mean you. I mean everybody that sells anything. These customers are uneducated sheep, most of them. Psychologically they're babies. When they see something bright and shiny and new they want it. They don't read their sales contracts. They don't have any idea of the interest they're paying. They're not even sure if they can afford the installments. The one thing they do know is that they want that shiny new gimmick. They're being seduced and swindled by every credit retailer in the nation. And behind the whole thing stand the credit wholesalers, the big banks like us. That is not a clean way to make money. But . . ." He paused because he realized he had everyone's rapt attention, "lending to businesses like Jet-Tech, to manu-facturers, to developers, to creators of things, that's another story. Lending like that keeps payrolls up. It keeps money circulating. It keeps the country moving ahead. It—"

"It allows them to make more big shiny new things to sell to morons," Burckhardt interrupted. "Jesus, Woody, off the soap box. We've got things to do here."

"You don't want to see the point, do you?" Palmer asked. "If we've got money to invest, let's do something decent with it."

"Who are we," Burckhardt snapped, "who are you, for that matter—Irma, for Christ's sake don't make notes of this nonsense—to stand up on your hind legs and buck the whole course of the national economy? Who named you the keeper of the consumer's budget? If these silly bastards want to dig deeper and deeper into debt, *vox populi vox dei*, sonny. We aren't in business to play Daddy to them. Quite the opposite. We make money by giving them what they want. If they want unlimited personal credit, that is what they get."

"It's your kind of attitude," Palmer responded, "that encourages them to dig that hole a little deeper each month. What is the consumer debt now? Two hundred and fifty billion? Where on God's earth are these poor idiots going to find the money to repay?"

"Oh, crap," Burckhardt said. "Woody, if I didn't know better—sorry, Irma—I'd wonder how you ever wandered into banking."

271

"Banking is as honorable as any other profession," Palmer said. "A very ancient profession, too. Only one other is older."

Harry Elder laughed mirthlessly. "Time. Return to your corners, gentlemen. And, incidentally, I think Woody has a point. If we could find a way to ease the risk on the Jet-Tech loan, I'd be for it."

"Yes?" Burckhardt was on his feet now. "You're another one, aren't you, Harry? If you can duck a fight, you'll duck it."

"Easy," Elder murmured. "Sit down, Lane."

Burckhardt's face was red now. His milky-blue eyes seemed to grow smaller. "Get this through your heads, you two," he said in a raspy voice. He seemed to be having difficulty with his breathing. "If millions of mouth-breathers in this glorious democracy of ours are stupid enough and greedy enough and self-indulgent enough to want to put their souls in hock"—he sucked in a tremendous gasp of air—"then I am not going to sit back and let every other lending institution on earth milk them dry. I'm going to get Ubco's share. The lion's share, God damn it!" His voice grew abruptly louder, almost out of control. "And no matter what kind of pressure Joe Loomis cooks up, he is not going to make me risk money on his schemes when there are so many millions of my fellow Americans crying their little hearts out for credit. No, sir."

"And that," Palmer heard himself say, "is not the coward's way out, is it?"

The skin around Burckhardt's eyes knotted. Deep wrinkles cut into his forehead. Beneath his jutting chin, the cords in his throat drew taut. He filled his lungs with air. Palmer could sense everyone sitting in nervous expectation.

Burckhardt turned away and walked to the window. He stood there for a moment, staring out blindly at the street below. After a while he turned back to them. His face seemed calm enough. He walked back to his chair and sat down, waving a hand at his secretary.

"Sorry, Irma. Start taking notes. Cliff, the deposit figures."

The meeting continued.

CHAPTER FORTY-TWO

Palmer walked the last couple to the front door at midnight. The man was Tim Carewe, third husband of Edith's Aunt Jane, a woman slightly older than Edith and just as tall. Because they lived in Rockland County, some fifty miles from New York City, they had taken a suite at the St. Regis rather than drive home late at night. This was about all Palmer could remember of them as he bade them good night and closed the door. He stood for a moment in the entry foyer of his home, feeling suddenly refreshed by the blast of chill outside air that had cooled the room for a moment. Then he made his way into the duplex living room and watched the fire in the immense grate.

"Mixed results," Edith said from the far end of the room, near the liquor closet and bar.

"Um?"

"This was in the nature of an experiment, darling. Could a party of eight fill this room? Answer: no."

"Sorry," Palmer mumbled.

"It's not your fault," Edith said, the words unevenly spaced as she laughed slightly. "I know better now. Although, I suppose, eight livelier people might have done a better job of it."

"If six of them are bankers and their wives," Palmer mused, staring into the flames, "you can hardly expect liveliness."

"Next party, by the way, we jump to twelve people. I think that will do it nicely."

Palmer glanced up. He saw that Edith was busily burying a liqueur pony glass in shaved ice. In a minute, he knew, she would fill the glass with Drambuie or Benedictine, let it chill and sip it. "Make another?" he asked.

"Right."

"Do I understand," he went on, "from what you've just said that they were bored tonight?"

"Bored? I don't know. It may very well be the room."

Palmer shook his head. "It's the people. It's me, as a matter of fact. Except for Jane and her husband, you didn't know any of the rest. I did. We were all right at dinner, but afterwards, when I let Burckhardt corner me and talk shop, the chill set in."

"What was all that about?" she asked, twisting another liqueur pony into the ice. "It didn't sound like shop as much as it did philosophy."

"I suppose," Palmer said, watching her pour the glasses half full, "its being philosophy was what made the old bird so testy. He's not equipped to argue philosophy, or thinks he isn't."

"He seemed to be accusing you of reactionary tendencies."

"It seems that I don't move with the times."

They were silent for a moment. From outside the house, some distance away, came the sound of a church bell striking twelve times. "Aren't they chilled enough?" Palmer asked.

Edith shook her head. "Of all the bankers I know," she said then, "I would least suspect you of being a reactionary. What times do you not move with?"

"Oh. One of these long, drawn-out, complicated questions to which we'll all know the answer in fifty years, I suspect. Meanwhile, the thing's highly academic, to begin with, because my objections are entirely futile."

"Tilting at windmills?"

He sat down on a tall bar stool. "Everyone I've talked to about it thinks I'm wrong." He stared at the container of shaved ice. The two buried liqueur glasses looked like eyes in the snow. They stared back at him.

"But you're not convinced."

"I'm completely convinced I'm right." He smiled lopsidedly. "I suppose I am wrong, from the pragmatic viewpoint. At least, I'm wrong this year and probably next."

"Do you just want to keep on talking," she asked, "or will you eventually let me in on it?"

"I thought you'd heard old Burckhardt. That voice of his reverberates."

"I was faithfully carrying on a discussion with the others."

"Well. It's this business about unlimited consumer credit." He sighed. "Surely they're cold now."

Edith removed a pony glass and handed it to Palmer. "If you like warm Drambuie."

Palmer sipped the cordial and found it cold enough. "You see," he began then, "there has to be a day of reckoning when all the debtors either pay up—which is impossible—or the economy deflates like a punctured balloon. A time of reckoning when accounts receivable are so overextended and the credit structure is so far beyond the cash position that the manufacturers call due the wholesalers, who call due the retailers, who call due the customers."

"But can't the customers pay, darling?"

"They're employed by the manufacturers, whose accounts receivables are so overextended that they can no longer, in all common sense, ship goods. They curtail production, lay off workers. An unemployed worker cannot pay his debts. You see?"

Edith shook her head and slowly withdrew her pony of cordial from the ice. "I thought automation would take care of all that."

Palmer laughed, a short, jeering bark so much like one of Burckhardt's that he paused for a moment to wonder when he'd picked up the mannerism. "The way we produce goods doesn't alter the credit cycle," he explained at last.

"Then we're doomed."

"I get so wound up in this stuff that I start to spout dogma." Palmer sighed and sipped his cordial. "Two things can save the situation. The Federal Reserve can tighten up on the banks. Then the banks can tighten up credit to retailers who, in turn, will curb consumer credit. Or consumers can police themselves and act like adults, not greedy children."

"Then," Edith announced, holding her drink against the light and studying it for a moment, "it's all up to the consumers."

"Apparently."

"And they will not act like adults," Edith said, "until they stop living in fear that tonight or on a particularly sunny day next week they'll all be blown to bits."

They sipped their drinks in silence. A log shifted position in the hearth and sent a shower of sparks up the flue. "I should think it isn't a topic one could dive into at a moment's notice," Edith said.

"It came up today, at a staff meeting. My colleagues must now consider me a crank on the subject."

"How do they feel?"

"I hadn't really discussed it with them before."

"Then with whom?"

"Oh, I don't know. I've had it out with our public-relations people."

"Mac Burns?" she asked.

"I think so. He and Miss Clary are abysmally ignorant of banking." Palmer watched the cordial in his glass and realized that the late hour and, possibly, the liquor he'd drunk throughout the evening, had loosened his tongue too much. It was not, he told himself, that he couldn't handle a discussion which referred to Virginia. It was rather, he saw now, that he'd been foolish even to introduce her name.

"She's your own p.r. person?"

You see, Palmer told himself; you see? Aloud then: "She's our liaison on the working level with Burns." He took a short, guarded breath and attempted a diversion. "Neither of them understands banking. It's amazing how people get to be experts these days. I met a man in Albany who knows all about atomic power. He's on a legislative committee involved with placement of power plants. After five minutes' talk, I saw that he knew as much about atomic power as anyone who'd read an article on it in a Sunday newspaper supplement. But he's an expert at Albany."

"Then who hired Miss Clary?" Edith asked, cutting back to the original thought.

Palmer shrugged. "She was there when I arrived."

"Is she attractive?"

Palmer laughed slightly. He had memorized the correct answer to this question early in his married life. "I hadn't really noticed," he said.

"How old is she?"

"Oh. Your age?"

"But what does she look like?"

"Brunette. Medium-short." He paused for an instant. "Why?"

Edith sipped her cordial. "Just curious. I've met Mac Burns, but I've never met Miss Clary. Miss?"

"She's called that. Actually, I think she's a widow."

"Really?"

Palmer nodded, refusing to be drawn any further into it than he already had. He had actually wondered about the same thing, why Virginia used her maiden name, but he had felt it in bad taste to ask her.

"Sounds very dramatic," Edith said then. "Mysterious black widow. What does she do at your shop?"

"Releases and such."

"Speeches?"

"First drafts on occasion."

"I'm impressed," Edith said. "Now I know where all those quotable attacks on the savings banks come from."

"Not quite." Palmer stood up and tipped more Drambuie into his glass. "I do my own final drafts."

Edith laughed softly. "Burckhardt's right, darling. You are hopelessly old-fashioned."

"Nothing of the sort. Bankers are, or should be, listened to. Their word is not, and should not be, lightly given. Unless he remains temperate, a banker who attacks other bankers demeans his opponent and throws suspicion on himself. I try to keep my speeches temperate."

"Very well put." Edith regarded him with a sly expression. "I was wrong, Woods, and so were you. You are your father's son after all."

Palmer stood up, gaining physical height, if nothing else. "Nothing of the kind," he said. "I'll tell you something about my father. If he were alive now, he'd side with Burckhardt. I know, because he and I used to have some of these same arguments."

"Sorry."

"And I'll tell you something else," Palmer went on, trying to hold his voice at a reasonably low level. "If I didn't feel the way I do about banking, I would have left it long ago. What do you think kept me in it? What keeps me in now?"

"You're good at it. And, Woods, what else would you do?"

Palmer shook his head sadly. He pushed his glass away from him and walked toward the hearth. He stared at the fire for a moment, reached for the poker and knocked the logs into a better position. Then he turned to face his wife.

"Everybody makes do with what they have at hand," he said then. His voice echoed peculiarly in the huge room. "Even the sons of the well-to-do. Even," he added, nodding at her, "their daughters. What I had at hand was banking. I made do with it. I tell myself it's an honorable profession. I believe it performs necessary functions. And when it ceases to do this, then what I have made of it becomes nothing. Does that make sense to you?"

"Sad sense."

"Yes, sad," he agreed. "Because banking is sloughing off its necessary functions as a snake sheds a tight, restricting skin. Banking is supposed to strengthen, to maintain, to protect. The chief function of banking is to conserve."

276

"It was," Edith said. "Functions change."

"Lungs breathe. The heart pumps. Some functions do not change. If they do, the result is death."

"Goodness. Woods, I had no idea you—"

"I had no idea, either," he cut in. "I always knew I felt this way. I just didn't know I could feel it so strongly. But this business today brought it all out again. I might as well tell you exactly what's happening."

"Yes."

"Jet-Tech International. They want an unprecedentedly large loan at unprecedentedly low rates. We're turning them down because we can make much more profit with the same money by getting little debtors deeper in debt. If Jet-Tech doesn't get the loan from us, they are prepared to take over the bank."

"You're not serious."

"They are. This savings-bank fight? It's a legitimate battle. But Jet-Tech is deliberately stirring it to fever pitch. By involving Burckhardt, by causing him to lose, they discredit him with his stockholders. Meanwhile, they're quietly buying up all the shares they can find."

"Lovely. Does Burckhardt know?"

"Yes."

Edith was silent for a moment. "The stock will go up?"

"It's moving already."

"Did you ever think," she said slowly, thoughtfully, "that Burckhardt can make a lovely profit on his holdings?"

"Yes, I've thought of it. Discarded the idea, too. Somebody else. Not Burckhardt."

"Somebody like you?"

Palmer stared at her. Her hazel eyes, beneath her blonde brows, were perfectly level and unmoving as they returned the stare. "Madam," he said at length, "you amaze me."

"Then you won't?" she asked.

"No. But not for that reason. Look." He hitched his stool closer to the bar. "If I buy Ubco for a quick profit, I put my lot in with Jet-Tech. My hands would be tied."

"But, Woods, what if they win? Can they?"

"They have an excellent chance."

She clapped her hands. "Darling, don't you see?"

"See what?"

"That what you should really buy is Jet-Tech. Immediately."

Palmer examined his half-full glass. Tomorrow, when news leaked that the loan was being turned down, Jet-Tech shares would drop three points or more. The day after tomorrow was the time to buy them. "Edith, where's last Sunday's *Times*?"

"I don't . . . It might be in the wood basket."

277

Palmer pawed through the logs and searched the kindling paper beneath them. "Here. Two weeks old. Doesn't matter." He found the financial section and scanned the big board review of the week. "Jet-Tech opened the week at 44. High for the week, 46 and an eighth. Closed the week at 43 and three-quarters." He stood up and carried the paper back to the bar. "After tomorrow, it should drop to 40 or thereabouts. Then, if they get control of Ubco, the stock can skyrocket. Ten points would be a conservative guess."

"Then do it."

He sat there without speaking for a moment.

"I know," Edith went on, "you have scruples." She inspected her empty glass and decided to bury it in ice again, filling it with cordial once more. "I know."

"It's a lot of things, Edith."

She shook her head. "Just scruples."

"Scruples have nothing to do with it. 'Has'? Are scruples plural?"

Edith frowned. "You could get around it by rephrasing. Uh . . . having scruples has nothing to do with it. Yes?"

"That's dishonest. You have measles, not scruples."

"I happen to know that measles are very plural."

Palmer took a deep breath. "All right. Having scruples has nothing to do with it. Here's what it is. Whatever Burckhardt feels about Joe Loomis, I know Jet-Tech is doing a worth-while job. Without organizations like it, where would we be in the so-called race for space?"

"But Jet-Tech's being on the side of the angels does not give them the right to steal a bank."

Palmer got up and walked toward the window wall. His footsteps made a hollow sound in that great room; they seemed to echo. He walked past the fire, thought of poking the logs again, decided not to and continued toward the window. When he got there, he gently pressed his forehead against the cold glass. Beyond, through the window, the cast-concrete façade with its sharp convolutions and twisted piercings gave him a fragmented view of the street, the headlight of a car, lamp in a window, an iron-fence finial.

It wasn't possible, Palmer told himself, to apply ethics to business. It merely confused the issue. It was unrealistic to think that one course was "right," while another was not. The only "right" in business was to show a profit without going to jail.

He turned around to face his wife. "I'm wrong," he said then.

"What, darling?" Her voice was faint across the length of the room.

"I'm wrong," he said, raising his voice. "They have whatever right they need to try taking us over."

"Yes? And?"

"And I have every right to try and stop them."

"Is that what you intend to do?"

"Yes," he murmured.

278

"I didn't hear you."

"Yes," Palmer said. Then, so loudly it was almost a shout: "Yes!"

He turned back to the window and found himself staring into the faces of a man and a woman who were peering through the pierced façade at him. After a shocked moment, they withdrew their faces and disappeared.

"You needn't shout," Edith said then.

CHAPTER FORTY-THREE

The meeting with Jet-Tech had been scheduled for the teak-and-green board room of the bank's main office downtown. Again, Palmer had not been invited but this time he stayed away. Instead, he spent most of the afternoon writing his Buffalo speech. The draft Virginia had given him was, as she freely admitted, a simple rewrite of the Syracuse one. Now, at ten minutes to five, Palmer had finished a new draft and given it to her.

She stood before his desk, scanning the first page, frowning slightly as she tried to decipher his handwriting on the lined yellow sheet. "What's this word? 'Convolutions'?"

"I think so."

"Looks more like 'convulsions.' Do they know what a convolution is in Buffalo?" She smiled softly at him. "They know what a convulsion is, I think."

"Go soak your head."

"I shall." She nodded very firmly. "I am to edit this as I retype it?"

"Miss Clary," Palmer began, "you are a publicist, not a typist."

"And you are an executive vice-president, not a speechwriter."

He opened his mouth to say something. The intercom emitted its discreet ping. "Yes?" he asked it.

"A Mr. Gauss to see you."

"Who?"

"A Mr. Heinz Gauss. He has no appointment."

"Good grief! Send him in." Palmer stood up and started for the door. "What do you know?"

"The scientific Heinz Gauss?" Virginia asked.

"The one I nabbed in Peenemünde." Palmer opened the door as Gauss got to it. "Gauss!" he exclaimed, reaching for the man's hand.

Heinz Gauss paused in the doorway, letting his hand be pumped. He stood a full head shorter than Palmer, a thin, small man in his early sixties, with receding black hair, dirty gray over the temples. As he watched Palmer with large, black eyes, his narrow, beaklike nose seemed to tremble slightly. His wide, thin-lipped mouth quivered, then stopped, then moved again, as though in the first inarticulate stages of a stammer. Palmer could see grayish-yellow scalp beneath the brushed-back strands of Gauss's hair.

"You haven't changed much," Palmer said.

"Oh. But I have, a great deal." When Palmer let his hand go, Gauss continued to stand there. Now he peered about the immense room. His glance settled on Virginia.

"This is Miss Clary, our public-relations officer."

Gauss straightened but his heels did not click. He bowed slightly. "A pleasure, Miss Clary."

Virginia walked toward the door. If it had not been for the fact that she obviously hoped to leave the room, Palmer saw, Gauss would not have relinquished his position in the doorway. Now he did so, side-stepping into the room.

"I'll have the revised draft later," Virginia said.

"You're not going home now?"

"No. I'm going to work on it here for a while."

"I'll drop by your office later."

"Fine."

Palmer closed the door and escorted Gauss to the chair in front of the desk. The little man sat down gingerly, as if trying to compress his buttocks so that they took up a minimum of space. Palmer sat in his own chair. "Cigarette?"

Gauss began to reach for the cigarette, then stopped, his hand halfway across the desk. "A sense of *déjà vu*," he murmured.

"How's that?"

"You were offering me cigarettes the last time we met."

"I was, wasn't I? And after all these years I'm at it again." Palmer smiled slightly. "What brings you to town?"

Gauss frowned as he took the cigarette and lighted it. "But you must know," he said. "This Jet-Tech thing. I am director of research."

Palmer felt a sensation inside his chest almost exactly as if someone had brushed against his heart with a cold rag. No word from Gauss in fifteen years. That was to be expected. But his sudden reappearance now made much too much sense. "You're in town with Barney Kinch, I expect."

"I have just come from the meeting. One whose outcome you probably know?"

"Yes." Palmer hitched himself closer to his desk. "If it's any comfort to you, I argued against the decision."

The German's eyes brightened. "Yes? But why?"

"Because I think we could have worked out something. Not what your people asked for, but something that would at least have gotten you some money."

"Some money." Gauss's thin mouth turned down at the corners. "Shall I tell you something for the sake of old times?"

"If you'd like."

"Half my experimental work budget for next year has been squandered on this God-awful Wotan booster."

"The one that keeps blowing up?" Palmer asked. "That yours?"

"*Mea culpa.*" The little man sat back more comfortably in the chair, as if the failure gave him certain rights. "It is a silly adventure, to begin with. These liquid-fuel engines are obsolescent before they come off the drawing boards. You don't think the other scientists are fooling around with such child's play any more, do you?"

Palmer shrugged. "I don't really keep up with much of that work," he admitted.

"But the Jet-Tech name is associated with this God-awful Wotan rocket," Gauss said. "So in the name of good public relations, I pour millions of R and D money into this sinkhole." He leaned forward. "This is only one reason I had hoped the loan would be approved."

Palmer girded himself to meet the inescapable request that would follow. "I'm as sorry as you."

The German nodded. "There are other reasons. I had hoped you would have been at the meeting with me. I brought some of our new toys. Ingenious things. Very exciting."

"Yes?"

"Nobody there understood what they could mean. You, I think, would have. You have scientific training, no?"

Palmer shook his head. "Very rudimentary."

"Nevertheless," the little man went on, "you understand the principle of the ion motor? Instead of getting thrust by expelling hot gases, it emits a stream of ions, electrified particles. All the companies have them. Only I have one that produces real thrust. Real, steady, palpable, dynamic thrust. Not down here on earth. The air is too dense. In space, where there is no air. Very exciting."

"Your own device?"

Gauss touched his chest. "My team. I am too old for startling break-throughs in science. Break-throughs are achieved by thirty-year-olds. But I can still show them where to drive the first wedge. And they listen."

"That can be just as satisfying."

"A moment ago," the German said, as if his visit had been painstakingly outlined in advance, "I said these liquid-fuel boosters were obsolescent. You understand the advantages of solid fuel?"

"For missiles. They can be fired faster."

"For space rockets, too. Solid fuel requires less gadgetry, fewer of all those

281

delicate little intestines and organs that malfunction so easily. We have something so new in solid fuel, so revolutionary, that it can take us beyond Mars . . . and back."

"Top secret?"

"The government, of course, knows." The little man raised his hands to the side of his head. "They fail to understand, really understand, what we can do with this fuel. It is sintered. Are you familiar with that term?"

" 'Sintered'? You bake it in little pieces?"

"Pellets the size of a moth ball. Each pellet burns exactly X seconds. Never more, never less. It has a hardened skin that compresses the combustion and amplifies its effect. We get more thrust from the same amount of fuel. You can store these pellets like the candy-coated gum balls you see in the penny machines. You let out a stream of them into the combustion chamber as slowly or as quickly as you wish. Fantastic control!"

"You sound as if you're halfway to the stars already."

"Not only to the stars. We are one of these God-awful diversified companies." The German pronounced the word "diversified" with slow, disdainful relish. "We have some electronics work of interesting promise. Microminiaturization. It is not my field, but I try to keep up with it. We have a short-wave transmitter the size of a dime. And a receiver the size of a match head. I showed these toys this afternoon. Nobody understood. I tried to explain. I said that we could build an amplifier so powerful it would take the electricity from a tiny solar battery and use it to send radio signals from Mars to Earth for years . . . years! And it could all be contained—amplifiers, battery, transmitter, receiver—in a thimble."

"What did Burckhardt say to that?"

"His mouth said nothing. His eyes told me I was a liar. I brought along a film of our new kerosene turbine engine. It is the size, roughly, of a console television set. Weight, eighty pounds. Horsepower, eighty-five. You understand what that fantastic weight-power ratio means? You realize that an automobile with an engine this light and this powerful can be made equally as light, thus fast, thus cheap. In the film, we install this engine in a Volkswagen. Four people get into the car. It takes off from a standing start up a twenty per cent grade. Lightning! And on cheap kerosene, not gasoline."

"That must have impressed our people."

"Yes. They asked how quickly we could get it in production." Gauss sighed. "Two years? Three? Even with the loan money, that long."

"They lost interest then," Palmer surmised.

"One of our plans struck a bit of fire. We have this miniaturized computer. Full digital type with million-character storage and a faster read-out than any comparable mechanism. It is suitable for inventory control. With additional storage, it handles retail bookkeeping of any conceivable kind. We sell it for fifty thousand dollars. The government won't let us rent it, of course.

But if we had the money, we would do our own financing. Retail stores could buy a computer on credit from us."

"Burckhardt liked that."

"Until we explained that for the first few years there would be no profit. We would have to plow it back into free training for each retail store's personnel."

"You did bring a bundle of goodies along, didn't you?" Palmer relaxed in his chair. If Gauss's mission was to beg for money, he was at least a fascinating beggar. "It must give you a great deal of satisfaction to be responsible for so many advanced ideas."

Matching his posture, the German leaned further back in his chair. He crossed an ankle over one knee and gestured expansively with his cigarette, holding it by the filter tip, like a pencil. It was almost impossible to recognize in him now the wary, humble little man who had first entered the room.

"I think," he said, "that we have been able to show the competition a few things." His face suddenly grew furtive. "Something we did not discuss this afternoon. But you'll appreciate it. We have a fuel cell not much larger than a loaf of bread. It works on any hydrocarbon at all, butane, gasoline, even light-grade oil. And it has an output of over a hundred watts. In conjunction with this," he continued, touching the palm of one hand with the index finger of the other, "we have been able to adapt our supermagnet concept to a one-pound electric motor that puts out eight horsepower. Can you believe this?" He nodded vigorously.

"At first blush," Palmer said, "you seem to have put your turbine engine out of business. Attach one of those motors to each wheel of a car and run them off the fuel cell."

"Precisely. I knew you would understand." The German smiled broadly. "So you see, we have not been wasting our time. Except with this God-awful Wotan."

"Yes, I can see that."

"But you can see what it adds up to?" Gauss asked. "The solid-fuel booster? The ion motor? The microminiaturized communications? The fuel cell? The supermotor? It is the beginning of a do-it-yourself space-exploration kit. The very essence of sophisticated equipment, small, light, allowing us to shift more payload into food for colonists. Once a landing is made, ground transportation is by means of this fuel cell and motor arrangement. The moon, for example, becomes friendly territory in a matter of a few days. And, from the moon, with its lower gravity, we reach for the other planets." He shook his hands in the air. "It is really within reach, all of it. Why waste time with synthetic space platforms? We have a natural one already, the moon. And Jet-Tech has the means to convert the moon into the biggest space platform we will ever need. It will be our springboard to the stars."

Neither man spoke for a moment. Palmer smiled slowly. "Poetic," he said. "And very impressive."

"Is it not?" The German nodded several times, his black eyes flashing. He grew silent then. After a few seconds his face went dead. He sighed. As if his body had been dipped in some powerful astringent, he seemed to shrink in size. He pulled in his arms, uncrossed his legs and pressed his knees tightly together. "All of this," he said in a shrunken voice from which all joy had been wrung out, "means money."

"Surely you can count on government funds."

"We move too quickly for such a trickle of money." Gauss's nostrils flared disdainfully. "Half a million here, half a million there. The solar system lies within our grip and we live like paupers on the dole."

Palmer grinned. "I like the way you throw that money around. Half a million here . . . half a million there. It has a nice ring."

"Oh. You joke." The German smiled shamefacedly. "I know I get excited about this. Partly it is because I know what we can do. And partly it is because I am the most God-awful impatient man in the universe. As you know, I am older than the rest of the Peenemünde group. I am sometimes older than God. I see myself lying in my coffin, dead, and still our work inches along on a pittance when it could take great soaring strides."

"And partly," Palmer said, still smiling to take the sting out of his words, "it's because you are a God-awful egotist. You want it all for yourself, don't you?"

Gauss paused, mouth open. His eyes went blank for a moment. Then he returned Palmer's smile, tentatively. "There is no point in, ah, disguising this. Even as a boy of twenty-one, fresh from the Kaiser Wilhelm Institute. All of us were grasping for the stars. We read Goddard's work, of course. The liquid-fuel rocket. The two-stage rocket. No one in America followed his experiments, but we did."

"Yes." Palmer cleared his throat dryly. "The V-2 showed that."

Gauss gestured erratically, a kind of churning motion in the air before his chest. "That came later, my friend. Years later, on orders. All this *schrecklichkeit* on orders. And I know, I know, many people died. But when time was running out for you, after the Russians' first sputnik, what carried your satellite into space? What basic difference was there between your old Redstone and our old V-2?"

Palmer sat there for a moment, remembering the raid on Peenemünde, the capture of men like Gauss who could now take credit for the first American satellite booster. He wondered how much credit he himself could take. He had never thought too much about it, even at the time of the first launching failures. In those days his only thought had been that, perhaps, he had helped to capture the wrong Germans.

"Gauss," he said then, "it's quitting time. Would you care to have a drink somewhere nearby?"

The German stood up even before Palmer had finished his question. "Capital suggestion," he said, turning toward the door.

On their way out, Palmer stopped for a moment. "Will you wait for me at the elevator? I have to check some late work."

He left Gauss in the long corridor that led toward the elevator door. The little man walked slowly from painting to painting, examining them in the illumination of the overhead spotlights that automatically switched on at sundown. Palmer detoured past Virginia's office and found her busily typing.

"You're supposed to edit, not rewrite."

"I started to, but there were so many changes the page was illegible." She looked up from her desk suddenly and smiled at him. "Herr Gauss?"

"I'm having a quick drink with him. It's the only way to ease him on his way." He looked around the empty office furtively. "Did you . . . have you any . . . I mean—"

"No plans for the evening," she cut in. "You?"

"Do you have a night line on your phone? I'll call you when I've gotten rid of Gauss."

"I don't know what number they've plugged me into. Look, we can just meet somewhere, can't we?"

"Where?"

She thought for a moment. "You wouldn't be likely to know anyone at this place. Or vice versa. It's a bar on Third." She gave him the address.

"It'll be an hour, probably," he said. "Is that all right?"

"No."

"I'm sorry. Why not?"

"Too long. Make it five minutes?"

He smiled. "Make it forty-five?"

"Go. Quickly."

He leaned over her. The faint, smoky perfume in her hair sent an abrupt tremor through his thigh. He started to kiss her cheek.

"Absolutely not," she said. "Madman."

"Good-by. Forty-five minutes."

When Palmer got to the elevator, Gauss looked, if anything, smaller and more humble. Perhaps it was a trick of the corridor, Palmer thought, the high ceiling that dwarfed anything human. The German's eyes were big and mournful. His long, sharp-edged nose seemed to tremble. "I am no good at this kind of thing," he said in a thin voice hardly above a whisper.

"What thing?"

"Begging."

Palmer pushed the elevator button. "Nonsense. They don't need you for that."

Gauss nodded quickly, several times. "But they do."

"I'm the wrong one to ask. I said my piece and was voted down. Now I have to abide by the decision of my colleagues. Loomis and Kinch understand that."

The German laughed suddenly, a kind of forlorn cackle. "They send the wrong man to see the wrong man. Typical."

At that moment the elevator doors opened. Palmer and Gauss stepped inside. "At any rate," Palmer said, "we can have a drink."

"Yes," the little man agreed. "That will be the only correct factor in the equation."

CHAPTER FORTY-FOUR

Palmer had picked a bar not too far from the one in which he was to meet Virginia. In the first fifteen minutes, Gauss had finished one Scotch and was well into his second. The liquor did nothing to cheer him up, Palmer noted. It served merely to dissolve the bonds that held his self-pity in check. Palmer sat across the booth table from the German and wondered how a man who took such pride in so many important scientific undertakings could still, despite it all, seem so desolate.

"Na," Gauss was saying. "Na, na. It has all passed me by, *alte freund.* I am past sixty. Very much past it. And what small luck I ever had has long run out. It is, *du kennst, ausgespielt,* played out, and me along with the luck."

"What's luck to do with science?"

"Everything. Ask what luck has to do with anything a man does? Paint pictures? Compose music? Write poems? Build rockets? The timing is everything, and all timing is luck."

"You've had your successes." Palmer saw that Gauss's glass was empty again. He signaled for a waiter.

"And who knows about them?" the German asked. "The whole world knows some of my colleagues. Who is there to know the name of Gauss? I will tell you." He chuckled dourly, a sound Palmer winced to hear. "My name is very famous in physics. Oh, yes. My last name. You have heard of Karl Friedrich Gauss? The mathematician? The pioneer in magnetism?"

"I can't say that I have. A relative of yours?"

"Everyone asks me that." Gauss sniffed. "There is a unit in physics, like the ohm or the watt or the ampere. It is the gauss, a measure of magnetic strength. You have certainly heard of the gauss. That was Karl Friedrich."

"Your grandfather?"

"My *garnicht!*" He looked up as the waiter brought his third drink. Gauss

286

bristled. "You bring Ballantine's?" he snapped. "I cannot drink any other Scotch."

"It's Ballantine's, sir."

"It had better be." Gauss fixed the waiter with a hard stare, lifted the glass and sipped it. "*Sehr gut,*" he barked. The waiter retreated. The German continued sipping his drink. As he did, his rigid posture relaxed. "Karl Friedrich Gauss. No relative, none whatsoever. My God how I tried to find a family connection with him. *Garnicht.* Have you any idea what it means to be a physicist saddled with such a name? It is like a poet born with the name of Goethe." He frowned and his thin nose quivered.

"It sounds as if you'd had a hard time," Palmer suggested, glancing at the clock over the bar. In twenty minutes he would have to get rid of this self-pitying old man.

"Nothing is easy," Gauss mumbled. A vast sigh escaped him. "From the beginning, the timing was bad. The luck was never there. And now, again, still, the timing is once more bad. The worst."

"I know," Palmer said. "You feel you're on the edge of a break-through but the money isn't there."

"Why?" Gauss burst out. "The money is always there for Von Braun. Why never for Gauss?"

"Perhaps, if you worked directly for the government . . ."

"*Nahrischkeit.* When first I came here the government took me under its wing. That immense, feathery wing beneath which so much *dreck* is swept. It was like trying to breathe in a sewer. Stifling. No imagination. No daring. No willingness to strike out in new directions. My God, I was desperate. A desperate man, growing old. After thirty, after thirty-five, in physics you are finished as an innovator. The startling insights come no more. You substitute experience and cunning for genius. You scavenge ideas. You put bits and pieces together, other people's bits, the leavings of younger men, and you make a little something of your own. They pat you on the head. *Alte hund,* so, so. To leave government work, I took the first offer that showed any promise. And again, the timing was wrong. The luck had disappeared."

"I thought your team had created all these new things at Jet-Tech."

"The toys I mentioned?" The German sipped his drink. "They are not bad. But in a year General Dynamics and Bell and G.E. and Union Carbide and Westinghouse and all the rest will have them, or better, if they do not already. And I sit here with empty pockets, unable to blaze my name across the skies. It is humiliating, at my age. Degrading. I am a scientist, not a beggar. This Jet-Tech is a . . . that thing . . . a jinx? Bad luck. No luck."

"You're an ambitious man," Palmer said slowly. "At your age, that's a good sign."

"A sign of sickness. It eats away inside me. Why this one? Why that one? Why not Gauss?"

"It can happen," Palmer told him. "You might, oh, do something that didn't need these great amounts of money. Or you might move to another organization, leave Jet-Tech."

"To become an elderly lackey? *Danke, nein.* At least at Jet-Tech I am top man. King of the dunghill." He laughed a shuddering kind of laugh and his eyes grew darker, hooded by his straggly brows for a moment as he stared down at the table. *"Der koenig von scheiss,"* he murmured. His thin, wide mouth, still twisted upward in a mocking smile, went dead and flat.

Palmer gestured to the waiter with a writing motion, while he mouthed the word "check." The little German touched a ring of water on the wooden table top between them and slowly extended the wetness into an arrowlike line. "Some things are ironic the moment they are uttered," he said, still in that dull, low voice, as if addressing no one but himself. *"Morgen, die ganze welt. Morgen* comes for some. For others, never. All a matter of timing. And now time, too, is *ausgespielt.* All gone. Nothing left but illusion. *Der koenig von scheiss."*

The waiter arrived at the table, folded the check and placed it face down before Palmer. Gauss looked up sharply. "What? Who asked this of you?" he demanded.

"This gentleman," the waiter explained.

"I'm due home," Palmer said. "Matter of fact, I'm overdue."

"Yes?" Gauss deflated slowly. "Yes, of course. I'm sorry to have kept you."

"Not at all. It was my idea to have this drink."

"And the money? The loan?"

"Gauss, you have to understand something," Palmer began. Then he stopped, seeing the waiter still there. He opened his wallet and laid a twenty-dollar bill on the unread check. As he did so, he saw Gauss's eyes hungrily following the motion. Incredible, Palmer thought as the waiter took the money away. Absolutely beyond belief. This man, he knew, could be paid no less than $30,000 a year, if not much more. He was a widower without children; he probably banked every cent he'd earned. And yet he had worked himself into such a state of imaginary poverty that he could no longer control outward appearances.

"I am on record," Palmer went on then, "in favor of a loan, not the loan you asked for, but something I'm sure you could have used to good effect. That is now ancient history, even though it's all happened within the last two days. The official decision was reported to Jet-Tech this afternoon and there it stands. Loomis might come back with a new proposal and reopen the negotiations. I sincerely hope he does. Do you understand? I want you to have the money. When there is something I can do about it, I will. At the moment, however, absolutely nothing more can be done . . . by me."

Gauss nodded slowly, wearily. "I know. Loomis tells me much the same thing. I am to wait. Eventually, the money will come."

"He said that? When?"

"Today. And many times before."

"How positive does he sound?" Palmer asked.

"Infinitely positive. You know these financial types." Gauss blinked. "His type, you understand. You are a different breed entirely, my old friend."

"Loomis is certain the money will come eventually?"

"Eventually." The German's thin mouth bit off the word as though it tasted bad. Then he was silent.

Palmer stood up. "Gauss, I'm afraid I'll have to be moving along now. It was nice talking with you, even if I couldn't help much." He stood there, waiting for the old man to rise. Instead, Gauss sat hunched forward at the table, eyes fixed on the ring and arrow of moisture. "Where are you staying in town?" Palmer asked, hoping to shake him out of the fugue he seemed to be in.

After a long moment, Palmer cleared his throat. The situation, he realized, could quickly get beyond him. He was sorry now that he'd fed Gauss three drinks . . . or any, for that matter. "Gauss?" he asked. "Are you all right?"

The little man blinked. Slowly his glance traveled up Palmer's body to his face. "I want to tell you something," he said then in a low, hoarse voice. "They did not send me. I pretended they did. But they do not even know I am here. They have no idea we know each other, even."

"This was all your idea?"

Gauss nodded. "Please."

"Yes?"

"Sit down. Please."

Palmer glanced at the wall clock. His meeting with Virginia was ten minutes off. "For only a minute or two," he said, sitting down across the table from Gauss. "Then I really must go."

"Of course." The German smiled slowly, not at Palmer, but at the symbol drawn on the table. "This is the male principle," he said, touching it with his finger. "It is also the symbol for iron. And for the planet Mars. Odd." He sat there, smiling and saying nothing, for another long moment.

"Gauss, I am in a rush."

"Yes. Yes. Yes." The old man seemed to gather himself together. "It is within my power," he said then in a stronger voice, "to make the name of Gauss more famous than Karl Friedrich ever could. They will call him 'that other Gauss.' And when they refer to Gauss, it will be to me, to Heinz Walther Gauss, *du kennst?*"

"I hope you are right."

Gauss shook his head. "Na. Na. You don't really like me, *meine alte freund*. You say words empty of feeling because you are in a hurry and I am delaying you—*nicht wahr?*—and I embarrass you with my God-awful egotism. But I know. I know I am right. It is within my grasp."

"What is it?" Palmer asked, wishing he had never invited this garrulous old man for a drink.

"I said the other Gauss had studied magnetism, yes?" the German began.

289

"I, too, as a younger man, became involved in a number of experiments in magnetism. You are familiar with Einstein's later hypotheses? The magnetic nature of the earth's gravitational field?"

"Not at all," Palmer admitted.

"I had no access to them in Germany," Gauss continued. "The man was a Jew. But when I came on his work after the war it was a situation of *déjà vu* again. I had been here before, in my fantasies. The certified Aryan and the expelled Jew. Do you know how much time I lost—the world lost—because I had no idea of Einstein's work?"

Gauss's index finger traced and retraced the symbol on the table top. "The situation is a plain, simple, elemental truth. At least, once Einstein explains it, you see how simple it is. And if the force of gravity is a magnetic force, it can, in theory, be counteracted by an equal and opposing magnetic force. You follow?"

Palmer nodded. "In practice, of course, it can't be done."

"In science there is no 'of course.'" Gauss shot a quick look at Palmer. "Attend this closely, now. The magnets necessary to counteract gravity would be too heavy to lift themselves from the earth. A neat problem. Add more magnetic force, add more weight, add more failure. This we can prove on paper, so no one has wasted his time trying to do it in a laboratory. Clear?"

"Clear."

"In the last few years," the old man went on, "we have a new field, cryogenics. We cool things as close to absolute zero as possible and study what happens to them. You know of this?"

"Vaguely. What is that, about four hundred degrees below regular zero?"

Gauss gestured impatiently. "Not important. Meanwhile, at Bell and Westinghouse, they have rethought the electromagnet and reduced its factors of inefficiency to a bare minimum. They have thus created supermagnets. But all magnets work on a ferrous core. Iron. Nickel. Cobalt. Any of the ferrous group. Yes?"

"If you say so."

The German shrugged. "It is a fact. Until recently. But." He lifted his finger from the table and pointed it at the ceiling. "Supercooling shows us that other metals, other non-metallic elements and certain alloys can become highly magnetic."

"I see," Palmer said. "More magnetic than the ferrous group?"

"The word," Gauss said, his voice becoming very quiet, "is *phenomenally* more magnetic. I borrowed one of our Jet-Tech cooling mechanisms. No one knew what I wanted it for. I also borrowed the circuitry design of various Bell and Westinghouse experiments. A peculiar thing happened. Only one other person knows this, one of my assistants, Carmer, a fairly unimaginative man. He helped me and he saw what I saw. But he has no idea what it means." The old man stopped and thought for a moment.

"Go on," Palmer said.

Gauss nodded. "Try to visualize this. The cooling chamber has a clear quartz window in it. You can watch what happens to the material you are cooling. The alloy is in the form of a bar, like a thick bolt, some four inches long and perhaps an inch and a half thick. It has electromagnetic windings, of course. I bring its temperature down to ten Kelvin, or minus two-sixty-three centigrade. I then introduce a phased pulsating current into the windings. I increase the strength of the current and adjust the phasing. And this is what I see—what Carmer and I see—through the quartz window. The magnet, core and windings, weighs about two pounds. It slowly rises from the bottom of the cooling chamber and hovers in the air."

"Against the pull of gravity?"

"Exactly. The first time, I grew so excited that I accidentally turned the potentiometer too quickly. The magnet flew up and hit the top of the cooling chamber. After that, in successive experiments, I could control it more positively."

"Let me understand this. You lay claim to having defeated the gravitational pull of the Earth."

Gauss nodded slowly. "You understand correctly."

"But . . ." Palmer stopped for a moment. Then: "But of what practical use is this, Gauss? Let's suppose you wanted to equip a vehicle with this principle. You couldn't keep its magnets supercooled. Not in the open air."

"True."

"Then of what use is this?"

"Precisely in what you have called a vehicle. A space vehicle."

Palmer frowned. "I just don't see it."

"Yes, you do." The old man smiled triumphantly. "You see it when I tell you that the cold in outer space is close to absolute zero."

"I . . . Is that true?"

"Of course it is true. Let me keep my vehicle's magnets supercool for a few seconds on Earth, just long enough to take off, to rise above the atmosphere into the supercool reaches of space, and I have no problem keeping them as cold as I wish for as long as I wish."

"But can a vehicle rise that quickly?"

"Are you aware that the Earth's gravitational field is stronger in some places than in others?"

"No, but it seems logical."

"There are definite lines of force much more powerful than the areas between," Gauss said. "Sit precisely over one of these lines and turn on full power. The vehicle *snaps* clear of Earth at a speed close to that of light. As you would flick a pea with the tip of your finger. *Snap!* At the speed of light!"

"But . . ." Palmer paused.

"Go ahead. But what?"

"The men inside the vehicle. They can't withstand acceleration like that."

"Ha!" For the first time that evening, the German's face actually lighted up. He slammed his open hand down on the table, obliterating the sign he had drawn on it. "I have you, my friend! You do believe me."

"Up to this point? I don't know enough to disbelieve you."

"You know enough to see that it makes sense?"

"Yes," Palmer admitted.

"You accept it," Gauss persisted. "You do accept it. You must. Otherwise you would not worry about the men inside the vehicle."

"That's true, I suppose."

"Now listen," the German told him. "Do not mistake my meaning when I say I do not give a bean for those men. Their welfare is totally unimportant to me. It is not that I am inhuman. But my problem was to develop a principle in physics, a principle I can now prove in practice. This I have done. And I have shown how the absolute cold of space makes the principle feasible outside a laboratory cooling chamber. I am a physicist, not a biologist. Let a biologist solve the problem of those men. Agreed?"

Palmer gave him a lopsided grin. "Don't fool yourself, Gauss. You are a cold-blooded old man." He leaned forward. "No one knows the significance of this experiment? The vehicle it makes possible?"

"Not even Carmer. I think he humors me. He sees nothing practical in this toy of mine."

"Without explaining it," Palmer said, "what if I told my people that you were on to something really big? How much would it cost you to push this thing to a conclusion?"

"Twenty million. Thirty." Gauss pursed his thin lips in a pouting movement. "They will not buy it, not without definite information, perhaps a demonstration. This I cannot do. The security risk would be tremendous."

"They're responsible men. They can keep a secret."

"From the Russians? It is not the Russians I worry about," the old man explained. "It is my distinguished fellow scientists of the free world. They are not going to steal this from me." His mournful eyes grew small and fierce. "I will not let this happen. I cannot. I have only a few years left to me. They cannot cheat me of what is mine."

"But, eventually, the whole world will know."

"Bravo! When Gauss announces it, Gauss wants the whole world to know. And to know it is Gauss who gives them this miracle."

Palmer thought for a moment. "Then what you're asking of us is twenty to thirty million dollars on a horse so dark no one can see what it looks like."

"Since I have told you this much, you can visit my laboratory and watch the experiment yourself. Then they can take your word for it."

"That's not the way bankers operate, Gauss, and well you know it." Palmer watched the old man and saw that he had started to shrink again in that super-self-pitying way of his. "You have an ingenious laboratory toy. I'm certain it works. Your word is good enough for me. But it will take a mint of money to translate that toy into something, a prototype vehicle perhaps, that proves its usefulness. And many millions more to solve the problem of protecting the men who ride in it. And then—"

"Robot control," Gauss interrupted in a low voice. "The prototype need not carry a man."

"You miss my point."

"Perhaps," the German said slowly, "it is because I do not want to understand your point. Or that I understand it all too well and do not want to assault my ears with it again." He got to his feet. "I have delayed you too long."

Palmer looked at the wall clock. He was ten minutes late for his rendezvous. He stood up. "Can you go on with this work, even without a special allocation of money?"

"It is not a question of 'can.'" Gauss pulled on his overcoat, his glance directed away from Palmer. "I *must* continue the work. I will sign false requisitions for material, lie about it, steal equipment."

"What if you got a government contract? What if you left Jet-Tech and set up the whole project under government supervision?"

Gauss nodded sardonically. "To the man who has already burned up millions of its dollars on the *verflüchte* Wotan booster, the government will not hand over millions more." He jammed his hat on his head. "In my mind's eye today, after I was told that the loan had been denied, I saw myself appealing to you. I was brilliant. Confident. I filled you with confidence in me. Now I see myself as you see me: a crazy old man with nothing on his brain but money. An aged failure. *Der koenig von scheiss.* So be it." He turned blindly in the direction of the door to the street.

"Gauss." Palmer shrugged into his coat as he followed the German out onto Third Avenue. "Gauss, hold up a second."

"You are late enough, my friend. Time is important. Timing is everything." The cold wind sweeping down the avenue from the north made the brim of Gauss's hat flicker. "You have been talking to an expert on bad timing. Ten years I lost because Einstein was a Jew. Never mind. I still have ten more years to live."

His smile was strange in the neon-lighted darkness. "With luck," he added in a mocking voice. He turned and walked across the avenue. Then he disappeared along a side street.

The wind made Palmer's cheeks smart. He turned his back to it. Needle-thin fingers of cold cut through the fabric of his overcoat and jacket, touching his flesh. After a moment the wind died down. But Palmer remained chilled, cold to the very center of his body, as he walked slowly toward his second encounter of the night.

CHAPTER FORTY-FIVE

She was sitting by herself in a booth toward the rear of the bar. Palmer saw her, after a moment of searching, and went directly to her. "I'm very sorry," he began as he sat down across from her, "but Gauss had a lot to tell me."

She had looked up as he first entered the bar. Seeing him, her glance had dropped to the drink she was holding in both hands. Now she seemed unable to look up at him again. "That's all right," she said in a somewhat muffled voice.

"Evidently not."

"It's all right," she insisted, still not looking at him.

"He's a fascinating specimen," Palmer said, "and I suppose if I hadn't something more important to do, I'd still be there, listening."

Slowly, her eyes came up to meet his. "If Gauss was important," she said in a flat voice, "you didn't have to leave."

"This is more important."

One corner of her mouth quirked up quickly, then down. Now that she had found it possible to look at him, Palmer noticed, she seemed unable to look away. With a faint shock of recognition, he saw that her huge, dark eyes were very much like the old German's, at least now. Then he understood that it was neither their similar size nor their color. It was the common element of self-pity, that moist, inward-turning look that Gauss had blatantly projected and that Virginia, now, was trying to hide.

"Yes," she said then, "I have been feeling very sorry for myself."

"How did you know I was thinking—?"

"Forget it," she cut in. "Just remember how difficult it is to hide your thoughts from a Celt." She made a small, disgusted face and leaned back against the rear of the booth, the synthetic leather upholstery pushing her dark, random curls sideways as she rested her head against it. "I was reviewing the relationship during the last hour or so. It didn't fare especially well at all. And then, when I saw you were going to be late, things deteriorated still further. Finally," she added, almost as an afterthought, "when I realized you just were not going to arrive, the whole affair died, not with a bang, but a whimper. Right there on the table in front of me. I was tidying up the remains for the undertaker when you appeared."

"Good God, I was only a few minutes late."

"Fifteen."

"Oh, look—"

"You know," she cut in again, "in fiction this scene pops up from time to time. And, when our hero finally puts in an appearance, all the heroine's dark, dismal brooding fades like a bad dream and everything's sunny and smiling again. The dear nearness of him does this. The mere fact that he finally shows up at all sends the idiot girl into raptures once more."

"Not you."

"Not me," she agreed. "The old head bone's getting a bit too brittle for that kind of gymnastics. However." She reached for his hand and patted it. "I'm glad you're here, anyway."

"I'm glad you're glad." He took her hand and held it.

"What on earth," she said then, "is so fascinating about some beat-up has-been Nazi that keeps you from an assignation with the most exciting woman in New York City?"

"If I told you, you wouldn't believe it."

"Try me."

"I will, sometime." Palmer squeezed her hand. "Why do you say he's a Nazi?"

"*Nein?*" she asked, sliding into a sauerkraut accent. "He vas nevah a membah of de pahty, yah? None of us Nazis vas Nazis. Unt ve didn't know vat vas goink on, *ja wohl?*"

He grinned at her. "You Irish are real dandy haters, aren't you?"

"There's this apocryphal story about a young Irish priest who took his first parish in Brooklyn," she said. "He had the gift of tongues, this bhoyo. Fantastic public speaker. But virulently anti-British. Every Sunday he'd conclude the sermon with a diatribe against the black-hearted scuts. People flocked from other parishes just to hear him speak. Finally, he came to the attention of the Powerhouse. That's Cardinal Spellman, to the likes of you. Spellman called him in and is reputed to have said: 'Me boy, we have marked you for higher things. But you'll get nowhere until you cut out this anti-British stuff. Why, man, it all happened forty years ago, the Throuble. If you can go a month of sermons without mentioning the British, I'm inviting you to help celebrate Mass at St. Pat's. Four Sundays from now, if you stop maligning the British.' Ah, now, and didn't the young father's eyes light up? He vowed a holy vow he would forget the British. And he kept the vow, too, so he did. T'wasn't easy. Always the temptation during a sermon to lash out at the murtherers. But he bit down the words and sweetness prevailed for three Sundays in a row. On the fourth, now, it was coming up on Good Friday in a week or so, and the good father was sermonizing about the Last Supper. 'There sat they all,' he told his flock, 'the Son of God and his Apostles. T'was a solemn meal, so it was, but for Jesus most solemn of all. He knew that one amongst them would bethray him. Just then, Judas Iscariot smiles at Our Lord, butter wouldn't melt on his lyin' tongue, and passing some sweet

295

to the Son of God, Judas says to Him: "Gor-blimey, guv'nr, 'ave a bit o' treacle wiv' yer crumpet.'"'"

Palmer's laugh startled a passing waiter so that the man stopped, turned and stood waiting for an order. After a moment, Palmer noticed him. "The same," he said, pointing to Virginia's empty glass, "and another for the lady."

"So don't talk about hating," Virginia concluded as the waiter left.

Palmer nodded for a moment, before speaking. "I had a sermon on much the same subject from Vic Culhane recently."

"Vic's a grand hater," Virginia said, still dusting her speech with bits of brogue. "Next to the Irish, the Italians are darlin' haters, so they are. And Vic's both."

"Actually, he was warning me about Mac Burns."

"Ah, well, now, there's a wee bit o' Lebanon in all of us, includin' all of us from the Emerald Isle."

"How much did you have to drink before I showed up?"

"Persons of the Lebanese persuasion," she said, "are a match in the Hate Department for individuals of the Gaelic nomination."

"Confess: you're stoned."

"Bagged, crocked, zonked." She sighed. "Not at all. I nursed one drink through the dragging hours waiting for you. See?" She pushed the empty glass toward him. "Notice how tiny the ice cubes are? Mere pebbles."

"Something's peculiar about you tonight."

"Just the aftereffects of a long hard look at myself."

"God," Palmer said gloomily. "I'll never be late for a date again."

"No, the examination began long before you were supposed to arrive. Actually, it started back at the office when I left you and your Buchenwald buddy chumming it up. I sat down at my desk and what I felt was jealousy. You hear that? I was jealous of that sad little sack monopolizing your time. Neither of us had so much as mentioned that we might see each other to-night. Get this. But I fondly hoped, because you tell me early in the day when you have some official or family function that evening and you hadn't said anything, that you and I would, uh, make it tonight. Which the advent of your Kraut friend now made highly disputable."

"I won't even pretend that I follow your reasoning."

"Don't. I'd know you were lying."

"But continue. I am always enthralled by the irrational mind at work."

"Thank you." She looked up as the waiter brought their drinks. "Prosit!" she snapped, clanging her glass against Palmer's. "Negst time ve vin!"

"Ah, cut it out."

"Anyway. So, I began to analyze this feeling of jealousy, or whatever it was. And from there, by easy stages suitable to a weak mind, I progressed to a long hard look at the game you and I are playing, what cards we hold and who can expect to win. I found that I hold nothing higher than a five. All I can do, with a great deal of aplomb and a cheerful grin, is lose."

"Virginia, I'm beginning to understand you, and it worries me."

"Should you live a hundred years, you would never understand me. I'm talking straight, Woods. Not banker talk . . . people talk. What I am trying to say is that you have nothing to lose. The worst that can happen to you is that you get laid."

"That's a lovely way of putting it."

She made a rueful face. "When you're talking to yourself, you tend to skip the amenities and get down to harsh facts. We're both adult adults, Woods. So forgive my verbal short cuts. But listen to what I'm saying."

"Go on."

"For a long time," she said, "I was quite sure I would never get married again. You set up too many hostages that way. I had both of mine taken from me. It's a withering experience, how withering you can only guess from this: it happened almost twenty years ago and I'm only able to talk about it now."

"This is the first time?"

"To anyone but my mother, yes." She watched him closely for a moment. "It has very little to do with you, my talking about it. I'm at ease with you. I consider you a friend, an ally, one of the few people I feel I can rely on. But the main reason I can talk about it is that I'm over it, finally. And the point is, I'm ready to think about getting married again, have been for some time now."

"Good."

"You don't know how good. But it has its grimmer aspects, too." She picked up her drink and stared into it for a moment before sipping. "I am now forty-one. On my good days, in a kind light, I can pass for thirty-five? Sometimes. And the number of men older than me—or almost—who are decent prospects for marriage is very small. It's small even if you include everyone eligible on simple grounds of being single. When you weed out the creepier specimens, the crypto-fairies, the obvious psychotics and the ones who, for no good reason, just aren't my type, you have reduced the field almost to invisibility."

"That was a fast trip. Perhaps your standards are too high."

"Yes, perhaps they are. I'm too new at this husband-hunting game to think high standards are bad."

Palmer nodded. "There's an intimation that, later, your standards may drop."

"They have already. Look at you."

"Ah, yes."

"You should be flattered, in a way. I have high standards and you meet all of them. You surpass most. You are the most terrific thing—look at him blush! —that could happen to a girl. Oh, but there's this one little thing. You're a little bit married."

"I am not blushing," Palmer insisted. "Girls always tell me these things."

"So they should." She smiled slowly at him. "But you create terrible problems for me, my married friend. If I intend to find a husband, I have to put you behind me. And if I can't put you behind me, I'll never find a husband."

"I've been behind you," Palmer said. "Mighty fine country."

"I'm getting too serious for you, aren't I?" she asked. "That's why you're cracking wise."

"That's why."

"Don't. Be serious with me for a moment."

"I'll try," he promised, "although the inevitable result of it will be that I get up from this booth and walk out of your life. Because every girl should be married."

Neither of them spoke for a while. "Stop looking at me that way," she said then.

"What way?"

"You know what way. Woods, please level with me. What do you see in me?"

Palmer thought for a moment, recognizing the fact that he would have to give a serious answer. "I see a beautiful girl . . . woman," he said then.

"Please."

"But I have to start with that. You aren't pretty, but you are beautiful. It means a great deal to me. Then I see a very intelligent woman, much too intelligent to have an easy time with men. You forgot that in your category of impossible single men . . . the stupid one who is afraid of you. Then, I see a . . . what's the next thing? A woman of stature, of professional ability, acknowledged, certified, capable of commanding a salary that puts her, I suppose, in the top one per cent of female wage earners. And, by the way, since we're leveling with each other, you're badly underpaid at Ubco. However. There's more to see in you. I'm a very poor judge of the emotions. You have to know your own to be able to understand another's. But you're a very warm person, very giving. You're almost unable to keep a shield in front of you. You keep dropping it before it properly protects you. That's bad for you, but very good for the man to whom you give all this emotional warmth. You . . . I think I . . . what I . . ." He stopped.

She took his hand. "If it's good for you, it can't really be bad for me."

Her fingers were warm on the back of his hand. Palmer turned his hand over and grasped hers, palm to palm. "It's very good for me. You wouldn't understand. I hardly do myself. I have a very cold, fishy head and heart. It's a proper banker's heart. But you warm it and melt it. I'm in pain when that happens. I don't want it. I want our relationship held at the physical level. That way, as you so correctly put it, the worst thing that can happen to me is that I get laid. But it starts to go beyond that. At first, it's simply that you're the only one I trust. That's still true. But it begins to get deeper than that. These things are treacherous, especially when you're as unused to dealing with them as I am. And now, of course, as I can see from tonight's little heart-to-heart, the whole thing's gone out of hand."

298

He could feel the slow pressure of her hand in his. She was watching him with one eyebrow raised, as though not quite believing any of what he was saying, or not wanting to. Now she shook her head slowly from side to side.

"You really have a grim opinion of yourself, don't you?" she asked.

"N–no. Do I?"

"In matters emotional. You consider yourself a kind of thief."

"I do not."

"Yes. You tell me what I give you. It sounds like a con game, you fleecing me out of something and giving me nothing in return. But it isn't that way."

"I?" Palmer asked. "What have I given you?"

"The same warmth you get from me." Her hand loosened in his and began to rub forward and back in a slow but urgent rhythm. He felt his palm grow warm.

"A lovely demonstration," he said. "But this is how people start fires."

"I once knew a Boy Scout who did it for me with sticks."

"Virginia," Palmer said, clasping her hand to stop the motion. "Listen to me. A moment ago you were complaining that I create terrible problems for you. Even without knowing that you were thinking of getting married again, I knew I was making trouble for you. Because I'm making trouble for me, too."

She made a face. "I'm sorry I started on it. Feeling sorry for yourself is a strong mood to fall into. I'm sorry I let it spill over. Now, then." She rapped the knuckles of his hand on the table top. "Let's just drag this thing back down to the physical level again, shall we?"

"And leave everything else hanging in mid-air?"

"Why not? Why should we be the only people in the world to settle something? Let the whole miserable thing hang there."

"Until your next mood."

"Right." She took a long sip of her drink. "Have you got a car?"

"Of my own? No."

"Me neither. And right now the only thing to do is get in a car and drive great, huge distances."

" 'Forget your troubles; come on, get happy?' "

"Great lyrics for a song."

" 'When you're down and out, lift up your head and shout, there's gonna be a great day?' " Palmer asked.

"I had no idea you were this talented."

"This is nothing," Palmer said, standing up. "I am now going to show you just how talented I am." He lifted her black cloth coat from the hook on which it was hung and held it out to her. "With nothing up either sleeve but a Hertz credit card, I am going to get us a car."

CHAPTER FORTY-SIX

The bright red Corvette had shown an alarming tendency to hit ninety miles an hour with insidious ease on the broad New England Thruway. The road had got them well past Stamford in much less than an hour, where they had turned off somewhat impulsively and, within minutes, had found a kind of inn-motel. In one large bed created by pushing two twin beds together, they had spent the time until midnight. Now Virginia insisted on taking the older Merritt Parkway back to New York. More sharply graded, narrower, with more stringent speed limits, it made the return trip longer.

"Did I ever tell you I hate sports cars?" Virginia asked.

Palmer glanced at the speedometer needle and found it hovering at seventy. He let up on the accelerator. "Why?"

"A man driving a sports car is just not interested in women."

"Is that a fact?"

"He's having a sexual relationship with the car, not the girl beside him."

"A form of sodomy, I take it?"

"And these Goddamned bucket seats make it impossible to cuddle up."

"There you have a point." Palmer checked his speed, now fifty-five. "These cars respond so fast you have to concentrate on what you're doing."

"Instead of on me."

"I think you will find, if you review the past few hours, that you have been concentrated on with intensity, not to say ferocity."

"Um. You were pretty ferocious in there. For an old man."

"Steady. Remember I'm driving."

"You won't let me forget it."

"It's just that, for an old man, I'm too young to die."

"I was only being funny."

"At the moment, I have a number of sore spots."

She began to stroke his thigh. "If you'd like to turn back, we still have a few hours coming to us at the motel. I could, uh, massage."

"Easy."

"I'm not that bad as a masseuse."

"Easy, damn it."

"Is this one of the sore spots?"

"Ai! Yes."

"Right here?"

"Please!"

"It doesn't seem so much sore as dead."

"You remind me," Palmer said, finding it difficult to speak in a normal tone, "of the man who killed his parents and then claimed special treatment because he was an orphan. Stop it."

"I'm wrong. It's not dead. See?"

"I'm going to pull over onto the grass in another second."

"Don't do that. You'll attract the cops."

He winced. "My God, your hands are cold. Stop. Look at the—" The speedometer needle had hit seventy again. "I mean it. Stop."

"Very well." She settled back in the bucket seat as far from him as she could. "You know what they say about cold hands."

"I know what they say about that sort of thing in a speeding auto."

"You just don't understand me." She chuckled softly to herself and drew her coat closer around her. "I'm trying to make up for twenty years in a few weeks."

"Are you trying to tell me that for twenty years you didn't—?"

"Not exactly that," she cut in, "because I had my small, grudging moments with self-protecting men. The whole thing was so bad that for months afterward I'd avoid sex. A year might pass. I would pretty well have figured out that I was not only frigid but totally congealed. Then I would pull myself together and fight it. I'd meet somebody, give him his head. It's amazing how ritualistic this is. The luncheon date. The dinner date. The night club or theater date. The dinner date at his apartment. The pass. The yes. The no. The whatever. It doesn't matter. Because either way it ends badly. Or did, for me. Now you . . ."

She was silent for a long moment. "Can I turn on the radio?" she asked then.

"No. Just keep talking. No props."

"I suppose I asked for that." She tried to tuck her legs up under her, but the bucket seat prevented it. "Well. Anyway, you. I can remember the first night at Mac's apartment very clearly. It was the first impulsive act I've ever, uh, committed? Is that the word? One minute I was thinking furiously, the old Clary brain rattling away as it always does opposite a man. The next minute I had stopped thinking and we were embracing and, you know, roller-coaster from there on in. And later, when the brain cut in again, clickety-click, the first thing I thought of was how wonderful it felt not to think."

"In short, you plead temporary insanity."

"Oh, you utterly miss the point. You understood it before, in the bar. You said I was too smart to have an easy time with men. I don't know about being smart. But I know many an evening I ruined because I sat there thinking. You're not supposed to do that with a member of the opposite sex, except at an office or something like that. But when there's just the two of you, and the reason you're there together is what my mother calls 'social,' then you're supposed to let yourself react emotionally. Let his signals come through. Transmit some of your own. Let life happen. That sort of thing."

"You do that."

"So it seems to you."

"Very much so."

"Because I'm able to react that way to you. You're the first in—I get sick at repeating this—twenty years. It's all very odd." She reached in her purse for cigarettes, lighted two and gave him one. Palmer opened his window an inch to let the smoke flow out of the small car. The cold wind cut at his left ear.

"Why odd?" he asked then.

"Because you don't give that way. One would think, wouldn't one, that it would take a very emotionally free person to unlock congealed me. You are not that person. You are another me. Only you've been in deep freeze so much longer."

"Going on forty-five years."

"I love the way you flatly admit it."

"It's true. I told you that, remember?"

"I didn't believe you," she said. "I still find it hard to believe. Why should you melt me? Ah, but, really, it's too simple, isn't it? We appreciate each other because neither of us makes a big thing of it. We underplay—because we don't know how to be normally emotional—and this makes both of us more comfortable."

"You make it sound like a piece of stagecraft."

She nodded vigorously. "That's what it is. We've both been acting all our lives, acting out lies to ourselves, acting out fake public personalities."

"Do you think I have a fake public personality?"

"Three that I know of."

"Not really."

"One, the banker. One, the husband and father. One, the lover. They're all different. And none of them are you."

"We are digging rather deeply tonight, eh?"

"The light, loverly touch?" she asked. "You and I are so rarely serious with each other. It's easier to make light of it."

He saw the speedometer needle inching upward, removed his toe from the accelerator and let the car ease back to fifty-five miles per hour. "All right, then," he said, "I have three fake personalities, none of them me. Tell me: what is the real me?"

"Hum." She wriggled sideways on the bucket seat to look at Palmer. "Something very sinister, very treacherous, or so you think."

"Me? Not me."

"You think so. Very sang froid, very calculating."

"You're wrong."

"A watcher, a listener, a waiter, a plotter, a pouncer."

"A yellow-breasted pouncer."

"There you go," she observed, "making light again. The true touch of Machiavelli. The smiler, indolent master of small talk, yet wary, casual but fully armed at all times."

"I'm none of those things."

"Those and more. You have thickly coiled schemes. I know you. You're planning right now to . . . to take over the bank."

"Had one once. Didn't like it."

"You didn't connive to get that bank. It was given you. All your life you've wanted to get something by chicanery, by outwitting the world."

"Absolute nonsense."

"No," she said. "Way down inside there you really believe it. You have an inner vision of yourself moving stealthily through high danger, cat-footed, alert, daring, a man to be reckoned with."

"Gee, doesn't everybody?"

"Only you've never outgrown it. Am I right? Say I'm right. Please?" She reached for his thigh and began to squeeze it. "Say it."

"Yes! You're right! Let go!"

"I knew you'd confess eventually." She swung around to face forward. "But, really, Woods, really and truly, please tell me what you're like. I don't mean what you're really like. Nobody knows that about himself. And, after all, I couldn't stand to know. Just . . . oh, you know, what you really want, what you're after."

Palmer slowed up for the toll booths ahead, scrabbled in his trousers pocket for change. "I know what I want," he muttered. "It's just that I can't get anyone to understand it." He braked to a halt, paid the toll-booth attendant and sped off across the state line into New York again. "Just violated the Mann Act," he announced crisply.

"A Federal rap," Virginia said. "But you've committed some local and state felonies, too, you know."

"Ha?"

"Fornication and circumlocution."

Palmer steered the car along the Hutchinson River Parkway now, watching the signs that would lead him back through Westchester into Manhattan. "I'm not trying to circumlocute," he announced then. "I'll talk."

"I notice you're keeping pretty quiet about the other rap."

"Well, you know, gentleman's code and all that."

"I wish I had a friend I could tell it all to," she mused. "Somebody who wouldn't judge or be shocked. Somebody who'd enjoy the details. Can I tell you? There was this great big huge bed in this motel. Two beds pushed together. And he—"

"Bedwise, Syracuse was better."

"Mac Burns's rug beats either of them."

"So it does. You're right." He sighed sharply. "Who's making light of things now?"

"But sex is worth laughing about. You can't do anything to spoil it when it's good. I mean the only way you can spoil it is by being utterly solemn about it. Do you think Mac suspects? I'm sorry. I'm interrupting you. You wanted to talk."

"He may," Palmer said, remembering the hints Burns had dropped in Albany. "I don't really much care if he does."

"Pooh. That's part of your act. Of course you care."

"You misunderstand. If he could prove anything, I'd care. Very much. But he can suspect his heart out and it wouldn't really bother me."

She was silent for a moment, her eyes fixed on the road ahead. "Why would you care so much if he could prove something? I know why, but I want to hear it from you."

"Because it would give him tremendous power over me."

"Why should that bother you?" she asked. "Don't other people have power over you?"

"Power I let them have. Burckhardt can tell me what to do and I do it, if I wish. If I don't wish, I can stop giving him this power just by walking away from Ubco."

"Ah. Who else have you given power to?"

"Various people. Burns. My family. Culhane. You."

"But you could take back the gift just by walking away from them," she said.

"Yes."

"Are you going to walk away from me?"

"I wouldn't like to."

"Would you walk away from your family?"

"No."

She stubbed out her cigarette in the dashboard ash tray. For a long moment, her deep-set, dark eyes stared straight ahead. On either side now, large apartment buildings loomed high over the parkway. To the left, ahead, the fluorescent glare of a huge shopping center brightened the night. The car shot down a long grade, gaining speed.

"Thank you," she said at last.

"You said you knew."

"I did. But thank you for being honest enough to confirm it." She reached into the ash tray, where the stub was still smoking faintly, and ground it out more thoroughly. "Of course," she pointed out, "you leave me no alternative."

"That's not true. You know the old story. There is always an alternative."

"Not in this case. There is absolutely no reason for me to see you ever again, except at the office, and there is every reason for me just to forget the whole affair as if it had never existed."

"That's true," he admitted. "But those are reasons, not choices. Let me show you what I mean."

"Please don't."

"You see, don't you, that if you decided to drop me, a whole other chain of alternatives would begin?"

"Yes. Please, let's forget it," she said.

"Only a moment more." He swung the car in a broad arc off the parkway and headed south along the Thruway toward Manhattan. "It's the indefiniteness of life that confuses people. The better logician you are, the further you can extend your chain of alternatives. The less intellect you have, the more positive a choice you can make. Your problem, as I think I said before, is that you're too bright."

"No." He could hear her breathing grow irregular. He glanced sideways at her and saw that she had turned her face away from him.

"It's true," he said then. "Stupid people can always be positive. They have so little ability to project alternatives that they never know what they've missed. And so they're happy."

"That's not . . . my problem," she said, the words coming out unsteadily. After a moment he saw her straighten up in the bucket seat.

"What is?"

"Oh. Nothing minor."

"Tell me."

"My problem," she said very quickly then, "is that I'm in love with you."

The Thruway, now the Major Deegan Expressway, led south through the Bronx to the Triborough Bridge. They passed Yankee Stadium, a dark unlit hulk on their left. An electric sign on it showed, first, that the time was 12:27 and, second, that the temperature was 28°. Palmer shot around a slower-moving car and pressed forward. Then he saw that the speedometer was up to seventy again. He slumped back in his seat and let the car slow down.

"God," he said then.

"The Devil. He has his little ways."

"His price is rather steep."

"The sin is cardinal," she said. "Do Protestants ever fall in love with people they shouldn't?"

"No comment."

"I can always ask some other Protestant."

"There aren't any more in New York."

"I'd forgotten," she said. "Well, I'll just have to—" She gestured abruptly. "I'm sorry I told you. It was self-indulgent. Self-centered. People in love are popularly supposed to give, give, give. It isn't so. They grab and hoard."

Palmer paid another toll at the bridge. A minute later they were moving down the East River Drive. "I can drop you at home and then turn in the car. Or vice versa."

"Vice versa. I want to grab and hoard a few more minutes." She lighted another cigarette. "See how unselfish love makes you? Oh. You winced. The word made you wince. 'Love.' Good God, I think I'm cracking up." She ground out the cigarette. "I'm embarrassed and awkward and disconnected. Why did you wince at 'love'? Why do I find myself needling you? You're obviously as horribly embarrassed as I am. I believe I . . . my mind's unhinged. Come unhinged. Demented. But you mustn't wince at four-letter words. Perhaps I'm drunk? I'm nattering. Shut up." She folded her arms and stared out the side window.

Thoroughly unnerved, Palmer took the wrong exit and soon found himself in the Sixties, moving farther westward from the Hertz station where he had rented the car. He swung downtown on Lexington and turned left again, moving east along a deserted block of fairly shabby brownstone houses, their uniform appearance broken here and there by a higher, newer, more expensive building. As he stopped for the traffic light at Second Avenue he heard running footsteps behind him. He glanced in the rear-view mirror and saw a young woman in a long, light-colored coat, running down the middle of the street, followed by a small child with a dog in tow.

"What on earth is this?" he asked, twisting around to watch them directly. Virginia turned to see what was happening.

The woman, coat flapping open in the chill breeze, reached their car and rapped on the window. The dog barked happily and the child holding it gasped for breath. Palmer rolled down the window.

"Can you give me a push?" the woman asked breathlessly.

"I . . . uh. This is a light car."

"I've got a Volkswagen. Please? I mean, I thought you might . . ." Her voice died away and she closed her mouth, breathing heavily through her nostrils. The dog dabbed his paws against her coat. "I'm half a block back. See?"

Palmer turned and saw the little car double-parked. "All right," he said. He reversed gears and began backing up. The young woman, the dog and the child—who seemed to be a girl about seven years old—followed his Corvette. The woman kept a hand on the car's fender, as if to guide it. "No one else has bothered to stop," she said then. "It's awfully nice of you."

"What seems to be wrong with your car?" Palmer asked, trying to ignore the fact that he had not, actually, stopped for her.

"Battery."

"You know how to do this now?" Palmer asked. "You put it in second and turn on the key and let out the clutch?"

"Yes. Yes, I know."

"And after I get you up to a little speed, you slowly let the clutch in?" he persisted. "Slowly."

"I know. The battery's gone bad before."

Having reached the Volkswagen, Palmer carefully backed around it, the woman still following him. "Get in the car, you two," she called to the child and dog. "Thanks again," she said to Palmer. "You wouldn't know what to do about the battery."

"There are all-night garages around. They'll charge it for a dollar or two."

"Is there any other way?"

"Drive around long enough to charge it yourself, from the generator. But it may not work. You may have a short. Better try the garage."

"Too expensive. I'm broke. Got thirty cents till the end of the week."

"What?"

She smiled and nodded. Then, after a moment she got into her car. Palmer nosed the Corvette behind the Volkswagen and shifted into low. He let his car move slowly ahead, picking up speed. A faint clashing came from the bumpers of the two cars. Then the Volkswagen shot ahead, the woman wig-wagging furiously. She beeped her horn four times and sped around the corner, through a red light, onto Second Avenue. By the time Palmer reached the corner, the Volkswagen had disappeared.

"Did you hear the same thing I did?" he asked then.

Virginia nodded. "She and her kid are obviously going to sleep in the car, if she can find a place to park."

"But it's freezing."

"Maybe her check comes through Monday morning."

"What check?"

"The alimony or support check."

"How do you kn—?"

"Forget it," she cut in, her voice dull and flat. "It's her crisis. She's young. If worse comes to worst she can sell the car. Assuming it's hers."

"But she seemed like a nice enough person."

"Ah, God, Woods, shut up."

Palmer turned east on Forty-eighth Street, checked in the car, refused the attendant's offer of a lift home and walked with Virginia to First Avenue.

"Why not take the lift? Cabs may be scarce," she said.

"He knows my name. He would drop us at two different places. Just common sense not to let him." Palmer hailed a passing cab which, though empty, ignored him.

"I see. Pardon me for asking."

"Virginia, look," Palmer began in a tone from which he tried to keep any sign of exasperation. "Don't think I'm some kind of stick. I understand what's been said and what it costs you to have said it. But I hope you understand why I'm not responding now."

"If ever."

"That's a good, old-fashioned snide remark, isn't it?"

"Woods." She paused, unable to speak for a moment. "It wasn't meant to be snide. Crude realism sometimes sounds that way. I meant, simply, that you may just not respond. To me. These things are not unheard of."

"All right. It's just that I hate to be thought of as unresponsive. It's too near the truth for comfort."

"Oh, my God." She walked several steps away from him and blew out a plume of breath into the cold night air. "Some people are thick. You're not. Some people are blind. You see. It's just that you have the wonderful faculty of seeing and understanding and doing nothing about it. That girl."

He stood there, waiting for her to finish the thought. Then: "What girl?"

"The girl with the child and the dog and the Volkswagen with the run-down battery and thirty cents till the end of the week. Wasn't it odd how quickly the car started?"

"I don't—"

"Of course you do. There's nothing wrong with the battery. If there were, and if she'd told the truth about its having happened before, then she wouldn't need to ask what to do about it so as to work her conversation around to the fact that she had no money. Woods, please don't tell me you didn't understand that. It's just that she's too proud to beg for money. At least, in front of the child."

"But she didn't—"

"Of course not. She got no response and instantly dropped it."

"I'm sure you're—"

"No, I'm not. She was plain enough. There's a cab."

Automatically, Palmer lifted his hand and signaled the cab. It slowed down for them and they got in. Virginia gave the driver her address, adding: "This gentleman has to go on from there."

For a moment, as they sat waiting for the light to turn green, neither of them spoke. Then, when the cab began to move again, she turned to Palmer and said: "Please accept my apology for everything."

He watched her for a moment, trying to understand her. The voice in which she had apologized had been flat, hurried, almost brusque, delivering an unpleasant thought because duty demanded it. But her eyes, he saw now, were more articulate. In them he read a kind of shame and something like fear. He took her hand.

"I will," he said. "Please accept mine."

"Everything tonight is too much," she said in that same quick, unaccented tone. "And that girl with her child was much too much. She was acting out the . . . the . . ." She shrugged, unable to complete the thought.

"Say it."

"The nightmare. Every woman alone has it. The primordial nightmare. I don't want to talk about it." She looked out of the cab. "We're almost there, anyway."

"Yes."

"I can't invite you up. You understand that."

"Yes."

"You understand I want to."

"Yes."

She took a deep breath and nodded. "I clasp you to me. The adder to the bosom. Knowing I have to let go."

"Virginia . . ."

"I wish to God I could stop maundering." She bit her lower lip and stared out the front window of the cab. "This corner, cabby. Don't turn in. I'll walk from here. Good night."

"Let me—"

"Good night," she said, opening the door on the wrong side, the side away from the curb.

"Lady," the cab driver began, "don't you know you—"

"Bug out, Jack," she told him.

She was standing in the street now. "Good night." She slammed the door and ran in front of the cab to the corner, the high black heels of her shoes reflecting points of light from the street lamps overhead. Palmer saw her slow to a walk as she gained the sidewalk. He watched the shift of her buttocks as she turned past the corner of a building and disappeared. The cab driver made a small, moist noise by sucking one of his teeth.

"Where to now?" he asked in a gelid tone.

Palmer sighed and thought for a moment. Then: "A friend of mine's car is stalled. It's a Volkswagen, double-parked somewhere between First and Third in the low Sixties. Will you zigzag through that area for a while?"

"Why not?" He shifted into gear and the cab shot forward, making the last of a changing light. "That young lady," he said then. "I mean, like she should know which side of a cab she should get out of."

Palmer remained silent, in the mistaken belief that he would discourage conversation by so doing.

"You'd be amazed," the driver said after a while. He waited, then went on: "The people who do that, like without thinking. Educated people."

Palmer lighted a cigarette and began to watch for the Volkswagen.

"I'n know." The driver laughed slightly. "Why sh'I expect educated people they should know better? I mean, the way they educate people these days? I mean, the cost keeps going up, up, up, but for the price you still don't buy no education."

Palmer leaned forward. "Turn here and start the zigzags."

"Right. I got a boy he's fifteen now. In two years he's gotta go to college. You're dirt without you got that degree. Earning power, spelled B.A. Without you got it, you got nothing. Now, he's a bright boy, no genius. Just a normal, bright boy. Got a neighty average so far. You know the average they need to get in C.C.N.Y., yet? Used to be a neighty was plenty good. Now, all of a sudden, eighty-seven. My boy is cooked. Any normal bright kid is cooked. But he's bright enough to dig around a little. Nobody wants to be a druggist. A kid who's bent that way, he wants he should be a doctor. But my boy is bright. He figures he'll settle now for pharmacy and get in while the getting-in's good."

The cab swung north on Third Avenue and after a pause turned east again on a side street. Palmer looked down the block but saw no Volkswagen.

"Trouble is," the driver continued then, "the schools. The teaching. I mean, they don't give the kids the things they need. My God, they start back with the friggen cave men, the Greeks, the Egyptians, the I-Don't-Know-Whats. Do the kids need this, I ast you? But the schools, they're in there real hard with the whole thing back to 1776. Why? Do kids need that? What is it so much? The books they read, do they need such books? Poetry? Shakespeare? Books you never heard of by guys you never heard of? Does this help the kid he should make a buck? Does it train him for a living?"

The cab crossed Second Avenue and continued toward the river.

"Cut it all out, for Christ's sake," the driver was saying. "Give the kids a break. What the hell do they go to school for? As a father I'm talking. The kids got a right to decent schooling. They got a right to—"

"Slow down," Palmer snapped. He could see the Volkswagen double-parked at the First Avenue end of the block. "Very slow." He took out his wallet and tore a sheet of paper from his notebook. Then he put all the ten-dollar bills he had—three—on top of the paper and folded the whole into a small packet. "Now pull up right next to the Volks," he ordered.

The woman and the child were sitting in the car as the cab stopped. The child was asleep, holding the sleeping dog in her arms, but the woman had been watching the cab. When Palmer opened the door nearest to her, she got out of her car.

"I think you dropped this," Palmer said.

"I don't—? Oh, the man with the Corvette."

"I think you dropped this," he repeated, holding out the packet to her.

She took it. "It doesn't look like—"

Palmer closed the cab door. "Get going, driver."

The driver gunned the motor and made the green light at First. He turned uptown and slowed the cab. "What was all that about?"

"Now take me to, ah, the Plaza."

"Sure." The cab turned west. "You live there, chief?"

"No."

"Just a quick one, huh?"

"No."

"Meeting somebody?"

"No." Palmer remained silent and, for some reason, so did the driver, all the way to the Plaza Hotel. Then Palmer paid him and said: "It's just a good place, at this time of night, to get a cab."

CHAPTER FORTY-SEVEN

The house with the pierced-screen façade was dark. Palmer paid off the driver and let himself into the entrance foyer. In total darkness, he hung up his coat, hat and muffler, feeling for the thick oak pegs on which to hang them.

He stood still then and listened for a moment. Somewhere in the innards of the house the gas heater clicked twice and its heavily muffled blower began to turn with a barely audible hum. Palmer bent down and untied his shoes. He stepped out of them and began to pad on stockinged feet in the direction of the free-rising staircase, wondering if it would be too foolhardy to try ascending it without any light.

As he moved past the entrance to the living room, he heard a soft, bitter snapping sound. He whirled and stared directly into two immense red eyes, glowing hellishly in the blackness.

His heart slammed against his ribs. The skin along his neck and shoulders crept sideways, as if trying to lift away from his body. Something snapped again and one of the eyes broke into two hot red chunks. Palmer sighed and relaxed.

He padded silently to the hearth, found the poker and knocked it carelessly against the glowing embers, breaking them into several smaller pieces, rather than the two huge coals that had frightened him. Palmer stopped suddenly, put away the poker and found a small, short log. He placed it on the embers, knelt before it and began to blow. The coals flickered orangely, strange shudders of passion twisting across their striated faces. The thin, dry bark of the log crackled. Palmer continued blowing softly.

All at once, with a faint puffing pop, the log burst into fat yellow flame. Palmer rocked up off his knees, squatting now as he grimaced into the sudden flare of light. He hunkered there for a long moment, then stood up and went to the bar, moving softly by flickering light across the great room, the bare floor cold to his stockinged feet. He poured an inch of Scotch in a big, square-bottomed glass and returned to the fire.

He sat down on the polished oak floor in front of the fire, tucking his feet up under his thighs, Hindu fashion. Even though it had been standing out for some time, the Scotch was faintly cold to his lips and tongue. Then it burned very gently as it sank down his throat. He could feel the friendly fire radiate outward as it reached his stomach. He took a second sip and was disappointed to find that the whisky had no power to re-create that first warming heat.

The log was burning briskly now, inner resin sputtering as it oozed out, sizzled for a moment in little frothy bubbles and burst finally into rich smoky flame. Palmer's eyes shifted back and forth across the length of the log as the flames rose and fell in uneven, never-to-be-repeated patterns.

Could they repeat? he wondered. Wasn't it mathematically possible for them to repeat? He could ask Gauss about that sometime.

If indeed, he reflected, Gauss would ever speak to him about anything again.

He sat there, sipping whisky and replaying in his mind the wild and oddly exciting conversation with Gauss. Some of those ideas had to be sound. Commercially sound. And, even if they weren't quite, at least in their present state, wasn't it the business of any bank with half an ounce of public interest to finance the development of such ideas?

He had, he knew, let Gauss down rather badly. Not that he'd ever given him reason to expect anything more.

Virginia, of course, was another matter. Apparently he had given her reason to expect something more.

He felt quite sure, as he sat watching the fire, that he had never said anything to her, given any hint that would lead her to believe that he could ever become seriously, totally, involved with her. The trouble was, with Virginia, that she rarely paid much attention to the actual words. Her instinct for inarticulate signals was too strong.

Any normally perceptive person could read those signals, given an incentive to do so and a bit of practice. It wasn't hard. Good poker players did it all the time. So, for that matter, did credit managers in stores. Loan officers in banks. Personnel people who hired employees.

Somehow, without words, he had given her the feeling that he was open to her, emotionally open. This, it seemed, had been dishonest of him. For it seemed, didn't it, that he was emotionally open to no one.

He felt a numbness in one leg and slowly straightened it, then the other, until he was sitting with both legs out before him, like a child. He felt the heat of the fire toasting the soles of his stockinged feet. A faint, ammoniac smell of hot wool made him pull back his feet from the flames.

There must have been a time, in his adult life, when Palmer had been open to someone else. As he sat before the fire, he supposed now that it had been that way with Edith when first they'd met. After all, proposing marriage to a girl argued some degree of emotional involvement.

He smiled slightly at the irony of the thought, then felt the smile die on his face as he wondered, perhaps for the first time in his life, if he had ever been in love with Edith.

The thought was monstrous. He felt it settle down before him with the idiot smile of a circus freak. He could see it in the flames, watching him—not closely—because it had only a casual interest in whether he believed it or not. Of course you loved your wife. At least when you married her. Didn't you?

It seemed to reach out from the fire and tap him on the knee with odious familiarity, a cretinoid version of Mac Burns's repellent friendliness. And, for all its birth in fire, its touch was clammy.

Palmer blinked. He lifted the glass to his lips and slowly sipped the whisky. Why had Virginia said that, that thing about all of it being an act? Why had she come to see it that way, the way he himself saw it? And if she had sensed that he played roles—always, always—why had she believed his unconscious signals, his tentative reachings, the signs that made her think he might love her?

Palmer finished his drink and sat there, eyes half glazed, staring into the jittery line of flames. He seemed hypnotized by them. Despite their heat, despite the dryness of his eyes, he did not blink again.

Palmer leaned back on one elbow, eyes still fascinated by the flames. He and his brother Hanley had played the pretending game by the hour, alone in Hanley's room, just the two of them, in the days when Hanley had been in high school and Father had still lived at home.

They had played many parts: Tom Swift, Bulldog Drummond, Petrie and Nayland Smith locked in combat with the insidious Fu Manchu, the heroes of a dozen E. Phillips Oppenheim romances, Philo Vance with his gold-tipped Regie cigarettes, lean, saturnine, silent men, dissembling their brilliance, revealing nothing to a world unworthy of revelation.

Hanley had been tremendous. He had no mind for the plotting; that had been Palmer's duty. But once the plot had been laid, Hanley would rise to the occasion, improvising, stalking the long, narrow room, smiling coldly, eyebrow raised, brave, cunning, tight-lipped, victorious.

As he stared into the fire, watching those old scenes in Hanley's room, Palmer supposed now that he was the only one in the whole world, really, who knew why Hanley had enlisted as a Naval aviation cadet almost a year before Pearl Harbor. It had been a Hanley kind of gesture, of course, but it had been for a reason no one knew but he.

The two of them had been quite different kinds of people, on the surface, and very much the same underneath. Hanley had been taller, more muscular, more clearly patterned on Father. As the elder, with the sickening burden of the first-born, he had got the full, unrelieved treatment, the paternal character-molding process. Hanley, Palmer realized now, had been bewildered by it all at first. Only later, when Palmer himself had grown to adolescence and begun his dogged, often silly, rebellion against his father, had Hanley realized that one could say no, one could resist. The revelation had appalled him. At twenty-five, with college behind him and a life in Father's bank ahead of him, Hanley had for the first time said no. It was his last time, too, of course.

The act of resistance, for a novice, can be fatal. And if the PBY crash had not done the job for Hanley, Palmer thought now, something else could have, a Zero kamikaze pilot, perhaps, or a U-boat torpedo. Suicide by enlistment. Not an uncommon crime.

He stirred and blinked. The flames were dying. The small, thin log had burned itself nearly out. It lay, in three pieces, amid the older, darker coals.

He wondered, as he watched the embers, if Hanley could have known what hurt he had done his younger brother when he fled from the bank into the iron embrace of war.

Probably not. *De mortuis nil nisi bonum.*

Palmer groaned slightly as he got to his feet. He carried his empty glass to the bar and stood there for a moment, trying to find out if he wanted another drink or not. Yes? No? Wasn't it possible to learn even that much about yourself?

He turned and surveyed the immense room, its farthest corners shadowed now, only the center vaguely illuminated by the dying fire. It is cowardly, he told himself, to blame what you don't feel on a dead brother and a dead father. It is cowardly and simple-minded and childish.

And if you betray everything and everyone, he thought, wife, mistress, even a chance acquaintance like Gauss, you cannot evade the blame by heaping it on the heads of ghosts.

He returned to the fireplace and, with the poker, smashed the large embers into tiny bits. The glow faded quickly. He watched it for a moment as the coals turned dull red, then winked out one by one. He put down the poker and made his way in near darkness to the foyer outside the room. He found the stairway and began to mount it slowly, step by step, feeling ahead of him with his stockinged feet, one hand on the rail for steadiness in the spiraling blackness.

He made slow progress. Had there been landings in the steady upward sweep of the staircase, he could have taken advantage of them, paused and gone on again. As it was, with each step exactly like the last, he was forced to stop quite frequently. Something was very obviously awry with his internal mechanism of balance. He could feel his body veer sharply to the right against the railing. Without visual points of reference, he seemed unable to keep erect.

After a while—ten or twelve steps—he gave up and stood there in the dark with his eyes closed, right hand clamped tightly to the railing, legs spread slightly apart for better balance.

His grip on the railing tightened. He could feel the palm of his hand grow damp with sweat. Carefully, he crossed his left hand in front of him and clasped the railing with it. The double hold twisted him slightly off balance. Sweat chilled his forehead.

The one, the only decision, he was thinking—his mind working at top speed, racing back and forth along the image junctures of memory—the only

314

time I ever made up my own mind, he thought, was when I gave up the bank and came to New York. And even that, he realized with panicky clarity, was a reaction to someone else, a dead someone else who was as powerful dead in his crypt at Rosehill as alive behind his desk at the bank.

Palmer's body was rocking unsteadily. He knew that what he ought first to do—calmly, rationally—was to stabilize himself again, untwist, take a new stance, relax and continue mounting the stairs.

A pure, shadowless white light flooded downward over him, like a bath of milk.

"Woods?"

With light now to see by, to pick up a physical frame of reference, the terrible vertigo dwindled. He straightened and dropped both hands from the railing.

"Are you all right?"

"A little too much to drink, perhaps," he said, taking the simplest explanation at hand and immediately realizing how much at her mercy it left him.

"You don't sound— Well, come up, darling. Don't stand there."

Edith stood at the light-switch panel, her blue and green tartan wool dressing gown thrown over her shoulders. Her hair was put up in a few small yellow curls. Her face looked chalky and blank, eyes washed out, eyebrows almost invisible, mouth a whitish pink. Faintly green shadows lay beneath her cheekbones.

"I'm sorry I wakened you."

"You didn't. I was reading. I heard you come in and do something with the fire. Then I fell asleep because I knew you were home."

"You didn't have to wait up. I told you I had no idea how long I'd be."

"Yes." Her hand dropped from the light switch. "But I never know what might—" She gestured cryptically. "This town is— I never know what might happen to you late at night."

"Nothing. I take cabs."

"And then," she went on, "after I'd fallen asleep, I woke up all at once because you were grunting or something. Groaning. It was a terrible sound, Woods. I didn't know— I mean, it sounded—" She shook her head.

"Like what?"

"It's silly," she said. "But men your age do have heart attacks."

"Ah, no. Please."

She sighed almost sharply. "And it's only that you have a load on and you panic in the dark on those stairs because you're too something to turn on the light."

"Too something?"

"Come to bed, Woods. We'll waken the children this way."

"I didn't turn on the light because I didn't want to waken you."

She led the way into their bedroom. "For some reason, you tried to get up those stairs in the dark rather than have me know how late it was."

315

"What reason could that be?"

She sat down on the edge of her bed. "Really, Woods, this is ludicrous. If anyone knows the reason, it's you. Now, go to bed."

"Without telling you the reason?"

She watched him coldly for a moment. "Don't start anything now, darling. I warn you."

He made a disgusted face as he pulled off his jacket and dropped it on a chair. With one yank, he pulled his tie loose. "All right," he said, unbuttoning his shirt. "Then I have a question for you."

"You've had nothing but."

"Can you ever revember—remember—something I did that was entirely, solely, all my own decision?"

"What?"

"I give up," he announced, removing his shirt. "All lines of communication are down. Between you and me. Between me and me. Central isn't answering. Nobody's on duty at the board." He began to feel almost light-headed with relief. She did not suspect, nor was she really interested in how he had spent the evening.

"Are you trying to act drunk? Is that it?"

He began to hum the music to an old song he could barely remember. As he pulled off his trousers and dropped them carelessly on the jacket, he half sang, half whispered: " 'Hello, Central, give me a line. I want Bryant Seven-O-Nine. Hello, who's this? It's, um, dum, dum. Well, dum-dum, dum-dum, dum-dum, dum. And something, something, something, for . . . Annie doesn't live here any more.' "

He changed into his pajamas, still humming very softly. "What ever happened," he asked suddenly, "to Skinnay Ennis? I used to be able to imitate him."

"I have no idea," Edith said. "Did you turn off the light over the stairs?"

"No. Some other poor soul may try to negotiate them before morning. Some fuddled burglar."

"Please turn it out, Woods."

"You remember the Hal Kemp orchestra? Trumpet section? Triple tonguing. Unison. Very effective. 'Got a date with an angel,' " he sang softly.

She turned away from him, burying her head in the pillow. He frowned. After a moment he sat down on the edge of his own bed and turned off the lamp on the night table. "Yes. All right. Good night," he said.

He sat there in the darkness, listening to her breathing, until it grew regular and deep. Then he stood up and went to the window.

Through the pierced-concrete façade he could see a street lamp, shining coldly. He thought of Virginia for a moment, then of Gauss. Finally, he lighted a cigarette, sat down at the window and thought about how long $30 would last a woman, her daughter and their dog.

CHAPTER FORTY-EIGHT

Brooklyn was bitterly cold. The night wind of January swept down across a stretch of the East River in which cakes of ice floated. The wind moaned in the small but elegant remodeled tenement buildings of the Heights section and howled across the open spaces around Borough Hall. By ten o'clock even the business district was empty of every moving thing but an occasional car. Except for the webbed bridge in the distance, this might be the "downtown" section of any small city, Palmer decided, so thoroughly had the bitter wind swept the streets.

His driver, a Brooklyn native, deftly threaded the car through several side streets and parked it in front of an imposing old building that, to judge by the Masonic devices cut in the granite façade, had once been a Shriners' hall. It could no longer be, Palmer thought as he got out of the car, if tonight's meeting were held here.

He stood for a moment in the chilling wind and looked slowly around him, making his first leisurely inspection of Brooklyn. An old city, he saw, much older now than Manhattan, which seemed bent on growing constantly younger by eating pieces of what had once been its youth.

"Won't need you until at least midnight, Jimmy," he told his driver. "You'd better find a warm place to wait."

"Nothing open around here this time of night, Mr. Palmer."

"Lock up and come in with me."

The two men mounted the broad stone stairs. The driver pushed open an immense, richly carved wooden door. They found themselves alone in a walnut-paneled foyer. Palmer listened for a moment, then heard the sound of laughter. He followed it several yards down a corridor to a pair of large walnut doors with heavily incised brass handles. He pushed down on one and opened the door a crack. He found himself staring into a yellow eye while, in the background, men continued laughing.

"Woody!" Both Burns's eyes and his entire, grinning face came into view as he opened the door. "Baby, you're almost late. I was considering biting a nail or three."

"Is there someplace my driver can wait?"

"Down the hall," Burns said, pointing. "First stairway on the right."

"See you later, Mr. Palmer," Jimmy said.

"Inside, Woody-doll." Burns escorted Palmer into the room and swung the door shut behind him. The laughter stopped.

Palmer looked around him. The room was easily 40 feet long, with a table that ran very nearly the full length. The ruins of dinner lay on a white tablecloth. Around the table sat a group of men in evening dress.

Palmer had never, to his knowledge, met any of them, but their faces were not entirely strange to him. Faces like theirs were to be found in Albany and in the corridor of the midtown hotel where Vic Culhane had his office. The same faces, or ones very like them, appeared regularly at the dinners Palmer had been attending these past months.

Despite variations from one set of features to another, they ran to certain physical types. If they were fat, the faces tended to be fat in a certain way, the suet concentrated below the nose, around the mouth, in heavy jowls and thick, powerful folds under the chin, as though at one time great heat had been applied, melting the fat and causing it to run to the bottom of the face. If they were lean, they were almost always well tanned—December and January in Miami Beach—with strong lines cut like deep parentheses around the mouth, violet-gray smears under the eyes and arrowlike creases dropping down and away from each nostril.

The fat faces bore smudgy nondescript noses, heads topped by yellowish scalp. The thin faces had sharp, dangerous noses under graying, close-cropped hair. Uniformly, the dinner jackets were of the latest style in a blue lighter than navy, skimpy in fit, with narrow shawl-like lapels. Uniformly, too, the shirts bore intricate white-on-white patterns. An occasional front bore a fine froth of ruffles, but this did not change the fact that these were much the same shirts such men would wear with business suits.

Burns had taken Palmer on a slow circuit of the table, introducing him to each of the nearly fifty men there. Now they found themselves back at the head—or foot?—of the table where they had started. Palmer could remember none of the names. They were, as always, roughly one-third Irish, one-third Italian and one-third Jewish. As he sat down next to Burns, waiters arrived to clear the remnants of dinner. Two waiters pushed a portable bar around the room, dispensing liqueurs, brandy, whisky and coffee.

"Two coffee royals," Burns told them.

Palmer watched one waiter fill two cups part way with coffee, while his partner brimmed each cup with brandy and set them in front of Burns and Palmer. "Not for me," Palmer said in an undertone. Conversation around the table had resumed. "Just some Scotch on ice."

Halfway down the table, the owner of one of the fat faces got to his feet and lightly tapped his water glass with a spoon. "Gentlemen," he said, "on behalf of our little dining club, I'd like to welcome Mr. Palmer, who you've all met personally by now. We're very sorry he couldn't join us for dinner, but the fact is his plane was late coming down here from Buffalo. We don't stand much on ceremony, so, without making what my Italian friends call a *tsimmes,* let me turn over the floor to him. From United Bank and Trust Company, Woods Palmer."

A polite round of applause greeted Palmer as he stood up, nodding and trying to smile. It had never been easy for him to smile at strangers, but by now he had almost got the knack of it.

"Gentlemen," he began. "Believe me when I say I am very sorry indeed that I couldn't join you for what looks to have been a very excellent dinner. I say that because I genuinely wish I had been spared the time to get to know all of you a little better and not, as you might suspect, because the dinners they serve on the plane leave something to be desired."

He paused, waiting out the laughter, and then went into a long, pointless joke Burns had told him several days ago. Although he did not consider it in any way funny, the audience at Buffalo had howled over it.

"You know, flying in one of these modern jets reminds me of the story about the time Boeing developed this tremendously fast airliner. It did two thousand miles an hour with ease. But at twenty-one hundred, the wings tore right off. They spent millions of dollars trying to correct the fault. Finally they invited leading aviation engineers from every nation to suggest possible answers. The Russians came, tried and failed. So did the British, the French and the Germans. Finally there were no visiting engineers left but this one little man from Israel." He paused so that the Jews in his audience could shift mental gears and prepare themselves for what might turn out to be an anti-Semitic joke. Burns had carefully explained to him that the essence of timing the joke was to pause at this point and get the Jews worried, along with the more sensitive listeners of other faiths.

"Well, they asked him what equipment and helpers he needed. 'Just a ladder,' he said, 'and an electric drill.' They were somewhat amazed at this modest request, but they complied. The Israeli engineer then climbed up the ladder and began to drill a line of tiny holes half an inch apart along the leading edge of the wings. Then he said: 'Let's take her up.' When the Israeli volunteered to fly with them, two brave pilots doubled their life insurance, strapped on extra parachutes and boarded the plane. As they taxied for take-off, the wings began to flap dangerously."

Palmer paused again, as Burns had instructed him. The hidden logic of the joke would now seem uncovered to the audience. They would know it was anti-Semitic. It was important that they be given time to reach this conclusion.

"But by some miracle the plane took to the air," Palmer continued. "The pilot gunned it up to six hundred miles an hour, twelve, two thousand. The critical point was at hand. Twenty-one hundred. And the wings held. The pilot landed the plane and bedlam broke loose. The Boeing people showered the little Israeli engineer with lavish praise and money. That night at a victory banquet, he was asked how he had gotten the inspiration for this scientific miracle. 'Well,' he said modestly. 'There was nothing much to it.'"

Palmer paused for the last time. Tension in his audience had reached its peak. The anti-Semites among them were ready to guffaw. The Jews were ready to laugh politely and briefly.

"He said: 'Actually I got the idea from the toilet paper back home. It's got holes like that and it won't tear off either.' "

The silence was total for an instant. Then laughter broke out at the far end of the table where two men got the pointless point of the story first. Laughter spread quickly to the rest of the table, laughter first of relief at the joke not being (quite) anti-Semitic and, second, at the loony illogic of it.

"I think," Palmer went on after a moment, "you would call that a shaggy toilet-paper joke." He paused again for the laugh Burns called the "bounce-back," the small remark that brought the audience out of the joke and into the immediate present again.

"You know," he continued then, "we bankers have a saying about toilet paper. If we ever wanted to change the brand in our public rest rooms, we'd have to get an enabling act from Albany . . . or Washington. That's how closely banks are regulated."

Palmer let his audience settle back now, paying for the joke in much the same manner that television viewers were forced to sit through commercials.

"That's what I'm here to discuss with you tonight," he said. He took a sip of water and launched into the main body of his speech, pretty much as he'd presented it at Buffalo and at Rochester. Although it covered the same ground as his original speech at Syracuse, he had rewritten its argumentation to avoid as much criticism of savings banks as possible.

Giving it again tonight, he realized how right he had been to change the speech. Brooklyn was, in some ways, a bastion of savings banking. Some of the businessmen here tonight were undoubtedly trustees of savings banks. And the savings banks in Brooklyn were among the hungriest for broader branch privileges. Ever since the war they had provided the mortgage money to build thousands of one-family homes farther out on Long Island. Their depositors had moved into these homes. But the banks were prevented from establishing branches on Long Island to serve their old depositors.

". . . seems eminently fair and equitable," Palmer said, moving into the last section of his speech, "that savings banks should have the right to follow their depositors. No one denies this principle. The intent of the law as it now stands is not to bar them forever, but to make the change in a gradual manner that will in no way upset the economy of the state.

"The proposed changes now urged by the savings banks are not unreasonable. It is only the speed with which they want the change accomplished that makes me wonder what effect it must have on the businesses who now depend for their financing on commercial banks.

"Gentlemen, when you deal with money you learn to move cautiously. A mistake is too costly to be remedied. In my opinion, that same prudent caution should also guide our solution of the savings banks' problem." Palmer paused. "And now, do you have any questions?"

A thin-faced man at the far end of the table raised his hand but began speaking before Palmer could officially recognize him. "Mr. Palmer," he said in a hoarse, powerful voice. "Prudence and caution are just great. But this branch bill, or something like it, has been coming up at Albany for five or ten years now. Don't you think we've been prudent and cautious long enough?"

The audience laughed and Palmer saw that they were laughing not out of vague good humor, but because they felt a point had been scored against him.

As long as two months ago, when Burns had first suggested this smaller, but more influential, gathering, Palmer had seen the problem it posed. The comparative intimacy of the group worked to the speaker's disadvantage. The audience was made up of friends or, at the very least, business and political bedfellows. He was the outsider, for all that he arrived under the protective aegis of Mac Burns. His slightest hesitation, his first attempt to hedge, would be instantly apparent in a group this size. And any attempt to put down a heckling questioner would immediately turn them actively against him.

"Have we?" Palmer asked in return. "We live in a fast-moving age. A jet plane takes me here from Buffalo in less than an hour. By the same token, bad things happen fast, too. Even in the more leisurely era of the late 1920's it took only a week to wipe out half the fortunes in America, bankrupt hundreds of thousands of small investors and give the stock market a black name for almost a generation.

"If you went to work like a burglar and deliberately tried to send our economy into a tailspin, it would take you years. But suddenly, overnight, everything could collapse. You and I are trained to think in terms of cycles, of chart lines that gently curve up and down. But in reality it just doesn't work that way. The soundness of the economy is something like the virtue of a woman. It can seem perfect for years. And then one word can destroy it."

He stood there, watching them openly now, looking from face to face. The thin ones looked dangerous, as they meant to look. But now even the fat ones had an air of menace. Palmer realized as he looked at them that it had, indeed, been some powerful form of heat that had melted the suet and sent it sliding to the bottom of their faces. It had been the heat of friction, the tremendous heat generated by a man who shoves and claws his way through many bodies to ultimate success.

"As far as I can see," one of the fat faces said then, "we need the savings banks' mortgage money as badly as we need the commercial banks' business financing. Would you care to comment on that?"

"Happy to." Palmer picked up his glass and saw, too late, that it was his Scotch, not his water. He sipped it and put it down again.

"I know some of you are involved in one-family home construction," he went on then. "What I'm about to say will not come as a nasty surprise to you. For the first time in the post-war period, your kind of housing is lagging behind apartment-house construction. It's unheard of. But it's true.

"I suggest that next year the gap will grow wider. Wider yet the year after that. I suggest that our whole economy is undergoing a subtle change. From the day the Pilgrims landed until just a few years ago, our economy was based on ownership. More and more that's beginning to change. People want the use of more things. But they're less interested in owning them.

"We saw the change first in the way people use money. The whole post-war boom in personal credit is nothing more than this: people want the use of money, but they no longer care to accumulate it. If you save for a car or a house or a color television set, you wait a long time before you can actually buy it. That won't do any more. Today, people want what they want *now*. They want to use it *now*. And if a bank or a finance company or a landlord is the real owner, they couldn't care less.

"All right," Palmer concluded. "If time-buying is a good way to get what you want now, then renting is an even better way. People rent damned near everything these days. Cars, trucks, fur coats, pictures, apartments, chairs and tables, summer cottages, part-time help, power tools, boats, you name it . . . somebody'll rent it to you. It's no wonder, then, that apartment construction is pulling ahead of one-family homes. There's where the future of the economy lies, in the service industries that rent shelter, transportation and the luxuries of life. And none of these industries can get its financing any-where but from a commercial bank."

There was a pause. Palmer realized that he had shaken them. He hadn't meant to dig that deeply into motivations, but he saw now that it was just as well he had. He realized, too, that he could dig very little deeper. The thoughtful, somewhat somber looks on their faces could easily turn to dis-belief if he told them how he really felt.

"Are you trying to tell us," one man asked then, "that there's no place in the economy for thrift?"

"No, sir, I am not." Palmer took a long, deep breath. "If you get that message, it's the public that's telling you, not me. Check your statistics. You'll find that although salaries go higher every year, the average savings account is no larger today than fifteen years ago. In fact, it's beginning to shrink."

"But, look," his questioner persisted, "that's just the cost of living, rising along with salaries."

"It certainly does that," Palmer agreed. "That's what discourages the aver-age wage earner. That's one of the reasons he wants his luxuries now, not later. He knows the dollar he saves today won't have the same buying power five years from now when he's accumulated enough to get, let's say, a car."

Once again the abrupt silence told Palmer he'd shaken them. The danger now, he told himself, was to avoid plunging them into such gloom that they got a feeling of being powerless to do anything about the situation.

322

"Seems to me," a small, thin man several chairs away now said, "that you're pretty pessimistic about the common sense of the average wage earner. We know he goes on buyers' strikes when the feeling hits him. He's not a complete moron."

"That's right," Palmer said. "He's not. But what is a buyers' strike, when you get right down to it? It isn't a blanket refusal to buy. It's the consumer saying to himself: 'I'm going to wait till the price gets better.' And meanwhile . . . what? Does he do without? He's got the same three problems he's always had: food, shelter and clothing. Inevitably the economy adjusts to his needs, the law of supply and demand. He can't stay out on strike forever and he doesn't. He's smart but, no matter how he feels, eventually he has no choice."

Palmer realized that he was now on the verge of going too far. In another mood, with more time to consider what he was saying, he himself might take issue with what he'd just said.

"I didn't want to get us off on a tangent," he said then. "My only point is that our economy is changing, in order to remain abundant. Since the changes *are* keeping it abundant, there's nothing wrong with the changes. But the changes are moving our economy further from pure thrift and closer to a more unlimited credit situation.

"Since this is so, it would seem intelligent—in fact, downright necessary— to give some small measure of protection to the financial institutions that will keep the wheels of our changing economy moving freely. I don't suggest we protect the commercial banks at the expense of the savings banks. I say only this: let's not unbalance the relationship between these two kinds of banks any further than it already is."

Palmer stood waiting for more questions. He could feel a subtle change in the atmosphere and he wasn't quite sure what it meant. When he had begun speaking, they had been friendly enough. When he'd finished, they'd been politely skeptical. A few moments after that, they'd begun to swarm to a kind of attack. Now they seemed to have paused while their mood changed. Several of them had an abstracted, inward-turning look about them, as if their minds were elsewhere. The next question, Palmer hoped, might tell him what had happened.

"Mr. Palmer." A small man, neither thin nor fat, with sparse gray-blond hair combed across his scalp MacArthur style, stirred uneasily in his chair. "In your opinion, what's the immediate future of some of these service industries, say the ones who operate through licensees?"

Palmer nodded and tried to keep from smiling with relief. Now he understood the change in mood. They had stopped being interested in an abstract way. As businessmen, they were now interested in specific business opportunities.

He launched into a brief summary and, after several more questions in the same vein, the chairman of the meeting rose to thank him.

323

"I think I speak for most of us," he said, "when I remark that the question of savings banking may still be moot in our minds, but your report on business has been downright fascinating. I take it you are on hand at your bank for discussions slightly more concrete than chin music?"

Palmer bowed. "Always," he assured them. "And so—"

"—is every other commercial banker," the chairman finished for him.

Palmer waited for the guffaws to subside. "Amen," he added then.

Driving back to Manhattan through the chilly night, Palmer sat silently beside Burns, wishing he had not offered to give him a ride. Burns talked steadily, pouring out seemingly encyclopedic information about most of the audience. But as they crossed the Brooklyn Bridge and turned to head up-town on the East River Drive, his conversation began to flag for the first time.

". . . owns a chain of appliance stores in Queens and Nassau," he was saying. "The guy sitting to the left of him, our left, that is, was Hymie Chwastenstein, one of the state senators from Brooklyn. He's got a piece of every real estate syndication deal on the island, but he— You're not even listening."

"R-r-right," Palmer announced.

"Look, you need these *schmegegies*. They don't need you."

"After tonight they do."

"Ah? I set you up for a political speech and you use it to scout new business. Is that the pitch?" Burns asked.

"Let's just say I gave them something to think about."

Burns shook his head. "When am I gonna learn you can't beat that pure Aryan Protestant stock for real business moxie?"

"Don't be sarcastic, for God's sake."

Burns made a face and settled back in the seat. "Whyn't you get yourself a real car, Woody-baby? This is the cheapest Caddy they make, for God's sake."

"I get it for free. You can't beat that price."

"Oh, but we're in a chipper mood tonight, aren't we?"

"I think I'm entitled to feel chipper," Palmer said. "Those boys were ready to flay me alive for a few minutes there."

Burns sighed heavily. "Woody-doll, I don't tell you how to play banker. Don't tell me how to play politician. You think you swung those characters to our side?"

"I don't know. But I started them wondering."

"About business, not about politics." Burns lighted a cigarette. In the dark-ened interior of the car the flame of his lighter picked out tiny sparks of glit-tering yellow in his eyes. "Business is logic and you were very logical with them. You hear about the iron logic of politics, but it's another of the lies they tell about it. Politics is a matter of commitments and commitments are not always made on a logical basis. If they were, if logic ruled the candidates and the voters, the outcome of every election would be cut and dried."

"We're not talking about the public postures of politicians, Mac. We're talking about their real business, the private business of getting rich."

"You're a novice," Burns told him. "Like any novice, you think you understand the whole game. I'm an old hand at politics, sweetie, and I still don't understand all the rules."

"Then how do you operate?"

"Take tonight," Burns explained. "It's a good example. Whatever you told them and whatever they told you, my nose tells me you pulled a boo-boo."

Palmer shifted impatiently. "How?"

"By being bright. By lecturing. By having smart answers. By knowing something they didn't. You get the picture, Woody? Humility-wise, you goofed."

Palmer laughed. "What a wordsmith."

Burns's answering laughter sounded strained. "You didn't defer to them. You weren't humble. You didn't get down on your knees every two minutes and kiss their collective ass for allowing you the supreme privilege of addressing them. These *schmendricks* have an image of themselves you wouldn't believe. In their own little bailiwicks they are little tin gods. These are not the high-level committee-chairman type of business executives, Woody, the kind you're used to dealing with. These are slum kids who made it big the hard way, the only way they could. And you'd better kowtow to the image they have of themselves, or they mark you lousy."

Palmer's jaw tightened. Damn him, he thought. He was right, of course. Burns could hardly miscalculate men like that. He was one of them.

"I see what you mean," he said then in a thin, controlled tone. "I wish you'd briefed me before I spoke, but I realize there was no time."

"Woody, you still don't get the picture," Burns remonstrated. "Humility is every speaker's stock in trade. You're arrogant with your kind of people because that's the way to out-snob them. But how many of your kind of people do you find in the average New York audience? In politics, generally? So, look: don't take chances. Get humble and stay humble."

"Mac," Palmer asked softly after a moment, "what are my kind of people?"

"Ah, God, it's late and we're almost home."

"I think you let it slip back there. Pure Aryan Protestant stock?"

"With money," Burns added glumly. "Hereditary money."

Palmer was silent for a moment. "You know," he said then, "this is sort of funny. I'm Burckhardt's contact with you because he doesn't like you. Now I find that you don't like me."

"Woody! Baby! You *know* better."

"Do I?"

"Of course you do," Burns assured him. He laid his hand on Palmer's knee and pressed hard. "We get along great and you know it."

The car pulled off the drive at Forty-second Street and sped up First Avenue toward Burns's apartment. The United Nations Buildings flashed past on the right and vanished as the driver gunned the car forward.

"I have a feeling about you," Palmer said then, watching the streets. "I think you fool yourself sometimes. A little while ago you said politics wasn't entirely logical. I don't think you are, either."

Burns shrugged. "Guilty."

Palmer saw that their car was now cruising in the Fifties. At any moment it would turn right and stop at Burns's apartment house. "You make commitments," Palmer said slowly, "as you yourself put it, not always on a logical basis. Your commitment to Ubco I can't possibly judge. I'm too close to it to be objective. But some of your other commitments, ones I can only guess at, don't seem entirely rational."

"Which ones?" Burns asked.

The car turned right and headed for the river. "I think," Palmer said, "at one time or another, you must have had dealings with people like Burckhardt." He was choosing his words with extreme care now. He could not let Burns know that he was certain of a connection with Jet-Tech. But he had to shake him, hard.

"Those kind of people—my kind, you seem to think—can be pretty impressive," Palmer said. The car turned right and entered the curving approach to Burns's building. "A man like Joe Loomis, for example," he added softly. "Terribly impressive. Ever met him?"

The car stopped and the doorman dashed out to meet it. Burns frowned. "Loomis?" he asked. "I wouldn't be surprised if I had. I meet a lot of people."

The man opened the car door and stood at attention, holding the handle. "Good evening, Mr. Burns, sir."

Burns got out of the car and stood under the porte-cochere for a moment. "I place him. He's the gentile Barney Baruch, isn't he?"

"Pure Aryan Protestant stock," Palmer said.

"Yeah?" Burns stood lost in thought for a moment. "Yeah," he said then. His face went dead, with a kind of somber impassiveness. Because he seemed to be staring at the toes of his shoes, Palmer could not watch his eyes. After a moment Burns looked up at Palmer and one corner of his mouth flattened to a tight line.

"Old buddy," he said then, "remind me sometime to tell you about your commitments. The wilder ones."

They watched each other for a moment and, in that instant, Palmer realized he had been more right than he knew about Burns. This was a man who could jettison logic under the heat of emotion, could act against his own interest, a Samson pulling the temple down about his own head.

"Good night, boychik," Burns said. A smile warped his mouth for a moment and was gone.

"Good night, Mac."

"Stay humble, doll."

326

"Likewise," Palmer said.

Secondary figures broke up the tableau. The doorman closed the car door. The driver released the brake and let the car purr off into the night. But nothing the subordinates did, by way of unconscious glossing over, made Palmer feel any less uneasy.

Chapter Forty-nine

Palmer was walking past the receptionist on the way back to his office at about ten in the morning. The bosomy girl was on the telephone. He heard her say: "Started? Right," and hang up the phone. "Oh, Mr. Palmer?"

He paused, halfway into his office. "Yes?"

"Mr. Burckhardt is on his way up in the elevator."

"Thank you."

Palmer walked into his office, sat down at his desk and continued editing the draft of a speech he would make in Utica that weekend. Virginia had patterned the draft after his own model, the one he had given in Brooklyn the other night. In the pessimistic light of several mornings after, Palmer saw that Burns had been, if not entirely correct, certainly more than halfway there. The speech wasn't really arrogant, but it was too smooth, too knowledgeable and entirely without deference to the audience.

He was penciling in a few lines of humility at the beginning—"I want to thank you all very much for taking time from your busy schedules and honoring me by this invitation to address you"—when Burckhardt strode into his office and closed the door sharply behind him.

Palmer looked up. The older man stood there for a moment, mastering something inside him that could have been anger or only shortness of breath. His naturally florid face looked redder than usual, making his teeth, when he bared them in a sketch of a smile, seem startlingly white and unreal.

"Good morning, Lane," Palmer said, getting to his feet.

Burckhardt grunted something and waved him back down. "Problems," he muttered.

Palmer indicated the chair across from him and watched Burckhardt sit in it. "What kind?"

"Seen the morning papers? The Albany stories?"

"*Times* and *Trib*," Palmer said. "Nothing much there."

"You ought to read the *Bulletin*, sonny," Burckhardt said in a low, harsh tone. He unbuttoned his overcoat and felt around inside until he produced a much folded copy of the tabloid. Palmer realized that Burckhardt had taken some pains to conceal from the world that he had read, or was at all interested in the contents of, the *Bulletin*. "Page four," the older man said, slapping the paper on the desk. "Don't you ever read the *Bulletin?*" he asked then, almost petulantly.

"Almost never. Should I?"

"The political column, always, every day." Burckhardt's breathing was calmer now, but not by very much. "You're from out of town, Woody, so there's some small excuse for you not knowing about the *Bulletin's* political coverage. But they always have the inside dope a day ahead of the other papers. Remember that."

Palmer nodded and read the item Burckhardt had marked.

"Albany is wondering," the column item read, "how long sweetness and light will continue beaming over the savings banks' branch bill. At the moment the upstaters are solidly against it, but there hasn't been Peep One out of the downstate Dems on behalf of the measure. With less than a month before the close of the session, insiders are wondering when fireworks will begin. Or is the word 'if'? Word seems to be that commercial-bank missionaries have convinced a few key leaders that Tammany should thumbs-down the new bid by the savings banks. Big question is, can the Tiger make city voters—traditionally in favor of more savings-bank branches—swallow a pill that bitter? Watch this one. It's got a short fuse."

Palmer put down the paper and looked at the older man. "Trial balloon?" he suggested.

Burckhardt shook his head slowly from side to side. "He knows something."

"But he could still be sending up balloons. This business here about city voters being traditionally for the savings banks. It's nonsense, isn't it?"

"Damned if I know. Aren't they?"

"I've never seen anything to convince me they give a hoot about it one way or the other," Palmer said.

Burckhardt stood up. As he walked toward the huge picture window, he let his overcoat drop on the chair behind him. "Something's up," he grunted, pacing aimlessly. "An item like this comes from something or someone. Put Burns on it. Have him find out what's behind the thing."

Palmer reached for his phone. "Get me Mac Burns," he said and hung up. Then, to Burckhardt: "Ubco shares rose nearly a point yesterday."

"Means nothing."

"The Dow-Jones average was down more than three. But a slow-moving bank stock like Ubco was up."

"Absolutely nothing."

"Have you heard from Loomis since your Jet-Tech meeting?" Palmer asked.

"No. Should I?"

"I thought he might make a more reasonable loan request."

"He hasn't. Nor would I expect him to."

"I would," Palmer said, "if he feels he hasn't cornered enough Ubco stock yet. But since there's been no new approach on a loan, I can only assume he—" The phone rang. ". . . he feels he's well on the way to control."

"Answer your Goddamned phone."

"Hello?"

"Woody-sweetie. *Wie gehts?*"

"The item in the *Bulletin* this morning."

"Yeah?" Burns sounded superlatively calm and easy this morning.

"How do you evaluate it?"

"Me? What can I tell you, doll? I don't bother to evaluate horse shit. You want me to?"

Palmer was about to tell him that Burckhardt felt the item merited more than routine attention, then realized he would only harden Burns's attitude by so doing. "Of course I do," he said instead. "The item came from somewhere, Mac."

"Somewhere in his hat."

"See what you can find out."

"Ah, crap, Woody. Why waste time?"

"Because you and I both know that the *Bulletin* has good sources."

"Yeah? What's it worth to you if the *Bulletin*, tomorrow morning, in the same space, says the non-partisan opposition to the savings-bank branch bill is going to defeat it without working up a sweat?"

"You can get them to print it?"

"Just ask me."

"Not I," Palmer demurred.

"I'm just illustrating a point, lover. Newspapermen print anything newsy within reason if you tell it to them with enough authority. Some savings-bank character fed him this pipe dream and made him believe it. I can feed him another and make him believe it, too. What's that prove?"

"Whoever gave him this morning's item," Palmer said in a clear, slow voice, "must carry as much authority as, uh, say, you do."

There was a pause at the other end of the line. Then: "You trying to tell me something, Woody?" Burns asked in a dead voice.

"Why? Do you get some kind of message?"

"Same one I got from you last night. If you have something to tell me, why don't you just out and say it?"

Palmer laughed. "I'd rather leak it to you, politico style. Mac, you're getting hypersensitive. There is no message."

"What're you doing for lunch, Woody?"

"Got a date."

"Break it?"

"Can't."

"Drink after dinner?"

"Another date. Unbreakable."

"Jesus. Who do I have to be to get a date with you? A chick?"

"Now I'm getting some kind of message, Mac."

"Message?" Burns asked innocently. "What message? There is no message."

"Touché."

"What about dinner?"

"You want to see me very badly, don't you?"

"That's right."

"Something you can't tell me over the phone?"

"Why?" Burns asked lazily, "is your line bugged?" He laughed softly. "How late is your after-dinner date, old buddy?"

Palmer thought for a moment. Burns was always fairly persistent when he wanted to meet, but rarely this much. "Where can I call you around eight tonight?" he asked then.

"Home. But I'm leaving for Albany at nine."

"All right," Palmer said. "I'll call and let you know when I can see you."

"Crazy," Burns said in mock admiration. "Talk to you, doll," he added by way of closing the conversation.

"Good-by." Palmer hung up and grimaced at Burckhardt. "He pooh-poohs it. Offered to plant an item directly countering it."

"Good. Let him." The older man walked back to a chair and sat down with a thud that forced him to exhale breath on the last word, turning it into a small explosion.

"Bad idea. I have difficulty following Burns, as a political mentor. But one thing he's taught me: never look like a winner. Play it humble."

"Uhn. What was that little argument between the two of you?" Burckhardt wanted to know. "Why can't you meet the man if he asks you?"

"I am," Palmer said, borrowing Burns's lazy, innocent air.

"But you made him beg for it."

"I don't think I've ever put this in plain words before, but I don't trust Mac Burns."

"Why?"

"I think he's working for Jet-Tech."

Burckhardt's milky-blue eyes widened. "Nonsense."

"It's only a hunch. But until he changes my mind for me, I'm going to be wary as hell of him."

"Don't be a Goddamned . . ." The older man floundered around for a phrase. "A Goddamned intelligence spy."

"I'm meeting him, aren't I?"

Burckhardt looked pained. He stood up slowly. In contrast with a few minutes before, his movements now were almost creaky. For a man who kept so blatantly in shape, Palmer saw, Burckhardt was beginning to act his age. The starch seemed to have dissolved out of him, but whether it was the slowly mounting tension of the weeks to come or the immediate tension of the item in the *Bulletin*, Palmer could not tell.

"I intend to get up to Albany next week," Palmer said then, realizing that he was mollifying the old bird, "when the Banks Committee reports the bill out on the floor. I'll be in Utica first and then in Rochester. I'll probably get back to Albany by Thursday."

Burckhardt nodded slowly. "I wish to hell I could keep up with it, Woody," he said in an undertone, as if afraid of being heard. "Last year I did all right. Took a lot out of me, but it was worth it. This year . . . ?" He turned toward the door, then wheeled back and stared fiercely at Palmer. "That's why I've got you, this year, sonny-boy," he snapped in a pretty fair imitation of the authentic Burckhardt style. "You better not bobble this. If I could stop them last year, old as I am, I expect you to clobber hell out of the bastards. And if you don't, my friend, you can say good-by to Ubco."

Palmer stood up as slowly as the older man had, but with a smooth display of leg-muscle strength, deliberately drawing out the movement to illustrate the contrast between them.

"I can say good-by right now," he suggested coldly.

"Don't get on your high horse, for Christ's sake."

"I'm serious."

"Ah, the hell you are." Burckhardt turned toward the door. "Jesus," he mumbled, more to himself than to Palmer, "never hire anybody who's independently wealthy." He stopped at the door and opened it. "On the other hand," he said then in a low but carrying voice, "if you clobber them, Woody, something very interesting will happen to you."

"What?"

Burckhardt closed the door. "I'm exercising my voluntary retirement clause at the end of this year."

"The hell you are," Palmer snapped back, grinning at him.

"The hell I'm not. Doctor's orders."

"What could a doctor ever make you do?"

"Slow up, for one thing." Burckhardt's hand, almost as if he hadn't noticed it, crept toward his left breast. "Relax, for another."

"And why, all of a sudden, are you taking his advice?"

Burckhardt's mouth twisted sideways. "Figure it out for yourself."

Palmer waved a hand at him in disbelief. "Lane, this is Palmer. The carrot works with donkeys, not with me."

"I'm retiring, Woody, and that's that."

"And the board will replace you with me." Palmer shook his head. "Look, I know all about motivating a staff to keep them hopping. Don't waste your time with me, Lane. I'm already hopping."

Burckhardt's grin was lopsided. "Then hop to it, sonny." He straightened up, opened the door and left.

Palmer stood there for a long moment, trying to decide whether or not the whole thing had been an act, including Burckhardt's pitiable feebleness. He soon came to the conclusion that, with Burckhardt, anything was possible. Sitting down, he dialed Virginia on the PBX phone.

"Public Relations, Miss Clary's office."

"Is she there?"

"One moment, please, Mr. Palmer," the girl said, stressing his name so that it carried to the next desk where Virginia sat.

"Yes, Mr. Palmer," Virginia said, coming on the line.

"Would you drop in a moment?"

When she came in the door of his office, he saw that she was wearing a new dress, or at least one he had never seen before. He signaled her to close the door behind her. He watched the way her breasts pushed out against the soft, knitted material of the dress as she twisted sideways.

"Want you to read an item and tell me what you think," he said as she sat down opposite him.

"The one in the *Bulletin* this morning?"

"God, you're too sharp for words."

She smoothed the dress down along her thighs. "Oh?"

"Stop it. What did you think of the item?"

She watched him for a moment, her large dark eyes traveling slowly from his face to his hands and back. "It's probably true."

"Mac Burns doesn't think so. Says it's just a plant by the opposition."

"I'm sure it is," she agreed. "That doesn't stop it from being true." She picked up the newspaper and tapped her knee with it. "They've hired Sydney Baron to do their p.r., you know. He's a very savvy operator."

"As savvy as Mac?"

"Probably. But no matter how good you are in the p.r. business, you murder yourself if you feed enough phony information to the press. You can get away with it a few times and then you're dead. That's why I feel the item's a plant, but true."

"I see. Is there any way to check it?"

"Not without a lot of trouble."

Palmer pushed his phone across the desk to her. "Go ahead. Take a lot of trouble."

Virginia thought for a moment. Then she punched the button that gave her a direct outgoing line, unmonitored by the switchboard, and dialed a number.

"Calling the *Bulletin?*" Palmer asked.

She shook her head. "My contacts are lousy there. I'm calling the *Star*. It's significant that they didn't run the item. If anybody planted it, they'd have tried the *Star* first to— Hello? Is Cathcart in town or up in Albany? I see. Thank you." She hung up for a moment, then dialed three numbers. "Person to person to Arthur J. Cathcart in Albany, New York. You can try him in the capitol press office." She gave the number she was calling from and sat there, waiting.

"I'm beginning to get it now," Palmer said.

"May I have a cigarette?" Palmer offered her the pack. "Light it for me, please?"

Palmer did so, smiling slightly, and handed the cigarette to her. She started to say something, then stopped, nodded twice and said, into the phone: "Arthur J.? Ginnie Clary. Awful. How's yourself? Is that a fact, now? You see what Jimmy had in his column this morning? About the savings banks' branch bill? Of course you read the *Bulletin*, Arthur. That's where you get your stories for tomorrow from. Arthur! Look, did anyone peddle that item to you first? Are you absolutely sure? What? Well, put him on."

She looked up at Palmer and winked. Covering the phone, she murmured: "Nobody tried to feed it to the *Star*. But the *Bulletin* guy is there now and—" She uncovered the phone.

"Hello, Jim. Fine. Fine but baffled. Jim, that savings-bank item this morning. Yes. No. I'd like to know the source, if you feel up to revealing it. Who? You're kidding. Why? Oh. Oh. Thanks, Jim. Don't get in any pinochle games with shifty Arthur. Good-by, dear."

She replaced the phone and frowned as she looked down at it. "Let me tell you," Palmer offered. "Mac Burns planted the item."

Her eyes lifted suddenly. "That's right," she said in an amazed tone.

"What reason did he give?"

"That he didn't want it to look like a shoo-in for our side. He wanted the issue to look in doubt."

"And on the strength of that the *Bulletin* printed it?"

"On the strength of that and their knowledge that there was more truth than poetry to the thing." She paused for a moment. "But here's the funny thing, Woods. Mac gave him the item two days ago, by phone from New York. That's why Jimmy believed it. He figured it this way: Burns is close to Culhane. He's calling from the city because he's just gotten wind that all is not well within the organization. It's not sure it can hold its legislators in line behind the commercial banks."

"He told you all this over the phone?"

"No. But I can guess the rest."

"Didn't it bother Jimmy that Burns is supposed to be on the commercial-bank side?"

"Not at all. Public-relations people do that, Woods. If they have a hot item —no matter who it helps or hurts—they may feed it to a favorite newspaper-man. He's indebted to them for an exclusive. At some future date, when they need a plug for a client, he comes through for them."

"I see." Palmer watched her inhale cigarette smoke and slowly let it out again. "So Burckhardt was right. In this town, only the paranoids usually are. Where there's smoke, by God, there's fire."

"It looks that way. Burns needs Jimmy, not just now but for years to come. He wouldn't plant a phony item and ruin the relationship."

333

Palmer nodded. He sank back in his chair and swiveled it left and right a few degrees as he thought. Then: "No. You're wrong. So's Burckhardt. I was right to begin with. It's a trial balloon. Burns is sending it up to see what happens. Meanwhile, he's busy making it come true. First he plants the seed of doubt in the minds of Tammany legislators. Then he gets to work convincing them that the item they read is true. That their voters are for more savings-bank branches. That they'd better reverse themselves and fight for the bill."

Virginia stared disgustedly at the tip of her cigarette. "I'm afraid it all makes great sense. Except . . . except why Mac is doing this to us."

"You know my theory. He's planned to do this from the beginning."

"Yes, I know your theory." She turned her glance toward him and studied his eyes for a moment. "I know all your theories. Will I see you tonight?"

"I thought—"

"That I wanted to call it all off? I do. But not yet."

"I'm glad to know it."

"You cold fish," she said sweetly. "You haven't given it a single thought since whenever it was . . . last Friday night."

"You're wrong about that."

"Tell me you've thought of nothing else."

"I've thought of a lot of things. And of you."

"How's my billing? Fifth from the top? Right after Fink's Mules?"

"Virginia," he said, "you give away your age too readily. Fink's Mules. Do you remember the whistling of Elmo Tanner? Henry Busse and his Shuffle Rhythm?"

"Darling, that's the new stuff. Did you ever see me do a hot Maxixe?"

"If you're free tonight you might show me."

"Where?"

"I don't know. I'm calling Burns at eight. He wants to see me for a minute or two."

"At his apartment?"

"Yes. Unfortunately, he's leaving for Albany at nine."

"That's terrible," she said. "You sort of hang around to finish your drink there. I'll call you at nine-fifteen. If he's left we can schedule a Maxixe lesson."

"I don't know," he mused. "I sort of wanted to brush up on my Black Bottom."

She got to her feet. "Sometimes your remarks border on the obscene."

"That's interesting country down there around the border."

She started for the door. "Your conversation is fascinating. Tiny intimations of obscenity lurk within its bland depths like . . . uh, truffles in *pâté*."

He stared thoughtfully at the middle distance. "Nobody knows," he announced calmly, "the truffles obscene."

She slammed the door slightly as she left. He wheeled about slowly in his swivel chair and let his eyes unfocus as they watched the closed door.

He thought about tonight, the two of them alone in Burns's apartment. Fragments of scenes jittered across the inner eye of his mind, projected on the blank door like a badly cut stag movie. He blinked and tried to change reels. One could not expect to have a calm, productive day if the morning featured short subjects like these.

He finally managed to suppress the recollections by thinking hard about what he would tell Edith as an excuse for coming home late tonight.

CHAPTER FIFTY

Palmer arrived at Burns's apartment shortly after eight-fifteen that night. He found the publicist freshly shaved and dressed, a small two-suiter case lying packed but open on the foyer table. "Help yourself to a drink, Woody," Burns said as he escorted him into the main room. "My car's picking me up in fifteen minutes. I have to be at Westchester Airport by nine-thirty."

"Is that where you get an Albany plane?"

"It's one of these small airlines," Burns explained, walking into his bedroom. "I don't mind, though. Little old planes are a hell of a lot safer than the new jets."

"Possibly." Palmer made himself a very light Scotch drink. "Want a drink?" he called into the bedroom.

"Crazy, dad," Burns said. "One for the road."

Palmer made him a stiff drink and set it on the counter of the bar. "What did you want to see me about, Mac?"

"Don't you figure it's time we had a talk?" Burns asked, coming back into the room. He carried a small sheaf of papers which he deposited on the foyer table. "Sort of buddy-to-buddy?"

"Any time, buddy."

"That's the ticket." Burns returned, picked up his drink and sat down on the couch. "Cheers."

"Cheers."

They drank. A silence dropped down over them. Palmer could hear the traffic from the East River Drive below them. He turned and looked out the window at the Queensboro Bridge, twinkling coldly in the up-draft of warmer traffic fumes.

"We checked the man on the *Bulletin*," he said then.

"Jimmy?" Burns sounded off-hand. "Any clues?"

"One." Palmer sighed softly, turned and sat down across from Burns. "The name of his source."

"Jimmy gave you that?" The yellow eyes looked mildly interested. "Oh. I get it. He told Ginnie Clary."

"But here's the funny part," Palmer went on. "I already knew."

"Did you." A polite statement, not a question.

Burns's hands moved sideways to pick up his drink. Light glittered in the facets of his cuff links. He made an amused face, his thin lower lip half pouting. "You're about as sharp as they come, huh, Woody?"

"Not half as sharp as you, Mac."

"I'm so sharp I want the name Jimmy gave you. Just to make sure there aren't any little tricks."

"He gave us the name of Mac Burns," Palmer said, letting some of his irritation curdle the edge of his voice. "Now that you know it's not a bluff, I'd like to hear a few well-chosen words from you on the subject."

Burns frowned studiously. "Well, to begin with, Jimmy has a big mouth." "Continue."

"That's for openers," Burns said. He was silent for a moment. "Woody, why do you think I wanted to see you tonight? I knew you'd get to the bottom of that item in the *Bulletin*. Or guess. Either way I wanted to explain it to you."

"Commendable. Now explain."

"When you've been in politics as long as I have," Burns went on smoothly, "you know that there's a certain point in a campaign where you need a touch of uncertainty. It makes your own people work harder and it lulls the opposition a little. More than that, it puts the people solidly behind you because you don't look big any more. And God knows they sympathize with an underdog."

"Interesting," Palmer said dryly. "You hope to convince them that the commercial banks, those bloated titans of capitalism, are underdogs."

"You can convince people of anything, doll."

"No."

"Oh, yes."

Palmer shook his head. "Don't distract me, Mac. Let's keep to the point. The *Bulletin's* political writer is no novice. The only way you got him to use the item was because he suspected it was true." He sipped his drink slowly. "Is it?"

Burns turned his hands palms up. "Damned if I know."

"That's a stupid answer," Palmer snapped. "And you're anything but stupid. Let's get to the basic point, Mac. If the item isn't true, the publication of it will go a long way toward making it come true. With your help. So the fundamental issue is this: why are you knifing us?"

"Knifing you?" Burns's tawny eyes grew round. "For Christ's sake, Woody, that's the second of these Goddamned innuendoes. I'm getting—"

"You call that innuendo?" Palmer interrupted. "How plain shall I make it?

336

I think Jet-Tech's gotten to you. It wouldn't surprise me to learn they had you in their pocket before Ubco ever retained you. Do you want it any plainer?"

Burns jumped to his feet and brushed past Palmer as he walked to the window. He turned with theatrical effect, framed by the window as if by a proscenium arch. His narrow face had grown even sharper. "Woody, I have a boiling point like anybody else. You push me too far and I'll—"

"What does it take to push you too far, Mac?"

"One more hare-brained accusation." Burns's lower lip looked as hard as a knotted muscle.

"I've got several. Give me a second to pick the right one."

Palmer watched Burns's normally sallow coloring. The winter months had caused his tan to fade, but beneath the skin a hot redness began to suffuse through Burns's cheeks and forehead.

"Palmer," Burns said then in a thin tone, "you've had a hard-on for me right from the beginning, like that constipated boss of yours. You never did trust me, did you?"

"Wrong. I trusted you until, oh, a few weeks ago." Palmer sipped his drink again. "Even so, I wasn't convinced until today. Until I finally figured out exactly why you planted that item."

"But that's not the reason," Burns burst out. "You're guessing, and you're guessing wrong. I've told you my reason. Why can't you believe it?"

"I'd like to."

"Trust me, Woody." Burns's thin hands went out in front of him, cuff links sparkling wildly. "My God, we've got to trust each other."

"I'll trust you when you level with me."

"I am."

"Try it," Palmer suggested. "Try a little plain talk. Tell me what's really happening inside the downstate organization."

Burns's mouth, open to say something, remained silently open. He watched Palmer for a moment. Then his mouth closed, his hands fell to his sides and he walked back to the couch. Sitting down, he resumed drinking. He laughed softly to himself. "Is it possible for one newcomer to be so bright?" he asked the air next to him on the couch. "Or is that Clary chick feeding him lines?"

"She feeds me information," Palmer said, "which is more than I get from my fifty-thousand-a-year counselor."

Burns put down his glass and hunched forward over his knees, his fingers linked and hanging between his legs as he stared at them with a mournful look. "So all right," he said in a softer voice. "The natives are a little restless downstate. The trouble's starting in Brooklyn and Queens."

"Ah. You're about to tell me that I'm responsible for all of it. My speech the other night soured them?"

"More or less," Burns agreed. "I don't know if the speech hurt that much. They were lined up against you before you ever showed there. But the speech didn't help a whole bunch."

"If I'd been meek and humble, they'd have swung into line?"

"N-no," Burns admitted grudgingly. "It'd take more than that."

"Outright offer of money?"

"Not that. But something like it."

Palmer sat back in his chair and watched the corn-colored top of Burns's head. For a moment he was tempted to ask if it would have made a difference to the audience in Brooklyn had he been either Catholic or Jewish. Although he was tempted, he realized that he could only ask that of a friend or ally, not of someone in as suspect a position as Burns.

"Then let me summarize a little, Mac," he said instead. "We still have our upstate Republican majority at Albany. But now we're losing our Democratic support. Is that it?"

"I wouldn't go that far. You haven't lost too much downstate yet."

"I'm glad to hear that. It means that even if we lose most of it, we can still stop the branch bill. The Republican majority will swamp it."

Burns lifted his head and stared gloomily at Palmer. "I haven't given you the whole picture, Woody," he said in a low voice. "I'm getting rumors from upstate that worry me."

Palmer sat foward. "What rumors? From whom?"

"Vic Culhane has men up there. The word we get is that some of the smaller commercial banks are swinging over into the savings-bank camp. They have nothing to lose because they're small. And they hate the big downstate commercial banks anyway."

"That doesn't make sense!" Palmer nearly shouted. "They depend on us. We do their correspondence banking for them. We buy their mortgages. We handle their investment portfolios. Good God, we get them World Series tickets, tickets for Broadway shows. When they come to town they loll around in a lavish private office of ours, transacting their own business. We do everything but burp them."

Burns smiled very softly. "You're their Big Daddy, aren't you?" he suggested. "And how does Junior ever feel about Big Daddy?" His eyes glittered. "Or wouldn't you know?"

Palmer let out a long, pent-up breath. He rubbed his left temple, feeling a vein or tendon or something twitch beneath his hand. "Tell me the whole thing, Mac."

Burns nodded. "I am. For real, now. This is the word we get. At the moment it doesn't amount to much. A few little banks upstate. But they show signs of getting together among themselves. And that, old buddy, would be the finish."

Palmer made a face. Burns glanced at his watch. "Shoving-off time, Woody. You stick around, finish your drink. I'll hop up to Albany and put out a few fires."

"Stay away from these little upstate banks."

"That's your department, baby."

338

"Right. I've got this swing through Utica and Rochester next week. I'll rent a car and do it on the road. Drop in and talk to them."

"You think that'll help?"

"Why not?"

"All right," Burns said, moving toward the entrance foyer. "But just to show you I'm on your side, sweetie, take a word of advice from your fifty-thousand-a-year counselor. Bring along a pair of slacks and a sports shirt. The older the better, but clean. Don't show up there in that J. Press sack suit with the thin tie and the tab-collar shirt. You dig?"

Palmer nodded. "The humility bit," he said with distaste.

"Old shoes, old sports jacket. You got a pipe?"

"No."

"Get one." Burns laughed. "Man, you should see your face now. You are a study." He closed and locked his two-suiter. "It's a lucky thing I like you, doll. Otherwise I'd be mad as hell at you."

"How come you like me so much, Mac?"

Burns opened the door. "Because, way down deep, old buddy, I'm just as arrogant as you." He smiled as he went out and closed the door behind him.

Palmer walked back into the living room, glancing at his watch. He had a lot of time before Virginia called him. He took his half-empty glass and poured a stiff shot of whisky into it, then stood at the window staring out at the bridge.

It led to Queens, and from there to Long Island, one of the storm centers of the whole savings-bank battle. And yet, Palmer asked himself, would it be much of a battle at all if Jet-Tech weren't stirring it up?

He lifted the glass to his lips and found that he was drinking almost straight whisky, barely chilled by the ice. But there was no reason, he told himself, why he should limit his intake. He had nothing ahead of him this evening but pleasure, a pleasure he would enjoy all the more if the acuteness of his inhibitions were blunted slightly by alcohol.

Palmer had not really wondered about Virginia's eagerness to see him again. In part this was because he had not really believed her the other night when she had said she would be better off not seeing him any more. It was probably, he reflected, a simple matter of resources. She had none. No strong prior emotional attachments. No genuine hope of them. She had launched herself into this affair much the way he had, on impulse, without preparation, from a position of total vulnerability.

If they ended the affair, Palmer saw now, she had nowhere to turn, nor did he. He had his family. But this was no more an emotional resource for him than her mother was for Virginia. Both of them had reached out for each other on the spur of the moment, led to the act by a combination of circumstances, by a similar hunger, by the small beginnings of a feeling of attraction. And, because their hunger was great, they dispensed with the polite formalities of prolonged flirtation.

339

Palmer watched what seemed in the darkness to be a small tugboat racing downriver, an immense plume of foam boiling up at its blunt bow as it shoved through the black water.

He smiled crookedly, thinking that, in their unwillingness to wait, he and Virginia were like the rest of the world, those millions who wanted their luxuries now and overextended themselves to satisfy their hunger quickly.

Palmer's eyes unfocused as he stared out the window. He was trying to look into, or listen to, or touch or smell the state of his emotions. He wondered if there were a way to know them as surely as a doctor with a stethoscope knew the beat of a heart. He asked himself if he felt . . . overextended? Was he really spending any emotion? Was his own supply of it diminished?

He closed his eyes and pressed his forehead against the cold glass. It would be a terrible confession, he realized now, if he had done everything—the lies to Edith, the adulterous betrayal of her, the pillage of Virginia's emotions—and felt, at heart, nothing.

There was a small, discreet knock at the door. Once, then twice. Palmer opened his eyes and wheeled around.

He felt an unreasoning surge of anger. Some idiot, some meddling idiot, was going to interrupt now, complicating his plans, making trouble. Some delivery boy, doorman, someone who— Or was it Burns?

Palmer's mouth flattened. If this was Burns, how could he answer Virginia's phone call later? Burns would answer the phone. Would she recognize his voice and hang up without speaking? Would she call back later? Or was the evening completely lost?

Palmer strode to the door. "Who is it?"

A mumbled sound, low-pitched and meaningless. He made an irritated face, fumbled with the lock and opened the door. Virginia stood there.

"I saw him leave. I've been watching this place like a private eye and it's cold outside."

Palmer found himself unable to speak. He pulled her inside and closed the door, then latched the chain. All he could do then was to look at her and feel a tremendous sense of relief sweep through him.

"Hey," she said. "Hello?"

Palmer swallowed. "Hello. I . . . I thought it . . . I thought he'd come back."

"Good Lord, I hope not." She cupped the side of his face in the palm of her hand, cold from the outside air. "I made discreet inquiries earlier in the day. He has a reservation on a nine-forty flight to Albany. Out of Westchester Airport."

"Wonderful."

"Did I frighten you? I'm sorry."

"No. I mean, yes. I was afraid it was someone else. And . . ." His voice died away. For a moment he decided to let his statement stand at that. Then

340

he understood, probably for the first time in his life, that it could do him no harm to tell her the truth, no harm to him and some good to her.

"And I was afraid," he went on in a stronger voice, "that something would prevent me from seeing you tonight." He held her by the waist. "I was very unhappy at the thought."

Her face, somewhat wary as she listened, softened now. "That's no way for a cold fish to feel," she said in a low, happy voice.

"It's the way I felt."

"How flattering." Her arms went around his neck. "How lovely." Her lips were cold against his, with the deep chill of the wintry outside air. As they kissed, he felt her mouth grow warm. A line of tension shot down his body and looped up through his groin. At the same time, he found himself wondering if he had been unhappy, or merely irritated. After a moment, however, he stopped wondering at all.

His fingers began to undo her coat, creeping between their bodies and working with excruciating slowness. As he freed the last button and swept the coat off her shoulders, the phone rang.

He stepped away from her. The phone rang twice more. "Outside call," she whispered. "Don't answer."

"He knows I'm here. If it's him," Palmer whispered.

"To hell with him, or any of his friends," Virginia suggested in a low voice. Her breath tickled the inner channel of his ear. "This always happens, anyway," she said. "Remember? Somebody always calls him when we're here. Forget it."

After the fifth ring the phone stopped. Palmer stood there for a moment, motionless, as if expecting it to ring again. Virginia opened his coat and slid it off onto the floor. "Come along," she said, taking his hand. "Quickly."

CHAPTER FIFTY-ONE

Palmer dozed for a very brief moment. Virginia lay motionless beside him for a while, and, when she stirred slightly, he awoke at once, but smoothly, without being startled. He lay perfectly still, eyes closed, his breathing regular but deep. When she stirred again, searching for something, he continued to lie without moving. He had no idea why.

After a moment he heard his lighter make its small, rasping click. Then he smelled cigarette smoke. "Are you awake?" she whispered very softly.

Palmer's breathing remained slow and deep. A few moments later she slid gently off the bed. He could hear her blow out what must be cigarette smoke. He opened his eyes a fraction of an inch and watched her naked body at the window a few feet away. She had pulled back one of the draperies and was staring at something outside. The diffused light through the open door from the living room illuminated her body without casting shadows, except for the deep cleft between her buttocks.

In a kind of watchful repose now, attention focused outside the room, unaware of his scrutiny, she seemed much different. He found himself wondering why.

It might be, Palmer told himself, that he rarely caught her in repose of any kind. Even when she was sitting—at a desk, for example—he could not possibly think of her as being at rest. Something about her, perhaps the movement of her eyes, or the way she spoke, told him that she was definitely in motion. And this, he decided, was nearly always true of her. She gave off a dynamic kind of tension.

But now, he realized, he could not see her eyes, nor would she speak, for fear of waking him. He was seeing her as she might be when alone in her room, one elbow on the wall next to the window, her weight resting entirely on one leg while the other crossed in front of it at a relaxed angle. He could see the sole of her foot, the concave line of the arch, the slight callous at the back of her heel. He noticed, for the first time, that her feet were very narrow, even the one that bore her weight.

She sighed softly and Palmer tried to evaluate the sound. He decided it was compounded of a certain past satisfaction and a present unwillingness to be alone and at rest. Of all the ways in which she resembled him, she was perhaps most similar in her inability to relax, completely relax and let every thought drop away.

Palmer thought now that perhaps this was an unhappy corollary of intelligence. He lay there, his eyes roving over her legs and back, indulging in the kind of half-thinking that follows pleasant exertion.

Although he enjoyed watching her body, he found his eyes closing. He could almost feel his thinking grow even drowsier and less linked to reality.

He wondered what it would be like to marry her.

There would be all the trouble of a divorce, of course. But Edith and he both came from a milieu where divorce was no novelty. His own parents had never married again, but his Uncle Hanley, now nearing seventy, had only recently married his third wife, a lady of fifty-five. Edith's younger sister, now single, had muddled her way through two marriages. Her Aunt Jane had been the focus of a particularly scandalous divorce. She had been named corespondent by the wife of another man, a fact which did nothing good for Jane's own marriage. She and her lover had got their divorces within a few months of each other but, for some reason, had felt no great urge to marry. The man drifted off with someone else. Jane remained single for a while and then married and divorced a man from New Orleans, all in less than a year. Finally, with an attorney from Boston whom no one really knew, she now seemed to have a lasting marriage. He was in some sort of government work now and . . .

Palmer pulled his thoughts back onto whatever poorly marked track they had been following. Edith, he told himself muzzily, would not make any great fuss about a divorce, nor would she set down impossibly stringent stipulations about his seeing the children.

Virginia would have to leave her job at the bank, of course. For that matter, Palmer realized, he might be asked to leave, too.

Hazily now, he began to analyze the condition of his estate. Assuming that half of it, in lump sum or scheduled pay-outs, would satisfy Edith—in addition to the house, and, of course, the various trust funds for herself and the children—was there enough left to live on? What could a man and woman live on, in comfort, as an absolute minimum? He had no idea. Ten thousand? Twenty? Would they travel a lot after he resigned his job? Probably. They might settle abroad. Spain, perhaps, or a Mediterranean island.

He tried to picture them on a curving, ancient beach, surrounded by the deep teal of the sea. He found it impossible to visualize. A city was the only feasible background for two people who could not, by any stretch of the imagination, hope to vegetate on some remote Riviera. City living was expensive. Forty thousand a year? And, Palmer told himself, he was going to live for at least thirty more years. That meant more than a million dollars of expense. He could never count on that much after a divorce. Lower sights. The interest on a quarter of a million would give him as much as $12,500 a year. At the same time, he would liquidate $12,500 of principal per year for a total annual income of $25,000. As interest on his diminishing principal grew smaller, he would liquidate larger amounts of principal, working toward total pauperism in thirty years. But, meanwhile, having $25,000 per annum on which to—

He forced his thoughts back on the track again. Drawing on principal was depressing enough, as a concept. There had to be another way.

Of course, if he and Virginia didn't marry after the divorce, his income from Ubco would generously cover everything. They would wait, patiently, for several years. Then, when they married, there could be no onus attached to it. He would remain at Ubco. He could certainly ask Virginia to wait a few years during which their meetings would continue to remain as discreet as they were now.

Palmer wondered what it would be like to be married to Virginia. He felt quite sure that her sexual appetite would remain keen. His own, he was certain, would match hers. Of course, there was a difference between a few hours of pleasure now and then and the prospect of decades of steady fornication.

Realizing that he had no real experience through which he might anticipate the effect of such a situation, Palmer felt a faint stirring of uneasiness. Life with Edith had always been, even at the beginning, sexually uneventful. Once a week, more or less, had been the tempo of their life together.

There had never been such a thing as spontaneous sex between them, Palmer recalled now. The thing had been put on almost a scheduled basis, usually falling on a Friday or a Saturday, since they could sleep late the next morning. None of this had been agreed upon, he remembered. It had just happened, through a process of trial and error, of his asking and of her refusing, politely, with many a good reason, except on a weekend. And then, of course, there were the unforeseen complications. Edith thought it unwise when either of them had a cold, for example, a touch of indigestion or a headache. Then, too, she had been active in a number of philanthropic organizations. The meetings and affairs of these groups, added to the P.-T.A. meetings that came later, soon put the whole business of fornication in a sub-category of their lives, on a par with seeing an occasional legitimate play or inviting relatives to dinner.

By the time they had come to New York, Palmer saw, the pattern had become so ingrained that, even without the charitable groups and the P.-T.A., life always presented a variety of activities more important than sex. Edith's supervision of the house remodeling, for example, had completely ruled out sex, except for one night in October, since their arrival in New York. His own absence during so many evenings, of course, had helped immeasurably, even before Virginia. But, as he lay there between wakefulness and sleep, Palmer found himself wondering whether he would have stayed out so often or so late if there had been anything vitally interesting to which he could hurry home.

He started to sigh, then checked himself, still enough awake to remember that he was supposed to be sleeping, as far as Virginia knew. He opened his eyes slightly and saw that she had hardly moved at all from the window.

As he watched her, Palmer compared her full, curving hips and ample breasts with Edith's boyish figure. Neither woman had any unnecessary fat, but Edith's breasts were small, with flat nipples set in small orange-brown circles. Virginia's breasts were quite full, startlingly so in a woman so much shorter than Edith, and her nipples stood erect in the center of large pink aureoles. Their erectness, of course, was only the result—

Palmer closed his eyes and tried to keep his thoughts in some kind of order. It was not possible, he saw now, to blame Edith for everything. She was, in her own Vogue-model way, a very attractive woman. The fact that she held no real sexual excitement for him was, in part, the result of all the evenings when he had returned home late and, before that, in Chicago, all those nights when he had let her put him off with ridiculous excuses. For the fact, Palmer understood now, was that he had never pressed the issue. Edith had no way of knowing, no more than he had until Virginia showed it to him, how strong his sexual appetite could be, or how important the satisfaction of it could become.

Which led one to wonder, Palmer told himself, how strong a drive sex really was. Was it strong enough, for example, to force him into leaving Edith? Was it so powerful that it could provide a reason for spending the rest of his life with Virginia? He felt the corners of his mouth twist very slightly. The drowsy stranger in his brain was quite amusing.

He came suddenly awake now, as though some thin, icy liquid had poured into his veins, sluicing through the luxuriously sluggish river there. Palmer could picture himself quite clearly. He lay there on one side, like a naked, fallen tree on which a parasitic version of himself had suddenly taken root. The stranger had feasted on him, the other self, sex-driven. But he was wide awake now. It was even an effort to keep his eyes shut.

Was it possible, he wondered, that anybody could have let his mind drift so far out of its own control that it slipped into the control of the testes? All that rubbishy nonsense, the carving up of the estate, the fiddling about with principal and interest. Could he have possibly, with any degree of serious-ness, actually pictured himself liquidating principal?

He let his eyes open part way, as if to reassure himself that he was back among real things again. He glanced at the window. Virginia seemed not to have moved.

Through all the teeming idiocy of his demented thoughts, her body had remained a few feet from him, almost as he remembered it last, weight shifted onto one foot, the shadowless light from the door turning the swelling mounds of her buttocks a soft pink and the valley between them a darker rose.

A thick, viscous flow of heat enveloped him. He swallowed, forcing saliva down his dry throat. He could feel the first stirrings in his groin and for an instant he was horrified, but only for an instant.

The syrupy heat surged lazily through his veins. He swung slowly off the bed in a kind of turning fall, his hands outstretched to cushion himself. He was on his hands and knees now. She had heard the sound. She was starting to turn toward him. Her breasts, swinging into the light, seemed to blind him for an instant like a great bursting light behind his eyes. He raised his head and slowly kissed the soft, smooth inner curve of her thigh.

345

Palmer had wanted to take her home by cab. But it was already six-thirty in the morning and so he agreed, reluctantly, to let her leave Burns's building ahead of him. After fifteen minutes spent in turning the apartment into a "clean house," Palmer made his way down the elevator to the basement and out a side-street door. He found a cab turning in off the East River Drive, with an irate driver who had taken a fare to Idlewild but had no return passenger. Palmer listened to the man's bitter complaints all the way to the house with the pierced-concrete façade.

He let the cab get out of sight before he entered the house. The street was silent, the air bitterly cold. The sky, although it showed faint signs of the dawning sun, hung like a dense, dull sheet of lead.

The same questionable light, almost as gray as the sky from which it came, filtered into the huge, empty living room as Palmer hung up his coat, hat and muffler. Everything about him looked stark. The warm natural oak of the curving staircase seemed muddy in this ugly light. On the second floor he paused for a moment to remove his shoes, wondering why life always imitated the comic strips.

He removed his outer clothes in the bathroom next to the master bedroom. He toyed with the, at first, wild idea of pretending he had just got up. It would not be too difficult if Edith were still asleep. All he really had to do was to muss up his bed, then return to the bathroom, turn on the shower and let it waken her as the day began.

He looked into the bedroom. Edith seemed to be sleeping. His bed had been turned back. He padded on bare feet to it, removing his undershirt as he did so. Then he rumpled his pillow and blankets with slow, careful motions.

Back in the bathroom, he took off his shorts and looked at himself for a moment in the full-length mirror. It had been Edith's idea to install one here. She felt sure it would go a long way toward helping both of them watch their weight. All it gave Palmer now was the startling information that he bore a livid bite just below his navel. He examined it more closely and found that it was not possible to tell, from the mark, what had actually caused it. Nodding almost sagely, he turned on the one-handled control of the shower,

346

setting it halfway between warm and cool. Hissing filled the room. He stepped into the shower and began to soap himself.

He had finished, dried himself and put on a bathrobe when Edith appeared at the door, drowsy, a frown producing two vertical wrinkles between her almost invisible eyebrows.

"Good morning," Palmer said softly.

"Um. When in God's name did you get in?"

He studied her light, hazel eyes. Without make-up they looked smaller, almost bleached out. Instinctively, he parried. "What's wrong? Did you fall asleep early?"

The non-sequitur confused Edith in her still-sleepy state. "I was still up at one. And you hadn't come in."

"You couldn't have been up at two," Palmer said then. "You were dead to the world."

If Edith noticed that he hadn't actually answered her original question, she gave no sign. Instead, she moved toward the double sink, hand stretched out for her toothbrush. When she began brushing her teeth, Palmer wet his shaving brush and worked up a lather in the soap cup. A faint odor of lavender mixed with the minty smell of toothpaste slowly filled the room. Waffle-surfaced glass panels in the wall glowed faintly orange as the thermostatic control adjusted them against the morning chill. Palmer lathered his face and began shaving. From time to time he glanced at his wife to see if she might be about to resume her questioning. After a while he watched her because he realized he hadn't seen her in quite this way for some time now. When they had been living at the hotel, the bathroom had had room for only one person at a time. Since they'd moved into this house, she had, for some reason, preceded him each morning.

The sensible flannel pajamas hung straight from her shoulders like a maternity jacket. In the soft pink-white glare of the overhead fluorescent fixtures, the green-and-blue Paisley pattern seemed darker than he remembered. She had pulled up the pajama bottoms as high as they would go. Her narrow bare feet and thin ankles looked pinched and cold, despite the radiant heat panels in the walls. As he watched her finish her teeth and wash her face now with some milky fluid from a tall blue bottle, Palmer saw that the motion of her upper trunk was making the pajama pants slide slowly down over her hips. The cuffs began to drape about her feet until only her toes were showing.

"You losing weight?" he asked. When she said nothing, he continued shaving in silence.

Finally: "I hadn't noticed." She dried her face and stepped on the scales. She hitched up her pajamas and stared mutely at the dial for a long time. "No," she announced then. "Why?"

"Either that or the elastic in those pajamas has had it."

"They're twelves," she said, returning to the mirror.

"So?"

347

"That's for length," she explained. "The waist's always been too wide."

"Oh."

"But I've only had this trouble with pajamas for the last twenty years or so," she added then. "It's peculiar of you to notice."

"Don't bark."

"Was that a bark? It sounded fairly even and reasonable to me."

He shaved without speaking for a moment holding his jaw tight as he finished off his chin. Then: "It sounded like a bark."

"Why?"

He gestured aimlessly with the razor. "Just did."

"Edgy this morning?"

"Not particularly."

"Bad night?"

"No worse than any other I've spent with Burns."

"Your branch bill," she said.

"Not mine. The savings banks'. Things are getting sticky upstate."

"That's nothing," she said, "to what's happening to things downstate."

"What?"

"In a room this size it's hard to believe you didn't hear me."

"I heard you. I just don't understand what it means."

"It means things are even stickier in New York City."

He turned to look at her. "What things?"

"All things." She finished making up her face.

"All things?"

"Woods, there is the most boring sort of echo in here." She started out of the room.

"Arf."

"And I can do without that implication too."

"What implication?"

"The female animal that barks," she said, "is the bitch." She left the room. He could hear her banging things in the bedroom. Something dropped on the closet floor with a tremendous clatter. Then the door of the closet slammed shut.

"Easy on the furniture," he called, wiping lather from his face.

She was out of the bedroom by the time he was ready to dress. He pulled on a pair of shorts before taking off his bathrobe, to make sure the bite was hidden. When he walked into the dining room a few minutes later it was deserted, the table unmade. He wandered into the kitchen. Mrs. Gage, in her quilted wrapper with the patchwork roses, was filling a kettle with cold water.

"Good morning. Where's Mrs. Palmer?"

The housekeeper watched him for a moment before answering. "Upstairs. Is my watch wrong? I've got seven-thirty."

He checked his own watch. "That's right."

"You're up early," she said. "Good morning."

Palmer produced an affable smile as he left the room. It didn't necessarily mean anything, he told himself, that he was up earlier than usual. He walked down the long, curving flight of stairs to the front door and opened it. The dead chill of a windless winter morning seemed to soak into him as he looked about the narrow space between the door and the pierced-concrete façade for two newspapers cleverly hidden there. Finding them, he hurried inside and started slowly up the stairs again, reading the Albany dispatch in the *Times*. There seemed to be quite a bit of disputed legislation at the moment, but not a line about the branch bill.

Palmer stood on the second-floor landing as he checked the *Herald-Tribune's* report. Following the newspaper's usual policy, two separate stories split the Albany news between them, one reporting facts, the other delving behind the news. As always, Palmer felt a faint sense of irritation at having to plow through two stories to get the jist of one. Toward the bottom of the interpretative story, however, as it broke to a smaller headline on a later page, he found a potpourri of short italic paragraphs rounding up a variety of rumors.

"No less a source than Victor S. 'Big Vic' Culhane is telling associates there's no truth to the rumored split in solid Tammany opposition to the savings banks' branch bill. His alter ego, publicist Mac Burns, seemingly pleased at events here, has pushed on into rural New York State for a quick swing through the western tier of counties."

Palmer panicked.

Teetering on the top step, he had barely enough presence to grab for the railing, letting both newspapers fall noisily to the floor as he did so. Then he scooped them up and went into the bedroom.

He threw the *Times* down on Edith's bed, then sat on his own, knees tightly pressed together as he tried to decide what to do with the *Herald-Tribune*. For a moment he was so unnerved that he found himself pushing the paper under his blanket. Then he got himself under control and stood up. Moving quietly, he went to the bedroom door, saw that no one was in the hall, and walked quickly down the stairs to the front door. Leaving it open, he walked out into the street. Two men in dark overcoats were walking toward him.

He waited until they had passed. By this time the below-freezing temperature had seeped through his shirt and trousers. He could feel a faint chilly tremor beginning at the pit of his stomach above the diaphragm. He stooped quickly and half-shoved, half-pitched the newspaper under a parked car two doors down the street. Then he hurried back into his house, closed the door and stood there for a while to get warm.

Very calmly now, his breathing hard but under control, he tried to decide which meaning of the item had panicked him more thoroughly, the fact that it proved Burns was really in Albany last night when Edith had been told he was in New York, or the fact that the sneaky little bastard had stolen a march on him and was visiting the rural bankers before Palmer got a chance to.

He started up the stairs for the third time in less than an hour, but now he could hear sounds of pre-breakfast activity. He was fated to solve the problem of the newspaper item in the company of his family, it seemed. He paused halfway up the stairs. He'd got rid of the paper. Edith would be unlikely to go to the trouble of getting another one. So much for that aspect of the problem. But what to do about Burns?

He entered the dining room, to see Gerri setting out silverware. "Hi," she said. "You look like somebody squashed a bug in the palm of your hand."

Palmer winced. "And good morning to you," he said.

Woody came heavily into the room, knotting his tie in place. He sat down at his place, finished off his juice in one long swallow and gasped for air. "Hi, Dad," he said then.

"Morning," Palmer said, trying to keep the sourness out of his voice. He sat down at the head of the table and felt a headache begin its steady pounding throb just above the nape of his neck. He sipped his juice, watching Woody reach for a piece of toast.

"Hold it," he snapped. "We're not all here, yet."

Woody shrugged and caught his sister's eye as she sat down. Whatever he was trying to signal he failed to communicate, since Gerri kept her eyes on her plate.

Tom came in from the kitchen at a slow pace, bent over double to tie a shoe lace as he hobbled along. "You can't do that," Palmer told him. "It's physically impossible."

Tom looked up with an abstracted air. "Huh?" He finished tying his shoe, slid into his seat and duplicated his brother's feat by downing a glass of orange juice in one smooth gulp. He didn't even gasp for air afterwards.

Palmer poured coffee for himself and handed the carafe to Gerri. "Fill your mother's cup."

"Hers runneth over," the girl muttered. "Gall and wormwood. Wormwood and gall."

Palmer closed his eyes for a moment. The headache had spread in the last few moments up the left side of his head to the top of his skull. He opened his eyes, to see Mrs. Gage carry in a chafing dish and set it before him. Palmer lifted the cover and looked at the scrambled eggs. He closed the cover quickly and sipped his coffee. The bitter hot liquid ran down his throat in a fiery thread, as if etching itself into the tender, dry flesh there. Palmer felt as if he had never used the throat before. After a moment, however, and several more sips of coffee, he felt somewhat better.

"Plates, please," he said, picking up the serving spoon.

As the children passed their plates, Edith came in with a platter of bacon, sat down at her place and picked up her coffee. "Thank you, Gerri," she said.

Palmer portioned out the eggs automatically. Years of experience made it possible for him to give each child the right amount—great gobs for Woody, very little for Tom—without thinking about it. "Edith?"

She shook her head. "Just coffee."

Palmer paused for a second. He had no desire to eat anything solid, but after a blameless night he usually ate a fairly substantial breakfast. He would have to do so now. He gave himself a spoonful of eggs, took one rasher of bacon and let both cool for a while on his plate as he tried to finish his coffee. The headache had now spread all the way to his forehead. He could feel it begin to slide sideways into the right half of his skull as well.

He eyed the food on his plate. Then he looked up in time to see Woody finish his eggs and silently pass his plate for a second helping. "Edith," Palmer said in a voice he tried to keep from sounding querulous, "do any of these children remember words like 'please' and 'thank you'?"

"May I have some more eggs, please, Dad?" Woody rattled off in a monotone.

"Thank you for the eggs, Daddy," Tom piped up.

Gerri was chewing thoughtfully. After thoroughly Fletcherizing her food, she swallowed, washed it down with a genteel sip of juice and dabbed at her mouth with a napkin. "I wish to express my profound gratitude," she began, "to both my beloved parents, and especially to the one who so deftly served me my—"

"I withdraw the question," Palmer cut in. He loaded Woody's plate with eggs and handed it to his son. Then he cut into his own scrambled eggs with the side of his fork and managed to convey a bit of them to his mouth.

"I saw the *Times* on my bed," Edith said at that moment. "Have you got the *Trib*?"

The eggs fell off Palmer's fork. He looked up mildly. "The boy only delivered the *Times*."

"Service is so utterly unreliable in New York," Edith said. "Tom, eat."

Musing, Tom continued to examine his reflection in the silver coffee carafe. He lifted the corner of his upper lip in scorn. Then he bugged his eyes, crossing them expertly. "Tom," Palmer said in the flat, almost harsh voice he knew from experience projected very clearly, "eat."

As his youngest son began eating, so did Palmer. The first mouthful of eggs tasted quite good, but the texture gave him some trouble. He liked his eggs scrambled soft. This morning their moistness made him feel suddenly queasy. He turned to Gerri. "What's happening at school?"

"The usual gooky stuff."

Palmer put his fork down as he prepared to deepen the distraction he had just invented. Children should be, and were, a comfort to one's old age, he thought. "To what particular classic of international repute are you referring?" he inquired in a tone that reminded him of Mr. Interlocutor.

"*Madame Bovary*, of course," Gerri said. "In French, yet."

"It's horrible enough in English," Woody put in suddenly. His deeper voice, against the high tones of his brother and sister, reminded Palmer of a Great Dane surrounded by chihuahuas.

"As I recall," Palmer said, pretending to return to his eggs, "it's a fascinating book and a milestone in literature."

"Millstone," Gerri remarked.

"Mills bomb," Woody added gratuitously.

"I mean, look," Gerri continued then, not wanting her older brother to take the conversational lead from her, "all this agony. I mean, she's married to an old foop. It's not as if she was once in love with him or anything. *Quel horeur*. But why carry on so? I mean Leon and she had a good thing there. He's younger than she is, but not by much. And Rodolphe is just the right age. I mean she's got it made. All this business of sinking into debt. Things like that just don't happen. If she couldn't stand Charles she could just up and leave him. I mean, if a marriage has had it, why—?"

"There is a little matter," Palmer said, surprised at the abrupt heaviness in his voice, as if he had caught himself trying to murder a fly by smashing it with a Mack truck, "of her religion forbidding divorce."

"Big deal," Gerri argued. "She could just move out. People do it all the time."

"And what would she live on?" Palmer asked. "In those days there was no question of a settlement or alimony. And they—"

"Let her get a job," Gerri cut in.

"Doing what? What was she trained to do?"

"Embroider."

"What?"

"Crochet. Tat."

Palmer glanced up at Edith. "Gerri," he said slowly, "do your teachers give you any particular background for reading these novels? Or is it just an exercise in reading French?"

"Rodolphe would have been happy to keep her handsomely," Gerri went on thoughtfully. "Or perhaps she'd have been better moving to Rouen and taking a job to be near Leon. Anything but live with Charles. I mean, why should anybody get so desperate in a marriage that the only way out is arsenic? I mean it doesn't make sense."

"Now you said something," Woody muttered.

"Or she could poison Charles," Tom put in then.

Palmer placed his fork beside his plate with a sharp click. The distraction, for what it was worth, had failed. "It's sad to think of poor Flaubert," he said, "muddling through without the kind of help you could have given him."

"Flo who?" Tom asked.

This sent his brother and sister into a kind of giggle duet, Gerri's high, clear laughter and Woody's heavy, hollow guffaws interweaving like a flute and a bassoon. Palmer rubbed his temple. "Excuse me," he said, getting up. "I'll be back in a second."

He looked at himself as he stood before the bathroom mirror and swallowed two aspirin. For a middle-aged man with troubles, he seemed deceptively fit. The skin across his cheekbones looked tighter than usual and a vein in his right temple pulsed visibly, but other than that, Palmer decided, after an athletic night in his mistress's bed and a morning with a nasty surprise, he looked oddly untouched. Ten minutes from now: coronary. He peered unhappily at his reflection. Was she his mistress? he wondered. It had to be the wrong word. Palmer wasn't even sure he could be called her lover. The old cliché relationships didn't work at all any more. And miserable Emma Bovary turned out, finally, to be the victim of unenlightened plot construction.

Hoping for a few moments of relative quiet—fifteen minutes would do—so that the aspirin could get to work, Palmer returned to the breakfast table in time to hear Edith saying:

". . . is a mark of how times have changed, Gerri. She couldn't vote. She couldn't hold property. She was her husband's property, like his house or his horse and buggy. She had no choice at all, except to stay with him."

"No wonder she killed herself," Gerri said.

"She had that choice," Edith agreed. "But nowadays we have a lot of others."

"She had other choices," Woody announced. "She could have run away to America. She could have had the marriage annulled. She—"

"You don't seem to understand what marriage was like in those days," Edith interrupted. "I suppose no one does, any more. People went into it for life."

"Like going into Alcatraz," Gerri mused.

"Some people think marriages were a lot happier then." Edith looked up at Palmer as he arrived at the table. "Now let's finish breakfast quietly. Your father has what looks like a terrible headache."

Palmer stared at her. "How did y—?"

"Of course," Gerri said, "marriages were arranged in those days. Nobody married for love. I expect that's what made the marriages happier." Industriously, she polished off the rest of her eggs in two forkfuls.

CHAPTER FIFTY-THREE

A few weeks later, Lincoln's birthday arrived, on a Friday. The usual subtle pressures that run through the business community whenever a holiday of this kind fell next to a weekend had no effect on the business of banking. Other offices might yield to the pressure and close, Palmer thought as he arrived at his office at eight forty-five, but Lincoln's birthday was not a recognized bank holiday. Since it was not celebrated by banks in the South, Union banks had to remain open for any correspondent business that might trickle up from the Confederacy.

Although Palmer had finished his *Times* on the ride down, he had brought it into the office so that he could study its Albany dispatch again. The state legislature, in a frenzy of sudden activity, had scheduled a brief token session this morning which would allow senators and assemblymen to head home for a longer weekend than usual. One of the two items of business left for this morning, Palmer had noted, was a meeting of the Banks Committee to discuss a curious amendment to the savings banks' branch bill. It had been Burns's idea, earlier in the week, to have such an amendment introduced. Palmer had not been entirely certain of Burns's motives, but on the surface the idea had seemed good.

The original bill hoped to give the savings banks unlimited branch privileges. They would have the right to apply for as many as they wished, but the state banking department would decide whether any of these branch applications were honored. Burns's idea was to limit the branches to an amount equal to the present number of offices each savings bank operated.

As Palmer reread the *Times'* story from Albany, he reflected on the beautiful unscrupulousness of the amendment Burns had got a Brooklyn assemblyman to introduce.

Ostensibly it seemed logical enough: no one really wanted unlimited branch privileges, did they? On examination, however, it was clearly designed to favor the bigger savings banks who had as many as five offices. They could then have ten, while the one-office banks would have only two. This possibility would create dissension in the savings-bank camp, playing big banks against little ones and damaging their hitherto united front.

Palmer walked to his picture window and watched the crowds of people hurrying down Fifth Avenue toward their various offices. The brisk February wind forced them to duck their heads as they walked into the teeth of it.

He wondered how many of the people fighting against the wind were depositors in savings banks. Probably one out of two, or three, he thought. Did they have any idea what kind of clever infighting was going on in Albany at this moment?

By trying to split savings-bank solidarity, he knew Burns hoped to weaken any co-ordinated opposition to the amendment. If it passed, it was a sign of strength for the commercial-bank cause. In Albany, as anywhere else in life, signs of strength are contagious.

Palmer returned to his desk and flipped the page of his calendar book to today's date. A scribbled note caught his eye. He peered at it doubtfully for a moment, trying to decipher his own hurried handwriting. He had written something like "2 uks to shrhls mtg." He examined the message more closely and decided that the first two words were "2 wks." Then he understood the note: Ubco's annual shareholder's meeting was scheduled two weeks from today. He leafed forward in the calendar and, by way of verification, found a "Shrhls mtg tdy" note on a Friday page two weeks hence.

Palmer sighed and sat down. Even in the solitary quiet of his office he could feel the pressures about him, the crackling silence before the pot boiled over.

Everything was crowding in too fast. Ubco's stock had advanced another point during a week in which Dow-Jones averages had trended down. Against a downward, sluggish market, trading in Ubco shares had been damnably brisk. At Palmer's suggestion, Burckhardt had had the usual proxy statements mailed inordinately early this year, hoping to minimize the number that fell into new, unfriendly hands, but this was a closing-the-barn-door maneuver that could only hope to neutralize a few thousand shares at the very most. At the same time, if Burns's test of strength in Albany failed, it would demonstrate even to friendly shareholders that Burckhardt was not in control of the savings-banks situation. Was he then the proper man to sit in control of Ubco?

A complex maneuver, Palmer decided. He would not like the job of co-ordinating the flanking attacks Joe Loomis had organized. An exceedingly tricky question of timing and emphasis, but with enough simple strength in each of its components to stand a fair chance of success.

So thinking, Palmer picked up his phone and dialed Virginia on the intercom system. "How's the head?" he greeted her.

"Um. Morning." Her voice sounded hoarse and somewhat faint.

"Can you come in soon?"

"As soon as they remove the oxygen tent."

He hung up and grinned at nothing more tangible than the fact that, although they had both been very drunk last night, he had no ill effects this morning. He assumed it was because he had got home at a fairly decent hour —eleven—so that Edith could have no reason for suspecting anything.

The fact that he had come home around eleven almost every night for several weeks, of course, might seem a bit strange to her. But then, Palmer reflected, he had explained how busy things were before the test amendment. Since the night, some weeks before, when he had stayed out all night, Palmer had resolutely cut off his evenings with Virginia at eleven. They had fallen into the habit of leaving the office somewhere between four and five each day, careful to give one or the other a half-hour start to avoid suspicion. The hours from then until eleven were satisfyingly misspent in Burns's apartment where, during his prolonged absence at Albany, they lived like two hermits, bringing in small bags of food and liquor through the basement.

Until now the hours before eleven, Palmer recalled, had been normally slow ones. In contrast to the hectic hours of the business day, they usually passed at a torpid pace. This was not true of the hours he spent with Virginia. Their routine was a simple one but it seemed to live on great gulps of time, swallowed in chunks.

She opened his office door now, closed it behind her and stood there for a moment, her huge eyes half closed against the cold, brilliant February sunlight slanting in through the overhead louvers. Palmer watched her move slowly across the room, circle his desk and bend over him. The faintly smoky scent of her perfume struck sexual reverberations like a muted gong. She kissed his cheek lightly, examined it for a trace of lipstick, then went back around the desk and sat down in the chair opposite him. She seemed unable to open her eyes completely. This had the effect of lightening the great dark caves in which they were set above her high cheekbones. She wrinkled her nose.

"Please don't look smug," she said then.

"Right. How shall I look?"

"And don't look handsome, for God's sake. Look seedy, like me."

"Right. Seedy. How's this?"

"You look about as seedy as an executive vice-president of a large bank."

"I'm improving."

"What did you call me in for?" she moaned.

"The light is much brighter here. We sadists deny ourselves nothing."

She managed to open her eyes. "You've got more than a streak of sadism in you at that. How did you get me to do all that business last night?"

"Not by twisting your arm."

"I'd like to go on record as saying that never before have I ever before done anything before like that before."

"It's hazy, but I recall you suggesting it originally."

She sighed deeply. "You're probably right. I seem able to act out the wildest of my fantasies with you. It's downright embarrassing."

"You didn't seem noticeably embarrassed."

She closed her eyes again. "I wasn't," she said in a small voice. "I'm not." She twisted in the chair, as if to find a more comfortable posture. "I said that just because it's the proper thing to say," she muttered. "Enough. You didn't call me in to find out what you already knew."

"I wanted to know where we could get word fast on this amendment. Do you have a friend at one of the wire services?"

"Why not call Burns?"

"He's never where I can find him. I have to leave word. Then he calls me back. I want somebody I can reach almost constantly."

"I can call the Albany press room," she suggested.

"Isn't there anyone here in town? I don't want to bother them up there when they're trying to file a story."

She opened her eyes unwillingly. With almost trancelike slowness, she extended her right hand, fingers outstretched. It hung in the air before her, rock steady. "See that tremor?" she asked then.

"No."

With a disgusted look, she slapped her hand on the desk top. "Nothing works. All right. We'll drop in at the *Star*. You can sit somewhere out of the way. I'll see if George Mallett or someone will let me sort of unobtrusively hang around the teletype printers and watch the wire out of Albany. Good enough?"

"I can't visualize you being unobtrusive. Let's face it. You protrude."

She smiled softly at him. "What I love most about you," she said, "is that you never seem to lose sight of that." She glanced at her watch. "It's too early now. We'll leave around ten. The *Star* man at Albany will be filing about ten-thirty, if there's anything to file."

But when they got to the *Star*, they learned that Mallett would not be there until after lunch. They stood for a moment in the waiting room, trying to decide what to do next.

"We could pop over to the *Times*," Virginia was saying, "if you'd—"

"Bubby!" someone called loudly. "Bubbeleh!"

Palmer turned to see a vaguely familiar man grinning at Virginia from the city-room doorway. He stood somewhat under six feet, but his well-padded frame made him look shorter, Palmer noted. The round face under tightly cropped hair was one he had seen before, with its fast-moving eyes and puffy underlip.

"Doll," Virginia said. "Say hello again to my boss, Woods Palmer. This is Kessler, the only *Star* photographer who is no gentleman."

"Hiya, Palmer. Still stealing the wrong German rocketeers?"

Palmer watched Kessler's candid eyes. They waited warily for a sign of recognition. "You!" Palmer said then. He extended his hand and found it caught in a trap that mashed his fingers for a wincing instant, then released them. The cigarette that drooped over the exact center of Kessler's lower lip bobbed up and down, sending a fine snowfall of ashes over the front of his sharply tailored suit as he spoke.

"Man, did you goof. You should of stolen the ones the Russkis got."

357

"Is he always like this?" Palmer asked Virginia.

"No. At the moment he's on good behavior."

"That's right," Kessler agreed. "Being around a woman inhibits me." He leered at Virginia.

"Listen, doll, you've got a TWX printer in the photo department. Does it get the Albany wire?"

Kessler shook his head. "City-side AP. Why? Which thieves you wanna keep tabs on up there?"

"There's an amendment vote this morning."

"Some more of that banking crud?" he asked peevishly. "Bubby, I've covered this town for fifteen years and I never yet got a juicy photo in a bank."

"If you did, the *Star* wouldn't print it," she said.

He nodded and turned to Palmer. "Ask her. She'll tell you I'm a frustrated cheesecake artist. In fifteen years the highest up a broad's thigh I ever got the *Star* to print was when Gussie Moran used to wear those short-short tennis shorts." He eyed Palmer. "How come you're slumming with your hired help?" he asked then. "Newspapermen usually come to you, not vice-versa."

"We're having an affair," Virginia explained.

"God help you, Palmer," Kessler stated flatly. "This chick is like one of those things they put in your drink at a high-class bar. Ice cube with a hole in it?"

"You sound," Palmer said, "as if you'd once got a bad chill."

"Once?" Kessler laughed. "Tell the man how many desks I've chased you around, honey."

"Why humiliate yourself?" Virginia asked.

He watched her for a moment with a lascivious grin, then shrugged. "I'll take you to the TWX, bubby, but your boss has to stay out here."

Palmer sat down on a long couch covered in cracked tan leatherette. He stared around him at framed front pages of the *Star*, then lighted a cigarette and settled back for a long wait. A moment later Kessler walked out through the waiting room, did an elaborate you-still-here? double-take, walked over to him and sat down.

"That's a very classy chick," he said, lighting a new cigarette. "How'd she get messed up with a married man?"

Palmer laughed in what he hoped was a sufficiently off-hand manner. "Fatal charm. Can't seem to control it."

"You think I think she's kidding," Kessler said in a morose voice.

"What?"

The photographer stared somberly at the floor. "I know that chick. Used to date her. Lot of the boys did. Best newspaper girl in the business, even if she isn't with it any more. But all her energy went into that. She didn't have any left to dig sex. Besides, she had the usual Catholic hang-up about getting laid out of wedlock. Believe me, I know."

"Now I know you're kidding," Palmer assured him.

358

"Because I'm Jewish?" Kessler grinned sourly. "Jewish chicks have the same hang-up, Palmer. This town is loaded with nice Jewish, Italian and Irish broads who settled for spinsterhood right after their first tussle with a guy. The hang-up is too fierce, a steel chastity belt. The only thing that unlocks it is a wedding ring. But when they wait too long the guy who unlocks it finds there's nothing much left for him."

Palmer crossed one leg over the other and thoughtfully honed the tip of his cigarette against the sole of his shoe until a glowing red point of hot ash remained. "I don't want you to think this isn't extremely interesting," he said then, "but I think you're out of your mind."

"Yeah? What makes you th—"

"And I also think you're off base talking to me about Virginia. She's got an odd sense of humor that you seem to take literally. I'll tell you the truth: I don't believe your vile canards about New York's women. Did you ever think that you just happen to know frigid ones?"

"Not possible."

"Maybe they hold a fatal fascination for you."

"I'm punishing myself?" Kessler asked. He made a low, soft laughing sound. "Daddy, for a banker, you come on real crazy. Now let's talk about debentures and revolving credit."

"What happened to sex?"

Kessler raised and lowered his eyebrows several times, seeming to indicate that although the subject was here to stay, he'd rather get off it. "I was testing you, Pops," he admitted. "My experience with bankers is strictly limited to conversations that begin: 'You are one hundred dollars overdrawn.' Invariably. Tell me: how come that little speech is always accompanied by a great big smile?"

"It's a sad story," Palmer said. "Bank employees smile when they say that because it puts them one up. Being one up is a perquisite of the job. High pay isn't. So an employee takes what small pleasures he can get."

"Fascinating, man. How do they stand on sex?"

Palmer found himself laughing almost helplessly for a moment. Then he saw Virginia coming through the city-room entrance toward him and the look on her face made him stop laughing. "Don't tell me," he said.

"Five against, two for, one abstaining," she announced. "The amendment is defeated. Decisively."

Palmer stood up slowly, holding his hat in his hands. "So much for a show of strength," he said in a flat voice.

She nodded. "It's a show, all right. Of their strength."

"And Mac's impeccable sense of timing."

Her eyes shifted sideways for a split second to indicate Kessler, still sitting there. "That's something we can talk about," she said.

"When Kessler's not around," Kessler added. The photographer got to his feet. "Someday," he said slowly, "one of Mac Burns's potential clients is not

359

gonna trust him, right from the beginning, and not hire him and Mac will not be able to pull any fast ones. On that day I will take your hat, carefully salt it and eat every last shred."

Palmer frowned at Virginia. "How much of our confidential business has gotten around town?"

Kessler shook his head. "Nobody's told me nothing, Daddy. I just know Mac Burns. And now you do, too." His eyes flicked back and forth between Palmer and the woman Virginia. "How does he do it? You come on like an intelligent guy. How can you fall for his line of crap?"

Palmer's immediate reaction was to give this man an answer. His second reaction was to say nothing. With a pleased sense of release, he found himself reverting to his original reaction. "The funny thing," he told Kessler, "is that I didn't trust him from the very beginning. I saw this double-cross coming long before he made his first move. I even know why he's doing it."

At this Kessler wheeled on Virginia. "What kind of boss you got, bubby?" He swung back to Palmer. "What's the answer? Hypnosis? Why'd you let him do it or don't you care?"

Palmer blinked. He paused for a moment, not out of the innate caution he had rejected a moment before, but because he was suddenly having trouble with his temper. "Let me get this straight," he said then, stalling to play for time. "Doesn't any newspaperman in New York like Mac Burns?"

"Only the ones on his payroll."

Palmer turned to Virginia. "And that's public knowledge, too?"

She nodded. "You'd be surprised how a little thing like that gets around."

"Is this—?" Palmer paused again. "Does any—?" He stopped and moistened his lips. "Is this a common practice in public relations?"

Kessler's sudden violent grin released a gigantic ash from the cigarette in his mouth. "Welcome to the big city, Pops."

"Not common," Virginia said. "But done here and there."

The photographer eyed Palmer for a long moment. "You're putting me on, Dad," he remarked then. "How else could a *dschlub* like Burns get anything in print?"

Palmer nodded curtly. He put his hat on his head and looked at Virginia. "Let's get back to the office. I have an Albany call to make."

Kessler jerked his thumb at a small anteroom. "Be my guest."

"There's no story in it," Palmer warned him.

"I just want to hear Mac the Knife get chopped up."

The photographer picked up a telephone in the anteroom and asked the operator for the *Star's* Albany tie line. "This is Kessler," he said after a moment. "Is Mac Burns lurking around there?" With a beatific smile, he handed the phone to Palmer.

"Hello?" Palmer listened to a variety of random sounds at the other end of the line. Then:

"Sweetheart? This is Mac. *Wie gehts?*"

"*Machts nichts gut*," Palmer said.

"Who is this?" The affability drained out of Burns's voice as if a flush-box chain had been pulled. "Kessler?"

"It's Palmer. I'm at the *Star*. We just read the amendment vote on the ticker."

"Woody-baby?" A pause. Then: "Fella, I'm as depressed as you are." Burns's voice struggled to get into a lower, more suitable key after the hail-fellow hilarity of his original greetings. "Hit me like a ton of bricks."

"A ton of something, Mac," Palmer said. "I called to hear your explanation. Make it brief. I have a statement to read you."

"What kind of sta—?"

"Explanation first."

"Well, what can I tell you? I had every expectation of winning, baby. You know that. But three of the upstate Republican members double-crossed us."

"Would they be any of the ones you visited with on your upstate tour?"

"Woody! I swear to Christ I don't know how y—"

"Mac, have you finished your explanation?"

"How the hell can you explain anything like this? Be reasonable, Woody. Three finks who should vote with the commercial banks decide to vote with the savings banks."

"And prove to the world how weak we are."

"The end of the world it ain't, sweetie. You know better than that. It's one cockamamie little amendment."

"End of explanation?"

"Yeah."

"Mac, I have a statement." Palmer held his hand palm up in front of him, as if reading from a paper. "Now hear this: the relationship between United Bank and Trust Company and Mac Burns is hereby terminated. Party of the second part will no longer represent himself as public-relations counsel to party of the first part. Signed this twelfth day of February by Woods Palmer, Jr., executive vice-president. How do you read me?"

"I don't underst—"

"You are fired, Mac. Sacked. Dismissed. You are no longer my p.r. man. I am no longer your client. Is that clear?"

"Does Burckha—?"

"And I am now free to do whatever I can to undo the chicanery, the betrayal of trust and the utter and complete treachery which you have inflicted—for money—on Ubco."

"Have you told Burck—?"

"People who hardly know me," Palmer interrupted again, "are moved to ask me why I ever trusted you from the beginning. I am moved to ask myself why, knowing what your game was, I let you damage us this much."

"Woody, has Bur—?"

"I may never be able to find either answer, Mac, but at least I will not have to listen to the questions any more. Good-by."

"Will you—?"

Palmer replaced the phone in its cradle with great gentleness. Then he turned to Kessler. "Entirely off the record, of course?"

"Of course." Kessler had lighted a fresh cigarette, which now dangled from the exact center of his mouth.

"Thank you for the use of the hall."

"My pleasure."

Palmer glanced at Virginia and indicated the outer door of the waiting room. "Shall we?" They nodded to the photographer and left him standing there, a fine rain of ash settling over his somewhat plump belly.

Downstairs, as they stepped out into the fresh wind of Forty-seventh Street, Virginia took his arm. "What a ham you are," she murmured.

"I didn't really overdo it, did I?"

"Firing your p.r. man over a long-distance wire of the *New York Star?* I wouldn't call that overdoing it."

"Do people listen in?"

"Only at both ends."

They reached Broadway, where a whirlwind of dirt forced them to close their eyes for a moment. "Funny thing," Palmer said then.

"Hysterical."

"No, funny that I wasn't really angry when I heard the news about the amendment. Nor when I started to talk to Burns."

"But now you're really good and mad?" she asked.

"Yes."

She squeezed his arm. "Let's get you a drink."

"At eleven in the morning?"

"I'll have one, too."

Palmer glanced around him at the sleazy late-morning vulgarities of Times Square. "Not around here."

"At Mac's apartment."

He smiled grimly. "I wouldn't be very good company."

She glanced up at him. "Just what are you angry at, Woods?"

"At myself."

"For not dumping Mac before this?"

He shook his head. "Worse than that."

"For what, then?"

"For standing around as if I were a bystander, not a participant. For pretending I didn't really have any responsibilities in any of this. For subconsciously hoping he'd successfully double-cross Ubco." He bared his teeth at her in a grin devoid of pleasure. "In a sense, for wanting him to win. For hating what Burckhardt's doing even more than I hate what Mac's doing."

The light turned green. They crossed the wide intersection and, as is always the case, found the light turning red again before they had covered more than half the distance. They ran the rest of the way to the curb.

"What brought all this on?" she asked then, slightly out of breath.

"Your friend, Kessler, asking me why I *let* Burns do this. And suggesting that perhaps I didn't really care one way or the other."

"Do you?"

"That's not the point. It was his attitude. Kessler's." He was striding east on Forty-seventh now, almost dragging her along. "His assumption that someone in my position is a kind of philosophical eunuch who really can't be bothered with the things men like Kessler hold dear. Integrity being the chief one."

They had crossed Sixth Avenue and were tearing along at a headlong pace. "Woods," she gasped, "where are we rushing?"

He slowed to a more normal walk. "It was his assumption," he said more quietly then, "that I was some kind of neuter. Remember? 'What kind of boss have you got?' Remember him asking that?"

"But surely he didn't mean that you—"

"I know what he meant."

"You're way overboard, Woods. You're reading things into this that aren't there."

"That's entirely possible. It was—" He stopped talking for a moment. Then he sighed. "You couldn't be expected to feel it the way I did. You didn't put in all those years under a father like mine, then volunteer—the irony of it—to work under a Burckhardt. I have a sore spot. Kessler found it without too much trouble."

"By accident," she said.

"How ever he found it, he managed to give it a good, stiff poke."

"And you leaped up as if stung by a bee, hopped to the phone and fired Mac. I always thought bankers moved so slowly."

"It's just that I suddenly realized why I'd been giving Mac such a free rein. You see, I've never really felt he was my responsibility." Palmer guided her across Fifth Avenue. They stood on the other corner, now, she waiting for a clue from him as to their next move, he not realizing they had stopped. "Burckhardt hired him, repented of it, felt he had a tiger by the tail and hired me to hold the beast for him. By the time I'd figured out some of it, I'd begun to resent Burckhardt almost as much as I used to resent my father. And somehow, I suppose, I took a secret joy in watching Burns double-cross him. Kessler was right. I really didn't care."

"But now?"

"Now I've somehow begun to feel it as a personal thing. I hate being under-estimated. It's insulting. It's especially insulting from a cut-rate Lebanese Machiavelli like Burns."

"I refuse to believe," she said, "that a chance remark by a big-mouth photographer could make you see the light."

363

"But that's what happened."

"That's not it at all." She frowned, stepped out onto the curb and hailed a passing taxi. "Get in."

The cab slowly made its way through heavy traffic north and east toward Burns's apartment house. "What really happened," Virginia told him then, "is that out of some idiotic strain of fair play that encircles your soul like a noose, you decided to give Burns one more chance. You agreed to this treacherous amendment of his."

"How silly."

"I agree, but that's exactly what you did. You refused to believe what you knew to be true. You hung on to the last shreds of your simpleton's faith in the goodness of man."

"Uhm."

"No one, you decided, could be as treacherous as the man you'd finally figured Mac Burns to be. But I tell you, Woods, this town is full of Mac Burnses. So is this world. And now, finally, you know it, too. That's why you're angry."

"I've calmed down considerably," he said, smiling and taking her hand.

"You said a funny thing before." She squeezed his hand almost absent-mindedly. "That thing about having a tiger by the tail."

"Is that funny?"

"Funny-tragic. You have the Tammany tiger by the tail, Woods. It's not as easy to let go of as a quick phone call to Burns."

"He's fired. Even he understands that."

"Then, darling, you don't understand tigers."

CHAPTER FIFTY-FOUR

By one o'clock, the slanting winter sun had crept across the floor of Burns's living room until it reached the thick, white rug. As if igniting the snowy fur, the sunlight now seemed to fill the entire room, reflected from the hot glare of white on which Virginia lay. Palmer got up, half blinded, and made his way to the bar. The sun felt hot on his naked body. He had never before experienced sex in blazing daylight. The light penetrated every crevice of her body, every fold, every hollow. Sex had taken on such jolting clarity and texture that it was almost like an entirely new sensation. He poured a small amount of whisky into each glass and carried them back to the rug.

"No ice?" she murmured, looking up at him.

"Too lazy."

From her prone, spread-eagled position, she slid sideways with sudden grace and bit his foot, hard. He winced. Whisky sloshed out of one glass and splashed on her breasts. "Cold!" she yelped. "You filthy beast."

He tipped the glass slightly as he poured a few more drops of whisky on her belly. "Beast," she muttered. "Wasting good whisky."

He knelt beside her. "We'd better not waste it, then."

They both heard the key in the door.

Palmer stood up. He pulled her to her feet. She turned toward the bedroom door. He watched her pick up clothing as she moved. He turned toward the front door. He could see it opening. When he glanced at the bedroom door, it was closed. Slowly, he stepped to the bar and put down the glasses. He saw that she had left some clothing on the sofa. It looked like his. He noticed a small whisky stain on the rug. Then he looked up at the front door.

"Sweetie, for a banker, you're really hung."

Burns's thin lower lip curled in mock admiration. He closed the door behind him. It made a sharp, reverberating click.

Palmer saw Burns put down his overnight case on the foyer table. He leafed through several letters stacked there. Then he turned to Palmer, still smiling. "Why don't you get dressed or something?"

Palmer turned to the bar, picked up the fuller of the two glasses and slowly sipped from it. "How'd you get back to town this quickly?" he asked then.

"One of those Mohawk Convairs to Newark. Helicopter to West Thirtieth Street. Cab here. Two hours."

"Amazing world we live in." Palmer finished the whisky. "Drink?"

He turned to find Burns moving slowly, noticingly, through the living room. The sun blazed in his corn-yellow hair. He stooped over the sofa and picked up a black brassière, examined the label. "Thirty-six C," he murmured. "What you'd call ample." His mobile mouth had set into a kind of benign, at-peace-with-the-world smile. He glanced at Palmer. "Now I begin to understand how you keep in condition, Woody-baby. Not an ounce of fat on you, huh?"

Palmer picked up his underwear shorts and put them on. "Will you step into the kitchen while she leaves?"

"I'm not supposed to know it's Ginnie?"

"Round one." Palmer shrugged into his undershirt. "Then I'd better give her her bra."

"Go right ahead. It's like, uh, lending support."

"Ha." Palmer knocked on the bedroom door. It opened a crack and he passed the brassière through. "He knows it's you," he said.

"It figures." She closed the door sharply.

"She sounds mad," Burns said affably. "But who is she mad at?"

Palmer sat down on the sofa. In methodical fashion, he put on his socks and adjusted the garters. "If I were she," he said, "I wouldn't know where to begin." He stood up, stepped into his trousers and sat down again to put on his shoes. Then he looked at Burns. "I don't either," he added.

"Just as long as you're not mad at me," Burns said. "After all, sweetie, you got good value out of my apartment."

The bedroom door opened and Virginia walked between the two men to the window. In the sunlight she opened her compact, inspected her face and put on lipstick. Then she turned to them. "Hello, Mac," she said.

"Lovely." Burns nodded. "Sorry about the timing."

Her eyebrows went up. "Oh?" She took a long, calming breath. "Well, I've got things to do at the office. Gentlemen, good-by."

Mac held up his hand. "You've got things to do here, too, Ginnie. What's the rush?"

"What sort of things?"

Burns half turned toward the bar. "We have to have a drink. And while we're drinking, we have a couple of business matters to discuss."

Tying his tie, Palmer's heart seemed to constrict. The meaning was too clear, too impossible to confuse. He got into his suit coat and brushed some white shreds of rug lint from his sleeves. "Let's postpone it," he said. "It's going to be a long day and a long evening. We're going to see each other at that wedding reception tonight, anyway."

"That's true," Burns said. "I forgot all about the reception. But, Woody, it's hardly the place to talk business." He had poured whisky into three glasses. Now he splashed water into each. "Let's drink," he said, as affably as a command can sound.

Silently, Palmer and Virginia accepted their glasses. Burns raised his. "My favorite toast," he said. "To love." He started to sip his drink, then found he was alone in doing do. " 'S'matter? You two are in love, aren't you?"

Virginia sat down in a chair near the window. The bright sunlight sank into her black hair and left nothing of itself but tiny, curving glints of fire. In shadow, her small face looked immobile. She held the drink in her lap without looking at it. "Why is it, Mac," she said then, "that in your mouth the word sounds so dirty?"

"Ah, for Christ's sake, kids," Burns said with sudden gaiety, "don't let's turn this into a wake. I know what these things are like. I've been married three times. I'm an expert."

"Would you care to explain what 'these things' are?" Palmer asked, not because he was at all interested, but out of a compelling need to postpone the real business at hand.

"These affairs," Burns said promptly. "You live through what I've lived through, kiddies, and you get to be an expert on sex and love and all that. If I had the time I could write a book. If there was any money in it."

366

"This is a new and revolting side of you, Mac," Virginia remarked. "Advice to the lovelorn."

"I am especially an expert on the extramarital affair," he said. He frowned and glanced at Palmer. His tawny eyes almost twinkled. "You marry a girl, right? She's attractive, like Edith. Slender, tender and tall. I happen to dig Edith the most. She walks, talks and looks like a couple of million in tax-free municipal debentures. I'm a sucker for that type of girl. And so were you, once, Woody. But I'm getting personal. This, uh, hypothetical guy marries this hypothetical girl. They make it big in the sack and they have the comfort of knowing it's super-legal, even patriotic. Then things happen. They see too much of each other. Things are just too legal. Of the two, the wife changes faster. At about the time she has her hubby squared away as number-one Fall Guy of all time, she gets knocked up. The final symptom sets in: the Great American Female Frustration. She finds out she can't be Amelia Earhart, Madame Curie and Claire Booth Luce all rolled up into one. All she can be is pregnant. For the next few years she can spend her time in the company of illiterate kids. If she's really off the deep end, now, she stops having 'em after the first. If she can somehow convince herself she's wrong to feel this way, she'll go for a second or a third or even a fourth kid, hating herself all the way. But, in either case, she knows what to blame for how she feels. It's that legal thing her hubby does to her. Her attitude toward it will never be the same again. And the first to find this out is hubby. It may take him years to decide what to do about it. Then he cheats. And, God Almighty, but this is what sex should be. It's wild, it's dirty, it's illegal and more satisfying than he ever remembered was possible. He feels so free he can hardly believe it. There is just no holding this lad." He lifted his glass again. "To love."

This time Palmer and Virginia sipped their drinks.

Burns laughed softly. "If I learned anything about sex, doing it the hard way, I learned that a mistress is one thing and a wife is something entirely different. Even if she starts as one and ends as the other, she's something different, the same girl. It's just two different things, like farina and . . . and baklava."

Virginia nodded, put down her drink and got up. "This piece of baklava has work back at the office. Good-by again."

"Jesus, am I that boring?" Burns asked. "All right. I'll get fascinating." He turned to Palmer. "Woods Palmer, Jr. The savings banks' branch bill is going to pass. Not by much, but by enough. The news that it's going to pass will get more and more believable as the weeks go by. By the time your shareholders meet, the rumor will be so strong you'll have a real rumpus on your hands. The questions from the floor are already written, Woody. I have a dozen of them ready to be asked by irate shareholders who will make Burckhardt look like the incompetent, bumbling horse's ass we both know him to be. Right?"

Palmer gestured with his glass. "This is your story."

"Right." Burns poured more whisky in his own glass. "More?" he asked Virginia, then Palmer. They both declined. "Next," he continued briskly, "we have the proposal sent to Burckhardt two weeks ago for inclusion in the agenda of the meeting. You know the proposal I mean?"

Palmer frowned. "I've heard of no proposal."

"A group of dissident shareholders propose to enlarge the board from seven to seventeen, by appointing ten new directors. Since the thing was filed in time, under the by-laws, it goes on the agenda. It comes up for a vote. And, Woody, you will not be terribly surprised, I hope, to find out that by the time of the meeting we're going to have a controlling number of shares?"

Palmer shook his head slowly. "Burckhardt hasn't mentioned this proposal," he said in a dull, puzzled voice. He made a sound somewhere between a chuckle and a clearing of the throat. "What on earth has gotten into that old bastard?"

"Fear," Burns suggested.

No one spoke for a long moment. Then Virginia walked to the bar and added some whisky to her glass. "I have a good idea of who these ten new directors will be." She turned to Palmer. "It's just the way you thought they'd do it," she told him. "The crazy thing is that they may win."

Palmer nodded. "I know." His voice sounded guilty to him and he went back over what she had said, trying to find out if she had been accusing him or if the guilt were all in his own mind.

"Don't blame him," Burns said then, solving the problem for Palmer. "He inherited this after it was already running in high gear. Nobody on earth could have stopped it."

"It's shot through with wishful thinking, Mac," Virginia said. "You haven't won yet, and you're not all that sure you will."

Burns smiled easily. "Ginnie, how did you get so smart?"

"Knowing you has been an education."

Burns jerked his sharp chin at Palmer. "Knowing him hasn't been dull, either." He laughed quietly for a moment. "All right. I'm not as sure of winning as I'd like to be. There's only one piece of the puzzle missing." He indicated a chair. "Sit down, lover. The going gets heavy from here on out."

She sat down next to Palmer on the sofa. He could feel the swelling softness of her thigh pressing against his. For once, the closeness of her body failed to arouse him. He knew his forehead was damp but he refused to touch it and reveal the tension he felt. Instead he tried to soften the look on his face to one of casual interest. He felt very tired. The sight of Burns going through his various acts, benign and understanding, tough and demanding, had begun to confuse him by the suddenness of the character changes. He sighed unsteadily. "Get on with it, Mac."

"The figurehead," Burns responded quickly. "The replacement for Big Daddy Burckhardt. The tried, true, dyed-in-the-wool banker's banker who will guarantee that Ubco continues on a sound footing under seasoned, younger management. That's the missing piece, Woody. You."

"You won't get our directors to buy me as a replacement."

"You can. You'll get help, of course. You won't be our only man on the inside."

"I have been waiting patiently to hear Cliff's name mentioned."

"You knew?" Burns asked.

"Suspected. Mr. Mergendahl is smooth."

"Not as smooth as we thought, huh?"

"Smooth enough to be the figurehead you need," Palmer said. He could feel the sweat building up on his face and chest. "Why not use him that way?"

Burns shook his head sadly. "You have so much to learn about p.r., sweetie. The first lesson is always this: appearances count. Never mind what goes on behind the scenes. It's the scenery that impresses people. How would it look to the public if we skipped over our executive v.p. and jumped a mere treasurer into the top spot? And when I say the public, I don't only mean our thousands of innocent shareholders, I mean our depositors, too."

"I love to hear you say 'our.' You do it very well."

Burns smiled in a pleased way. "With you as replacement, Woody, Burckhardt's departure is simply a routine retirement, followed by a promotion for you. Happens every day. It's great scenery. I've painted it a dozen times in my life. Never fails to please the audience."

"I'd make a rotten replacement."

"Gee, no. I think you'd be a smash hit."

"Even if you could get me to stand still for this," Palmer said, "you'd never be sure of me from then on in. What makes you think I'd go along with you? What makes you think I'd okay that wild loan to Jet-Tech?"

"You're for it, aren't you?"

"I was for the principle of doing it." Palmer leaned forward. "But none of that's important, Mac. The only thing that concerns you is that I won't do it. Won't let myself be used to dump Burckhardt. Won't replace him. Won't okay the loan."

Burns spread his narrow hands palms up on either side of him, as if helpless in the grip of higher forces. With simple directness he said: "I tell you you will."

Palmer watched him silently for a moment. Then he blinked. "You'll try to use this business here today as blackmail." He sat back in the sofa. "Won't work. Your word against mine. All you have is a dirty story to tell. It may strain things between Edith and me. It may even impress a few directors. But I'll deny it. I'll ruin your credibility by telling them how you've double-crossed us from the beginning. They'll stop believing you soon enough."

"You're willing to gamble your job and your marriage on it, huh?"

"And her job," Palmer added, indicating Virginia, "and her reputation."

"You're a hell of a big spender, Woody." Burns's lower lip curled sarcastically. "Your job means nothing to you, as far as money is concerned. The marriage you were ready to dump anyway. So whose chips are you playing with?"

"I th—" Virginia's voice died in a harsh welter of throat sounds. She coughed slightly. "I think it's a good bet," she said then. "I don't care whose chips he uses, he can outface you."

"Not that easily," Burns said.

"It isn't hard," Palmer told him, "when I'm only fighting hearsay."

Burns snapped his fingers. "Kids, I'm so excited and upset and all that, I forgot the main part." He walked to the hi-fi phonograph console and knelt beside it, reaching in back for something. Instantly, Palmer knew what was coming. Whether by instinct, by some subconscious understanding of the way Burns's mind worked, or out of his earlier G-2 training, he was quite certain, with the leaden sureness of a man standing in the path of an avalanche, what Burns would take out of its hiding place.

Smaller than a shoebox, the black container trailed a thin wire behind it as Burns placed it gently on top of the console and flipped open its lid.

"One and seven-eighths inches per second?" Palmer heard himself ask.

Burns turned slowly to face him, his yellow eyebrows high. "You're guessing, aren't you?"

"Just figuring something out," Palmer explained. He paused for a moment. "You've got enough tape for about five hours. How did you turn it on and—?" He stopped. "The telephone." He turned to Virginia. "Do you remember the telephone calls we didn't answer?"

She nodded. "But how—?"

"Another phone call turned it off, after we left. We wouldn't be there to hear it." Palmer found himself sitting forward on the edge of the sofa. Now he settled back. "Ingenious. But a random outside call would confuse the machine."

"Happened a couple of times," Burns admitted. "I monitored the tapes two mornings ago. I missed some sessions on account of stray phone calls. But I didn't miss all of them," he added with a thin smile.

He pressed a button and the tape reels began to turn slowly. Then he walked away from the machine, unbuttoning his collar. "Gotta change my shirt," he murmured. "That's a duplicate tape, kids, with the dead stuff edited out. The original's in my office. Happy listening."

He walked into his bedroom, leaving the recorder turning. After a moment it began to emit a low hissing sound. Palmer could hear sounds of movement, then a knocking on the door.

"Decent?" he heard his voice say. It sounded hollow, but the muffled, flat intonation of his Midwest accent was unmistakable.

"Always," Virginia's voice replied. The small loud-speaker turned her voice

370

into a tinny replica. "I would like to bottle that look of yours. I would like to cork the bottle and open it only when I needed moral support."

"There is nothing moral about my support."

"Exactly. It's a little late to ask, but I take it you like me."

"Yes, I do."

"You said that without stammering."

"Don't be incisive, on top of everything else. You've done enough for me this evening without that."

"And here I thought all along that you were doing something for me."

"Oh, look, there must be a dozen other men in your life who'd jump at the chance to—"

"How do you know so much about me and the dozens of men in my life?"

"I don't. But you're very attractive."

"Thank you. I'm going to astound you."

"Again?"

"Look, I . . . What do I call you? In the office, I know what to say. But what about here?"

"For a long time I was called Junior. Don't ever try it."

"Look . . . Woods . . . Woody?"

"Go on. Suffer."

"Woods, I have this astounding confession. At least it's astounding to me. I calculated it while I was showering. This hasn't happened to me in almost two years."

"You're right. It's astounding."

"Isn't it? And it wasn't because I didn't want to, several times."

Listening to the recording, Palmer shifted uncomfortably on the sofa and darted a quick glance at Virginia. She had been watching him, but quickly looked away.

"What a judgment on New York men," Palmer's voice rasped from the tiny machine.

"I'll tell you about the New York men I've met sometime. But not now. I have the feeling we ought to vacate the premises."

"Separately."

"Very separately. I'll go first. I'll clean up the place a bit before I do."

"No. I'll do that."

"It's all right."

"I'll do it," his voice insisted. "I'm much better at it than you."

"I'm so good," Palmer interrupted the tape, "that I completely missed this lovely little machine."

"One kiss this way," Virginia's recorded voice begged. "When I'm dressed it won't be the same."

The tape went dead for a moment. There was the suddenly sharper, momentary hiss of an amateur splice running over the recording head. Palmer

371

glanced at Virginia again and this time they watched each other for a long moment.

"Why did you do that?" her voice asked from the recorder.

"Hm?"

"Take your hand away from there."

"Good God, did I? Um. Here is this lovely thing here."

"Yes, it's there."

"How is it these days?"

"Just the way you left it. You're quite hirsute, for a blond."

Hearing her comment now, Palmer made a face. Virginia looked away as the tape rasped on.

"Prop up your head," her recorded voice suggested. "The rug isn't all that soft."

Palmer got to his feet and walked slowly toward the tape machine, not listening to it for a moment, trying instead to evaluate the importance of the recordings. The voices were recognizable. His name was established firmly by the dialogue. Their condition—nakedness—was also affirmed. And—

"I wish to hell," Virginia's voice complained through the squawky speaker, "that we could be like ordinary illicit lovers. The girl falls asleep. The man tiptoes about the bedroom, getting dressed. In the morning, she awakes to find him gone and money on the dresser. Instead, you kip off and I'm left to examine my own entrails."

Palmer pressed the machine's "off" button. He stared at the motionless reels for a moment. Then he pressed the rewind button and listened as their two voices, speeded up and reversed, made a meaningless, high-pitched jumble of their love, two undersized monkeys in heat.

"You want that copy?" Burns asked, walking into the room. He stood there fitting in cuff links. They glittered boldly in the hot sunlight. "There are some choicer parts later on you might want to review at your leisure."

"I have a feeling," Virginia said somberly, "that neither of us will have much leisure in the next few weeks."

"Then it's all agreed," Burns said. He unzipped his fly, tucked in his shirt and fastened his trousers and belt.

Palmer watched the last of the tape rewind. He listened to the loose end flap for a moment. Then he turned off the machine. He started to lift out the full reel, then stopped. "Who helped you with this thing, Mac?"

"Nobody."

"I mean the telephone relay. The wiring, all that."

"But nobody, sweetie," Burns assured him. "This thing's been rigged for years. Handy in a lot of odd circumstances."

Palmer stood there silently, trying to anticipate the next possibilities. He could pocket this tape without too much trouble. Could he, perhaps, force Burns to call his own office and have the original tape delivered here?

"Take it, old buddy," Burns said. "The original is locked away in my wall safe at the office." Then, with that disconcerting habit of outguessing his antagonist: "Nobody knows the combination but me."

Palmer went to the picture window. The afternoon traffic along the drive was sparse. Slanting sun glittered on the roofs of passing cars and against the windows of other cars crossing the Queensboro Bridge. A police helicopter churned by overhead.

The next set of choices was clear. Submit to Burns, Palmer told himself, or face public disgrace. But where Burns's mind could not readily lead him was into the tangled undergrowth of Palmer's reaction to public disgrace. It was true, now, Palmer reflected, that Edith would have grounds for a New York divorce, which meant a fantastically punitive support-alimony settlement. He would be left with rather less than half of his holdings, possibly a third. The affiliation with Ubco would, of course, vanish instantly, Virginia's job with it. It would be a full, tabloid-treatment divorce, complete with tape recordings played in the courtroom, headlines for several weeks, juicy hints of political scandal, illicit love nest, all the ingredients for maximum newspaper exposure.

It would be hard to withstand, Palmer told himself, but like anything else, it would come to an end eventually. And after that he would still be left in a position most people would call comfortable. There would be enough money for a long time, if budgeted properly. He would have to move, probably to another country, but this would help keep his expenses on a modest scale. He would be denied free access to his children but they would soon be old enough to need no guardian. Then they could pick up the threads of their relationship, whatever it was, with their father.

The whole thing seemed, the more he thought about it, if not enjoyable, at least bearable.

He turned away from the window and waited a moment for his irises to adjust to the dimmer light. Burns and Virginia were both watching him. A lot of people would be in the months ahead, if he took the more difficult choice. A lot of things would be thought and said about him, none of them complimentary. But was any of this to be thought of as shame?

Palmer moved slowly from the window. He had to be very careful about his own motives, he realized. He had to be very sure, for example, that he was not so tenaciously caught up in guilt that he would welcome public disgrace as a way of expiating his sins. It was too bad, he saw now, that he understood so little about himself. It would be a major error to make a wrong decision for emotional—and therefore wrong—reasons.

"Can I summarize?" he asked Burns.

"If you need to, lover."

"Be Jet-Tech's pawn in the maneuvering ahead. Or have you take your recordings to my employers and my wife."

"Not just recordings, Woody. I have witnesses to comings and goings. The doormen, the janitors in the basement. After all, somebody had to make the calls that turned on the recorder. You understand."

"What you've put together, then, is a kind of instant divorce package."

"Very good, sweetie. Very well put." Burns stepped to a mirror over the bar and adjusted his tie. "You're overlooking a couple of things in the Jet-Tech package, though. You understand we couldn't raise you to chairman of the board at your age. We'd bump Burckhardt back to, uh, some meaningless title like chairman of the executive committee or something. You'd be president and chief executive officer. And your salary, old buddy, will go to about, oh, whatever you'd like over and above a hundred gees a year. You say two hundred, you got it. You want stock options, they're yours. This character Loomis is nothing if not a gent."

"One might almost say the same about you, too, Mac, dear," Virginia added.

Palmer walked into the foyer and put on his overcoat. He came back into the room carrying Virginia's bright-red cloth coat. "How far does Loomis' boundless generosity extend?" he asked then. "I have this accomplice here who ought to get something for herself, too."

"You name it, sweetie," Burns said.

"You name it, sweetie," Palmer told Virginia.

The spot of intense red made by the sunlight on her coat touched everyone's cheeks with a kind of hectic pink. "I'm overwhelmed," she muttered, getting into the coat as Palmer held it for her.

"So what's the word, kids?" Burns asked then.

Palmer put on his hat. "You're pushing, Mac."

"I'm in a position to."

"That's true. But, then, why push? Or are things as locked up, cut and dried, as they seem?"

"You of all people know they are," Burns assured him. "I'm pushing because I have a deadline."

"Suppose I give you my answer tonight, at the wedding reception."

Burns pursed his thin lips unpleasantly. "Baby," he said. The word hovered in the air for a moment. "Baby, you know that if I want to force a decision right this second, I have the leverage to do it."

"But you'd rather have a decision given freely and in good will."

Burns looked unhappy for a moment. "I'll see you at the reception, Woody. But you can't stall beyond that. Understood?"

Palmer nodded. He took Virginia's arm. "Let's leave here together by the front elevator."

"Mr. Palmer! You take a girl's breath away."

Jauntily, Palmer led the way out of the apartment.

374

"I don't really want to go," Edith was saying. She sat before her dressing-table mirror, listlessly applying foundation to her face. Already the fine network of almost invisible lines had blended into a smooth, youthful mask.

Palmer walked in from the bathroom, where he had completed his second shave of the day. He knew that his beard was too light in color really to show, but after the early evening hours he could easily feel a roughness if he brushed a hand over his cheek and this, rather than any outward sign, had caused him to reshave.

"It may even be fun," he said encouragingly. "There'll be celebrities, other than us, that is. And the food will be delicious."

"If you like Jewish food," Edith added *sotto voce* through a mouth closed to allow the addition of lipstick.

"I detect a disapproving note."

Edith sighed. "It's possible to like Jews and loathe Jewish food. It's overcooked and underseasoned. Some of my best friends hate Jewish food."

Because he was bent on getting her into a better frame of mind, Palmer chuckled at the remark. "Reminds me of a joke Burns told me."

Edith arched her eyebrows. "Is that how you spend your time with him?"

"This Chinese restaurant opened in Brooklyn," Palmer went on quickly. "The first patron looked over the menu and said: 'How come all you've got is pizza, lasagna, manicotti and eggplant parmigiana? You call that Chinese food?' The waiter shrugged and said: 'What can we do? We're located in a Jewish neighborhood.'"

Edith finished making up her mouth and turned her attention to her eyes. "That joke," she said in a slow, faraway voice, concentrating on her eyes instead of her thoughts, "is only funny to a New Yorker. If you're trying to put me in a good humor, spare the comedy."

"Why on earth would I want you in a good humor?" Palmer asked, too nettled to mind his words. "I like you just the way you are."

"That's my darling," she muttered, carefully drawing a dark-brown line along the base of her eyelashes. "Tell me one thing and I'll go to the Plaza, if not happily, at least without noticeable rancor."

"Ask me."

"Tell me we can arrive at nine and leave at ten."

"We can arrive at nine, but I can't leave at ten."

"Can I?" she pursued.

"If you wish."

"Agreed." She was working on the tips of her lashes now, building them up and out in dark sweeps. As Palmer watched, her face took on accent and interest. She was changing from one person, pale, laundered, almost nunlike, to a beautiful woman. He leaned against the wall beside the mirror and continued his inspection.

Since a rather lavish buffet dinner had been planned, the invitations to the Plaza called for seven-thirty attendance. When the Palmers arrived at nine, however, they found the large room only half filled. The buffet tables—such was the experience of the catering staff—were only now beginning to be loaded with an assortment of food.

Palmer handed his engraved invitation to a uniformed hotel captain, who advanced a step or two into the room and said, in a quiet but penetrating voice: "Mr. and Mrs. Woods Palmer, Jr.," reading the calligraphed inscription on the thick vellum card.

Immediately a small knot of people near the door looked up from a private conversation and smiled brilliantly at the Palmers. As if on cue, a seven-piece band broke into a complex cha-cha, complete with pistol-shot bongo beats and the sibilant percussion of maracas.

A pleasant-faced man in the group advanced a step. Although they had met only once before, in Albany, Palmer knew him fairly well through intermediaries. The lieutenant governor's sparse, crew-cut hair revealed a scalp as pink as human skin can attain without artificial aid. An engineer by profession, he had taught at one of the local colleges for several years before entering politics. Something of the professor remained, Palmer noted, if only his ability to retain a fairly coherent sense of organization when discussing political affairs. He was also one of the few professional politicians Palmer had met whose face over the years had set into upward lines, rather than the down-trending cuts and wrinkles of a man with permanent worries. Above his blue eyes, almost as milky in color as Burckhardt's, the lieutenant governor's forehead was creased horizontally by what seemed now, to Palmer, to be the signs of a humorous cynicism.

"Woods," he said in a low, dry, measured voice, "it's good of you to come."

"Governor, this is my wife, Edith."

"A very great pleasure, Mrs. Palmer. Let me introduce you to my wife, Cyma. Honey, Mr. and Mrs. Palmer, from United Bank." The small woman produced the harassed smile common to most mothers of the bride.

"How do you do, Mrs. Adler," Edith said. "This must be quite an occasion for you. All the planning that goes into one of these things."

Mrs. Adler twisted her narrow shoulders in a self-deprecatory gesture. "I don't have that many daughters to give away," she said. She turned to the girl standing beside her. "This is the bride. Mim, Mr. and Mrs. Palmer. My daughter, Miranda, and this is her husband."

The girl looked barely old enough to be legally married. Palmer smiled at her and got an odd, tired smile in return. He felt Adler touch his arm and move him adroitly past the receiving group, murmuring: "The child of my old age."

"How many others do you have?" Palmer asked.

They were moving in the direction of the bar. "Two boys. Both in their thirties and each with two kids. Mim's still in college. There's quite a gap in age between her and the boys."

"Miranda," Palmer said. "Prospero's daughter. That makes you the wizard, doesn't it?"

Adler's mouth twisted sideways, as if smothering a remark. "The old magician now produces champagne," he said, gesturing to the bartenders.

"My daughter's eleven, and surrounded by boys on each side," Palmer said, taking two glasses.

"When the time comes for her wedding, my friend," Adler said, "you'll bless the day you became a banker." His eyes roamed the room. A group of newcomers stood at the door. "Why she couldn't just elope and leave me with a few dollars in the savings bank, I don't know."

Palmer laughed. "As a depositor, do you take a lively interest in the savings-bank branch bill?"

"With what this thing's costing, I have no further money to be interested in." Adler grinned ruefully. "I've got to say hello again. Enjoy." He left for the door and Palmer wandered over to Edith, handing her the champagne. They lifted their glasses slightly to the newly married couple.

"Much happiness," Edith said.

The girl's cheeks, almost pure white, looked blue under her eyes. She nodded. "Thank you, Mrs. Palmer." As the newcomers were introduced, the Palmers moved off to one side of the room.

"Imagine that," Edith said. "She's under such tension the blood seems to have drained entirely out of her, but she remembers our name."

"A politician's daughter never forgets."

"Tell me who some of these people are, darling."

"Adler? He's unique. He's reputed to be honest. He may be at that. Seemed pretty shook up over the cost of this shindig."

"Is Mac Burns here yet? I don't see him."

"Mac will arrive late," Palmer predicted, "with a gorgeous girl on his arm. It's a trademark. But there's Whatshisname, the U.S. senator."

"Which one?"

"He's either the upstate or the downstate one, I forget which. The woman he's talking to is the Governor's wife. That means His Excellency is here, but closeted away somewhere, politicking."

"That couple who just came in?"

"My God, Edith, you ought to know what our Mayor looks like."

"And the big man just behind them? What an odd face. One would almost call him intelligent."

"Victor S. Culhane. Of whom I have spoken before, dear."

"Big Vic? Thrilling."

"Would you like to meet him?"

"No, indeed."

"Are you ready to eat?"

"Not yet."

"More wine?"

"I still have this."

"Then let's dance."

"No one else is, darling."

"Would you like me to entertain you with card tricks?" Palmer asked.

"Can you?"

He gave her a sour smile. "These things are always in the eye of the beholder."

"Meaning?"

"Meaning one who will not be entertained, cannot be entertained."

"Oh, look!"

Palmer followed her glance and saw a couple in their late sixties march out on the floor and begin dancing a cha-cha. For a moment, Palmer could not place what was wrong with their dancing. He was aware only that although they seemed to be doing the right things, something was terribly amiss. The woman's eyes were fixed resolutely on a point about a foot in front of her face and her mouth moved almost surreptitiously. Then Palmer realized that she was counting and also, apparently, watching a particular clip of film reeling past her mind's eye, probably a mental image of a dance instructor at work. The man had thrown pride away and was openly watching his own feet with a kind of dazed expression, as if a magician were alternately hiding and revealing them under a row of shells. Both of them continued to step, pause, back up and move ahead with a curious air of fierce concentration mixed in some strange way with an imitation of casualness. Now and then one would lag enough behind the beat so that they realized something had gone wrong. With a determined effort, they would hop ahead to the next part of the step, skipping a beat in order to recover the lost one. More often, however, Palmer noticed, they both tended to lag or speed by less than a beat, and remain calmly unaware of it.

"I don't think we can top that," he told Edith in a low voice.

"Could anyone?" she asked. Then, softly: "Here are the Burckhardts."

Palmer watched the arrivals make their way rather quickly through the reception line, accept champagne, touch glasses with the lieutenant governor and look around them for familiar faces. Burckhardt saw Palmer almost at once and immediately led his wife over.

"Evening, Edith. Woody."

Before the couples had fully paid each other their respects, Burckhardt took Palmer's elbow and swiveled him ninety degrees sideways, forming a separate conversation group. "Where the hell were you today?" he muttered angrily.

"With Burns."

"In Albany?"

"Here. He came back by about one, full of excuses."

"Never trust a Greek." Burckhardt took a long, unsteady breath that did nothing to calm him. "And what in Christ's name have you got to say for yourself, sonny?"

"Just that I think we've trusted Burns one step too far."

"That's the kind of half-assed crap I'd expect from you," the older man said, moving in as close to Palmer's ear as he could and keeping his voice to a kind of harsh purr. "What do you plan to do about it, besides stand around here swilling cheap champagne?"

"Didn't you get any of the Bollinger?" Palmer asked, giving Burckhardt a wide stare.

"Look, boy." Burckhardt's voice was so close to his ear that Palmer felt as though he had leaned against some heavy piece of machinery, vibrating furiously through the bones of his skull. "That bastard double-crossed us," the older man informed him. "I depended on you to keep him in line. I still haven't figured out whether you're stupid or crooked. Which is it?"

"What would you rather it be?"

Burckhardt stepped back and fixed his hot blue eyes on Palmer. "For your sake, stupidity."

"You know it wasn't," Palmer replied as pleasantly as he knew how. "You had warnings from me more than a month ago. You ignored them."

"I had no warning this amendment idea of his would backfire. Or was it your idea, too?"

"His. But I went along with it. In the absence of any orders to the contrary from you, I continued to back your man Burns."

Burckhardt's eyes narrowed. "What happens if I don't tell you to breathe, Woody? You just turn blue and die?"

Palmer smiled amiably. "You're suffering what all lone wolves suffer, Lane. If you could bring yourself to delegate authority, you wouldn't get in these corners. But now, I'm afraid, it's too late."

"The hell it is," Burckhardt snapped.

"I hope you're right."

"I'm going to do what I should've done in the first place," Burckhardt said. "I'm going to pack a little black bag full of coarse green notes and get up there to Albany and buy what you fancy fellows have been trying to finesse for me. The hell with finesse. It's time for cash."

"It's time to get off the subject," Palmer told him. "Here comes Madigan."

They both looked up to see a stocky man in his mid-fifties bearing down on them, Jim Madigan, the executive officer of Murray Hill Savings Bank. The room had begun to fill now and Madigan had some difficulty shouldering his way between people. He grinned broadly.

"I didn't know you boys had arrived," he said, pumping their hands in turn. "I've been chatting with the Governor and I thought you'd certainly pay your respects."

"Later," Burckhardt barked. "Jeez, Jim, you look lousy. Putting on weight?"

Madigan's grin widened and he patted Burckhardt's flat belly. "Old Iron Gut. When you going to retire and enjoy life, Lane?"

"Whenever you bastards stop shaking the tin cup for more branches."

Palmer returned Madigan's grin but turned slightly so as to take himself out of the group. Under the pretext of conferring with Edith and Mrs. Burckhardt, he slipped further away. After a moment, now in the clear, he started for the bar, carrying his glasses and those of the ladies.

The elderly couple were now doing a mambo in the same wind-up-doll style. Some younger couples had joined them. Heartened by this sign, the band seemed ready to stretch the medley into an all-night session. As Palmer moved carefully between standing groups of people, he concentrated on passing conversation.

". . . absolutely lousy. I heard him three nights running at Grossinger's and he used the same jokes over and over again."

"He killed 'em at the Fountainbleu, though. They were . . ."

". . . just a small taxpayer, Charlie. Store on the ground floor, terrace apartments overhead."

"How much action you got left? I could maybe go for a ten per cent participation if you . . ."

". . . she's still there, still doing the same act. She must be my age by now, but she's still packing 'em in."

"Does she still twirl her knockers up on her shoulder? I remember . . ."

". . . deserves it, if anybody does. He's delivered plenty for the organization over the last twenty years."

"But an appellate judgeship, Harry. Can you actually see him in . . . ?"

". . . no idea he really meant it. Then, later, he came to my room."

"You're kidding, sweetie. He hasn't been able to satisfy a woman in . . ."

". . . twelve-thousand-a-year job if . . ."

". . . five-thousand plurality . . ."

". . . try some Scotch instead?"

Palmer turned and saw that Vic Culhane had addressed the question to him. "Is that what you're drinking, Vic?"

"Champagne's too tricky for me."

Palmer nodded. "I wouldn't think anything would be too tricky for an operator like you."

Culhane smiled slowly. He pulled in his abdomen and, in the process, seemed to reach the height of seven feet. "Mac tells me you may be helping him out. That's a pretty tricky proposition, too."

"Is that a warning?"

"A compliment, if anything. Mac underestimates the whole world. I told him that, in your case, he'd be making a mistake."

Palmer shook his head. "With the cards he's holding, he can't lose the trick."

"One trick doesn't make a rubber."

"One trick can win it, though."

Culhane squinted at him. "Say, what the hell are we talking about now?"

"Bridge?" Palmer asked. Then, to the bartender: "Scotch on ice."

"Rocksville," the bartender murmured. "Right you are."

". . . introduce me to him, Al. I mean, sort of casual."

Palmer turned to see the stranger who had breathed this almost in his ear and saw two men begin making their way to the Mayor. Palmer turned back to Culhane and smiled wryly. "Are all wedding receptions like this?"

"Isn't everything?" Culhane asked.

They stood with their backs to the bar and watched the crowd grow larger. One of the officers of the Chase Manhattan Bank was talking animatedly to an I.L.G.W.U. official. Behind them, on the edge of the dance floor, Burckhardt and Madigan were still conferring with each other. To their left, Edith and someone high up at New York University were discussing something. Palmer sighed and sipped his whisky. The band played a long "chaser" phrase and stopped playing.

"I'm pleased to see Mim married, anyway," Culhane observed.

"She seems like a quiet girl."

"I remember her as a baby, right after the war. Between her two brothers and her father, she didn't get much chance to do any real talking."

Palmer thought for a moment. "That's one of the things that amazes me about this city," he said then. "At least the political side of it. It's a family affair. Everybody knows everybody else's wife and kids."

". . . him to get off his dead ass and start promoting signatures. The petitions have to be filed by . . ."

Three men walked past Palmer and the rest of the conversation was lost to him. He sipped his whisky. The reception group at the door had begun to disintegrate now. The bridegroom, whose name Palmer had yet to learn, had disappeared some time ago, as had the lieutenant governor, leaving Mrs. Adler and her daughter to handle latecomers. In the absence of band music now, Palmer sensed a kind of hush. None of the conversations stopped, but the tone in which they were carried on had been modulated to a more discreet level. Without music, eavesdropping would be much easier.

"Well," Palmer said then, almost reluctantly, "I'd better bring champagne to the ladies." He ordered two glasses from the bartender.

"Pair of bubblies," the man said. "Right you are."

Palmer finished his whisky and took the filled wine glasses. "Nice talking to you, Vic."

"Same here. When's your daughter due for this kind of shindig."

"Years and years."

"Maybe by then you'll be right in the thick of it."

"If I last that long."

Culhane's mouth twisted slightly. "Woody, you I don't underestimate."

Palmer made his way very slowly through the crowd, guarding the filled glasses as he side-stepped his way toward Edith.

". . . topping out next month and he's already in hock. Before he can rent, he'll have to give away most of it for ready cash."

"What's the lending rate to him now? Eighteen per cent? He's in such a box, I . . ."

". . . air-conditioned T-Bird with a built-in bar. I said I . . ."

". . . convertible debentures at four and a half . . ."

". . . an ass like two mounds of whipped . . ."

"Here, dear," Palmer said, handing Edith a glass. "Where's Mrs. B.?"

"Somewhere. I was having the most fascinating conversation with . . ."

". . . forty-three credit cards and not one of them will . . ."

"I guess I'd better drink her wine, then," Palmer said.

"On top of Scotch?"

"It's my last drink of the evening," Palmer announced.

"It's the last time you'll be able to make it to the bar and back, anyway. Did you ever see such a crush? These people are—"

Someone bumped into the bass drum, knocking the hi-sock cymbal end over end. It tumbled off the bandstand in a fury of shimmering crashes. Conversation stopped cold. Everyone seemed to pivot toward the bandstand and, for a moment, the room was almost at peace. In that instant, there was a movement at the door. Palmer's eyes swung sideways and saw Mac Burns enter the room. At his side, in a red silk sheath, walked Virginia Clary. Her arm was in his.

"I see what you mean," Edith murmured. "The well-timed entrance. Who's the slinky thing with him?"

"Slinky? Her?"

"I couldn't think of a better description. Did he pick her because she's shorter than him?"

"That's my p.r. director."

"The . . . the one who writes your speeches?"

"She used to."

"Imagine that in a bank." Edith watched them pay their respects to the bride and her mother. "Times have changed."

"She doesn't look that way in the office," Palmer assured her.

"That's Miss Clare?" Edith asked. Burns and Virginia were moving slowly toward Palmer now, although they didn't seem to have seen him.

"Clary. Virginia Clary. Used to be with the *Times*. And the *Trib*."

"Both? It hardly seems possible in a girl that—" Edith stopped for a moment. "But she isn't that young, is she?"

"Pardon?"

"At a distance she looked quite young."

"I don't know."

"Early forties," Edith said. "They seem to be heading for us."

"Don't get too chummy with Burns. I happen to be hopping mad at him."

"How do you feel about Miss Clary?"

"Curious as to her choice of escorts."

"Isn't she free to choose?"

"It's just a little odd, choosing Burns."

"Perhaps they're having an affair," Edith suggested as the two people in question drew slowly closer.

"Good grief, no!" Palmer exploded.

"So positive?"

"I'm not positive," he retrieved quickly, "it's just so unlikely." At that moment Virginia caught sight of him. The arm linked with Burns tightened slowly until she was pressing against her escort.

"I've seen unlikelier," Edith murmured.

Burns saw them now, and pantomimed an immense, wonderfully surprised hello. He led Virginia to them. "Woody . . . and my favorite blonde. How are you, dear?" he asked Edith. Then, without waiting for a reply: "Edith Palmer, Virginia Clary, Ubco's stalwart p.r. lady."

After less than a second, Edith extended her hand. "I can't say I've heard all about you," she told Virginia. "But I do know you're the genius who writes Woods's speeches."

Virginia shook her hand. "I used to be," she said in a soft voice.

"Pardon me?"

"I used to be," Virginia said in a louder tone. "I've been demoted."

"Woods doesn't take kindly to other people being as smart as he is."

"Who does?" Burns asked genially.

"Oh, that reminds me," Edith said, "I'm not supposed to get too chummy with you, Mr. Burns. My husband is hopping mad at you. Why?"

"You mean he didn't tell you?" Burns asked with the same amiable grin. His sharp nose swiveled sideways to point at Palmer.

". . . told me I as good as had the contract in the palm of my hand," a man near Palmer said.

"I didn't want to bore her," Palmer told Burns.

"A little matter of politics," Burns said to Edith. "You wouldn't be interested."

"On the contrary. I'm always interested."

Virginia moved closer to Burns until their bodies touched. She patted Burns's hand. "You have more stamina than I do," she said.

"I should think you'd have more than your share," Edith told her, "working with these two." She paused for a moment, then glanced around her. "You don't have your champagne?"

"I'll get some," Burns said and immediately left the three of them.

". . . have a Caddy if you gave me one, Morris. Since I got my Rolls, I—"

"Hoo-ha, a Rolls yet. Next you'll change your name to Kane or . . ."

Palmer became acutely aware of the fact that neither he nor the two women had spoken for a rather long moment. He glanced hastily around the room. "Mac doesn't seem to have gotten very far," he said. "Who are those two he's talking with?"

Virginia followed his glance. "Upstate Republicans."

"I didn't realize Mac talked to anyone but Democrats," Edith said.

"Everyone talks to everyone," Virginia said. "It's a cardinal rule of politics. Keep talking. Keep friendly. Keep the lines of communication open."

"A wonderful rule," Edith mused. "I mean, not just in politics."

". . . piece of the action back in '56 and it pays me, like, a couple of bills a month."

"But the show closed already. Oh, you mean the record royalties and . . ."

"We don't seem to be obeying the rule," Edith remarked then. "Tell me, Miss Clary: have you been with the bank long?"

"Not— I'm finishing my second year." Virginia glanced at Palmer. "Can it be that long?"

"I'm a newcomer myself. Is it two years?"

She thought for a moment. "It must be. It doesn't feel like it, but it must be."

They fell silent again. Palmer looked for Burns and found him chatting with a former governor of the state. "I hope you're not thirsty," Palmer said. "Mac's paused again."

"Why don't you hunt him down," Edith suggested. "We'll wait for you."

"I—"

"Go ahead, darling. Miss Clary and I can find things to talk about."

"I'm sure he'll be along in—"

"Look there," she said. "Now the senator's side-tracked him." She handed Palmer her empty glass. "We'll either be here or . . ." She looked around her. "Or at the first table."

Palmer glanced at Virginia and failed to read the peculiar look in her eyes. "Be right back." Feeling sick at the pit of his stomach, he left.

". . . hooked me for twenty thou a year in alimony, but it was . . ."

". . . name this hospital wing after my folks, if I kick in about . . ."

". . . can run a Puerto Rican on the ticket. Spics vote, don't . . . ?"

He found Burns at the bar, deep in a private conversation with Vic Culhane. "Mac," Palmer said, "thanks a lot."

Burns turned toward him with a slow, insolent smile. "I wonder what the hell they'll find to talk about, Woody-baby. That wife of yours is pretty sharp, isn't she?"

Palmer ordered three glasses of champagne. "How did you talk Virginia into coming with you?"

"Charm. You ought to be glad I'm playing decoy, lover."

Palmer started to take the filled glasses, then changed his mind. "Bartender, send a waiter over with these, and a bottle? It's the first table on the right." He stared at Burns for a moment and then left.

The place had become so crowded that people were forced to stand at the door, waiting for an opening. Waiting patiently there were two men Palmer recognized as United Nations delegates, although not from any major nation. He began to force his way slowly through the packed groups of people.

". . . opened at ten and an eighth and by the close it dropped to six. Is that . . . ?"

". . . clothes at Saks are too dowdy. There's this place in Miami at the . . ."

". . . fascinating to women, I should think." Palmer was surprised to recognize Edith's voice. He caught sight of her several feet to his right, standing next to an empty table.

". . . so much that," Virginia was saying, "as it is his aura of being almost out of control, almost about to crash. I suppose that's what attracts women."

"But it's so much play-acting, of course," Edith replied.

"Yes, but to a certain kind of woman even the play-acting is impressive."

"Somehow you don't sound as if you're that certain kind of woman."

"I tell myself I'm not."

"Better than that," Edith said almost solemnly. "I say you're not."

Neither of the women spoke for a moment. They seemed not to have seen Palmer. Even separated from them by a few feet of space and a row of people, Palmer could feel the muted tension.

"Is my husband difficult to work for?" Edith asked suddenly.

"Wh— I don't think I'd say that."

"What would you say about him?"

Virginia paused. "As his employee, speaking to his wife," she said then in a thin, edgy voice, "I don't believe I would say anything . . . at all."

"Ah." Edith smiled pleasantly and, turning, saw Palmer. "Here he is. But without the wine. Darling?"

"I'm having a waiter bring it."

She glanced at her tiny watch, a small, tight cluster of diamonds on her wrist. "He won't get here in time, darling. It's ten o'clock."

"You're leaving?" Virginia said.

"I am, at any rate," Edith explained. She glanced at Palmer. "I think you ought to stay."

"I'm afraid so."

"Well, then." Edith stood up straighter.

"I'll get you to the car," Palmer said, taking her hand. "Stay close to me in this crush."

"Good night, Miss Clary. I'm terribly pleased to have met you."

"Thank you, Mrs. Palmer. It has been a pleasure."

Edith looked at her for a moment. "I think," she said in a musing voice, "we both did that rather well."

Chapter Fifty-six

Palmer did not return for nearly half an hour. It took him several minutes to have the car called but, after putting Edith in it and bidding her good night, he did not immediately return to the reception. Instead he lingered on the long sweeping East steps of the Plaza and breathed cold air until his eyes watered. He glanced north toward the park and saw the row of hansom cabs, steam spurting in thin jets from the horses' nostrils. After a while the cold penetrated his clothing and he went inside again. The heat was welcome at first, but rapidly grew too much for him. He sank into a chair in the lobby and felt the tall-ceilinged room tilt slightly. The combination of champagne and Scotch, for a moment, seemed to undo him. Then he sighed and got slowly to his feet. He caught sight of himself in an antique glass mirror, a tall, thin man with a furtive face. He stopped, straightened up and frowned at himself. Immediately he looked more promising. A bellhop was watching him.

Palmer transferred the frown from the mirror to the bellhop, who instantly looked away. Nodding, Palmer retraced his steps and sat down in the small chamber next to the room in which the reception was being held. He could hear the haggling babble of voices almost as clearly out here as inside. Beneath them, the thock, pung, thock-thock-thock of the bongo drums produced a staccato accompaniment.

He tried as best he could, in his present state, to evaluate Edith's behavior. Nothing she had said, he decided, really came to much. But if this were true, he told himself, why did it all make him so uneasy?

He sat forward on the narrow, red velours bench, elbows on his knees, and tried to play back her remarks about, and to, Virginia. Instead of performing this act, his mind wandered slightly under the insidious influence of the music from the other room. The trumpet, under full mute, gave off thin, nagging sparks of sound, jagged spears of complaint, smothering in the percussive wash of rhythm. After a stabbing minor run of notes, the trumpet seemed to drown. The piano rolled meaningless arpeggios over its body.

Palmer straightened up and felt for his cigarettes. He found a thin silver case, large enough to hold ten smokes, in the side pocket of his dinner jacket. There were no matches. Holding an unlighted cigarette between his fingers, he stared at it for a long time, trying to summon up Edith's words.

The attempt reminded him of the immense superiority of electronic devices over the human mind. A minor collection of transistors and electromagnets had already defeated him today, in Burns's apartment. It was possible, he thought rather hazily, that tape recorders would eventually conquer the entire planet, creating vast electronic enterprises of superhuman memory and agility. If Heinz Gauss were to be believed, monstrous electromagnets could even defeat the elemental force of gravity that held humans to their own patch of earth. Palmer wondered in a vague way what the potty old man was up to at the—

A match flared in front of his eyes. Palmer looked up, saw the waiter holding the match and held his cigarette in the flame. "Thank you."

"Yes, sir. Some wine, sir?"

Palmer winced. "Scotch on ice, please."

"Yes, sir. On the rocks." The waiter disappeared.

Palmer inhaled cigarette smoke. Was it possible, he wondered, that Edith not only knew about his affair, but knew Virginia was the woman? If Edith had made an accurate series of guesses, what did she plan to do about them? Would she look for confirmation? How long would it take her to realize the part Burns had played, the information he held?

A drink appeared before him. He thanked the waiter and slowly sipped the whisky. The cool, astringent taste seemed to straighten out his thinking. Even though he recognized this as a dangerous illusion, Palmer welcomed it.

No, he told himself, though she might suspect something, she could not possibly suspect everything. But when she saw—as she inevitably had to—the role he would soon be playing in Jet-Tech's take-over of Ubco, she would realize that some powerful kind of leverage was being applied to him. She would have little difficulty identifying it.

Within an hour or two, at the most, he had to give Burns his answer. Palmer stood up, glass in hand, and walked to the doorway of the reception room. The tables around the dance floor were filled with people nervously picking at plates of food. A few couples on the floor made sinuous patterns to the Caribbean beat of the band. The elderly pair, foreheads beaded, continued to prance with imperfect mechanical skill through an ingenious maze of steps.

Palmer wondered why he had delayed giving Burns his answer. It was so obvious to both of them what the answer had to be.

He watched an upstate banker, the representative of a powerful chain of commercial banks, telling a long story or joke to a New York building contractor currently suspected of involvement in a Title I scandal, a Democratic congressman from Brooklyn and Jim Madigan, of the Murray Hill bank. At this distance, several yards, they looked like a band of brothers. After the story had ended, the contractor picked up their empty plates and took them to the buffet table for refilling.

Palmer found himself wondering if he would ever understand the peculiar allegiances of politics. As anyone did who kept reasonably well informed, he knew that wherever politicians met—in state legislatures or the houses of Congress in Washington—their personal feelings for each other were one thing and their political allegiances, which might make them enemies, were another. Democrat might gleefully trample on Republican while a legislature was in session. But if they were friends, as most of them were, these displays of political animosity disappeared after hours. Palmer asked himself suddenly whether this was such a sound idea.

There was something typically American in the loose-knit amiability of it, the steadfast refusal to remain serious. Like the code of Omertá, which bound even warring Mafia members to silence, the code of the non-serious protected politicians from grave harm at each other's hands. Scandals broke. Peculations were revealed, but rarely by other politicians except those out of office. The whole thing, Palmer reflected, was a private club. Anyone had the right to form such tight private associations, but they did not quite fit the classic picture of a democracy. Nothing in modern politics did, Palmer reminded himself. The infant days of the Republic, when political contests smoldered with personal hostility, harsh polemic charges and the kind of partisanship that pervaded every corner of a politician's life, were dead.

". . . fifty thousand front money till the mortgage closing, then . . ."

". . . district never was any good. Too many egghead voters trying to . . ."

". . . drop by my place around midnight," Burns murmured in his ear. Palmer blinked and looked sideways at Burns. "Do we have to?" he asked.

"We really do, Woody-baby."

"I can give you my answer here."

"But I can't give you your instructions here, can I, doll?"

Palmer said nothing for a moment, trying to digest the idea of "instructions." "I don't see Virginia."

"She's around. Want me to find her for you?"

Palmer shook his head. "I can do that for myself."

"You sure can, lover." Burns laughed pleasantly and went away.

". . . rather have a Negro in that spot. Looks better on the ticket if he . . ."

". . . what can you give a woman who has everything, Paddy? So I had the back yard bulldozed and put in one of those faggot Jap gardens with the . . ."

Palmer sipped his whisky, moving slowly along one wall as he did so, his eyes searching the room for the red silk sheath.

Was it possible, he mused, that no one anywhere was free of the kind of "instructions" Burns mentioned? Did everyone serve someone else? Wouldn't you think, he asked himself, that a man of independent wealth could have solved the problem of independent action? Or was it in the nature of action—in the moment of choosing it last summer when Burckhardt offered him the job—that you put yourself at the mercy of "instructions"?

Was it really impossible, at this stage of the world's slow unraveling, to function in response only to the dictates of a single conscience?

The band's seemingly endless Latin American medley braked suddenly to a halt with a wild thud of bongos. After a pause, the music began again, a slow, wheeling waltz. Palmer saw the red dress across the room, beside the buffet table.

He made his way to Virginia, finding her in the company of a man he had never met. The two of them were talking rather earnestly as they moved along the table, filling their plates. She turned as Palmer touched her shoulder.

"Mr. P!" She sounded slightly edgy. "I thought you'd gone home. Say hello to Syd Baron, the p.r. genius behind the savings banks."

Palmer shook the man's hand and said: "This is old-folks music, Miss Clary. Shall we?"

Virginia gestured with her half-filled plate. "I was just—"

Palmer relieved her of the plate, put it down and led Virginia onto the floor. They moved into the looping rhythms of the waltz, turning slowly in one spot for a long moment.

"What was he telling you?" he asked.

Virginia shook her head. "Nothing important." Her eyes, a few inches from his, regarded him speculatively. "You all right?"

"How all right would you expect me to be?"

"Um. You have a point."

"I also have a date at midnight with Burns. I'm to tell him my decision and he, as he delicately put it a moment ago, is to give me my instructions."

"He assumes you'll say yes."

"No other assumption makes much sense," Palmer said.

She nodded. "I was hoping you'd see it that way."

Palmer held her away from him, trying to get an entire picture, rather than a close-up of an eye or mouth. "You'd hoped?"

"Otherwise he'd have destroyed you."

"That's not possible."

"You're indestructible?"

"Something like it." Palmer wondered how much of his own fantasies she had suspected. "I had a picture of letting him do his worst," he said then, pulling her close to him so that he could speak softly into her ear. "I saw myself after it was all over, divested of job and family, but with more than enough money to live comfortably somewhere."

"Some island in the sun?"

"That sort of thing," he admitted. "With you."

"A gorgeous thought. Hopelessly impractical."

"Most gorgeous thoughts are." They wheeled slowly for a moment in silence. "Why are they?" he asked then. "Why is this one hopeless?"

"Not to waste time, because you'd never do it."

"I thought of doing it. I thought quite a bit about doing it."

"You thought too much about doing it," she told him.

"You sound very positive."

"You thought about the two of us in bed for the rest of our lives," she murmured in his ear. "You thought of how delirious it would be for a while. Then you wondered what came after that. Just the two of us, Crusoe and Friday, all other ties cut off—friends, family—only the slightly umbilical tie of sex. And you wondered how long it would take for even that to shrivel."

"You have an obscenely graphic mind."

"I know how you think. Unfortunately, it's pretty much the way I think when I'm in a cold and calculating mood."

"As you are right now," he told her. "I'm starting to freeze at the touch."

"So you'll be a smart boy and say yes to Mac," she said.

"You're pushing."

"I admit it."

"Why?" he asked.

"Because I think I know what's best."

"For whom?"

The music stopped. They stood motionless for a moment in the middle of the dance floor. After a pause the band began a slow fox trot and Palmer was dismayed to find that it was the same Gershwin tune to which he and Virginia had danced once before.

"Do you rememb—?"

"Oh, shut up," she said, moving her pelvis in against him as they danced. "Woods," she said at last, her breath stirring his ear. "Is there anything wrong with your replacing Burckhardt? Aren't you eminently qualified for it? Isn't this the chance to do the things you've wanted Ubco to do? Weren't you in favor of the loan all along?"

" 'Treat me rough,' " Palmer quoted, " 'muss my hair.' " He swayed slightly and realized he was not as steady on his feet as he'd imagined. " 'Don't you dare to handle me with care.' "

"Woods."

" 'I'm no innocent child, baby. Keep on treating me wild . . . baby.' " He laughed peculiarly. The room seemed to tilt. "I can see it all. Slim, balding Woods Palmer, Jr., master of fat, bulging Ubco. Nestled away in his p.r. department, the quasi-umbilical link, kept supple by illicit guilt. And behind Palmer, in all his superior splendor, the towering figure of Mac Burns or Loomis or someone like him, a man of parts, part schemer, part fixer, part pimp."

She stopped dancing. He stopped talking. "Go on," she said in a flat voice.

390

"Nothing personal, doll-baby," he added, smiling in a hideously amiable imitation of Burns. "Or is there?"

Virginia turned and walked off the floor.

Chapter Fifty-seven

He found himself walking east on Fifty-ninth Street. He had no clear idea how he had got there.

Although March was only a few days off, the night wind was bitterly cold. It seemed to bore through his dress overcoat—really more of a topcoat—with an icy anger. He paused for a moment after crossing Madison Avenue and stared into the window of a toy store. He examined, in turn, a scale model of a Sten gun, a Bofors anti-aircraft cannon, a Thompson submachine gun, an M-1 Garand, a late-model Lueger, a Schmeisser machine pistol, and what the paratroops called a grease gun, the light-weight magazine-loading submachine gun with folding wire stock.

No accuracy, Palmer recalled. He felt the window come up hard against his nose and forehead. He stared at the grease gun. No accuracy, but what fire power. With one of those, in a board room, it wouldn't matter if his father or Loomis or Burckhardt or any other constipated old bastard thought he was in charge. The fire power spoke louder.

Dimly, Palmer realized that he was feeling and thinking very oddly. He tried to straighten up, freeing himself from the chill support of the glass window. He saw a sign over the display of guns: "World War II Replicas." World War III, he decided, would be fought with some of Heinz Gauss's weird laser rays, or supersonic beams or anti-gravity magnets. Why blow up the enemy with H-bombs? Send them hurtling off the face of the earth with Anti-G.

He stumbled, pulled himself erect, and walked quickly eastward into the teeth of the wind.

Of course, he told himself as he crossed Park Avenue, Virginia was absolutely right. He not only had no choice in the matter, but the one choice open to him was actually good for him. But why did she have to be right? Why, he asked himself, couldn't she be bravely wrong?

Tell him to go to hell, Woods, he pictured her saying. Tell him you're no patsy, no figurehead, no cat's-paw. Let him do his damnedest, Woods. Whatever happens, I have you and you have me. Any other way . . .

391

I now pronounce you mouse and wife.

He paused at the corner of Lexington Avenue and tried to get his bearings. Bloomingdale's was dark except for its gaily lighted windows. He headed for them, an oasis of friendliness, and as he reached the first one, all the window lights snapped off for the night.

Jackpot.

Palmer wheeled east again and headed for Third Avenue. He had a mission that lay to the east, he remembered that much. To the east lay the rest of the evening's work. Burns's apartment: the obligatory scene.

But how much, really, did Edith know?

". . . cleaned out in Vegas betting straight red. I dropped maybe . . ."

". . . cockamamie chicken-shit crumbum with fifty votes to deliver on . . ."

The voices echoed strangely in his head. He reached Third Avenue and plunged on eastward. The cold wind brought with it a faint scent of river water, recently released from winter ice.

". . . yentzing this p.r. broad in his office while his wife was . . ."

". . . accept your resignation in the best interests of the . . ."

Palmer blinked and stood still. The voices were very real despite the fact that he knew they were a hallucination. He did not actually hear them, he realized, as much as he felt them take place in his head, not as spoken words but as remarkably vivid states of mind. He took a long breath of the wind, until his lungs ached. Then he continued walking east.

". . . completes the signing of the documents, Mr. Loomis, and now . . ."

". . . hardly think Mr. Burns is board of directors caliber, but if you . . ."

He reached Second Avenue and stared for a long moment at the upsweeping approaches to the Queensboro Bridge. For a moment he played with the idea of walking across the river instead of meeting Burns.

"Except that there's nothing on the other side either," one of the voices remarked.

Palmer opened the door of a Nedick's and sat down at the counter. "Black coffee."

"Scuppa scoff, no moo," the counterman said.

Palmer winced. All evening, he felt, he had been giving beverage orders in fairly ordinary English, only to have the bartender or waiter or counterman turn them into an elusive kind of Choctaw.

"What do I say if I want milk?" he asked. "Moo me?"

The counterman and the only other customer there laughed politely. Palmer accepted his coffee and surrounded the cup with his fingers, trying to warm them. After a moment he began to sip the acrid liquid.

". . . saw that old biddy about an hour ago," the counterman was telling his other customer.

"She hit you up for coffee and?"

"Nah. She knows better by now. Poking around in the trash basket outside, looking for newspapers."

The customer laughed. "That old bat can't read."

"Not to read," the counterman explained. "To wrap around her. 'S cold outside."

"Jeez, what a kook."

The counterman began to giggle. "She got a surprise. Like something bit her, yet. I mean, she digs that crow claw of hers down in the trash. I was watching from inside here. Saw it all. She digs her hand down in the trash and, like, she snags a finger on the lid of an open can or something. Christ! You'd a thought a snake bit her. She starts screaming and hollering and dancing around trying to get her hand loose. But this tin is hooked in good, all right. Finally she shakes loose and goes running off down the street."

The two of them chuckled happily at the picture. "That oughta stop her from looting trash baskets," the customer said.

"Bleeding like a stuck pig."

"Really hooked into something, huh?"

"Sliced her good."

Palmer listened to their mirth, downed the last of his coffee and laid a dime on the counter. He stood up and left. The wind banged against him, seemingly with less force now that he had the hot coffee inside him. He walked east, downhill slightly, until he reached Sutton Place. Then he began walking south.

This town, he thought. These people. These cold-hearted, cutthroat people.

At Fifty-seventh Street, he stopped for a moment and leaned against a traffic light to steady himself. Despite the coffee he still felt dizzy. As he stood there he heard a siren in the distance. It grew louder, then faded reluctantly away.

This town. Violent town.

He pushed himself erect and kept on going.

Burns's apartment was empty. After Palmer let himself in he searched from room to room, stumbling slightly as he moved. Then he locked the door and took off his coat. The heat of the apartment was too much. He cranked open both movable sections of the picture window and let icy blasts of air sluice through the living room.

Then he sat down on the end of the couch and took off his tight dress pumps. Padding about in stockinged feet, he examined the insides of the phonograph console and thoroughly, if unsteadily, searched the rest of the living room for microphones or other bits of recording apparatus. By the time Burns's key turned in the lock, Palmer was back on the couch smiling slightly at nothing. The cold air pouring into his face seemed to do him a great deal of good.

"Surprise, sweetie," Burns said. "Look who I brought."

Palmer glanced up, almost idly, and saw Virginia. "It," he said very slowly, "figures."

". . . installed a refrigerator in the back bar of the T-Bird and it's . . ."

Palmer closed his eyes tight. He had to stop materializing these voices. "What, Woody?" Burns asked.

"Nothing." Palmer opened his eyes and watched Virginia. "The fair Miss Clary."

"The calmer Mr. Palmer," she said. "At least, you look calmer."

"You walked away from me."

"You insulted me."

"Did not. Insulted Mac Burns."

"How'd you do that, Woody?" Burns asked. He was pouring three drinks.

"Inferred you were a pimp." Palmer smiled so pleasantly that his jaw ached.

Burns stopped pouring whisky. For a moment he made no move. Then he finished pouring. "Would you like to explain the inference, old buddy?"

"If you're making me a drink, don't make me a drink."

"All right. Now, about the remark."

"Personal interchange between me and my, uh, inamorata."

"Involving me, though."

"Tangentially." Palmer sighed. "Did you bring along the parchment and the pin?"

"What?"

"Don't I prick my finger and sign in blood?"

"Woods," Virginia said, "are you really that stoned?"

"Not wounded, sire, but dead." Palmer stood up and began pacing the room in his stockinged feet. "You two," he said after a moment.

"How's that?" Burns asked.

"Never mind. No sense crying over spilt." Palmer stopped pacing for a moment. "Go ahead, drink. Drink."

Burns gave Virginia her glass and raised his. "To a, uh, mutually beneficial relationship and all that jazz." They sipped their whisky. "Can I have your decision, baby?" he asked Palmer.

"You may."

"Correcting my English?"

"Bad habit."

"You'll shake it, huh?"

Palmer shrugged. The room began to tilt slightly on an axis formed by Burns's upright body. "Steady down, Mac."

Virginia frowned. "Woods, are you—?"

"All right?" he finished for her. "I am in tune with the world, Miss Clary the Fair: that is, I am all wrong."

She turned to Burns. "I think you'd better see that he gets home as soon—"

"You do that very fair, Miss Clary," Palmer cut in. "The sympathy bit. Tell me. How much rehearsal time have you two had over the last few months?"

"Woods, you're going to say something I'll—"

Palmer cut her off with a violent exhalation of breath. For a moment the room was silent. He chuckled softly. "If you think," he began then, "that I spent all those dead years in Chicago, watching my father die, only to end up here as a kind of Gilded Nonesuch, making your looting of Ubco look legitimate, you have sadly misjudged me and my motives."

". . . went to work for this father image, Burckhardt, the . . ."

Palmer turned away from them. By an effort of will he stopped the voices again. He turned back in time to see Burns smiling.

"You smile, sir?" Palmer asked.

"Come on, Woody. This is getting out of hand. All I want is your word on this. If you feel so strongly, I won't press you. All I want is, uh, what would you call it . . . tacit co-operation? Just relax, in other words, and let it happen. Let yourself become president of Ubco. Is that hard to take?"

"You do rehearse," Palmer said. "It's almost the same way Miss Clary put it to me."

"I can't help if she talks sense, too," Burns argued.

"You still have that peculiar smile on your hot little lips," Palmer pointed out. He took a step toward Burns. The left side of the room lifted very slightly, then settled again.

"All right, Woody. Let's shake on it, buddy."

"Am I a figure of fun?" Palmer wanted to know. He was now less than a yard from Burns. He could smell the man's after-shave lotion.

"Nobody said anyth—"

"I am," Palmer concluded. "Otherwise you'd stop smiling."

Burns took a step toward him and put out his hand. "Woody, be a good boy. Let's shake."

Palmer watched the gems in Burns's outstretched cuff link glitter almost evilly. His eyes swung up to Burns's pallid face, then sideways to Virginia. She watched him for a moment, seeing something odd. She took a step away from him. Her eyes shifted warily to Burns, back to Palmer.

"Woods," she said, "why don't—?"

"Why does everyone start their sentences with my name?" Palmer demanded.

"Woody," Burns said, "come on, old buddy. Let's be friends again."

"With you?"

Palmer blinked at the force in his voice. The question had come out almost as a shout. He took a breath and felt a fluttering below his lungs.

"With you, you filthy, scheming bastard?" he asked.

". . . played you for a patsy from the start . . ."

". . . dangled this broad under your nose like a choice hunk of . . ."

Palmer heard himself project an inarticulate noise, part grunt, part howl. "Shut up!" he yelled. The unheard voices fell silent. "Mac Burns!" he shouted. "Third-rate mind in a fourth-rate cesspool. Ornament of the public-relations profession. Paranoid, junior grade. Prince of pimps. Protector of the Unfaith." He raised his left hand to prod Burns's chest with his finger.

Burns flinched and threw up a hand, as if to defend himself.

"No you don't!" Palmer said. Everything slowed down abruptly. Burns's hand seemed to be bunching into a fist.

Palmer felt his right arm grow taut. The elbow moved back and down. His right hand moved up and out. The fingers tensed. The muscle in his right forearm tightened.

His arm looped sideways. He could feel his body falling into the movement, supporting it. Burns's eyes widened. The fist hit Burns between his sharp chin and his ear.

Palmer could feel the jawbone rattle against his knuckles. He saw Burns's face go greenish-white. Then it sank out of view.

Palmer looked down. Burns lay curled, foetus-like, on the sensuously thick white rug. His eyelids fluttered for a moment. Then he lay perfectly still.

A line of deep-red blood rilled up out of the corner of his mouth, ran swiftly down his chin and began to spill into the thick pile of the rug.

Palmer stepped back. The air had thinned. His lungs could not suck enough oxygen from it. He gasped in breath after breath.

After a long moment, he could feel the frenzy in his lungs begin to subside. His mouth was dry and bitter-tasting. The fingers of his right hand felt dead.

He listened closely. The room was silent. Even the wordless voices had stopped. He looked at Virginia. Her huge eyes seemed wide enough to blot out her face.

He knelt beside Burns and pushed his hand under the man's chin, lifting it away from the rug. The round blood stain on the rug was as brilliant as new paint. He felt the sweat-moistened skin of Burns's throat. A faint throb fluttered against his finger tips. He stood up and looked around the room again.

His glance brushed across Virginia's face, went past, returned. Her eyes lifted from Burns to his face. "Is he all right?" she asked. Her voice sounded like a spade digging into sand.

Palmer nodded. "Will you—?" His voice clicked tight shut. He tried to swallow. Nothing happened.

"I'll look," she said, moving slowly toward the bathroom. Palmer watched the narrow point of her black velvet slipper brush the rug near the blood spot. He could hear her rummaging in Burns's medicine cabinet.

When she came back she was holding a small white pharmacist's box. She handed it without comment to Palmer. He lifted the cardboard lid and saw a row of four gauze-wrapped ampules. His hand was shaking badly. He tried to read the legend printed on small paper bands around each ampule. "Crush glass between fingers and . . ."

Palmer got his arms under Burns's armpits. He struggled for a moment, then wrestled Burns onto the sofa. Gasping for breath, Palmer fumbled with Burns's collar, trying to undo his dress tie. His fingers trembled almost uncontrollably. After a long moment he realized it was a clip-on tie. He removed it and managed to take out the first two shirt studs. Then he broke one of the ampules. A harsh ammoniacal smell filled the air. Palmer waved the reeking gauze under Burns's nose.

Burns mumbled something and tried to pull his pale white face away from the broken ampule. After a moment his eyes opened briefly. "Stop," he grunted. "Stop."

Palmer took away the ampule and dropped it in an ash tray. It missed, falling to the floor instead. Some powerful perfume meant to mask the ammonia stench now lingered in the air around him. He sat down in a chair opposite the sofa and waited.

After a while Virginia came up behind Palmer. She lifted his right hand to look at the fingers. Even with her own hand as a support, his fingers quivered noticeably. "How do they feel?" she asked.

Palmer shook his head. "Numb."

"Try moving them back and forth."

He did. Each movement hurt, but not unbearably. The pain held no interest for him, but the sharp tremor that shook his whole hand and forearm did.

"They don't seem broken," Virginia said. "I'm giving you a drink."

Palmer refused it, then took it in his left hand. He stared at it for a moment, downed some of the whisky. It made him feel no calmer. He put the glass away on an end table, missing it by several inches. The glass fell to the white rug and remained upright without spilling a drop.

The unreality of it seemed to panic Palmer. Normally glasses spilled, didn't they? He rested his elbows on his knees and covered his face with his hands, trying to master the flutter in his diaphragm that seemed to make the rest of him tremble, too.

". . . one thing you never forget, never. No matter how they smile or how friendly they are, you never . . ."

Palmer's jaw tightened at the sound of the voice, by far the most real of those he had been hallucinating. Then he realized it was Burns's voice. He took his hands away from his face and watched Burns's mouth move painfully as the words came out.

". . . should never forget it for one Goddamned second. Scratch a Protestant and you find a killer." Burns felt his jaw. His lips were very pale. Then he lifted himself partly off the sofa, supported on one elbow, and looked past Palmer as if he were not sitting there. "And a Catholic-hater," he told Virginia. "To a Protestant we're cockroaches. Don't ever think otherwise."

Palmer took a long breath, trying to steady himself. "Mac," he said, speaking slowly, "I have never in my—"

"You know it as well as I do," Burns said to Virginia. "They've run this country on the blood and bone of the people they hate. It's their guilt makes them hate us. Any psychiatrist'll tell you that. Ask any of them. Ask a Protestant psychiatrist, if you can find one."

"Mac," she said, "lie back and rest, will you?"

"Two hundred years of it," Burns said. His voice had grown stronger, but it remained at a quiet level, as though proceeding directly from long-muffled feelings rather than new thoughts. "In my neighborhood out in Los Angeles we fought with the Mexicans and the Italians because they were somebody to fight with, but all of us fought the Protestants. We all hated them. They all hated us. We were vermin. They were the Master Race. Protestant rulers of the world. Rulers of the—"

"Lie back and stop talking," Virginia cut in. "You got a clout on the jaw, you loony."

"Two hundred years of it," Burns said. "With their General Motors and their Jet-Techs and their Westinghouses and their banks. Good God, their banks. That solid white Protestant wall. All that Protestant money . . . billions of it. They own it, they lend it, you pay it back. For two hundred years you and I have had their stinking heel in our face with their—"

"Will you act like a man with a sore jaw?" Virginia asked. "How about a drink?"

"I got a sore jaw," Burns agreed. In his somber intensity he pronounced it "saw jawr," forgetting years of self-training. "I got a sore belly full of their exclusive country clubs and restricted hotels and resorts and their finishing schools and their Ivy League colleges with Jew quotas and Catholic quotas and their Goddamned renting covenants and dining clubs and racket clubs and Junior Epworth Daughters of the American Great I Am and all the rest of the bed sheets they hid behind.

"Listen to me," Burns went on. "You'll learn. Even a smart cookie like you. Vic says I'm crazy. He thinks we can do business with them. Bullshit we can do business with them. There's only one way they respect us, only one way we can keep them in line. That's with *our* foot in *their* face!" Suddenly he was shouting. "And, sister, that time is Goddamned near at hand. If you th—"

"Mac, Mac, Mac." She put a hand on his shoulder and pushed him back into the sofa. "Shut up. Please?"

Burns sat up almost at once and swung his feet onto the floor. He gently felt his jaw. "If you think," he told Virginia, "that what we have here in New York City happened overnight, you're crazy. We bled for this, baby, for every inch of it. And don't think they didn't set us against each other, Italian against Irish against Jew against Negro against Puerto Rican. But now we got it." His hand twitched. Palmer saw him extend it palm up and violently grasp air in a tight fist.

"We got it right here, baby. The Protestants will never get this town back from the people who live in it. Not with all their sixty-thousand-dollar Westchester homes, not with their key-game split-levels in Fairfield County and

398

their crappy little fortresses on the North Shore. We own our own town, sweetheart. And we own some other towns, too. Ask any Polack in Chicago. Ask any guinea in San Francisco. Hell, out there in California we even own the bank." His eyes swung sideways to Palmer, recognizing him for the first time. "Hello, Palmer," he said. "Hello, loser."

Palmer watched him for a moment. Then he laughed, a sound too brief to indicate mirth. His right arm went up, hand outstretched, palm down. "Heil Burns," he said.

Burns's face, white with shock, grew suddenly red. He started to stand up, then fell back on the sofa. He grimaced and felt his forehead. "You bastard," he mumbled.

Palmer stood up and walked into the kitchen. He found a small towel, wrapped four ice cubes in it and brought it back to Burns. "Cool off a little," he said, handing him the improvised ice bag. "I'm sorry I hit you. It's the first time I've lost my temper in years."

"You hear?" Burns asked Virginia. He laid the ice bag on his forehead and winced. "You hear what he's really sorry about? About losing his Goddamned Protestant temper. About showing us what he's really like."

"His hand is going to hurt long after your jaw stops throbbing," Virginia pointed out. "Why don't you calm down and try to forget the whole thing?"

Burns frowned. "I'll have a lump the size of—" His eyes grew wider. "I'll have a Goddamned black-and-blue mark there for—" He moaned and shifted the ice bag to his jaw.

"Just to make you happier," Palmer added, "see if any of your teeth are loose. You were bleeding before."

"Where? Where?"

Palmer pointed to the rug. "Can't you taste it?"

Burns swallowed hastily. Palmer could see him moving his tongue gingerly from molar to molar. "You'll never forget this," Burns said then. "You're finished in this town. I wouldn't have you fronting for me now if you got down on your knees and licked my shoes."

"Mac, please," Virginia told him. "Try and collect yourself."

Burns snorted. "I'm collected." He stood up and walked to the picture window, slowly, like an old man. He stared out the window for a long moment. After a while, the hand holding the ice bag dropped to his side. His back grew straighter. He turned around and moved almost briskly toward the bar, where he dumped the ice and towel into a teak bowl. Then he turned to Palmer. "You'd better leave."

Palmer stood up. "I'm only sorry for having lost my temper. Hitting you was very satisfying."

"Go on, blow."

Palmer nodded. "Something else was satisfying, too."

"Seeing me bleed?"

"The experience—the unique one—of hearing the truth from you. Of finally learning how you really feel about something."

Burns turned to Virginia. "You hear? Is that *chutzbah?* You ever?"

"But it's a little appalling to realize what it takes to get you to tell the truth," Palmer said. "You've done nothing but lie to me and play-act from the first time we met. Some of the lies I recognized. Some I will probably never know the truth of. One time, one single time, just now, I finally found the real Mac Burns. And look what it took to find him."

"You'll find more of him," Burns promised. "I wish tomorrow was a weekday, Palmer. But Monday morning, you'll see plenty of the real Mac Burns."

Palmer sat down on the sofa and put on his shoes. Then he walked into the entry alcove, put on his coat and came back into the living room for a moment.

"If I felt the way you did," he told Burns, "I'd wonder how binding an agreement could be between the Protestants at Jet-Tech and a person like you."

"The Masked Avenger of Beirut," Virginia put in. "Mac, this is all so silly. He's going to walk out now and the whole mess will start to putrefy. It doesn't have to."

"Apparently it does," Palmer told her. "This man has stopped functioning rationally."

"You hear?" Burns asked Virginia. "Did I say *chutzbah?* Is there a stronger word? His kind drive us crazy. Then they accuse us of being irrational."

"Mac," Palmer said, "I cannot wipe out the last two hundred years. But I will not be charged with guilt by association. And I will not allow you to excuse your own chicanery by crying about Protestant discrimination. You asked for that punch. I'm only sorry I was mixed-up enough to give it to you."

"Go on. Get out."

"Virginia, can I give you a lift?"

"Who, me? Scarlet Mary? P.R.'s gift to organized prostitution?"

Palmer stared at her for a moment. Then he turned toward the door. "Speaking as one American citizen to two others," he said, "the hell with both of you."

"Woods."

He turned back. "Do you want a lift or don't you?"

"I'm going to stay for a while and try to calm this boy down."

He turned for the door again and hesitated. The signs and symbols seemed to shift back and forth in his mind between reality and dream. Had he really suspected her? How could he have suspected her? Whose side was she on? Were there any sides? Or was it just the typically circular mess life kept bringing to him, like a proud cat with a dead mouse.

"I'm sorry about that, too," he said then, not looking at her. "About the inferences I made. At least, I think I'm sorry."

"You fink," she said. "Go home."

"I'll talk to you Monday. Or something."

"Or something." She took his arm and walked with him to the entrance alcove. "I've got to calm this idiot down," she murmured in his ear. "He's hurt enough to pull the whole temple down on his head, Philistines and all."

"Tell him," Palmer said, raising his voice so that Burns could hear him, "that he ought to worry as much about his supposed friends as his supposed enemies." Then, in a whisper: "If it won't take long, I'll wait for you somewhere."

She shook her head. "Didn't you see that corner we passed tonight?" she asked in a small voice. "From here on we are just friends."

"What?"

"Good night. Go home. Good night."

"Look, I—"

She put her finger tips on his mouth. "Good night, Woods."

"What did I—"

"Not you," she whispered. "Nothing you did, although you did plenty."

"Then wh—?"

"It's just that . . ." She paused. Then she opened the door for him and pushed him out into the corridor. "Don't give my regards to Edith," she murmured. "Good night."

Chapter Fifty-eight

The cabby was driving too quickly up Third Avenue. Instead of holding the car to the twenty-two miles per hour at which the traffic lights were timed, he was speeding ahead and braking sharply at each cross street to wait the few seconds it took for the light to change to green.

Palmer found himself fascinated by the way in which the driver seemed to get no message at all from the fact that he always ran into a red light that eventually turned green. On the verge of explaining this simple phenomenon to the cabby, Palmer decided against it. As if to repay his diffidence, the driver put on a tremendous burst of speed, the cab's overtaxed differential whining in protest. This caused the car to reach the next red light so far ahead of the changing cycle that fully fifteen seconds elapsed before the light turned green.

Waiting, Palmer was distracted by the sight of a man standing next to a mailbox and slowly thumping it. Behind a three days' growth of grayish beard, the man's toothless mouth brought his nose and chin close together. Palmer cranked down the window to hear what the man was saying.

". . . rot-ten, lous-y, stink-ing . . ." He kept time to the iambs by giving the mailbox a smart wallop that produced a muffled boom.

". . . I don't, e-ver, want to, see them, e-ver, ay-gen . . ." The strong rhythm began to grow almost hypnotic.

Although the light had turned green, both Palmer and the cabby were now completely fascinated by the performance.

". . . peo-ple, ne-ver, e-ver, know the, right, right, right, right way." Boom, boom.

The man looked up to see Palmer and the cabby watching him. With the airy gesture of a man totally at peace with the world, he grinned broadly. Palmer caught sight of pink gums spotted with brownish sores.

"In other words," the man said, "they can't do nothing to me no more."

The cabby jumped slightly, slammed the cab into gear and roared off up Third Avenue. "They sure can't," he remarked.

"Not much more left to do," Palmer said.

"Poor bastard." The driver wheeled abruptly left and headed west on a side street. "I ain't got that many years to go," he mused, "before I'll be talking to myself on street corners."

"Christ."

"None of us ain't," the cabby added morosely. "None of us."

He was silent for the rest of the ride. Palmer left the cab and unlocked the door of the house with the pierced-concrete façade. He pushed the knob with such a weak effort that the door moved inward less than an inch. Damned old clown, he thought, ought to be locked up somewhere. Society had a responsibility to hide its more obvious mistakes.

With what seemed like too much of an effort for the task, he summoned up enough strength to push the door open. The knuckles of his hand ached at the pressure. He stepped inside and closed the door slowly, grateful for warmth after the cold outside air. He stood there in the dark, nursing his bruised hand. After a moment he hung up his coat and hat, took off his shoes and moved silently to the wall switch. He turned on the stairwell light and slowly went up the free-floating oak steps to the second floor. Once there, he switched off the stairwell light and moved cautiously through the darkness to the kitchen.

After closing the kitchen door behind him, he turned on a light and sank down on one of the stools, too tired for a moment to move. The climb up the stairs had, for the first time that he could remember, winded him.

Finally, he opened the refrigerator and poured himself a glass of milk. As he sipped it he heard someone stirring beyond the kitchen door. With a sinking sensation he knew that Edith was awake and, very probably, putting on her robe. After a moment the kitchen door swung open.

She had removed all her make-up. A broad, brilliant turquoise ribbon held her pale hair back from her forehead and kept it from the skin of her face, which had been covered with a thin layer of some humectant cream that Palmer knew from experience stayed peculiarly wet to the touch all night long.

Edith looked at him for a moment without any particular expression except a slight narrowing of her hazel eyes caused by her sudden transition from darkness into a lighted room. Then she moved to the table and picked up Palmer's shoes, which he had somehow placed next to the glass of milk. She bent over and laid the shoes on the floor.

"It only took ten years to break Woody of that habit," she said then. "I imagine there's hope for you." She paused. "You look awful."

"I feel awful."

"Scotch and champagne?"

"And treachery."

She blinked. "From . . . from Mac Burns?"

"Very astute guess. I can't even say it came as an immense shock." Palmer picked up his milk. "He's been on the Jet-Tech payroll since the beginning, even before I came into the picture."

"What's happened to your hand?" she asked then.

Palmer frowned. "What?"

"Woods, your right hand, as well you know. You've been favoring it ever since I walked in. And the knuckles are puffy and red."

Palmer shrugged wearily. "I punched him."

"Burckhardt?"

"Burckh—?" Palmer stared at her. "What on earth gave you the idea th—?"

"He's really the one who's landed you in this kettle of fish," she pointed out. "I see. You picked the wrong target. Burns."

He was silent for a moment, too tired to respond. Then: "Perhaps."

"So this great public-spirited savings-bank fight has been phony from the beginning."

"Not at all. Just the additional weight Jet-Tech threw on their side."

"But all your work. All those late-night meetings, those jaunts over most of upstate New York, all the evenings and nights and days you weren't here . . . all a lot of waste motion."

He nodded slowly, head beginning to droop with fatigue. "Wheel spinning."

"Woods, I thought you were too bright to be taken in like that."

He lifted his head to look at her. "Edith." He stopped. "Look." He gestured aimlessly with a hand that dropped into his lap again. "When I got to New York, the . . . the game had already begun. The cards were dealt."

"I see." She took the empty glass from his hand and put it on the table. "By that you mean the savings-bank game. Those cards."

He nodded without speaking.

"But apparently there was another game being played," Edith said then. "Didn't you think that perhaps . . ." Her voice died away and she was silent.

403

"Hunh?"

"Nothing." She sat down across the table from him. "But, then, what about that wo—" She stopped abruptly.

"What?"

Edith shook her head. "Not important. Some other time."

Palmer saw her studying him for a moment. He tried to sit up straighter, as if this could in some way help him pass whatever inspection was being held. But his body was not strong enough to make the effort. Although he felt as if he could hardly move, he was by no means sleepy. If there was a way to prolong this moment of inaction into an infinite period of time, he would be content to sit here and wait, but for what he was waiting, Palmer had no idea.

"None of that is important," Edith said then in a slow, inward-turning way, as if addressing herself alone. "But one thing is. What are you going to do?"

Palmer tried to shrug. His great lethargy kept him motionless. "Bow out?" he suggested. "Admit the big town has me f-fl-flummoxed?"

Edith's face was perfectly still. "What would you like to do, if you could?"

Palmer's eyebrows flickered up, then settled wearily again. "Beat them."

"For Burckhardt's sake?"

Palmer made a soft lip noise. "He's finished, whatever I do. Beyond help. And I'm not about to help him even if I could."

"Then why do you want to beat them?"

He took in a long, slow breath of air. "It would give me great joy." He smiled meaninglessly. "Great juvenile joy, I admit." He breathed out almost lazily the pent-up air in his lungs. "Wishful thinking. Only fairytales end that way."

"Then what will we do?"

"We?"

"If you're bowing out. What will the family do? Leave New York? Leave this house?"

Palmer closed his eyes. "I hadn't thought."

"That's clear enough."

The sharp edge to her voice forced him to open his eyes. "I'm sorry."

"But to just give up . . ." She sat perfectly still, looking down at her hands as they cradled the empty milk-coated glass. Then: "Woods, if you didn't like the cards you were dealt, why did you play the game?"

"Didn't know they were stacked." He grinned in a silly way.

"Maybe they're just the wrong cards."

"With Joe Loomis dealing . . . yes."

"Who is—?"

"Jet-Tech." Palmer grimaced. "Septuagenarian mastermind." He laughed softly. "Master mechanic of the loaded deck."

"Is it—?" She stopped.

404

"Is what?"

"Nothing."

"God damn it, Edith. You keep starting questions and never finishing them."

"I wondered. Is it possible, is it too late . . . to just . . ." She made small twirling motions with her hands. "Just deal out a new game? With your own cards?"

"How?"

"I haven't the—"

"You're running the metaphor into the ground," Palmer said. "It is not, after all, a card game. Is it?"

"But it resembles one. And if your opponent has stacked the deck, you demand a new deal with a new deck."

"I am in no position to force anyone to accede to anything." He could feel small flashes of irritation inside him, directed at his wife but patently meant for himself, for his own helplessness. The odd thing, Palmer noticed, was that this anger warmed him. The great tottering lethargy that weighed him down seemed to shift suddenly. He felt without weight.

"Is something . . . are you feeling all right?" she asked.

"It's just— I'm suddenly weightless or—" He broke off with a self-conscious laugh. In that brief instant he remembered Heinz Gauss. "Look here," he said.

"Yes?"

"I mean . . ." He was silent again.

"What is it?"

"It reminded me of my anti-gravitational friend."

"Woods, what on earth are you talking about?"

"The inventor of the latter-day Gauss Effect."

Edith stood up and put the milk glass on the sink drainboard. "It's terribly late, darling. I think we'd better get to sleep."

Palmer snapped his fingers. "Not just yet."

She turned to face him. "What has gotten into you, Woods?"

"But, God, it's tricky."

"Woods."

"Yes, yes, I'll explain. It's in two steps." With a sudden burst of new energy, he jumped off the stool and began to pad back and forth in his stockinged feet. "The first is not too hard. The second is a bitch." He yanked his bow tie open and removed the top stud from his shirt. "Good God," he said, laughing again, "it might even work."

"Woods, it's the middle of the night."

He glanced at his watch. "Can't do a damned thing till morning."

"Then shall we go to bed?"

He shook his head violently. "Hours to plan it down to the—" He stopped and turned to her. "Edith, can you put up a pot of coffee?"

"If I get an inkling of what you—"

405

"Right!" he burst in. "Absolutely. You start. I'll explain."

Watching him, Edith mechanically took out the electric coffeemaker and began to fill it with water. "I'm listening."

"Right." Palmer paced to the door and back. "We'll take the coffee into that study or den or whatever of mine. All the reference stuff is there, isn't it?"

"What sort of reference stuff?"

"Directory of Directors. Armed Forces Procurement Manuals. Is Washington in the same time zone we—? Of course it is. Good. Fine. How's the coffee coming?"

"I don't think you really need it."

"I need it. This has to be put together like a Swiss watch."

"This?"

"I keep forgetting," he said, stopping for a moment in mid-stride. He rubbed his hands together so vigorously his knuckles throbbed with pain. He hardly noticed the sensation. He flexed the fingers of both hands and wiggled them in the air.

"You are about to witness a deck-stacking such as the likes of which you have never—" He broke off the impossible sentence and began pacing again. "Complete new deck of cards. Entirely different game."

"What's the name of the game?"

He wiggled his fingers at her. "Showdown," he said.

CHAPTER FIFTY-NINE

The first rays of late winter sun hit the pierced-concrete façade shortly after seven-thirty in the morning. It was not until an hour later, as he looked up from the pile of books and papers spread across his study desk, that Palmer noticed the change from night to day.

Edith had gone to bed at three, after making a second pot of coffee. Finishing the last of it, with its slightly boiled taste from being kept warm too long, Palmer shoved his fingers through his hair and pushed himself away from the desk. He could hear the children's voices somewhere in the house. He picked up the sheets of paper and stared at them.

With the cold touch of daylight, the whole plan seemed doomed to failure. Palmer tried to pour another cup of coffee from the empty pot. Then he re-read the sheets of paper on which he had outlined each step in the two-phase plan. Uneasy with doubt, he stood up and walked around his chair to loosen his leg and back muscles. The same fatigue that had borne him down on his return home earlier began now to stiffen his walk. His dress shirt clung damply to his back. The edges of his cuffs were soiled. Palmer tried to stretch and found that he was losing energy rapidly. He glanced at his watch and saw that he could not begin making phone calls until nine-thirty, an hour from now. He sat down at the desk and propped up his chin on the palms of his hands. He heard Gerri shout something that sounded like "Tie your own shoes!" A moment later he was asleep.

When Edith woke him, Palmer's first sensation was one of intense gritti-ness. ". . . undressed and go to bed," he heard her say.

He groaned softly. He seemed surrounded by sand, packed down into his eyes and collar. He tried to open his eyes. "Time?" he muttered.

"Ten o'clock, Woods. Will you please—?"

He sat up straight, wide awake. "Lost half an hour," he grunted. "God almighty. Have Mrs. Gage make 'nother pot of coffee."

"Woods."

He turned to look at her. Despite the fact that she had had only a few hours of sleep, she looked reprovingly fresh. She had made up her face and got dressed. The whole effect made him feel even grittier. "Will you?" he asked.

"Darling, it's Saturday. You're not going to be able to—"

"Never mind that. Burns can wait till Monday, but I can't. Fresh coffee?"

"Will you get some sleep later?"

"Later. And please keep the kids out of here."

"Have any of them bothered you?"

"No. But. All right. Please? Coffee?"

"In a minute." She picked up the coffeemaker and took it away.

Palmer lighted a cigarette. The smoke sickened him for a moment or two. Then he felt the quick jolt of adrenalin triggered off by nicotine. Because the effect would only last a short while, he immediately got to work.

He put in a person-to-person call to the Midwestern city where Jet-Tech's research division was located. The operator got no one at the laboratory. Local information could not at first find a home telephone for Heinz Gauss. The operator located the number in a nearby suburb and, eventually, Gauss himself answered the ring.

"My problem," Palmer began after salutations, "is that I can't get you out of my mind."

"So? I would have thought you had long forgotten about me, my friend."

"I probably would have," Palmer admitted, "if I hadn't begun to feel re-sponsible for the whole damned mess."

"In a way you are, of course. You brought me here in the first place, no?"

"That's the point." Palmer paused. He reminded himself that he was not dealing with a bumpkin. A little fake altruism would go a long way. At the same time, Gauss must not suspect any of his real motives.

"Something's come up," Palmer continued. "Not at the bank. With a friend outside the banking industry. He's . . . well, we needn't go into that now. I took the liberty of telling him a little about your frustrations and so forth and so on. I mentioned no names. But because he's in a position to do something about it he's probably guessed whom I meant."

"You didn't jeopar—?"

"I was very discreet. And he will be even more so. It's his business. If I told you his name you'd understand at once. The main point is this: if you want to leave, he can guarantee—I mean guarantee—a post of the same or even higher responsibility, with a great deal more freedom and a budget that is almost unlimited."

"Are you speaking of Westingh—?"

"I am not speaking of anything at this point. He said only what I have relayed to you. Now. How does it strike you?"

"But without knowing the name of the other company, how can I say anything?"

Palmer sighed in exasperation. The call was taking altogether too long on a line that might be tapped. He had other calls to make before he could— "Gauss, no one is asking you to commit yourself blindly. I am asking for a reaction to the general idea. Are you in favor of it?"

"But of course I am in favor."

"Fine."

"How soon do you think I c—?"

"No idea," Palmer cut in. Once he had heard this sign of Gauss's eagerness, he wanted only to end the conversation and leave the German in tantalizing suspense. "I'm very pleased at your reaction. With a little work we may be able to liberate you." Palmer laughed. "Again, that is."

"Is it a matter of days? Weeks? Months? I must kn—"

"As soon as I know, you will," Palmer promised. "I have to say good-by now, Gauss. But it's really *auf Wiedersehen*." He hung up quickly and puffed at his neglected cigarette.

The time was now well after ten-fifteen. Palmer placed another person-to-person call—this time to a New England city. Again he went through the same problem of tracing the man's home telephone to a suburb. A woman answered the phone.

"Long distance calling General Hagen," the operator announced.

"He's . . . who is calling, please?"

"Woods Palmer," Palmer said.

"Just a second. I'll see if . . ." The woman's voice trailed off.

Palmer decided that even if Hagen were asleep, it was high time he'd got up. How old would he be now, fifty-eight or nine? Not old enough to loaf in bed this late.

"Hello?" a sleepy voice said.

"General Hagen?" the operator asked.

408

"Speaking."

"Go ahead, sir."

Palmer opened his mouth. "Which Woods Palmer is this?" Hagen put in first.

"How many do you know, Eddie?"

"Christ. I forgot about your dad. Sorry to hear about it, Woody."

"It's long past. I'm in New York now."

"I know you're in New York. Half a dozen times I was in town and meant to look you up, but I figured you were too Goddamned busy stealing money to find time for a beat-up old tin-hat buddy. How they treating you?"

"Eddie, did an old Army buddy ever call you out of the clear blue sky to *offer* you a favor?"

"N-no," Hagen said cautiously. "And neither are you."

"Wrong. Have you replaced Aaronson yet?"

"You know I haven't."

"Tough to find a man of that stature."

"Don't rub it in. Who have you got in your hip pocket?"

"A man with some fantastic ideas. He has laboratory proof. Something very hot."

"Does he have a name? Or are you afraid I wouldn't recognize it?"

"I'm afraid you can't pay him what he's worth."

"We're not that small."

"If you can't start him at seventy with stock options, let's just move along to how your family is, and what you're shooting eighteen holes in."

"Hell, that's too high."

"Not for what he has."

"Can he take it with him if he leaves?"

"It's been private research up to now," Palmer explained.

"Still and all, we don't want any lawsuits later on."

"Your caution is commendable. Let's forget the whole thing. How's Margaret?"

"Never mind Margaret. What's his Goddamned name?"

"An old friend, Eddie. I brought him to you by jeep once."

"You're kidding. Which of the three?"

"The oldest one."

Hagen was silent for a moment. "I see." Another pause. "Somebody's been selling you a load of sauerbraten, Woody. He isn't even worth thirty grand without options."

Palmer grinned. The lower counter-offer was what he had been waiting to hear. "Okay," he said cheerfully. "Next time you're down this way, Eddie, give me a ring. Like to see you sometime. Give my regards to Mar—"

"Crap. Forty thousand. No options."

Ten minutes later the conversation closed at fifty. Palmer consulted his work sheets and dialed a number direct. "Jane, this is Woods Palmer."

"Darling, is everything all right?" Edith's aunt asked.

"Everything is fine. Everyone's in perfect health. Edith sends her love. Is Tim there?"

"Good Lord, no. He's in Pasco."

"Pasco, Washington?"

"At the . . . uh, the hotel in town. It's the one he always stays at in Pasco. I haven't the slightest idea what it's called but it's—"

"It's only seven in the morning out there, isn't it?"

"Darling, I wouldn't know. I've never called him."

"Is he likely to be up that early?"

"Probably. Are you—? You're not planning to call him?"

"I am."

"Whatever for, darling?"

"It's a business thing, Jane."

"How bizarre."

"Very. Well, thank you, dear. Edith will be calling you soon. Good-by for now."

"Good-by, darling. Woods? Woods?"

Palmer broke the connection and quickly got a dial tone to keep Jane from calling back. After a moment, he dialed long distance and gave the operator what information he could about Tim Carewe's whereabouts in Pasco.

At the second hotel she tried the desk clerk sleepily admitted the presence of such a person. After several rings, Jane's husband answered the phone. Palmer began talking before the operator could.

"Woods Palmer, Tim."

"What in hell's name are you doing in Pasco?"

"I'm in New York. I—"

"You're calling from New York?" Tim asked in confusion. The operator clicked off.

"I'm sorry if I woke you."

"I've been awake for hours," Tim interrupted. "Minutes, anyway. Look, is this about Jane? Is something—?"

"Not at all. I just spoke to her. She told me where to reach you. She's fine. You see, I have to get some information and the only one I know who'd have it at his finger tips is you. It's about a . . . where do I begin? A man, a scientist. Enemy alien, now U.S. citizen. Privately employed by a firm with large government contracts. He wants to accept an offer from another firm, also a government-contract situation. Is there anything to stop him beyond his own contractual obligations?"

Silence at the other end of the line. Then: "What's this to do with you?"

"Both firms do business with us."

"That's not much of a reason, old man."

"Tim, is what I'm asking for secret information?" Palmer asked impatiently.

"Not at all. I'm just terribly interested when a top research man wants to flit from job to job."

"Flit? He's been in this one spot for almost fifteen years."

"Reason for change?"

"More money, more freedom."

"I hardly think he—"

"Tim, what I'm asking, basically, is whether he has the same right any other citizen does. Or is there some joker in the deal that binds him to his job?"

"It's a free country, old man. Even for him. But I should tell you that any move on a high level immediately excites interest at the Pentagon and on the Hill. It isn't as if he's a machinist or a welder."

Palmer smiled slightly. "I wouldn't want to tip over any apple carts," he lied, "but at the same time, I hardly think he's quite that important."

"You'd be in no position to know," Carewe told him. Palmer could almost see the smug face he wore when saying it. "Most civilians couldn't know, you see. Frequently, even the scientist involved has no idea exactly where he fits into the total effort. Only a few people know that and, of course, they're not about to disclose such information."

"Are you one of them?"

"But surely you know better than to ask such a question."

A crisp, almost British note had crept into Tim's diction. Palmer had already learned what he wanted to know, but he could not resist baiting the man. "Then you might . . . stand in the way of such a move?" he asked.

"I most assuredly might. I should not like to think," Tim added, shifting into a hyper-British subjunctive, "that one of my own kin would suggest any other alternative."

"I believe I am your nevvew, twice removed," Palmer put in, "as the Limeys would say." He paused. "At any rate, Uncle Tim, thank you for your time."

"No need to get . . . er . . ."

"Smarmy," Palmer suggested. "Quite. And thanks again. Any message for Jane?"

"Tell her she's got a nut for a nephew," Tim said in plain American.

"Ha. Good-by." Palmer hung up and began rereading his work sheets. As matters now stood he had a commitment in principle from Gauss and a definite offer from Hagen. The government might or might not raise a fuss. If Tim's department kept hands off, Phase Two would be more difficult. But if Tim tried to stop Gauss from moving to a new job, Phase Two would be a snap.

He glanced at his watch. Because of delays in making his calls, it was now almost eleven o'clock. He picked up the phone and dialed Heinz Gauss directly.

"Hallo?"

"Gauss, Palmer again."

411

"I am glad that you called back. You left so much up in the air."

"It's no longer hanging. As soon as you can get out of your contract with Jet-Tech, you have a new one, for five years, starting at fifty thousand with stock options."

"But you— Stock options? Fifty thousand?" The German paused. "But with which company?"

"I'll tell you all that on Monday at lunch."

"You are coming here to see me?"

"I can't do that," Palmer explained. "The height of indiscretion. And there'll be another man meeting us for lunch, your new employer. What do you say to the Club, downtown here in New York? You can fly out Monday morning and take a helicopter from Idlewild to the Wall Street heliport. I'll meet you there."

"Please. Everything is happening too quickly. I must know about it more."

"And you will. At lunch on Monday."

"What excuse can I give them for—?"

"Look here," Palmer cut in sharply. "You don't have to account to them for every second of your time, do you?"

"Of course not." Gauss's sudden gruffness tried to atone for his previous uncertainty. "Not at all," he assured Palmer.

"There's one thing I should tell you in advance, however," Palmer said then. "The, uh, experiments you mentioned. Since they are your own work, you'd be free to resume them elsewhere, wouldn't you?"

"But, Palmer, you did not discuss them with the new company?"

"Certainly not. But they are a crucial factor in the transaction."

"I have my records," Gauss said. "They are personal records. Even if I left them behind, they would mean nothing to another. And, in any event, I remember all pertinent data."

"Do you recall what morning planes there are to New York?"

"At nine o'clock, I believe, and at eleven."

"Take the nine A.M. That's ten, New York time. You'll reach Idlewild at eleven-thirty and the Wall Street heliport by noon. Look for me."

"Must this proceed at such an accelerated tempo, my friend?"

"I believe this," Palmer began in what he hoped was not too solemn a tone. "I believe that every day in which your work is hampered, cut back or suppressed is one more day in which other scientists can steal a march on you."

"Very well put," Gauss said dryly. "But I have a great craving to know why, so suddenly, you take such an interest in my affairs?"

"Many reasons. I've already explained that I feel responsible for some of your problems. But I won't deny that I have a selfish motive."

"So. And this selfish motive?"

"The man who will meet us for lunch on Monday is an old friend of mine. His firm has had several bad breaks. I know, because we are his bank, that the company's trying to turn around on a new track. This space-age technology business moves so quickly that today's success can be tomorrow's headache. They're in grave need of one good break. I think you can be the break they need. I saw a way of settling two obligations at once. That's the size of it."

"Mm. I think I can begin to guess the identity of our luncheon guest."

"Let's leave it at that. You're too smart for me."

"Just this," Gauss insisted. "Did he recently lose a good man?"

"The latest in a string of bad breaks."

"So. Then he is an old friend of mine, too, *nicht wahr?*"

"*Montag, meine alte freund, Montag*," Palmer parried.

"I see." For a few moments, Gauss said nothing. Then: "Very interesting. I begin to think that perhaps I might like this very much."

"We'll have to work out procedures for releasing you from your Jet-Tech contract."

"The last of the five-year contracts expired last year. Since then, with the Wotan failures at Canaveral, I have been on ninety-day . . . ah, what are they called? Options?"

"Gauss, I must say good-by now."

The German chuckled. "Not *auf Wiedersehen?*"

"*Naturliche. Auf Wiedersehen.*"

"*Bis Montag.*"

Palmer hung up and grimaced at the dead phone. You would think, he told himself, that speaking German would be as distasteful to Gauss as to him, if only because it brought back their original relationship. But no German ever really got over the certain knowledge that his native tongue was the superior language. It was, after all, the language of the Master Race.

Palmer surveyed his work sheet and drew a large X through a section labeled "SECOND GAUSS CALL . . . SELFISH MOTIVE #1 . . . company needs one good break." He also X-ed out a section headed: "FIRST HAGEN CALL . . . mention Aaronson . . . keep calling deal off." Then he picked up the phone again and dialed Hagen's number. The General himself answered.

"Eddie, Palmer again. Can you have lunch with me in New York on Monday?"

"You're balmy, Woods. I have a few things to do up here, you know."

"To meet the man I mentioned."

"I've met him."

"He needs reassuring about things like freedom to pursue his own lines of experimentation and such."

"Reassure him. I'll back you up."

"You know his type. Rank-conscious. One look at you and he'd be heel-clicking."

"Old Army buddy, for a favor you're supposedly doing me, this is getting to be a fat pain in the ass."

"All right, Eddie. It's just that I didn't want the deal muffed."

"Any danger of it?"

"You don't think you're the only bidder in the auction?"

Hagen was silent for a moment. "What is this, the hurry-up con?"

"That's right," Palmer said, trying to sound sarcastic. "And when you open the envelope full of money it'll be nothing but torn-up paper. Eddie, if you want out, say so. But please say so now."

"Jesus. What time and where?"

"Twelve-thirty. The Club downtown."

"Or would Macy's window be a little more private."

"Yes or no."

"Go to hell. See you Monday."

"See you." Palmer hung up just as Edith came in with a cup of coffee. "An hour just to make that?"

"I don't even want you to drink this much, Woods. You've got to catch up on your sleep sometime soon."

"Soon." Palmer sighed heavily and sipped the coffee. Then he set the cup down with a click. "Will you make a phone call?"

"To whom?"

Palmer pulled the Manhattan directory toward him and began paging through it. "You're calling for General Hagen and you want a good table near the window for twelve-thirty Monday."

"Am I supposed to be Eddie's secretary?"

"You're simply calling *for* him."

"Is he a member?"

"That's the whole point of it. I'm not. He is. Clear?"

Her hazel eyes narrowed slightly. "I'm not at all sure you know what you're doing. And I have the horrible feeling you aren't sure, either."

"Make the call."

"Now?"

"Phase One is over. The sooner you make the call, the sooner Phase Two begins."

"After I make the call, will you go to bed?"

"Why are you so solicitous of my health?"

"Isn't every loyal, dutiful wife?"

He looked up, trying to read her meaning. They watched each other for a long, silent moment. Then she picked up the phone.

"Let's go," she said.

CHAPTER SIXTY

To Palmer the next forty-eight hours seemed to last much longer than that. While living through them, he had little time for a detached view. Phase Two had too many elements to leave him much time for reflection. Instead, he plunged forward, deliberately building momentum, snatching sleep when he could, juggling time to fit the pattern of his work sheets. Later, when he had time to analyze this burst of activity, about the only concrete symbol of it he could find was his telephone bill, for a sum well over $300, most of it in long-distance calls.

At Edith's insistence, he had finally gone to sleep after lunch on Saturday, setting his alarm for seven in the evening. At that time—six in the Midwest—he began placing his Chicago calls.

Most of the people he talked to were dressing for a dinner at home or elsewhere. They were interested but rushed, exactly the state of mind Palmer had counted on since, being rushed, they would have no time to discuss the situation in depth with him. Nearly all of them were what Palmer's father had called "the boys," business associates of one sort or another, men whose companies were banking customers, other bankers in correspondent institutions, brokers used by Palmer or his father through the years to lay off large stock sales by spreading them geographically, poker or hunting cronies of the elder Palmer and a number of Palmer's own friends.

In all, he completed more than thirty such calls and, in every case, stripped of the salutations, the queries about health and business, the mildly obscene references, the family regards and the other trappings of business conversation, they boiled down to this key speech, which Palmer had written out in several versions:

"Bill" (or Jack or Phil or, in one case, Gibbsy), Palmer would eventually say, "I seem to recall you went big for Jet-Tech on that sell-off last June. Holding much of it?"

Here the versions varied, depending on the response Palmer got. If the man no longer had substantial holdings of Jet-Tech stock, Palmer would express relief and congratulations, ending the conversation as quickly as possible on a hinted note of "big trouble" when the market opened tomorrow, or, at the latest, Tuesday. If the man had a number of Jet-Tech shares, Palmer would grow somewhat more explicit. In a worried tone, he would express disappointment at the news and point out that, although he was bound to secrecy, he felt that the ties of friendship had to be honored, even if only to the extent of a hint that had to be understandably vague. "I'm selling mine when the market opens Monday," this version of the key speech would conclude, "because by Tuesday afternoon, it'll be a bargain-hunter's dream."

By ten o'clock Saturday night, Palmer finished his Chicago and Rocky Mountain Time Zone calls and moved into the West Coast area, where it was now seven in the evening. The calls he made took him until well past midnight, at which time he placed a call to the Pasco hotel, in Washington State, where Jane's husband should, by now, be retiring with a good book. When the room clerk there reported that no one answered, Palmer asked that the call be left in.

Edith prevailed on him to get to bed again at about one o'clock Sunday morning, but when the telephone rang at four he bounced quickly out of bed to answer it on the bedroom extension.

"No, no, nothing's wrong, Tim. I'm sorry I left the call in. It was an oversight. What time is it out there, one in the morning?"

"I've been helping brigadier generals get pie-eyed drunk," Tim informed him. "And I am in no mood for any of your subtleties, Woods. Has this got to do with the Kraut job-hopper?"

"Afraid so. He's determined to do it. The tough thing is that I don't even know which side I'm on. We bank for both companies. The old one needs him, but so does the new one. And I'm afraid the old one's been guilty of gross negligence in its contractual relationship with him. He's on ninety-day options and, of course, this gives him no feeling of job security whatsoever."

"The hell you say." Tim was silent for a moment. "He probably isn't worth a long-term contract. They wouldn't risk losing a really first-rate man."

"The other company seems eager enough to get him."

"Woods, will you tell me why you bother me with all this at one in the morning? Why, in fact, you bother me with it at all? In due course the matter will come to the attention of the proper authorities. I see no reason for you to try short-cutting protocol in this slapdash fashion."

"No short cut intended, Tim. Just information."

Jane's husband groaned softly. "What information, Woods? And make it brief."

"If you'd rather, I can call you tomorrow. Or you can call me"—Palmer paused a moment—"collect," he added, grinning.

"See here," Tim burst out. "Will you kindly state your—?"

"Certainly," Palmer cut in soothingly, "certainly. Mind you, if this is classified information the general public is not entitled to, why—"

"Get on with it, man!"

"Of course," Palmer assured him. He reached quickly for the most outrageous request he could make. "What I'd like to know is how high a priority these Wotan launchings have. I mean, they've been fizzling so regularly, I should imagine the whole project had been back-dated, if not scratched. So what I want to kn—"

"Woods." Tim's voice, perfectly dead, cut in with a dull thudding sound. "Have you been drinking?"

"Matter of fact, I was asleep when your call came in."

" '*Your* call!' " Tim exploded.

"Yes, of course, quite right. Sorry."

"Woods, go back to sleep or go to hell, but in any event hang up."

"Tim, have I put my foot in it?" Palmer asked innocently.

"Good night." With a grinding clash, the line went dead.

Palmer returned to his bed, smiling in the darkness. "What was all that?" Edith asked sleepily.

"Just stirring up the animals."

After lying in bed until five, without regaining sleep, Palmer got up. He spent the next few hours crossing off items on his work sheets and making condensed versions of what remained to be done. A number of out-of-town calls which he had failed to complete the previous evening would have to be placed again. He would have to make certain that incoming calls were screened. Try as he might, Tim Carewe must not get through to him. By mid-morning Jane's husband would certainly begin to realize that something rather important was afoot. So far Palmer's teasing had kept him enough off base that he had been unable to ask any really damning questions. But the key word "Wotan" would eventually trigger off a spate of queries, none of which Palmer wanted to be put in the position of having to answer.

But perhaps the most important job remaining for the balance of the day was a call Palmer would have to make to Burns, as late Sunday evening as possible. He spent some time during the afternoon working out various ways in which the conversation would go. When he actually placed the call, Palmer was pleased to find so few of the stumbling blocks he had anticipated.

". . . calling to ask how your jaw feels."

"Great. Is that all?"

"Not entirely."

"You didn't call to apologize," Burns stated flatly. "Your kind never does."

"You have quite a view of 'my kind,' don't you?"

"Yes, I do," Burns agreed. "We have a name for you. You're a Wap."

"A what?"

"White, Anglo-Saxon Protestant."

"Like Joe Loomis?"

"All right, Palmer, is that all?"

"Apparently there are Waps and Waps. Some Waps you trust."

"That'll be the day."

"Pretty much why I called. I've been worrying about you."

"You should. Tomorrow morning I blow you apart."

"I've been worrying about what you'll do to yourself, Mac. The same thing keeps coming to mind. All your eggs in one basket."

"What?"

"Do I have to explain it, Mac? You're an intelligent man. You've got an undercover deal with one group of Waps and an above-board deal with another. But you've put all your eggs in Jet-Tech's basket, an undercover deal no one has to honor."

"Let me do my own worrying, Palmer."

"You don't do enough of it. Put yourself in Loomis' shoes for a moment. What does he see in you? A smart operator who can do him some good. Of what use are you once you've done your job? What public agreement binds him to you? Now, Ubco retains you openly. It's a matter of public record. If we don't like what you've done, if we want to get rid of you, we have to buy off the rest of your contract. Does Loomis? Does he really have to do anything for you when your usefulness is ended? Does he have to do any more than say good-by?"

Burns said nothing for a moment. Then: "Stop worrying. I'm smart enough to keep a step ahead of the game."

"If anybody is, you are. But, Mac, I hope it won't come as a terrible shock when I tell you that the name of the game has changed."

"Talk sense."

"The game. The one we've all been playing. I've just changed it."

"What?"

"I've told you as much as I can, Mac. But I can give you one hint: place a phone call to Loomis tomorrow afternoon about half-past three."

"Why?"

"By then it should all be clear. And, look, once you understand what the new game is, don't hesitate to call me back. If you've been a good boy in the meanwhile, I can always use a player with your brains."

"Palmer, who do you th—?"

"I mean it," Palmer insisted. "You're too valuable to have as an enemy. Tomorrow afternoon, when you see what's happened, take a look at all those eggs in that one little basket. Then call me."

"What happens at three-thir—?"

"Not at," Palmer corrected him, "by. It still gives you time to start blowing me up, if you want to by then. So long."

He broke the connection and began calling a few New York people he could trust, people he had done business with when he had been in Chicago, bankers and brokers for the most part, but one or two businessmen as well. In Chicago and on the West Coast, the rumor would already have spread at Saturday-night social events. As he talked to New Yorkers now, automatically feeling his way into the key statement, Palmer found himself replaying the conversation with Burns, testing it for flaws. He found it, on the whole, satisfactory. He could not be absolutely certain, but he felt fairly sure it would

418

pique Burns's curiosity enough to keep him from doing anything during the morning with his blackmail information. By the time he saw the signs of what was happening and realized that the mysterious three-thirty deadline was the time the market closed, it would be too late.

Palmer got to sleep around midnight on Sunday and again got up at five the next morning. By now the lack of sleep, the constant conversations, the uncertainties, the hints and innuendoes, the steady revision of work sheets, the painstaking evaluation and re-evaluation of each discussion, the testing of tones of voice and scraps of phrases, all began to revolve pinwheel fashion in his head. He got out of bed and stumbled into his study, where he prepared a final draft of what remained on his work sheet, reducing it to a 3"-by-5" file card he placed in his wallet. At about six o'clock he got in the tub and lay back in tepid water, trying to let its warmth soothe the tension in his neck and shoulders.

Edith found him there, asleep, at seven. Her short, sharp scream of surprise woke him so abruptly that he floundered helplessly for a moment in the still warm water. "What the hell?"

"Woods, you idiot. You were asleep."

He blinked uncertainly at her. "Time's it?"

"Seven." She watched him for a moment. "You've lost weight lately."

"Have I?"

"I can practically count your ribs."

"Um."

"What is that, that thing down there?"

Palmer looked at his abdomen and, for a moment, was confused. "Which thing?"

"That mark. There."

He immediately remembered the bite Virginia had given him near his navel. Reacting very slowly, in the role of a man who is about to get a surprise, he examined his abdomen and saw that the mark had faded somewhat to a kind of amoeboid brownish splotch that no longer resembled a bite. He professed to miss it. "What mark?"

"There." She reached over and prodded it. "Does it hurt?"

"This?" He stared stupidly at it. "What the hell do you suppose—? A bug or something?"

"I haven't the slightest idea. I suppose a belt buckle might do that, if you were fat." She leaned back against the far wall of the bathroom. "Where on earth would you find a bug that could do that? Not here."

He shrugged. The tepid water rippled violently. "One of those upstate hotels."

"That was weeks ago. You would have noticed it by now."

"I haven't spent a great deal of time contemplating my navel."

Edith started to say something, then repressed it. "Do you think you're clean enough?"

"Yes. Yes. Quite." He struggled to get up out of the tub. The sudden change in his body's apparent weight out of the water made him lurch sideways. He reached wildly for support. Edith grasped his hand and steadied him.

"Are you all right?"

"Fine." He stepped out of the tub and opened the drain.

"You've been going at it pretty hard."

He nodded, drying himself with a towel. His skin felt puckered and tender. The sudden coolness of the air, after the warm water, made him shiver. "After today, I'll be just fine," he said.

He glanced up to find her examining him closely. After a moment he lifted his eyebrows in a kind of what-are-you-looking-at? expression. She shook her head slowly.

"I suppose," she mused, more to herself than to him, "there's no doubt it's a bite?"

CHAPTER SIXTY-ONE

Battery Park, jutting like a blunt peninsula into the harbor at the foot of Manhattan, looked smeary with haze, even in the direct light of the noon sun. A chill, steady wind blew from the general direction of Bedloe's Island, where Palmer could just about make out the gray-green thrust of the Statue of Liberty, disappearing like a phantom in successive layers of haze and smoke. After a moment, the car he was in moved on with the traffic.

The heliport waiting area was entirely unprotected from the wind. Palmer got out of the car and tried to light a cigarette but the flame of his Zippo flared like a blowtorch in the heavy wind, burning his hand. He dropped the lighter in his pocket and threw the cigarette into the choppy waves that splashed against the heliport's bulkhead. As he watched the wind-driven water slam against the wall, a particularly high wave sent spray against his face, a hail of tiny salt drops. It deposited a condom and a ragged bit of orange peel at his feet. Palmer stared at these mementos of New York City for a moment, then turned and walked to the other side of the heliport.

On the whole, Palmer decided as he stood there in the driving wind, it hadn't gone too badly. The market had opened at nine-thirty with Jet-Tech at forty-five. Trading in the stock had been slow to pick up. But at eleven-thirty, when he had stopped by a street-level brokerage house to check the board, volume had picked up a bit more than it might on a normal day. So far, some 10,000 shares had been traded and the price had moved downward seven-eighths of a point.

Another high wave spattered salt spray across his face. He turned sideways and faced toward the city itself, away from the direction in which Gauss's helicopter would come.

Of course, Palmer told himself, if the S.E.C. got wind of what he had done, there could be a nasty scandal. From the beginning, however, he had counted on two things to keep him out of the S.E.C.'s line of fire. One, and perhaps the most important, was that he had been making his phone calls to people he could trust, men he knew personally and who, in turn, knew the importance of keeping their mouths shut. Most of them, at one time or another, had had to face S.E.C. questioning. They understood perfectly the kind of answers that would satisfy the Commission without implicating anyone else and, of course, without putting themselves in jeopardy.

But just as important, Palmer realized, was the fact that if his plan worked, S.E.C. would be too busy buzzing around the corpus of Jet-Tech's holdings, probing for soft spots and finding the usual ripe-for-plucking situations every major corporation had—that no one would wonder how the sell-off had been triggered. That there was an immense soft spot somewhere, Palmer never doubted. Jet-Tech's dogged insistence on a half-billion-dollar loan showed more than a desire for expansion money. It showed a pressing need to refund indebtedness that was being called due.

Leaning sideways against a high concrete block wall, Palmer stared along the rough, unpainted surface to the cluster of financial district buildings groping upward through the haze. In one of them, Ubco's head office, Burckhardt would still have no idea of what was about to happen. In another, the Stock Exchange, out-of-town sell orders would be filtering in now from points west. In a third, the suite of offices that were Jet-Tech's New York operational base, a few people would have begun to react uneasily.

They would in all likelihood be second-echelon officers whose stock options had been handed them when shares were trading at forty-four or -five. Such men watched every downward tick of the stock as if it were Poe's razor-edged pendulum, inching closer to their throats. Any downward movement of a point or more that seemed substantial enough to be fairly permanent could at a single stroke render their options so much waste paper.

More to the point, if they had not yet exercised their options, the downward turn could cost them money. Further, Palmer recalled, grinning slightly, if they were in the six-month period after purchase of stock, when the S.E.C. forbade them to unload it, a down-tick not only cost money but there would be nothing they could do to prevent the loss. And so, as it had to increasing numbers of men everywhere of late, loss of incentive would come to Jet-Tech's second managerial echelon.

Palmer's grin broadened slightly. On the whole, he had so far handled the thing fairly well. Even if it failed by a narrow margin to create the kind

421

of havoc he hoped for it, even if it failed to divert Joe Loomis' head-long grab for control of Ubco, it would at the very least create a great many problems.

He stared at the towers of the financial district and nothing he could do, no determined effort of will, could stop him from feeling inordinately satisfied with himself in the way a country yokel is pleased to have bested a city slicker. Even as he sensed this feeling, and fought against it out of a determination not to give himself fake airs, he knew that in part he had to be right. He had proved himself as adept in this jungle as any of the others and, perhaps, by the end of today or tomorrow, he would have proved himself superior.

Behind him Palmer heard the muffled chopping of a helicopter. He turned in time to see one sweep past and circle the tip of the island, heading north up the Hudson, probably bound for the Thirtieth Street heliport. The other flight, he decided, would not be far behind. It lacked a minute or two yet of its announced arrival time.

Now Palmer could hear the sound of another helicopter in the distance, the peculiar harsh throb of its immense rotors hacking the air into puffing blasts of noise. He stared across the river in the direction of Brooklyn.

He could see the helicopter now, swinging out in a wide slanting arc as it closed for a landing. One of the ground-control men, in neat coveralls, strolled out onto the small concrete landing pad and stared up at the helicopter, making long, sweeping motions with his right arm.

A downward rush of air rattled the brim of Palmer's hat. He clung to it for a moment as the helicopter settled on the pad. Then the engine died and the rotor slowly spun itself into immobility. The third passenger out of the door was Heinz Gauss.

The little man stared about him for a moment, his large eyes twitching sideways. Palmer could never remember him looking quite so nervous and guilt-ridden, even on that day at Peenemünde when he had first been apprehended. Palmer waved to the German and walked to meet him. They shook hands silently in the cold wind. Gauss carried nothing but a battered brown leather brief case with greenish brass clasps.

The bank's Sixty Special Cadillac was waiting outside. Palmer ushered Gauss into the car and gave the driver the address of the Club, a few blocks away. As the car started, Palmer shook his head slowly at Gauss.

"I'm glad you could make it, Harry," Palmer said. "How are those choppers?"

Gauss frowned in misery and gestured helplessly for a moment. "Not bad," he said then, apparently trying to choose a phrase that did little to reveal his German accent.

Realizing that he could not really trust Gauss with the kind of play-acting necessary to keep his identity and national origin a secret from the driver, Palmer launched into a long and involved discussion of the light-frame, one-family house-construction picture on Long Island, complete with average figures on principal, interest, term, features of the various open-end kinds of mortgages and tract financing. In the clogged lunchtime traffic, the ride took more than ten minutes.

". . . simultaneous lines of credit from his lumber and masonry suppliers," Palmer rattled away, "which completes his initial FHA stages and frees his capital for sales promotion. But once he reaches shell stage on the— Oh, here we are. Right here will do, Jimmy," he added to the driver.

They got out of the car at exactly twelve-thirty, hurried through the ancient lobby and ascended without speaking in the wheezing old elevator. In the Club's waiting room, Palmer nodded to the attendant.

"General Hagen's table," he said.

The man smiled and led the way into the dining room. Behind him as he walked, Palmer could hear Gauss murmur: "Ach, I was right."

In her role as Hagen's secretary, Edith had ordered a table near the corner windows. As Palmer and Gauss entered the big room, one person sat at that table, a short, thin man with an almost completely bald head who, when he stood up, looked much like a successful and retired jockey.

In point of fact, Eddie Hagen had been one of Billy Mitchel's young protégés, in the 1920's, whose Army career had suffered greatly because of his loyalty to the unlucky general. Frozen in captain's grade from 1934 until Pearl Harbor, Hagen had finally transferred out of the Air Corps and into Intelligence, where, with the start of World War II, he had quickly risen to one-star status. After retirement, Hagen had become honorary board chairman of a small company manufacturing bomb-sight components. Although he had been hired simply to ease the way for more government contracts, Hagen had taken his job seriously and begun recruiting young men from nearby M.I.T. The company's product line now encompassed automation components, various electronic "black box" equipment, robot assemblies of several kinds and telemetry apparatus. By now, the firm ranked eighth or ninth on the list of private aero-space contractors, a position it had no right to hold by virtue of its size, which was still fairly small, but rather by the quality of its products and Hagen's ability to sell them to his friends in Washington.

He nodded to Palmer and drew himself up a little straighter as he faced Gauss. "Doctor," he said gravely, "a pleasure to see you again."

They sat down at the table, Palmer inwardly pleased that Hagen had taken exactly the right opening tack. Nothing could have pleased a German more than to be addressed by his rank.

"General," Gauss said, "a distinct pleasure."

They began to reminisce, Hagen demonstrating a startling knowledge of Gauss's activities since the war. Palmer's attention drifted. His glance slid sideways to nearby tables. Two brokers were watching him with open interest. On the pretense of looking for a waiter, Palmer turned around in his chair. His glance swept the room. Loomis' corner table was empty, but next to it Archie Nicos sipped a drink with thoughtful slowness while the two other investment bankers with him carried on a veiled conversation.

Nearer the door, Palmer saw one of the trust-department vice-presidents of Chase Manhattan and, a few tables away, two men from Manufacturers Hanover, lunching with one of the officers of the Federal Reserve. Directly across the room, Palmer was startled for a moment to see George Mallett of the *Star*, in deep discussion with three Merrill Lynch partners. Nearer to his own table, Palmer saw some men he failed to recognize. He stole a second glance at them.

". . . Lehman Brothers," Hagen said in an undertone. Then he resumed his conversation with Gauss.

Palmer smiled slightly. Hagen had always had the ability to carry on at least two separate lines of thought simultaneously. Palmer saw a waiter heading his way. He turned to his menu. "Broiled swordfish?" he asked his companions.

They broke off their reminiscences to look at him. "It's only Monday, Woody," Hagen said dryly. "I think the occasion merits the filet mignon. Doctor?"

"*Ja.* Fine."

"Medium?" Palmer asked.

"Fine. Very good." Gauss turned back to Hagen. "The boosters, at first, were the source of the problem, you understand. The ball valve design did not function with complete predictability at low temperatures. The first modification we tried was—"

"Steaks for all of us," Palmer told the waiter. "How do you like yours, General?"

"Rare."

"Two medium, one rare. And three double Scotch on ice to begin. Doctor?" Palmer asked.

"Yes, *bitte.*"

Palmer watched the waiter leave. In so doing, he caught sight of two Lazard Freres partners walking into the dining room with a man from Chemical Bank between them. Palmer sat back in relaxed satisfaction. The brethren were gathering. Today's playlet had an all-star audience.

With dessert, the constant flow of technical talk between Hagen and Gauss slowed somewhat. Hagen glanced up from his Camembert and grinned at Palmer. "We seem to talk the same language, Woody." Then, to Gauss: "How soon can you start?"

By now the room was completely filled. Several of the earlier diners had left, to be replaced by other brokers and bankers. The news that Eddie Hagen and Jet-Tech's head of research had had a long and friendly lunch together would now begin to seep with amazing speed through the spongy soil of

424

Wall Street. It was time to stage-manage a firm, happy handshake, and bring down the curtain.

Palmer managed to do this by glancing at his watch and saying: "Good grief, General, I promised this man to have him back at the heliport in fifteen minutes. Can we make it?"

Hagen suppressed a smile as he got to his feet. He put out his hand with such ostentation that Palmer was afraid for a moment the gesture was too broad. "Doctor," Hagen said as he pumped the German's hand, "I don't care what it takes in money, but the first thing I want you to build is that cryogenic anti-G demonstrator. This I have to see."

"You will," Gauss promised, beaming.

"Then we have a deal?"

"Oh, yes!" Gauss almost shouted. "Yes, of course."

"Danke, meine freund."

"Bitte, bitte schoen."

As Palmer led the way to the elevators, he felt Hagen's hand on his arm, slowing him a pace. "I don't know what you're really up to, you tricky bastard," Hagen murmured in his ear, "but I think you really did do me a favor."

"Naturliche," Palmer whispered.

"Up yours, too," Hagen grunted. "Meanwhile, I'll go back in there and have another cup of coffee, looking very satisfied with myself and life and all that crap. Right?"

"And if anybody asks you anything," Palmer murmured, "clam up."

"Don't teach your grandmother to suck eggs," Hagen retorted. "And, look, old Army buddy, remember me when I need a little plant-expansion loan or two. Or three."

"That's right, grandmother."

"Once more, Doctor," Hagen said loudly to Gauss, "a very great pleasure. *Auf Wiedersehen.*"

This time Gauss actually brought his heels together. If his trouser cuffs had not got in the way, Palmer noted, the click would have been resounding.

They rode down the elevator as silently as they had come. The silence continued on the ride back to the heliport. After Palmer escorted the German through the ticket line, bought his boarding pass and took him into the waiting area, he broke the silence to say: "You should be back home by three-thirty New York time, two-thirty out there."

Gauss nodded nervously. "Look," he said then. He paused and wet his lips. His sad eyes looked moist. "We really have an agreement, the General and I?"

"His handshake is as binding as a contract. However, if I know the General, you'll get a copy of the contract in tomorrow's mail."

Gauss brightened momentarily. Then he looked depressed again. "I must tell them at Jet-Tech," he muttered.

"If you have any reservations, simply sign your copies of the contract and mail them back to the General. In a day or two he'll return your file copy, with his company's signatures. That makes it legal and binding. Then tell Jet-Tech."

"Ah." Gauss seemed at peace now. He stared up at the sky in a business-like manner, then turned and looked for a moment at the skyline. He frowned. "Messy," he said. "No sense of form."

Palmer shrugged. "That's part of New York's charm."

"For me, no." Gauss drew himself up to his full 5'4" and paced importantly a few feet toward the river's edge. "The General's research headquarters are in New England, *nicht wahr?* I seem to recall the town as rather old and traditional? I participated in a seminar at the university there several years ago. Now that, that place, that is charming to me."

"Very," Palmer agreed.

They stood silently as a helicopter landed and disgorged its passengers. One of the ground-control men waved to a uniformed ticket agent, who opened a rope and ushered the new passengers aboard.

Gauss turned to stare at the skyline again. He shook his head. "I do not understand how one lives here," he said. A wave larger than the rest hit the bulkhead behind him and dashed spray over his shoes, together with an oily scrap of brownish paper. Gauss made a face. Then he extended his hand rather stiffly. "A pleasure."

Palmer shook it. "Good luck."

Gauss smiled thinly. "One makes one's own," he said. Then he turned and boarded the helicopter.

Heil Hitler, Palmer thought. Without waiting to watch the take-off, he turned and walked off the pad, through the ticket office and into the Sixty Special. For all he cared at this point, the helicopter could tilt, side-slip and sink like a thrashing beetle beneath the greasy brown-green waters of New York Harbor. The curtain was down. The playlet had ended. The cocky, sniveling little German who had been his leading man could now fall off the face of the earth.

CHAPTER SIXTY-TWO

It was two-thirty when Palmer reached his office on Fifth Avenue. He sat down behind the desk at one end of his tremendous room and was about to pick up the phone when he noticed a sheaf of messages. Beginning at five minutes to nine that morning, and at hourly intervals thereafter, Burckhardt had called, eventually leaving five messages in all. Jane's husband, Tim, had called, once at eleven. Edith had called shortly thereafter. At two-fifteen George Mallett of the *Star* had called, evidently having got to a phone as quickly as he could after seeing Palmer at lunch. A few minutes after one, Burns had called twice, five minutes apart. And Palmer's personal broker had begun calling at the same time.

Palmer punched the button that gave him an outside line and dialed his broker's own direct line, thus cutting out any possible switchboard eavesdropping.

"It's me, Pete," Palmer announced.

"And about time, too," the broker said in a low voice. "It's hit thirty-nine."

"That's six points down. What's your guess by the end of the day?"

"No more real action. We haven't had any big-block dumping yet."

"You won't till the trend is fully established," Palmer guessed. "Perhaps by noon tomorrow."

"Don't be surprised if it rallies a few points at the close today."

"Bargain hunters?"

"Yeah. It'll take some strong pressure to hold this downward trend."

"The pressure's been applied," Palmer told him.

"When?"

"About an hour ago."

"No signs of it in the trading."

"It hasn't spread around the Street yet. You'll get wind of it."

"What is it?" the broker asked.

"Rather not say. Rather you tell me."

"We're being cute?"

"Let me know when you hear," Palmer said. "And let me know the minute you see signs of big blocks being offered."

"What's your estimate, Woody?"

"What am I, a broker?"

"Ha." The line went dead.

Palmer sat there smiling slightly. Then he punched Burckhardt's button and waited. After a moment it glowed green.

"Yes?"

"Lane, did you call me?"

"Wh—? You damned fool! Where in Christ's name have you been?"

"Downtown. I almost dropped in on you."

"I know you were downtown. Everybody knows it. Four people called to tell me where they saw you having lunch. What the hell are you pulling?"

"Nothing I need any help with."

"Listen, you snotty bastard, when I ask a question, I—"

"If I thought you could help, I'd ask," Palmer cut in. "I honestly can't trust you not to blow the whole thing. You're too impetuous."

"Who do you th—?"

427

A button on an incoming line glowed green as the intercom pinged. The light began to blink in a slow, insistent rhythm. "Another call coming in," Palmer announced cheerfully.

"I don't give a sh—"

"Impetuous," Palmer interrupted. "And I call that a very tactful euphemism. Just relax. I'll wake you when it's over."

"Palmer, you little—"

"Call you later, Lane." Palmer punched the other button, cutting off Burckhardt. "Yes?"

"A Mr. Mallett calling, sir."

"Put him on. George?"

"You dodging me?" Mallett asked.

"Just got in this minute. My boss was chewing my ear."

"Have a good lunch?"

"Excellent," Palmer said. "How was yours?"

"Spicy. Were your ears burning?"

"Should they have been?"

"Tell me it was just an old Army reunion."

"It was, in a way."

"Is Gauss going to work for Hagen?"

"You'd better ask one of them."

"I have. Hagen has no comment. Gauss isn't in town."

"Why don't you try the government agency that supervises this sort of thing."

"Anyone in particular?" the reporter asked.

"A Mr. Carewe. Tim Carewe. He might know something."

"For the record?" Mallett asked. "He wouldn't talk, would he?"

"Bother him anyway."

"I'd rather bother you."

"If you bother Tim," Palmer promised, "I'll lay out the thing in enough detail, off the record, so that you can know what questions to ask Hagen and Loomis and Gauss."

"In other words, you want this Carewe guy bothered. And you're willing to finger the other lads as a pay-off."

"That is not the kind of language one expects from a *Star* man."

"I'll give it a whirl," Mallett said.

"Right. Good-by."

Palmer punched his direct outside-line button again and dialed Mac Burns. The time was now a quarter to three. "Just returning your call, Mac."

"Lover, why didn't you tell me you had Lebanese blood?"

"Is that your idea of a compliment?"

Burns chuckled. "I couldn't wait till the market closed. I got the idea real fast when it started to happen. All I want to know is how you did it."

"Did what?"

428

"Crazy. Look, I just sent you something by messenger. It should be there any minute."

"What is it?"

"A reel of tape. It's yours."

"I'm touched, Mac."

"And I'm flabbergasted. The calls are piling up, sweetie. Lemme call you back tonight sometime. Better yet: have dinner with me."

"Mac, when you switch allegiances, you don't waste any time. I'm still a Wap."

"Don't kid me, boychik. With that kind of mind?"

"It's the same mind it was before. Just working on a different idea. I don't know about dinner. Call me around five."

"Great. Gotta run. Bye."

Palmer hung up and watched the button go dark. He checked the time of Burns's first phone message and realized that the call had been placed before Burns could possibly have heard of the luncheon meeting. In other words, Palmer decided, Burns had first called in response to the sudden drop in Jet-Tech's market price. He probably hadn't yet heard about Gauss. One of the calls he had said were piling up now would probably bring news of the luncheon.

Palmer closed his eyes and leaned back in his chair. It should not be too hard to out-think Burns, he told himself. The effusive greeting, the warm rapprochement attempt, had not been generated by anything more than the stock sell-off. Burns had analyzed the situation and decided that this was Palmer's answer to the threat of being exposed. Therefore, Burns would think, neutralize Palmer by sending him the tape recording in question. This would relieve the pressure on the stock and Burns would devise some other way of getting Palmer in the Jet-Tech camp, probably through— What was the old saying? Easier to catch flies with honey than vinegar?

The intercom emitted its crystal ping again. "Yes?"

"Package just delivered, sir."

"Bring it in, please."

Palmer pressed a blank button he had had wired directly to Virginia Clary. "Have you got a tape recorder anywhere in the building?" he asked without preamble.

"I— Yes, I think so."

"Have it brought in and come in yourself."

"Are you in your office?"

"As quickly as you can, please."

By ten after three Palmer had threaded Burns's tape in the machine. He and Virginia stood there watching it unreel. A thin, scratchy noise came from the speaker.

"Turn it up," Virginia suggested.

"Perhaps I ought just to send it over to WQXR for broadcast purposes."

429

"Um."

After a moment Palmer could hear their voices. He listened for a moment. Then he frowned and put the recorder into fast forward speed, watching the tape carefully as it reeled past. It took a few minutes for it to transfer to the take-up reel. "Peculiar," Palmer said. "Not a splice on it."

"Should there be?"

"The original tape covers many evenings and afternoons of recording. The machine in Burns's apartment had tiny three-inch reels. But this tape fills a seven-inch reel, which means it represents three or four of the smaller ones. To put them together they'd have to be spliced. This tape has no splices. Therefore . . ."

"Therefore, it's a re-recording, not the original."

"There's that brilliant Clary mind again."

"Did Mac represent it as the original? How did you get him to part with it?"

"My secret. Point is, he didn't part with the original. He just wants to fool me into thinking he did."

"Meaning?"

"Meaning I was right about Mac. He doesn't really know how serious his trouble is. If he'd known about my luncheon, he'd know the situation was now irreversible and even a phony bribe like this couldn't possibly save it."

"Woods, I have no idea what you're talking about."

"I know." He looked up from the tape machine. "I'm sorry. I haven't even talked to you since Friday night. This is all gibberish to you, isn't it?"

"I spent a very quiet weekend at home. Next to the phone."

"I'm sorry."

She avoided his glance. "It got to the point where my mother told me, point-blank: 'Virginia, whoever he is he doesn't want to talk to you.' She's shockingly bright sometimes."

"It wasn't that I didn't want to talk to you. It was just that I—"

"Didn't," Virginia finished for him.

"When this is over I'll tell you exactly what I did over the weekend. Then you'll—"

"When what is over?"

"This thing I'm in the middle of now." Palmer picked up both reels and reversed them. Then he fed the tape through the recording head and pushed the "Record" button. "I'm erasing this tape," he said. "It isn't the only one in existence, but there's no point leaving it as it is."

"Are our voices being recorded now?"

"Level's too low. It's just wiping the tape clear."

"Then may I make something in the nature of a statement?"

He glanced sideways at her. "Please don't. By this time tomorrow, or Wednesday morning at the latest, I'll be able to explain the whole thing."

"If you're going to tell George Mallett, you might as well tell me."

"How did y—?"

"He called to ask me whether you were in the habit of breaking a promise."

"Just a few minutes ago?"

She nodded. "I told him I had always considered you a model of faithfulness." There was a longish silence. "But apparently you don't think of me in those same terms," she went on then. "I'm not to be trusted with information you're about to tell the *Star*."

"Off the record, only," Palmer explained hastily.

"Lovely." She was watching the rust-brown tape reel through the recorder. After a moment she seemed to force her glance up and away from the tape. She stared at him then with the same fixed attention she had given the machine. In the afternoon light, filtered through the overhead louvers, her eyes were set in deep caves of dark violet. Palmer could see his own reflection in her pupils.

"Do you really think—?" She broke off. "Of course you do."

"Think what?"

"Nothing." Her full lower lip thinned out flat and tight for an instant. Then one corner of her mouth quirked downward. "I'll say it anyway. You still think I was in cahoots with Mac, don't you?"

"I never thought you w—"

"Yes, you did. You all but said so on Friday night."

"I said and did a great many wild things that night. I'd been drinking."

"*In vino veritas* and all that," Virginia said. "Did you know I studied both Latin and Greek? Nothing like a well-rounded education. That, of course, was before I took up whoring as a profession."

He sighed sharply. "I'm sorry for what I said. For what I thought. I know it wasn't that way. It just seemed so to a drunken man."

She nodded again. "I can see how it might. But that doesn't explain why you didn't call me during the weekend and tell me so. I sat around the house about one jump ahead of the overdose-of-sleeping-tablets routine. You can't imagine how low I felt. And the silly thing is that one rotten phone call would have cured me. That's the kind of idiotic position I get myself into, Woods. You'd think a woman my age would know better."

"I'm really sorry. I—"

"And, of course, it doesn't explain why you won't trust me now," she pointed out. He started to say something and she held up her hand, palm out, almost touching his mouth. "I don't want to hear about it anyway," she said. "It's the principle, not the money. If you're finished with the recorder, I'll have it picked up."

"Look, will it help things if you sit here when I talk to Mallett? Then you'll know exactly what he'll know."

She shook her head. "I have a thousand things to do."

"Then let's have a drink after work."

"No."

"I do trust you, you know. You're the one I really do trust."

431

"Yes." She watched the end of the tape reel through and flap against the take-up reel. "I'll have this thing picked up." She started for the door.

"Virginia?"

She turned. "Maybe I'll be over this by tomorrow. Or Wednesday. God knows I don't have the pride I used to."

"Will you please come back here?"

She continued toward the door. "I'm really quite sure you'd rather talk to me tomorrow. And I'm perfectly willing to wait till then."

"The hell you are."

She turned slowly on one toe, reached for the door and swung it open. "I'll have that machine picked up, Mr. Palmer," she announced in a loud voice. Then she walked out, closing the door behind her.

Immediately the intercom sounded. Palmer watched Burckhardt's button pulse and glow. He ignored it, stripping off the tape and dropping the full reel in his pocket. After a minute another light began to blink, indicating a call on his direct private wire. He answered the call.

"Ticked up half a point," Palmer's broker said. "Then, at thirty-nine and a half, the bottom suddenly blew out of it. The market's closed but the tape's late on Jet-Tech. At the moment it's reporting at thirty-four. What happened?"

"You still haven't heard?"

"Must you be so cagey? Is it this business about the German scientist?"

"So you did hear?" Palmer persisted.

"It's all over the Street. But should it have this kind of effect?"

"Pete, the effect is only beginning to be felt."

"But why?"

"Gee, Pete," Palmer said, "I thought you were the broker." He cut the connection and, still ignoring Burckhardt's light, pressed down the button for another incoming call.

"A Mr. Mallett, sir."

"Put him on." Palmer felt in his pocket for one of his card-sized work sheets. "George, did you make that call?"

"For whatever good it did me, yes. The poor guy hung up on me, finally."

"Why 'poor guy'?"

"He sounded so harassed I almost felt sorry for him."

"Tim Carewe harassed? About this business with Gauss?"

"What else? He had nothing to say for publication. He said our Washington bureau would get a press release on the matter within a few hours. Then he hung up in the middle of my next question."

"Terrific!"

"Do you figure, as a big taxpayer, that you're entitled to pull the wings off public servants?"

"Tim gets paid to be harassed. What I'm enthusiastic about is that his agency will make a statement on the question. When that breaks, you'll have your story all wrapped up for you."

"Fine," Mallett said without notable joy. "Just begin anywhere at all. Only begin."

"Off the—"

"Record," the reporter agreed wearily. "Spiel."

"I suppose it begins with the Wotan booster fiasco," Palmer said, deciphering the tiny notes he had written on his 3"-by-5" card. "Gauss felt all along that his research budget was being skimped and his development program was being held back. At the same time, the Wotan business cost Jet-Tech a lot of prestige. Quite a bit of their outstanding paper was being called due anyway, and this didn't help. They asked us for a loan so large I can't even mention the sum. Just call it unprecedented. We turned it down. Gauss felt pretty hopeless about things. He came to me for help. He said I owed him something because I'd been the one who shanghaied him over to the U.S. in the first place. It seemed to me he had a point. I sort of cast around and came up with Hagen, who'd just lost Aaronson, anyway, and badly needed a research director with real scope. The rest you've already figured out."

"That's the whole thing?"

"The whole thing."

Palmer could hear Mallett's breathing for a moment. Then he realized the reporter was laughing softly. "George?"

"Don't mind me," Mallett explained. "It's just that I can enjoy a good joke as well as the next guy."

"Is it that funny?"

"The part we haven't talked about is hilarious. The savings banks' branch-bill part."

"I don't get the connection. Do you?" Palmer asked blandly.

There was a pause. Then: "I don't know," Mallett mused. "Maybe my desk will buy this yarn the way you tell it. If I can get any corroboration from the principals involved or from Carewe's agency. If it goes through that way it'll stay off the political desk. Otherwise . . ." He laughed quietly again. "Some of our Albany boys are pretty sharp."

"It doesn't seem to be on their beat, does it?"

"I suppose that's what you've counted on all along." Mallett sniffed. "Okay. I'll write it your way. If you're lucky it'll print that way. The only thing I'd really like to know, off the well-known record, is whose gray cells dreamed this up? It's too sneaky for Ginnie Clary and too complicated for Mac Burns."

"I have no idea what you're talking about, George, but it sounds sort of snide."

Mallett made a lip noise. "I think maybe you owe me a lunch when this blows over. I'd like to get to know you better, huh?"

"Definitely."

Another button was blinking green now. "See you," the reporter said. Palmer pressed down the new call. "A Mr. Loomis on the line, sir," said the Ubco operator.

433

"Tell him I'm not here," Palmer said.

He slowly tore his little file card into bits. He threw them in his ash tray and set them on fire. After they had turned to curly bits of ash, Palmer sat very still watching the row of intercom buttons. None of them was lighted now.

Palmer nodded and leaned back in his chair. After a minute he closed his eyes and tried to relax.

CHAPTER SIXTY-THREE

At five o'clock the bank's switchboard closed for the night. The first incoming night call, at Palmer's request, had been linked to Virginia Clary's extension. None were put through to his desk. And yet, at five-thirty, the button for his private wire glowed green. Thinking it was his broker, he pressed the button and said:

"Yes, Pete?"

"Do I sound like a Pete?" Mac Burns asked.

Palmer blinked. No one in New York had this number except his brokers here and in Chicago. He had also, earlier today, given the number to Edith so that she could get through to him in case Tim Carewe, unable to reach Palmer, had called his home.

In the instant after Burns spoke, Palmer's eyes raced aimlessly across his desk, staring without seeing at dozens of unanswered telephone messages. Did Virginia know this number? Probably. Probably Burckhardt did too, for that matter. Almost anyone at Ubco who had been in his office might have noted the number. Burns himself could have, for that matter. Palmer abruptly realized that his pause had stretched on too long.

"How does a Pete sound?" he asked then.

"Listen, lover, have we got a date?"

"As a matter of fact, it depends on what we have to talk about."

"Mucho things, sweetie," Burns said.

"God, a linguist. Tell me: why do you sound so ebullient?"

"Any reason I shouldn't?" Burns persisted.

"I can think of dozens."

"Because my *kishkes* are hanging out all over the arena?" Burns asked. "Because you shivved me good, baby? Because I have not seen knifework like this since the time I had my appendix carved?"

"Please, no flattery."

"No anesthetic, either," Burns pointed out. "Man, when you cut, you really cut. I didn't get the news about the Nazi switch artist till four this afternoon. Nice friends you got."

"He's no friend."

"Not any more. Wait'll he finds out how you used him."

"Why, Mac. He was unhappy at Jet-Tech. Whoever got him a new job did him a favor."

"And Eddie Hagen? Does he realize where you put him?"

"General Hagen has himself a new head of research. Whoever did that for him got him out of a spot."

"And put him right in front of a Senate investigating committee," Burns said.

Palmer sat up straight. "I don't get it."

"Hagen will. And Gauss. And a bunch of Jet-Tech top brass."

"Are you saying they'll be subpoenaed?"

"My Washington man just got off the phone with me, boychik. He tells me the agency that oversees these kind of things is hopping mad. They've scheduled a press conference in half an hour. They're going to cry foul and demand an investigation."

"They have a right to," Palmer said.

"What's to keep the boys from mentioning your name at such a hearing?"

"Nothing, I suppose."

"Well?" Burns demanded.

"Well, what? It's a free country, Mac. If they want to tell the senators that I allegedly brought them together in the interests of helping a man with a lot to offer our national defense effort—a man who was stymied in his present position—I can't really stop them. Nor would I try."

"The senators can see it another way, lover. They can see you pulling a man out of the vital Wotan project just when he was most needed."

"If you mean Gauss," Palmer said, "I think he'll report the story just the other way around. He'll probably say the Wotan failures were due to Jet-Tech's penny-pinching, their inability to back him up properly. There aren't ten men in the world who could prove him wrong. As a matter of fact, he's probably right."

Burns paused for a long time. Then he chuckled lightly. "I just took off my hat to you, Woody-baby," he said. "I doffed the old *chapeau*. A regular chess player, aren't you?"

"You're forgetting the stalemate play," Palmer observed. "The one where Jet-Tech tells the senators that I had ulterior motives for what I'm alleged to have done. Can you see them making that move?"

"That's not a stalemate move, doll, that's just plain suicide for them."

"Exactly. Now, if you'd like, I'll give you a chance to rewind the tape and see if I made any damaging admissions. Go ahead. I'll wait."

435

This time Burns guffawed with delight. "Christ, you're rich. I don't have to play back the tape. The minute I heard your first 'allegedly' I shut off the recorder. Like I said, sweetie, the *chapeau* is off to you."

With an effort Palmer restrained himself from changing the "like" to "as." Although he had probably impressed Burns and won him over as an ally, the man was still too volatile to be shaken violently. "Then this conversation can take the place of a meeting later on tonight?"

"Not by me it can't. I have things to discuss."

"Are you at your apartment now?"

"Yeah. How soon can you get here?" Burns asked.

"How long will our meeting take?"

"Hours, probably."

"Then I'll stop by my place for dinner. I'll see you at, oh, eight."

"Eat with me, sweetie."

"No need to trouble yourself, Mac."

"Really. I have a hot tray from Chambord. Tonight I'll make it two."

Palmer made a face. "What's on the menu?"

"You name it. Medallion of beef? *Truit amandine?* A sensational *canelloni?* Let me do the ordering."

Palmer smiled slightly. "I'll be there in an hour." He hung up and sat for a moment, analyzing the conversation. It was possible that he had tipped Burns far enough off balance to make him react spontaneously.

It had been clear to Palmer for some time now that, for Burns, the world was made up of two kinds of people: idiots and himself. Burns treated everyone with a combination of suave condescension, veiled pity and obvious distrust. But Palmer had gambled on the fact that his own scheme, if it worked, would impress Burns enough to create respect. It was certain enough that Burns could respect no one unless he proved equally wily. For this reason, too, Burns worked badly with anyone he felt to be his mental inferior, a category that included nearly everyone. Now, perhaps, Palmer felt, this had changed.

He stood up and walked out of his room, pacing down the wide, high-ceilinged hall to the office in which Virginia worked. He could hear a typewriter going. He looked in the room and saw her hunched over the machine, pecking rapidly at it with three or four fingers. Her carefully careless hair seemed less careful and more careless than usual. Palmer suspected she had been absent-mindedly running her fingers through it as she worked.

"What's the hot scoop?"

The typing stopped. She sat there with her back to him, perfectly still. Then, after a moment, the tension in her back began to ease. She sat up straight and, without turning toward him, said: "Newspapermen do not use the term 'scoop.' Only amateurs and dilettantes. And bankers."

"Do I get a peek at your face?"

"No. I've broken out in great ruddy boils."

"The old complaint?"

"If you mean stupidity, yes."

He walked past the desk at which she was sitting, then turned to confront her face to face. She looked tired. The shadows around her eyes had shifted in color from violet to blackish-blue.

"Hell. No boils."

She shrugged.

He watched her for a moment, while she avoided his glance. He tried to find in her face that great, warming glow she had given off so many times before, the almost palpable heat of curiosity or compassion or lust or tenderness or anger or any of the other things she had shared with him. It crossed his mind that her face tonight was only a mask, cleverly cast, and the phrase "death mask" shot across one corner of his thoughts, but not quickly enough for him to ignore it.

He sat down on a corner of her desk. "Do you have time to listen to me?"

She closed her eyes for a moment, then opened them. "Of course."

"About this weekend and today and all of that?"

She nodded. "Except that I can save you a great deal of time. George Mallett called me about five and read me the first few graphs of a story he'd just written."

Palmer leaned forward. "Do you remember it in any detail?"

"I'm afraid so."

"Can you tell me what it said?"

She turned to look at him for the first time. Her glance seemed vaguely reproachful in a confused way, as if she felt reproach but was trying to hide it. "Can you trust my memory?"

"Ee."

She made a meaningless, throwing-away gesture with both hands. "I'm sorry. I remember now. You said you trusted me after all. Isn't that right? Yes, that's right. Well, let's see." Her voice rattled on in what Palmer decided was a deliberate monotone. "It was all about the thing with Gauss and Hagen and Jet-Tech. And your name didn't come into it at all and neither did Ubco. And you can relax and take a breath now. George is a friend. He's a decent person. He's another one you can trust. In short, he's a loser. Like me. And you're a winner. I forgot to buy some kind of trophy to present you. I thought of it, but I forgot to do anything about it. That's what makes losers: no follow-through. That's one thing that makes losers. Another is being trustful. When you pick yourself up and place yourself gently in someone else's hands, trustingly, you immediately begin the process of losing. Especially when you have no business putting yourself in his hands, nor were you invited to in so many words, especially then."

She stopped at last and looked up at him. "Do you have time to buy me a drink?"

He nodded. "Where's your coat?"

437

"I'll get it. I'm not doddering yet."

"I didn't—"

"If only I could keep myself from saying things like that."

After walking silently for several blocks, they sat down in a bar that turned out to be the same one in which Palmer and Gauss had met once before. Virginia looked around her for a moment, then ordered a double Scotch from the waiter.

"You must forgive me," she said when the drinks had come. "I'm permanently off-guard with you. I shouldn't be, but I am. I say things to you I don't even tell myself."

"I wish you could forgive me for whatever it is I did to you."

"I have." She sipped her drink tentatively, then drank half of it. "What you did was to be married even before we met. You are forgiven. Do you know the thing that happens to single women when they reach my age? The business of wanting to have a baby before menopause sets in. Did anyone ever blurt that out to you half so charmingly?"

"No. But you're not exactly in their position, are you?"

"You mean because I once had a child?" She smiled very broadly and when she relaxed her mouth the lips did not return to their normal position immediately. They seemed stuck for a moment. Then they relaxed in sections, oddly. "But it's exactly as if Jeannie had never been born. It's been almost twenty years. I might at this point be a grandmother. If. All of which boils down to a single sturdy thought: in an accident like that, the luckiest is when there are no survivors."

"I don't think you—"

"I don't. You're right. I'm really better off alive. I do believe that. I very devoutly believe that. After all, it's the only choice I have. The new baby would be as pretty as Jeannie. I could make another beauty. Some women feel so strongly about it that they say—but only say—they wouldn't even insist on being married. Of course, there you are. I would insist. You see? Which accounts for the no-survivors theory."

"Men have proposed to you since then."

"Have they, now?"

Palmer nodded. "I'm certain they have."

"Well, so they have. You're quite acute. They've proposed in droves. In groves of droves. At least three of them."

"Why didn't you marry one of them?"

"He wasn't you." She finished her drink rapidly. "I loathe hearing things like that come out. I have to stop. Let's talk about, uh, about, uh, about sex." She looked around and signaled the waiter. "Another for me. Single this time. About sex," she went on to Palmer, "the inexhaustible subject. I wonder why I was so good with you? Was I good with you? Tell me I was, because otherwise I was nothing. Lie to me if you have to. Go ahead."

"Virginia, please stop this."

"Say: 'Virginia, you were great in bed.' Try that one."

"Will you pl—"

"Not direct enough for you? Say: 'Virginia, you are a great lay.' Hm?"

"Virginia, you are a great boob. Shut up and drink."

"Yes, of course, Mr. Palmer, sir," she said, pausing at each comma.

"Let's start," Palmer said, taking a long, slow breath, "with the assumption that the first careless rapture is past."

"And the careful rupture begins."

"Shut up." He frowned at her. "People who talk too much and too easily get in too much trouble. You have no idea how irritating it is to find out, finally, that my father was right. Where the hell was I?"

"You were about to tell me," she said, "that while you no longer harbored any lunacies about getting a divorce and marrying me, there was absolutely no reason why I couldn't settle down with you to a long affair, concluded finally by gray hair, dentures, madness and death. Yes?"

"I had no such idea."

"Please have it. Please ask me. I might even agree to it."

"Virginia, can't you stop talking for a while?"

"Can't you just picture it? You by the fire, emaciated, hard of hearing, rheumy of eye, with those liverish spots of ancient skin and a slight tremor. Me, kneeling arthritically at your feet, raddled hair, sunken cheeks, pendulous paps, decayed teeth. The Sinners' Twilight. Passion's Finale. Adultery Rewarded. One could hardly, with so little flesh there, call it a carnal relationship. My God, Woods, I wonder what old people do do? Are they free of it at last? Tell me?"

"If you don't mind, I'll tell you what I want to, not what you want me to."

"Very masterful. Well put." She reached across and caressed his cheek. "I must remember to see you in a new light. Boy financier. Wall Street Wonder. Youthful Machiavelli of the Business World. Continue. Dominate. Proceed."

"All I wanted to say," Palmer went on after a moment, "is that whatever derailed us these past few days shouldn't have. And if we could—"

"Why should you struggle in the toils of doubt?" she asked. She lifted her new drink to Palmer. "I just happen to know what derailed us." She put down her drink and seemed to forget it. "The confrontation scene. Mistress Meets Matron. Virtue Vanquishes Vice. All I had to do, Woods, darling, was to meet your wife and pass what was apparently the time of day with her. Shall I tell you about Mrs. Palmer, Mr. Palmer? Woman of resource? Inner power? Great guile? Insidious insight? Modern Mother and Mate? Details on Page Three? Do tell me why I babble on in this embarrassing way. Oh, look. It's so simple. I don't know if she loves you or hates you or what, but you cannot shake her loose. She doesn't intend to be discarded. And I'm with her. There, but for the grace of God, go I. We read each other's signals, she and I. There is nothing between you and me but the limber, dangerous link of sex. There is, between you and your wife, fantastically strong, triple-forged, vanadium-steel bonds. You are cut from the same, very exclusive bolt of cloth. By the same tailor. My God, Woods, you even look alike. Here." She pushed her new drink across to him. "Take it."

"I'll order another for myself."

"I'm not going to drink it. You drink it."

"I thought—"

"You thought I wanted to get stoned." She smiled sweetly. "Let me set you straight. This is much too serious to be solved by whisky."

Palmer picked up her drink and sipped it. "In other words," he said then, "you want to call it quits."

"I want to certify a death that took place late Friday night and Saturday morning. Will you sign the certificate?"

"And if I don't believe what it says?"

"Go on," she chided him. "You're so relieved you can hardly breathe. Imagine. How easy I'm making it for you. Could a woman be more of a gentleman?"

"The only trouble is that I don't believe you."

She nodded vigorously. "Nicely put. Flattery by denial."

"Will you stop play-acting?" he asked in a fierce undertone.

"Anything you say. I'm in a very pliant mood. There isn't anything I wouldn't do for you tonight, Woods. I'd even go to bed with you. But it would be awful. Is Mac's apartment free? I'll show you what I mean."

"He's waiting there for me. We have something to discuss."

"Too bad. How about Hertz Rent a Rendezvous? We could drive up to that motel in Connecticut." She stood up suddenly. A man at a nearby table looked at her, then looked away. "Please, Woods. Sign my certificate. Please."

He took her hand and tried to pull her back down into the booth. "Please try to control yourself," he said.

"I am in perfect control." The same man glanced at her again and this time the rest of the people at his table did, too. Virginia looked at him. "Perfect control, I assure you," she told the man.

"Wild," he said appreciatively.

She turned back to Palmer. "Agreed?"

"I don't—"

"Have any choice," she finished for him. "I have a clincher for you. On Friday night," she continued, sitting down again and lowering her voice, "I was offered a job with the savings banks. That was early in the evening. I said no. By Monday, so lucid had my weekend experience been, I called the man who made the offer and said yes. I start whenever I want to. They're preparing a three-year contract. The salary is higher than Ubco pays. As a matter of fact, I won't believe the figure till I see my first paycheck. But money is only a minor inducement." She reached across and took his hand. Her own felt cold.

Her fingers squeezed hard. "There are others. I've decided, for instance,

440

that I'm not really a commercial-bank girl at heart. Early upbringing. Poor girl from East Harlem. Ubco . . . A World She Never Made. I intend to be happier with the opposition. They're more my kind of people. They don't own the country and the world. Ubco always scared me. The power! But even that is only a minor inducement, too." She took his other hand and held them both very tightly. "Most important, darling. I'll be far away from you. So." She put his hands down very carefully on the table, stood up and stepped into the aisle. "So you see the way it is."

"You have no contract with Ubco?"

"None. Never deemed worthy of one, I suppose."

"The savings banks can't win, you know."

"You and Mac will see to that. He's your boy again, isn't he? He always gravitates to power. But I don't care if we win or lose. Note the 'we.'" I'm not changing jobs—or turning coat, if you will—out of any such convictions. I just simply want to get away from you. Because if I stay at Ubco we'll drift in and out of bed with each other. Some nights you'll go home. Some nights you'll meet me. You'll leave early, before eleven, the way you've been doing these past weeks. Ha. Caught you." She sat down again.

"I hardly hoped you hadn't noticed."

"Pretty insulting if I hadn't, hm?"

He smiled tentatively at her. "You haven't signed anything with the savings banks yet. Let's talk about it for a minute."

She shook her head. "Let's talk about marriage instead." She watched his face for a moment. "See how much of a gentleman I am, Woods? How I side-tracked you from trying to argue me out of my decision? Suppose you had? Suppose you'd exerted your not inconsiderable hold over me—and I freely admit that there isn't anything in the world too degrading or self-destructive or even obscene that I wouldn't do for you if asked. Suppose you'd talked me into staying with Ubco. How angry you would have been if you'd succeeded."

"Doesn't seem much chance of that," Palmer said. "Skip it."

"Not at all. Ginnie Clary has thoughts to utter. And don't, for God's sake, sulk. You have so little to sulk about, you bastard." She took his hand again and brought it to her mouth, rubbing her lips across it with slow emphasis.

"Don't." Palmer pulled his hand away and looked at the faint double line of lipstick. "Either be impossible or be loving. Don't be both at the same time."

"I can only be what I am," she said. For a moment they watched each other almost warily. Then a corner of her mouth turned up derisively. "For a man married as long as you," she said then, "you really don't understand marriage at all, do you?"

"But you do."

"Unfortunately, I do. It's a changing thing, from couple to couple. And with any one couple it changes from year to year. But it always ends up the same way. Whatever it began as—legalized lust or social convention or some lint-headed thought of raising kids—it always ends in the same thing: a compact between two dying people who cannot face death alone."

Palmer made a face. "Ginnie Clary has such pleasant thoughts to utter."

"You might find your condition much easier to endure if you face a few of these rough-edged night thoughts from time to time."

"Rough-edged? That one is covered with slivers of glass."

She laughed softly. "It may well be. But you know how true it is. We all do on our side of forty. Serutan Country. Downhillsville. But those who face it squarest are single bodies like me."

"In order to face something that squarely," he muttered, "you almost have to stick your neck way out."

"Yes. But that way you learn so many useful things. Like who you are. And do you have any real affinity for what you're doing."

"Oh," he said softly. "Affinity?"

Her face went blank for a moment as she watched him. "I mean for the job, Woods. I mean for Ubco. I didn't mean . . ." She gestured vaguely. "I'm a poor kid from a slum. There are a lot of us clawing our way out and up. You find out what the rules are and who makes them. Then you abide by the rules. Vic Culhane has made it pretty much on his own terms. He's at ease with what he's become. Mac Burns has made it, he believes, on the terms handed him by those who make them. He hates having had to make it that way, which is why he really hasn't made it at all. Even with his bleached hair. I . . . I thought I'd pretty well made it sort of off the back rail, a carom shot, the way Negro prize fighters and Jewish scientists and Italian crooners make it. You know. There are certain allowable categories. Jews have a somewhat wider range, actually. They don't have to be scientists. They can be musicians or comics or trial lawyers, too. So here I was, all set with Ubco. Except that what I'm involved with turns out to be something I don't really understand or like or need. I may end up leaving the savings banks, too. But at the moment I seem to be a banking expert, thanks to you, I suppose, and it does pay well."

"These rules," Palmer asked. "What are they? Who makes them?"

"Doll-baby," Virginia said in a reverberating imitation of Burns. "Don't you really know? *You* make the rules."

"Me?"

"You and your people."

He nodded slowly. "Us Waps."

"I didn't know you'd heard the term."

He smiled crookedly. "The underground's gotten careless. Some of the code books have fallen into enemy hands."

"Well." She looked momentarily confused. Then she shook her head slightly as if to clear it. "Anyway. It's all fairly simple. I don't belong with Ubco. So I'm getting out."

"That's crap."

"No. It's true."

"Just polite, issue-evading crap."

"No. It isn't the whole truth, but it's true."

"Then let's get the rest of it on the record," Palmer suggested.

"No need to."

"I think there is."

"You'll hate hearing it. I'll hate saying it."

Palmer lifted his hands for an instant. "All right. Let's get over the hard part fast. You want to get married. I can't marry you. Next step."

"Last stop." She patted his hand. "Good-by."

"It's so useless," he burst out then. "So wasteful."

She got to her feet and looked down at him. Her hand went to his hair, smoothing it back for an instant. The touch of her fingers on his temple felt like a breath of chill wind. "I should be very direct and cruel," she said in an undertone. "I should say that what you're feeling is injured ego. But it wouldn't help you to know. So I'll put it truthfully in this way: I am too much involved with you on too basic a level to endure the proximity of working in the same office. Having to see you even for a minute or two each day, having to hear or overhear your voice, having to listen to others mention your name, having to see it typed on a sheet of paper . . . this kind of thing is already killing me. Good-by, darling."

He stood up. "Can we—?"

"No, we cannot. I don't know how strong you th–think I am." Her voice broke and she turned quickly away.

"Look, if I could—"

"You can't." She tried to keep her voice level. "And, anyway, Woods, it's all a . . . a m–masterstroke. Sheer genius. You see? You must see. If I'm working for the savings banks . . ." Her voice died away for a moment. She swallowed once, with difficulty. "If I'm there and you're with Ubco . . . I mean, the tape recordings," she added, suddenly out of breath.

"What?"

"Th–they can't be used. They'd incriminate a savings-bank representative. Me. You idiot, they're useless to Burns." An immense sob seemed to bubble up through her throat. Her eyes widened in horror. Before Palmer could reach for her hand she ran to the door and disappeared outside. Moving as quickly as he could without drawing undue attention to himself by running, Palmer followed her. When he reached the street, she was getting into a cab. He watched her long, smooth calves, swelling upward from narrow ankles. Then the cab door slammed and she was gone.

He stood, coatless, in the cold evening air. Would it have been better, he wondered, to have run through the bar? Would the several seconds thus gained have allowed him time to stop her?

CHAPTER SIXTY-FOUR

As he turned the corner that led to the porte-cochere of Burns's building, Palmer stopped for a moment and leaned against the glossy white-faced brick, feeling its spiny texture against his cheek, wondering how he could take another step.

Ahead of him, a few hundred feet beyond a railing, ran the murmuring traffic of the East River Drive and, beyond it, the swift rush of the river itself. He could smell its faintly musky mixture of brine and moisture and complicated pollution.

He could remember being almost as confused as he was now, but never before at a time when he needed so desperately to have a clear, cold mind. He felt he could never match Burns's adept maneuverability. The man was a master conspirator, not only with a mind for it, but with a positive pleasure in creating intrigue. Palmer realized that he himself was an amateur and without even the amateur's love of the game. He could conspire well enough, in a plodding, workmanlike way, if pushed to it by extreme provocation. But nothing in his life had fitted him for the natural, almost casual approach to chicanery.

As he stood there gathering his wits, Palmer remembered other planets which scientists thought might have different atmospheres from that of Earth. Methane could be the "air" breathed by creatures on other planets, inhaled as naturally as Earthlings breathed oxygen. The choking fumes would be dangerously alien to explorers from Earth, just as the New York atmosphere of intrigue was alien at first to one from another city.

But most of us learn to breathe here, Palmer thought. And flourish.

So thinking, he walked on into Burns's building. As he rode up in the elevator he gingerly approached for a moment the things Virginia had told him, gingerly because he knew how destructive to his clear-headedness they would be. By the time he had reached Burns's floor, however, he had patched up a kind of uneasy peace with Virginia, at least in his mind, by telling himself that she would feel differently about it tomorrow and that, in any case, her decision couldn't really be final.

He would talk to her about it in the morning. Things would change.

Burns was not waiting at the door of his apartment. Instead the door was open and, as Palmer rang the bell, he could hear Burns shout something unintelligible from inside. Palmer walked in and closed the door behind him.

"Great timing, baby!" Burns yelled. "Food just arrived."

Palmer sniffed the air as he took off his hat and coat. "Smells fine."

He walked through the living room to the kitchenette, where Burns was setting dishes around a small alcove table. "You like cold *laban?*"

"Never tried it," Palmer said. "What's it like?"

"Like the only thing that cuts through real Lebanese food."

"Pardon?"

"I decided not to order from Chambord." Burns straightened up and grinned somewhat recklessly at him. "I had them send everything up from a little place in the Thirties. Best Lebanese eating west of Beirut." He indicated an assortment of small white cardboard cartons. "The works, Woody. We start with a little taste of brain salad, very nourishing. If you don't like that, I've got *baba gannouj* . . . sort of a mixed-up eggplant thing. The side dish is *hourus bitahini*, chickpeas mashed in sesame oil, real crazy. The kebabs are *kibbi* with *urohamasa*. I got 'em broiling in the rotisserie. For dessert, doll, we have *mubalbiah*, kind of a custard. And the *laban*, of course. It's yoghurt, but loaded with olive oil and dried mint."

Palmer stood motionless for a long moment. Then he sat down at the table. "If I don't like *laban*," he said matter-of-factly, "have you got any beer?"

They began eating. "I got a banker joke for you," Burns announced, waving a long slice of pickle.

"Commercial or savings?"

"You know about the Irish banks," Burns continued. "They're mostly still owned by the English. So this English banker in his morning coat and cane arrives in Dublin for the annual inspection. He goes right to the bank and walks in, see? It's twelve o'clock. Nobody's there. The door's wide open, the cash drawers are wide open, even the vault door's wide open. Money lying around. Nobody there, not a soul. Now he's really angry. He marches over to the burglar alarm and pulls it. All hell busts loose. Bells! Sirens! Deafening! He runs out to the sidewalk. Nobody stops. People just walk right by without even looking at him. All of a sudden, across the street, the door of a pub opens up and a waiter starts crossing over to the bank carrying a tray with four pints of ale on it." Burns stopped talking.

"Yes?" Palmer asked.

"Yes, what? Laugh, you bastard."

Palmer frowned, then got the joke. "They . . . they use the burglar alarm . . . ?"

"To ring for the waiter," Burns finished. He burst into raucous laughter.

Palmer smiled in a pained way. "Is there any more of that *gannouj?*"

"Christ. Tell you a joke."

"Try it on Vic Culhane."

"He told it to me," Burns admitted. "Jesus, Woody, get with it. This is supposed to be a love feast."

"Bury-the-hatchet-type thing?"

"I'm trying to make up for the tape recording, doll."

Palmer made a face and kept on avidly eating. He swallowed some of the sharp, spicy yoghurt. "You're right about this stuff. It's the only thing that cuts the food."

"You don't like the food?"

"I've already made a pig of myself over it. It's great."

"All right. Good." Burns lighted a cigarette and blew out a great deal of smoke, squinting at Palmer through it. "Look, Woody, I'm trying to ease tension. I'm usually superb at the job. A few days ago I swore to hang you up by the crown jewels. Then you pulled the rug out from under me, Joe Loomis and the whole frigging scheme. Now we're supposed to be working back toward a meeting of the minds. After all, I held off on the tape recordings long enough for you to pull the stunt with the Kraut. So meet me. Talk to me. Tell me how much you love me."

Palmer shook his head. "We'll get a lot further if we don't lie to each other. I'm uncomfortable about you because I don't trust you. You're unhappy with me because you really don't like anybody that can outsmart you, even once."

"Not so. I hate losers, old buddy. But I dig winners the most."

"That's true enough, I guess." Palmer cut into another broiled ball of chopped meat. "That far I can trust you . . . to pick the winning side."

Burns's smile was crooked. "Which fight are we talking about? The branch bill at Albany or the stock fight for Ubco?"

"Is that still on?" Palmer asked with mock innocence.

"Nobody's called it yet."

"I should think," Palmer mused, "that Loomis would be having his hands full by tomorrow with his own dissident stockholders. Once Washington starts asking questions, some kind of rump committee will try to spring him from Jet-Tech."

Burns nodded. "That far ahead I also thought."

"Which is why we're having this love feast."

Burns turned his hands palms up. "If you know that much about how my mind works, how come you still can't trust me?"

"Because I'm human, Mac. My foot's going to slip sometime. When it does, you'll double-cross me. Again."

Burns's tawny eyes widened. "A fine friend. How do I know you won't cross me?"

"You don't."

Burns thought for a moment, then stood up and went into the living room. He returned in a few moments with five flat boxes of recording tape. "It's all here," he said. "I mean the original tape, not the re-recordings. I don't have another inch of it anywhere. You believe me?"

446

Palmer took the reels of tape and hefted them for a moment. "That's a touching gesture, Mac."

"It was meant to be. Now do you trust me?"

"Considering that if Virginia Clary goes over to the other side those tapes are worthless anyway," Palmer said, "yes."

Burns sat down slowly, his eyes on Palmer. "You're too much, baby," he said then. "When did she tell you? Tonight?"

"Yes."

"And loused up my big gesture."

"Sad." Palmer began to eat the custard. "So now we both know how much we trust each other, Mac. It's a stand-off, New York style. If you're willing to settle for it, let's get to work."

CHAPTER SIXTY-FIVE

Loose ends. Palmer grimaced as he closed his eyes for a moment. The glare of the fluorescent light over the desk in his study had begun to make his vision blur.

After a while he opened his eyes again and reread the notes on his desk, checking for loose ends in the plans he and Burns had concluded earlier tonight. He glanced at his watch and found that it was well past three in the morning. If he wanted to be certain that all his loose ends were securely knotted in place by the end of the day that faced him, he knew he had to get some sleep.

Sighing, Palmer reached for the telephone and dialed Burns's office. A woman answered in a draggy voice: "Atherton, Cragie and Moon."

"Is this the p.r. division? Is Mac Burns there?"

Her voice became more distinct. "This is p.r. May I help you?"

"This is Mr. Palmer. Give me Mr. Burns."

"Right away, Mr. Palmer." She stressed his name so markedly that Palmer could visualize Burns, in the same room, looking up suddenly and making for the phone.

"You still up, lover?"

"Apparently you've got your staff up, too. Or is she an extra-curricular attraction?"

"Strictly business. The cartoon's finished. The copy's finished. We have no time—" Burns broke off to cough hackingly. "—no time to get type set for

447

this, so we're using one of the IBM typewriters in the office. One of the art-department boys is hand-lettering the display type."

"Let's hear the copy, Mac."

"Yeah." A confused background mumble. "Not that, *schmuck*," Burns snapped. "The revised one that— Gimme. Okay, Woody?"

"Go ahead."

"All right, the headline will read, uh, where is it . . . 'SOCIALIST BANKS ARE BLEEDING YOU DRY!' Only great, huh?"

"Christ," Palmer grunted. "Never mind. Keep going."

"Okay. Then the big cartoon under it. This big, fat, sloppy bank labeled 'Savings Bank' with a hammer-and-sickle flag flying from it. There's a big hose running into one window. The hose comes from a pump. A senator type with frock coat and string tie is pumping the pump. He's labeled 'State Legislature.' From the pump the hose goes to a great big hypodermic needle that's stuck in the arm of a little skinny John Q. Public *schmendrick*. Couple drops of blood leaking from the needle. He looks beat. Pockets turned inside out. The usual cornball hoke. And there are lines around the bank showing that it's getting fatter every second. You like?"

"Terrible."

"Baby!"

"I mean it," Palmer insisted. "Change the headline from 'SOCIALIST' to 'SOCIALISTIC.' We're less liable that way. Take off the hammer-and-sickle flag. See if you can do without the drops of blood, for God's sake. When you do all that I'll still hate it, but we have no choice."

"Right. Now the copy."

"Go."

"Uh . . . it starts off: 'If you think creeping socialism is somebody else's nightmare, not yours, think twice. Socialist tendencies are right at work in the very heart of our state, right where it hurts most—your pocketbook.' Paragraph. Then we tack in that one-paragraph description from the Syracuse speech, the one you liked. Blah, blah, blah. Then the copy goes on: 'Don't let socialist banks bleed you dry. Don't let the pampered, privileged savings banks grow fat on your thrift.' Paragraph. 'You pay taxes. Why shouldn't savings banks pay taxes?' Paragraph. 'You invest in America. Why shouldn't savings banks invest in America?' Paragraph. 'You believe in private enter-prise. Why shouldn't the savings banks?' Paragraph. 'Don't let the savings-bank fungus, imported from a foreign country, eat away at the heart of your state and your nation.' Paragraph. Pretty foul shit, huh, Woody? Anyway, here's the closer: 'Wake up to what's happening. Tell your State Senator and State Assemblyman to vote for private enterprise, not creeping socialism.' Para-graph. 'Tell them to vote NO on the Savings Banks' Branch Bill.' Then it's signed 'Independent Citizens' Committee for Private Enterprise,' with a suite number in a hotel."

"Did you reserve the suite?" Palmer asked.

"Two hours ago."

Palmer drew a line through an item on his sheets of paper. "What name?"

"Jimmy Fogel."

Palmer made a note. "Is he trustworthy?"

"No. Greedy, yes. I'll have this layout upstate and in his hands by eight this morning. He'll have it at the newspaper by eight-thirty. They'll hit the stands no later than three P.M."

"Doesn't this Fogel character suspect anything?"

"He's getting five thousand bucks for the job. That's ten times the monthly retainer I pay him. In other words, he has ten months to get back in everybody's good graces after this bomb goes off."

Palmer made another note. "What's the ad costing?"

"Two gees. It's a full page and we're paying a premium for back-page placement."

Palmer noted the new cost figure. "What makes you think the upstate paper will accept the ad?"

"Fogel. He's got something on one of the editors. Photos of the poor son of a bitch with two faggots from New York."

"What kind of photos?"

Burns laughed. "I got ladies with me here, doll. Let's just call the poses good enough for inclusion in a textbook, you might say."

Palmer closed his eyes again. "Will you take the ad upstate? Are you going to stick around to make certain Fogel comes through?"

"Not me, boychik. I stay right here in New York. One of my people makes the trip, hands over the ad, turns tail and runs home again like a thief. That's the way it's got to be."

"Good night, Mac," Palmer said. "Call me at the office when you know anything."

He hung up the phone, switched off the fluorescent light and opened his eyes in the half-darkness.

As he made his way to his bedroom, Palmer could hear Edith's slow, steady breathing. She seemed to be enjoying a smooth, unruffled dream. He watched her face for a moment, impassive, calm.

Then he sat down on the edge of his bed and rubbed his eyes before lying back full length. He wondered for a moment what kind of dreams he would have tonight.

CHAPTER SIXTY-SIX

The market opened on Tuesday with a slight but general upswing. By ten the tape had already begun to lag on Jet-Tech trading. By eleven the most reliable quotation Palmer's broker had been able to get was thirty-five, down ten from its pre-Palmer price of forty-five.

A girl from Virginia Clary's office brought Palmer the first editions of the afternoon papers at eleven, while he was talking to his broker. Both the *Journal-American* and the *World-Telegram* carried United Press International stories out of Washington on the press conference called by Tim Carewe's agency. Although the statement was by no means as strong as Palmer had been led to expect, it nevertheless covered all the ground he had hoped it would. The *Journal's* headline failed to get the real meat of it: "CALL FOR WOTAN-SCIENTIST PROBE." But the *Telegram* managed to condense the gist properly: "SPACE AGENCY FLAYS SCIENTIST SWITCH: TO QUIZ JET-TECH WOTAN FLOPS."

Although Palmer's telephone had been ringing fairly steadily since nine in the morning, he had left instructions that only newspapermen were to be put through. Burns used his private line three times, once to report contact with Fogel, once to report that the ad layout had been delivered to the newspaper and once to say that the ad had been engraved and was now being stereotyped for the first press run.

Shortly after eleven, Palmer's secretary brought in his telephone messages, among which were five from Burckhardt, calling from his Connecticut home.

Frowning, Palmer punched the Burckhardt button on his intercom. When no one answered, he placed a call to the Connecticut number. It was answered by one of the maids.

"No sir, Mr. Palmer, he left about half an hour ago."

As Palmer replaced the phone it immediately rang. He picked it up again. "Palmer."

"George Mallett. I'm calling for a favor."

"The answer is yes," Palmer said.

The reporter laughed. "I just got a call from one of my colleagues at Albany. Here's the favor: tell me, so I can tell him, what you know about a guy named Jimmy Fogel."

Palmer sat back in his chair and tried to relax. Part of telling a convincing lie was in betraying as little muscular tension as possible, especially as it affected the voice. "Jimmy Fogel?" he repeated. "That's easy, George. Nothing."

"Never heard of him?"

"Never. Is he a banker?"

"Maybe. He's been known to bank a crap game now and then."

"Albany gent?"

Mallett laughed again. "You're awful," he said. "You do the whole thing as naturally as a belch. Don't you have any nerves at all?"

Palmer quickly calculated his chances if he admitted even part of the truth, off the record, to the reporter. He decided this was one time he could trust no one. The possibilities were too juicy even for the *Star* to resist. "Am I supposed to know this fellow, George?" he asked then.

"I don't know. I'm just a messenger boy on this one. Maybe you don't know him. Maybe Mac Burns does. You two back in bed together?"

"We have never, as you so elegantly put it, fallen out of bed. I fired him once and then changed my mind," Palmer responded. "As far as I know, Mr. Burns is still being retained by Ubco as special public-relations counsel." He paused very briefly. "What's the matter with this Fogel?"

"Nothing money won't make up for. If you really don't know, I guess I'm not at liberty to tell you. But it'll be out by the end of the day."

"Some political thing?"

"Yeah." The reporter stopped for a moment. "They just gave me a note. Jet-Tech's hit thirty-two. That's a four-year low."

"Terrible. I hope you don't own any, George."

"Me?" He chuckled softly. "I got up from my lunch table yesterday—you remember that memorable lunch?—and sold all I owned. When do you think I ought to buy it back?"

"Buy a good stock, George. Buy Ubco."

The door to Palmer's office opened and Burckhardt stood there, glaring at him. Palmer nodded and said into the phone: "My boss just came in, George. Anything else?"

"I'll hang up and let you two talk," the reporter said. "The poor old duffer probably hasn't an idea in the world of what's really happening."

"That's possible, George. So long."

Palmer hung up the phone. "Who was that?" Burckhardt demanded.

"Mallett of the *Star*. I'm sorry you couldn't reach me, Lane. The lines were only open to newspapermen."

"The lines—?" Burckhardt's milky-blue eyes narrowed to a ferocious squint. His normally ruddy face turned violently red. With an effort he calmly closed the door behind him and advanced to the center of the enormous room. "I'll be Goddamned," he announced in a terribly calm voice. "The chief executive officer of the bank can't talk to his hired flunky. But any two-bit poop-snooper can get right through to you." He turned slowly until he faced Palmer. "All right, start talking."

"About what?" Palmer said in a mild voice. "Did you notice that trading of Ubco shares has slowed to a crawl? Suddenly no one's buying them."

"Everybody who was buying them," Burckhardt muttered, "is too busy worrying about their Jet-Tech holdings. Just what kind of mess have you gotten us into?"

"We're in no mess. Jet-Tech is."

Burckhardt pulled in a deep, ragged breath. "It's bound to rub off on Ubco, you stinking idiot!" he shouted. His eyes widened. "Do you realize what can happen to us then?"

Palmer watched the faint fringe of blasted capillaries that tangled in the corners of Burckhardt's eyes. The yellowish cast of his eyeballs clashed wildly with the fierce blue irises. "Sit down, Lane," he said then. "Please."

"Don't patronize me, you little fart." The older man paced energetically toward the immense window at the far end of the room. "I want to know what you think you were doing. By what colossal nerve did you give yourself the right to jeopardize the reputation of something I've put my whole life into?"

Palmer took out his cigarettes and shoved them across the desk to Burckhardt. "Don't be angry," he said in a slow, reasonable voice. "There just wasn't time for a full explanation before. In any event, we both know what your reaction would have been if you'd known in advance."

"The same as it is now, you little—"

"Calm down and sit down!" Palmer snapped. "I don't intend to take any more abuse."

The two men watched each other for a moment with a kind of tired wariness. Then Burckhardt sat down across from Palmer and lighted a cigarette. "Since you're not going to be with Ubco much longer," he said in a deliberately flat voice, "I don't suppose it's worth busting an artery over you."

Palmer smiled pleasantly. "Nothing's worth it. You've been presented with a *fait accompli*. Naturally, you're angry. Last week you had your back to the wall. This bank was about to be yanked out from under you. The Jet-Tech people had a lock on me, Lane. They were demanding that I front for them in the take-over."

"What kind of—?"

"Not important," Palmer cut in. "It was powerful persuasion. I'd have had a lot of trouble refusing their demand. With me fronting, they would have moved their directors on the board, dumped you upstairs to some honorary chairmanship and gone about securing that fantastic loan of theirs, or an even wilder one. As things stand now, Loomis has his hands so full with his own problems he's in no position to make any moves at our stockholder meeting."

Burckhardt sat silently for a moment, taking short puffs on his cigarette,

452

not inhaling, but simply filling the air around him with a great amount of smoke.

"And the savings banks?" he barked then.

Unable to tell how much Burckhardt knew, Palmer answered evasively. "You don't think the Jet-Tech crowd will have any heart left for their Albany battles."

"And that little Greek bastard they planted on me?"

Palmer made a face. "Lebanese. It's easy to see why you never got along with Burns. Do you hate all the foreign-born or just him?"

"I know plenty," Burckhardt stated flatly. "Do business with dozens of 'em. The minute I laid eyes on Burns I knew what I was up against. Look." He hitched himself closer to the desk in a kind of confidential posture. "Would any white man do what he did?"

Palmer's mouth pushed out sideways in a pained grimace. "The miracle to me," he said after a moment, "is how you manage to get along in this town feeling that way."

"Never mind about that. The Harps and Sheenies have their town and I have mine."

"It's the same town."

"It's not!" Burckhardt almost shouted. "I let them have all the silly political games they play with the Wops and the Spics and Niggers. That doesn't concern me. When they want money, though . . ." He grinned savagely. "When they want money, little boy, they come to where the money is."

" 'A might fortress is our God,' " Palmer quoted, " 'a bulwark never failing.' "

Burckhardt stared at him. "What?"

"When was the last time you went to church?" Palmer asked. "As long ago as I?"

"Will you stop—"

"Got it!" Palmer crowed. He hummed for a moment, then quoted again: " 'And though this world, with devils filled, should threaten to undo us; we will not fear, for God hath willed His truth to triumph through us.' "

Burckhardt ground out his cigarette with thrusting twists of his powerful fingers. "That's what's always been the matter with you," he said nastily. "You can't stand up on your hind legs and say your piece like a man. You sneak around corners and quote Scripture and make snide little remarks. God damn it, Woody, what kind of mollycoddle did your old man make?"

Palmer felt himself standing up. He had no recollection of wanting to rise, but once he was on his feet he could hear his own voice raised as high as Burckhardt's. "You want straight talk?"

"For once in your life."

Palmer was leaning across his desk. His face was less than a foot from Burckhardt's. "Since when did you ever listen to the truth?" he asked. "You're too busy striking poses, you old fraud. What kind of banker are you supposed to be, anyway? What the hell do you really know about it? You're another of these big-mouthed, pea-brained charlatans the country's too full of as it is. The only thing you know is how to shove hard. The minute you come against somebody with even half a brain, you're dead. Joe Loomis cut you up in stinking little shreds and left you for bait, you miserable old fake. I pasted you back together so that you look like a man again. And all you can do is holler about it like a snot-nosed kid. If you want to sit quietly and let me finish the patching-up job, all right. But if you open that sewer-mouth at me one more time, I'll leave you for the maggots."

Palmer felt the room shift alarmingly. He sat down and steadied himself. His intercom pinged softly. He ignored it.

After a while, when both men had their breathing under control, Burckhardt took another of Palmer's cigarettes, lighted it and walked slowly to the immense plate-glass window. He stared out at Fifth Avenue for a long moment. When he turned back, Palmer could not see the expression on his face, silhouetted against the outside glare.

"What," Burckhardt began slowly, his voice almost hushed, "do you plan to do about the savings banks?"

Palmer shrugged. "The situation's developing," he said impatiently. "No need to go into details. We'll panic the Banks Committee so they pigeonhole the resolution for another year."

"Will it work?"

Palmer squinted at the older man. It was difficult to talk to the detailless outline of a man, without expression or even gesture. Palmer stood up and moved slowly toward the window, hoping to force Burckhardt to turn sideways and allow the light to reach his face. "It'll work," Palmer said. "It's costing enough."

"How much?" The two syllables fell without weight or force.

"It's up to seven thousand now. Probably ten before we're done. Not counting Burns's out-of-pocket expenses."

"Burns."

"Yes, Burns."

"You and Burns," the older man said.

"Any objection?"

Burckhardt turned slightly so that Palmer could see the absolutely blank expression on his face. "I don't know," Burckhardt said.

"What don't you know?"

The older man gestured faintly. "Anything."

Palmer watched him more closely now. There was a draggy tempo to the sparse movements Burckhardt made. His lips hardly flickered as he spoke. His eyes remained fixed almost straight ahead. "That doesn't sound like you," Palmer commented.

Burckhardt's lower lip slowly shoved up in a that's-how-it-is expression. "Okay."

"Okay what?" Palmer persisted.

"Nothing." Burckhardt turned away and took a step toward the door. Then he paused and slowly, almost ponderously for a man of his litheness, turned back. "You hurt," he said then. "I guess I laid myself open for it, but, brother, you hurt."

A peculiar emotion began to well up in Palmer. For a moment he was afraid it would be remorse. Then he recognized it for something slightly different: pity. He felt the muscles of his face react woodenly as he tried to force them into a more friendly expression. "That's nothing," he said at last. "I floored Burns. Knocked him cold the other night. Now he's my buddy, for as far as I can trust him. Are you?"

Burckhardt stood motionless for a while, giving the impression that he was waiting for some kind of feeling to come to him. At last he said: "Ever meet anybody who buddied up to his gravedigger?"

Palmer shook his head. "I'm your plastic surgeon, not your gravedigger."

The older man laughed softly, a curiously disembodied sound like dry palms rubbing together. "Hell of an operation, Woody."

Palmer's private phone rang. He walked to the desk and answered it. After a moment he said "Thanks, Pete," and hung up. He faced Burckhardt. "Jet-Tech's hit twenty-nine. Lowest in twelve years."

Burckhardt's mouth moved sluggishly. It seemed to frame and then reject a series of phrases. Finally he said: "Congratulations."

"Do you own any, Lane?"

"No."

"You won't be tempted to buy some at the bargain prices?"

"No."

"That's good. We can't have a situation where they catch an Ubco officer taking a position in Jet-Tech stock."

Burckhardt nodded and started for the door, moving with a kind of heavy-footed stolidness, as if he had suddenly gained thirty pounds in the last few minutes. At the door he paused. "Any other instructions?"

"Just to try a different attitude."

"Not happy enough for you?"

"Listen," Palmer said. "I know you. You never delegate responsibility because you trust nobody but yourself. You're happiest that way. Now learn to be happy another way. It's as simple as that."

"Too old to try."

"Don't con me, Lane."

The older man's mouth moved silently for a moment. "It's funny how poor my judgment was. I thought I knew you inside out. All I ever saw in you was a Daddy's Boy." Then his eyes narrowed in perplexity. "Whose boy are you, anyway?"

"My own," Palmer said, so softly he seemed to be addressing himself.

"Whose?"

Palmer cleared his throat. "My own," he said more distinctly.

455

Burckhardt stood there in the doorway for a moment, his face working slowly as if digesting the idea Palmer had voiced. Then he opened the door. "I hope you're pleased with how it feels to be your own man," he said then. "I used to be."

CHAPTER SIXTY-SEVEN

Palmer awoke at six-thirty, shut off the alarm and stumbled into his study. He sank down at the desk and examined a sheet of paper on which he had scribbled the events of the day.

The stockholder meeting began at ten today and ended by noon. If all went well he would be elected a director, pursuant to a decision made several months ago, thus placing him at the directors' lunch and meeting thereafter. But he had no way of knowing, with any real certainty, whether all would go well.

In the last few days he had heard no murmur from the Loomis forces, squeezed between their own dissident stockholders and a pending Senate subcommittee investigation. Chances were, he mused sleepily as he rechecked the list, that the meeting today would go smoothly. But he was so close to winning that he was dissatisfied with any plan whose outcome was left to chance. There had to be a way to turn chance into certainty. He sat and thought for a long time as, slowly, the rest of his family awoke and began their day.

At eight o'clock a phone call took him from the breakfast table. "I just spent another five gees," Mac Burns told him.

Palmer chewed and swallowed the piece of toast in his mouth. "On Fogel?"

"Sent him to Europe for two months. Long enough?"

"I thought everything had gone smoothly in Albany."

"Like silk. But don't you feel happier just knowing Fogel's on a Pan Am jet this very moment?"

"Um." Palmer brushed crumbs from his lips. "Any word from the Banks Committee?"

"I'll know by lunch."

"How does it look?"

"Like they're scared of the branch bill and want to dump it."

"Lovely. Talk to you later, Mac."

Palmer slipped back into his seat at the breakfast table in time to hear Edith tell Gerri: ". . . definitely none of your business."

"Why isn't it?" the girl wanted to know.

Palmer watched the girl's gray eyes sweep up for a moment to glance at him, then lower again to her plate of scrambled eggs. "What's none of her business?" Palmer asked.

Edith eyed him cautioningly. "Your business."

"Hm?"

"I just wondered out loud," Gerri explained, "why Mr. Burns calls you at such weird hours. And Mom said—"

"She's right," Palmer cut in. "My business is not your business." He buttered another slice of toast. "On the other hand, your business is my business. Unfair?"

"And how," Woody said, his low-pitched voice gruff with some past but remembered intrusion into his privacy.

"You see?" Palmer asked Edith. "Not only do these children look miserable and behave miserably, but deep down inside they are consistent, homogeneous clots of misery. Or is the word 'lump'?"

"Lumps of laziness," Gerri suggested. "Clots of carelessness. But morsels of misery."

"Thank you." Palmer broke his toast and began eating it.

"What's she talking about?" Tom asked.

"It's better not knowing," Edith said. "If you—"

The telephone rang again. They sat quietly and listened to Mrs. Gage take her time answering. On the fourth ring she did. "For you again, Mr. Palmer."

"Woody." Burckhardt's usually hard, forceful voice sounded oddly tentative, but Palmer couldn't tell whether it was anything more than early-morning fuzziness. "I have to see you before the meeting."

"Why don't we meet in your office at nine-thirty?" Palmer suggested.

"No good. Some of the directors will expect to be invited there to gas with me. What about nine, your office? Then I'll ride you downtown to the meeting. We'll talk on the way."

Palmer considered this for a moment. He decided he did not want any of the directors seeing him linked this closely, still, with Burckhardt. "Won't work," he said at length. "I'm not going to my office. I've got to finish three or four chores," he lied, "and then go direct to the meeting."

"Then for Christ's sake let's talk now," Burckhardt said.

"I'm eating breakfast. Can I call you back?"

"I'm leaving here in fifteen minutes."

Burckhardt said nothing for a long moment, apparently realizing how he had mouse-trapped himself. "All right," he said finally and hung up.

Palmer returned to the table as Woody was complaining about something. ". . . expect you to go to every dance but why should I? It's bad enough they

457

have one every lousy week. Why do I have to spend a lot of money on some dopey girl just so people don't think I'm some kind of grind?"

Palmer tried to fit the complaint into a known category. With Woody this was not too difficult. "You come up for a raise in May," he said at last. "I think your reputation at school won't suffer too badly if you wait till then."

" 'S'what you think." Woody moodily poked at his eggs. "What I was sort of working out was an advance against future allowances. You see—"

"If you get your raise now," Palmer cut in, "what happens after May? How do you pay back the advance?"

Woody brightened considerably. "I've got that all worked out," he said. "After June this stupid social season ends. No more drain on the exchequer. I have a surplus out of which I can repay the advance."

Palmer kept his face blank. He ate a forkful of eggs, making a point of chewing them thoroughly. Then he turned to Edith. "Think he can remember the idea from now till summer?"

"We'll remind him."

Palmer nodded. "Then let's try it. But—" He held up his hand to stave off requests from Gerri and Tom. "It applies only to Palmers over the age of fourteen."

"Great," Woody said. "Thanks."

"I think," Palmer said to Edith, meeting her glance for a brief instant, "we ought to decide what Woody's going to be doing this summer that gives him this tremendous financial surplus. Working?"

Edith considered her glass of orange juice. "I'd half thought we might spend the summer at the Michigan place."

"You four," Palmer said. "It would be a fairly complicated commute for me."

"I'd thought," she said, "you might want to take off a month."

"I don't see how I—" Palmer stopped, looked down at his plate and thought for a moment. "I guess we'd better talk about it tonight, after the meeting's out of the way."

"Fine," Edith said quickly with a relieved air.

Palmer glanced at his watch. Eight-twenty. He stood up. "This won't take long." He went into his study, consulted his notes, looked up a number and dialed it.

"Yes?" The thin, chipper voice of an old man.

"Mr. Loomis? This is Woods Palmer."

"One moment. I'll see if Mr. Loomis is at home."

Palmer sat down at his study desk and reached for a half-empty pack of cigarettes. The original idea for the phone call had come to him in the middle of the night as a result of being awakened by a bad dream. He had thought so much of the idea at the time that he had got up, made a note of it and developed it further on arising. Now he was no longer as proud of the thought as he had been, but anything, any means of approaching Loomis was worth trying at this point. The main thing was to offer something, not ask for it. And the important thing was to spring it at the last moment, scant hours before the meeting, to prevent Loomis from thinking too long about it.

"Good morning, Mr. Palmer," another spry old voice said.

"Thank you for coming to the phone, Mr. Loomis," Palmer began. "I had an idea for you, a helpful one."

"That would be a refreshing change." Loomis' voice had gone thin with sarcasm. "Before you tell me about it, will I see you at the stockholders' meeting this morning?"

"Yes, you will."

"And, again before I hear the idea, what will it cost me?"

Palmer laughed in a manner he hoped sounded easy. "Why not listen to the idea first. Then perhaps you might have one of your own I might like to hear."

"Proceed."

Palmer fumbled a match against the striking surface of the matchbook and lighted a cigarette. "Have any of your people come up with a workable way to silence the senatorial investigation?"

"No. But you have?"

"Possibly."

"And I get the idea with no strings?"

Palmer blew smoke at the fluorescent lamp. "Of course."

"Just a gift from one gentleman to another?" Loomis persisted.

"Pretty much that way."

"But I, sir, am no gentleman. And you, sir, are a banker."

Palmer laughed again, more naturally. "The idea is simple enough. Why not have a talk with General Hagen?"

"To what end?"

"Merger."

There was silence at the other end of the line. Then: "Have you discussed this with Eddie Hagen?"

"No."

"You just, ah, out of the goodness of your heart, so to speak, came up with the idea?" Loomis asked.

"Not entirely," Palmer admitted. "I'd been wondering for several days now what I'd do to extricate myself if I were in your shoes. This seems a workable way."

"Hagen's your friend. What do you think his reaction would be?"

"No idea. You and I might discuss it at lunch, after the meeting."

"Ye-es." Then, more to himself than to Palmer, Loomis said: "Very interesting. If we merged, Gauss would still be working for Jet-Tech and the investigating subcommittee would have little left to investigate." Loomis paused for a long moment. "I can't say I always approve of the way your mind works, Mr. Palmer, but I sometimes admire the results."

"Pretty much the way I feel about your mind, Mr. Loomis," Palmer responded. "Tell me, sir, do you feel you have a choice as to how you'll conduct yourself at the stockholders' meeting today?"

"Ye-es. I can open up swinging and raise general hell. I have the votes."

"My idea of successful hell-raising," Palmer said, "is when your own home base is so secure that you can afford to raise hell away from home. Is that your idea, too, Mr. Loomis?"

"Let's not fool around," the other man said. "I'll promise a peaceful meeting if you promise Eddie Hagen's serious consideration of a merger."

"Sounds *quid pro quo*. Let's agree on it."

"With one rider," Loomis added. "Ubco must renew consideration of the Jet-Tech loan application."

"At the same principal and terms?"

"I leave that to your discretion."

"Then it won't be the same principal and terms," Palmer warned him.

"Mr. Palmer, the matter is in your hands."

"Thank you, Mr. Loomis."

"You're welcome, Mr. Palmer."

"We'll talk about it later today, Mr. Loomis."

"I look forward to it, Mr. Palmer."

"Good-by, sir."

"Good-by."

Palmer hung up the phone, ground out his cigarette and bounced up out of his chair. He was grinning as he walked back into the dining room.

". . . goopy sex-hygiene lectures and all that," Woody was complaining.

"If anybody needs them," Gerri retorted, "you do, buster."

"Look who's talking," her brother hooted.

"What's sex hygiene?" Tom asked.

"Hold it," Palmer said. He turned to his elder son. "Woody, is this another subtle lead-in to a question of money? Because if you and some girl—"

"Woods!" Edith interrupted.

Woody's face grew bright pink. He hid as much of it as he could by lowering it to make a studious examination of his plate. "Lay off, Pop," he muttered. "I was just telling about the silly way these girls carry on in class. Is there some other school in town I can transfer to next fall?"

"Some vocational high school," Gerri kindly suggested.

"Doesn't anybody shut her up?" Woody asked.

"I think sex-hygiene lectures are a big waste of time," Gerri announced. "We just started them. After class one of the girls filled in the rest of the course in five fast minutes. Even the details like wrapping film and all that junk."

Palmer frowned. "Details like what?"

"That transparent stuff you wrap sandwiches in," Gerri explained. "It's all the rage with the teen-agers. Right, Woody?"

Her brother's face had now grown a darker shade of pink. "Dry up," he growled.

"The rage for what?" Palmer asked.

Edith stood up and began collecting plates. "Finished, Tom?" she asked briskly.

The younger boy shook his head. "The rage for what?" he echoed.

"The poor man's contraceptive device," Gerri informed him. "Costs nothing, easy to come by and—"

"Halt." Palmer stared from one child to the next and ended by looking at Edith. "Do other families have to go through this at breakfast?" he wanted to know. "She's your daughter."

Edith gave him a broad, fake grin. "How can you expect to keep up with the latest advances of modern technology?"

Palmer's eyes widened slightly. "It cost the chemical companies millions in R and D money to develop . . ." He stopped and looked at his fork helplessly. "And these science-minded kids simply . . ." He stopped again. Then he turned to Gerri. "Where do you get all this lovely information?"

The girl gestured airily. "The study period after our sex-hygiene class."

"Well, keep it to yourself in the— No. Never mind." Palmer rubbed his cheek hard. "I guess we're better off knowing what you know." He glanced at his watch again and immediately stood up. "If you ladies and gentlemen here in Obstetrics will allow me, I have an urgent call in Surgery." He nodded to each of them in turn and left the room.

He glanced out the study window and saw, through the pierced-concrete façade, that the bank's Sixty Special was already double-parked in front of the house. The driver had arrived five minutes before his normal time, Palmer noted. As a matter of fact, he recalled, this had happened every morning since Tuesday, when he and Burckhardt had had their showdown. Banks were fairly quiet, restrained places, but their grapevine systems functioned with the speed of light.

Palmer relaxed in the back of the Cadillac as the car swung east and slipped into the downtown lanes of the East River Drive. He scanned the *Times* and was pleased to note that the Jet-Tech investigation had been relegated to the business section of the paper where, he saw, it merited a small headline near the bottom of the page. He shifted his attention to the market listings and confirmed the fact that Jet-Tech stock had leveled off at thirty-one while Ubco shares had dropped half a point. Since no one was feverishly buying them any more, their price might slowly drift back over the next weeks to where it had been half a year before.

In the downtown financial section, Palmer stopped the car two blocks from Ubco's main office and dismissed the driver. Then he stepped into a cigar store, bought a pack of cigarettes and got two dollars' worth of change. In the store's single phone booth he called Eddie Hagen at his New England office.

"This is a pay phone," he explained when he had got through to Hagen. "I just had a curious feeler from Jet-Tech."

"Where, buddy?" Hagen asked. "What tender portion of the anatomy?"

"Hold tight," Palmer said. "They'd like to talk merger with you."

"Hah?"

"Sure. Gets them off the hook with the Senate subcommittee. Gets you off, too."

"Jet-Tech couldn't swallow us," Hagen said. "They've got indigestion from overeating already. And your outfit won't pay for the Tums."

"We may reopen the question of a loan."

"What kind of merger idea did they suggest? Stock transfer?"

"No details. Just interested willingness."

Hagen was silent for a moment. "We could use their computers. But, otherwise, we don't match. The product mix is lousy. We compete on several items."

"Don't talk production to me, Eddie. I'm just carrying a message. Why not talk to them? Once can't hurt."

"As the willing virgin said," Hagen added. "You remember what happened to her? She got screwed."

"Yes or no, Eddie?"

"How the hell can I say?" Hagen snapped. "I've got a board to confer with."

"Can I tell the Jet-Tech people you'll discuss it with your board?"

"What the hell, why not? Tell 'em. But, Woody?"

"Yes?"

"Your last favor landed me up to my navel in hot soup, old Army buddy. This time I want protection."

"What kind?"

"If I sit down with Jet-Tech, I want them to understand that the whole fate of their Ubco loan depends on how nice they are to me."

"Christ, Eddie. This is starting to get out of hand."

"Yes or no?" Hagen asked.

"Qualified yes. I have a board of directors, too."

"Okay. Tell Jet-Tech to call me. Loomis?"

"Most likely."

"Remind me to wear my iron jock to the meeting. Good-by, dear old Army buddy."

"Good-by, greedy friend."

Palmer walked slowly up Broad Street. The nine o'clock traffic had all but disappeared now. No great hordes of people belched up out of the subway stairs. The financial district had begun to clot slowly with large chauffeur-driven Cadillacs, Lincolns, Rolls-Royces, and an occasional Mercedes, here and there a low-slung Jaguar driven by its owner.

The sky was coldly clear overhead. It showed in small, irregular patches of ice blue between dull, upthrusting buildings. Palmer stood at a corner for a moment, listening to what sounded like the beating of gigantic wings. He looked up, squinting into the bright sky, and saw the churning flash of a helicopter rising high overhead. It hovered for a moment, checking in mid-flight and hanging from its slow-beating rotors like a hawk wheeling cautiously as it took aim. Then, with a buoyant sideways jolt, it slid upwards and disappeared. After a moment the throb of its great metal wings grew faint beneath the impatient honking of the traffic.

Palmer glanced around at the buildings, old ones shabby in their hoary coats of Manhattan soot, new ones already scabbed in places by the action of New York's caustic air. Palmer took a breath and sorted out the typical smells of this town and this place, the faintly briny, vaguely rotting odor of the river and the sweetish fetor of exhaust fumes. It was not the kind of air the average human being could take, an atmosphere hostile to most forms of Earth life.

He walked slowly for a moment toward Ubco's main office, wondering whether he or anyone else in this town could long exist in such an alien atmosphere. Instantly, because of some crossed neural connection in his memory, he thought of Virginia.

He had stepped into a sidewalk phone booth and dialed the number of his office before, slowly, he replaced the phone on its hook. He would call her after the meeting, he decided, or, better yet, go back uptown afterwards and invite her for a drink. He had no clear idea of what they would talk about. The decisions all seemed made. But he would feel better if he invited her. Even if she refused, he would feel better.

He caught sight of Ubco's main office through the glass walls of the phone booth. A Fleetwood had stopped at the entrance and two elderly gentlemen were being escorted into the bank. For a moment Palmer wondered if the building had some rear entrance through which he might make an appearance, alone, beholden to no one, his own man.

He leaned for a moment against the wall of the booth. Another car had driven up to Ubco's entrance, depositing three elderly directors.

Palmer found himself wondering how many of these aged gentlemen had an idea of what lay beneath the surface of what would, as usual, be a smoothly run, almost somnolent meeting. Aside from a handful, did any of them suspect? Did they smell treachery, lying, blackmail, subornation, bribery and the delicately wrought web of pressure, counter-pressure, maneuver and counter-maneuver which Palmer had been forced to weave?

Did they, behind the bland young face of their executive vice-president, see anything more than a properly prudent, well-brought-up white Protestant, one of their own kind? Did they see the schemer, the liar, the adulterer? Did any of them pierce the actor's smooth façade to see the other roles he played?

As he stood there in the booth, Palmer realized that none of them would see any of this when they looked at him. Not even Burckhardt and Loomis understood every detail, every lie, every bit of chicanery. All they would see was what they were supposed to see, one of their own kind.

Abruptly, Palmer understood that they would be right. He was one of their own kind. At last.

He left the phone booth and walked even more slowly toward the bank. A girl in high-heeled black patent-leather pumps hurried across his path, late for work. He watched the smooth pulsing throb of her calf muscles as she crossed the street, the complicated shifting of her buttocks, swelling and curving with each step.

Palmer turned away. He began to wander in the opposite direction, moving farther and farther from the bank.

At an intersection he darted suddenly across the traffic. A maddened horn brayed in his ear. He walked on, blindly, block after block. The river stench was thick in his nostrils.

At another intersection some faint instinct for self-preservation made him look up. Battery Park lay immediately ahead. He plunged out of the last sooty canyon and walked swiftly toward the water.

Very old people and very young ones moved through the treeless park. The old ones sat and watched two ships slowly negotiate the harbor, outward bound. The children gravitated toward a popcorn-and-candy vendor. Palmer stood at the scaly iron railing and stared south into the heart of the harbor.

He watched the two ships carefully revolve through small, stately arcs of movement, controlled by tugboats. To his left, indistinctly, Palmer caught a glimpse of a light-green plinth. He stared hard and, for a moment, was able to distinguish the peaky crown of the Statue of Liberty before the smoke and mist closed down over her.

Palmer turned his back on the harbor and stared instead at the nervous, slashed skyline, profile of some terrible uneasiness charted on a graph. His eye traced the violent upswings and the dark depressions of the soul. It was all there, he decided. And not a level stretch anywhere.

He asked himself how long he could stand it. He asked himself if, together, he and Edith could manage to thrive in this frightening city. He remembered soft lakes and the gently rolling woods of Michigan. He asked himself about the summer. He got no answers.

High above the jutting crags of the financial district, a thrusting slab of new white carried a flashing electric sign that reported temperature and time. Palmer watched it for a moment: 41. 9:45. 41. 9:45. 41. 9:46.

He glanced down at his hands and saw that small, sharp shreds of blackish rust had come off on his palms. He brushed them together and felt the gift of the city.

But, Christ, he thought, no one retires at my age. I don't play the piano or collect stamps or make oil paintings.

He had a tremendous urge to call Virginia again. He looked around him for a phone booth and, finding none, walked quickly out of the park. As he entered the high canyons of the city once more, he felt almost unbearably relieved. The tight, enclosing spaces comforted him. The narrow, channeled vistas were almost soothing.

He walked past three phone booths on his way to the bank. As he entered, the doorman gave him a small, tight salute. Palmer smiled, nodded and paused for a moment under the high ceiling of this gold and green immensity of space. He could hear an IBM machine at work. The off-beat rhythm of the operation suggested to him that the machine was computing and printing quarterly dividend cards for savings accounts.

The smile on his face died slowly. He walked toward the elevator at the far end of the lobby, aware of the fact that most of the employees were openly watching him now that they suspected his real power. He also knew, as he walked, that he gave them a fairly confidence-inspiring picture. He looked like he belonged in a bank.

It was, after all, the best, if not the only, thing he could do.